I0523133

Ah Jubah!

Ah Jubah!

A PleaPrayerPromise

from

Asiri Odu

ỌYA'S TORNADO

Publisher's note: *Ah Jubah!* is a political and historical novel that addresses complex and confounding issues in innovative ways. Neither Asiri Odu nor Ọya's Tornado advocate violence, apart from self-defense. The myriad actions undertaken by the characters of *Ah Jubah!* reflect the diverse strategies that revolutionaries have employed throughout time and will continue to employ to fight racists, racism, and racist oppression and, even more important, to manifest their destinies.

Copyright © 2015 Ọya's Tornado
All rights reserved

This book is a publication of
OYA'S TORNADO
Books To Blow Your Mind
Orífín, Ilé Àjẹ́
oyastornado@yahoo.com

OYA'S TORNADO™, *Books To Blow Your Mind*™, and all associated tornado logos are trademarks of Ọya's Tornado.

Original poems and songs appear courtesy of the genius and the kind permission of Aseret Sin.
All rights reserved

No part of this book may be reproduced or utilized in any form or by any means, electronic or mechanical, including photocopying and recording, or by any information storage and retrieval system, without permission in writing from the publisher.

Manufactured in the United States of America

ISBN: 9780991073047

10 9 8 7 6 5 4 3 2 1

First Edition

For the warriors of wood, iron, and words

Yaa Asante Waa
Queen Nzingah
Marimba Ani
Boukman
Odùduwà
Steel Pulse
Ishmael Reed
Fred Hampton
The Maji Maji
Sam Greenlee
Nyabinghi
Lumumba
Abbey Lincoln
The Black Panther Party
The Black Liberation Army
Teresa N. Washington
John A. Williams
X Clan
Ṣàngó
Allah
Ògún
Zumbi
Ògbóni
Bobby Wright
Fannie Lou Hamer
The Deacons for Defense
Fela Anikulapo Kuti
Toni Morrison
Yemọja
Killarmy
Bob Marley
Robert Williams
Sarraounia Aben Soro
Mummar al-Quaddafi
Thomas Sankara
Assata Shakur
Angela Davis
The Kandake
Dead Prez
and many more
including, hopefully,
You

A NOTE ON THE TITLE

"Jubah" is a Pan-African concept, and, as such, it boasts numerous spellings and meanings.

In East Africa "Juba" is a personal name, and it is also the name of the capital of South Sudan. The river "Jubba" flows from Ethiopia to Somalia, and "Jubba" is the name of a Somalian airline.

In West Africa among the Yoruba "júbà" means to pay homage. "A júbà" means, "we/they pay homage"; the phrase could also be interpreted as a statement of surprise or delight that celebratory ritual invocation is taking place or will be enacted.

In African America the concept boasts many spellings, including Juba, Jubah, Juber, Jubba, and Jibber, and multiple meanings. "Juba" may signify a personal name, the title of a song, a type of dance, or a dish, but its mention most often invokes the ritual ceremony of praise, pain, exultation, conjuration, invocation, and revitalization that has been an integral aspect of African America since the first enslaved Africans bowed over a pot or stole away to the woods.

African Americans are comprised of Africans who were stolen from every region of the Continent, including its islands, so it is logical that the African America "Juba" incorporates both East and West African meanings and expands them.

Employing the African methodology of embracing and evolving ancient rituals and wisdom, this book offers the reader an exploration of the power and profundity that is encoded covertly and extolled overtly through the multifold Pan-African force that is best defined as the response it elicits, *Ah Jubah!*

A NOTE TO THE READER

This is not a book for the weak
This is not a book for deceivers
This is not a book for believers

This is not a book for self-haters

If you are enamored of and rally to support
the unnatural and/or the abominable
if you find it easy, fun, or necessary
to excuse atrocities
this book is not for you

This novel revolutionary manual
is for the warriors
who refuse to bow and scrape
who will not pervert or truncate
their power and glory and gifts

This book is for the Suns
who shine and who live
to ensure others glow and grow

This is a book by and for the courageous

This is a book by and for the Gods

She rose. Like the moon, with the moon, she rose shining. Her body, awash in moonglow, glistened. She let the moon's beams guide her over the plush veldts of emerald green grass, around trees that would never be cut because they would never be seen, except by her, and over streams made iridescent with the scales of slumbering fish. She followed the path opened by the moon.

Because she was the color of the night she melded into its perfection and was indistinguishable from it. The pounding of her feet matched time with the beating of the Earth's heart. Crows offered her tender caws of encouragement. Black pumas stretched on sturdy branches and nodded in approval of her mission. Her Mother gauged her progress from Ahstah.

She altered her path and adjusted her stride so that her toes could better grip the moistening soil and loosening grass. She felt the pull of the river. She heard the plankton, fish, and crocodiles feasting, jilting, and floating as they made the silt that would nourish the Nubah. She quickened her pace. Her full eyes narrowed to slits with her blissful contemplation of her destiny. A sheen of sweat covered her skin. Her buttocks, firm and high, contracted their muscles and vibrated with each step. Her young breasts bobbed; her nipples led the way. Her clitoris sprang forth, a maroon star.

At the riverside, she reclined and watched the moon ascend. When she and the moon reached their apexes, she felt a vibration deep and strong enough to reposition her bones.

She rocked as the Earth's vibration massaged her buttocks, thighs, knees, and soul. With her palms on the Earth, she rose.

Her star stretched to kiss her ocean. Her emi and the Earth's coalesced.

Ahhh

She kneaded her breasts at the moment of entry.

                                          Ahhh

                                                  She stroked her
lips and massaged her thighs.

                                        Ahhh

                                             She grew still and let the Earth's
rhythms transport her.

                                        Ahhhh

                                           On the sacred throbbing Earth, she came into
herself.

She turned toward the window and inhaled dawn's dewy air. She felt a
tremor rock her 3-year-old body.

"Ahh!"

A cool burgundy current of electricity charged her clitoris. She moved,
changed position to her side . . . and it was gone! She rolled slowly onto her
back.

"Ahhh!"

She wanted the throbbing to continue its self-directed pulse forever. She
laid still and became 1 with time, space, place, and ecstasy.

The child with cinnamon skin wrapped in pink sheets which were
tucked under a pink coverlet, situated under a pink canopy, surrounded by 3
bedrooms, a kitchen, 2 bathrooms, a basement, a living room, and a foyer,
all stationed on a emicenter over which the Kankakee stoked fires to warm
new life, acquainted herself with her power.

Having no words for her center of contentment or the contentment, she
represented feeling with sound

                                        "Ah"

                                            and held her body as still as the buried
bones of her ancestors.

Her clitoris, 4 inches long, flexible, and rich with semen stores, curved
into her vagina and found its home. She reclined at the riverside all night
long, enjoying her totality. She thanked her Mother with unspoken praises
that reverberated through the Earth.

She begot herself within her self.

After giving birth, she took her child, the shining, tiny, onyx gift of Ah
who was a replica of her Mother and her self, into the baobab den that
would be their home. There, on the carpet of plush grass, she taught her
daughter the language of the mind, the pulse song of the clitoris, and the
praises to the Earth, the Mother, the Waters, and the Cosmos.

In the next room, the mother dreamt of her Babygirl loving herself in mirror-smooth river water. She sighed, smiled, and turned in her sleep.

"Ah," she moaned along with her bliss-filled 3 year old. She wanted so much for this Babygirl

"Ah"

to know her love, her self, her peace, and her power.

She had dragged herself out of a cotton field and traveled from the banks of the Mississippi to those of the Illinois. She had a man but had given up on bliss until

"Ah!"

She rolled over on her back and greeted the morning in the same fashion as her daughter.

The Ah birthed themselves until they were an multigenerational family of 12 cooking herbs for nourishment and healing and perfecting the arts of education, elevation, and spiritual revelation in the baobab den. They used their mouths only to eat because their minds were channels of fluid communication and tomes of ageless wisdom. All they did was done in harmony. They dreamt the same dreams.

Every 3rd day when the sun was ¾ past its apex, they went to Ahstah. They rose in unified Blackness to sojourn with and learn from the Mother.

You and your powers comprise the soul of this planet: The power of the cosmos thrives in you young Gods.

What of those who came before us, Mother?

The Ahtlna. They had 23 emi, and their powers and capacities were vast, but so too was their potential for destruction. With so much power, a reversion occurred. They raped, emptied, and dulled minds, as overt spiritual stimulation resulted in moral degradation.

You are the first of your kind. You own 12 emi. Through your labors you have unlimited potential to evolve and expand. You are able to marshal all the powers of the cosmos and are capable of infinite growth. Indeed, soon you will create your complement.

When an Ah gave birth to a child with testes, the collective exclaimed audibly and mentally.

They called it Aha. It was of the way.

"These men ain't shit."

"God, did Montez wig out again?"

Azure passed the spliff to Alteveze and topped off their glasses of chardonnay. Alteveze had insisted on drinking from the oversized hand blown goblets so that they could get drunk as quickly as possible.

"I took him straight outta his momma's crib into mine—what was I thinking?" Alteveze was a study of disappointment. Her flashed dreds trembled as she spoke. Altezeve's peachstone skin had grown dull with stress, but her naturally arched, thick eyebrows maintained their vitality and expanded and contracted as her mood changed from vexation to rage to frustration.

"Oh. Another male," Azure, nonplussed, received the joint and inhaled.

"Why can't these boys, these males, cross the bridge into manhood?"

"Alteveze, these brothas are marked by slavery's curse: If they're not out studdin, they're grimacing from the psychic knife scars on they balls. It's easier for them to remain irresponsible lil boyz than to struggle on into manhood. We have to help them cross over." The filigree brass filings that capped the 2 braids that trekked down her hairline echoed her sentiment. Azure sounded sensible, reasonable, but both she and Alteveze both knew Azure wasn't going that route.

"Sorry," she brushed away ash from her jeans, "but fuck that last part. I mean, that's all I been doing since I been in the game. But this is the umpteenth brotha who decided my trim so good, he would rather crawl up into my womb than let me birth a child."

"Weeelll," Azure looked suggestively at her sista, and her large afro-puff rose slightly, "that might be awright."

"Shut up fool!" they laughed and sipped. Azure went to fetch some apples, grapes, and cheese to cushion the wine.

"Seriously, God," Alteveze called into the kitchenette, "he even quote Parliament Funkadelic. Somethin bout, you spend your whole life trying to get back into the hole you came out of, or some such shit."

"My, *that's* not a male-oriented thought at all!"

"What we supposed to do?"

"Open wide and shut the fuck up."

Azure set the snacks on her narrow glass coffee table that was really just round display-self glass placed on a large pot that she had thrown using the black clay from a creek near her apartment.

"Well, aside from his lack of philosophical depth, what's really wrong with Montez? He got a good lil job, he gives you anything you want. Everybody know—'Montez love him some Veze!'" they laughed and slapped their hands high and hard.

"It's true but the brotha doesn't have any goals or dreams. I mean, he could spend his whole life up unda me."

"Right," Azure nodded looking serious, "or up over."

"There *you* go," she giggled and struck her own jab against her friend's celibacy: "I'ma get you some dick for xmas cause that's all on yo wig."

"Don't waste your time," Azure dismissed the suggestion with an extended suck of her teeth.

"For real though: He just ain't doin nothin with his life. He gon sell cars the rest of his life?"

"I understand. Brother has no drive—pardon the pun," Azure paused and watched as Alteveze gobbled hunk after hunk of bleu cheese. "You think I bought that cheese just for yo lips?"

Alteveze answered by curling the offending lips and reaching for cheddar. "But I feel you, Veze. You want a man by your side: a complement and a warrior."

"Damn right."

"Well, uhh, what about Saddiq? I mean, he in school, and"

"Girl, please!"

Alteveze cocked her head to the side, "You know he ain't serious. He just a kick-about and ain't no tellin who *he* up under right now."

Azure smiled and thought, I sure am glad I decided to take an extended leave of absence from "love." What a monumental waste of time. "Well, sistagirl, whatchu gon do?"

"Refill my glass," and she did.

"Montez is alright. He's stable. Make a good daddy and provider."

"Damn, that sounds dull."

"Then stick with drama king Saddiq."

"Yeh, so I can write all of his essays for him and introduce him to my friends so he can sample new pussy and kick my ass when my friend's pussy ain't good enough. I don't want a drama king or a numb ass," Alteveze sighed. "I'm alright by mydamnself."

"Well," she nodded at Thomas Sankara who was gazing at them from her warriors' shrine, "maybe that's how you gon be."

"Humph. By mydamnself."

She knelt in the shrine. The paint made of ground oyster shells and lime shone pewter blue in the moonlight.

"Aro Aro Aro"	She clasped the left hand of her Ìyá in her own.
"Ẹ̀jọ̀ titi Ọ̀run"	They kneeled and greeted the Earth with their heads.
"Ẹ̀jọ̀ titi Ayé"	At the ojúbọ they bent and tasted the Earth packed bone hard yet fecund with blood, prayer, praise, and lamentation.

"Ọmọ Ìyàlájẹ́, your education with me is nearing its end," she gazed into her daughter's eyes. "Your apo ìkà is filled with power, destiny waits in your womb, wisdom finds its home in your head. You have the bird; you have the calabash as do we all. Your strength is in ìrókò; you rest in Àjẹ́ Kòbàlé. By the womb of Imọlẹ̀, your path is well lit."

"Àṣẹ"

"The Ancestors will always walk with you."

                                                    "Àṣẹ"

"Your outer head will not spoil your inner head."

                                                    "Àṣẹ"

"Ọmọ Ìyàlájẹ́, you will always be as effective as salt."

                                                    "Àṣẹ."

Ìyá took to her mat. With her legs V-ed and her palms facing the curling thatch, she took a black feather and swept Ọmọ Ìyàlájẹ́'s brow. She swept the 16 cowries resting in their tray. Ọmọ Ìyàlájẹ́'s eyes closed as the road of knowing opened. Her Ẹlẹ́da sparked. She looked back on 36 seasons of training.

"Never pluck the leaves from the limbs, Ọmọ Ìyàlájẹ́; it is an offense. Always take those golden leaves kissing Imọlẹ̀ or those caught in a spider's web."

They had traveled beyond the Ọráńyàn staff about 2000 paces into the bush of Ifẹ̀. Ọmọ Ìyàlájẹ́ listened to the calling parrots as they brushed the earth with their red dipped feathers in search of grub worms. She watched Ìyá's gnarled hands collect the leaves. Such weathered hands! Hands she had witnessed crack a coconut to pour forth milk. Hands she had seen pulling forth from the womb the tiniest premature baby so that she could ensure its life after the mother's death. Hands that trembled 3 feet over packed earth that hid a clay pot that was filled with ṣẹgi beads. She fingered those beads now adorning her waist. "Ayé has given you a gift," the elder had said. Now the knowing hands opened and allowed the golden leaves to float into her palms.

"Steep them in ogogoro and sip before you sleep."

Amp was sucking her ear. Like, French-kissing her ear. He was high. He had a soft, black, big Afro; it was a magnificent frame for his smoked cedar skin. She felt the brush of his high cheekbones. Cheekbones of the child of 2 cultures.

"Wait," she tried to pull away, "I gotta find Tina."

"No baby," he purred and pulled her to his chest.

Boy, she thought, he's pretty strong.

"Mmm," he licked his lips, "how old did you say you was?"

"13."

Hands, fingers, legs, arms, tongue were all over her still-boyish frame. She was lost in sensation. His control of her body was masterful.

He paused his explorations to ask, "You smoke weed?"

"Úhn ùn."

He paused, looked at her with all the seriousness he could muster, and exclaimed, "Well, I do!" and burst out laughing.

She slipped into his laughter with the ease and grace of a Greg Louganis dive.

He's beautiful and he likes me! Everyone say I'm ugly but he likes me. Maybe he'll be my boyfriend . . . but he's all the way here in Champagne. How will we see each other? Maybe he has a ca

"You know how old I am?" He mumble-murmured in her ear interrupting her thoughts.

She was eager to learn more about him, "How old?"

"18," his smile was dazzling. "Come on. I wanna show you some pictures of my family."

The pictures were a blur. Once he got her firmly ensconced on the bed, he fingered her vagina, and she felt like a magician was pulling rabbits, lions, snakes and whole new species of life out of her.

"Oooohh," she swooned.

She didn't know any more than she did when she was 3 and felt her clitoris vibrating of its own accord: She knew it felt good.

"But Raheem, I am not a semen receptacle. You have to recognize me as your complement. My role transcends helpmate."

"You've been reading too many books. This feminist, excuse me, *womanist* crap has poisoned your brain. Allah has laid down your path," he stood over her and looked down, "You, like your womb, are to be productive, hidden, and silent."

"I'll be damned," she mumbled and offered a hint of an eyeroll. After a pause, she gazed up at him, "My vibrations roar with your own if you listen."

"Hadizat, we don't have time for gyrations into oblivion. You are the seat of our power as the source of my children. But I am the executor of our estate," Raheem made an expansive gesture with his arms that encompassed both their home and her being. He paused to ensure he had Hadizat's full attention: "Allah has decreed me your only vibration."

She glanced between her legs as if in conference with her crotch but said nothing.

The deeper his faith is getting, the quicker his mind is going. Hadizat shook her head. He sounds just like a recording of Imam Razak. He hasn't had an original independent thought in 3 months.

She had lost respect for him, but she had to try again to reach him.

"Raheem, I need passion, spontaneity, energy. . . . We used to have all that. Don't you remember?" She reached for his hand, but his eyes closed and his face followed.

Hadizat sighed, rose, and walked into their bedroom. She emerged with a poem, "I wrote this for you." She stroked his arm and Stonehenge softened a bit. "Sit down, please. Close your eyes and listen."

Exchange Rates

You wind round my mind
tapestry of synthetic lies
laced in lead linked in iron
Onyx was once the only hue
anointing the gold of my soul
Adorned with you I was whole
But you traded the throbbing for the lifeless
strangling gray of static

My vibrations surge in overdrive
                     not automatic

Remember when I used to with you
ride the top of all rhythms
electrified by the force of souls
Now I am alone
wondering what they promised you in kind
to convince you to pawn your soul.

"Hadizat," his voice sounded like steel scraping granite, and it matched the jabs of his index finger, "let me remind you that all verses must praise Allah who gives us grace in all things. Your poem is blasphemous and dirty." He wrinkled his brow, "I didn't know this was in you."

"Perhaps because I'm all covered up, graces and vices," she gestured to the long mauve gown she was wearing. "But no matter what, I'm still a whore." The eyes she had fallen in love with before she met his mind looked at her mouth as if she had 3 lips.

She tried again to move him, "When you walked out of Temple #2 3 years ago, you reminded me of a photo Askia has of Muslim brothers in Senegal. They wear long beautiful robes that complement their slightly tarnished auras. When I saw you, you were coming towards me in a sky blue dress. Framed so beautifully against the verdant Earth and the cerulean sky—you were the Earth and the sky in 1. My only desire was to remove the sky blue cloth and witness your midnight perfection."

"Your mind is a labyrinth of alleys," he snarled.

"I didn't hear you complain last night."

"I never knew"

               "You never listened."

                     "I married a slut."

She rose and strutted away, swaying her immaculate brown ass under multitudinous yards of mauve silk, "Well, she's leaving you."

"You were never with the Faith."

"My faith was in you."

Amp led her into a completely dark room. She vaguely remembered Tina as she kissed him in the pitch dark with her eyes wide open. He encircled her waist with his arms. He had filled her ears with saliva and had her clitoris humming like a jaw's harp. She felt like a live wire.

Then the throbbing stopped.

He bent her at the waist. The washing machine was cold against her cheek. She reached back to feel what was nudging her. Long, hard, draped in ribbed latex. His penis, she thought. He's gonna—

She held onto the washing machine for her life because the edge of the whole world was forcing its way into her vagina. She yelped as he plowed, plowed, plowed making way, clearing a path in 13 year old virgin territory that even Ògún would have left fallow.

The washing machine shook from the outside force of 13 year old hands backed by 18 year old thrusts as methodical and persistent as a lynch mob.

She didn't weep. She was too stunned. She grew analytical. Analyzing, separating, as was separate, the pleasures of fondling versus the pain of— this other thing.

When she was reunited with Tina, she collapsed at her cousin's feet in a heap.

She walked the road to Nupe. She was leaving Ògún. So dull, so violent, so taciturn. Now, Ṣàngó! And she conjured him. The long braids that begged her fingertips for touches. Gold glistening in his ear lobes and against skin that could only be the color of eternity. Always wearing red and such stylish clothes! I won't, I refuse to remain in Ògún's dungeon. Ṣàngó loves me and I him. The wetness between her thighs was both lubricant and accelerant: She walked faster.

When he first saw her, he saw himself. It wasn't narcissism that attracted him. Her aura and vibration mesmerized him. He heard a humming.

MMMmmmahahahahhhhh

"Ìyawó mi, wá nibi."

Then he touched her, and the humming seemed to chorus with the earth under their feet. Vibration charged the air. "The ancestors are singing for us," he smiled

"I hear them."

Her hair was braided in an elaborate coiffure of a globe shimmering with gold filings. He caressed the beaded ball and then her forehead and then her cheeks. He stroked her lips with his fingertips. He submerged his nose into the myrrh of her bosom and inhaled so deeply she felt a breeze in her spine.

He led her to his repose room, and, as she reclined on the pelts and cushions and cloths, he removed, inhaled, and draped each of her cloths around his neck. He slid her waistbeads over the perfectly rounded mounds of her behind and placed them on his shrine. Then he turned to Àràká with the concentration of a novitiate at the crossroads.

She awoke to find her limbs locked by muscular hands and gouged by fingernails. Her mothers held her legs and arms with the intensity of crabs keeping another in a barrel. She wondered, Why are they holding me so tightly?

"Ama," her mother stood above her, "you are about to become a woman. You are 13 and must now prepare for marriage. During the Bathing, you, my daughter, will make me proud."

Mama Akyem came toward her with a triangular piece of a mirror—a gift granted from the sale of slaves—she was proud to exclaim. The original hand mirror had been oval in shape and encased in a frame of fake silver that was admired away after a week.

Ama glimpsed her face in the mirror as Akyem knelt between her spread legs.

She was too shocked to scream. The pain was so devastating that Ama killed her self. The orgasmic spark she felt immediately prior to the torturous cutting were the last things she felt.

3 weeks later Ama ran into the forest. The night before she left, she tried to tell her mother that her Mother was calling her but she could not speak. Perhaps she should have felt sad leaving her mother as she did, but she could no longer feel.

Àjẹ́ Kòbàlé Loves Cloth
And Wears All Her Garments At Once
Cast for Ọya, when she was called Àràká
when she needed a hiding place for her soul.
My Bark And Leaves Appear Thin
But They Shield My Soul
is the 1 who cast for Ọya, who was known as Àràká
when she was going to Ọyọ́ to meet her lover.
But what would she meet on the road?
"How can my path be good?" she asked.
Àràká was preparing to travel to meet Ṣàngó.
Her Ẹlẹ́da was shining.

She put 2 & 3 together and consulted Ifá.
She was told to sacrifice 2 cloths: 1 green, 1 gold,
as well as eko, palm oil, and salt to Àwọn Ìyá Wa
to make her journey successful.
She was told to crown the sacrifice
with the red feather of a gray parrot.
Àràká was told to offer 8,000 cowries at orítamẹẹ́tà.
Àràká heard.
Àràká made the sacrifice.
On her journey, Àràká wore a red cloth of the finest material;
it flowed about her body like woven blood.
Her hair was braided and beaded in the shape of a fan.
She was honored as royalty at every town in which she stopped.
Àràká was treated with honor because her power
was known, feared, and revered in her terrain.
But when she reached Lokanja, she was unknown.
The king's messenger reported the beautiful traveler.
Olokanja demanded she be brought forth in chains.
Àràká submitted to the chains.
Àràká submitted without fear.
She faced Olokanja in all her wealth, weight, and wrath.
He gazed on this woman in red and saw a new wife.
Olokanja dismissed his servants and
unlocked Àràká's chains with his own hands.
He demanded Àràká remove her red cloth.
Àràká said, "King, leave me to walk my way.
"My husband is waiting for me."
Olokanja laughed and replied, "Yes, I am waiting!"
Olokanja laughed.
He began ripping the cloth from Àràká's body.
Àràká stood forth naked, her body shining.
Her waistbeads tinkled.
Olokanja heard the beads' song and felt his penis being summoned.
As he reached for her breasts, spit met his face.
Eeeehhh! Àràká spit on Olokanja!
Olokanja raised his hand to strike the impudent woman
and he struck wind!
Kai!
Where had Àràká gone?
Olokanja looked everywhere.
He saw nothing but an Àjẹ́ Kòbàlé tree stirred by a breeze.
The tree tinkled like Àràká's beads.
Olokanja began stripping the green leaves.

"1 will release this woman," he said.
He began raping leaves in handfuls.
With his ninth handful, he heard a screaming.
"What is that?"
He turned around to see a red tornado coming to dance with him.
They danced.
The tornado wrapped him in a complete embrace
from the inside out.
Olokanja's limbs were scattered to each corner of his kingdom.
His head remained at the roots of the Àjẹ́ Kòbàlé.
The tornado left and Àràká returned.
She was dressed in gold: the hue of her soul.
She wore a crown of red parrot's feathers.
She claimed the head of Olokanja and the town of Lokanja.
Alayé! The citizens hailed her.
Ọya! Ọya, oooo! They cried.
Àràká summoned Olokanja's servants.
Àràká told them to bury Olokanja's head under the Àjẹ́ Kòbàlé
so that he can forever fertilize the tree he defiled
and replenish the leaves he destroyed.
Àràká told his citizens to bring forth Olokanja's wealth.
They placed his gold, his silver, his cowries, his bronzes, his lapis
lazuli, his coral, his pearls, his cloths, his steeds, his cattle, his
slaves—everything he once claimed he owned—around the tree.
Àràká liberated the people Olokanja had enslaved.
She gave them half of Olokanja's wealth.
She gave them administrative power over Lokanja.
Àràká waved a parrot's feather
over the other half of Olokanja's wealth.
Like the wind, Àràká arrived with the wealth in Ọ̀yọ́.
She met Ṣàngó.
Àràká matched her wealth with Ṣàngó's own.
Àràká matched her power with his own.
She is more than his equal.
She is more than a conqueror.

Ọya O! Ọya O!
The wife is fiercer than the husband.
Ọya outwits the king in killing strategy
Ìyá Ọya! Alayé Àràká Ọya O!

This is what they sang
This is what they sang for Ọya

When she was known as Àràká
When she needed a hiding place for her soul.
Àjẹ́. Àjẹ́ Kòbàlé.

"Ọmọ Ìyàlájẹ́, mark this ẹsẹ well. This is the last ẹsẹ I will teach you."
Ọmọ Ìyàlájẹ́ added the texts, lessons, and leaves to her soul.

"This bush, as you see," Ìyá gestured about her compound, "grows everywhere. It is lulayọ̀ jàre. Take the petals of 1 flower and 3 roots of the plant. Parch and grind them. Add baobab seeds and red pepper and wrap in an ìrókò leaf. Steep in a shallow bowl of the patient's urine for 8 days. On the 9th day, take a small amount on your index finger. Place your medicated finger on the cervix of the woman and she will lose the pregnancy.

"To seal the womb completely, prepare only the petals and roots, then recite this incantation:
We open the door of the home when we wish
We prepare the hearth as we wish
If a visitor comes, he does not stay
We control our home with lulayọ̀ jàre"

Ìyá stood before her daughter who was cradling pigeons, leaves, and roots. She offered them and knelt in learning, "This is how you rid yourself or another of an unwanted person: He will run until he dies. . ."
"This is how to summon someone who has travelled far from you. . ."
"This is how to traverse miles in mere seconds. . ."
"Here is what you do to position a child in the womb for birth. . ."
For 36 seasons she learned the fundamentals; for 27 more seasons she did the Work.

When this child rested in her mother's womb, Ìyá had seen her potential, recognized her path. She took the child as her own and filled her head and soul with pure wisdom. Every moment of the child's conscious and unconscious life was a moment packed with education. Ìyá devised an intensive curriculum because time was short and raiders were plucking and picking people from their homes as if human beings had become mangos to sale at a market—mere commodities.
Ìyá ferreted out secret sites for study; she needed privacy because she wanted the child's Àjẹ́ to be expertly directed. Ìyá taught her daughter with the same devotion and intensity with which her Mothers had educated her. The child's mind was fertile. She used her analytical acumen to build on the lessons her Ìyá taught her. She made her own discoveries, created her own medicines, and performed her own practical experiments as well.
Near the end of the rainy season, the women trekked far into the bush

and found an intricately curled vine boasting proud violet flowers with amber accents. "Here it is," Ìyá offered kola and egg and incantation. She removed a body-length section of the vine. "This plant only grows at this time of year. At no other. You can use this vine to tie the hands, mind, and feet of a person who wants to do you harm. They will see you and become confused: Their mind will scatter and their tongue will cease to work. This is how it is used. . ."

"This bark," she held 3 finger strips of the gray bark, "made into a tea will cure fever." Ìyá reached up and plucked a leaf from the same tree, "Adding this leaf will add delirium to the fever."

When they returned to the ojúbọ, Ìyá prepared bathwater of Àjẹ́ Kòbàlé, verbena hastata, hyacinth, and ground amethyst. Ìyá scrubbed Ọmọ Ìyàlájẹ́'s body while chanting sacred words of power. When her bath was complete, Ìyá wrapped her body in a white cotton cloth and stretched her out on the bed. "Now, you will undergo a process of expansion. When your inner eyes come forth, you will be able to see beyond what is said and into what is truly felt. When your inner eyes come forth, your mind will be able to stand in for your body anywhere, no matter where you are physically."

"When the sun and moon are ¾ past their apex, take to your back, clear your mind of all. Join us."

They sat facing each other with only the vibrations of the emi between them. There at the cresting of the Ormolu River, the 1 owned by Ọya, she told her apprentice, "Your training and education with me are complete. I have taught you all I know. Let us listen to Our Mothers." She cast the cowries.

"There are chains in your eyes. And water." She gazed at Ọmọ Ìyàlájẹ́ and then through her, beyond her. "You will witness what our people have not the heart to imagine.

"1 grove of water. 1 tomb of soil damp with our blood. 1 chain binding your hands, 1 chain binding your feet, dragging you across the water.

"You will bear 1 daughter who will bear 1 daughter who will bear 1 daughter who will bear 1 daughter. Their names will be riddles, yet all will continue the way. Ọmọ Ìyàlájẹ́, yes, that is your name for it is who you are. You are my spiritual daughter, my child, the Child of the Mother of Phenomenal Power. Your daughters may not remember this name but it is enough that you will all continue to *be* Ọmọ Ìyàlájẹ́.

"The name you will carry in your heart and tongue beyond the Ethiopic is the same as Yewájọbí, the Mother of All. This is significant because you will undergo another birth. You will go through a death canal but you will make it a womb of life, as Yemọja intends.

"You will die in a land so foreign"

                    "No!" She could not believe her

people's most feared taboo, to be cursed with burial away from and thus be cut off from the Ancestors and Ancients, would befall her.

"Eewọ Òrìṣà!" She snapped her fingers over her head 3 times in hopes of undoing her Ìyá's utterance.

A gnarled hand rose and demanded silence. The path had been cleared and lit long ago. There were new taboos now, and when the beast had finished its work, broken taboos would become as common as clouds.

"The land of your death is not as important as your way of life. You, my own," Ìyá cradled her daughter's head in her hands and looked directly into her progeny's eyes, "will always be with us and we with you," she paused so her daughter could absorb this truth.

"When you emerge from the water, you will be called a name not recognized in this land, but it is the title of the primordial Mother Creator: Ah-Ni. You will enter that accursed land in the way of Yewájọbí Yemọja, the Mother who strolls the sea floor. You will clothe the land of your exile with your vision, with our vision. Your progeny will clothe that land with blood. They will be warriors of water, wood, and lead."

"Ògún."

"Yes, but in a new way. New warriors."

"Your spirit is waiting with them. You must join. Yewájọbí Yemọja is waiting. She has spoken."

"Cynthia, listen: I can see your heart beating. I can see your every internal organ. Your womb, your"

"Kandace," she curled her lips, made crescent moons of her eyebrows, and looked sideways at this deep brown woman with shoals natural kinky hair that she had styled into 2 twists running to the back of her head. It was the hair, then, out wild a lá Angela Davis circa 1966—no, more like Chaka Khan, because there was a seductive wildness in this woman, that had initially caused Cynthia to shun Kandace. "Lord, she had thought, "they let *that* into grad school?" But Cynthia came to understand that Hattiesburg was the citadel of Hattie Forrest, wife of Nathaniel Bedford Forrest, founder of the Ku Klux Klan. It didn't matter how you wore your hair, to a racist, a nigger was a nigger.

When Cynthia first drove from her home in Itta Bena, Mississippi to Hattiesburg and entered Forrest County, she felt a weight of oppression that never lifted until she left the county. After 2 months of the hate-weighted gravity, she sought out the wild child. Running from such statements as, "Sure, I used to be a racist. . ." and "Wanna hear a nigger joke?" Running from the mocking emptiness that crouched in all the corners of her home. Running from the Black Bourgeoisie who used the myth of class to camouflage the fact that they really just hated their melanin, and fleeing general Caucasia, Cynthia sought out, begged for the presence of Kandace.

Kandace wasn't difficult to find. Both women had been pushed out of the urban area and into the "bottoms." They lived in different sections of the same roach ridden dilapidated housing complex, not because it was what they could afford; clean housing in the city was cheaper. But as Stevie Wonder reported, while you might have cash you can't cash in your race.

Cynthia found Kandace's home roach-free due to full crevice and joint calking and an arsenal of insecticides that had left her with hallucinogenic side effects for months.

Cynthia was surprised to find the mothers, sons, and daughters of the complex circulating through Kandace's home. The sons and daughters came for tutoring. The mothers came to learn how to read (some of the school children in their early teens did also).

During Cynthia's first visit, she found Kandace deep in discussion with 2 teen boys about the fact that first human being of the world was an African woman. During the discussion, Kandace smiled at Cynthia a knowing smile that asked rhetorically, "Now, who did you think *you* was?" But her mouth never said it, and her eyes sparkled with, "Welcome."

As the only 2 African Americans in the entire graduate program, they only had themselves, but in their neighborhood, they found and fortified a world. They tutored and enlightened members of their community. They critiqued each other's poems and supported 1 another's efforts to publish. They swayed next to old heads and sugar daddies at record spins. They jetted to New Orleans to relax with Kandace's family and to Itta Bena for Cynthia's family throwdowns. Their friendship grew into the sisterhood that Kandace had been awaiting her whole life. So she embraced it and poured her truth into it.

"I know it may sound crazy, but it's true," her eyes pleaded for understanding. "I can"

"Listen," Cynthia waved away her friend's confession, "all that mess you smoked and dropped at FAMU done scrambled your brain. You just havin a flashback!" Cynthia laughed, perhaps, a little too loudly. As she looked at Kandace, Cynthia's marble eyes—that's what Kandace called them, they were so wide, round and glassy—were as still as stones.

"Think so? Watch this," Kandace remained in her cross-legged seating position on the rug; however, instead of looking up at her friend who was sitting on the bed, she levitated until she was eye-level with Cynthia. Her thick twists rippled and undulated as if stirred by their own breeze. A breeze Cynthia didn't feel.

"Goddamn girl," Kandace opened her eyes at the whisper of her friend. She looked at the unfiltered honey-hued skin that was decorated with freckles that were as dark as she was all over. Kandace's normally narrow and slanted eyes were now bucked. Please, please, her eyes begged. You are my only friend. *Please* understand me. I can't hold this in any longer.

"Listen, I, uh, Ah, I gotta go," she reached for her jacket and purse with 1 hand while keeping her eyes trained on Kandace as if she were a cotton mouth moccasin. "I just remembered! I uhh"

"No, Cynthia," she descended and while she didn't touch Cynthia, Kandace held out a hand of friendship. "Please. You're the only 1 I can share this with. We've been so tight lately."

"Now, listen. I like you and everything-but-but—Damn! Why you wanna spring this on me? I-I don't want to deal with this shit!"

Kandace paused, Cynthia was about to bolt. She drew a deep breath, "Cynthia. You've known and trusted me all of this time. I need you to know and trust me on this level."

"I'm sorry. I'm not ready for this. I mean, I thought you was—well—normal."

"This is who I am, who I've always been," Kandace shrugged.

"But how did you learn that? To levitate?"

"When I was a child, this beautiful Mother would come and we would ride"

"What a broom?!

"No," she chuckled. She had to watch her words, but Cyn was with her. "The vibrations in the air. They're always there, waiting, it's just that most people can't feel or harness them.

"Cynthia, I can see the wind! Before a storm its red as blood. Like tidal waves of blood!" She poured forth her long stored waters and released them into the deepest safest vault she knew: the ears of her sister.

"Well, I've heard if you born with a caul you will see spirits and if you put sow milk in your eyes you can see the wind . . . I even heard about the Flying Africans but damn! Seems like you have all those powers."

"I don't know how I was born because they knocked my Momma out. She said when she woke up they had me swaddled in a blanket. She said she would always regret having a C-section because of the pain—she couldn't bend over or pick me up for months!—the difficulty she had in breastfeeding me, and the connections we didn't have because she was knocked out. So, I had the most Western birth you could imagine, and I ain't never been up under a hog, but I've been like this all of my life."

"This is unbelievable," Cynthia was still looking like a petrified doe. If it wasn't for the pomade on her short cropped hair, it would have stood on end, but there seemed to be more awe than fear in her widened eyes.

"When I was young and would get angry, I could do all kinds of things. Make people hurt themselves, make it rain. I can—" she paused not wanting to get too deep too soon, "I can do anything. And I'm not alone." Kandace strode off to her bedroom. "Comere, girl," she beckoned, "look at this."

"This" was 2 books on Àjẹ́ by Teresa N. Washington. The books detailed various people who could do everything she could, and their rich spiritual, literary, mythical, and historical traditions.

Cynthia flipped through 1 of the books. It included praisesongs to Àjẹ́, discussions about their military skills, and the evolution of those skills during slavery. She skimmed pages about African American, Jamaican, Kongolese, Ghanaian, Haitian, Cuban, and Mexican conjurers and 2-headed doctors who had Àjẹ́ and had used it to liberate their communities.

"You got a whole family: Aunts, Mommas, Sisters and Brothers with your same and similar powers in various degrees," Cynthia read aloud a passage about a woman who worked her wonders with a lodestone and a man who had conjured a whole family of racists using the blood of his slain daughter.

"Well, everybody can't do everything. Some people are born with certain skills. Others can gain abilities through initiation or medicinal preparations. But I think that 1 person doing all the things I can do is rare by any standard."

"But this book is talking about conjurers, rootwork, and all this stuff," Cynthia was engrossed in the book, "this is old Black American wisdom tooth knowledge."

"Same Àjẹ́," Kandace nodded.

"How come we don't hear about these folk like we used to?"

"Maybe the power has gotten weaker over the generations. You know, as Zora Neale Hurston acknowledged, 'we's a mingled people.' So much raping of our mothers may have diluted the force. Or maybe, like in my case, the Àjẹ́ has become more concentrated in fewer people. Look at this," Kandace grabbed *The Gẹ̀lẹ̀dẹ́ Spectacle* by Babatunde Lawal and flipped to some photographs. "This is a festival they have to appease us," she pointed at a shot of a Gẹ̀lẹ̀dẹ́ masker. "Look at these mothers sanctioning and validating the festival," she gazed at the 2 women in white, her cheek almost brushing her friend's. She was so relieved by her successful sharing that she didn't perceive the current flowing from Cynthia to herself. Therefore, Kandace was stunned when Cynthia turned her marble eyes to her friend and asked,

"Can you teach me?"

Hawa gazed with love at Danta and thought about the first time she met him. She had decided to get up, go out, and take a walk to unwind. She ended up with a hoe in her hand and sweat stinging her eyes as she and Dear weeded the garden. Manual labor was invigorating to Hawa's body and spirit, and by pretending the weeds were her principal, colleagues, and members of the Board of Education, she felt she was solving 2 problems at once.

5th grade special ed was a particularly rough row to hoe, especially because most of her students were not remedial or academically challenged. They were, however, African American, predominately poor, and some were too talkative (bad conduct), others were too advanced for their classes (insubordinate), and a few were introspective (insolent). So, to justify teaching precocious students in a special education setting, Hawa told herself that these Black Pearls were truly special, and she tailored the curriculum to suit these rare gems. When her students excelled in the culturally grounded aptitude tests she'd devised for them she knew she had the secret to success.

In addition to following the Board of Education's curriculum, which would in no way prepare the students for 6th grade or for life, she infused personalized, intensive training sessions into her lesson plans.

Hawa deciphered through a battery of tests that 20% of the students were auditorily inclined, 40% were visually inclined, 33% were tactilely adept, while the remaining 7% were multistyled. Hawa's goal was to facilitate the adaptation of at least 1 other learning style in each her charges so that they would all be multistyled learners who would excel in any educational setting.

She exhausted herself crafting style-specific audio-visual aids, practical examinations, guest lectures, and field trips. General instruction was undertaken in quality circles in which children with different learning styles worked and learned together. The students took turns leading their groups. Everything from mathematics and algebra, Ralph and Charlene's *forte*; to the life sciences at which Bertha, Romaine, Cetaval, and C.L. excelled; to mechanics and electronics, which Shantanique and Ivory enjoyed; to literary and language arts, which was the passion of Meliquan, Jarvion, and Rose, Hawa incorporated into the designated curriculum so that the students got what was mandated but they also got what they needed and much more.

It was arduous work, especially given the various racisms flourishing in Mississippi. Because no jobs were available in Bliss Bluff or the surrounding towns, she commuted to Corinth. Obtaining the job and keeping it meant undergoing a constant battery of performance and qualification tests. Because of her status as SSOS (Sole Sista on Staff) she was also subjected to random intrusive checks, condescension, and overt racist harassment and attacks. Her students' progress and their glowing faces made a dangerous and otherwise thankless job a joy.

Bliss Bluff was her maternal and ancestral home. Rather than live in Jackson or Memphis, Hawa returned to Bliss Bluff after she earned her degree and teaching certification because she wanted to fulfill many dreams: be near her feisty mothers, raise a garden, build her dream home, and teach. Originally she wanted to prepare the family's 180 acres of land for the children that she would have who would inherit it, but she'd nearly given up on having children because the prospect of finding a suitable father or complement or even impregnator seemed so slim. Her students became her children.

The day she met Danta, she and her grandmother Tynell, who was widely known as Mother Dear, were working methodically, moving from tomatoes to butterbeans to goobers to corn. The work was hot, sweaty, and necessary. Hawa rose, straightening her back and stretching at the end of her row. She gazed out across the field as she wiped the sweat and grit from her face. She did a double take: What she thought was a mirage was in fact a man leisurely strolling on the land over which she flew as a child with knees pumping and braids dancing in the wind.

Dear followed her gaze, "That's some strange nigga. Said he want to buy some land back there in the holla."

"I asked you to stop using that word, Dear," Hawa offered a gentle but stern scolding. She returned to the mirageman, "The land by Q.T.'s place?"

"Un hún. Tol im we don't sell land," Tynell looked at her grandbaby, standing alone as always, the distant woods framing her chestnut skin. She'd hoped some good doctor would have claimed her. But now, Hawa had moved to a place where cousins thrived but worthy bachelors were as plentiful as dodo birds. "Asked him what he wanted to plant or build. And this fool said a sanctuary."

"What?"

"Un hún," she affirmed. "Asked im how big and he said, 'Big enough for my soul'."

"Sho nuf?" She waved back at the man who waved in greeting and was coming towards them.

"Said he just wanted to go and meditate some times."

"Whachu tell him?"

"He free. Long's he ain't into no mess," Dear knew Hawa would take to this nut. Look at her now: love just waitin behind her eyes.

"What he say his name is?"

"Somethin like Danny or Dante. I don't right recollect. Ask him when he come." Well, Wa grown. Hmp, we couldn't tell her nothin when she was a child. Tynell shrugged, smiled, and bent over her row.

Deep red bone brother bout 5 inches taller than Hawa came and introduced himself by the time the women had weeded another row. Said, "Good afternoon. I'm Danta. I live in Pontotoc," with a Louisiana accent.

On Saturday, they drove to Memphis. That night on Beale Street, garish with whores, tourists, and 101 street corner musicians, the Technicolor bulbs lit up his face, but his real glow was from within. The moon emerged from the clouds to bear witness. She had wanted to have her fortune read that night, "1 part fun; 2 parts curiosity," she giggled. But he told her not to bother, that the woman turning cards had no shining.

"1 day, when you're ready, I'll read your life," and his smile was a massage for her soul.

After 7 months of knowing a man who strolled into her life like a gift, Hawa felt she was ready for her reading.

There, at the base of the river, clothed in emerald green grass and bordered in blood-tinted black soil, the Ah constructed Ta Ntr. They perfected and expanded the arts of the way: astral and physical flight, telepathy, telekinesis, mental and physical healing, form-taking and shape-changing, seeing through barriers, minute sound perception, touches of life and death, rhythmic and vibrational mental stimulation.

The Ah first embodied and then exceeded perfection, and Ahni guided their efforts. The Ah undertook the spiritual recording of their works, and they studied the lives of their forerunners, the Ahtlna, and learned from their errors and from their achievements.

Some of the Ahtlna had survived the transition and were living and creating in a region they called Dah. The Ah visited with the Ahtlna regularly. On 1 visit, the Ah found the Ahtlna creating terracotta images so that their progeny would have tactile references to facilitate their contact with their ancestors. Many of the Ah remained with the Ahtlna to learn these arts.

1 group of 12 Ah went north of Dah and created a settlement called Zim. At Zim the Ah erected an entire city in the image of Ah complete with obsidian and granite carved representations of the planets, nebula and galaxies of Ahstah and of Ahni, the Great Mother, and of their divine and human forms.

In the heart of the Continent, a group of Ah settled and erected Kng. The Ah of Kng specialized in interrelations with nature. These Ah listened to molecules, atoms, flora, fauna, and the Earth to understand their various spirits, characteristics, and powers. The Ah then combined the forces and energies of the life forms of the planet to create medicines that their progeny would still be using thousands of seasons later.

The progeny of the progeny of the progeny of the first Ah followed the River Nubah far south to its spreading delta. There Ah founded Kmt, which was also sculpted in the image of Ahni but with monuments 300 times the size of those of Zim. The Ah of Kmt brought with them the written language of Ta Ntr, but they transformed it and used the script to enliven each structure that they erected. The works at Kmt ensured that, no matter the emilevel of their distant progeny, the Ah would always have access to their sources of self.

1 group of Ah traveled southeast from Kmt and followed the green river which was bordered by stiff grass. At the mouth of this river, the Ah founded Tbk. At Tbk Ah recorded the wisdom, works, and terrestrial and

cosmic histories of the Ah in mental, spiritual, and cosmic libraries. The comprehensive knowledge of Ah was housed in Tbk.

The Ah and Aha of these 6 settlements were connected mentally, physically, and spiritually. Consequently, the settlements grew like sextuplets: They all resembled each other, but each boasted its own specialization. And Ta Ntr was the radiant source and center of power where all skills, wisdom, and powers converged.

"Christian men are out. Too zealous and hypocritical. Since I ain't a Valkyrie virgin, I don't respect their views or their pagan rituals. Like Easter, a time to rejoice and rape."

"Word, and xmas? Indiscriminant fucking and unchecked drinking and gluttony just to celebrate the winter solstice is a bit much."

"It's because they have no spirit that they tried to make their heathenism a religion."

"Alteveze, have you seen this book called *No Meek Messiah*?" Azure was getting excited. On this cool autumn day in Nashville, leaves spun and drifted before gathering into communities of kaleidoscopic beauty. She wanted to jump into the piles of leaves and play like a child, but she focused on the build.

"No. I haven't seen it."

"I couldn't afford the book so I chilled in Kemetic Visions bookshop and perused it like the big dog: It's hilarious; a great read! When we go together, I'll show it to you. You gots to check out *Nile Valley Contributions to Civilization*, too, and this film called *Zeitgeist*. These books and the film all discuss how Jesus is really Horus, the son of Ast/Isis and Ausar/Osiris. Girl they just flat out plagiarized and perverted, in 333 C.E., an African spiritual system that was over 10000 years old."

"Hmp. They debased a holistic spiritual system and turned it into a religion: a tool ideological, economic, social domination."

"Damn. Then where did our dead go?"

"What?" She didn't follow the shift in thought. She furrowed her brow, and Alteveze looked from Azure's shrine to her friend's countenance.

"All those ancestors who was waitin on heaven."

Azure nodded with understanding, "There was 1 elder I read about named Uncle Silas. He was enslaved, and, you know, some oppressors would force the Africans to attend bogus church services where they heard shit like, 'Don't steal your master's chickens,' 'Slaves be obedient to your masters,' and 'Q: What was you put on Earth to do? A: To make a crop.'"

"Right, right."

"Well, Elder Silas busted out during 1 of these indoctrination sessions and asked, 'Is us slaves gonna be free when we get to heaven?'"

"Aw, he straight called em out like that?!" Alteveze started crackin up.

"Just like that, and he repeated his query, 'I said, is us slaves gonna be free when we get to heaven?'" Azure was really feelin it. She stood up and implored of her dresser a question which was really an answer, "'Is we gon be free when we get to heaven?' And don't you know," she sat back down, "the cracker reverend sputtered and faltered and never answered the question."

"The elder was hip. He knew the god and heaven that the beasts created were propaganda."

"And any of us in the beast's heaven *gots* to be choppin pearly white cotton."

"Damn, they have truly dealt with us. Take our philosophy and culture, bleach and twist it and then call *us* heathens and pagans."

"You asked where the ancestors at?"

"Yeh?"

"Well, songs like 'I'll Fly Away,' 'Old Ship of Zion,' 'Motherless Child,' 'River Jordan,' they wasn't necessarily talkin bout going to heaven."

"Word?"

"I think they was talkin bout goin back to Africa."

Hadizat acquisitioned funds from Temple # 9 for a hajj to Mecca. That G plus her brother's G and her own placed her on the shores of West Africa 1 month after her break with Raheem.

Before settling in Mali, Hadizat toured Senegal and The Gambia. She truly returned through the door of no return at Gorée Island. But something was calling her to Mali. She didn't know what, especially since she didn't speak Bambara, Fula, Dogon, or French. However, before she answered Mali's call, she answered Djibril's.

Djibril was a graduate student at Cheikh Anta Diop University in Senegal. She loved him so deeply that while she was with him, she forgot all about Mali.

He was charming, intelligent, and, like many of his countrymen rather than bowing to an alien Arab mandate, he practiced an Africanized Islam that fit and reflected his culture. Hadizat appreciated African Islam's versatility and openness. Djibril, for example, kept his prayer beads alongside his mojos. Hadizat came to love and respect the man and his culture.

It was on the second meeting with his family that trouble arose. After a dinner of chicken and rice in coconut milk laced with pepper, honey, and curry prepared by her ever-smiling Djibril, Hadizat relaxed and read *Osiris Rising* on the veranda.

"Hadizat, there is someone you must meet!" Djibril came to her with his usual warmth and tenderness.

Hadizat smiled at the woman, who was perhaps 30 years old. Like

Djibril, this woman was dressed in a royal blue buba and wrappa. "This is Rhamatoulaye. Rhamatoulaye, Hadizat."

"Bonsoir."

"Comment allez-vous?"

"Bien bien. Et toi?"

"Ça va."

Hadizat said just about everything she knew in French as she greeted the beautiful woman.

"I will be pleased to welcome you to our family," Rhama smiled.

"Thank you, my sister." Hadizat embraced Rhama's open ocher-tone arms.

"Djibril has told me much about you."

"Are you his sister who had been in Bamako?"

"Uh? Yes? I was there with my family. You see, my father died."

"Oh, Rhama," Hadizat remembered her own father who had held down the streets of Detroit in radical majesty and lamented, "I am so sorry. Please accept my condolences. I too have lost my father and—" The bottom dropped out of Hadizat's world: *my* family? *my* father?

"Yes, uh thank you," Rhama filled the gap in communication and examined the widening eyes of Hadizat. "But this is also a time of joy because I have a new 'sister' as you say. We will bear many beautiful children for our husband," Rhamatoulaye embraced Hadizat.

"Uhh—"

Djibril's smile was as gorgeous as the day she met him. But his smile was not enticing enough to pull her into polygamy.

"I can't pull you up like this! It's like you weigh twice your actual weight," Kandace let go of Cynthia's forearms and sank down to the bed.

"Kan, please, I wanna do like you," Cynthia pleaded.

"Let's try this," Kandace laid flat on her back against the maroon, black, and gold coverlet. "Lay on top of me."

"Hey now!"

           "Listen, you know it ain't like that. How long I been dealing with Lerone? Hmp," she rolled her eyes before rolling over like she'd given up. "You the 1 wanna fly."

After 3 heartbeats, Kandace felt a tap on her shoulder blade.

Cynthia's legs were atop Kandace's. Their feet were entwined. Their nipples kissed through their blouses. Each sister had a chin cradled in a shoulder. Without a word their breaths became synchronous. The inhalation in the ear of 1 was the exhalation down the canal and to the drum of the other. After 34 breaths, Kandace and Cynthia felt a vibration. It seemed a golden cord had linked them and in the linking had electrified their clitorises. Before either could orgasm, they rose 16 inches off of the bed.

We've done it!
Oh my—Ahhh
You feel it too?
Yeeeeeeees
I didn't do it.
No, I know
When I was a child (the 2 said as 1) and sometimes now nnnnnnnggghh (the current came again).
After the surge calmed:
Wait, Kandace, I   we   how?
Yes, we're reading each other's thoughts, Listen.
AAAAHHhhhhhaaahhhhahahahhahahhhhhaaaa
The women levitated in orgasmic bliss for 3 hours.

"Bitch, you can't play that shit with me!" Jahmai could barely contain his alcohol-induced rage.

"Nigga, you mad! Butt fuckin insane! Now I'm fuckin *Ralph*? For WHAT!? He's an alcoholic and smells like a wet dog and we BOTH know he only interested in gray girls."

"What was he doin in my house?!"

"We BOTH pay bills muthafucka—Don't try it!" Chaka rolled her eyes and offered Jahmai her back.

"WHAT WAS HE DOIN IN MY HOUSE, WOMAN!?!"

"We was vibin. He was checkin out my paintings. Said his father was an artist. Gon give me a canvas his old man made."

"Before or after you give him some pussy?"

"Why? You gon kill me?" Chaka glared at Jahmai who was standing between her legs sharpening her butterfly knife. She flipped onto her back, kicked her legs once and rolled to the other side of the bed and picked up the bottle of red wine he'd finished ¾ of.

"Unfortunately, you the only nigga I've been fucking since we met. And it looks like you the only 1 on the horizon for now." As she tilted the bottle to her lips the back of her neck was clipped. The wine glass he threw knocked her head forward. She bumped her lip and tasted blood.

She lurched forward as if she were wracked with pain and confusion. By acting like she accidentally upset the bottle, she was able to grab and grip it. Shaking her shoulders as if she were weeping, she listened, judging his movements. He was coming. In 1 motion, she righted herself, aimed at his head, and hurled the bottle.

Wine drops sparkled like garnets as they danced from the bottle. For a moment, all motion seemed to stopped. Even the burgundy rain and spinning bottle seemed to pause. Jahmai watched the liquid stones spray and hang and fall. He was too mesmerized to duck.

Chaka rubbed the egg-shaped knot on Jahmai's head. He offered her kisses that ran from her lips to her neck to her navel. She cradled his head between her thighs. Her labia kissed his tongue.

"Oh baby!"

"I'm sorry."

"Me too ooohh aaahhh"

Jahmai nibbled, and, against her will, Chaka arched her back, thrusting her vagina deeper into his mouth. She was riding waves of pleasure while consumed with the fear that he'd bite her clitoris off.

Laughing later over a Giordano's deep dish pizza, she looked at this jealous violent man that she loved and prepared to leave him.

By the time Ama made it to the great green lake, she wasn't sure if she was still on the same Earth she'd left. For 3 weeks, she ran through the bush, securing only fragments of sleep. Her Mother was calling. Missing pieces of her self were waiting. A cord of belonging kept pulling. She ran until she tumbled into the lake.

The crocodiles gave her room. They stilled their communications and examined Ama's damaged body and soul.

Her waist beads—her only adornment left—swayed in the water. The wrappa that she had tied around herself prior to her departure had been snatched away by bushes and sapling trees. Instead of a wrappa she was now the owner of twigs, leaves, ticks, thorns, and leeches.

Kofi, the youngest learner at 14, waded to the newcomer. Her feet were so swollen they looked like pillows that were tufted with thorns, grasses and twigs, Kofi knelt beside her and submerged her feet in the cooling curing water. She looked at him with eyes as expressive as stones.

He plucked the twigs and thorns from her body and replaced the blood of wounds with healing water. Kofi cared for her body with a mother's tenderness and cried the tears she could not.

For 3 years, she didn't have sex. I'll re-virgin myself. She thought. But her body didn't love itself as it had before. At first she thought Amp had killed it. But he just scared it. It came 1 morning as she faced her window. Dawn, dew, and vibration rippled between her pink sheets to reacquaint her with rapture.

Ahhh!

That night, Àràká reached Ṣàngó exhausted and exhilarated. She met him in his room of repose. He was reclining and singing a song to himself as he twisted his hair.

For a few minutes, Àràká gazed at him unobserved. He *knows* he's fine, she thought and smirked. As if he heard her thought he turned towards her.

The low ember in his eye was stoked. When he rose and stood before her she knew the song he had been humming was about her.

After they bonded their love, Àràká held him and whispered:

Tuláàsi la fi í fẹ̀ràn Ṣàngó
Tìpàtípà la fi í fẹ̀ràn eni to ju ni lo

Tuláàsi la fi í fẹ̀ràn Ṣàngó
Tìpàtípà la fi í fẹ̀ràn eni to ju ni lo

Ṣàngó laughed and kissed the rise of his wife's breasts.

"My love," Àràká rose from the fur couch, "I've something for you."

Àràká stepped to her bag and unwrapped a magnificent staff. The bottom was a foot carved of teak. Red, white, and black cloths and evidence of sacrifice and libation streaked the shaft. The rounded head of the staff was bedecked with a profusion of iron studs.

"Consider this a gift from our husband." Àràká's eyes shined as she presented him the weapon.

"How do I use it?" He marveled at Ògún's craftsmanship.

"When you strike a man with this staff, he will shatter into 7 pieces; a woman will scatter into 9 pieces."

"Haa!" Ṣàngó charged and played at striking Àràká.

"Striking the owner will take the holder into oblivion," Àràká's eyes became iron: She was as serious as smallpox.

After a heartbeat, she brightened and pulled out piece after piece of weaponry. The objects included those crafted especially for her by Ògún and those pieces she'd granted herself.

After discussing each implement with Ṣàngó, Àràká took up her cowries.

"I will divine for us so that we can determine how to best secure our love," Àràká pulled an ọ̀pẹ̀lẹ̀ divining chain, ọpọ́n Ifá divining tray, iyérosun, and other implements of power from her bag.

"My wife, you are wisdom embodied." Ṣàngó stroked the handle of a saber and mused, "Ògún is not particularly sharp, but he is no fool. He'll be coming." He leaned in and blew on the ọ̀pẹ̀lẹ̀.

"You are the Empress. Your knowledge, foresight, and perceptions are especially keen at this time: You could do this reading for yourself," he winked. "Crossing you," Danta offered Hawa the full weight of his gaze, "is the Sun. Opulence and power and unification await you. And look!" Hawa leaned closer to see the Knight of Cups, "you will marry soon." After caressing her left hand, Danta continued, "The Star indicates a mixing of past and present influences." He paused, closed his eyes, and went inside,

"There is a woman in your world who is riddled by misfortune. You will help to make her whole. Hawa, your creativity, willpower, and ingenuity, seen here in the Magician, are your guides to actualization." He stared into Hawa's eyes, "You will educate a nation."

The shock in her eyes was easy to read, so he reiterated, "Yes. You will educate a nation," and then he added, "with me right by your side."

He took both of her hands in hers and kissed them. "Hawa, our union is not by accident; it is, like the nation we will educate, by design."

Danta coaxed the African black soap from a black gel to a brown lather to rich foamy white bubbles. Stray bubbles fought with the candles' flames and lost with a hiss and sputter. With his left hand, Danta poured water down the part in the middle of Hawa's head. He lathered her Afro to a crinkly sponginess. Next he scrubbed her neck. He worked circles of bubbles on Hawa's breasts, arms and back.

It was difficult for Hawa not to orgasm when Danta lathered his hands and shampooed her pubic hair and vagina. "Mmmm . . . ooooo . . . Ahhhh," she sighed. No other words were spoken. When her buttocks, toes, and thighs were all shiny brown and bubble laced, Danta rinsed her and dried her with terrycloth pats perfect for a baby.

Hawa sat on an ottoman and luxuriated in peace. Danta sat behind her and oiled her hair with tea tree and argan oil. Danta picked and patted the hair of his love to spherical perfection and then helped her to her feet: "We're going for a little ride."

Hawa walked to the clearing that Danta pointed to. As soon as she touched her feet to its earth, she felt tremors. Hawa sank to her knees and placed her palms on the Earth, "Oh, oh my!" She felt vibrations ripple from the land to her knees and her palms.

She sat down: "Mmmm," Hawa moaned.

The power grew stronger and she hoped it would last until Danta came. She reclined and widened her legs a bit to better enjoy the textures of grass-clothed silk and vibration.

"Aaahhhh"

Upon closing her eyes, she saw soul-red swirls like DNA double helixes. She followed these figures and relaxed in their movements.

Until he sighed and shifted, Hawa didn't know Danta was lying next to her.

"What is this?" she inquired without opening her eyes or changing her position.

"It's an emicenter.

"Emicenter? What is that?"

"Èmí is a Yoruba word. It means soul."

"So this is a soul center?" Hawa turned toward Danta.

"Yes, in a manner of speaking. You see," Danta positioned himself on his side so that he could gaze into Hawa's eyes, "our Mother, the Earth, who has given us life, also has life and soul, and she vibrates in specific regions throughout the world. The Ancients have always known how to enhance and expand their own spiritual energies by harnessing the power of emicenters."

"Now I know why you came to Bliss Bluff," her eyes narrowed to slits of pleasure.

"Yes, for the emicenter, and for much, much more. I came here for you and for a Work of cosmic importance." He paused and allowed the numming of the Mother to nurture his spirit.

"Hawa, before we become 1, there is a trial we should undertake."

Only the crickets and frogs responded. Hawa listened to her man and to the Earth.

"Remove your robe."

They both sat naked on the Earth. Hawa looked up and noticed the big dipper, little dipper, Orion's belt. She looked down and saw a knife, a ceramic bowl she had thrown, and 2 rings of filigreed gold and silver studded with onyx orbs.

"We are going to ask 1 another questions, and over this emicenter, we can't lie. Shall you go first, or shall I?"

"You."

"How did you get this scar." He fingered her right thigh between her vagina and hip bone.

"Sydney cut me. Wow, that was about 6 years ago," she frowned. She had forgotten the attack and the scar.

"Why?"

"He was jealous of me and felt inadequate . . . I didn't know how common his type was." Hawa was glad she had survived and met Danta.

"What is your dream, your goal in life?"

"To advance the liberation of my people."

"How many men have you had intercourse with?"

She closed her eyes. Afraid. Then she said, "Over 100." Her eyes remained closed.

"Why?"

"I used to think," she stroked a few blades of grass, "that nobody could really want or love me."

"Baby," his voice caught and he paused to stroke her jaw. "Tell me about your parents. How is your relationship with them?"

"My mothers. They gave me a foundation of independence and empowerment, but as I grew older I realized that they did not give me the tools I needed to a be a woman. They didn't teach me that my vagina is sacred. That I am sacred. That I am to be respected.

"My father didn't think children were worthy of respect, and girl children were nothing to him. He was raised by parents whose disciplinary skills came straight from the plantation overseer. But the violence he lashed me with was psychological and verbal. He called me ugly and little ugly, as if those were my names. The fact that I am his spit and image helped me realize that he was projecting his self-hatred onto me.

"My parents divorced when I was about 3 or 4. I remember how excited and relieved I was when Mom said Dad wouldn't be living with us anymore. I yelled out 'Yeaaaa!!!' But the damage had been done.

"You know," she continued after a paused filled with desolation, "that's why they call them your 'formative years.' When you're a toddler, you are developing your consciousness and character based on your environment and the providers of the foundation of your existence. My dad warped and crumbled my foundation. And he did it methodically.

"Honestly, I don't know if I can fully heal from that damage."

Danta had never heard her sound so bereft of life and hope. The more she spoke about her father and her childhood, the more her soul seemed to seep out of her body.

Danta held her with the ferocity of a mother. He didn't say a word, but Hawa knew that he was trying to love all of the pain, sadness, and confusion of that disrespected distraught child out of the woman he adored.

He knew he didn't need to tell her again how beautiful she was. How the nearly imperceptible angles that the corners of her eyes made highlighted her surging divinity. He did not need to tell her again that her lips looked like Mande sculpture brought to life or that the flaring of her nostrils in anger never failed to arose him. He didn't need to tell her again. But he told her. He showed her. He proved to her her power. He made it a point to fill her with the truth of her beauty and divinity when they ate, when the made love, when the sat quietly and watched the sunset, when they planned their shared future of community evolution. He showed and proved to her that her father was a liar and a coward and that she was a literal gift from the Gods.

After he relaxed his embrace and they wiped away 1 another's tears, Danta asked, "Will you be faithful to me?" because the 100+ was still in his mind.

"Oh," she opened her eyes to gaze at him, "oh, yes. Yes."

"What do you think when you think of me?"

"My Danta is the most together man on Earth. His spirit is 1 of harmony. His soul is as solid as onyx. He inspires me. He is the lost and found Afrikan. My husband, lover, brother, confidant, God, life."

"I wanted for so long to share this. I mean, not the powers like we did, but just my truth of Àjẹ́. Imagine: Anytime I hinted about this to anyone they looked sideways outta they eyes at me."

"Well, you gotta admit, you are not the most common woman around."

"We are all uncommon. A people who have survived all we have? Phenomenal. But my phenomenalness never did help me keep a man!" Kandace and Cynthia laughed.

"It would take a helluva man to stand by your side." Kandace's assent was silent. It was difficult to admit that there was no warrior-partner in this world for her.

"Well, sista," Cynthia inquired, "what you gon do with this power?"

"I don't know." She was a bit surprised by the question; she hadn't really thought about doing anything at all with it other than finding a way to live with it.

"Well, we need to figure out how this can help you in life." Cynthia tilted her head sidewise and gazed at her friend, "Now I understand why you be looking all spaced out sometimes."

Kandace laughed and she was joined by the ancestors.

"Does it help you with academics? I mean, do you flow faster when writing or does it help you researching?"

"Maybe it could . . . especially with historical research. It's like, I know there are ancestors listening to us now. They are always present. I just never really asked for their assistance before." The ancestors smiled, thinking of how they had guided Kandace throughout her life. Keeping her from harmful and hurting people, steering her out of dangerous situations, leading her to deep books and to understanding people. They smiled.

"Well, Kan, what do you wanna do in life?"

"I want to be a writer and educator."

"On what levels? I mean, we're about to have our M.A.s. What's your next move?"

"Well, whatever I do, I want it to touch both my children, spiritually speaking of course, and my ancestors."

"Certainly sounds like the work of a medium." Cynthia rose to her feet, "Let me make us some tea. You want Tiger Spice or Ginseng?"

"What about chamomile?"

"Cleaned out," she chuckled from the kitchen, "by a growing God named Kan-Kan."

Kandace began to think about Cynthia's questions. She had never thought about working with the ancestors on a conscious level. She thought about the beautiful traveler again. She would come and just stand beside Kandace's bed. When Kandace woke up, without a word and without an instrument, she and the woman rode. She could smell the nutmeg of her now, see her shoulder blades flexing under the sheer copper material. The ginger scent in her hair filled Kandace's nose. Yes, her first friend. The woman filled her mind, filled her self.

"Hope Tiger Spice is okay. I made it how you like it," Cynthia arrived with 2 thick white steaming mugs. Kandace inhaled the spicy tea. Cardamom, black pepper, and cinnamon soothed and invigorated her.

"You made a good point. I've been so busy camouflagin this for so long—even trying to change myself at 1 time—that I never thought about harnessing this force."

"That's why I'm here," Cynthia gave her a teasing elbow. "Aren't you writing about witchcraft for your thesis?"

"Yeh. I want to show the lack of veracity of the 'witch' concept and reveal the hypocritical, hyper-sexual, pseudo-religious nature of the 'witch' trials." She shook her head and looked back through the annals of time, "Christianity sho has killed lotsa folk."

"True. How much information is there about uh-Ah-Àjẹ́?" She had to concentrate on the dip down slide up rhythm of the word.

"There are Washington's books and a few other studies. But Washington's work is the most definitive. Other scholars approach the force from a Eurocentric or Christian-oriented perspective which skews and prejudices their assertions, or they cut and paste Washington's findings without giving her credit—which is both odd and dishonest. I mean, you can tell this woman struggled to undertake the research and bring these truths to light.

"She makes it clear that we Africans cannot understand our selves, forces, and powers if our points of entry and tools and terms of interpretation are Caucasian. Washington makes it clear: Witchcraft and Àjẹ́ have as much in common as wax fruit and real fruit, respectively."

Cynthia laughed so hard she almost spilled her tea, "Love the comparison!"

After listening to the rhythms created by Monk's manipulation of time, Cynthia asked, "Have you considered doing a comparative analysis of witchcraft and Àjẹ́?"

"Not, sister," Kandace winked, "until I started vibin with you."

"Check it, you can vibe with the ancestors and they can hip you. Don't know how you gon quote em," Kandace and Cynthia thought about this for a second and they both chuckled. "But maybe they can lead you to sources."

"Maybe even lead me to the Source. Cyn, I sho preciate cha!" Kandace jotted a few notes regarding the comparative analysis and then asked, "Tell me about your research on Black Abolitionists. Are you making progress?"

"It's going well. I've already written about 50 pages, 2 chapters. I've analyzed the Caribbean and Cuba and South America. The information you shared with me about Boukman, Nanny, Court and the Corromante-Creoles, St. Vincent, and Hyacinth will set my work off.

"We all know about Prophet Nat, Vesey, and Prosser, but the other abolitionists, the everyday abolitions, have been forgotten or ignored. I will unearth their texts. The tens of thousands of brothers and sisters on the plantation who would poison ol massah, set fires, get pissed off and up and chop the overseer down with a hoe, *their* truths need to be re-membered to the whole," Cynthia became illuminated from within the more she discussed her research. Her freckles seemed to glow most of all.

"Word. The everyday abolitionists. Those who got no awards, who went on no book signing tours, who received no applause but who manifested with spiritual and physical Àjẹ́ to free themselves every day in numerous ways," Kandace nodded.

"Exactly. For example, the sister who got so pissed off, she threw massah's infant chap into a pot of boiling lye. These types of personal revolutions were common, but it takes digging to find them."

"Ancestors just waiting for their verses to be sung."

"You know, from the works approved for our (mis)education, it's like without Garrison and Lincoln we would still be moaning lamenting slaves, but we were affecting our freedom every second. We had too!

"You know Garrison, Stowe, Brown an nem, they were in it for economic reasons or for self-glorification or to satisfy their voyeurism. But we HAD to manifest—or die, or acquiesce in social death and become the walking coffins that the oppressors intended for us to be."

"Yours is such a necessary study, Cyn, but where and how will you get the information you need—so much of this is undocumented?"

"Those WPA Freedom Narratives, girl!!! You notice that like a lot of conscious scholars I don't use the term 'ex-slave.' The obvious point of importance is that these elders are free!"

"So true. The term 'ex-slave' is used to position our ancestors and us in eternal conceptual if not literal slave status and slavery—as if a condition imposed on us by some beast is the only destiny we will ever have."

"Same goes for 'ex-con.' After they have paid their 'debt to society,' aren't they simply citizens?"

"Word."

"But the Freedom Narratives are a rich source. Now, some of them evince shielding, dissembling, and outright lies, especially if the interviewer was racist. Some of these beasts would introduce their interviewee with statements like this: 'Aunty Chloris was a surprisingly clean darkie. I was astonished to find her house was spotless. You could find the old wench everyday sittin on her porch.' Now, what kinda responses will 'Aunty Chloris' give to questions like, 'Do you miss slavery?' and 'Tell us bout the good ol days'?

"Right, finished before it's started," Kandace nodded.

"But many told the truth, especially those interviewed by African

Americans. You know, Zora Neale Hurston did some interviewing for them too."

"Zora was everywhere!"

"But the information is there, in fact, a book tellingly titled *The Unwritten History of Slavery* is published as part of the WPA's collection and includes many accounts of everyday abolitionists. Newspaper articles are also helpful. And Angela Davis did SO much work!"

"*Women Race and Class.*"

"Even locked down, the Ancestors were tickling her memory."

It got to the point where she had to get drunk or high to fuck. Because all the slims kept weed and juice, well, it was easy to engage. An everyday thing.

After Amp considerably stilled her vibrations and Chris gave her the big "bone and disown" she just was like, fuck it, lemme get mine. And she did, but from select slims. She and her girls had a saying, "Don't let the outer shell fool ya!" Not because bruhs had no convro, but because a rock-hard body on a 6'4" frame might mean a solid 4" prick.

She recalled Slab, also called Marcus, who was fffoine! 6' tall, chocolate to the bone, chiseled cheekbones, and a poetry-inspiring ass. He was new at the center, only been on point abouta week. She checked him ballin and hoped to snag him before 1 of her homies did. Slab was on the same vibe. Before she vamped to cook dinner, she snagged the digits. She and Slab spent all night havin phone sex.

The next morning, she skipped school cuz he HAD to come over. She showered, dressed in her Levis and button down and black sweater and kissed Moms good bye. She waited behind the Paxton's house until she saw Moms take the corner. She ran back to the crib, renewed her Chantilly, not forgetting to perfume the sheets lightly, and he knocked.

When they started tonguin, she felt, literally felt, that somethin was wrong. Once they undressed, she witnessed the incongruity and held herself back from a disgusted DAMN!

All of 3" of glorious rod stood up beckoning her—hard as a flashlight.

I skipped school for this!?!

Then it was suppressing the laughter that threatened to explode from her belly, throat and lips right into his face.

She told Rasheeda about it over a joint or 2 or 3. The more they smoked the funnier and shorter his dick would get. By the time the moon apexed, nigga had a pussy.

"'Ahni, motherdaughter, you've returned.' This is what father says."

"Baba, thank you," sand bit her knees and tears made tracks through the dust on her cheeks as she realized she had come so far only to come home.

She gazed into the Old Man's eyes and saw her father's loving tenderness shining on her.

Hadizat's father had been killed in the Detroit riots.

Rhaman had owned 12th. His pimpstroll alone, dignified yet so damn dap, was enough to solidify his control. He stayed sharp in bordering-on-flashy-though-never-outlandish vines. Denim, silks, pinstripes, baggies topped with Dobbs and sealed with Stacy's: He epitomized "revolutionary but gangster." The way he held down the stroll and his threads alone could have earned him respect. But as a warrior, a Panther, and progeny of 1 of Fard's followers, well, Rhaman was the ultraeverybrotha.

Whether distributing arms to cells, milk to grade schools, or exhorting at a rally, the King always delivered and was counted on as a community father. So when the feds tainted the breakfast program's milk with a laxative so lethal it killed 3 kindergartners and Hadizat and her brother Hussein were confined to their beds for 3 weeks force-swallowing grape juice and liquefied eggs to stay alive, King Rhaman took up arms.

While his retaliation was valiant (the bodies of 3 FBI agents were found decorating a lamp post on 12th Street) it could not fill the cavernous absence in which his assassination immersed his children.

7 months after Rhaman was assassinated while walking out his front door, his wife Sadia, who was serving a 25 to life sentence for conspiracy against Amerikkka's government and accessory to the murder of a pig, was lynched by prison guards for organizing a riot and breakout. With their parents' deaths, Hadizat and Hussein became Baby Panthers wards.

Maat and Tiye cared for them with and as their own children, but Hadizat and Hussein never bridged the void of their parents' deaths. Both sank into Islam. Hussein became a devout Sunni Muslim, and he was proud to contribute to his sister's assumed pilgrimage, having earned the title of Al-Hajj himself. He was happy his sister was growing closer in the faith and making her hajj. He thought their father would be proud.

As Hadizat gazed into the Old Man's indigo-rimmed irises, she saw her father's spirit shining therein. She wept as his gentle weathered hand caressed her cheek.

"My father says he's been expecting you: coming across the sea. Leaving in chains, returning on wings," Badu's smile glistened with tears he could not help but shed as he watched the woman he loved be reunited with her Self.

Badu had fallen into Hadizat's eyes 3 months before at a Mamadou Seck concert; he remained captivated by her eyes and knew he always would be.

During the concert, he noticed her eyes boasted the devouring yearning space of eyes that had looked in every gaily wrapped box or pissy sunken cardboard container for the gift of fulfillment. Badu stared at this gazelle-brown woman with little girl eyes that looked near tears although she was clapping and dancing with the crowd. Risking his pride, Badu walked in front of her and stared straight into the wide eyes and held them with his own. They made their own music from that moment on.

He rushed to dress because he was late for work at the cement factory. While dressing, Badu prayed this fascinating and perplexing woman would do as she had promised: relax until his 8 hour shift was completed.

Hadizat rolled over and was about to pray in thankful recognition of the peace of promise, but having often been the sport of quickly appeased gods, she did not. She went to the cupboard and found a bag of dates which she munched as she sipped coffee. She wrote poems for about 3 hours and, finally, hating to wash off the cologne of their, well, maybe, love, she showered.

Badu returned with a band of djeli who stationed themselves outside the door and windows of his flat and sang praises in Bambara and English about an ebony ibis, about sweet cream and dreams, about ancestors sighing with joy. The space around Hadizat's delighted eyes filled.

Their first 3 months together was a blissful time of learning, balancing, testing, trying, and trusting. When she told Badu about Djibril and Rhamatoulaye, she laughed but he patted her shoulder and said, "Well, I think you'll like Djenneba much better." He didn't understand Hadizat's abhorrence for man-sharing, a position rooted in centuries of loss, selling, raping, mating, kidnapping, and utter desolation and depravation. However, after he spent 12 hours searching for her to reveal his joke, he understood.

Badu found Hadizat at the 3000 nightclub in the arms of a handsome Mallam. She was twisting her hips like a wet woman trying to get dry. Badu's dragging her off the dancefloor moved the Mallam to show his power, and it took the entire male contingency of the nightclub to separate the men.

That night, Badu wore out Hadizat's back, ass, breasts, even her fingertips to drench her body and spirit and mind with the fact of his forever. In return, he found stinging scratches singing on his back and pectorals during his morning shower. Bending to soap his calves and feet was torture for his back. Even his knuckles were sore from gripping her, squeezing her, pleasing her. Did he force all of his love into her or pull out all of her and pour her into himself? Both Badu and Hadizat agreed that 1 is enough, all jokes aside.

He translated her poetry into Bambara and French. She had jambalaya, garlic bread, and baobab juice waiting for him when he came home. They drank too much, created their own jokes, danced in the streets, and prepared to save the world.

Hadizat had been pondering pregnancy. She didn't know if it would be an intrusion on their union or the supreme manifestation thereof. 1 night, while she was pondering her wonderful dilemma, Badu said, "My father wants to meet you."

"Oh? When did you talk to him?"

"Now."

"Badu, is this," she caressed his penis, now soft from loving, "the 'father' in question?"

Badu rose on 1 elbow to face her fully, "Our meeting has been foretold. I don't understand it all but you, Hadizat, are Ahni; you are Mother, Sister, Wife to me and my father. You and I will travel to Dogon country Tuesday. My village is called Hantu."

"What?"

"Hantu."

"Time and place."

"Oh," he smiled, "you know it?"

"No . . . I thought you were Bambara."

"No, I am Dogon."

"$360°$."

"Yes, Badu." And so, they went.

Jahmai went to Sam's Shoes clean. He was wearing his melon suit with an ecru dress shirt and multihued floral tie tacked with his gold and diamond stick pin. He'd shined his Stacy Adams that morning: he knew he was sharp. Humming softly to himself, he donned the black Godfather brim Chaka gave him on Valentine's Day.

As he went through his elaborate toilette, Chaka gave him some distance. She acted like she was preparing for school, but her lessons would be taking the form of a practical test.

He blasted Follow For Now's "Fire and Snakes" and sent gravel and dust flying from their driveway as he backed up before peeling out and speeding towards Sam's Shoes.

"Cain't go nowhere with a cut lip and a black eye," she fumed. But before she could get too pissed she recalled Flavor Flav's accusation and revised it, "Yeah, Chuck! He don put a black eye in the gang!" she laughed and succeeded in stoking the fire of her bruised jaw. "Cain't go nowhere anyway, without him, my hawk/man always scoping me out and making all these damn off-the-wall accusations. Fuck this."

She'd studied *Mules and Men* and recalled laughing with Jahmai over the jazz session significations that framed the folktales—but she had been captivated by the conjure.

Runnin feet.

Gripping her blue satin housecoat between her knees, she knelt on the grass at the driveway's edge and with a stiff white piece of cardboard she lifted his right footprint from the sandy gravel. His footprint was easy to distinguish next to the tire tracks of his '79 Monte Carlo. While lifting the track, she recalled the last time she went to reclaim him from his mother. They had a row that left him with a knot on the temple and her with a bruised pelvic bone. Same broomstick. His mother had given her a "gift" when she came to pick up Jahmai that night: a kufi filled with salt.

"Y'all ain't the only Geechees round this bitch!" she muttered as she transferred the last of the dirt and gravel onto the board.

She placed the dirt into the iron skillet that she'd scoured and left to dry the night before. To the dirt she added red pepper and a red wasp nest. Chaka turned on the stove, rolled her hips, and hummed "Billie's Blues."

By the time she got to bragging with Billie about the gifts her mother gave her to manifest her destiny, Chaka had rolled the track into the left foot of 1 of Jahmai's red thick and thins that she retrieved from the hamper.

She removed her robe and slipped into a pair of jeans, her favorite Jimi Hendrix t-shirt, and her combat boots. She fired up her Grand Am and drove towards a fishing spot on the Illinois.

After parking the car, she ran to the river's edge, tossed the sock over her left shoulder and said, "Run! Run til ya die, damn you!" Chaka winked at an old gray man who was so astonished by her actions he didn't notice he had a bite.

Ah nations were flourishing.

The Kng had taken communication with flora and fauna to new levels. Every animal, fish, and insect shared survival skills, auditory and visual secrets, and spiritual wisdom which the Kng logged and replicated. The swiftness, camouflage coloring, and precision of the cheetah were shared along with the regenerative skill of the starfish.

The Kng worked with their cosmic kin the Mọlẹ̀ to become mobile light while on Earth, not only in the cosmos. They gained mastery of the Mọlẹ̀'s cosmic-terrestrial gifts and created astounding technological, form altering, and power transforming devices. The Kng also discerned that the soil used to cover the bodies of the Ah who had joined the Mother could be used to make potent medicines. They devised formulae to reproduce melanin and serotonin and to stimulate weak emi. The Kng found the mirror of their souls as they gazed upon and interacted with nature.

Spurred by the foundation provided by the Ahtlna, the Dah established relationships with the multitudinous spirits and energies of the Earth and the sea. The Dah along with their ancestral guardians explicated the origins of existence through intricately articulated cosmological, ontological, mathematical, chemical, and scientific computations. Their advances were the result of their combining the forces of Àṣẹ and Àjẹ́ and serotonin and melanin. The Dah would go on to use these spiritual and biochemical forces to create the Way of Knowing called Da Fa, which would be an essential touchstone for the Ah after emi levels had diminished.

The Zim, southeast of the Kng, were masters of carving stone and wood and shaping terracotta. They fashioned soul shelters from and within the Earth and crafted confidants, images, doubles of themselves. Harnessing the souls and powers within themselves and their creative media, the Zim developed communication between themselves and their soul-sanctuaries so that the edifices were as spiritually-endowed as their creators.

The library of mental, vibrational, spiritual, and technical wisdom was flourishing at Tbk, where the histories of the 6 original settlements and the celestial origins of the Mother were housed. The origins of the Ah, of the Ahtlna, and the coming of Ahni and the way of Ah were recreated and documented in the cosmological teachings of the Dah and the script of Kmt. All of the works of the 6 emisites was held at Tbk. Every minute, new knowledge flowed in from each of the sites. Information as to modes of travel, healing, spirit work, architecture, the movements of Ahni, the goals of Ah were stored at Tbk for coming generations.

At Kmt, east of Tbk, were the physical copies of original records of the Coming. The 2 massive libraries stationed at the opposite ends of the Continent's great green river were unique. The libraries at Kmt were some of the most magnificent structures imaginable, and their towering pillars, dwarfing walls, and massive statues were all also texts whose timeless wisdom was engraved for all eternity. By contrast, the library of Tbk was not only portable but was maintained by every member of the community. Every family was a custodian of a library that was as eternal and expansive as that of Kmt.

Ta Ntr was the source of terrestrial Àṣẹ and Àjẹ́, creation, physical regeneration, human immortalization, and emi magnification: Ta Ntr was the source of inspiration for and the foundation of all the emisites. Ta Ntr was the terrestrial womb that birthed, renewed, recharged, and realigned each Ah.

Ta Ntr was also where the shrinking of the clitoris was first noted. After successive 3" births, there was an Ah born with a 2" long clitoris. The other emisites were noticing similar phenomena. Ahni informed the Ah that this transition, which would be followed in future generations by testicle expansion and penile growth in the Aha, was only 1 aspect of the changes to come.

The entire planet is undergoing transformative change. Even the sun's enriching and melanin-boosting rays will decline. The ecological changes signal the coming of an aberrant entity who will jeopardize not only Ah creations, but existence as a whole.

The Ah were perplexed, Untold seasons of work to be destroyed?

No, not destroyed, but as a result of the diligent work of the aberration, the difference between you and your progeny, yet thousands of seasons unborn, will be as wide as the Ethiopic. The majority will not have a fraction of your cipher. Many will intentionally deny, devalue, and destroy their emi. When this occurs, many of you will have joined me. Some of you will return to guide, as the Ahtlna are doing with you. But your present task is to leave records, paths, directions to the way, precisely as you are doing.

Prepare our progeny because everything that we have created and built they will see through a cracked and warped mirror. Many will not understand that the talents that you have used and are using to create art, architecture, mathematics, writing, geometry, astronomy, agriculture, science, and so much more as you build this world, are also skills that they have or can develop or can expand. Few of Ah progeny will access and apply their inherent intellect and even fewer will embrace and develop their personal divinity. In fact, many will be taught that they are less than human beings and will act in accord with that training.

Our progeny will be faced with the task of rebirthing themselves. Like seeds cast on stone, they will have to struggle to find ways to grow. These seeds, rather than soil and rain, will have to use asphalt for soil, tears for water, and sardonic smiles as sunlight.

Many of our young will die physical deaths and many of those who survive will live lives of social death. But there will be a few whose minds are fertile and whose souls are resplendent. They will access and activate the wisdom of the sites you are now constructing, and eventually they will construct new sites of powerful potent emi.

As you are aware, 6 new emisites are developing; each will have its own specialization. Zalah, which will be formed in the North, will be experts of weaponry and war. In the West, Gnah will be erected and will perfect the manufacture of protective spiritual adornment. Yah will be stationed in the South near the green river. The Yah will specialize in covert spiritual-terrestrial weaponry. The Dgn will be the masters of the seas and of the cosmos, for these 2 realms will provide essential pathways of liberation and elevation for our progeny.

The mutant will begin its rise and work when the green river in the south dies and the land of that region becomes moving stone. We have much to do to prepare for the transition. Return now and continue planting the seeds of evolution.

So they created AIDS and have been doling out this disease since 1967?! I always wondered how a disease originally relegated to Caucasian homosexual males could become pandemic in populations of Africana women. And how, concurrent with the heralded end of apartheid, HIV/AIDS came to ravage 85% of the Africans of South Africa.

Azure let the *Africa Today* news magazine fall open on her lap as she put her head back on her worn brown couch. She wanted to kill—to go to the Department of Defense and the Centers for Disease Control and cut down the sick scientists with the sickle of divine retribution. But, she thought, they are already dead. They and their ancestors were born dead. That is why they have done this: created this monstrous disease and intentionally infected millions of innocent men, women, and children.

Azure sat up, turned the page, and began reading an article about a Cameroonian physician who had created a natural cure for AIDS when the phone rang.

She placed her glass of mango juice on a cork coaster, held the magazine with 1 hand, and caught the phone on the 3rd ring.

"Peace."

"God, have you seen this new magazine called *Africa Today*?"

"Òrìṣà, that's what I'm reading now, and the same fucking information is in this month's *Third Eye*."

"This is nothing but genocide."

"And they're coming for us, the sisters. They're using our men as weapons of mass destruction against us. There are men on the down low who are infecting sisters, men who've been living a gay lifestyle while in prison infecting sisters, and think about all the songs out now and the videos."

"Exactly, many are shot right in prison! Others are straight pornography and the glorification of indiscriminate sex and hypersexuality."

"Caucasians have this sick mentality that criminalizes sexuality, so they decided to create the ultimate punishment for sex: AIDS. And they are infecting the most fecund people on the planet."

"Sex is promoted 24/7 on our television programs, videos, and in our music."

"Yeh, no AIDS awareness campaigns or public service announcements, no free condoms distributed at nightclubs, just 'come get dis aaaassssssss!'"

"And we Black women are the focus of their efforts because in taking us out, they slay 7 generations," she paused letting it digest.

"If we don't protect and defend ourselves, by 2030 we won't be here."

"New World Order—all expendables and undesirables must go!"

"But 1 of their own is blowing the whistle. We have to get Cantwell's book *AIDS and the Doctors of Death* and Ed Hooper's *The River*, too."

"I've got some more things you'll like to check out," Alteveze said, "like this booklet called *Psychiatry's Betrayal* which details the racism that forms the foundation of Caucasian medical establishment.

"There is also a deep book called *Medical Apartheid* that systematically explores the hundreds of heinous experiments performed on us. Many times while reading that book I stopped to weep. It's by Harriet A. Washington."

"Dorothy Roberts' *Killing the Black Body* is also required reading;

Roberts focuses on genocidal tactics in women's reproductive medicine."

"You know, Toni Morrison's *Home* is centered on the rescue and healing of a girl whose vagina and womb were used as an experimental test site and wastebin by her employer."

"*Home* is so profound. Through Ycidra's harming and healing, Morrison also emphasizes the destructive design of Caucasian medical practices and highlights the holistic affirming methodology of African medicine. Morrison also reveals that there is no atrocity that gives Caucasians pause: There is nothing they won't do to us."

"True. I went for a routine pap smear at Shinally and after the nurses had me wide open and strapped in the stirrups, a group of 20 medical students filed into the room."

"Say what?!" Azure stared at her phone as if could see Alteveze on its screen.

"With neither my knowledge nor my permission, my vagina and womb became a mandatory testing and teaching site."

Azure was ready to go to war NOW in her sister's defense, "When the fuck did this happen?"

"This was about 3 months ago."

"Why didn't you tell me?! We could have"

"I was so angry and ashamed . . . I just wanted to forget it."

"So what happened?"

"They tried to convince me to submit to their gang rapexamination and even held me down. They didn't let me up until I started screaming and threatening to kick everybody's ass and started swinging."

For 9 heartbeats Azure was speechless, then she whispered, "I can't believe they subjected you to that. I can't believe you didn't tell me. They need to be dealt with." Her mind was strolling through Shinally's halls, "They *will* be dealt with."

"We have more pressing issues before us," Alteveze tried to brush the episode off, and Azure let her, for now. "Millions of us are dying from the medical apartheid of HIV/AIDS. Azure, why aren't our leaders discussing these issues? Why aren't they hipping folks and why are our media organs focused on movies and videos that promote sex?"

"Many of us are enemies of progress and agents of destruction. Many of us are cowards too, especially here in the 'Ville."

"Well, we gon do our part, and we gon do it next Thursday during Nommo. We gon use the airwaves to disseminate this information and have a call-in discussion."

"You think we can get away with that?"

"We have to. We don't have a choice. Enlightenment or death."

"Word life. We gon shine on em."

"Listen," Alteveze whipped out a notebook and pen and placed her phone on speaker, "I wanna make some flyers to promote the show. Lemme see . . . how can we capture attention?"

"Draw a noose held by a gray's hand and put a brother in the middle."

"The caption: 'Lynching in the New Millennium: New Methods, Same Victims'."

"Yeh, 'If you're Black and wanna live, Listen!'"

"Tight!"

"Az, let's meet to discuss these other sources."

"Okay, tomorrow morning."

"10:00 at Café Noir."

"We can begin gaining our audience there."

"Alright, God. In Peace."

"With Peace."

After spending the evening in UI's library, Chaka decided to get a broasted chicken dinner rather than try to cook. Fact is, she wasn't ready to face what did or did not await her at home.

"Kool!" shouted Jackie before Chaka could get in the door good. Jackie called her Kool not only because that's who and what she was but also because her favorite affirmation when she started working there was "Kool and the Gang." Chaka smiled hearing her nickname: She loved coming here.

"Hey, baby! How you been doin? Where you been all this time?" The most memorable voice on Grand. Sounded like Satan himself threw the coals down his throat.

"Ol Lee! Reverend Lee! You a Baaaaahhhdddd Maaaannnhhh!" She sang his praisesong and checked him out. He was about 1/4 full of Milwaukee's Best now, and holding. Lee had become her father. With his growing hands, wisdom, and alcoholic's baby-time tenderness, Chaka loved him dearly. But everyone at Umoja Market, not matter their alleged or confirmed mental state or arrest record, was family to her.

"Poppa, I'm fine," she caressed his hand, "I been around," Lee ain't pissed himself yet today, but the mishap of yesterday was humming. "Rev, when are we going to Drew?"

"Dhalin, anytime you ready. You know, it's down in Drew, Missipp I learned to box." Lee stood on his shaky legs and channeled Ali in his prime. Ali's belt, stance, babyface and muscles suffused the aura of Lee and shimmered over his thin, beaten, flyweight frame. If you listened you could hear the chants rising: "Ali! Bumbaye! Ali! Bumbaye! Ali! Bumbaye!"

Jackie, the chef of Umoja Market, revealed that Lee used to be a fine man. Strong and stout-hearted. But he got caught with a man's wife, and the enraged brother balanced himself on Lee's throat with the aid of a crowbar and almost shattered his larynx—thus the coal-cool voice: husky and low and sweet, like Lee himself. Chaka looked at Lee's rheumy eyes and his lean body, *Yeh, I bet you was really somethin, Daddy.*

Lee had worked construction, but he turned to the more serious work of imbibing alcohol when 1 night while crossing Lincoln—"on the green light too, girl!"—Jackie had explained, a Caucasian woman, drunk as 9 sailors, ran a red light and carried Lee 3 blocks. When he stopped being her hood ornament, he had a femur that stuck out from his leg like Madagascar from the Continent. Without malice or vengeance in his heart, Lee settled down and committed slow suicide via cheap beer.

Like her adopted father, Chaka had, herself, recently traded in 1 form of suicide for another. During her junior year, when Chaka got real and stopped the partying and giggling of frosh and soph students, she also began an intensive study of cocaine (sponsored by Chaz, 1 of the more furtive members of Namibia–Angola Connection who ran Grand and 59th, including Umoja). When Chaz saw Chaka working for the Ph.D. in free C, he dammed the flow. As a result, Chaka worked at Umoja so that her fellowship would remain untouched as her wages went up her nose.

Meeting and loving Jahmai put an end to these relationships (human and chemical), all except for her love of Jackie, Lee, and T-Bone.

"Jack, where's T-Bone?"

"Look," Jackie pointed to the window and everyone looked and laughed. T-Bone was marching in the middle of the busy intersection as if he were a soldier in a time warp. Legs stiff, back straight, arms swinging, pivots perfectly executed: It was T-Bone against the traffic; and make it so bad, T-Bone was winning. Cars darted away from him, swerved around him, and the intersection lit up with blaring horns and vicious invectives to which T-Bone was oblivious.

"That nigga crazy, Baby Girl," Lee looked at Chaka and explained. "He ain't got no sense."

Actually, T-Bone was sittin on plenny much knowledge. With his sing-song voice and rhythmic flow, he could issue cipher sufficient to dumbfound a professor of philosophy for days. Chaka watched him at his ritual. He would cross the intersection 5 times and then go around Umoja 3 times clockwise 4 times counter-clockwise before he would enter the door. That was how he greeted each new moon.

Everyone said T-Bone was crazy, and he did receive government checks to back up that assertion. However, Chaka thought he was a 2-headed doctor who had been out-Hoodooed by the beast of America.

"And you? Yo drunk ass be pissin on yourself in an hour. Who worse?" Jackie asked Lee.

"Jackie, you know me. I'm a Baaaahhhhddd Maaaaahhhhnnnn!" Ali rose again.

"Well," said Jackie while she rolled out a huge trash barrel from under the counter, "take out this baaahd trash so you can have your liquid dinner later." Lee, T-Bone, Smitty and a few other brothers came to Umoja to do chores and earn a few dollars to satisfy their needs.

"Oh rubadubdub! what have we heee-ah?"

"Mister T-BONE!"

"Oooh, yes ma'am!" They slapped palms. She and T-Bone had grown tight; they had shared many pints of Seagram's while Chaka waited in the back of the store for Chaz or his brother Mizzan to come on wit da come on. Sometimes Chi State and UI students would come to cop and stop to try and discern why Chaka was drinking behind a certified crazy dude with plaits down his shoulders and skin as smooth and rich as black strap molasses.

"Whoop, whoop, Whoopi!" Pete yodeled while perched like a vulture behind the cash register. T-Bone twitched, hated to be likened to Goldberg.

"Oh, yes, ma'am," he replied. "Little girl, how can we help you?" T-Bone flashed his bone-white teeth at Pete and then extended his hand to rub Pete's bald head, "Oh!" T-Bone enthused, "rubadubdub, little girl!" Pete submitted to regendering with the same laughter that rose from the bellies of everyone in Umoja.

Chaka knew Umoja would never change. Even if the bodies lost breath, their spirits would joan on.

"Chaaakkkaaahh" Pete turned his attention to her, his Kenyan accent sounding like enchanting music coming from a dilapidated guitar, "When you gon let me"

"Killimongana," she used his own slang against him, "keep yo rabid mind offa me. Only thing I'll do for you is shovel dirt on yo coffin."

"Pete! Don't play with Chaka! She married now."

"Yeesss," Pete narrowed his eyes and scanned her body, "How *is* Missssster Chaka?"

"Tired from last night."

"OOOOhhh! Kool!" Jackie chuckled.

"MMMmmmm uuuummmmPPP!"

"Sho wish it was me!"

While all the signifying was going on, a chalk-white woman with hair dyed a violent violet red came in to pay for her gas. It was clear from her carriage and demeanor that she had picked the wrong part of town to enter when she stepped into the gallery of the ghetto wordsmiths.

"Oh boys and girlssss," T-Bone intoned. "What do we have heeeah?" everyone wondered the same with T-Bone. "Look at the way its actin," everyone followed T-Bone's directive and looked. They peeped the woman's nervous movements and darting eyes. "All that chemical done soaked its brain," T-Bone offered his assessment of the toxins in her hair dye. As her trembling hands fumbled with and finally dropped her wallet,

T-Bown shared his summation: "Yes, boys and girls," he nodded to the gallery, "the bitch *is* crazy." There was nothing else to do. With forks uplifted and balancing macaroni and cheese, bottles of soda draining into mouths, money changing hands, and pots of food being checked, everyone who heard T-Bone's pronouncements (all of Umoja) fell out. There was no way to stop laughing. Even Lee, who had a serious distaste for T-Bone was bent over, his husky chuckles raining invisible gold nuggets between his legs.

Everything calmed down as the woman scampered away. Chaka seized the moment to ask Jackie for some advice, "Jack-Jack!" Chaka cried.

"Kool!"

She leaned her head near the older woman and asked with all possible discretion, "Whatchu know about Hoodoo?"

"*Hoo*doo!?" Jackie shouted. "Why? You wanna kill somebody? I ain't gon tell you shit," she turned back to her collards.

"Girl Hoodooed me once—" Lee began reminiscing.

"Nigga, you *is* Hoodoo."

"And look like who dun it."

"Yes, ma'am, you dooo."

"She bled in my food," Lee continued, "and I couldn't leave her alone."

"You sure you didn't Hoodoo her?" Jackie's gold tooth flashed.

"Naw, Miss Jackie, naw," he protested.

"Well, I picked up some books." Chaka revisited the issue but with a deflection, "Wanna do some uh research."

"Gon mess around and kill somebody, girl!" Jackie looked Chaka full in the face, seriousness underlying the laughter in her large brown eyes. Jackie had gotten her hair finger waved and it complemented her soft round face and caramel-tone skin. Now that Jackie was engaged, she moved her wide and voluptuous hips around the kitchen with relaxed zazz.

Later, when Jackie took her break, she told Chaka to see Daniel's wife Patricia who'd just come from Liberia. She knew the Work.

Chaka ate her chicken breast, potato wedge, and roll and started reading *Jambalaya*. It was 10:00 pm when she returned to her duplex.

Since she moved to Rosedale with her uncle and his wife, she learned 3 things: she loved her uncle, she knew why Salan married him, and she knew why Salan was so tired. He would wear you out! When her mother could no longer support her, Uncle D said he'd be proud to take her in. She'd always admired him. As a child she'd sit in his lap for hours. He was always so intrigued by what her dolls had done that day; or the way she had dressed Monet, her teddy bear; or her recitation of school lessons. He would squeeze her and she'd declare him her No. 1 Daddy. She cried out "Daddy" the first time he came to her, just as she was dressing for a walk through her new neighborhood. What could she say? She and her uncle were, well, lovers, and it thrilled her? That she would call him, yearned for him, glad to be Salan's second?

Life with Uncle D was an adventure! 1 day he told her to get dressed cuz he wanted her to meet a friend. His friend Tony was quiet, too quiet. Even when she and Uncle D got so high they were just tripping off of Tony's crib—which was surprisingly opulent—she dug Tony checkin them out, her really, like a hawk, like she was somethin good to eat. It was kinda highblowin, actually. Fool ain't said a word since, "Good afternoon." Why were they here with this strange ass dude anyway?

Uncle D led her upstairs to a plush bedroom decorated in gold and sea foam blue and turned on the radio. She undressed but left on her lacy fire-red panty and bra set, which she knew provided a seductive contrast to her deep mahogany skin.

She relaxed on the bed and smiled as Ray, Goodman, and Brown asked where she had gotten her body. She answered the trio by gyrating her hips as she lay face-down on the bed. Her clitoris pulsed from the mixture of bass, asti spumanti, and red hair sess.

She was in her own sphere, high as a pine! She swiveled her head left and saw Uncle D and Tony staring at her like she was a delicious aromatic meal in a steel cage and they were starving dogs. She turned her head right and smiled.

She continued her horizontal slow drag while the R&B crooners marveled along with Tony and Uncle D at the masterpiece that was her lace-framed ass.

She gasped. Someone ripped off her panties, bent her until her back arched, and started sucking her anus. She'd never felt that before. She arched to meet the tender lips. After 5 minutes, and in 1 motion, he turned her over and sucked her vagina and tickled her clitoris. She was amazed and a little scared. Tony had come out of a stone cold sex bag! He lapped her waters like she was the last oasis in the Sahara.

"Man, save some for me." She felt him come, come like a cloud. Like the rain. Her Daddy. Tony moved to her breasts while Uncle D took Tony's former position. She was so overwhelmed with ecstacy she could do nothing but come over and over again while the men took turns caressing, twisting, sucking, and fucking her over and over and over and over.

Uncle D never grabbed her by the scruff of her neck and whispered anything like, "You bettah not tell nobody!" cuz there was no reason to. She felt free with him, just like when she was a child playing hide and go get it.

"1-2-3-4-5-6-7-8" Her 4 year old legs pushed and sluiced through the wind. She crept into a shed and positioned herself between tractor tires. She heard the door creak. Lil Man fell on her, callin himself kissing. Her Now-n-Later giggles tickled his lips. He lay beside her and she parted her legs. She didn't care to touch him, only to be touched—there! 1 finger sent her spinning, whirling into bliss.

Lil Man extricated his fingers from the moist, smooth labia, cotton, and terry cloth to unzip his pants. She turned on her belly and felt the grass cushion her cheek. She pressed herself to the ground. Uh! She felt the ground which seemed to hum and reach to her. "Aaahhh," she sighed.

Lil Man thought he was being beckoned but there was nothing he could do to surpass the Earth's demonstration of love. She rubbed her body into the ground and felt fingers grabbing her arm trying to turn her. The feeling was gone!

"Gotcha!" They heard the bam bam pam of feet running to base.

"Les go," he said, but she yearned for more Earth.

She squatted to pull her panties and jumper back into their proper places as Lil Man zipped his pants. They dusted themselves free of dirt and grass blades and prepared to leave. After a quick kiss, Lil Man told her to go first.

Wind again! Free! Home Free!

Lil Man was it.

That night on the trundle bed her clitoris vibrated under her whispers to Lil Man, Lil Man, Lil Man.

"From Lil Man to Uncle D," she giggled and hugged herself, glad to have come to Rosedale.

She slipped the Àjẹ́ Kòbàlé leaves into the ogogoro filled vessel. Each night she sipped the spiritually-charged liquor, bathed with the medicine-enriched black soap, and meditated. At first she was unable to travel. She would just lie on her bed pondering her defect. She so wanted and needed this elevation that her soul ached.

1 night, just as she rested her head and inhaled, her spirit rose. She was so startled she fell back into herself, "Ìyá said this might happen." She closed her eyes, breathed deeply and relaxed. She slept soundly. The next night, she was prepared. When her spirit rose she managed her ascent and stayed alight.

Seeing her home through astral vision was a shock. At first she thought her shrines were on fire, but she realized that she was seeing the ẹmí of the Gods. She was mesmerized by their shimmering flickering auras. Ọ̀ṣun boasted a blue cloud that radiated yellow and white rays. Ògún's energy was a swirl of black, forest green, and maroon. Ajé Ṣaluga was awash in a delicate periwinkle that morphed into an indigo as deep as the ocean. The broken vessels from which she had fed the Mothers glowed red, brown, amber, and russet. Ọbàtálá appeared to be engulfed in white, but the perceptive eye saw that the white was a commingling of infinite interlocked iridescent rainbows. Rivers of red, black, and white currents emanated from

Èṣù. Ọmọ Ìyàlájẹ́ was astounded by the catalyzation of Àṣẹ, Àjẹ́, ètutu, ẹbọ, ìjúbà, and libation.

"Iba a ṣe, Èṣù Larooye, Ìyá, Baba, Ọmọ oto." She began the ìjúbà, the song of praise and homage, and the shrine tripled in size. Its power surged like the Ethiopic.

"Oh Ẹlẹ́gbára, who transforms yesterday's proverbs into novel utterances!

"Owner of the Power!

"You who can do and undo. Don't undo me oooo! Don't misguide the movements of my feet, don't falsify the words of my mouth."

Ọmọ Ìyàlájẹ́ heard the hhhuuuuunnnnn before she felt it. Her soul started trembling. She wrapped her spirit around Èṣù and basked in the God's power.

"Oh Èṣù, Baba Ẹlẹ́gbà, I bear you sacrifice," could she pour libation in an astral state? She extended her hand.

Gold blinded her, she stopped, brought the outstretched hand to her face, and saw ochre threads and tiny shoots of the deepest blue, deeper than that of lapis lazuli. She examined her aura for 3 minutes before she resumed pouring libation and making sacrifice to all the Òrìṣà.

She gazed at the wrappa she'd worn that day. Even tossed across a chair it was still shimmering with her energy. By gazing upon her energy, she knew her Òrìṣà was Yemọja.

Yemọja, The Mother of Us All: Yewájọbí. Fierce guardian who births all waters, who birthed all Òrìṣà. Many are her daughters. Daughter Olókun, Daughter Ọ̀sun, Daughter Àràká, Daughter Ṣaluga. The black, gray, and blue frothy water that she would take away and that would take her away: Yemọja, she smiled, I see you and feel you glow in my skin; I feel your fluid in my veins.

A woman with blue black skin glowing beneath the sea. Her legs spread giving ocean Ocean. Her hair a crinkled fan 9 hands high and 9 wide. The shells around her waist larger than those she's spitting conchs and cowries laughing bubbles. Her fan is silver and oyster fringed in pearls whispering ṣẹgi ṣẹgi ṣẹgi; ṣewele ṣewele ṣewele. Whiiiiiiisk. Fish fly into nets, children are adorned, water diamonds shine in their hair, run down their bodies. Fish gather around her and dance. Whooosh 3 vessels capsize, pale skins and weak bones sink—a feast. Ancestors are waiting with Yemọja, waiting for the retribution they must have. Shrrring!

Yemọja astride Crocodile Waaka. This, she says, is your Home. Shrrringgg. You will always have a home, she smiles at her children because Waaka's spikes are tickling her—Ahhh—right there. Who can take the crown from the child of the Chief of Deep Waters? This is where Òrìṣà speaks of a home.

Yes child, she saw the hues of Àjẹ́ and Àṣẹ before she recognized her Ìyá. Her wisdom, strength, and power were magnified and rendered her ageless. Yes child, she continued. I knew you would cross over tonight. Now the *real* lessons begin.

"How many children do you have?"

"All of them," Okay. She thought, let me be more precise. Hawa focused her questions to ensure she made the most of her round of unification questioning.

"How many times has your semen produced a child."

"Once."

"Where's the child? the mother?"

"Here in Bliss Bluff."

"Do you love her?"

"Dearly."

"And me too?"

"Of course."

I guess that is what pulled him here, she thought with a snarl, but she asked, "Do you think I can handle polygamy? Do you think *you* can handle it?" she bucked her eyes in daring.

"No."

"Danta! Why have you hidden this from me?" She was hot.

"I didn't know, and you never asked."

"How could you not know?"

"You got pregnant just last week."

She didn't breathe. She didn't know what to say or think, so she said and thought nothing. If it were true, there would be ample time to rejoice. She pursed her lips and plunged ahead.

"Have you ever had sex with a man?"

"Yes."

"What was it like?"

"Rape."

He didn't breathe. Couldn't breathe. He couldn't control his rememory, and he found himself back at Parchman still sore from the rock and bottle pelting that accompanied the protest against racist economic and housing policies and legislation in the Mississippi Delta. Cold water flats, no water flats, flats with crumbling walls and roofs. Flats not repaired since they were built in the 1800s. State taxes and revenues going only towards maintaining the affluent areas born of white flight. And the latest scam: Pay checks can be cashed right in the casinos. As the attorney of the Community Action Agency, Danta prepared to sue the state of Mississippi for discrimination and civil rights violations. He also organized the protest, received the permit #912779, and led the march.

Danta was held without charges for three months. He was given excuse after excuse as authorities led him deeper into the prison industrial complex. He was a lawyer who was unable to defend himself or hire counsel. Every attempt he made to liberate himself was blocked. He learned the meaning of the "just us" system. He sucked his teeth recalling the sleepless nights he invested in passing the bar.

The stale shit and ammoniac urine that decorated his cell assaulted his nose, seeped into his prison clothes, and colonized the folds of his skin. Lice had established a mighty settlement upon his thin mattress and they erected outposts on his loins. But the biggest hairiest beast he'd ever seen staked a claim on his body.

Danta jumped from the slamming of metal bars into concrete casements and from the series of staccato metallic punches that signified lights out. "He told me a story, before the raping." Danta sounded like he was sitting in the cell. Even though they were outside in the fresh Mississippi air, Hawa heard the flat echo produced by close concrete walls.

In the darkened cell, the voice of the hairy subhuman washed centuries of depravity over Danta's body: "'Many of the slave masters loved dark meat. That's no secret. Some loved ass, some breasts. But some liked the legs, third legs, and the asses and holes they came with.

"'My great grandpa did his duty to God and country, boy, and had 2 children by his wife, but it was his body servant, his hand nigger, that he just couldn't leave lone.' This was followed by the most appalling, spiritless laugh I've ever heard.

"'Yeh, boy, I usda be ashamed uh the stories they told me bout him. But I know now. I usda fuck Bertha, my girl, in the ass, and lil boys, too; but that didn't satisfy me. It was like killin flies—too easy. But man to man combat . . . feelin the power of a buck trapped underneath ya? Oh Yeeeeh. And the mo dey fight, da better.

"'All them lashes, cat-uh-9 tails, clippins of ears and limbs cuttins, all of em give you a RISE! Best part uh da lynchin is to find out who gets da cock.' He even sounded like he was in some dilapidated shed about to rape a man he'd just whipped or at a lynching bee clamoring to hold the penis of a victim so the lynchers could slice it off."

"'We gots a whole trunk fulla cocks and fingers, and ears at the ol homestead. But it ain't nothing like a live 1.' I heard him removing his clothes and my mind scurried like a rat in a maze seeking modes of self-defense. There were none. I never felt so vulnerable, so betrayed by life, so forlorn. 'All dem books you niggas read don't tell ya bout that, do they boy? House niggas, drivers, some couldn't wait to bend over, was wet as pussy. But it ain't nothin like catchin it fightin, boy. Put some REAL stimulatin lashes down. All that screamin in sheds wasn't always rawhide, but it was always a bull, always a bull. Jus like dis heah.'"

"There's no way to describe 300 pounds of beast coming for you during lights out. There's no 1 to call because this is your punishment. This is your punishment for having the nerve to defend the rights and lives of your people," Danta's voice was without timber, pitch, or feeling.

"The pain was so brutal that I heard rather than felt it. It was the sound of wet mattress being ripped apart. I couldn't see, hear, or feel anything except what was in the place my mind took me. It was a white place. Cloudy, misty, and barren. I was drifting there like a feather, oblivious, until a strong wind blew away the clouds. When the clouds dissipated, I found myself in the deepest pocket of the only hell a man can know.

"When I was released, my rectum muscles and rectal cavity were ruptured. I had to have 6 surgeries to correct the damage.

"I fear nothing now. I've seen hell, felt it. I know it. Lived it and got over it. I was in a daze for 3 years. Functioning just enough to survive. I abandoned all rallies, protests, everything. What was the point? That was my answer, 'What is the point?' I shut everything down and out.

"Although I was healed and HIV/AIDS negative, the rape played itself out in my head every hour. Every man I saw was a potential victim or a possible rapist. I couldn't look at women at all. The shame was too great.

"3 years after I was released I hanged myself: But the rafter broke. I don't believe the bullshit cliché that everything happens for a reason, but I did realize that I had to overcome this damage. All of it. I had to heal myself. I knew that that was my mission. I had to, somehow, find a way to love myself and my people enough to live and to continue the struggle."

Danta would not look at Hawa. He didn't have to. There were no words. There were arms. Enfolding. Holding. The only thoughts in Hawa's mind were, How many ways can I love this man, hold this man, whole this man?

Kofi stood up with tears drying on his cheeks. He looked from the cerulean blue sky to the verdant wealth displayed by the ìrókò, baobab and silk cotton trees. He felt the spiritual force of the elders even before his gaze reached them. He smelled the fecundity of the Earth's loam. He marveled at the birds and animals singing, hunting, and frolicking all around him. Everything is so filled to bursting with life and rejuvenation. And yet, here is 1, his eyes and thoughts rested on Ama, whose spirit wavers between death and stasis. But there is life waiting in the rear of those eyes. I see it. I feel it.

He broke his contemplations to lay hands on Ama. He began with her torn, mangled, and cut feet. He pulled them from the waters in which they had been soaking, massaged them, and wrapped them with poultices of life everlasting and oríjì leaves mixed with ground charcoal and palm oil.

As he massaged and lathered her ankles and calves, he chanted, "I won't hurt you; I won't hurt you, daughter. I won't hurt you." It became a mantra. Did she understand Bambara, Lodagbaa, Ewe, More, or Hausa? He didn't know. So he rendered his promise in each of these languages: The language of his hands needed no translation.

He arrived at her knees with his hands cupped and his palms as gentle as clouds. As his fingers worked up to her thighs, he heard his grandmother's voice simultaneous to feeling the resistance in the young loins, "Son, careful, this is the place of breach."

Ama's eyes were as lively as freshly dug graves. She had no thoughts, but there was peace in the emptiness. A young comforter was bathing her. She couldn't feel him but noticed his motions. She closed her eyes and was there, the house of blood, mirrors, and unspeakable anguish. Mothers everywhere were hunched and straining, scarring their knees, flexing their biceps taut with the breaking down of a child's resistance. She clasped her legs. Too late then, but now?

Kofi looked in Ama's eyes and saw a flicker of rage.

Everything was gone now. She relaxed and her tears flowed.

Those tears are life, Kofi rejoiced. She has opened the door!

She received the cooling healing water. It trickled in streams between the young strands of her pubic hair before it kissed her labia majora.

Kofi cupped the water in his hands. Again and again and again he reached back and poured forth. Reached back and poured forth. The site of excision received alms and apology, alms and apology. The crusted small bloody stump, that often in its earlier full whole form raised Ama with the sun, remembered its peak, its head. The crust fell away and was chased by tears.

Ama returned to stasis as Kofi continued. He bathed her bead-adorned waist, her breast buds, and her reed thin arms.

The crocodiles cut through the water. They gathered at Ama's feet. In semi-circle, they shared the waters of their daughter.

Cupping water first to Ama's crusted eyes and face then to her shorn head, Kofi finally trickled the water onto her lips and then, into her mouth. He rose to search for food, leaving Ama with the crocodiles and the water.

"Being good to someone is just like being mean to someone. Risky. You don't get anything for it." *Sula*

She hung Toni Morrison's wry wisdom on the wall directly facing her bed. Cattycorner, Audre Lorde was asserting that "if nobody's really gonna dig you too tough anyway, it really doesn't matter what you dare to explore." *Zami*

On her mirror above her reflection: "Be the 30 mile woman, a friend of your own mind."

When Jahmai returned after 1 of their rows, he read the quotations and was charmed, not by their meanings but by Chaka's attempt to cleanse herself of him, which was an obvious exercise in futility since he was back. His eyes laughed and she heard them. She would be reading when they had sex.

She'd not called Sam's yet and was a bit afraid of what knowledge she'd gain by doing so. Would his cocky-ass voice shoot over the phone lines? Flowing with the power of being able to sell even wet napkins. . .

Or—what?

He should be getting off in 3 hours. Maybe I should go a DB&L. She chuckled recalling Charlene's phrase; Drive By and Look, which she used when they would go out hunting her free-flowing Renaldo.

"Lene, girl," she murmured, "I sho wish you was here now. You'd be impressed, I think." Charlene had power, came from power. She knew and did the Work.

She and Charlene wrote and shared their songs and poetry. Both loved men, too much, and they were so tight they were thought to be zami. UI never knew how much lovin went on in rooms 102 and 104. They tried to make each fucker a lover and rarely succeeded. Lene had graduated and returned to Ka, Virginia, but Chaka had stayed in Chi-Town, wrapping up her program. Jahmai, her reason for staying, was now dead to her. She would finish her course requirements and make a move.

She drove to Rush Street thinking about the man she used to love. He'd hipped her to Sly, P-Funk, Bootsy. She shared Lenny Kravitz, Jim Morrison and books books books. Hurston, Morrison, Walker, Reed, Bobby Wright, Ben-Jochannan. Chaka didn't yet know how scarce literature lovin brothers were.

Once as he sat her down to listen to Sly's "Poet" and he shared some art he'd done to complement the piece, he revealed how deep Sly was and how deep Sly had made him. She smiled at him in that superior way she'd perfected for him and said, "You wasn't deep, baby. You was just high." She'd told him she had only heard the tame tunes like "Dance to the Music," "Family Affair," and "Everyday People" cuz her family wasn't sittin up high and fuckin up they children's futures. He just smiled. She eventually became a bigger fan of Sly than he was.

She couldn't listen to Sly now, though, too many memories. She selected *America Eats Its Young* on her audio player because "Just Because You Win the Fight Don't Make You Right" was rich with meaning. When "If You Don't Like the Effect, Don't Produce the Cause" finished she noticed the Carlo was not in Sam's parking lot.

"I'll check Mom's crib, get some castles and go back home."

As she neared his mother's home she thought to herself, Had the nerve to throw an old shoe at me. Salt in a hat. "Girl, fuck them," she muttered. "Why you goin through all this? You just curious or you feelin guilty?"

The Carlo wasn't at his mom's either. From West 63rd she turned left on Western Ave. White Castle was, thankfully, not packed as she pulled in.

"2 fish castles, fries, and a large Sprite—easy on the ice," she ordered while gazing across the street. "Hmp! I didn't know that was there."

"Ma'am?" the attendant asked through the speaker.

"Oh, no, uh, sorry, not you." Chaka had spotted a botanica across the street. I'll pop over there when I finish eating, she resolved.

As soon as she pulled into the botanica's parking lot, a sienna-hued hand flipped the "Yes, We're Open" sign over to "Sorry, We're Closed." Chaka continued munching and made a mental note to come back and buy some incense and an uncrossing candle.

As Chaka was throwing away her trash, the botanica's door opened and a woman stepped out. She was wearing an embroidered tie and dye with matching gèlè of gold, navy, and ocher.

"Chaka?"

"Patricia?"

They'd never met but had heard so much about each other, from drive to dress to men, they knew each other.

"I've been wanting," they said simultaneously and stopped and laughed.

"Come inside," Patricia welcomed her.

The botanica was well-stocked with *real* products.

"This is impressive, Patricia, some of these botanicas are a real disappointment," Chaka examined a bottle of 4 thieves vinegar.

"Yes," Liberia's rhythms wove her every word into a poem, "many are fronts fa drugs n such."

"You said you wanted to talk to me?"

"Well, Jackie tol me you wanted to discuss some things."

"Uh, yeah, well, it's like this"

"Wait, come in de back.'

After passing through a beaded curtain, Chaka found herself in the middle of a shrine. "This is where de real work goes on. An everythin from fever grass to sassafras to dungoyaro is growin here," Patricia gestured toward a small tiered green room. "The owner, Mama Talice, is tryin tuh grow baobab and kola nut trees in her home." Patricia's laughter was amethyst fragments falling on silver.

"I want to know the Work." Chaka explained, "I come from a family of workers, down south. I've been reading and studying a little and I have even put—uh—something—into action recently."

"Well, I was on my way out. I have to pick up my 2 year old daughter."

"What's her name?"

"Ha name is Chaka, like ya own."

"Are you serious?" Chaka was delighted. "Is it a Liberian name?"

"No, it's"

"Yes, of course, Zulu—but why"

"I always admired the warrior spirit of Chaka Khan!" The women laughed and 2 lands, 4 ethnic groups, and innumerable warriors and artists joined them.

"I sense somthin in you," Patricia examined the woman and her aura, "a movin confusion. Come by tomorrow, hear? I'll do a reading so you can know yo direction."

"What time?"

"Come bout this time so we can have privacy."

"I'll see you tomorrow. Thank you, Patricia." Chaka was surprised by the sense of relief she felt.

Desegregated Eastville High was all Black as a result of white-flight. Among people who said "urrang" for "earring" and "ur" for "ear" and "har" for "hair," she was informed that she "talked white." Unwilling to twist her tongue into Rosedale's countriness, she seasoned her speech with "bitches," "muthafuckas," and "n shits." She fit right in.

She met some of the dappest brothas, and they kept her high. She came to enjoy "primos"—weed laced with cocaine. Rather than a wholesome family sit down, she'd get high, drink a 40, and have some "chinaman" (shrimp fried rice) while sitting on a park bench.

Because school was so weak, with a little effort, and little was all she was willing to put forth, she stayed at the top of her class.

She was going to graduate soon, 1 more year. She looked back on a life of fucking, smoking, and drinking. She couldn't recall a day in the past 5 years that she wasn't high on something. She grew depressed.

She thought back to her last conversation with Shay, her handlah back home. Shay was sad to see her leave for Rosedale

"but I'm glad too, girl. Cuz ain't shit here."

"True."

As Shay passed her the joint she concluded, "Ain't shit to do here but get high and fuck."

"Umph."

Shay made it sound hard, like it was, and bitter, like she grew to be. Shay had 2 girls now. She, on the other hand, had had 2 abortions. Uncle D was by her side though it all. But damn!

"Somthins gotta give." She leaned back and let the herb do its job. "What Shay don't know is that our options everywhere is limited as fuck." She'd smoked the joint down to the roach and switched the nub to her roach killers: her long babyfinger and thumb nails. Having finished the joint, she stretched out and sought numbness. Because she had found other stimulations, she'd forgotten that original vibration that coursed from the center of her body. Instead of loving and feeling herself in the dawn, she would roll over on Uncle D or whoever.

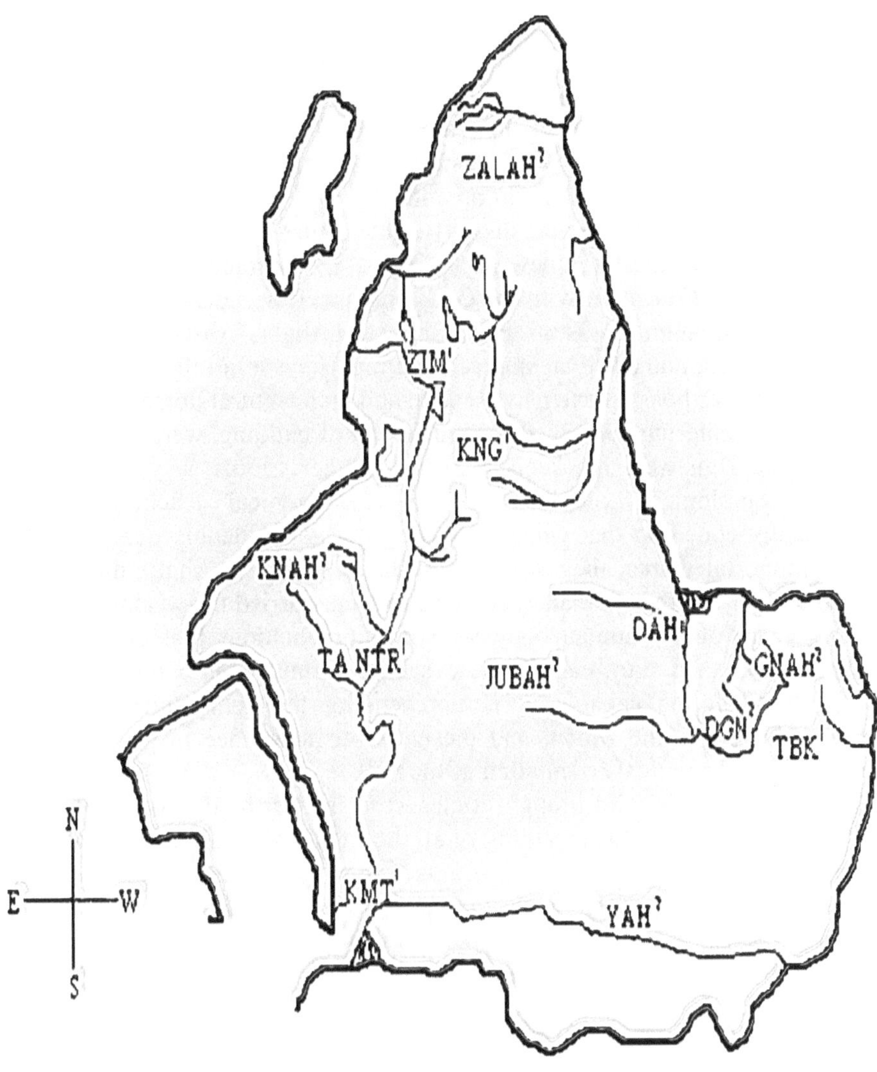

The 6 original emisites were flourishing and so were the 6 sister sites. Each of the 12 nations was a reflection of the infinite force of Ahni. And every site was a testament to the immeasurable power of Ah.

Ta Ntr was the mother-site of all. All skills and knowledge—architecture, juba, spiritwork, rootwork, travel modes, science, philosophy, mathematics, telepathy, iron smelting and gold fashioning, hunting, and written, oral, and spiritual wisdom—flowed to and from Ta Ntr.

The master ironsmiths resided at Knah. From the depths of the Earth, the Knah mined and at their forges they shaped the ore that became hunting weapons, cutting and carving tools, and cooking implements. With rhythmic bellows, the strength of elephants, and surgical precision, they made iron sing and dance.

The Knah shared their knowledge and skills with all, and while smithing flourished the Continent over, the Zalah deep in the North took the work to new heights. Their spears and tools boasted a poetic grace born of the balance of form and function. The Gnah on the western coast became master goldsmiths. With their adornments, the Gnah sought to replicate both the necessity of the sun and the divinity of the soul.

While the Ah mastered new disciplines, the way remained the constant unifying force. Education with the Gods and ancestors, gifts from the souls of plants and animals, astral flight, physical flight, Ah-wide telepathic communication, and spiritual studies were mainstays at all the emisites and each of the sites boasted extensive textual and architectural libraries.

The Ah, entering their 2nd thousand season of building, were as stable as the sun. In Dgn were the keepers of the Mother's tools, way, and texts. Their cosmological, ontological, and cosmogonical teachings were specifically coded so that when their progeny, yet millennia unborn, read these immortal works, they would gain direct access to Ahni's directives and the way. The master mathematicians of Kng married the wisdom etched in the DNA of the human body with the computations that ordered the cosmos, and then they carved these sacred formulae onto bones: Their progeny would be capable of comprehending the communicative flow among the Earth, the Moon, and the entire cosmos once they attained a complete mathematical articulation of the Self.

When Ahstah's orbit brought it closest to the Earth, all Ah gathered at Jubah, for at this site, the creativity of all the sites coalesced into the apex of celebration. The Jubah created drums from hides harvested from the elephant burial ground at Zalah. Drums were 34 feet high and 34 feet in diameter. When beaten with the elephant's shin bones, the rhythmic thunder of the drums called all organisms to join in the songs and dances and praises to Ahni and Ah.

Every element—from beaten gold knockers reproducing lightning's own chorus, to the animals that joined Ah to witness the flights, whirls, cloud leaps and swirls, to the flora that lent their expertise in catalyzing the power of the soil, to the amoeba revealing the secrets of multiplication and division—all forms and forces joined in the celebration of life.

While the Ah continued to self-birth and out-numbered Aha 2:1, with the receding of the clitoris and the blossoming of the penis and testes, Ah and Aha began coupling.

Ah traveled to visit, teach at, learn from, and remain in Ah sites that held specific interests for them. There was a constant flow of ideas, inventions, and knowledge as well as spiritual and biological coupling and creation. When they reached their apex in the 3000th season of building, Ahni discussed the coming of Yurugu.

"Welcome to Nommo!"
"I'm, Azure"
　　　"and I'm Alteveze"
　　　　　"and we manifest the power of the word!"
"Àṣẹ. Àṣẹ. Our number is 252-7119, and our program is not complete without your Nommo. So please call us."
"Tonight we ask our Ancestors to open our powers of understanding as we discuss an issue that threatens the entire Pan-African world: HIV/AIDS—its creation, manipulation, and dissemination. In our goal to better understand these issues, we are going to share with you information that we've gathered from a number of sources, including the 92 minute documentary *The Origin of AIDS*; Andrew Goliszek's book *In the Name of Science*, Alan Cantwell's book *AIDS and the Doctors of Death*; and documents released courtesy of the Freedom of Information Act.

"The world was introduced to AIDS through the male homosexual community—its first documented victims. The facts that the disease was ravaging gay communities, that it had no cure, that its modes of transmission were not fully known, and that it destroyed the human immune system were cooked in the media's pot of perversion to produce a disease that was not only a 'gay plague' but also a plague that *you* could get—*if* you followed a less than righteous lifestyle.

"Even though the media used a Caucasian heterosexual woman who acquired AIDS from her dentist and a Caucasian hemophiliac child who acquired the disease from a blood transfusion to put 'a human face' on HIV/AIDS (others who had died were apparently deemed nonhuman), the virus' association with degeneracy and debauchery remained.

"HIV/AIDS became not only a physical death sentence but it also became a license for the media to dig into the victims' personal lives in search of lurid details that could become headline news. Even the statement that an individual 'died from complications related to the AIDS virus' was designed to lead 1 to the conclusion that a lifestyle of lasciviousness led to the individual being rightly cursed with the dreaded 'gay plague.'

"You may have never known or cared about the sexual orientation of your favorite actor, singer, athlete, reporter, or writer until HIV/AIDS got a hold of him or her and the media drug that person's character from the hospice to the sewer of Christian hypocrisy.

"But to understand the origin of what was introduced to the world as a 'gay plague' and has now become a 'black plague' fittingly associated with 'black' (signifying evil, vile, beyond redemption, and a human being of African origin) people, 1 need not look to biblical scriptures or godly rage. 1 can simply look to the evil that masquerades in the west as 'science.'

"In 1978, under the guise of testing the efficacy of an experimental hepatitis B vaccine, the Centers for Disease Control (CDC) working with the National Institutes of Health (NIH) injected 'promiscuous homosexual' male test subjects of New York with a concoction manufactured by Merck that physician Wolf Szmuness of Colombia University School of Public Health created by developing the pooled blood serum of gay men infected with hepatitis B in the genetic material of chimpanzees.

"Several weeks after receiving Szmuness' 'experimental vaccine,' test subjects were diagnosed diseases that are now known as the hallmarks of HIV/AIDS infection, most notably Kaposi's sarcoma. Despite or, perhaps, because of the developments among the New York test subjects, in 1980 the CDC expanded its hepatitis B vaccine trials to Los Angeles, San Francisco, Chicago, St. Louis, and Denver.

"In 1981 the CDC acknowledged the existence of AIDS and confirmed that there were 26 known cases of the disease. Those infected were all previously healthy gay men who were residing in New York, San Francisco, and Los Angeles—the cities where the CDC conducted its experimental trials in 1978 and 1980. By 1982, 30% of the participants of the CDC's trials were HIV/AIDS positive.

"Since the 1980's, scientists and physicians have reaped billions of dollars in their proclaimed struggle to understand and cure a disease that it appears they created using criminally unhygienic and contaminated processes. And it appears they were not content to create 1 devastating disease; they used the parent virus to give birth to various lethal offspring, from the various members of the HIV family to the quick-killing Ebola, Marburg, and Lassa viruses.

"There are 2 recognized types of HIV: HIV 1 and HIV 2, and there are diverse mutations of these 2 viruses. HIV 1 is found largely in the U.S., Europe, and Central Africa, while HIV 2 is prevalent in West Africa. HIV 2's West African predominance appears to be indicative a race-specific viral construction, 1 perhaps tailored to African genetic structures.

"In addition to understanding the significance of HIV 1 and HIV 2 in the realm of medical genocide, which we will explore a bit later in the program, we must also examine the ways by which HIV 1, a disease originally rooted in the American homosexual, Caucasian, male demographic can reach pandemic levels among African American women.

"How a disease can move from the homosexual Caucasian male demographic to that of African American women within 2 decades has never been addressed by any study I have seen. The unspoken answer from the Caucasian medical community is promiscuity. But the sexual habits of the world's populations have not changed. Gay men have not started lusting after Africana women. So how did the disease "jump" demographic groups?

"1 factor in America could be the incarceration rates of African American and Latino and Chicano men, which are at all-time highs. The United States incarcerates more people than England, Germany, Canada, and France combined. At present, more than 1 million brothers are incarcerated, and many of them hold that having sex with men while imprisoned 'does not count.' These men enter into various liaisons while confined and never reveal their exploits to their female partners upon release. Because in this patriarchal society many women are convinced that they are incomplete without men, many women do everything to keep men, including not insisting on condoms or on testing for STDs and HIV.

"However, downlow brothers switching lanes, IV drug use, and accidental infections cannot account for the pandemic level of HIV infection among African American women age 18–40. We must also look to seemingly innocuous sources, such as yearly visits to gynecologists and implanted contraceptive devices, as possible routes of infection.

"Depo-Provera is an injectable contraceptive that is also used for chemical castration. It has consistently been tested on and injected into women in developing nations and on poor American women without their consent. Racist Israelis injected Ethiopian women with the drug without the women's consent—the women were told the drug was a vaccination.

Dorothy Roberts' book *Killing the Black Body* reveals that Caucasians have marketed Depo-Provera as the go-to contraception for African American, Native American, and South American women; women in Thailand and Mexico; and African women in South Africa and France. The reason for the Caucasian medical establishment's promotion and distribution of Depo-Provera to women of color goes far beyond the evil of population control. A study published in the medical journal *The Lancet* revealed that Depo-Provera increases the likelihood of a woman to contract HIV by 40%!

"The makers and distributers of the HIV-linked injectable contraception refuse to stop administering Depo-Provera to the millions of women it has been forced upon. The excuse they give is that the poor downtrodden women of Africa don't have many options for birth control. But the truth is that through Depo-Provera, the beast can reduce the population of Africana peoples with a double whammy—HIV-tainted contraception."

"Our first caller is Sahai. Peace: You're speaking with Nommo."

"Alteveze, Azure: thank you so much for sharing these life-saving truths with us. You sisters are true consciousness-raising warriors."

"Thank you for the recognition, Sahai."

"It doesn't take a Ph.D. to see that HIV/AIDS is melanin-directed, if not from its creation then its dissemination. But I am inspired by the information that you are sharing with us because it changes our perspective on this disease and its victims. Rather than seeing members of various communities as pariahs or sexual deviants, what emerges is a picture of people simply living their lives who are being attacked and killed in the most cowardly way possible.

"Many people would be loath to believe that their general practitioner, gynecologist, obstetrician, proctologist, cardiologist, or hematologist is using them as a test subject. Many would laugh or be incensed at such accusations. But the truth of the medical community's manipulation and desecration of our living and dead bodies is all too well documented. And the United States' government has authorized and funded experiments that have been conducted on various ethnic groups in this country and abroad. What we are really discussing here is a national pathology that has resulted in global crimes against humanity.

"It is frightening to know what the beasts have been able to do—and it is chilling to consider what they are doing right now. Thank you sisters for enlightening us tonight. I know there is much more to come."

"Sahai, we so appreciate the wisdom you have shared with us. Our goal is to drop knowledge that will encourage people to do their own research, to draw their own conclusions, and to approach with extreme caution medical services and members medical establishments."

"This is important, Alteveze, because mass inoculations are thought to be the primary route of HIV/AIDS transmission. A stirring 92 minute documentary—and make sure you view the full length hour and a half doc, not an edited version—titled *The Origin of AIDS* discusses the possible creation of a strain of HIV/AIDS in the Kongo by physician Hilary Koprowski and virologist Paul Osterrieth who were trying to create a polio vaccine using the kidneys of chimpanzees. Koprowski and Osterrieth used entire populations in Central Africa as tests subjects for their polio vaccine. 10 years after they had been given the polio vaccine, Central Africans began dying of AIDS. 1 can trace the first HIV/AIDS infections in the 1960s directly to Koprowski and Osterrieth's the mass inoculations in the 1950s.

"The documentary hypothesizes that the HIV/AIDS pandemic in Haiti could be traced to the Haitians who traveled to the Kongo to fill the positions vacated by fleeing Belgians in 1960. These Haitians naturally married Kongolese or sought medical services in the Kongo only to find, later, that they were infected with the disease now called HIV/AIDS.

"The documentary also offers information that connects America to the Kongo. Osterrieth, the virologist who created the virus-causing vaccine, not only worked in secret because he was cognizant of the diseases he could create by using chimpanzee tissue, but he sent finished vials of his lethal concoction to Koprowski's lab in Philadelphia. It would have been easy, and expedient from a Caucasian supremacist position, for Koprowski to share his virus with Szmuness, the NIH, and/or the CDC. And HIV 1's prevalence in Central Africa and North America, bears out the contention that the virus was shared."

"Powerful information, Azure. And speaking of expedience, it is widely-held that the World Health Organization infected millions of Africana people with HIV/AIDS during its smallpox eradication campaign which ran from 1967-1980. The WHO focused its campaign in the Kongo, Burundi, Rwanda, Zambia, Tanzania, Uganda, Malawi; Brazil (which has the highest population of Africana people in the Western Hemisphere and was the only Latin American country included in the WHO's campaign); and Haiti (the first free Africana country in the Western Hemisphere). The staggering rates of HIV/AIDS in these regions corresponds directly to the WHO's smallpox campaign."

"In addition to avoiding mass vaccination campaigns, we must call out and fight against governmental manipulations that link mass inoculations with 'compulsory' education. Citing an alleged outbreak of hepatitis C, Caucasian medical intuitions in America undertook the forcible mandatory testing and vaccination of children in so-called 'high-risk' areas. If 1 refused to test or vaccinate 1's child, 1's child could not attend school.

"In March of 1996, Yahweh, a religious leader in an African American community in Memphis TN, organized a protest against the board of education for its refusal to admit to school children from that community who had not received the Hepatitis C vaccine."

"Hmp, this makes me think of Shinally Medical College, right next door, always soliciting African Americans to participate in some test or other, and even promoting this same Hepatitis C vaccination that the brothers and sisters in Memphis fought against."

"Clearly, it's Nation Time."

"Our next caller is Dr. Northerly."

"Good evening."

"Peace."

"I'm not a regular listener, but I saw so many flyers in Shinally, I had to tune in. I'm a pediatrician in Shinally's Clinical Research Center.

"Here at Shinally, we've always tried to combat Tuskegeephobia, which is what we call the fear induced in African Americans from their knowledge that the American medical establishment has used them as guinea pigs. Our goal is to advance the study and prevention of African American health problems. Incendiary information such as what you've shared tonight will set back our work significantly!"

"Well, I suppose our planning this 'incendiary' program and not killing African Americans through seemingly innocuous clinical trials, such as those conducted at Shinally, reveals our true level of community concern."

"Northerly we are not an economically motivated outfit thriving off of federal grants and Black bodies. Our entire motivation is to stop the genocide of the Pan-African nation."

"Listen, it is a known fact that AIDS came from the green monkey disease. The SIV II virus in Afr"

"Northerly, we are not here to entertain lies and misinformation. Were homosexual Caucasian men going to Africa to copulate with green monkeys?!?" Alteveze was heated.

"This green monkey nonsense is just an attempt to cover the dirt of Osterrieth and Koprowski," Azure rolled her eyes.

"Northerly, you should rejoice! Being situated in the heart of our community and using us to perfect weapons of mass destruction to kill us has been more than successful," Alteveze offered the caller mock applause.

"I've not accomplished anything! I want as much as you to protect the Black community and eradicate this dreaded disease!"

"Yes, of course you do."

"Don't patronize me! Your program will instill fear in everyone!"

"Yes, and fear will precipitate action, even if the only actions are staying away from Shinally, except in case of dire emergency and using products from the Earth in treating ills."

"Exactly, Azure. The Earth has a cure for every human illness. In Ghana, Kenya, and Cameroon pharmacologists are developing or have developed cures for AIDS. 1 Ghanaian herbalist's cure for AIDS was so successful, he was killed. We need our traditional physicians, our 2 headed doctors, to return to the field and find the cures waiting in the Earth."

"Hogwash! Such primitive beliefs will contribute to the spread AIDS— no 1 will be tested, people will transfer viruses back and forth!"

"How?"

"Sex. Drugs."

"So now we have it. Northerly, your argument dates back to the era of Caucasian encroachment on Africa and its enslavement, colonization, and continued raping of the people and Continent."

"A group of savages whose lives were a merry-go-round of plagues due to their inability to establish a healthy civilization witnessed a people clothed in the beauty of skin as pure and smooth as the night sky. These people not only practiced excellent hygiene and boasted impeccable morals, but their lives were in harmony with the world and cosmos: they understood, as John Henrik Clarke points out, that the word 'civilization' is rooted in the word 'civil,' which means to be peaceful and at harmony with the Earth and all its inhabitants.

"The mutant couldn't understand such balance, harmony, and power. It could only see lack in its pale skin and bestiality. But rather than attempt to advance itself, the Caucasian decided to pervert or destroy millions of peaceful peoples and cultures around the world. HIV/AIDS is merely the latest assault. If you are looking for vile primitive beasts, Northerly, you need look no further than within yourself and your peoples."

"Azure, we've lost the caller."

"And yet, we've lost nothing."

"Well said, Azure."

"Before we return to the phone lines, I will share information with you about various experiments the US government and its agencies have conducted on its citizens and on any human beings unlucky enough to be in the United States' clutches. This information is readily available to everyone thanks to the Freedom of Information Act and can be found in numerous books and websites. What becomes clear when perusing this data is the government's lack of regard and respect for *any* human life. These demented pseudo-scientists will experiment on anyone in their vicinity—except, of course, themselves.

"Throughout the 1840s, J. Marion Sims, the so-called 'father of gynecology,' performed medical experiments on enslaved Africana women without anesthesia. These women would routinely die of infection soon after surgery. Based on his belief that the movement of newborns' skull bones during protracted births causes trismus, Sims used a shoemaker's awl to move the skull bones of babies born to enslaved mothers.

"In the late 19th and early 20th centuries, there are more than 40 reports of experimental infections with gonorrhea. Some researchers even applied gonorrhea cultures to the eyes of children using sticks. In 1895 in New York City, pediatrician Henry Heiman infected 2 mentally disabled boys aged 4 and 16 with gonorrhea to study the disease.

"In 1896, Dr. Arthur Wentworth performed spinal taps on 29 children at Boston's Children's Hospital to determine if the procedure was harmful.

"From 1913 to 1951 Dr. Leo Stanley, chief surgeon of San Quentin Prison, performed testicular transplants on prisoners at San Quentin. Stanley transplanted the testicles of recently executed inmates as well as the testicles of goats, boars, and rams into prisoners.

In 1950, Dr. Joseph Stokes of the University of Pennsylvania infected 200 female prisoners with viral hepatitis. From the 1950s to 1972, mentally disabled children at Willowbrook State School in Staten Island were also intentionally infected with viral hepatitis.

"In 1952, Chester M. Southam injected live cancer cells into prisoners of the Ohio State Prison. In 1963, Southam performed the same procedure on 22 elderly female patients at the Brooklyn Jewish Chronic Disease Hospital in order to study their immunological response. Southam did not obtain informed consent from the patients. Although he temporarily lost his medical license, he was later rewarded by being elected the vice-president of the American Cancer Society in 1965.

"From 1963 to 1966, New York University researcher Saul Krugman promised parents of mentally disabled children enrollment into the Willowbrook State School in Staten Island, New York, a residential mental institution for children, in exchange for allowing Krugman to perform procedures he called 'vaccinations.' Krugman was actually infecting the children with viral hepatitis by making them ingest an extract made from the feces of infected patients.

"While many of us are familiar with the Tuskegee studies in which, from 1932 to 1972, 400 African American men were denied treatment for syphilis so the disease' effects on the men, their wives, and children could be studied. However, we may not know that from 1946 to 1948 the National Institutes of Health and the organization that would become the World Health Organization infected Guatemalan prison inmates, mental patients, and soldiers with syphilis. Approximately 700 Guatemalans, including children, were infected and studied. And, in 1911 Dr. Hideyo Noguchi of the Rockefeller Institute for Medical Research injected 146 hospital patients, including some children, with syphilis.

"Many of these heinous experiments, like the Tuskegee Study, were overseen by the Centers for Disease Control, which, a journalist wrote, 'sees the poor, the black, the illiterate and the defenseless in American society as a vast experimental resource for the government.'"

The CDC, WHO, and NIH have also worked in conjunction with the American military to create weapons of mass destruction and to test them on and use them to destroy certain populations.

"A 1975 military manual observed that it would be possible to develop 'ethnic chemical weapons' designed to 'exploit naturally occurring differences in vulnerability among specific populations.' Here, 1 should think of Hanta, HIV 2, and Middle East Respiratory Syndrome."

In February, 1987, a lawsuit by the Foundation for Economic Trends, a Washington, D.C. environmental group, forced the Department of Defense (DOD) to admit to the operation of biological research programs at 127 sites all over the country, including universities, foundations and corporations.'"

"We will take a quick break for station identification. Stay with us."

This is 88.9 Double You, Emm, El, Aay, your edutainment station, broadcasting from the campus of Malare University, Nashville, TN.

"Peace unto you Black Nation, as we prepare for war. You are tuned in to Nommo with Alteveze and Azure. The number is 252-7119. Please join this important conversation."

"Previously we discussed the controversy over mandatory hepatitis testing and vaccination in Black communities. *Frontline*, a newsmagazine based in Atlanta, reports cases of cholera, hepatitis B, and tuberculosis and other diseases mysteriously popping up in Black communities.

"Like Shinally's Dr. Northerly, the U.S. government attributes this resurgence of formerly eradicated diseases to Black nastiness. However, there have been cases of TB that were, listen, non-responsive to treatment. The appearance of these mutated disease strains coincides with genetic-engineering advances and mandatory 'screening' initiatives that are imposed on certain communities and populations."

"Azure," Alteveze tapped her hand, "We must also note here the infection of millions of Haitians with cholera by United Nation's aid workers who came to 'assist' Haitians following the earthquake of 2010.

"The goal of Caucasian global supremacists is simple: increase their dwindling numbers and decrease the populations of the melanin-rich people of this world. This is why population control organizations are focused on countries in Latin America, the Caribbean, Africa and Asia, not Bosnia, Russia, Czechoslovakia, France, and Britain, because the European, or properly, Caucasoid life form has a lower birth-rate than *hue*man beings.

"Indeed, certain Caucasians are fighting to make abortion illegal so that Caucasian women will be forced to bring more of them into the world. This is why HIV/AIDS is surging at pandemic levels among Africana populations but has been stabilized among Caucasians. This is not about lifestyle, self-control, morals, or righteousness. It is about genocide."

"So true, Azure, and Africans are not the only victims. In 1768 Caucasians gave Native Americans blankets infected with smallpox, this was repeated in during the 'Trail of Tears' in 1838 and 1839 when Andrew Jackson forced the Cherokee to relocate from their lands east of the Mississippi River to what is now called Oklahoma. More recently the Hanta virus has killed approximately 200 Native Americans."

"Cambodian, Vietnamese, and Japanese people have all been victims of US germ warfare. And Caucasian gynecologists sterilized thousands of Native American and African American women without their knowledge or consent. California recently outlawed the sterilization of women in prisons—1 must wonder why was this even occurring."

"We, the masses, must refuse to be tortured and defiled by mutants. We must say, 'No More!'"

"No mo!"

"Sydney, peace and awareness, you're with Nommo."

"Peace, daughters. Thank you for taking my call.

"My people are from Alabama. They were pickers, migrant workers. We traveled all over Alabama. But this white man knew when we would return home to Notasulga and he always came to visit us. His name was Dr. Haskins, and he was real interested in me. Always listening to my heart, checkin my eyes, limbs, and skin. I was afraid of him at first cuz white folks was rare, comin to the house in all, and his smell was worse than wet chickens. I hated to go near him, but he always come. 'Regular as the reaper,' Momma would say.

"I am blind. I've been blind since birth. Once when he checked my eyes, Momma asked im, 'Can you cure im? Can you make im see?' I was about 6 and I prayed he could. But he laughed and said, 'Mary, I'm not god, just 1 of his representatives. I can't work miracles.'

"Daddy and Momma wanted other children after me, but they couldn't have any. 1 night I heard my folks whisperin bout something that wasn't normal. That's what Momma was saying, 'This thang ain't normal.' I didn't know what they was talkin about, but I knew sometimes Daddy and Momma had sores. Sometimes Daddy was in so much pain, he would cry out in the night. It was horrible to hear my daddy scream," Sydney's voice cracked like thin glass exposed to frost.

"1 time, Daddy and Momma left me with Miss Lolly to go to Mobile for free penicillin," Sydney choked up. "They came back. Said Haskins met em there an tol em they was sposed to be in Tchula, not Mobile."

"Have strength, Elder."

"You can't imagine how my daddy suffered in his last days. . . When he finally died, the casket was closed. H-h-his nose had rotted off."

"My word," Alteveze's hands were trembling.

"So I know y'all's speakin the truth, the facts. I'm 70 now. I've never had children. I'm sterile. My wife left me. She run off and had a child but she come on back as her man left her. We raised her child as our own.

"I never had spite against nobody. But I know, sure as I'm blind, they can create AIDS and anything else they want. My own self proves that."

"Elder Sydney, we appreciate your revelations. I know it wasn't easy for you to share this, but it is elders like you who can educate us with your experience," Azure's voice cracked.

"Elder, stay strong and keep teaching your truth."

"You girls are doing important work. I would be proud to call you my own. I hope that because of your work tonight, we can save some lives."

"Àṣẹ and Amen, Father."

"You are tuned into Nommo—the power of the word by which we declare, No Mo! No Moe hueman guinea pigs. No mo slaying of our mothers and fathers of our progeny and prophets. No More under-handed tricks. No more turning our other cheeks to the reality of our oppressors' bestiality only to be slapped again. No more.

"Sons and Daughters of Boukman of Nat Turner of Denmark Vesey of Gabriel Prosser of Patrice Lumumba of Winnie Mandela of Sojourner Truth of Ida B. Wells Barnett of MahuLisa of Consciousness and Evolution of Odù stand up and love your selves and souls by refusing to be oppressed any longer. No more slavery. No more neo-slavery. No more genocide. The only freedom is that we take! The only evolution is that we create. Listen, for 200 years they've been trying to exterminate us: No More."

"We urge you to do your own research. You can see the documentary, *The Origin of AIDS* free online. You can also access Tom Curtis' groundbreaking *Rolling Stone* article also titled "The Origin of AIDS" online for free. Also insightful is Edward Hooper's *The River*, Andrew Goliszek's *In the Name of Science*, and Harriet A. Washington's *Medical Apartheid*. In everything it does, the beast evinces pride. So it publishes all its evil. Arm yourselves with the ultimate weapon: knowledge."

"Never believe the death an oppressor has planned for you is the 1 you must succumb to."

"Our next caller is Derrick. Peace, Derrick."

"Peace, sisters. My mind is blown by the information you've shared. You know, the elders say that the beast is awake and thinking of ways to kill us as we party, sleep, fu"

"Please, brother"

"my bad, sisters, have sex, and get high, but this is a new level of assault. If these beasts are successful, we will be extinct by 2050!"

"If not before, which is the plan."

"But let's keep in mind the word 'undesirable.' We'll still have some toms floating around. . . Quite a few, in fact," Alteveze mused.

"Queens, this is a monumental global attack and its results so far have been devastating," Derrick lamented.

"Derrick, you're right. The attack we face is multipronged and the agents of destruction are numerous. In the 1990s, AIDS infection rates were soaring and so was the '0 Population Growth' movement. Today, with millions of Africana peoples having died and currently infected with HIV/AIDS, the hue and cry about population growth has ceased.

"While the catch phrases change, objectives and outcomes have not. African nations are now under attack by Ebola, which wreaks immediate havoc and is capable of decimating nations in mere months. Ebola and its brother Marburg are digging many graves in Central and West Africa.

"Ebola, Marburg, and Lassa are all part of the HIV/AIDS family and were created using similar processes. Indeed, Gorbee Logan, a Liberian physician practicing in Tubmanburg successfully treats Ebola victims with lamivudine, which is, not surprisingly, used to treat not only HIV but also hepatitis B. Logan states that his decision to use HIV drugs to treat Ebola was rooted in the fact that 'Ebola is a brainchild of HIV. . . . It's a destructive strain of HIV.' To determine the parentage of HIV we need look to the laboratories of individuals like Szmuness and to agencies of mass distribution that include the CDC and WHO, the World Health Organization."

"Derrick and Alteveze, we do not yet have the tools to fight Marburg, Lassa, and Ebola, but we have some tools to fight HIV/AIDS. First and foremost, we must know and protect our HIV statuses. With over-the-counter test kits available, there is no excuse for not knowing your status and that of your partner. If you are negative, stay negative; protect your life, destiny, and future. If you are positive, be honest. Condoms can break, but your word cannot. Discuss your status with your partner long before sex, and consult with a physician you *trust* and obtain lifesaving antiretroviral drugs. *Always—no matter your status—insist on safe sex.*"

"Excellent points, Azure. I think we also need to undertake grassroots education and protection plans that focus on our pre-teen youths. A documentary about the pandemic level of HIV/AIDS infection in the rural American south was stunning because it revealed that our children are in the throes of a living death. But what really shocked me is that rather than educate and protect the children, the schools' awareness programs only discuss abstinence.

"The human body's hormones surge during puberty because the drive to create life is the ultimate directive. Teaching abstinence is so ineffective it's a joke. Indeed, in the documentary, after a teacher gave a speech about abstinence—not safe sex, condom application, or full disclosure, but abstinence—a young man raised his hand and asked, 'What do you do if after you have sex you tell your partner that you have HIV and she says that she has it too?' The teacher was silent and offered no answer, because she was told she could only preach abstinence."

"Our children are grappling with issues of astounding and life-changing and life-taking depth and the would-be educators offer them solutions that solve nothing or silence. This is criminal."

"It is as if the school boards are promoting HIV/AIDS transmission by restricting their teaching to abstinence. It as if they are saying, 'If you are not abstinent, you deserve to get AIDS.' This, like the entire educational system, is miseducation by design.

"We have to be responsible for ourselves on all levels. We have to establish values that are not rooted in our oppressors' avarice, deception, and immediate gratification. We are failing our children—and ourselves—if we continue to allow the schools to continue to miseducate them."

"Excellent points, Alteveze. We have to realize the fact that the nation that made it illegal for us to read and write, that criminalized our education, will not now educate us—not unless they are educating us to destroy ourselves. . . Our education and our health care are *our* responsibilities.

"We also need to remove the sexual stigma from the disease because HIV/AIDS was not created in the genitals; it was created in a laboratory. What is more, sex is only 1 of its many routes of transmission. HIV/AIDS is not a punishment for having sex. Sex is a natural, healthy, necessary aspect of life; indeed, it is the source of life. Having a healthy sex life—no matter your sexual orientation—is as important as being holistically healthy.

"Being disgusted by sex and considering having sex an offense that merits punishment is only logical for a people who have a historical abhorrence for the life-making genitals: The hatred of the womb, vagina, menses, and to a lesser extent, the penis, testes, and semen, is the foundation of Christianity.

"We have to liberate our minds from their religious shackles to understand our genitals, bodies, and roles on this Earth and in the cosmos."

"Peace unto you, brother. Your speaking with Nommo."

"Peace and accolades, my sisters. Thank you for letting me speak. I, uh, don't want to give my name."

"It's alright brother."

"I am a 22 year old college student, and I have HIV."

"Take your time."

"I started experimenting with bisexuality 4 years ago as a freshman. My physics prof, well, you could say, initiated me. I was failing, see? I wanted to do some extra credit work to salvage my grade. He invited me to a tutorial. He and I were there—only—along with enough wine and weed to help me forget where I was and what I was doing.

"I went to the dorm and must've showered an hour, tears blending with the water and blood and . . . But, well, my college career was set, just by bending over. He, uh, promised me anything I wanted. I knew about AIDS but hell, 19 and strong, I *knew* I was invincible. And I had a *fiiiiine* sister!"

"Oh no"

"Yes, I, I—"

"Take your time; take your time."

"I tried to tell myself I wasn't gay—but it became—so easy. And, uh, I enjoyed it. I did. When I pledged, I found out I wasn't the only 1. Many of us were switching lanes. It was wild. Sometimes, right after 'fag bashing,' we would gang rape pledgees—ain't that a bitch?" his laughter sounded like it was rising from a grave. "Sometimes I d-d-on't know who I am.

"I can't believe that I dragged Co—my lady—into this," his voice broke and, along with it, the dam of emotions, "I'm scared to tell her, but I have to." His sobs moved to tears the studio audience and the families gathered around their radios.

"I just want to say this," the young man gathered himself: "Nothing is what it appears. Wear a condom until you're ready to have children. Even if you think you and your partner are monogamous, co-test at least once a month: You never really know what another person is doing . . . Please, please don't end up li, li,"

"Hold on brother, it's gonna be alright. You are strong to have come through what you have endured. Strong. Strong to share these hard truths with your community tonight. And we ARE your community, your kin, your blood. But you've got to use the same strength and courage to sit down and tell your lady what has happened and the results of your decisions."

"I know. I will. But I'm so scared."

"She decided to have a relationship with you," Azure sympathized, "but she did not decide to have HIV/AIDS. You have to tell her the truth because it may be her truth now too."

"Consider using your plight to continue educating. You've educated us here tonight, and you've made an excellent point: co-test! With personal HIV testing kits available at your local pharmacy, there is no reason not to know your status and to protect yourself and others. And there's no reason to let physicians fool with your blood or ask you invasive and ridiculous questions about your sexual life. With the personal tests you have no excuse not to control your fate."

"My brother, we wish you courage on your journey forward."

"Yours is a reality we have to face, not ignore. There will be many of us singing different verses of your song."

"Different melodies and lyrics"

"Same tune . . . I understand. I will try to be strong, and I will definitely tell the truth."

After a moment of silence Alteveze growled, "You know, it takes courage, Azure."

"Yes, real courage to come forward and testify"

"No, I mean courage to scatter lives and play god!"

"Well, the beast thinks it is god. This country was founded by masons and deists. Freemasons worship Nimrod, the African architech who built the tower of Babel, and Solomon, the wisest man of his time, who was another African master architech. The deists believe god created the world and vamped and left them to oversee everything and everyone. Deism is 1 of the many ways by which these mutants have tried to justify their existence and their oppression and slaughter of billions of innocents.

"Caucasians created the construct of race in their attempt to make the *absence* of melanin, which is a genetic deficiency, the measure of excellence. But what motivates them, Alteveze, is the lack they feel and signify because of their melanin deficiency."

"Those without melanin specialize in oppressing and killing those with melanin. They also enslave bodies, and, more important, they chain minds. This is done via religioous and cultural indoctrination. The beasts' ideological twisting and trapping have been so successful that many of us believe we have to be like the beast to succeed. Many of our leaders—heads of state, university professors, community leaders, and chiefs—actually surpass the beast in crushing minds and spirits."

"Those Tuskegee experiements went on under the mutual control of knee-grows and beast doctors, and there could be no slave master without slave catchers and factors," Alteveze noted.

"But morally bankrupt knee-grows didn't shoot whole communities of Africans into rivers because they lost the Civil War—confederate soliders did that. They didn't organize lynching bees. They did not create AIDS. So, while we often struggle to best our oppressors in oppressing, there is no comparison."

"It is also clear there is no limit to the methods the beast will devise to torture and kill African people and amputate our arc of existence. I want to share with you information from *Psychiatry's Betrayal*, an exposé published by the Citizen's Commission on Human Rights. It details numerous crimes against humanity that have gone unanswered:

"Margret Sanger, a eugenicist and the founder of Planned Parenthood of America proposed in 1939 a plan to stop the population growth of Africans in the U.S. Her plan to 'exterminate the Negro population' involved having Black ministers preach throughout the South that 'sterilization was a solution to poverty.' Sanger's objective and mission help us to put Planned Parenthood's mission and objective into proper perspective.

"*Pychiatry's Betrayal* also reveals that in the 1950s in New Orleans Black prisoners were used for psychosurgery experiments which involved electrodes being implanted into the brain. The experiments were conducted by psychiatrists Dr. Robert Heath from Tulane University and Australia's Dr. Harry Baily, who boasted in a lecture to nurses 20 years later that the 2 psychiatrists had used Blacks because it was 'cheaper to use niggers than cats because they were everywhere and cheap experimental animals.'"

"At this time, we'll take another call. Dr. Sims of Malare University! Peace and welcome to Nommo."

"In peace, Azure and Alteveze. On behalf of the Pan-African Nation, thank you. The information you have shared is vital to our existence.

"As a literature professor, I think it is imporant to acknowledge that our artists have used their craft to liberate, conscientize, and elevate. Ycidra, the protagonist of Toni Morrison's *Home*, is subjected to gruesome gynocological experiments at the hands of her employer. There is a clear line of continuity connecting Ycidra's struggle and the findings of Harriet A. Washington's *Medical Apartheid*."

"Alteveze and I were also discussing the significance of Ycidra's harming and healing, Dr. Sims!"

"The collective conscientization of students, professors, researchers and artists is definitely by design. And as it concerns the information you just read from *Psychiatry's Betrayal*, Ralph Ellison's protagonist in *Invisible Man* was subjected to electroshock therapy after the paint plant explosion."

"Sure was!" Alteveze was hunched over taking notes.

"Etheridge Knight also used his art to inform us about injustices being committed. Knight's poem "Hardrock Returns from the Hospital of the Criminally Insane" concerns an incarcerated brother who is lobotomized.

"Our artists have always used their gifts to tell our oppressors, 'yes, we see, we see you, and we see what you are doing to us.' Another example of artists using art to speak empowering truths is Gil Scott Heron's "Tuskegee 626." And Stetsasonic's *Blood, Sweat and Tears*, discusses the painting of projects with a chemically treated paint that caused psychological disturbances and the government distributing poisoned commodity cheese that led to nausea, vomitting, and death.

"This show has inspired me! I want to share my lyrical Nommo with you."

"Shine on us, Sun!"

The Texturization of a Nation

Dark n lovely will do you in
Seep into your brain change your mind
contribute to womb bruising ovarian contusions
Sister, they're knockin on your spirit
to let em in will do you in

Sportin waves will wash away your soul
Leave you dazed, brother
like project paint left
children seeing visions of hell
trying to kill themselves
like that tainted cheese
that not even rats would grease
that we lined up for
and wound up in windin sheets
like the children in Atlanta who never came home
like we thought we was free
like we started enjoying trees
until jails in Jackson Missip
started birthing Strange Fruit
without soil, limbs, or leaves
Now they created AIDS to number our days
and our leadurrs ain't murmured a thing
1
2
Check Onetwoonetwo

We need time
1 time for your mind
2 times for your Nation
                    Time
                    Nation
                    Time
                         to take gun or pen or juju in hand
                              Whatever it takes to blast
                                   these beasts from our sphere
                         Take time like the ancestors took to
                    fight against seasonings, cuffings, quarterings
               sufferation, ruination, scarification
as riddled, deep, and Black as the Rosetta Stone
as complex as Ishango bones
as perfect as Nabta Playa stones
We got styles from Zumbi to Nanny
from Hurston to Knight to Nat
to scatter dey ass
Just ask yo mommas
 we'll teach you if you don't know
the most expeditious manner by which
to demolish an ofay's soul.

"Nomo, Nommo, No More, No Moe!"

"Professor Sims, your mind is as beautiful as your soul is rich as your cipher is deep."

"Nation, we close this program, but not our fight against genocide, or our minds, or our evolution and revolution."

"From Azure"

"From Alteveze"

"Peace."

"Mmmm mm! Girl, you threw down on this lasagna! Where'd you learn to make this?"

"Hell, a cookbook! I'll try anything once," the fresh basil, oregano, and thyme she ground that afternoon perfumed her entire home and accented the rich aroma of her mozzarella, smoked provolone, and ricotta cheese blend.

"My question is, why am I so receptive? I mean, is this thing latent in me or what?"

"Well," Kandace sliced another forkful of lasagna, "from my understanding, Àjẹ́ is a force that is manifest to some degree in all Africana women. I guess the power depends on the person."

Cynthia drained her Beaujolais and topped off both glasses as she mused, "Okay, like some women can levitate or fly."

"Right. Depends on the person and the inclination and the spirit."

"And some women can read minds."

"See inside bodies and wombs"

"Some can be healers"

"Or killers, I mean, you've heard of Nanny?"

"Hún ùn."

"Girl, Nanny led Jamaica to independence from slavery in 1739! Her 500 Jamaican troops defeated a British army of 5,000. Her warriors were initiated into the revolt and bonded by Àjẹ́. Nanny invoked Nana Bùrúkù: 'Wicked Mother who cuts life and does not use a knife. Cut this evil on the plantation.' That is 1 of Nana Bùrúkù's praisesongs: it's in Mason's *Orin Òrìṣà*—important book. But Nanny showed herself to be a true embodiment of Nana Bùrúkù. They say her booty protected her from bullets."

"The power of the *boo*tay."

"And she could catch bullets in her hands."

"You believe that?"

"Well," Kandace shrugged, "if you don't believe in certain things, you know exactly what you cannot do, you've set your limits. But if you leave room and respect for everything, there's nothing closed unto you. At any rate, being able to deflect bullets is a well-documented African technology. There is very little that we cannot do. Naw," Kandace decided to embrace the truth, "we can do anything.

"You see, Àjẹ́ is everything. Odù is the Womb of Creation, The Owner of the Pot of Existence. She is also the embodiment of the Mother Earth or Imọlẹ̀ and of the Mother of Waters, Yemọja. In fact, both Odù and Yemọja share the same praisename, Yewájọbí, 'the Mother of all Òrìṣà and all living things.'

"As the Mother of All she is the Owner of All. Everything we create on Earth is an offering from her pot that will go back into her pot. Everything—literature, music, dance, insurrection, spiritual evolutions—everything—especially ourselves and progeny—are part of and 1 with Odù."

"Humph. Creative Mothers," Cynthia mused, "like Toni Morrison."

"Exactly. Cassandra Wilson"

"Ella Fitzgerald"

"Sojourner Truth"

"Alright now!"

"Harriet Tubman"

"Betye Sarr"

"Nina Simone!!!"

"Nikki Giovanni"

"I mean. . ." forks and garlic bread clattered to the table as the women rose and riffed, "We can flyyyyy like birds in the skyyyyy!"

The women sank to the couch laughing and on high. They felt as if an epiphany were occurring in their souls.

"In many African societies, women control the markets and wield vast social and political power. Among the Yoruba of Nigeria, women are instrumental to political and social development, and this exercise of power is not limited to a few women. Because all Yoruba women are recognized, traditionally, as having Àjẹ́, they are all inherently empowered. This was long before the advent of any concept of feminism. Indeed, feminism is nowhere near as empowering as the original African social structure, which benefited both men and women and wasn't predicated on dichotomy. Àjẹ́ is not a political power move. It is as natural and as necessary as the womb."

"As our mothers."

"That's the correlation! In Yoruba, Àwọn Ìyá Wa means our mothers, and àgbàláàgbà means old and wise 1."

"Hell, that ain't nothin by Big Momma and Mu Deah."

"Or Bird Women, Owner of the Birds."

"Ol Bird!"

"See how it go? To paraphrase Giovanni, we so hip even our errors correct. We really don't know how deep our powers go. We restin in, relyin on, and receivin wisdom we don't even recognize. Been made ashamed of our sources and forces, but we must reclaim them. Harness them. Manifest our destiny with them."

After polishing off their lasagna, Cynthia and Kandace maxed out on Kandace's porch and watched as the copper sun sank into violet and turquoise clouds. "Such an inspiring sunset!" Cynthia sighed. "So, how are things going in Rassmuss' class?"

"Well, honestly, I dreaded the thought of Early American anything, but I've learned a lot. The problem is that Rassmuss and I keep butting heads. Just last week he insinuated that Olaudah Equiano didn't exist because he doubted it was possible for an African to master English as Equiano had. You know I went off!"

"I heard about you, girl; you have guts! Terry told me you sat up and said that Rassmuss was following the lead of other academic racists in making all Africans either super-Africans or non-existent 1's invented by whites. Terry say, he was just lookin at you like, damn, does she know he's the department chair?"

"Hell yeah I know; that's precisely why I had to call his ass out! Imagine!"

"Be careful. You don't want no beast on your back . . . or standing in front of you blocking your degree."

"I'm gon let my integrity lead me. Fuck these racists," and she dismissed them with a wave of her hand. "Tell me, how is your thesis coming?"

"It's coming along well. Now I'm analyzing the strategies the abolitionists used; I'm especially interested Pan-African continuity."

"I've got some information on African rituals and military strategies that you might find useful. You know, during their recent wars, Liberian and Sierra Leonean soldiers used technology to make themselves invisible, to deflect bullets, and to alter their matter."

"Hmp," Cynthia mused, "Maybe they used the same technology as Nanny. This is deep. By the time I include the all of this power, I'll have an insurrection encyclopedia. Danes is already moaning about length."

"Fuck them. What do they know? Like you can really *elucidate* in 70 pages. This is our WORK."

"Most important work: Bridging the ancestors and the living."

"Speaking of living, Cyn, what is up with you and Samuel. Y'all still kickin it?"

She sucked her teeth, "Ain't much to kick. I mean, can he compare with what I'm learning with you?"

"You can share with him," Kandace got up from the settee and moved inside to the stereo. She was uncomfortable. She didn't want to replace Samuel or make him appear obsolete. "Pull him into your new sphere," she suggested as she dug in her crates and selected Sly Stone's *There's a Riot Goin On*, D'Angelo's *Black Messiah*, Miles' *Kind of Blue*, Mal Waldron's *1 and 2*, Rahsaan Roland Kirk's *Blacknuss*, and Cannonball's *Somethin' Else* and powered up her record player. The album: a music lovers best, and sometimes only, friend.

"He's a good man. Stable, educated, kind"

"and dull"

"and those types of
brothers are becoming more and more rare. I mean, look at some of the causes I've been sponsoring around here."

Barely audible under Sly's "Spaced Cowboy" Kandace heard 1 word: "Lerone."

"Shut up! I heard your ass. You don't know *what* Lerone got that makes me, uh, patient with him. . ." she lifted her left eyebrow suggestively.

"Lord! Hammercy!" They laughed and enjoyed the music, outwardly; inwardly, each mused the dearth of male complements. And the pickins would get slimmer when they earned their masters degrees. Brothers seemed more terrified of the letters PhD than HIV. What's an educated warrior woman to do?

"But what about your thesis, Kan? How is it going?"

"I'm working on the conclusion now. I've enjoyed the process: researching the ludicrous accusations and testimonies; learning more about the depth of Àjẹ́; and the analyzing, writing, and rewriting."

"So what is your assessment of the witch trials? Were there any Àjẹ́ among them?"

"Those people were massacred for no reason at all other than the titillation of some sick priests. There were no Àjẹ́ among them. The cultural differences alone are phenomenal. Caucasians cooking children and using their fat for power rituals, kissing the devil's ass, sexing any and everything—that has nothing to do with Àjẹ́."

"Hmm, seems more like excuses to wallow in their perversions."

"Exactly. Àjẹ́ is natural but"

"they ain't."

"Let's just make it plain. African spiritual systems don't have concepts inherent evil, original sin, or the devil: These fictions are outgrowths of Caucasian psychopathology.

"Speaking of the devil," Cynthia mused, "Caucasians called Èṣù the devil, but the Òrìṣà is everything but a devil: The God is male and female, divine linguist, mediator, trickster, signifier."

"And Èṣù's is reincarnated in the African American 'Devil,' who is also not at all evil but is a trickster who tests your skills, wit, and intelligence."

"Hurston really represented in *Mules and Men*."

"Say that twice. But back to these witches," Kandace was warming to the subject, "the most oft-referred to concept is sex: from fucking strange spirits to fucking animals to fucking objects. 1 researcher stated that the broomstick women used to 'fly' with was nothing but a dildo and that 'flying' was code for orgasm. They were fascinated with incubus and succubus spirits that come and sex you."

"The bitches was lonely."

"And horny."

"You know Kan, it is interesting that these witch trials ended with the influx of enslaved Africans. It is like we gave the vapid Caucasian mind something other than its females to focus on."

"Maybe all those 'bucks' reduced the need for broomsticks. . ."

"Hmm, the broomstick embodied. . ." Kandace mused, "Indeed, these so-called witches described the devil as a big black man. Seems the enslavement of Africans was a boon to Caucasians in many respects. What a sick and sad group of people," she shook her head.

"If my theory is correct that African men, the African penis, in particular, refocused Caucasian attention while giving them a sexual outlet, why would the Caucasian man allow the physical "bewitching" of the Caucasian woman?"

"Well, he wouldn't necessarily have to allow anything. There were lots of single and widow women to allow whatever they wanted. But many men would look the other way if impotence were a factor, or disinterest in sex, or over-interest in the African woman. Also, many Caucasian men get off watching their women have sex and/or be raped. Additionally, homosexuality has been a part of European culture since they were rooting in the Caucasus caves.

"You're right. I was reading these freedom narratives and 1 elder said all this mess about Blacks going with whites and whites going with Blacks was nonsense cuz this stuff has always been going on. Now you know he wasn't talkin bout Black women and gray men cuz ain't nobody ever got lynched for that, unless it was the woman refusing and getting killed. He was talking about gray women and Black men."

"I want you to share your sources with me."

"Nothin but a thang sister, nothin but a thang," Cynthia started writing down the books and articles she would gather for her comrade. "What I find interesting about your work is that you're clearing your own path, and your research will help you understand more about yourself and Àjẹ́."

"You know, the beautiful thing about Àjẹ́ is that it is sanctioned, overseen, and administered by a Great Mother who disseminates the knowledge and power to Our Mothers, so Àjẹ́'s social-spiritual articulation is reflected in every Africana community and in the vast majority of our families. But what is most important is the methodology. The work of Àjẹ́ is to ensure justice and impart justice wherever, whenever, and however necessary. It is truly a situation of a Grand Mother helping her progeny actualize. And Àjẹ́ never convict anyone without a fair trial, but once convicted, umm mm! I mean, such balance and diligence are nowhere evidenced in witchcraft or wicca or any Western government or organized religion.

"Certainly not America's so-called justice system. But Cyn, I have a very deep and perplexing issue I need to broach."

Cynthia turned to face Kandace who looked concerned.

"I thought you said you had some pee-can pie and," Cynthia started laughing, "and, and, I just been sittin here spillin my intellectual guts and and"

"You should have majored in drama or better yet, cuh-luh-hown-in! clown!" She got up to get the pecan pie.

"And Miss Cyn," now it was the full-tom special, "Ah sho hope it's some cream cheeeeze in da midduh."

"Won't be nothin in the middle if you don't stop clowning and help me make some coffee."

"All right now, don't make me send no incubus to you tonight. . ." Kandace threatened.

Cynthia paused, "He gon be big and black?"

"Naw," she widened her eyes innocently, "I figured that with reverse perverse discrimination you'd want him little and white."

"In less than a year, we're gonna be Masters of the Arts. What you wanna do with your degree?"

She held up her hand to signal a pause as she finished swallowing. "You know, I honestly don't know. What can you do with an M.A. in English but teach or go for the Ph.D.?"

"Write! you a writer girl! You've published in AWA and BLA! Well, I'll be damned, you on yo way!"

She laughed at Cyn's impromptu rap. "But, I don't wanna write books about books for the rest of my life."

"I feel you."

"I love literary analysis: That's my passion. But I want to write my own novels to motivate, stimulate, and inspire—and, yes, be torn apart by critics!" The friends shared a knowing chuckle.

"Well, I'm looking into Ph.D. programs."

"Really? All the politricks, racism, backbiting. . ."

"Well, my goal is to start an Africana Studies Program."

"Where?"

"Wilberforce."

"Where else? I should have known. You and the Force."

"That's my alma mater! And why are the biggest Africana studies programs housed in Euro-universities: We need knowledge of self."

"You're right, but many of those African-oriented programs at Euro-unies are only training grounds for neocolonizers. They train those crackers to speak a little lang to spy in African countries.

"And if Wilberforce is anything like FAMU, you'll find that those neo-negroes think *being* Black is enough knowledge of self. These students want to get as far from Blackness and as close to an MBA as possible.

"But I respect your vision and goal, Cyn. We need more people who are committed to our education and evolution." Kandace smiled at her friend who was still beaming with the thought of returning to Wilberforce. "As for me, if the opportunity arose, I would go straight to the Motherland."

"Where?"

"Nigeria."

"Of course, the continued path. You would be able to write your ass off there, and you would learn so much about Àjẹ́. I wouldn't mind going to the west side myself. I would love to learn about African spiritual-military technology at the Source."

"We need to be lookin into grants, right?"

"Yeh, I don't want to owe Uncle Sam shit."

Kandace got up and put the needle into the groove of *Bitches Brew*. Miles washed over them like indigo rain.

"Funny you played that," Cynthia mused. "You know what I really wanna do?"

"What?"

"Open a soul food restaurant."

Kandace cringed inside. She saw a vision of Cynthia transformed into a mammy, bowin and scrapin foe huh whi/te chirrins! But externally she responded by raising her left eyebrow.

"Dig it," Cynthia was already there, in the kitchen, judging from the glaze on her eyes, "the prices will be so high no peeps can step in there and the siddity Black folks wouldn't dare: Imagine being accosted by chittlins!"

The eyebrow remained peaked.

"Dig the menu: Hog maws, head cheese, cornbread, cracklin bread, smothered pork chops, greens seasoned with huge rubbery hunks a fatback! *Clean* white tables, white linen, *good* crystal, *real* silver. Top shelf.

"All the upper crust of the gray society will come. Slummin without the slums! And for a little while, they can brag on their knowledge of 'nigra' culture and cuisine.

"I figure I can stay open for a month before I shut it down."

"What? Why shut it down? They'd love it and loooove dem sum Cynthia."

"How long you think I can stay opened when poorly cleaned chittlins and once cooked poke salad are complimentary with each order?" The gleam in her eyes was now dazzling.

"Oh—oh—oh shit! You talkin bout some down-home Àjẹ́, girl!"

"Hell yeah! I look like Aunt Jemima to you? Well, even if I do, I ain't ja mamma!!!!!"

Miles offered his approval of Cynthia's plan with luscious lipwork.

"This work yuh done, its tearin at chuh heart. Do yuh want to undo da work uh get ove da guilt?"

"I don't know . . . If I stay where I am, I'll be in the same place . . . I . . . I just wanna be free."

"Yuh got tuh choose: freedom uh guilt."

"I," she hesitated, "I choose me."

No 1 had seen Jahmai since the Thursday morning Chaka made the running feet. His mother was calling, checking for him so much Chaka had had her calls forwarded to voicemail. Chaka knew the cause, not the effect. And all she wanted was amnesia.

"Can't go forward till yuh choose. Yuh spirit so twisted it pinched me when yuh come through da door. Maybe you wan test power. Now, power testin you," Patricia laughed, but gently; her voice was soothing, like drifting autumn leaves. This Chaka, she thought, she wear her heart pun her sleeve. Just as yuh can read Alapaha in her cheeks, she wears da shimmerings uh long-shed tears.

"Wanna see where he at?"

"Yes."

Patricia led Chaka to a clay bowl filled with water and a hint of bluing. As they knelt in front of the bowl, Patricia said. "Say his full name."

"Jahmai Maurice Sanders."

"Jahmai Maurice Sanders! Jahmai Maurice Sanders! Lover of violence an power! Bringer of strife an vexation. Jahmai Maurice Sanders. Ìyá Yemọja give us yuh clarity of vision," now chanting, Patricia sank all the way back into Liberia. "We gaze in da eyes uh yuh womb. Ìyá mi, show us da footpat! Reveal da footsteps. Reveal yuh son."

Incense smoke curled over the water.

She relaxed and looked at Chaka, whose nose-tip was almost touching the water, "Don look so hahd. Patience."

When she relaxed back on her haunches like Patricia, Chaka saw a man being eaten by a car. Terror dammed her lungs. When she could exhale, she saw Jahmai was actually hunched over and struggling with the car's smoking engine. His melon-hued suit was streaked with oil. He stretched, extended fully, and cocked his head as if he'd been called by someone across the highway. But the only sound came from the cars that whizzed past him. He began to walk as if he were trying to catch up with some debtor—or his fate.

"You some strong," Patricia nodded in recognition of Chaka's Work. "He be in Cairo soon."

"Cairo, Egypt!?!'"

"Naw. Cairo, Ill-nois," she chuckled, "He won't stop. Runnin feet. Sister, he'll run till he dies. Yuh use somethin with wings and red pepper." It was a statement, not a question.

She tore her eyes away from the smoky water and gazed at Patricia. "Yeh. I used a red wasp nest." She lowered her eyes and licked her lips. "Can we make him stop but stay in Cairo?"

"Sure yuh can."

"How?

"That's what yuh got tuh fine out."

How do you dam the flow of the Ethiopic? Chaka sat down and faced East and the Òrìṣà.

"O, Yemọja, Ìyá Yewájọbí, Yemaya. Mother of Fishes, cool and cooling Mother, protecting force who calms her children. Ìyá wielding the fan that composes and soothes. Ìyá wielding the fan of destruction and destitution. Ìyá àgbàláàgbà who brought us to this place, whose influence we have used and are using and will use."

"Àṣẹ"

"Great guiding force who gives us the will to live through and victoriously surmount our oppressors' worst evil."

"Àṣẹ"

"Ìyá whose back became our bridge to re-member self to Self. O Ìyàmi! Please help me. Show me the way forward."

"Àṣẹ"

"Great Mother, I come on behalf of your son, Jahmai Maurice Sanders. He is your son, recognize him. Recognize him: Ìyá, witness in him your flesh, waters, and bones. Ìyá Yemọja, I ask you to let his feet rest. Let your son find solace in Cairo. Let your son stop and re-evaluate his life from where he now stands."

"Àṣẹ"

"Ìyá, Ogunte, Òṣùpá: Ẹ jọwọ́, ẹ rànlọ́wọ́ ọmọkùnrin yin."

"Àṣẹ"

"Ẹ fun o àláàfía ati ọgbọ́n."

"Àṣẹ"

"Mother, use your fan to cool his feet; your son has learned."

"Àṣẹ"

A tremor of peace washed over the botanica. Chaka was fully reclined; her face glistened with wide-tracked tears that traveled to become dark splotches on the cerulean hem of Yemọja's gown.

Patricia gazed at Chaka who had gone so deep she had spoken Yoruba and knew she could have given Jahmai running feet with just her thoughts.

Jahmai was walking towards her. She quickened her pace to meet him. Finally, she could explain everything to him. That she loved him, truly, but she just couldn't stand the violence—going to class bruised or hiding like a shamed lil girl. No, she didn't want to get back together, but they could talk and maybe be friends.

He looked haggard, she thought, like he hasn't slept or bathed in weeks. His head bobbed with each step. She couldn't see his eyes because the round windows of his glasses were smeared with grime and fogged with sweat, but she saw his smile.

"Jahmai," he faltered and craned forward towards her voice, "we need to talk. Listen, there's so mu—" he kept moving. Since the initial falter he didn't break his stride. Chaka realized that he wasn't smiling but grimacing with concentration.

"Jahmai! JAHMAI!" she ran to catch up with him. "Jahmai, our mother called: She's worried about you," Chaka caressed his shoulder and stopped. It's like touching stone. Stone. Cold. Stone. And then she began trekking: always about 4 paces behind him, never able to catch up with him.

Clok, clok, clok, clok, she felt her feet turn to stone. Clok, clok, clok. Her thighs, clok, her pelvis, clok, her fingers, clok, her hands, clok, clok, clok, her arms. She heard her soul, squeezed to the limit with no place left in her body to live, begin to whistle, as it drained out of her third eye.

She woke up panting, sweating, terrified, I can't go to sleep again. No way. If I do, it'll continue. She rolled over and turned on the light. "That's what it feels like. I did that."

She lit 3 Ancient Times incense sticks. Chaka squatted and reached under the bed. She hand her hand until she felt cold stone. A shiver caressed her soul. With a sharp intake of breath, she extracted a clear crystal bowl, inside of which was sediment and just a kiss of water.

She washed and rinsed the bowl and then filled it with cold clear spring water. After adding a mist of Volupte and touching the bowl to her third eye, her heart, and her pelvis in blessing, she slid the bowl back under her bed. After logging the date, time and content of the dream, Chaka sank into the mattress. She had trapped the dream in ink, confined it to paper. She had freshened the water for her head. She felt peaceful but still apprehensive as she closed her eyes and eased into the crickets' mating calls.

The yellow sky held her attention. She'd heard about such a sky preceding tornadoes, but had never seen 1. After seeing the house—brown brick with black shutters—and viewing the white ringed tree, she was immediately inside. Hump! A traditional funeral! She immediately thought of her Aint Amy who took her everywhere.

Once Amy took 12-year-old Chaka with her to visit Gloss, her lover who was also her second cousin. While Chaka and her cousins were playing they heard crashes, bashes, and cussing. Aint Amy and she rode back home in silence. Aint Amy's face was so heavily bandaged from the pistol whipping that Gloss had given her that Chaka was surprised Aint Amy could see to drive. The bandages were soaking both her blood and her tears.

Another time Aint Amy took her to "check up" on a boyfriend who just happened to be in the middle of fucking some woman. Chaka watched, silent and wide eyed, as her aunt kicked both their naked asses. Curses dirtied the air like meningitis. This time, soiled sheets soaked the tears.

Long before the love battles, Aint Amy had taken her to oversee the preparation and laying out of Great Aint Syllva, the community evangelist of Alapaha, and, in doing so, had taken her to her first and only in-house funeral. Therefore, Chaka was not surprised to see Amy seated in the front row of blue aluminum chairs. She was decked out in a white lace dress; her bosom was overflowing, and a low backline revealed her supple ebony skin. Her white veiled hat was cocked at a jaunty angle over her right eye, white stockings and white pumps encrusted with pearls shined on her legs and feet. There was Momma in a white satin 2-piece suit and crowned with a hat rippling with feathers. Her Daddy was also bedecked in white from his snakeskin draped feet to his silk suit to his stingy brim. Her parents died when she was a child and she recognized them from the photographs that graced her Great Aunt's living room mantle. Aint May, her only living relative after Aint Amy died of a heart attack, was sitting on the front row in a white voile suit with thin navy piping.

Although her family did not appear to be dressed for a funeral, Chaka was not disturbed by the incongruity. She was more embarrassed that she was wearing a fuchsia hoochie-mama dress and black 5 inch platforms.

She drifted toward the casket by a force she could not control, as if she were on a moving sidewalk. The casket was open, but at the wrong end. Or the body was turned the wrong way. Approaching the casket's closed end, she gazed at the rich cedar wood and brass handles and rubbed the smooth varnished grain. The head is here. Why is this side closed? she wondered.

It seemed to take her days to reach the opened end of the coffin, but she felt no shock when she did. She felt no shock at all seeing ragged black gabardine slacks with gray pinstripes frayed round the calves. The slim scarred legs seemed to still be struggling to hold on to their horribly run black thick-n-thin socks. And the legs had to do the holding because the cracked ankles ended, not in feet, but in bloody stumps.

She heard screaming. She turned to comfort her family and found only sparkling, brilliant, empty white chairs. There was the tornado dancing in the front yard. She woke up to find she was the 1 screaming.

She sat up and instead of seeing Sula's quote she was looking at Jahmai's frayed Godfather. His long slim fingers made 4 jagged arches as he leaned against the wall. He looked deeply into her bloodshot, bucked, tearing eyes and asked, "Sleep well?" with his right eyebrow raised.

"......" He may be real. Don't say nothin! He may be a dream. Don't speak. He knows. Don't speak! He KNOWS. Keep yo lips together, girl.

He moved toward the bed and she jumped—defensive. Like a cat, she prepared her posture and weaponry.

"Heh heh heh heh," He chuckled. "Heheheheheheheh"

He may be a dreamhemayberealadreamrealdream

Jahmai reached under the bed and pulled out the bronze-hued satin panties she'd thought she'd lost at the laundromat. The panties were barely distinguishable as they were folded in a tight square with needles crisscrossing all the way through. He fished in the closet and extracted a knot of colorful cloth that was stitched with both their hairs and sprinkled with their blood. He grabbed her arm

He's definitely real

and dragged her to the bathroom, the kitchen, the study, and the living room, where he pulled out root after root after root after root.

"I told you, you can't put no root on me, Man. I told you it'd backfire. I told you, you'd get the thing you want but you'd have to keep rejuvenatin the roots and then they'd come back on you 7-fold!" The words rushed forth, "Why'd you do this? I told you, you cain't put no roots on me, my spirit won't accept it!" He *really* loves me, she thought.

"I really love you," he said.

Jahmai dug up more roots from around the doorstep, at the head of the driveway, and in the back yard to the left of the back door. He tossed the collection of knotted cloth, pins, hair, roots, paper, rum and perfume at her feet and stood before her: "You gave me the runnin feet." He looked at the sky. Night was conceding a hazy mauve and violet blue defeat to dawn. He gazed at the horizon a long time, as if glad he was no longer chasing it.

"I took it off you too. With my mouth. I begged."

"I was in Cairo," he started undressing, removing the funky, streaked, ripped suit. "I lost 3 days of work," he took in the contours of Chaka's body, "and finn ta to lose a 4th." By his eyes, she was the last woman in the world. She stood in the yard naked and glistening with sweat.

Jahmai embraced Chaka, first with his eyes, then with his hands, his arms, his thighs, "This the only root I need to hold you. Comere, come feel this root I'm gonna put on you. Put it on you . . . in you . . . this root. Plant it, this root, in you deep as the ocean, Momma—Ahhhhh—yeahhhh."

Hawa had been nervous about Danta meeting her cousins. When Herk, Duck, Pooh and Bun showed up—everyone checked out everyone else— like stags will do. Then Pooh asked, "Shoulduh congratulate ya or take ya to a shrink?" and all the spaces filled themselves.

As usual, Conch threw down: fried catfish; hushpuppies; chicken tenders; greens; fries; barbecue beef ribs; crisp whiting; golden fried trout; strawberry, coconut, pecan cake; red velvet cake; and pecan, and chocolate, and sweet potato pies all beckoned from the kitchen. Conch stepped back, admired her work, and said, "Wa, call the men in. They gon run off with yo husband."

Hawa stepped on the porch and simply dug the way she felt: secure, protected, respected. She was surrounded by the people whom she loved and who loved her. She looked up and admired the stars, smelled the honeysuckle perfuming the night, and sighed. Her next inhalation brought a much more pungent aroma—1 that smelled like college, imminent sex, any food stuffs handy, and strawberry trees dancing in car windows. She opened her eyes and followed the scent of homegrown to her husband.

"Yo man heah pretty shaap," exhaled Bobby.

"We'd seen im round." Duck's eyes were pink when he arrived, and were now a rich maroon. He passed her the joint. She dragged, always stunned that weed was so harsh on her throat.

"I ain't nevah met a real lawyer. Needed 1 coupla times, though."

"Member when you and Dink stole that gas!"

Husky laughter filled the night.

"Girl, that was all Dink! You know I was sleep. Had that sleepin disease," Herk defended himself.

"Called weed."

"Called Nita."

The joint was now a roach, the only insect lovingly handled and kissed to glowing orgasm.

"Dinner's ready y'all."

"Shucky ducky."

"Quack-quack."

When her cousins broke for the house, she stroked Danta's thigh and said, "Baby, I didn't know you knew ol' skunny bo bo."

"Who?" His eyebrows became crescent moons, his eyes, harvest moons.

"Weed." Her love was comin down.

"I don't." His wasn't. "I'm hungry! Let's go."

Hawa watched him. So straight and serious and spiritually attuned. Now, trying not to look high. She giggled. She knew she'd be in for it tonight. Let me stop now—she thought. I'm already wet. Must be years since I puffed. But around my loves, I won't get paranoid. As the smell of catfish and barbecue serenaded her nose, it dawned on her that she was also hungry. She followed Danta.

"Wa! Get in here and fix dis boy's plate!" She sped up to see Conch offering her man a hill of food.

"Cee! you gon kill im!"

"Ain't no tellin when you gon eat like this again," Conch murmured to Danta in pseudo-confidentiality.

"Well," Hawa dished up her own plate and tried not to marvel at the altered distances and robust colors the food had acquired, "you the 1 taught me how to cook."

"Yo Momma sho couldn't," Conch teased Valeria whose culinary skills were dubious at best.

"Don't I serve you right, Daddy?" Hawa cooed to Danta.

"Mm hmm!" Danta answered with his mouth full.

"Just like the devil," Tynell murmured. The room rocked with laughter. Duck lost control of his drink and vodka and orange juice splashed on the floor.

Valeria pursed her lips and scolded, "All right now. Let's not tear up the house," her soprano sotte voce plea for order made the laughter increase. Hawa, feeling completely free for the first time in years, radiated as she popped a piece of catfish in her mouth and went to get a towel for Duck.

It was after the meal and Leroy's re-enactment of the Devil and Jack's strength contest and the Devil's creation of the neologism used by Danta, above, that Danta retrieved his guitar from beside the sofa to provide the bottom to Hawa's "Shuga Man."

I ain't never needed no body
Each road a life I strolled all on my alone
But my Mommas recognized my wealth
They came up with a plan
Sent me 1 Shuga Man
Shuga Manhan
My Shuga Man
When the nites get stone cold
And my spirit get empty—like a picked cotton boll
He covers me all up in his soul
The Gods sent me
My own Òrìṣà that my arms can hold
Shuga Man
Shuga Manhannnn
Shuga Man
Shuga Man
If all my friends turn dey backs on me
If a rain of pain strive to wash me out in misery
He swoop right down on da top a me
pushin sure and pure love under the neath of me
Shhhhugahhh Man
    Shuga Man
Brown Shuga Man
Ain't nevah needed nobody
    I can hold myself
When these jealous muthafuckas wan test me
    Aw, I place dey heads on my shelf
Oh, my Mommas recognized all my wealth
    yes they did
Sent me a warrior who can whole all of me from my soul to my self
Shuga Man
Don't fly away from me Daddy, no
Let me be the wind fore the storm you blow
Listen to the ancestors moan as we roll
Shuga Man

"Baby, that was beautiful! Fantastic!" Valeria beamed.

"You been hidin your gifts from us, girl!" Hawa's stepfather Earl embraced her and kissed her cheek.

"I don't like all dat cussin tho!" Tynell waved her hand as if the dispel the language.

"You remind me of Billie Holiday," Conch said.

"Bring Ella to my mind," added Peaches.

"Danta, you know you way around that box! Hawa never told us you played guitar," Earl clapped him on his shoulder.

"It's a surprise," Hawa gushed. "Danta has so many gifts and so much love, it's like I have my own star."

"Yes, your own Sun," Valeria smiled and sang the first song Hawa remembered her singing. Danta picked out the melody right on time.

You are sunshine, my only sunshine
You make me happy, when skies are gray
You'll never know, dear, how much I love you
So please don't take my sunshine away

Valeria finished the song with a 30-year-old baby in her lap. Hawa tried to imagine her baby self smiling into her mother's face.

"Get up now! Time for you to have your own babies," Tynell scolded.

"Yeh, Hawa, my kids be too old to play with yourn," Mildred observed as she watched 7-year-old Martique eat his sweet potato pie and feed his 3-year-old sister Dawn.

The night was like a fresh sheet of paper before the hand and the pen: all possibilities were open and all were explored: Lying, jookin, eatin, boogyin, bluesin. Danta and Hawa performed Betty Wright's "Tonight is the Night (You Make Me a Woman)." Hollas and whistles echoed off the walls as Hawa made her rendition extra special for her husband. Then, more dancin and laughin and squeezin. More cussin, trippin, kissin, ass slappin and sneakin out to indulge.

Tyrone Davis' "If I Could Turn Back the Hands of Time" started glitching, much to the vociferous dismay of all the dancers. While Danta went to the system to correct the problem, Cuttin' Frank saw his opportunity, and he seized it.

"I'm gon really turn back the hands of time for you!" He moved to the center of the living room, his trademark overalls sporting the crease that Miss Nellie had starched with love to perfection. "The blues that Tyrone Davis jazzed up for you has its roots in men working like mules. Long before there were any high-tech contraptions and programmed beats, we made the beats with the Earth, with the trees, with our shoulders, and with iron, steel!" Cuttin Frank stood up, grabbed his 10 pound hammer and became John Henry. As he drove down the boss man down along with the crosstie, Hawa grabbed her phone to record what may never be seen again. Hawa wondered if everyone could appreciate the rich and rare gift of hearing "John Henry" from the mouth of 1 of its shapers.

When Cuttin Frank concluded his rendition and his standing ovation settled, he continued, "We worked like mules to build this country. Drivers stood over us with guns and whips in the early days," he paused to let the conditions under which we built this nation sink into the minds of the youth. "But it wasn't all sufferin," he hinted at a smile, just enough to make his gold tooth sparkle. "We created songs to live and love and laugh by as well." With this, Cuttin Frank stomp-clapped out a rhythm to "Uncle Bud." Everyone joined his beat and the house got to rockin. When Cuttin Frank sang all the verses he knew, Leroy took the floor and contributed his knowledge. His verses were raunchier than his elder's and equally popular.

When the word warriors finished spreadin their jenk and the house filled with the rhythms of John Lee Hooker's "Crawling King Snake," Hawa tipped outside with a plate of fish, chicken, raw eggs, beer, wine, and a sampling of cakes and pies. Hooker's nimble fingers, plucking all manner of double entendre from his guitar, provided the throbbing downbeat for her footsteps as she approached the Wicked Tree.

This tree was Great Grand Mother Dona's healing tree. With 1 leaf passed through the ailing's mouth and her own, and charged by secret and sacred words—she removed any aliment. Dear used to keep a side-turned tractor tire next to the trunk filled with water and enlivened with 1 catfish. In praise. In remembrance. Hawa kicked off her shoes and placed her sacrifice at the ancestors' lips. With her forehead cushioned in the roots, Hawa wept and whispered, "Thank you, Thank you, Thank you, Thank you." When she felt a mother's breeze caress her nape, she touched her head to the Earth and returned to her living blood.

The choices presented themselves like a collection of insults: Exotic Dancing, College, Single Motherhood. After deciding not to return for her audition at 6T9 because of her inability to dance in high heels, she turned to her second choice: College. She'd graduated with honors in literature, history, and creative and dramatic arts. She had won essay contests, and was on the honor roll consecutively for 4 years. Uncle D and Salan beamed with pride as she gave the salutatorian speech and accepted her diploma. After abandoning her dreams of private dancing, she applied and was accepted to Howard. She was also awarded a full tuition scholarship. She didn't know what she'd study, but she tried to be optimistic.

It never dawned on her to be amazed that she had been high every day of her high school years and that even the racist teachers admired her, even though she stunned them with her queries: "But if this class is *World*

Civilizations, where's the information about Africa?" or, more succinctly, "This book is racist."

Public Enemy, Paris, and X Clan started expanding her consciousness over the summer. She decided that when she got to Howard she would find a deep conscious brother who was a melding of Posdenus of De La Soul and Malcolm X.

While the future offered some promise, the present was bleak. All of her friends now had at least 1 child. This was cute for a while. Originally, she wanted a boy. She would name him Casanova Capone Monet Love—and of course, he would be the flyest child in kindergarten. But the rigors of childrearing moved her to postpone pregnancy. For now, her nights were filled with old lovers, weed, and cruisin or Uncle D. During the day she worked at a chain clothing store: at least she would have some cold school clothes.

By the time July came to a steaming end, she was more than ready for Howard. Her former handlahs were now tired teen moms. The old lovers were more old than loving, and many were frustrated or dead-beat baby-daddies. Her romps with Uncle D had long lost their mystique. She felt empty.

She remembered once Uncle D sat her and talked to her when she was a wee lil girl, maybe 3.5. He talked about how he had been such a miserable and lonely child, and how worthless he'd often felt. He told her, "When I was going off to college, I thought, 'Nobody there knows me. They don't know David Preston from Hot Coffee, Mississippi. Nobody knows me or what anybody thinks of me. I can be anybody I want to be. I can change and be a new me'." She thought about this. There was nothing in her life that shamed her—but she wanted to, needed to, make some changes. She wanted to be proud of her friends and her life, instead of harboring "relative secrets." Most of all she wanted a life deeper than worrying where the next box of pampers or the next bag of weed was coming from.

She thought Howard would be Revolution Central with Fred Hamptons organizing and electrifying, deep committed sisters, conscious professors, political collectives, ciphers, poetry readings. Earthborn and intellectual highs.

She found some of this but mostly as a front to fuck, con, and exhibit 1's parents' money. There were few deep brothers but many a "hey babeee" artist. The sisters were locked in struggles over fashion, men, and lace-front wigs and weaves.

She established her own clique, partially in revolt against the Greek fraternities and sororities, partially in disappointment for not having witnessed the consciousness she'd dreamed of, and partially because a group of disaffected girls gravitated to her. She created the SatelLITES:

Loving, Intelligent, Tastefully Erotic Sisters. The Lites freely indulged in weed, wine, and men, and they were academically tight.

The AKAs hated them because the Lites' raw charm was more enticing than their daddies' money and their washed-out skin. The Deltas, who were wannabe Lites masquerading as AKAs, despised their integrity. The Zetas didn't count. The few conscious sisters on campus just shook their heads and awaited the awakening; the brothas came for the Lite of their lives.

No party started until the Lite shined. They came high, took over the drinks and the dancefloor (upon which they broke it all the way down). The Qs protected them as lil sisters, the Sigmas were always gripping, and the A Phis, largely given to homosexuality, were irrelevant. The Kappas, the established males of the Deltas, were the Lites conquering ground. These tall, buff brothas were renamed Pure Gold, Satan's Son, Little Clown, Massive, and I'll Be Damned! as each of them went "on line" with the Lite.

The Deltas, seeing their long-time slims snatched by ghetto upstarts, undertook tactics from slander to threats to regain their hold. The Lites were unfazed; they would fall into a ΔΣT party wielding cigarettes and "lite" thangs up. The Kappas would leave with them for private gatherings on different levels. Finished.

She enjoyed the hell outta frosh year. Sophomore year, she put sisters on line and crossed them, kicked it steady with both Satan's Son and Gold and had Soul, her Ghetto Superstar, on the side. Her grades were tight too: scholarship intact.

Then Soul lent her *Two Thousand Seasons*.

The Lite did a 180°. Armah and Diop, coupled with a class on African politics, set off the Light of Consciousness. The Lites went from partying and getting drunk to holding lectures and poetry readings and mounting plays. "More God Than Greek" started a uproar:

We've forsaken our propensity for innovation, silenced our power of the word. Lusting after perversions, we reach back only as far as Greece. We gobble the leavings of beasts and poison the Gods starving within.

We shake canes now instead of rattlin chains. Our pimpstroll is the crippled child of the slave coffle. We proudly inflict upon ourselves brandings, burnings, rapings. We get up for the ass stroke, thrusting, crushing, rushing, to prove to who what? That we don't love or know ourselves.

The Sahara's gone from green to gold. How many seasons saw Gods slashed and sold? And now, bold, you, confused negro retro pseudo greek freak/n on yo knees don't even know that

*behind the pale skin of the dog parading as god you seek are
the rhythms of Earth and Cosmos, U God Me.*

*When the light of your lucifer no longer shines, when you
realize the theft and lies behind the prize of the pale greek thief,
it will be Me: the Sun of Man you will seek.*

By the time she dropped the knowledge, she was a junior and had
started spending more and more time outside the campus gates with Soul in
the hood.

Soul held weekly community symposia and ran a tutoring and
counseling program for students throughout the week. He'd "done time" in
Howard, as he said. While he supported her academic mission, he
supplemented Howard's curriculum with his own. "Queen, check this out."
"This" could be an introduction to an underground conscious hip hop crew,
to Kemetic philosophy, or to an Ntozake Shange poem. After she graduated,
as valedictorian and with honors, she moved into Banneker Estates, a
rundown project, with Soul. Their community service work and her M.A.
study of African political science were intertwined and often
indistinguishable.

Soul expected to find her working on her M.A. thesis, when he came
home. Instead he found his woman weeping.

Rape? Theft? Assault? What violation had his skinny Queen crying? He
took her head between his large palms and held it to his chest. His smell—
sandalwood and myrrh—made her weep more. He looked into her eyes.

"What shall we name our baby?"

There on the rug she purchased at a flea market for $30, that she called
the tree of life, he re-planted his seed again and again and again.

"Ast. Ast. Ast."

Her scalp was near his nose; she felt his deep inhalations. In front of the
A Street Temple, he stood behind her, holding her, and said, "I love the way
your hair smells in the sun."

The next year as they lay in bed—she: doing some homework, he:
reading *The Famished Road*—she leapt up and ran to the bathroom. He
listened and heard his clippers. He crept to the bathroom and saw clumps of
TCB straightened hair falling like black snow on the white porcelain sink
and blue tile floor. Her concentration was intense. The clippers rode like
butter over her expertly molded head. When she had done the best should
could do, he finished her work, evened everything, lined her up, and
swabbed her neck down with alcohol. As she showered, he carefully
collected the hair and burned it.

Glistening, naked, and truly clean, she admired her reflection. He stood behind her, radiating in her glow, and said, "I was wondering when you was gonna cut that dead shit off."

The first thing you see is a mass of black curls, a veritable cap of them, glistening like satin. Then you see her perfect golden brown face. She is trying to smile. Her fists are in 2 perfect little balls. She has on a little pink dress. She is about 3 months old. She is the baby girl of the whole family. This is a favorite picture.

There is a picture of her in a gingham blue check dress decorated with red-haired Raggedy Ann images (Raggedy Ann was her favorite character). She hated having to take that picture because her Mother had fluffed her soft black hair into a buoyant cloud.

"It's so pretty, Baby!"

"I don't like Afros, Mommy," she said because self-hatred had already started changing her mind. All day she turned her lips down, so her smile is tentative on the picture. It seems she is overwhelmed by the buoyant hair on her head.

There is a picture of her with tiny "catch-n-catch," decorated with multi-hued rubber bands. She is in Arkansas, and she is smiling and running with arms open to embrace the world!

Before the picture was taken, she embraced the ritual with her Grandmother who, after she had adorned the last plait intoned, "Now, say, 'mo hair, better hair, longer hair.'"

"Mo hair, better hair, longer hair," she repeated, after Dear, knowing the ritual invocation would work.

And it would have, but she would wrap a huge terry cloth towel over her head, run to the large oval mirror framed in gold and admire her looped pastel hair. Tryna be barbie, or cher, 1.

And it would have worked, but she went from jherri curl to press-n-curl. She sported a long, flowing, greasy mane, that worked—til it went outta style, then a perm, too soon and too strong, burnt the sides of her hair out. To this she added Dark n Lovely's honey blonde.

"You look like 1 of those *hard* women," was her mother's measured critique.

Her hair was hard, stiff and tufted. She sculpted it with Stiff Stuff, and gilded it with spray paint. Her hair was as unhealthy as she was.

Her ritual frying, dying, and lying was scarring her scalp and her soul, but what is a beautiful New Afrikan trapped in Babylon to do?

Her hair finally recovered and started to grow. Long. Here's a shot of her at the Gulf of Mexico lookin like Janet with the wind blowing in her hair. Here she is sitting under a massive, slick, black beehive "wrap."

She had her own styles, her own identity but she couldn't find them because they were hidden under someone else's lyes.

"You have a beautiful pea-shaped head," he admired. Yes, Momma molded my head well, she smiled. Then she showered and emerged feeling new. She'd shaved years of trauma from her head and trapped the strands in a plastic Ziploc for remembrance. He caressed her head as they made love. She felt free! Sun free, free enough to stretch her arms in Arkansas!

But.

Should I grow it out? This ball fade is in. She had waves: "Sportin Waves!" in fact. What would happen if she grew it out? Could she get/keep a man? Would folk stare at, laugh at, admonish her? She stared at her perfectly shaped head in the mirror and decided.

"Baby Damballah," that was her answer when her department chair asked her what she called her hairstyle, "Baby Damballah." To achieve it, she would section small square parts and braid them. Later, she rolled them round a pencil. Baby Serpent Gods protecting her head.

As her hair grew, she experimented. She twisted variations on goddess braids. She fashioned bold knots, and cornrows, just like when I was a lil girl. Her mothers stopped asking, "When you gon press it out?" and started asking, "Can you do mine like that?" She would smile. Sometimes, she pulled her hair back and let it burst into a black crown-cloud. But she loved it best free, like her, and smiling in the Arkansas Sun!

"You sho got a head a hair on you!" The sun loved to kiss her hair.

There is a picture of her in Morocco. Strangely, in this racist country, where Arabs scream "Nigger!!" just like in America, she has freedom of hair. She loves this photo, because she looks exactly like her Mother. She is promising; there's a covenant in her smile. There is a black cloud on her head: It is symbolic of the origin of life and the depths of her power. She is wrapped in a blanket because it is cold, but she is shining. She outshines the minaret of the mosque. Her clitoral vibration is a call to prayer that crescendos in her hair. Look out! She's bout to come up a cloud!

She loosened the 4 snake thick plaits that trailed from her crown to her nape to peer out, tufted, over her shoulders, neck and back. Her hair had lost the crispness and shine she liked it to have. So she loosened it and prepared for the ritual: Washing My Hair. She liked uninterrupted peace and good music to boom as she felt the water cascade over her head and penetrate to her scalp.

Between her fingers, her hair was like loose shoals of partially combed cotton. So much of it! Yet, she hated losing 1 strand! She shampooed, wishing Milk Plus Six hadn't been discontinued (she still searched for it, reaching in back of dusty surplus store shelves for even an old bottle). She lathered her hair, twice, into a white cloud with a black base, lathering even her ears in her intensity. She lathered until the hair crinkled and shined and held water like coal miners clutched diamonds.

She rinsed her hair, which was springy and dense like a virgin forest, and massaged conditioner from her roots through to the end of each strong spiral. After rinsing and a towel wrap to absorb water, she oiled her scalp, added a leave-in conditioner and braided 6 massive Damballah in preparation for whatever style her mind could dream up.

She loosened her plaits with her fingers. As she looked at her reflection, she thought of how in Ghana people said she looked like a Fulani. Especially when she framed 4 huge twists that rode to the back of her head like Damballah-Hwedo squared with 2 skinny braids that ran from her widow's peak to her ears (good for breaking edges). Perhaps she was a Fulani, because she and Tracy had been handling *that* style since they were about 5. But there was 1 man, who, when she wore her beautiful high cotton boll, would religiously point to her head, and in the full depth and breadth of African negativity and hatred of natural hair, ask, "What is *that*?"

"My Crown." That was her answer, but what she wanted to say was: "The answer to self-hatred and negation" or "The manifestation of 360° of Manifest Blackness" or "Ask yo Momma." But she would simply smile a very private smile and say, "My Crown." She would go on, passion and power vibratin in her wake.

She would think about the few times that she was bold enough to "freestyle" on the oppressive African campus. With her hair fully fluffed out she strolled and sang "Sweet Thing," not only in praise of Chaka Khan, but also because that is who she was, "A Sweet Thing" (Kitu Kitamu). Each time she revealed her cloud, she was openly admired. 1 boy toasted her in front of her boyfriend, 1 sister broke the pose from the picture she was taking to exclaim, "Heeey!!!" She was too surprised and delighted to say anything else.

Now the plaits were loosened. She loved it this way, the huge rolls and ripples and crinkles fanning and undulating, whipping, standing and falling all over her head. She loved it like this. The Hair was a living thing. Like masses of butterflies resting and preparing for flight, flying. Altogether, her hair was like a heart. Parted in the center, the ripples came round and kissed her cheeks, tickled her ears.

He came in the bathroom; his face was hidden by her hair, but she knew he was there.

It is like the Ethiopic. Waves crashing and falling around her face. It is the ocean and it is also the sky. Yes, Eternity is this Woman's Hair. Eternity. I want to make love to her with her hair like this, he thought. "I want to make love to you with your hair like this," he said. She laughed and doves cooed in their nests. What will her hair say to me when I lose my fingers and knuckles in it? When I bury my nose in it? Can I find the source of this force? Let me try, he resolved. "Let me try," he said.

He paused as they giggled and fondled their way to the bed . . . Is her hair smiling? Yes, and it is a very private smile.

They made love with light because he liked to witness her in bliss. As he sank into the rhythms of ecstasy, he was shocked to find that her hair was squeezing his finger shafts. In time with his thrusts, her hair pulsed and throbbed, sighed and shuddered. Finally, with the two of them, it climaxed. He was lost in admiration for right there in the palms of his hands breathed a miniature cosmos, and it was smiling a very private smile.

Badu's nephew, Narmah, brought Hadizat, Badu, and the Old Man cool water from an earthen jug that bore the face of an ancestor; the water of life poured from the mouth.

"Hadizat, I have been waiting for you. I have much to show you."

Badu acted as translator. Seamlessly and in a pitch just lower than his elder's, he transformed the lyrical Dogon into English.

"Ahhhhh. That is the origin. It is the first word uttered by creation's Creator when she prepared the Pot and fertilized the Womb of All. Ahhhhh. This is what Mother said when she created all the planets, and the nebula, and the galaxies, and the stars, and this Earth and its land masses. Ahhhh and her daughter came on feet of ebony and brass up the great Womb of the Continent. Ahhh. She realized as she sat on the labia of the Womb giving birth, that she was Ahni. Her Daughter was Ahni, and her Daughter's Daughter was Ahni. When she witnessed her perfected reflection in triplicate—the recognition of Ahni, whose eye and Womb she was under and in, the eye and Womb her daughter was under and in, the eye and Womb her Daughter cast upon and held within, she said, "Ahhhh." This is the first sound. The essence of being, recognition of spirit, force and power. Ahhh is the vibration of the Womb of Origins.

Ah is the land of origins. Ah are also the original people. Ahni is the creator of all. Ah means totality; Ni means creator. You, child, are the manifestation of the Creator of Totality and the Totality of all Creation: Ahni.

"To gaze upon the Mother's home, our home, Ahstah, look here to Sigi Tolo," he raised his right hand and eyes to the sky studded with stars, "and then follow the 3 eyes south. There is the sphere of our origins.

"Ahtlna was the first civilization that Ahni created here. The Ahtlna made of this land a spectacular space of spiritual, telepathic, and astral power. When they thought, they built. With their thoughts they directed rivers, trees, metals; any and all elements would lend and bend themselves to their design. However, with 23 emi, their cipher was so strong and they developed so quickly that indolence set in. They ceased building and creation morphed into destruction. Their fragmentation and decadence caused fracturing within the Earth. Water took them under. However, the works of Ahtlna have never been forgotten, and many of their reincarnations join us here.

"When this planet righted itself, Ahni came forth again. She brought a new generation of Ah with 12 emi. They were also self-generating and while not as empowered as the Ahtlna, their force was phenomenal. With 12 rather than 23 emi, they would not slip into ennui but would work consistently to shine. We are the progeny of these Gods, and we are not alone. Our people are many, both here and in your home across the sea.

"We call those of us who were exiled and enslaved Tahn. The work that had been forgotten, foregone, and stalled here by all but a few of us Ancient Ones, you Tahn carry on to new levels. We have been witnessing your works. We see you shining.

"In many ways, you Tahn mirror the Ahtlna, but by inversion. Unlike the Ahtlna, with infinity seemingly at their disposal, you Tahn seem to have nothing. But you actually have everything. You have what you are, The Tahn: The Shining."

The Old Man wet his throat as did Badu. Ahni sat transfixed; she was astounded by what the Old Man was sharing.

"Ahni, our connections are both ancient and historic. My father's father told me that when he was an adolescent, his work consisted of 2 endeavors: alerting the village when the raiders were coming and signaling returnees who made it back home. You see, with our emilevel, our skill set is diverse. Many of us can transform ourselves into stones, the wind, insects, or flowers. Others can fly just as you see the buzzard fly. Some of us can communicate with and learn from flora, while others can commune with fauna. My grandfather, like everyone in our community, put his skills to work to assist those of us who had been stolen.

"Jaba and Maata are 2 ancestors who gained acclaim for their skills. They could fly physically and astrally; they could make themselves invisible; they could pass through matter, alter their matter; they could not be wounded; they could communicate between themselves and with others telepathically.

During the time of upheaval, Jaba and his sister, Maata allowed themselves to be captured. Once taken to America, they mentally and physically conferred with emideep comrades and shared their knowledge and skills. Jaba and Maata traveled to different communities to teach material equivalents of their spiritual powers to enslaved Africans.

"Father," Ahni started, her voice trembling, "my ancestors told these stories, stories of Flying Africans. I always wondered what happened to them, the 1's who flew back. Did they make it? Did they reach Africa? And what happened when they did?"

"Yes child. My father's father shined in the air so they knew that a safe land welcomed them. That was his work," the elder smiled at Ahni.

"Hundreds returned. Many went back to the lands of oppression to continue their work with the Tahn. Many of the Flying Ah were never in Africa but came straight from Ahni and returned to her. Many were killed and were reborn to continue the Work. Some were too devastated by what they endured to return, for every horror to be imagined on the Earth, the Tahn experienced! The searings, the rapings, the sodomy, the brandings, the lashings, the amputations, the beheadings, the forced building of an entire nation so that they could bear the privilege of being shunned in that nation," the Old 1 began to weep. "In this era of blissful forgetfulness, some of us know that to forget is to die. We will never forget.

"We have witnessed your rise from unimaginable atrocity. We have celebrated your religious innovations—the taking of an infinity and concentrating it into an approved imitation. We rejoice that you are now reveling in your true force. We've heard the power of the rhythms and rhymes encoded in your music so that only the spiritually inclined can fathom your messaging. Yes, we heard the call of the Tahn. We have witnessed the reformation of Kmt in Washington, D.C., your technological inventions and innovations such as refrigeration, the steam engine, the light bulb, the oil pan, the thermostat, so many technological advances! And of course, your physical, political, spiritual, and artistic thrusts for freedom, we have watched, echoed, listened, guided, and followed you.

Narmah came again, now bearing a covered, glazed clay pot. Beginning with the Old Man, each of the 3 took honey with 2 fingers. The child left.

"Ahni, this is the first of infinite discussions we shall have. The ways of Ah are yours and are opened unto you. You had been existing but you will begin thriving now—on all levels.

"You have 7 emi access naturally and normally but most of your cipher have been suppressed into a dormant stage."

"Why has that happened?"

"You have been living in the land of a spirit-crushing people, in a land that they fashioned from and maintained by oppression. But it is your spirit, your shining, your destiny—Ah destiny—that has led you here.

"Previously you sought solace in Nation of Islam and Sunni Islam. But you could find no peace in them."

Ahni nodded her head, "The teachings just didn't fit my soul."

"Your divinity rejected spiritual enslavement. Islam is a tool for control as is Christianity. They are not spiritual oases but all too transparent mirages. These—religions—are institutions of cultural, economic, and ideological control and spiritual excision. Only those devoid of spirit find fulfillment in them, thus your dissatisfaction.

"Both systems are truncated, perverted, bastardizations of the way of Ahni. The melanin deficient who have no cipher stole precepts and concepts they had not the acumen to comprehend and twisted and distorted the way into a tool of destruction.

It is tragic that, instead of recognizing that these things are antiway, many believe in and embrace them as the only way. But I'm getting ahead of myself," the Old Man chuckled. "Daughter, we have time," he enfolded her hands into his, "We *are* time."

Narmah, as if reading the Old 1's mind, or as if he were an extension of the elder, brought in food. Curried chicken with almond slices and spinach, rice with coconut milk and plantains were arranged on a platter. After the repast, the child brought the trio a calabash of honey wine.

"Father, you've prepared a tremendous feast for me. Food for my mind, body, and soul."

"And you've exercised my tongue beyond reason!" Badu jokingly scolded his elder.

"Well, a young man such as yourself cannot work too hard! Your father would be ashamed of you if he were here to witness your laziness." As the 2 men joked, Ahni was astounded. This elder was not father but *grand*father?! He looked so young! The Old Man winked at Ahni, rose, collected the dishes, and bid the couple good night.

She smiled at Badu. She wanted very much to hold him, to smell his unadorned flesh.

"Ahni." Badu's smile reflected the intensity of her own, "How do you like your new name?"

"I feel like I've stepped into my soul and it fits perfectly," she spoke from a source of sincerity, a lost-found reservoir of identity. "But I have a spectacular amount of growing to do to fill my shoes."

"Don't worry. We are with you." She looked into his eyes and felt just that, that Badu and the Old Man had always been and would always be with her.

Badu sat beside Ahni and smiled, "It's 1 thing to fall in love; it's another to have the Work as the love of your life. How do you feel?"

After a moment of thought, she replied, "Except for 1 issue, I feel completely at peace. I feel I've waited 300 years for this."

"I just wanted to know from your lips," Badu caressed her shoulder. "But please," he continued, "what is the issue disturbing your mind?"

"Why are so many Caucasians here?" Badu nodded slowly.

"You are astute, Ahni." He sighed. "They are like a plague. They come to buy spirituality," his voice was too resonant with sadness for any degree of chagrin to inhabit his words.

"There were some among us, elders advanced in years who held great knowledge but who lacked wisdom and understanding. Like the Ahtlna, they began a retrogressive slide. These elders opened many of the doors of the cosmic wisdom of Ah to various Yurugu. These elders hoped to use knowledge to build bridges of understanding between Ah and Ogo. They forgot that understanding and uniting are not Ogo's way. Once these mutants understood the depth of the information our elders shared with them, they published their findings—not for holistic evolution, to build their names, careers, and bank accounts. Now hundreds and thousands of Yurugu journey here: nesting, infesting, reeking, and leeching. They come seeking, as they did in Kmt, what they can never attain nor understand, yet will eternally covet and hope to destroy.

"We are ridden with tourists as the nasty are ridden with roaches. They've come, smelling like horses or, alternatively, glue, to investigate, interview, retire, and revel in their myths of superiority. With our misguided senses of hospitality—and with a pitiful lust of euros and dollars—we have tolerated and amused these entities. As a result, Dgn is now as fragmented as Kmt was before its destruction. Yet there will be a difference between Dgn and Kmt: Dgn will bury these beasts in the sand."

"You've had a long and exciting day, Ahni. I want you to rest well, for our work is infinite."

Ahni and Badu sank into the bed and into each other's arms and minds.

That night Badu entered Ahni's dreams. He took her on a tour of Dogon, starting with his family's compound and his ancestors' graves.

This is the resting place of my mother and father. Father was not like our family. Mother met him on Senegal; he was a fisherman. He lived mostly in Senegal. He would come here about 1 week every 2 months. Mother lived both here and in Senegal. The Old Man saw to my upbringing.

My father died 7 years ago when his vessel capsized during a storm. My mother died when the vessel she hired to search for my father's boat sank. Ahni stopped as a wave of grief engulfed her. She grabbed Badu's shoulders and the realization hit her. Yes, he confirmed, my father summoned her to join him. They are together. They are working with Ahni on Ahstah.

This is the Old Man's wife, my Grand Mother. Her name is Annar. She saw you coming before she died. She is with our children.

He took her to 1 large egg-shaped mound outside the village. She paused before observing, This is a larger version of the mound in our room. Yes. This is our home of the Mother. Many come here for fertility. But some come to meditate, rejuvenate, or confer with Ahni.

When she woke, she sensed fulfillment and resonance. The vibrations were her own and Badu's who was inside her. She arched her back to engulf him and wove her right arm around his waist feeling the rhythms of his muscles and the contour of his torso rising and falling in rhythm with his pelvis and her own. She urged him deeper. Her left hand was in his right hand—fingers laced, palms kissing.

She was called Daughter by everyone although she responded to no 1 verbally. No 1 thought her rude. Daughter's silence was as accepted as her glistening presence. She became 1 with the community. She joined her age-mates hunting and fishing although she herself ate no meat. Daughter washed her clothes and dishes and body in the river with her new people. But the majority of her time was spent with Kofi and the Elders.

It was not unusual to find Daughter lying on Wakynam's back, her head facing her right shoulder, her arms on either side of Wakynam's neck her toes cutting twin paths through the water.

They dismembered me, Wakynam revealed. That is why I took this form. Protection. Recollection. I created a place where healing gives birth to totality.

I was the first person cut in my village, Singbeh told Daughter. In that era, it was the men who held their daughters down and hacked them. After I was butchered, I heard Wakynam's call. I was the first to join her. From the moment I healed, I have summoned boys and girls to come and reclaim wholeness.

I was scheduled to be cut, divulged Nankrom, along with all the other boys of my age group. But when I watched my twin brother bleed to death while the cutting continued, I screamed, fought, and ran. I brought shame on my father. He banished me, but my brother's spirit and I will ever be grateful for Wakynam for providing us, all of us, with a home.

They revealed their histories, offered their truths, uncovered old wounds, and shared healing methods. Daughter knew she was home.

Kofi—his eyes as bright with love as hers were large and pain-laced—was her constant companion. He was undergoing rigorous training to become 1 with the circle. Most of his mates only saw the glitter shining a nation away on the coast. The rest had little stamina for such training. But Kofi bore the blood of keepers of the way and trod his life-path with pride.

Their training was multi-tiered. On the elders' instructions, Kofi and Daughter went deep into the bush, near the foot of the mountain in search of particular healing plants. Armed with tools that ranged from tweezers to machetes, they cut bark strips, collected seeds, leaves, and roots that could not be found near the village, and they planted, replenished, and transplanted flora.

Sometimes Kofi would finger a plant with wonder, "I dreamt of this flower, Daughter; it can cure malaria."

Daughter would nod her head, smile at Kofi's forgetfulness, and add the plant to their basket. Sometimes she summoned Kofi or took a handful of roots to him. After inhaling the roots, medicines revealed themselves.

Smells like tumbayo.

"Yes" tumbayo, but stronger. It is a different species, Kofi had to remind himself that Daughter needed no words. This may be good for many aliments.

Catarrh, yaws, worms—

Yes! Depending upon the dosage. We must show the Elders.

Other times, their training took them to the lagoon where they floated for hours with only their noses visible just above the surface. They went on physical and astral excursions. They would lose themselves in tree branches and listen to Wakynam share history.

The crocodile is our favored form for it suits our purpose, clime, history, and cause. In the past, long ago, thousands of seasons gone, we could take any form. Our bodies were as malleable as our minds. We were representative of everything in the cosmos, and all could be found in us.

Our minds, not feet or cars or airplanes, our minds took us where we wanted to go. Like *that*!

That was a jaw snapping that echoed off the baobab trees far in the distance.

Mother, what happened? Where have these powers gone?

They are still within many of us, but there is a drive to crush the power. Indeed, the reason that so many of us have been mutilated is because certain people know that the clitoris is a pod of power. Daughter, initially, women impregnated themselves. Clitorises were long and filled with biological and cosmic power.

In time, the clitoris shrank to its present length. Its biological properties were transferred to the testes and penis. But the cosmic power remained within the clitoris; in some, the force became concentrated and even more powerful.

The weak among us began devolving and following the paths of those without melanin. They demanded the subjugation of women physically, spiritually, culturally, and biologically. Husbands began hacking power from their wives. Mothers began butchering their daughters. In an attempt to reify a false construct of power, father's removed their son's foreskins.

Kumba is a land where what has been excised can be re-membered, where the fragmented can heal and be made whole. It is a land where sources of self can be developed without fear or shame or contrived restrictions.

What differences have you noted between Kumba and your village, Daughter?

In Mapu there is a labor division. My mother and the other women take care of the homes: wash dishes and clothes, care for children, prepare meals. The women also plant and harvest crops, and many women trade.

And the men? your father?

Father stays mostly in the town hall in the day, discussing issues. He comes home, drinks palm wine or apketeshi, and relaxes with his friends. Sometimes men hunt and fish, but if they don't, women buy meat and fish with money they make from their trading.

But here in Kumba, women and men hunt, collect flora, and fish together. There is no division of labor. We all wash clothes and take turns cooking.

I wonder what the people of my village would think of Kumba, Daughter mused. Sometimes, I wish my mother and father could see me now.

You are missing them.

I now have a sister, an infant. I worry. . .

Return, Daughter. You will go in peace and you will return in peace, with whomever you return. Will Kofi accompany you?

Kofi felt her question his mind.

Yes, of course I must accompany you.

Go see your sister whose spirit is summoning you. We are always here.

With a machete apiece, fresh and dried fruit, 2 thick leather water bags, dried fish, and 2 cover cloths apiece, Kofi and Daughter set out 3 days after their discussion with Wakynam.

Since having come to Kumba, Daughter had fully healed and had matured into a beautiful and wise young woman, and yet, her mind was silent as they embarked on their journey. Daughter strode forward, mashing her feelings into the dirt path.

"Daughter, look!" Kofi pointed up. Daughter's eyes followed his finger and she gazed at an expansive cumulonimbus cloud.

It has the same gray streaks as your aura when you came to us.

Daughter felt like she was being pressed into a tight space. Her breathing became constricted. She stumbled on a root. Blood trickled from her right foot into the red dust.

Kofi stooped to aid her. She sat down and he cleaned her foot with water. He gathered timitan leaves, crushed them, and pressed them to the wound to disinfect the cut and speed healing.

She stared from her foot to the cloud.

Shall we go back?

No.

Holding hands, not to support Daughter, who would have been disappointed if Kofi thought her weak, but to comfort and bond, the pair continued their journey.

Around the ìrókò wrapped in white cloth deep in the back courtyard were the festivities. Roasted mutton, fried fish, grilled chicken, okro stew, palmwine, paw paw, mangoes, olives, ogogoro, and rice yam were brought out. Stews swollen with crabs, shrimp, and fish and seasoned with ginger, nutmeg, efirin, red, white, and black pepper and salt were brought out. Spice! Àràká and Ṣàngó must have spice!

The newlyweds, decked out in red garments and gold adornments, sat amidst their friends and family. Ọ̀ṣun emerged from her compound in a flowing sheer blue dress. She looked a reflection of the twilight sky. She congratulated Ṣàngó and welcomed the new wife to the home with dignity and only a tinge of jealousy. Ọbà, the shy but skilled 1, was adorned in a dress of silver chain mail. She embraced Àràká in welcome.

Ògún, having lost this woman amongst women, this complement of complements, strutted into the courtyard unsure of himself. When he saw Ṣàngó, his mood changed, abruptly, so much so that the drummers and flutists paused. In fact, everyone halted at the sounds issuing from his mouth. Ògún was laughing? Ògún was laughing!

"Fire breathing coward!" he slapped Ṣàngó on the back.

"Metal brained bastard!" Ṣàngó retorted.

"I've yet to see another force move as fast as you! Your flight alone put fear into me." The signifying between the men turned the crowd's astonishment into a higher level of celebration. The musicians fell upon their instruments with gusto.

"If I'd held a mirror up to your face that day, I'm sure you would have broken my record," Ṣàngó was comfortable as victor-via-warrior-wife and joked freely.

"Ah, the music is sweet," Ògún murmured. He turned from Ṣàngó, gazed around, and snatched Ọbà and led her to the dancing arena. Soon the courtyard was alive with singing and laughing and intricate dance steps. Ọ̀ṣun, who had been moving with grace and reserve began to roll her hips with abandon. Ṣàngó and Ògún soon found themselves facing 1 another. Everyone cleared a space so the 2 rivals could battle in choreo-aesthetics. Àràká chuckled as she looked at them, her men. The meeting 9 weeks ago was quite different, she smiled.

Ògún entered the clearing like an earthquake, roaring and wielding 2 clubs a spear and a machete. Àràká and Ṣàngó stood side by side. Àràká's eyes gleamed, glistened, and reflected the clanking metal. Her nature rose. He is so powerful. She cut her eye at her lover and saw his knees shaking with fear.

Ògún's weaponry was spinning and whistling like the Niger set to boil. Àràká glanced at Ṣàngó to gage his level of preparation but—he was gone. Her love was in the wind! Àràká turned to Ògún and smiled.

"Woman! It's me and you!" Ògún growled.

"Shut up and fight."

Àràká brought out her club and stood with her left leg slightly bent at the knee and her right leg prepared to thrust her forward, forth. Ògún tossed aside his 7 foot spear and his hatchet with its gleaming curved 3 foot blade. They were mere toys. He summoned his own instrument, the twin of Àràká's.

Cha!!! The clubs met with a wrangling clash of 2 irresistible forces. Àràká did a front-flip over Ògún's head; she was as agile in the air as a dove. She felt a tremor in her clitoris.

"Ah!" she purred. My husband is truly my equal. "It is a shame you didn't recognize my power, Ògún. I loved you in ọrun and here, but you wanted me as your whipping post. Fool! Cross fool! We could have birthed the world anew."

Sweating and holding his stance, Ògún cried, "Woman, come back to my home, *our* home. I will decorate it as you wish, come and bear my children. Àràká, my love for you is vast! There is no secret, no knowledge I withheld from you. Look! The very staff that you would use to kill me I made for you. Come to me," his arms opened for her.

Àràká's eyes of steel softened. But no, Ògún had none of Ṣàngó's flash none of his charm. The earlobes dipped in gold tinkling as his body rocked with hers, shuddering as he thrust upward. Caressing the staff of power, she recalled the braids inlaid with cowries and coral snaking across her lover's shoulders. And Ògún? Yes, he was the strongest of all. Why those arms are like elephant thighs; his neck as thick as the trunk of a baobab. But the man is oblivious to human passions. He would come to me like a lion to its mate and then back to that damn forge!

"You were more than enough in ọrun, but here? Your charms are as rusty tin."

"Àràká, I warn you, don't vex me!"

"Damn you and your warning!" Her ire was invoked. "My own Mother never beat me as you did!" with that recollection, a warrior's fire ruptured in Àràká. She lunged low and struck upwards. Ògún, with his legs parted wide, seemed receptive to the blow.

CHIIINNNnnnnn

The staffs connected again—flaming ingots flew through the air.

"Àràká! You would destroy my manhood?"

"Baby, I will scatter your legacy. I will pour the waters of the Ethiopic on your forge's fire!"

"You and which 601 Ìrúnmọlẹ̀?" Ògún laughed and the sky shook.

"Ìyàmi Òṣòròngà."

"Little girl, I bedded your mother to beget you!"

Enlisting a 3 pronged attack, Àràká's teeth of Àjẹ́ sucked Ògún's intestines as her mind entered his and introduced puling static. She took to the air. Áàjálayé.

Ògún's roar of pain was the trumpeting of a million elephants. He clutched his stomach and his eyes rolled around in their sockets.

Àràká, with her lance on high, zoomed down from the heights prepared to make ultimate contact. What!? She felt her teeth strike metal, her mind was forced back into its own domain. She smiled and descended upon her prepared opponent.

Ògún dipped down and struck upward with the might of a moving mountain.

Shlllaaang!!!

They backed up, squared off, and faced each other again. Their chests were heaving in time; their eyes were locked in an unblinking stare. Each mind was thinking its twin's thought. Ògún rushed forward and struck a left-sided blow for his pride simultaneous to Àràká's twin left-sided blow for her freedom.

Both connected.

When the smoked cleared, there were 2 piles of stones: 1 of 7, 1 of 9. Each was pile smoking and red-centered.

When Ṣàngó heard silence, he crept back to the clearing. When he saw the smoldering stones, he ran to get Òsanyìn, the healer.

The Crippled King laughed long and hard when he heard Ṣàngó's exposition. His laughter was so light that only the birds lighting in nearby branches heard him. As he hopped with 1 leg and a cane to the scene, he wheezed to Ṣàngó, "Oh, mighty 1! Where were you at the time of this battle?" Òsanyìn's eyes crinkled with mirth.

"Fool, Heal my wife or you will have only a head to roll about on like Èjìogbè!"

"Patience, patience," Òsanyìn, still rippling in delight squatted and brought forth 4 sacred seeds. He ground them in his calabash and spit in the concoction.

Òsanyìn sprinkled the mixture over the 7 stone pile and chanted, "Blacksmith of Ọ̀run! He who walks all over the Earth! Ally of the man with a quick hand. He who kills the husband on the forge of fire (here, he winked at Ṣàngó). He kills the wife on the hearth!

Ògún, didé!!"

Ògún stood as if he'd just come for a visit and was waiting for a seat.

Òsanyìn stood over the 9 stones and chanted, "The wife who is more severe than the husband. Àràká! Known in ọrun as Àràká Áàjálayé!

Whirlwind that uproots trees. Àjẹ́ so fierce none may behold her face. Swirling hurricane of many colors. Àràká who upstages Ṣàngó in severity (another wink)! Didé, Áàjálayé, arise!!!

Àràká was restored—cool, calm, and composed.

Ọ̀sanyìn stepped back, gazed at the resurrected duo and declared: "Ògún meéje; Àràká mẹsàn-án." And he dipped and hobbled back into the forest.

Gazing at Ògún and Ṣàngó, now dancing, Àràká laughed.

Ẹ fọ̀ wọ̀ mi, wọ̀ mí o!
Ẹ fọ̀ wọ̀ mi, wọ̀ mí o!

That wasn't coming from the flutes. Àjẹ́ was summoning her. Àràká rose and left the party.

By the time she returned, the moon was making its descent. She crept into the sleeping compound and noticed that all traces of the party were gone.

Àràká bathed, and the cold water was refreshing. She didn't dry herself completely but let the night air kiss and cool her skin as she made her way to her husband.

She curled into Ṣàngó like a baby in the womb, but something was wrong. He wasn't receptive. Hard as Ògún.

"Everything before was preparation for this moment. There are 2 councils you will now meet."

Ìyá was almost chanting as she and her acolyte soared over the thatched roofs and tree tops, "The first is the council of Àjẹ́. After that, you will meet Ìyáńlá privately."

The women ascended as silently as the dawn. Could they have been seen, they would have appeared to be standing, their heads slightly inclined. When they reached the stratosphere, they drifted to a stop. They stood in front of a magnificent crossroads.

"Orítà mérìndìnlógún."

"Yes. 8 roads go to the cosmos. 8 roads go to the Earth."

At the center of the crossroads, 16 hues became 1: the pure Blackness of the cosmos. The women entered and became 1 with the center.

As they rose, the atmosphere became lighter and the journey smoother. The women arrived at a grand meeting hall. The space was beyond luxurious. A waterfall of cosmic matter rolled forth spewing wisdom, brilliance, and immortality. On either side was lush emerald grass interspersed with flowers of violet-red, marine, magenta, and dusk-kissed pink. Low couches of velvet as deep and plush as the snow of Killemanjaro rose from the ground. Terrestrial and spiritual animals gamboled and grazed. Here was a gazelle, there an elephant of azure. A golden goat and a mauve monkey were deep in conversation. Butterflies with children's faces fluttered by. Stars visited, glowing and throbbing as they shared wisdom.

Chatting orally and astrally in multitudinous frequencies were the Ìrúnmọlẹ̀. Ọṣun wore a sea foam blue tunic that was so sheer it could have been sewn from the sky. She laughed and brass chimes tinkled. Her skin, blue-black and resplendent, glowed. Her hair, woven with brass filings was braided into a crown of hearts. Ògún, sporting an iridescent amber and black suit, conferred with Ọ̀ṣun. Around his waist was a belt of power. A scythe and machete laid gracefully on each of his hips. Next to them was an anvil and hammer. Just inside his thighs were a knife with a needle-sharp point and a hatchet. Jutting in front of his pelvis, the head resting on his own penis' shaft was its magnificent twin. Its head was studded with diamonds, the shaft consisted of the purest and hardest obsidian.

In a suit of clover woven so fine there was no seam, no gap, no break in its rhythm, was Ọ̀sanyìn. On his right side stood a brass staff crested by 16 golden birds who surveyed the gathering; in his left hand he carried a calabash of pewter that contained the 4 seeds of life. He was conversing with the Ọọ̀ni of Ifẹ̀.

Èṣù, transmogrifying each minute, was decked out in black platform boots and a black and red jumpsuit. The flair of his cuffs and sleeves undulated with his every gesture. The right side of his garment was red, and the material was as fluid as blood; the left side of his apparel was the melanin richness of orítà mérìndìnlógún. Instead of a seam uniting the red and black sides of his suit, ties of silver twinkled down his midsection. Èṣù's penis jutted from his body as sleek and black as the night. The head was 7 inches in diameter, the shaft a full foot in length. When Èṣù became no bigger than a mouse, his massive penis retained its size.

Olódùmarè was seated on a plush red chaise entwined around and within Òṣùmàrè, who radiated with 16 hues coursing through her body. The loving, squeezing, undulating pair was busy creating a new galaxy.

The Ìyálóde and the Apèènà spoke in high voices attracting Èṣù and Egúngún to their conversation. Ọṣọ́ọ̀si broke away from meditations with Ìyá Orò and the Aláàfin Ọ̀yọ́ to broach an issue with Ìyá Mápò.

Out of the corner of her eye, she saw a figure coming. She was stunning. Her dress could only be described as a controllment of the sea. Slate blue and frothing, the dress moved of its own accord. The garment was mesmerizing. Yes! There were iridescent golden, silver, and vermilion fish darting throughout the dress. Yemọja smiled and her seashell teeth tinkled. Hair. She had hair for days—a thick and spiraling black cloud glistening with diamond water droplets.

Ọmọ Ìyàlájẹ́ was mesmerized by this woman. She was her mother. She had her face. She was her daughter. By gazing at her she was looking through curvilinear time at all the lineage of her being, all being, all time.

She embraced her Self and fell into Her arms for 3 eternities. During her plummet, Yemọja revealed All to her. All. She awakened

in a world of spine splintering agony. Chained Africans were screaming, writhing, and being branded. Sons, mothers, daughters, and fathers were stacked like timber in pens. Women, children, and men were being raped under the enraged eye of the sun. Heads of decapitated warriors threatened from poles. A mutant walked by wearing a belt of black penises.

She was aghast. What world is this? How did such a state befall my people? What work am I to undertake in this abyss? How did these skinless beasts come to destroy my people? Her mind was clouded with questions as thick as the smoke rising from the branded beaten bodies.

Why not kill all these skinless slavers, these beasts?

And what of our own slavers? Her second mind queried. What of those of us strolling and grinning alongside these aberrations? There they are, her mind directed her vision, holding their own mothers to receive a red hot brand; holding still their sons so that their anuses can be penetrated.

They deserve astonishing deaths.

She sprang like a panther and sank her teeth into the jugular of the beast nearest her. A rain of blows engulfed her like a tidal wave. She regained consciousness in agony. Her cheeks were streaked like a child's as her tears cut paths through the dirt and soot on her face, but her eyes were fire. She lunged at another mutant, but she was beaten, manacled, and dragged through the courtyard by her hair. Groin punches, kidney kicks, and razor lashings propelled her into a dungeon where hundreds of her waited in chains.

While the Ah were consumed with their ceaseless efforts, everyone stopped and bore witness as the first sign that had been foretold came to pass: The green river cresting the Continent became sluggish and brackish and finally stood still.

Gnarled and water-starved brambles fought for life along a narrow and shallow bog that had previously flowed with vitality. The drying sun of the day and the stunning cold at night ended the gropings of roots living on the river's banks and killed shoots still glowing in the Earth's womb. Shuddering and weeping flora folded their arms across 1 another's backs in mourning. Dust rushed to wrap the surviving plants in its comforting embrace. That embrace became a blanket that not only absorbed all moisturizing tears but also clogged and choked and buried all that had thrived at and in the river.

The undulating burble of life that the river had laughed as it rolled across the Continent was replaced with the infernal sigh of trillions of powder-fine stones that eddied, valleyed, fanned, frolicked, and killed everything they touched. The result was land upon which nothing could grow—except more sand. Waves and waves of sand; golden dunes and alabaster rifts and valleys. Minute grains that multiplied into snakes, mazes, and fans of yet more sun burnished sand. Ecru, auburn, and sienna mounds moved across the land in a celebratory funeral train that forever mourned the loss of water while celebrating the triumph of death.

The next sign to come to pass was the reduction in the sun's intensity and in the sun's and Earth's radio, magnetic, and micro waves and ultra-violet rays. Most of the Ah regulated their biochemical rhythms to the ecological changes. However, some did not have the emi capacity for such adjustment. Consequently, there was an increase in textile manufacturing, the harnessing of fire for warmth, and the construction of ecologically attuned dwellings that used the heat of the day to provide warmth at night and, conversely, used the cool of the night to make homes comfortable during the day.

The planet cooled by $30°$ over a period of 300 years. The appearance of snow on Ta Ntr's mountain was the most ominous sign of all.

And then, it came.

It had a humanoid form but was, in every respect, different from the Ah. The outer covering of the entity was almost non-existent and was so thin that nearly all its internal organs and veins could be seen. Its translucent skin was covered with fur like that of a baboon, but sparser. With this fur, the beast's biology attempted to compensate for its lack of protecting and empowering melanin.

Its genotypic and phenotypic structures showed ample evidence of cross-breeding with another organism. But even more disturbing, although quite logical, was that the entity had absolutely no vibration.

The Ah were a people conversant with mountains, stars, planets, streams, grass blades, nebula, clouds, leopards, molecules—all life forms: They had never before encountered something that was living yet had no inner life, no vibration, no spirit, at all.

Here, sharing their space was a soulless form? They had never imagined the like. There was no astral potential. A scan revealed its pituitary and pineal glands to be as biospiritually barren as the sand that now promenaded across the Continent's basin.

The entity revealed that its species had erected nothing on any scale but was residing in clusters of caves a continent away. Apparently the snow now cresting Ta Ntr's mountain was abundant there. The Ah, never having cause to visit areas of utter desolation, had noted the spot mentioned by the thing and had dismissed it as fruitless. There was no emi, Ahni's rays were not strong there, and all existence there was either fragile or brutal.

The thing said that when its kind had devoured all life in the immediate vicinity, they ventured out of the caves in search of food. As they sought life to feed upon, the herd journeyed far from the caves, farther than they had gone before. Many of them were killed on the journey by stronger animals, by disease, or by stronger members of the herd who would corner, slay, and devour weaker members.

After migrating several years in this fashion, the beasts arrived at a cape that jutted toward the Continent of Ah. They were dazzled by the edifices, harmony, and productivity of civilization. After a discussion, the mutants hollowed out a rotted tree trunk and sent across the waters the entity now before the Ah.

They have been able to do so much with their lands! We do nothing. It thought, straining the tendons in its neck to better view the immense monuments and architecture of Kmt. Even their outcoverings are jeweled! It pains my eyes to gaze upon them; they shine so!

How do they keep their teeth so long? it marveled. I thought that after 1's genitals developed, 1's teeth should have turned black and fallen out, yet theirs are brilliant and strong.

Everything here is orderly. Our grunts, groans, and brays are not heard here. But here is a sound that is married to feeling that I cannot describe. That sound and feeling is everywhere, engulfs everything. There is also a *force* all about them and this land, the air . . .

That edifice is fantastic, like steps to the sky, and so beautifully decorated! I've never seen such colors, such stones! How are they able perfectly carve and expertly position such immense stones and structures? I must tour this land!

It is completely ignorant.

Did you notice that it has no soul, no emi?

The scent of this thing is unbearable! It smells like 5 types of feces! I can't stand this. I must take leave. Many Ah agreed and vacated.

Speaking its language, an Ah asked: "What created you?"

"Our soft ones birth us. At first when they dripped red, we would kill them. Ha. Ha. Ha. Ha."

The Ah raised a collective left eyebrow.

"The dying ones would tell us of our origins. The first 1 of us was ranging and rooting with our ancestors who have big bellies that sway near the ground. In the same way as all our kind before, our ancestor sucked the teat with the brood and ate feces, roots, and carcasses along with the brood. But he had deformities that would not allow him to keep up with his family when they went on their rangings.

1 day his frustration was so great he refused to eat his breakfast of feces or roll in the mire. His family left him in his despair and went to root for food. Our ancestor examined the long, awkward extremities dangling where his family had short limbs. He was preparing to hack off his limbs with a jagged rock so that he would be the same as his family when a cougar leaped from a tree and prepared to attack him. His fear was so great, he stood up! The cat, upon seeing such a tall opponent, fled. When our ancestor later caught up with his family, he was walking shakily on his extended legs. His family grunted in amazement.

"Our ancestor noticed various differences and similarities between himself and his family. For example, their skin and hair were the same, but his hair grew quicker and thinner and his skin was thinner than their own. Copulating organs were the same though, and when he felt the need to copulate he, like all the others turned upon the form nearest to him and entered an available cavity. But the most striking similarity was his desire to eat—eat his family members. This insatiable urge came over him the day he witnessed his mother eat 2 of her most recent litter. He followed his mother's example by eating her." It grinned and phlegm-green saliva glistened on the black stumps in its mouth.

The Ah decided not to discuss their origins or any aspect of their work with it.

"You are welcome here for 3 suns."

On the outskirts of the city was the waste processing plant. A group of Ah guided Yurugu to the site and its eyes lit up. There was no need to ask it if the accommodations were to its liking.

So this is it: Yurugu. A scanning revealed internal organs similar to Ah, but its DNA was compromised: Myriad mutations danced on its helixes. Its biochemical, physical, and intellectual capacities were all either diminished or stunted. The beast was absent all melanin and serotonin. There was no possibility for esoteric communication, education, or elevation.

"Can you imagine," 1 of the Ah said at a meeting concerning Ogo, "being descended from hogs? I wonder what genetic aberrations will surface in its future generations."

"Actually, there is the possibility of genetic upgrading," said 1 Ah from Kmt. "If our genes crossed with its, the result would be increased melanin and serotonin."

"Perhaps," a Kng scientist mused, "but there is also the potential for disaster. The product of the experiment could be a most devious, crude, heinous entity with powerful spiritual capability."

"I would think twice before attempting to 'complete' Yurugu, for it is, as Ahni has said, inherently incomplete," an Ah from Dgn reasoned.

"We already have progeny with reduced emi. How can we justify attempts to enhance or evolve a beast that will precipitate our destruction when we have so much work to do to prepare our unborn?"

"Perhaps if we could alter its genetic structure, we could alter its negativity and the lessen its capacity for destruction."

"Our focus must be the protection and elevation of Ah," an artist from Jubah was resolute.

"We must thoroughly comprehend them to protect ourselves. Perhaps a group of us should follow it home," the Ah of Kmt suggested.

"A good idea."

"Necessary."

The Ah decided on a 3 pronged expedition. 1 group would accompany Ogo back to its herd. Another group would confer with Ahni about Yurugu. A third group would tour the Earth to see what other entities were developing.

I did not discuss its origin to you because I wanted Yurugu to reveal to you its truth from its own mouth.

During my creation of the various human beings who people this planet, I incrementally reduced the dominant genotypic and phenotypic attributes of the Ah. These reductions resulted in diverse types of human beings with unique cultural and physical traits. However, the beings that were created from only recessive genes and mutated genetic recombinations are marked with physical melanin deficiencies and genetical and chromosomal abnormalities. Not only do they have no souls and no capacity for spiritual development, but some boast an extraordinary capability for destruction and devolution.

It may seem ironic, but this entity, known as Yurugu or Ogo because it is an aberration, an anomaly, will, with its works of destruction and degeneration, provide the catalyst and impetus for the Ah to fully manifest their divinity.

The nations you have built here, like those we have established on all planets throughout the cosmos are, stupendous educational centers. It is clear what we can do without encumbrance, but what can we do when facing insurmountable odds? How will we respond when tossed into a bottomless pit of abomination? When Yurugu's destructions have fragmented and demoralized this planet and all of its inhabitants, how will we institute recreation and foment revolution? This is the wisdom we must obtain to ensure the continuity of the cosmos.

Yurugu will push our progeny beyond their limits; and there, in an apparent oblivion, our offspring will reach into the limitless Self and into the cosmos and grasp and craft essential restorative tools, many of which are intangible and will ever elude Yurugu. When our progeny / our selves take up these tools, the identities that they construct from their inherent divinity will confirm to Ogo, for all eternity, that its existence is nothing more than a living death for which there is no burial, no end.

I am sure that you have noticed a diminishment of some powers and an increase of others. Be not alarmed. I'm preparing Ah for the future. Many Ah will retain full emispan; however, a significant number of Ah will become more inclined to the methodologies of Yurugu for 2 purposes: to aid Yurugu and to aid Ah.

Yurugu will undertake a campaign of global physical and psychological rape that will leave many Ah lost. After divorcing themselves from their spiritual inheritance and adopting the ways of Ogo, many Ah will be incapable of mental, personal, communal, or spiritual evolution. They will be as barren as Ogo. No seed planted in them will grow because they will have excised their spirits from their selves.

A time will come when we and what we have built will exist only as fables and myths in the minds of our progeny. These brilliant edifices and sites of power will be covered by sand, water, and weeds as Yurugu bends the Earth and its inhabitants to its will.

The Ah who will struggle to re-member our works to our progeny will be branded esoteric or backward. At the same time that Yurugu will help divorce the spirit and soul from Ah, it will be rummaging through the remains of our 12 sites hoping to seek and suck knowledge like the parasite it is, but it will understand nothing.

Yurugu will pervert the meaning of your words and philosophies and babble lies about what Ah has erected. It will actually claim to have founded and built Kmt. All of the Ah doubled over with laughter at this, and the mirth that rose from their bellies and sprang from their mouths was so resonant it gave birth to 99,999 planets.

Yes, my Gods, and to reify its lies, Yurugu will physically extract our living libraries and place them in their barren halls. Yurugu does not understand that the physical books are copies of the spiritual tomes embedded in all Ah bones and souls.

While Ogo struggles to revise and recast reality, misled Ah progeny will be striving to master the ludicrous distractions of Yurugu. Millions of Ah will be forced to attend institutions called "schools" where they will undergo intensive training to memorize the lies Yurugu will weave about its origins and contributions to this planet. These centers will be bastions of the study of deception, and Yurugu will make this training compulsory in the demented fragmented world it will dominate.

Mother, what can we do? How can we fight these atrocities?

There is nothing to fight, Ahni smiled. There are cycles in evolution, and this phase is of particular importance because it will reveal to us our resilience and our ability to rebound. What we learn from these struggles will help us fortify and sustain the cosmos.

Yurugu devoured, defecated, and redevoured its destiny, and it will attempt to force the Ah and Tahn to do the same. It will convince the Ah to do the unthinkable: to excise and toss away the nodule of power, the clitoris. Yes, she nodded as the Gods gasped, in cultures where the hatred of females is part of the worldview, males will demand all external female genitalia be hacked off. All Ah cocked their heads in disbelief. What is more, in their efforts to force their aberrant construct of gender on the world, males will excise the foreskins of their penises.

The horror of excision will leave females in a morass of psychosexual trauma. Forming healthy sexual relationships with the self and others will be nearly impossible. Even worse, women's lives will consist of cycles of spiraling agony as they struggle to pass urine and menstrual blood through a tiny hole and are forced to submit to excruciatingly painful sex with men. Childbirth will be the equivalent of a death sentence for many women.

In addition to males starting life with the trauma of an unnecessary, painful, and slow-to-heal surgery, the excision of the foreskin will reduce sexual sensitivity and stimulation; this will move many men to violently force their penises into any orifice of any person—or animal—in their vicinity. As Yurugu's reign reaches its apex, sexual violence will be as common as clouds, and millions will act exactly as Yurugu did when it was rooting in caves and eating and copulating with its porcine kin.

This information stunned the Ah into a contemplative state so complete that the cosmos stilled its rotations and revolutions of 9 full seconds.

Ahni continued to describe the train of atrocities that would roll over the planet: Ogo will convince the millions who will come to populate this world that it—an aberration devoid of creative abilities—is the supreme life form on this planet and a representative of a divine being.

What?!?

Yes. It will convince multitudes that by prostrating before an image of Yurugu or by praying to a mythical Yurugu in a fantasy land in the sky called "heaven," that they can live in clouds and walk on streets of gold.

Hun?!?

They will create stories and books that they will decree "holy." They will create so-called "chosen" races among their dead selves.

Many Ah will subscribe to this miseducation and become champions of Yurugu's propaganda and lies. Forms of thought control called Christianity and Islam will reign in the world and massacres will follow. Ogo will twist the minds of millions. However, even while inundated by the vapid rhetoric of the void, Ah and emi will flow. Indeed, the chief emissary of their imaginary god will bow to the feet of a statue of me every night.

Ogo is now among you, recognize. It will enslave Ah, torture, kill, and experiment on Ah in attempts to reproduce melanin. At the same time that it is trying to manufacture melanin and steal Ah knowledge, it will be teaching the world that its true creators, you, are the embodiment of evil.

Ah's greatest lessons will be taught during this period. We will be the victims of numerous attempts at genocide and unspeakable atrocities. However, the stream of usurpations that Ogo will unleash will result in the rise of a phenomenal manifestation of Ah called Tahn.

They will be called Tahn because they will be the Ah who are duped, deceived, and lured away, but who, despite all they have suffered, shine.

They will be sold. Yes, she affirmed to her stunned progeny, these divine human beings will be exchanged for iron bars, liquor, and shiny trinkets, or they will be stolen, snatched as they travel to and from farms, markets, and rivers. Yurugu will endeavor to strip not only the divinity but also the humanity from these Ah who will subjected to an industrialized form of physical and psychological torture that Yurugu will call slavery.

However, the atrocities that they suffer and surmount will be the impetus for the Tahn's deification. Many of you will witness the shining here with me. Many of you will return to participate in this monumental work: You will be the Tahn who shine and kindle numinosity in others.

Ogo is incapable of shining, but it has diverse degrees of negativity and depravity that it will develop and exploit. Utilizing the principles of divide and rule and destroy, it will create an allure that will alternately discombobulate and attract many people of this world. We shall witness Ogo's religious thrustings, shaky erections, and pseudo-scientific gropings. We shall watch as multitudes stand in awe of foolishness, express admiration for hypocrisy, and offer obeisance to figments of imagination. Then we shall watch a famished Yurugu devour himself.

She turned ink into blood. She re-membered all and everything that had been dismembered and disremembered. Although there was no vibration outside, her inner power rocked all in her vicinity. Her divine destiny led her to the path: With her 2 hands and the might of Ògún, she cleared it. The Loa danced in her womb. Òrìṣà whispered in her ears. She continued her testament to the unborn patiently waiting daughter.

The child inside her womb rolled over as she rolled over on her side. Soul fit his body to hers as surely as orí directs 1's head.

"Mmmm," She felt the favored tremor. She smiled and prepared for immeasurable pleasure. It had been years since she felt the bliss. She never forgot her first gift. Her first loving of self by self. She once discussed the feeling with Soul. His facial expression did not reveal if he thought her sick or an unconscious masturbator. After she changed the topic to a more mundane 1, she saw his relief. So she asked him again, point-blank, what he thought of her self-stimulating clitoris. After a pause, he admitted jealousy.

She didn't even know if the feeling were her own or if other women knew this power. The few times she felt safe enough to reveal her bliss with sisters she was greeted only with eyebrows raised in admiration.

aaahahahhAAHHH

She squeezed her thighs so tightly she felt the muscles burn. *If I can stay this way, it can go on forever.*

Soul awoke and attempted to turn her over, but she could not be moved.

"Baby, you okay?" Her resistance surprised him.

"It's happening. Its . . . Ahhhh . . . No, don't touch me!"

She felt the wall he erected, but she just had to feel this love and let her daughter feel it too. *Babygirl, do you feel it? It's yours too.*

When the throbs ebbed and released her to this world, she rolled over to Soul. She was very wet and even more aroused than usual in the mornings. His erect penis demolished the wall his anger had built. He mounted her, in careful respect of the baby.

She closed her eyes and waited to receive his gift. He placed the head of his penis inside of her and then stilled all movement. When she opened her eyes in inquiry, he asked, "How can I compete with you and—*you*?"

"You don't have to compete," she stroked his strong jaw and contracted her vaginal lips. "Join us."

They joined: 3 in 1. His movement was gentle but insistent and methodical. She opened her legs wide urging him deeper. He altered his thrusts from circular to quick and shallow. She was about to have another orgasm when he pulled out. Cool air rushed in. Before she could form her lips into protest, she felt a soft lapping. Her clitoris loved the idea of a duet and vibrated like a 100 watt speaker riddled with bass heavy hip hop. He inserted his thumb into her vagina and danced it Damballah while he sucked her clitoris. She came smiling. When her trembling subsided, Soul guided her hips until she was on top of him. She arched her back to receive him fully. As she squeezed her vaginal walls and glided him inside from head to medium shaft, she encircled his back with her arms and sucked his lips. She rose to ride him properly and watched a smile glow on his face. His eyes were closed. She wondered what he was thinking about when he grabbed her shoulder and molded his body into hers. Her nipples kissed his own. He thrust inside her with the resolve of a Black Power salute. She felt his forearms tremble. She felt the tickling hair of his scrotum.

Their love making continued in the shower until the water ran cold. They emerged pruned, exhausted and exhilarated. As Soul dressed hurriedly and charged out the door, she laughed at making her man late for work.

She rubbed her belly and smiled, "Glorious 1, you will certainly have a better childhood than your mother did."

Her mother gave everything she could to keep her alive. But subsistence was not enough. When she hit 13 she had her mother sign approval for her to work in the shirt factory across town. They hired teenagers for cleaning up and piecework. The first night after an 8 hour day of hand stitching hems, her fingers were locked into claws. Her mother massaged her hands with warmed olive oil and fed her.

Her mother asked, "Well, are you going back tomorrow?"

"Yes," she murmured, already asleep.

Her mother was proud of this child who had the presence of mind, integrity, and strength to work rather than wait or, worse, beg.

The child curled her body around her anointed hands and prayed for a better life. Within a year she was living with Uncle D.

When she was she 15, she and Uncle D spent the summer in Helena, Arkansas where he tried to organize and manage a collective of exploited blues musicians.

Helena had only a catfish plant and black berries. She chose black berries and after she plucked them, she sold them at the plantation homes.

She met Dean that summer, and between blackberry cobbler, Uncle D, golden fried catfish, juke joints, and record spins they found time to attempt a young love.

She and Dean fell into house parties, sipped moonshine, and slow dragged splinters up 1 another's backs. They christened his 98 and once, at midnight, they explored 1 another while backed against the trunk of an oak tree. Dean was her first real boyfriend partially because he satisfied her so thoroughly she didn't have energy or desire to drift away to a curious but busy Uncle D. With Dean she felt special. The lips mocked as big and ugly, he sucked like Godiva chocolate. The child dismissed as hideous, who looked for reflections of her beauty in the eyes of penises, developed with Dean a burgeoning love that found its fullest manifestation with Soul.

"Let me get up and get busy." She fanned all the memories of the past away and began to prepare her lecture on collective communal labor and activism as the path to liberation and elevation for the Africana community. When she rose from her bed, her vision faded to black. Static filled her head and ears until she lost all control of her limbs. As her consciousness returned, she heard the radio playing. She was glad that she passed out right next to the bed upon which she had fallen.

She passed out often as a pre-teen and teen. Sometimes simply standing up would leave her inert. Once she passed out while running the 800; on another occasion she collapsed as she planted her right foot to high jump. For 3 minutes she laid prone on the ground. As she regained consciousness, her only thought was why no 1 cared enough to help her.

As her consciousness and body realigned, she noted that the baby was fine. She felt her frolicking. She hadn't passed out for years. Why now?

What did it mean? Probably just the pregnancy. The static cleared out of her head. She owned her body again. She got up to return to her work and remembered something she'd completely forgotten. Once when she was sleeping, a woman came and took her hand and road piggy-back style around the ceiling of her room and all over the house. The woman never spoke to her; she would just take her on exploratory missions around her home. They circled the ceiling and enjoyed the breezes they created. On another occasion, the woman parted the gold carpet in the living room and there, 6 inches below the floor was a swimming pool. Like fish, they dove and splashed. Now, her work forgotten, she sat and tried to remember who this was, her first playmate.

"Backlash!" Azure slammed the door and pitched her book bag across the room. "Can you believe this shit? They banned us from the radio! On what fucking grounds?"

"What grounds Ameri-kay-kay-kay need to get into our asses other than Blackness?"

"I bet that fucking Northerly complained."

"Azure, our own can sell us out. That's how we been trained."

"Well, on the fa reala, we did our part and I'm so glad you suggested recording the show. We may be whited out but the word ain't."

"Not no moe!"

"Nommo!"

"Listen, let's make an event up outta this shit. Let's make copies of the program before the recording disappears. Then let's sell it, cheap."

"Yeh, The Show that Shook the 'Ville."

"Right, the message will move! I'll talk to Ekundayo at Kemetic Visions bookshop about stocking some CDs."

"Let's put up flyers too, advertising the CDs and the knowledge. Oh," Azure's eyes lit up, "we need to buy all the *Africa Todays* and *Third Eyes* we can and make photocopies and scan them and save them. I have a feeling they will soon get whited out like we did."

"Word."

"Listen, I've been writing my ass off! I'm on a new lyrical level."

"Me too," Alteveze nodded.

"Me and you, The Family, Acey Duecy, Saddiq, King David, we got some baaad verbal artistry. Let's ask Ekundayo about some space to hold some readings."

"Giiiiirl, they don't know we fin to take this shit to the next stage."

"Fin?" Azure raised her left eyebrow.

"Hell yeh! Fin!"

"You a sho nuff college student!"

"Sho you right."

For Our God Fathers

Dangerous, endangered
Going the way of de in de un an do do
Dead to the world
Brotha, you ain't know
they got both yo heads in a noose
while you knock boots
and paper chase
the oppressor's sole objective is
to get you gone
You sittin on a corner cuttin white cocaine
with red wine and bitter black tears
and the beast is sizing you up and stretchin you out
You so deluded you extend your extremities
What's that about?
Yo windin sheet ain't ready yet
That tree can't hold yo soul
and it don't need no mo limbs
Use your arms and legs
to embrace
a warrior's weaponry
roll out to the burbs
and choke breath out of
architects of death
Stop facilitiatin your misery
Manifest your inner divinity
Be the God that
You are, father
Stop livin yo oppressors' dream

~~~~~Saddiq


## Colour Struck

Zora told ya but ya didn't listen
Blackness has myriad manifestations
infinite possibilities

You say i'm Black
~~~~~

i say
    how Black am i
               to you maybe i'm
       blue Black
       dusty Black
       rusty Black
       true Black
           or perhaps to you i'm
       nigga wench can't be raped Black
       filthy evil bitch Black
       video ho Black
       coon can Black
       coon dick Black
           then again i could be
       caught by the klan Black
       dragged to death Black
       resurrected and fighting back Black
       cracker crunchin in the night Black
       Ease in and slit ya neck Black
       Show ya my indifferent back Black

Just how Black
am i
devils lied on Sharmeka Moffitt Black?
children in Atlanta didn't come home Black?
brothas lynched in county jails Black?
caucasian heaven ain't nothing but a hell Black?

i can't fit on no numerical scale from 1 to 10 Black
i'm a cosmos from my soul to the skin Black
i like my coffee like i like my men Black

i greet the sun naked every day let the rays kiss me completely
Magnify my Melanin.
Fuck a tan line.
The more the sun strokes me the more aligned
my soul and mind become with my body
The more i recognize that i am the Infinite

So, yes, i am
       Alkebu-Lan Black
       Kemet Black
       Odùduwà Black

> Asase Yaa Black
> Ast Black
> Ausar Lord of Perfect Black Black
> Nzambi Black
> Nyame Black
> Nyabinghi Black

Clarke tried ta tell ya and ya didn't listen:
enslaving portuguese
reprobate british
thieving greek
asiatic weak
vicious french
perverted arabic
terms don't define me

> The Mothers don't give birth to adjectives
> our wombs mold Gods at 1 with infinity
> but without divine vision you can't see
> so i'mma tell ya how Black
> i can be
> Accept and give life to your seeds Black
> Give you easily more than you need Black
> Gots a whole universe up my sleeve Black

> I'm the Creator you gon meet in heaven Black
> The Devil you'll play skins with in hell Black

i'm the ink that signifies the page Black
Ancestors springing from the grave Black
i come from my momma's womb and not a crayon box Black

Don't hate me
cause an assimilado ideology diluted your Ancient Properties Black
The tragedies of aroons, attos, and eoles, don't move me Black
i ain't never lusted after mules Black
why not get yo mind out that light brown bag Black
who taught you recessive genes is supreme Black
fine tooth comb is for the slack Black
no dead white bones llowed in this rich Earth Black

All existence emanates from me
but it is a few things i ain't nevah gone be
passin
color struck

hi yellow
afro asiatic
mediocre
or light(weight) enuff for you
i'm too damn Black
i'm goin on the lam Black
i'm deep in the night ram Black
i'm can't stand the smell of
caucazoids, ham, or cracker backers Black
i'm Hoodoo Black
Juba Black
Soul Black
Pure Melanin to the bone Black

> But the main thing I am
> right now
> is worlds beyond you Black

~~~~~Azure

Ruminations

Sometimes I wonder if

WHEN THE REVOLUTION COOOOOMMMMEESSS

we will still be here.

~~~~~Alteveze

Ruinations

Everything has changed
since i been away
but niggas still
the same
once was slavery's bell round the neck
it's now ma bell on the hip pressed up against the ear
niggas whispering into speaking into freaking into lil black boxes
no fear
massah can never lose
you
totin him on yo hip

i no longer know where i am going here
sometimes i get turned around
i look to my folks for direction
niggas is still
headed towards a booty call
bowing at the church of confused beast-lovers
or at the shop of beauty which kills effortless supremacy
with cancer-causing white lyes

Everything has changed here
except racism and deluded negroes
who act like it doesn't exist
and confused kneegrows
who actually think they can
Only time they raisin a fist is to be handcuffed to a
European miss/ter or another pale oppress/her

Niggas still
reaching for greek
guess it's too hard to be God
Boogyin down in oz
forget about your troubles
just get on down
fuck the ancestors' struggles
get down get down
bleach and perm on the double
just get on down

Aint no change
Niggas is still
                    so i move
                          in fear
There are new masks covering the old ones
We've been wearing both so long
we have forgotten what we truly look like
feel like
how strong hairs reflect the mind
how a warrior bedecked
in the armour of midnight strikes
We need to get to working that root
that is the skin
getting not over

but in
      to ourselves
But how can we when
niggas is still
believing in black magic and a white god
refusing to accept they been Who(?)doed

                     ~~~~~The Family

I.D.

My name is Oblivion
I am the average Caucasian
you meet on the street
at the grocery store
in your school
at the gas station
at the liquor store

There is nothing left
in and for me but hate

You can see it in my eyes
You can read it in my internet comments
You can smell it on my breath
It is manifest
 in my lack of a future
 in my fear of my cave-dwelling past

I am infected by the most virulent
of viruses

The evil
that I created millennia ago
once I realized
the depth of my void
the poverty of my soul.

                    ~~~~~Lil X

"Alteveze! We sparked the wisdom!"

"Girl, that shit was tight. The Family got some deep vibes."

"Yeh, and those verses from the audience blew me away! My ears are still vibrating. Who was that young brother?"

"Lil X. I talked with him after the reading. He lives in Carver Homes."

"Seems like he was just waiting for something like this to spit his lit. His presence gave me an idea," Azure was on high, "We need more folk from the hood in our sphere. "

"I agree with you."

"We can get some of these young warriors who would be slangin or drinkin to write rhymes, stories, plays, whatever the spirit inspires in them."

"Exactly," Alteveze turned as Saddiq entered the room. "Maybe we can even publish some of this stuff."

"In peace, Òrìṣà."

"At peace, God. What you think?"

"We need to be about this every week. We gotta let Beast Inc. know that we know the time and are pulling the whole community's coattail."

"Excuse me, y'all, while I make us some tea."

After she set the water boiling and placed the chamomile bags in the empty cups, Azure reached for the honey, but it wasn't on the counter where she usually put it. She had every cupboard door open before she found the jar in the cabinet with the canned goods. *Why and when did I put this here?* she wondered. *I guess I been moving so fast.* . . .

"How'd y'all do on Roberts' test?" she called into the living room.

"That was a mutha!"

"Say what? Saddiq, it was easy! I said, 'let's have a study group.' But noooo! You gotta be Bobby Bad Ass. Keep on and you'll be taking pictures of me and Azure at *our* graduation."

"Yeh you'll follow Mack and Syd on the 5 year plan.

"Me and ol Rob tight now," Saddiq grinned with confidence.

"Maybe," Alteveze cocked an eye, "but he ain't givin out no grades."

"Y'all ever thought about," Azure passed her friends honeyed tea.

"Thanks Azure. Could you slide that crumb cake on over here?"

"how many Caucasian profs we got?" she finished her thought.

"Well, it's common knowledge they near bout the only grays you have to see for 4 years," Alteveze shrugged.

"But," Azure implored, "why them? Why here? Where are our graduates?"

"The situation is the same at most HBCU's. The graduates wanna be academic dons or high rolling businessmen. They ain't interested in givin back personally, just in pimping themselves on Malare." Saddiq sipped his tea and shook his head.

"The other issue is the university and its actual mission. It doesn't exist to train revolutionaries and promote revolution. We are being trained to support the status quo and to labor devotedly for Caucasia. This is why we have certain types of professors and a certain type of curriculum. This is why we don't have an Africana Studies program." Azure stood up to properly break it down, "We got the most noted Black special book collection in the world, we got wisdom-keepers on the ground and in the vicinity, but I'm taking Psychology 440, Interpreting Texts 401, and Mentoring 500 as electives in my last year cause I already took the 2 Africana literature courses Malare offers."

"Sounds like a C-O-N spiracy!" Saddiq stage-whispered and chuckled. "But seriously: this is why we have to educate ourselves about the fact that we are responsible for crafting an education that elevates us."

"True dat, Diq," Azure nodded. "You know, maybe we can build on these poetry readings and eventually establish an Afrikan wisdom center in the community."

"Hmm. A *real* Freedom School. Freeing the deaf, dumb, and blind of their mental slave shackles," Alteveze was inspired.

"Word. We need institutions that mold and support African Gods as opposed to mass-producing malcontent wannabees.

"I'm interested in brothas like Lil X. He is young," Azure nodded her head, agreeing with herself, "but he has hella potential. We can't let the system crush shinin like that."

"Isn't he gang-affiliated?" Saddiq asked. "I mean, he was wavin all types a flags. . ."

"Couldn't find more red on a fire truck. . . ." Alteveze agreed.

Azure gazed into her friends' probing eyes. She paused, wondering how her next thought would be taken, wondering about the depth of the trinity's consciousness. "I think we need more participation from gang members."

"Azure, now, 1 or 2 brothas might be alright. But . . . Shit! You got a death wish?"

"Just for killin 2 birds with 1 stone," Azure chewed her left thumb's cuticle, her mind was weeks away, at the next reading. "Whachall doin tomorrow?" She flipped the vibe, changed the tempo. She didn't wanna argue or justify, she needed to act.

"I'm studyin for Wright's test."

"Why? That's 3 weeks away?"

"Yeah, but I'm 6 weeks behind," Saddiq explained and the trio laughed.

"Maybe you on a 6 year plan," Alteveze winked.

"I'm goin to see Lil X."

"What time?" Alteveze was momma-quick, "I'll go with you."

"No, don't change your plans. Study. I can handle it."

"Listen, Azure," Alteveze locked eyes with her sister, "call me before you go and when you come back."

"I will," Azure reassured her, "but, Sista, don't worry."

"Boy, you betta get yo butt in here and clean this mess, and that quick! Leavin yo junk all over the floor! Y'all done got that to the bad, thinkin I'm a maid or somethin' round here. Saddia, go answer the door for me."

Azure greeted the little girl who was a soft brown miniature of her big brother and followed her into the living room. "Thank you Little 1."

Saddia smiled in response.

The supple brown leather furniture was arranged with an eye for lighting, comfort, and accessibility. The walls were decorated with original artworks including a stunning AFRICOBRA piece of the Black Panthers that centered the room.

Azure navigated around a profusion of CDs, jeans, shoes, and toys until she stood before a middle-aged woman with a teenager's supple skin who sported a daishiki and a gold tooth.

"Yes? What you want?"

"Good morning, ma'am," She tried to be polite, but not too "proper." "My name is Azure. I'm lookin for Lil X."

Sylvia Wilson looked Azure up and down, from her fro to her pressed black denim suit. She was neat but not fancy. Ms Wilson smiled at the visitor and called over her shoulder, "Zave, here somebody for you." Turning to Azure she said, "Come on in and have a seat. I got some greens on the stove that I have to tend to—uh—Azure. Saddia, Simone, Siddar, y'all clean up that mess up now!"

"Aw man!" this from the little boy, Siddar, whose twin was Simone.

"Alright now. . ." Momma threatened with a raised left eyebrow. The children bent over the disarray and Lil X, aka, Xavier, emerged.

"Hey!" he smiled at her, "you're the woman from the poetry reading."

"I'm Azure," she introduced herself and returned his smile. "Brother, we were all impressed with your work. You write a lot?"

"Yeh, ain't doin shit else."

"Why not?"

"Bad ass got kicked outta school for fightin," this from Momma in the kitchen.

"You must fight a lot. I mean, it takes like 4 fights for you to get expelled, right?"

"Well, I got the boot after my first brawl."

"Xavier, how old are you?"

"17."

"How far did you get in school?"

"I was in my junior year."

"Well, you gon transfer, get your GED, or what?"

"What I need that shit for? Too much hassle, and I make plenny ends."

"Doin what?"

"What I can." He shrugged as he gestured to the house. The furniture was high quality. The matching bronze and glass center and end tables were expensive. The imitation Indian rug Azure'd bought at the swap meet found its original on the floor.

"But in your poems. . ." It wasn't that she was surprised, but she just wanted to get this paradoxical existence straight in her head.

"Azure, that's poetry. I mean, it's a message; it's about alternatives, truths. But we gots to eat. They done cut welfare down and fin to cut it out."

"Miss Clarise over on Vine gotta go to those literacy and GED classes *evry* day. If she miss 1 day—for any reason—whomp, no more food, no more shelter. That woman got 4 kids and the baby got sickle cell. What she gon do if he has a crisis?"

"Ummm MMM! This is too much. There are already too many of us dying. Well," Azure mused, "they think it's too many of us any way."

"You right about that sister, brought us here to build this nation and then tell us to get the hell out or kill us out now that building's finished." Sylvia paused and the silence rested. Azure could hear the children laughing in a back room. "I don't have to go to those classes cause I not only finished high school but did 2 years at NCU. They can't force me to do 1 thing. Azure," she emerged from the kitchen, "who you work for?"

"I'm a student at Malare ma'am. I write poetry, and we had a reading last night. That's how I met Xavier."

"Yeah? Ol Zave was a good student," Sylvia said with pride—and with confidence since Azure had made it clear that she didn't work for any agency and wasn't an agent. "But always fighting. I guess he like me in that sense. His Daddy too."

"Are you a warrior too, Ms—"

"Call me Sylvia or Sister Sly, if you like: that's what everyone called me when I was a member of SNCC. I joined after they took up self-defense! We didn't play!" From her tone it was clear that Sister Sly back in the day stayed armed and was prepared to kill for freedom.

"Awww shhh," she caught herself, "ucky, now!!! That's alright!"

"Yeah, we were really struggling for the cause then. When I think of how everything has crumbled . . . Well, I guess revolutions have peaks and valleys too," Sylvia returned to the kitchen though it was clear she wanted to say more. I need to sit down and vibe with Sister Sly, Azure thought.

Azure turned to Xavier, "So, who you be fightin?"

"BGD."

"You VL?"

"5 up high, 6 must die," he stacked his signs to emphasize his point.

Azure had some VLs in her family. While she respected the origin of the organization, she was angry about the loss of lives and lack of direction: Kick our youths out of school or miseducate them so much they drop out then infuse the hood with drugs so that gangs seem like the only option.

"I'd like to see some of your work. How about the rest of the People? Any of them write?"

Azure's usage of the word "People," a term for members of the Vice Lord Nation, surprised Xavier. "Why? Y'all gon have another reading soon?"

"Um hmm. Bout a month. After midterms."

"Azure. . ." He wasn't calling her but saying her name.

She looked at him. Damn, he has some beautiful eyelashes.

"That's a kinda blue right? Like Spanish 'azul'."

"Yeah." She smiled.

"Well, nobody will fuck with you. You with me. But don't be wearing no lotta blue round here."

"Say what?! You don't have to school me. Goin to Malare don't make you *that* stupid!" She smiled.

"Girl! Don't be starin in nobody face like that! You raised better than that!" Lil X shouted at his baby sister, Simone, who had entered the living room and stood by his side openly staring at Azure.

"No, it's alright," she held out her hand to the little girl. Simone stepped forward and took her hand. "What's your name?"

"Simone, what's yours?"

"Azure."

Simone stepped closer then reached out with both hands towards Azure's hair, "Your hair is like a cloud." And she submerged her hands into the Afro that Azure styled back from her forehead.

"Yes it is," she laughed. "You like it?"

"Yes!" She ran into the kitchen, "Mommy, I want a cloud! I want a cloud! Mommy!"

Afralo

Babygirl
The rich Black cloud on your head
matches the softness in my heart
          the strength of my womb
I toted you like the jewel you are
kicks and finger tips grippin me

inside
     outside calling
Mommy,
Come see!
All the clouds wanna be
beautiful
Like me.
       Afralo.

She could be my own daughter, Azure mused.

"Still wanna see the poems?" His voice called her into the future, "Follow me."

She checked out his stride as he walked to his room. He is 1 of our warriors! Not a butter-fat pseudo-intellectual academic suffering from ennui like all too many of the brothers at Malare. No, this brother—at 17—was a head taller than her, bowlegged, and built like he hunts every day. He does, she mused.

"Gimme alla dat noise! Y'all get the hell outta here!"

The children were playing hot box with 2 empty cassette tape cases as bases and a rolled up t-shirt as the ball. "Here," he thrust some dollars into his siblings' hands, "y'all go buy some candy."

"Lil X, you know these children are our future," she was shocked at his tone.

"Yeah, and the future is hard. They gotta be tough. The future is as fucked up as the past and the present. That's what I write about."

"To change it?"

"Naw, to cope."

He cleared off a space on the bed and she sat down.

"Mind if I close the door? I—well—my family isn't really hip to my work."

"Yeh, it's cool. But your mom is cool as a fan. In fact, I'd like to vibe with her." He cocked an eyebrow at her as if to say, Whaaat!? But he didn't say anything as he shut the door and lit 3 sticks of sandalwood incense.

He went to a dresser and removed the 2 bottom drawers and began rifling through red and black notebooks. He set some aside in 1 pile and dismissed others. "Here it is!" Lil X brandished a chrome .44.

"Need to clean it," Azure observed. After 7 heartbeats she divulged, "You know, my old man, he's in for murder."

"Straight? What's his name?"

"Lil Loco."

"Say what!?! Lil Loco? From Hyde?"

"Mm hmm."

"But he, he killed Big Red," he stared at her with his head cocked at a nearly 45° angle. "Man, Red was just like a daddy to me!"

"Lil Loco is like a husband to me. I used to be a Queen: GTO."

"Awww shit! Hell fuck ass naw! I thought you was cool," his voice rose an octave. He held the gun lightly. "You a mark or what?" He asked her, but he could have been addressing the gun because he wouldn't look at her.

"How can I violate anybody when that shit is in my *distant* past. I'm in school. Graduate soon."

"Maybe not . . . Azure." He and the gun looked directly at her as he rolled her name off of his tongue like it was phlegm.

"Why you think I told you? Oh, so you bad! Go on an shoot me. You got the heart?"

He sucked his teeth, "Yeh, I got the heart, but I don't wanna fuck up my room." He lowered the .44 and sat it and himself beside her on the bed.

"Xavier, I told you about myself and Lil Loco to show and prove there's more than 1 way to live. You ain't gotta follow Red or Loco or me. You got to clear your own road and make your way out of the trap. If not, it'll trap you. . ." She changed her focus. "Man, you are so talented! I look at you and see a warrior going to waste. Where the fuck you think I'd be if I was still GTO."

"Dead."

He picked up the gun and went with it to a bookshelf facing the bed. He put the gun on the top-most shelf, out of the children's reach, and pulled down a mickey mouse doll. "You got a lotta heart to max out in my sphere and reveal that you a GTO," he let his gaze rest on her for a full 3 seconds.

"*Former* GTO," she clarified. "But, yeh, I grew up on MacArthur."

"Humph!" He pulled the head off of the doll and Azure thought that that was 1 good way to kill that racist son of a bitch. He brought out a package of 1.5s and a bag of sess with a rich perfume she smelled through the plastic.

"Well, you a big shot now," he began the expert rolling of a medium-sized spliff, "Ms. College Thang!"

"I go see Loco every 2 weeks."

They both scooted back on the bed so that their backs were braced against the wall. Their feet dangled over the edge; the notebooks sat between them.

"-it?" he had taken a deep drag and holding the sess in his lungs, offered Azure a toke.

She inhaled.

This shit is too much like back in the day. Project bricks, weed leaves, and hard legs. Can't believe this shit. What the fuck would Alteveze say? She laughed.

"You touched that quick? Musta been a while," he rasped through plumes of smoke

"No, I, well, yeah. Comon brother, let's vibe.

Marijuana's levitation and Xavier's rhythms relaxed her. The brotha has talent! Real and raw. He read her 3 pieces: 1 about the futility of selling dope, 1 an ode to his fallen soldiers, 1 about shooting a rival drug dealer who was actually himself. Azure gazed at him while he read; his real spirit took over his façade. It was hard to imagine him killing anyone.

"I wish I was writing like you at 17."

"Oh yeah," his voice had grown husky, his eyes were slitted. "What was you doin?"

"What there was to do."

"What was that?" He lowered is eyelids to take in the soft V her jeans made between her thighs. His eyelashes, like that, are like a prayer. She needed to feel them sweeping her cheeks.

"Read another 1 *little* brother." He cocked his eyebrow at her and chuckled. I need to check this here vibration. This CHILD is 17; I'm 22. These brothers grow too fast, live too hard, die too soon. Hell, he grown. Passed life expectancy 2 years ago. Hump, by today's standards, he uh O.G. So what does that make me, going into my seventh year of celibacy. . . She hid a wince as a current coursed through her that was not a by-product of the weed.

"You write raps too?"

"Some but the structure is too limiting. I like to use rhyme unexpectedly. But yeah, I started out freestylin. Check this out":

Classy queen your power's vibratin in me
I already taste the flow of your honey rich sea
You make my soul fall down to its knees
Let this sun glow on your soul and in your body

So it wasn't just her, wasn't just the weed. He felt it too, she thought. What she said aloud was:

Lil handlah hard leg you too young fa me
Plus momma's in the kitchen cookin collard greens.

They laughed and sealed their friendship. Azure stayed at Xavier's place till 7 and greased back on fried chicken, greens, and yams with chocolate pie for dessert.

"Listen, Azure, I gotta handle some bidness, and you know blocks is finna get hot: Lemme walk you home."

"Azure, you welcome here any time!" Sylvia smiled and Azure felt adopted.

"Thank you Ma'am. Saddia, Simone, Siddar, see you later."

"Tell ya straighter!" they sang and Azure wondered how that phrase had come around again.

"Almighty!"

"5 to the sky."

"XL!"

"Red Dog!"

As the men greeted 1 another with the gangster pound, Red Dog looked Azure up and down and said to Xavier, "You must think you a don."

"I am," Xavier said as he adjusted his nuts and strutted away.

What would Loco say?

They came to the Cool Spot and a brotha in a Bulls jacket approached with slow swag. He and Lil X gave a handshake that ended with the thumb, index, and middle fingers out-stretched.

"Peeps, Rollie checkin."

"Round?"

"VLT."

"All is Well."

"Brown, meet Azure, she goes to Malare."

"Well aaaallllRRIIGHTT! Big X done marked the spizzot."

"Naw, man, we on anotha tip."

"Well, excuse the fuck up outta me." The brother had a rough goatee and pockmarked skin. He exuded a compelling blend of violence, apathy, and misogyny as he dismissed Xavier to turn his attentions to Azure, "But uh, um, Miss Lady, I may have somethin you can use." He weighted his penis and sac as if they were so heavy they were burdensome.

"Yeah?" She clocked him dead in the eye, "you write?"

"Naw, but I can read tween yo lines," and as Xavier and Azure went away, Brown shouted, "DAMN!"

She and Xavier strolled on. He wondered how she was handling the "compliments" she was receiving. She was tripping off of how much she had missed. The college community was so stuffy, smug, and fake sometimes. She felt alive just strolling and digging and being dug.

"Wait," she stopped 70 yards south of the Cool Spot. Xavier stopped and looked at her wondering if she had left something behind at his house.

"Do you feel that?"

"What?"

"Comere," he came and stood close to her, facing her, so close he could smell her breath. It was the scent of chocolate. He wondered if the taste was on her lips. He continued to look at her eyes, but she wasn't looking at him. She was inside.

"Don't you feel it?"

He stopped looking at, stopped concentrating on, this woman he was falling in love with and tried to feel what she was feeling.

"Yeh," a vibration was fighting its way through the sidewalk littered with Colt 45 tall boys, Old English 800 bottles, cigarette butts, and hamburger wrappers, "something like a low voltage charge."

"Xavier," she had stopped looking inward and now focused on the lean young man who was standing so close to her she could feel his body heat. She lowered her eyes and lips and said, "I think this is some kind of force."

"It is probably just electric lines, gas lines, or something," he wondered what her hair felt like, what it was like to get lost in her hair, her mind.

"No, this is something else," she looked up and caught him in the wonder of her hair. "This is natural. From the Earth." She would investigate later. Darkness was embracing them like a hand slipping into a glove.

"Can I ask you a personal question?"

"I've killed 5 niggas, but I ain't shed no blood in over a year."

"Well, I wanted to ask about your father. I can read your signs." She motioned to his left hand which had a 5 point star with darkened points.

"My Daddy? Dead up. Went to Nam and came back and took the war to the real enemy. He went to the top of Pickadilly and picked off 16 dillies fore a sniper shot him."

"Got damn!" She stopped and looked him straight in the face. "*That's* your ole man, Raymond Wilson?"

"Mm hmm."

"Ooo! He straight up took beasts *out*," Azure was beside herself, "Man, he's 1 of my heroes. Lot's a folks *talk* bout puttin head out, but who really has the heart to do it? Your father had hella heart!" Her reverie and reverence were complete.

"I feel you but. . ."

She became inundated in the absence that surrounded Xavier: "You need him." They paused in silence. "I'm sorry," she mentally kicked herself for her exuberance. "You musta been what? I was 10 when I heard."

"5, I was 5," Xavier's pimpstroll was much less pronounced now. She witnessed the void the revolution left.

"What about your people?" He asked her.

"Oh, they around. My Mom works at Urban League. Dad's remarried." His family was far more interesting, "You write about your Daddy?"

"Nope."

They made it to her apartment, and Azure put the key in the lock, "Listen, you got time to come in?" Her eyes were shining, "I wanna show you something."

"No, I Ah. . ."

"Duty callin?"

"Word."

"In peace, Xavier."

"Peace."

She unlocked the door but was accosted before she could step inside:

"Sista, what the fuck you doin with that nigga? Don't you see that lil punk's in a gang? You could get killed. Or that nigga be done come through here and cleaned us out!"

Azure turned and looked at her neighbor Jerome, and as she began to think of an appropriate response to his tirade, she decided to have better things on her mind. She opened her door and inhaled deeply the scent of her self.

"Sista, you betta check yoself be"

SLAM!

She took a bottle of gin to her warriors' shine. Harriet, Ida, Banneker, Ann Wade, Highland Garnett, El Hajj, King, Chaney, Huey, Bobby, Bambara, Dona Wade, Lumumba, Nkrumah, George Jackson, Garvey, Toussaint, Nat, Sarraounia, Vesey, Prosser, Doc, Baraka, George Wade, Betty, Lil Loco, Shaka, Gran Mat, Emmett, Raymond Wilson, Henry Wade, Du Bois, Aminat, Ast, Mariah Wade, Unka El, Yaa Asante Waa, Rufe, Saro-Wiwa, Sam Greenlee, Abbey Lincoln, Queen Aminat, Kwame Ture, Colin Ferguson, Fannie Lou, Zora, Wright, Ras Tafari, Nzingha, Garvey, Boukman, the 54th, Toni Morrison, Fela, Sly, George Clinton, Steel Pulse, Assata, Afeni, Zaki, Ben Okri, Fred Hampton, Elijah Muhammed, Fard, Abubakari II, Menelik II, and more.

Photographs, Ve Ve, miniature temples, symbols, colors, a sickle, a pregnant woman's torso, a cut noose, Kongo's flag, a butterfly knife, Ghana's flag, her cousin Mike's bandana, a hammer, her Mu Deah's favorite brush, a miniature shot gun, news clippings, a 2-headed axe, book titles, shackles, an anvil, scarves, hair picks, a machete, and 1 black leather glove molded with clay into a fist. She poured gin and words of homage to the living and transmigrated warriors on the shrine. She lit red, black and green candles so the warriors could help her to see where the struggle now lie. Azure meditated and conferred with her guardians, our guardians.

When she eased out of her meditative state, she rose to call Alteveze.

"We gon blow Juneteenth out this year!"

"Peace."

"Peace, Sister. I interrupt something?" The phone had rung 7 times and Alteveze's voice sounded husky.

"No," rustling adjustments, "you all right?"

"Guess who Lil X daddy is?"

"Who?"

"Raymond Wilson."

"Oh, Damn 2 times! No wonder the brotha so deep."

"But he was only 5 when Pops went out like the warrior he was, so it was and still is hard for him. His mom was a member of the revolutionized SNCC!"

"All those revolutionaries!" Alteveze mused in a cadence unique to her Midwestern hometown.

"But Lil X deep in the game. Straight VL."

"What?"

"Vice Lord."

"Sounds like a gang. But, girl, all I know is Crips and Bloods."

"Crips and Bloods is West Coast, they babies in the game. VLs, BGDs, and Blackstone Rangers the original hard legs. In fact, they usta be all about community uplift and what not. But Hoover, as in J. E. as opposed to the King, put salt in all the gangs.

"Now, *King* Hoover is a co-founder and chairman of the BGDs, that's Black Gangster Disciples, now known as GDs. But," Azure realized that her exposition was way over Alteveze's head, "well, Lil X, he like a Blood to break it down in West Coast terminology."

"Well, you done slipped into all types of unbeknownst knowledge and what not, but the essence is that the brotha's a banger and slanger, right?"

"Right. So how did the study session go?"

"Girl, how you think, Saddiq ain't got no focus."

"Depends on my view." Saddiq seemed to be whispering in Alteveze's ear but his voice was clear over the phone.

"Mm hmm, I hear how it went, and I see who got focus on what, too. Lemme let you go," she laughed.

"Tomorrow."

"9?"

"I'm there."

"In Peace."

When Azure woke up the next morning she was dizzy, groggy, and nauseous. She walked to the bathroom wondering what was wrong and vomited yellow bile into the sink.

"Sadie's Place is open for business!!"

Cynthia and Kandace slapped both palms and laced their fingers.

"I can't believe you got the loans so easily!" Kandace narrowed an eye and smiled, "You must have some Àjẹ́ tucked away your damnski!"

"Yeah, we were granted more than enough money, and with what we earn, we won't be worried about nothing!" Cynthia laughed.

"Hell of a graduation present."

"You put the add in the *Metro*?"

"Full color spread! You didn't see it?" Kandace asked.

"Naw, I been straightening the health inspector, fire marshall and grocers. I don't understand this shit. Somebody *must* a worked a root as easy as its been."

Cynthia pulled the shades back. The place was beautiful. The color scheme was eggshell and gold. The walls were eggshell with heavy crown molding. The hardwood maple floor was polished to a high gloss. Each table was adorned in white linen with interwoven gold threads. Scalloped gold-edged linen napkins were fanned in frosted water goblets. Down home blues and classic jazz music were everlastingly programmed on the computerized audio system.

"It was our luck that those Cambodians got arrested for hiring undocumented workers. Hin Sheu was so eager to cover his losses he offered the space for next to nothin.

"Of the $20,000 we got from the bank, I only had to put down $2,000."

"We saved money buying and making the furnishings ourselves too."

"Creativity comes in handy," Cynthia and Kandace both loved to design and to sew, "No 1 would believe we made the drapes, tablecloths, and napkins. Place looks sharp!"

The women took in the restaurant and admired their work, "Floors are washed."

"Fridge's stocked."

"Help's comin at 6."

"Soup's on at 7."

"Let's get to those greens and chittlins."

Business boomed. Sadie's Place had a funky elegance and high prices, ensuring exclusive clientele. The allure of 2 attractive young Black women was also helpful for business—including the business of feeding fantasies.

Kandace and Cynthia decided that the best serving staff would be Caucasian college students, as long as they were clean, neat, and quiet. Cynthia liked the idea of Caucasians dishing out death to each other.

No 1 could believe that poke salad—tender, steamed, and well-seasoned with curry, fatback slabs, bay leaf, and fresh ground ginger—was *gratis*. The salad accompanied honey-drenched bricks of buttery cornbread and spicy chittlins—which were also endless.

Fried chicken breast fillet in white wine and honey sauce with yams and shells and cheese was the house specialty. But the butterfly pork chops smothered in pepper sauce and served with biscuits, collards, and fried corn was the crowd favorite. Grilled hog head cheese slabs over dirty rice with oxtail soup, roasted pig's feet standing in a bed of fried green onions accompanied by pinto beans, and Sadie's mega gumbo with dandelion leaf stew were also popular. Potato, chocolate, and lemon pies, and peach and blackberry cobblers were for dessert. Every night at 9, "Sadie" stepped out to greet the crowd.

"We're officially the bomb! The mayor and his wife praised our food on the 10:00 news! We're booked solid for 4 weeks!"

"I figure in 8 more weeks we'll have 70 Gs.

"Well, how you wanna work it? You know Cantrell and J.C.D. are meeting here in 6 weeks for a private party for 60. The week after that is the FOP luncheon, and the Policeman's Benevolent Society's dinner is the following week."

"The net from that will put us over the top."

"Well, what you wanna do? You wanna be neo-mammies forever?" Kandace turned her attention from the reeking hog intestines to gaze at her sister.

"Hold the chittlins."

Kan chucked and said, "I'll call KLM and reserve the tickets." Just then, the phone rang. Both women were up to their elbows in offal.

"I'll get it," Cynthia removed her heavy duty rubber gloves; rinsed, soaped, and rinsed her hands; dried them on a paper towel; and jogged to the phone which was still ringing. "Hello? . . . Oh Hello Mr. Perkins! . . . Yes, thank you . . . Oh, Danny's getting married? Congratulations! . . . Sure . . . the 16th? No problem . . . See you then—if not before! . . . Bye-bye."

"Listen."

"I know, Perkins' wedding reception; 2 days after the business meeting. Perfect. We can close on the 18th and be in"

"The 18th? But won't they—well, perish before then?"

"Don't worry: You know pork digests slowly, and I'm gonna alter their biochemical compositions. There won't be a grave dug until we've touched down."

"SadieeeEEE! Ooo, Sadie Mae! Come on out here!"

"What the—" The restaurant was jumping. B.B. King's crooning filled the establishment. He and Lucille rode and writhed just under the garrulous laughter of 50 greasy, swine-hued men. Having eaten to bursting, they drank for a settling digestive burp only to stuff themselves again. Now the men, led by mayor Billy Ray Wallace and his key crony Eugene Cantrell, had decided it was time for some nigger-baiting and hopefully catching.

"Girl, that's you. It's your place. Go on; I'll watch the pies," as Kandace watched Cynthia greet their guests with sassy banter, she felt a presence at her elbow.

"Ma'am, should I circulate the free rounds again?"

"Yes," the girl was looking tired—well, she'd rest soon, long time. "Then," Kandace searched the girl's name tag "uh, Cindy, take a break. And tell the others to break as well. Y'all come eat anything you want. Just dessert and drinks left."

"Yes, ma'am."

Not long ago it'd be *my* mouth fulla ma'ams to her lil ass. I don't even need to read her thoughts to know her mind. All these crackers plottin! Joe sneakin roun and writin down recipes. Hmp! Put em right insida his mind. He'll cook a killer feast for his whole family next week. And that Sue steals the other's tips and schemin on the cash register. Come next month, take what you want, bitch. "Nigger bitch" "Black nigger" fine, think it all you want, but you'll never say it and you don't have to, don't have to.

When she peeked around the kitchen alcove to see how Cynthia was fairing; she found her sister sitting on Cantrell's lap.

"Whall, this here just like my foefathas! Fine wench too! Kaw Kaw kaw kawkawkawkaw kaw kaw kaw kawk a w ka w ak k."

"Sadie, you cook like this all over the house?"

 The men rippled with laughter again.

"Go ask yo mamma."

"Oh yeah! She a hot 1, Cant!

"Like to get em while dey ey ey yyy ggrrg ggrrgg ggggg rrrr," Cantrell's face went from crimson to maroon. He clutched at his neck and drew blood.

"He chokin!

"Who know duh heimluk?"

"Ohhh maaaahhh gaawwwddd!"

Now's who's laughin? Can't believe this shit! Fools think this is 1799? Still talking and livin shit. Damn! The pies! Save him Cynthia, she projected, $5,000 bonus tonight! Drunk sick bastard! Should kill em all here—now. Hell, we *are* killin em here and now. These numb fuckas nevah stop to think that we never eat nothin here.

When she decided he'd suffered enough, Cynthia stopped acting like she was too shocked to move and grabbed Cantrell from behind and placed her hands in a fist under his diaphragm, which was difficult to locate under his serpentine rolls of flab. Her Heimlich was efficient and effective and sent chittlins, saliva, and bile flying in the faces of Cantrell's friends.

"You saved em Sadie!" the mayor gushed, "You saved ol Cant!"

"No, he wasn't gonna die. Just needed to do what he's doin now: Sit down quietly. Cindy, bring Mr. Cantrell something cold to drink and a cool cloth."

Night air will cool the pies.

"Brang dranks fuh all us!!!"

"Whiskey!!"

You'd think they finish their meal with sobriety, gratitude, and reflection. Noooo: Fools rowdier than before.

"Put some mo salad and chittlins raht here! I got my secon win! And turn up dat blues! Believe tha's 1 of my boys sangin," Cantrell shouted.

Enjoy it. Kandace shook her head and walked back in to the kitchen. Dance the saggy white bottom all night. These are the real witches and wizards if there are any. Those women in the 1600s didn't stand a chance against these muthas. Yeh, you had to kiss the devil's ass alright: If you weren't on Cotton or Increase Mather's good side, you found your side on a stake.

All those Caucasian women tried and killed in the court of catch 22: they were guilty through silence; they were guilty through a quick dunking, or they were murdered via a long 1. It never crossed anyone's mind that these dreaded "witches" didn't have the power to free themselves or slay their persecutors.

Taking hallucinogenic drugs to "fly" and meet the "devil," or what was more often the case, using an ointment to lubricate their vaginas and masturbating with a broomstick and meeting the "devil" through orgasm. If it wasn't a broomstick used to "fly" to Satan, he came with a dick "as long as the handle of an oven fork." Or the member was like a "spindle hugely enlarged." On other occasions, his penis must have been like a cucumber, a carrot, or a zucchini. 1 woman testified the penis was "a good finger long." Seems like the underlying confession was "I was so horny; I *had* to get some satisfaction!" But this simple human need was dressed in religious hypocrisy and fairy tale foolishness.

A lonely deprived woman became a succubus. A rapist, an incubus. What really intrigued me, Kandace continued her musings as she crowned each pie slice with a dollop of whipped cream, was William Woods' *A Casebook of Witchcraft* which discusses a visitation of an incubus who resembled "holie bishop Slyvanus" and who made his sexual victim cry out so loud in pleasure that the whole village came to find the offender. Also telling is the "magic staffe" of St. Bernard which was a repellant/substitute for a roving incubus: When a wench complained of being "visited regularly by the devil, St. Bernard "tooke hir his staffe and bid hir laie it in bed beside hir." The "bedstaff" was so effective, the wench traded the devil's dick for the rod of a "saint."

It is not surprising that this era saw a rise in accounts of "midwives and whores who murder children" by thrusting needles in the infants' heads. Perhaps this was the most efficient way to get rid of the unholy spawn of bishops and priests.

The devil was never more popular than he was during this time. Caucasian men and women lined up to kiss the devil's black ass, and, if they were lucky, they could ride his ebony shaft all night long.

There is no mention of anything even remotely resembling Àjẹ́ in any of these accounts because Àjẹ́ is actual and it acts covertly. Àjẹ́ moved masters to hang themselves and mistresses to throw themselves off of roofs. Àjẹ́ lit the fires that burned whole plantations to the ground. It poisoned pots of food for dining rooms filled with oppressors—just like we're doing right now. Àjẹ́ is everything that witchcraft is not. Àjẹ́ is everything that witchcraft could never be.

"The language is so harsh in your concluding chapter, Kandace," Dr. Smythe's tone was bristling with aggression.

Silence.

"Do you think so condemnatory a tone is fitting?" he charged.

"Tone is a subjective concept: What rankles some delights others."

"Yes, yes, but . . ."

"What I find most compelling," Dr. Whitlow interjected, "is your discussion of Àjẹ́ and most particularly, your assertion that Àjẹ́ enslaved in the new world may have instigated the Inquisition."

"There are temples for Ast (misnamed Isis and later disempowered as the Virgin Mary) all over Europe. The city of Paris is named for Ast. This God, like all African Gods, has endured centuries of desecration and ethnic cleansing. If nothing else, my theory that Ast and her enslaved daughters used the witch concept and witch trials to destroy their defilers and reduce the Caucasian world population adds a layer of complexity and logic to an otherwise inexplicably asinine set of events.

"Enslaved Africans killing their oppressors is well-documented. But, what could be more effective than Àjẹ́ using the methodology of the Signifying Monkey who pits the jungle's 2 strongest animals against 1 another and chuckles over their corpses. Caucasian men killed scores of Caucasian women. For every woman they killed, they killed generations of Caucasian offspring. The Inquisition served no purpose other than a purpose for Àjẹ́ when examined politically."

"Well," Dr. Smythe shook his oversized head and dandruff flew," I still feel the tone is too accusatory. At times I felt a chill course through me. What I want to say is, this work has merit and can make a significant contribution to this field, but you leave no room for Cauc—" he shook his head as if to banish his origins, "*white* sympathy."

"I wasn't aware that that was a requirement."

Dr. Janepes thought a change of topic was in order: "Kandace, I am wondering if there are any instances of white and black women working together?"

"I found none. The oppressor does not help the oppressed. Caucasian women needed the African women to remain in the box of subjugation that Caucasians fashioned for them. The very concept of Caucasian womanhood hinged on the enslavement, subjugation, and vilification of the African woman. Without the living comparison these women provided to the Caucasian imagination as hyper-sexual, evil, dirty, etc. there could be no virginal, pristine, frigid plantation mistress myth.

"The inability and even refusal of Caucasian women to see African women as equals who were worthy of forming bonds and forging alliances is apparent in the abolitionist literature in which the protagonists are all visually Caucasian but legally Black (i.e., quadroon and octoroon victims of 1 or 2 drops). Blackness could not be dealt with on its own terms holistically. However, bleached Blackness served an important purpose, it became these writers' admission ticket and justification for voyeurism. The voyeuristic inclination is apparent in all would-be "Black" characters created by Caucasian America's writers, including and especially Lydia Marie Childs and Harriet Beecher Stowe."

The perceived need to "humanize" Blackness by depicting it as being as near to Caucasian as possible significantly informed African American writing and self-perception as well, Kandace mused. Harriet Wilson's *Our Nig*, the first novel published by an African American, is replete with tragic mulatto overtones. The same inferiority complex forms the foundation William Wells Brown's *Clotel* and is also evident in Charles Chesnutt's *The Marrow of Tradition* and Harriet Jacobs' autobiography. Rarely did early American fiction writers of any ethnicity depict a wholly African character who was intelligent, caring, worthy of respect, and heroic. Never could such a character be a woman.

This pattern of privileging recessive genes reached its apex during the Harlem Renaissance, Kandace mused while cutting slices of pie. Not only did this era see the triumph of tragic mulatto literature but it also spawned artists who strove to be tragic mulattos because the lighter you and your characters, the more publishing opportunities you had. Wallace Thurman broke these molds with *The Blacker the Berry* which focuses on the struggles of a sister who is richly melanin-endowed, but Thurman was also writing about himself and voicing pains that many ignored.

"Antebellum literature does not reflect bonding between African and Caucasian women," Kandace returned to her recollection of her defense, "The fear of the 'exotic' 'stealing' the master precluded such bonding. While it was stated that Caucasian women attended the rituals of Marie Leveau in New Orleans, researchers posit that these women came to procure something for a price, abortifacients, for example. They were not sharing spiritual knowledge; they certainly were not helping plot insurrections."

"I understand what you're saying. White women would have lost everything in the event of an insurrection," admitted Dr. Janepes. "They wouldn't have overthrown their own system."

"Well, you have temerity, I'll say that!" Smythe had turned ecru, then red, then an odd mélange of colors that could only be described as vomit orange-green.

"I have a question," Dr. Glint cleared her throat.

Now, this trick hasn't even read the thesis and hasn't said 1 word to me since she agreed to be on my committee. I had really hoped this "sista" would have at least had helpful commentary, but she's been a blank page— in all respects.

"My question is more personal."

"Yes?"

"Are you Àjẹ́?"

                         "Yes."

The lips pursing into an easy smile spoke the volumes that did not come from her mouth. If there was an element of discomfort in the room before it had now been elevated to naked dread.

"You may cross yourselves if you like. Making a symbolic cross from head to heart to shoulders is merely re-membering the Ankh—the Kmtic sign of life and the 4 points of the sun of BaKongo cosmology. Remember, the pope bows to my Mother, nightly.

"Is this a defense or a. . ."

"An inquisition-in-inverse?" Kandace completed Janepes' thought and laughed. The tension heightened. Her degree was assured with her 297 page, meticulously researched and referenced M.A. thesis. The committee had never seen anything like it.

"Don't worry, I've had Àjẹ́ from birth, and I've not killed anyone— yet," Kandace winked.

At this point all the Caucasian examiners turned red. Roxanne Glint, the pseudo-sister, turned a deeper shade of black, much to her chagrin.

"Well, thank you, Kandace. Please step outside and we'll call you in with our decision."

Like I can't hear what y'all gon say. Like it matters anyway.

"Cynthia, we need to publish our theses."

"Okay. Are the pies ready?"

"Am I Black?"

I gotta write this fast, got to get this down quick cause this gon be the only chance that I get. Big Sal, who do the laundry, gon be round here at 7:45, and we got it worked out so that either this gon be in your hands or you gon be in mine. I don't know exactly what you gon do with this, Lil Wom, if I ain't able to make it. But when you get this, you gon have all of you: All that I can give. You have a whole ocean to you, Lil Wom, that you don't know yet. This here is comin through the Waters. Just look to the water if you don't understand all in here. It's 3:45 now and we got a little time to talk, but the tide is comin.

My Momma, yo Gran-Momma come straight from Africa, and she was 1 of the last batch of Africans brought here to merica. She call herself Yemoja and we all called her Ja-Ja, well, I called her Ma Ja. Whitefolks called her Ann, wouldn't call her Yemoja. Momma Ja say they try to take her home from her mind by callin her Ann and Annie. But she say they don't know she is Ah-Ni who strolls the sea with Yemoja. She say she called Wade on account of when the ship carryin her from home got up on the merican shore, a wind picked up and threw her over the side of the ship.

Ma Ja say she was under the water breathin and tryin to die, havin seen this land. But she say the more she breathe, the more she live—like she breathin air, like she belong in water. She say she saw men without skin jump in to get her—2 of em—and saw them thrashin toward her. Momma Ja say a crocodile come and attack these men, but she not scared, she was standin straight up and lookin at the fishes. The fishes was givin her air and wouldn't let her die and she knew the crocodile wouldn't hurt her cause it was her. The fish got up under her feet and carried her the 2 miles to the shore. As the fishes carried her, the crocodile came to her and said that she had work to do and life to live and pain to feel. Momma say this was Crocodile Waaka and it tol her not to be scared cause their mother would be watchin over her. Anytime times got hard, all Momma Ja had to do was look to water and know she wasn't alone. Crocodile Waaka tol her never forget who she was and not to let her daughter forget neither.

Then Momma Ja say the fishes was gone and she start glidin straight to the shore. The sun had been high in the sky when she flew off the boat and now it was dusk. She say the sellin was going on—right by the seaside— and everyone saw her comin. First hair, then eyes, neck, then bosom and waist then thighs, knees, and ankles. Whitefolks say, Here come Ann, Annie Wade, and put her right up for sale, like it was the commonest thing in the world, for the woman they had scratched off as dead to come sailing straight up to the shore. But she say it took a while for her to be sol. The way she come and look, with seaweed jewelry and bubblin breath and eyes that look so empty folk knew they was too full, the only 1 to look seriously at her was a trader who was takin a load a Africans to Missippi. Momma Ja say he say he gon roughin that smoove skin a hern up and take that uppity look out uh her eyes. But he couldn't. Nobody without skin could change that of Momma Ja's, not with Momma's Momma lookin after her.

This the histry of yo Momma's Momma—the way Momma Ja would tell me when she would do my hair.

She was the color of night sky: pure. And I mean to tell you her skin was as smooth, like she had sailed that lantic ocean with her own limbs. I look a lot like Ma Ja—cheek bones you could set a saucer on and I got her full dark lips too. Got the same thunderhead hair. I favors Ma Ja right smart, and this is a wondrous thing considering the man who put me into Momma: low down skinless dog.

The first time, the man dat claimed he owned Momma strung him up and beat the shit out of him on account of he had wanted Momma to bring pure stock only, which is why he bought her an put her with Daddy. Daddy said that that cracker shoulda been killed, that the only way is to kill evil is to kill it dead. Daddy took Momma to Ma Jule to try to Work the child out of Momma, but the baby come on through anyway. As soon as it saw light it died.

Ma Ja didn't like to talk about this too much, and I didn't ask her about it no great lot either. She did like to talk about her home, though, and Jubateenth.

She talked about our relatives; she say we is Moyalajeh. And she talk about Africa and all she learned from her mother, her Iyah, and how she learned her destiny. She talk about how Yemoja, the mother of all waters, show herself to her: When she would go to the river to draw water, the fishes would come to her and stand pon top the water and kind a dance for her. She say, her, fishes, and water go way back, back to Crocodile Waaka. Now I don't understand all this in full, and you probably can't either. But this from the mouth of your Momma's Momma—and even if we don't understand all, maybe your children or their children will.

Ma Ja talk about how her granddaddy would weave cloth with the family colors: blue for peace, red for power, purple for divinity and a brown so deep it's like black for ourselves. She say gold united everyone and everything—gold, the color of the soul. Ma Ja would create dyes in our family colors from different tree barks and roots and berries. She would dye cloth and design us clothes. We'd be dressed alike for special days, like Jubateenth.

Ma Ja love to talk about the Jubateenth! She say about 3 years after she was drug here, the war started. She say bukrah war coalesce with that we had *been* fightin. She say a lot of the suicides bukrah committed in anguish about the war was really us fightin in any and every way we could, from smothering infant oppressors to throwin mistresses off balconies.

Momma say when freedom was declared, buckra didn't want us to know. Some of us was still enslaved years after mancipation! But when Ma Ja and nem got the word, whew! Say first they went and chopped down the biggest greenest tree they could find and soaked it in water for 3 days which allowed them time for preparations. Food? She say it was 6 goats and 2 cows 4 hogs ain't no tellin how many chickens and turkeys, pies and cakes and all like dat. On the third day, with that log ready, you talk about a ruckus raised—Juba!

Momma say they pulled out drum and fife and bones of all kinds; those who didn't have no instrument, well, Momma say they made music outta theyselves. Momma would sing out clear wid her eyes real wide and far off and her body just a movin and hands a pattin:

Juba left and Juba right
Juba gon come out tonight
Juba up and Juba down
And Juba all around the town
Juba dis and Juba dat
Juba killed dat Yaller cat
Juba front and Juba back
Juba come out to attack
Oh, Juba
Juba, Juba, Juba, Juba!

After Juberlee, Momma Ja and Daddy moved from Pisgah, Mississippi to Bliss Bluff. Bliss Bluff was near bout an all-Black town, so that made it mo bettah. They built a house of pines with they own hands up on 80 acres they bought wid they own money. They was good farmers and made they way through life. Momma say they tried to have chillen but they never seemed to take root in her belly, not til I come along.

Now, the Daddy I call Daddy is my Daddy, but he ain't the man put me in Momma. Momma tell me the man I call Daddy is named Mosa, and he was as dark as Momma and built like Ol John Henry himself. Massah put them together for profit, but Mosa, he love Momma and she love him. But the man who put me in Momma is the same man who jumped on her before.

She say it was early in the evenin when she had took her horse to town to get some rations. Momma say she felt strange that whole ride to town, say she usually go with Daddy but he was breakin in some new ground foe plantin time. Didn't neither 1 of them think it'd be no trouble, but when Momma got good and on her way, that strange feelin kept gettin worse. As she was comin out of Fugitt's store she felt somethin kinda drop inside her, she say. It was duskin dark outside when she got on her horse with her goods. She was a quarter of the way home when she saw it come from behind a copse of trees. She say it look so unnatural, that skinless thing, that she froze. When she recognized who it was, Momma say she felt like she was shot back in time cause how did it get to Bliss Bluff? She couldn't figure out what era she was in or where she was but she knew she was in trouble.

Momma didn't like to talk about this much, and when she did speak on it, she spit all the time. It made her sick. She say he look bout like a bald dog on hind legs, and his arms was too long for his body. She say it look like his eyes didn't have no color at all. Momma Ja say before she could spur her horse, he ran up quick and pulled her by her leg off the horse. Momma's fightin and screamin riled the horse and he galloped straight home. When Daddy saw it, he ran, jumped on it, and headed straight out to Fugitt's. He found Momma in some bushes, she wasn't makin no sound at all, she was on her knees, with her hands cupped up under her chin. Her smooth face just wet and in her hands she caught her tears and she was lookin and listenin to her hands. She was talkin to her water, you see. She looked up and told Daddy who it was.

When she woke up she felt groggy. She could have returned to sleep but she had slept for so long she decided to roll and roll until her feet swept the floor. Is it dusk or dawn? How'd I sleep like this? Where is everybody? She kicked around for her slippers and found and pushed her feet into them. She stood up. As she walked to her wrapper, her joints protested with pops and creaks.

"Umph, I'm stiff as a board. Or I'm getting old," she chuckled. She unfolded her blue cloth wrapper, wrapped it around her body.

She stepped outside, stretched, and looked for answers in the sky. The stars are coming out. So its dusk. The Sta—That's what I dreamt about!

This dream-waking-dream epiphany is always a trip. I dreamt I was on a hill looking at the stars through a wooden instrument. Oh! As soon as I focused on a dynamic cluster of stars I understood I was looking at a woman! A gorgeous mother in the sky! So perfect and serene and still and Oh. My. Oh.

"Ahhh, she is looking back at me!

"She is staring right at me!

"She. Is. Me."

She walked between her and Badu's and the old Man's home. She'd never taken this path physically. But she knew it well and stepped with confidence. There's an immense silk cotton tree here. A bottle tree on the left. There it is. Brilliant blue glass bottles shining on an acacia tree. And here's a white clothed pillar. For a second the pillar was bathed in fire. Her eyes widened. She blinked. It was white again. Without thinking she kicked off her slippers and trekked on. She arrived at a clearing.

Badu and the Old Man were seated before a huge egg-shaped mound of earth that was white from centuries of millet-rich libation. Behind this mound was a smaller mound, also glowing from libation.

Badu and the Old Man faced each other. Ahni removed her cloth and straddled the smaller mound. She felt her blood come. She nourished the mound as it nourished her.

After the sky dawned its most alluring gown, Ahni tilted her head to the cosmos. Ahstah bathed her in a luminous glow.

Open your eyes and witness your Self.

Ahni opened her eyes and saw a woman within a woman within the Earth within the cosmos. She was home.

Yes, Daughter, you are within and of me I am within and of you.

She felt—yes—ibis feathers brush her face. So soft was the touch she was moved to tears. As the arms of night clouds embraced her she felt tears anoint her forehead and run to join their sister streams. She closed her eyes and witnessed herself embracing her self.

How exquisite.

Her legs were wrapped around her waist; her arms embraced her shoulders.

I have a gift for you.

She felt the light of peace drench her. So softly now coming stronger.

ahahahahahahahahahaAHAHAHAHAHAHHAHAHAHHHHHAAAA

The vibration, the rhythm, the life flowed among Mother and Daughter Sisters Lovers LoveHers entwined in the first sound, first feeling. Her clitoris responded, rising meeting its twin. She held her self with all of her power.

Ah birthing by the river. Ah depicting their souls in stone. Ah coaxing and creating perfection with leaves. A collective of Ah flying through the cosmos. Ah cavorting with constellations. Ah in juba—a blinding shining. Ah channeling the Continent's green river. Ah circumnavigating the globe. Ah adorned in beads, lapis lazuli, coral, gold, crowning buildings with electrum capstones. Ahstronomers and Ahstronauts whose knowledge of the cosmos is as intimate as it is complete. Massive libraries constructed from and decorated with tomes of knowledge and filled with volumes of wisdom, the very architecture a text. Gang symbols, Ve Ve, Medu Netcher, Nsibidi, Shumom, all the writings of all of the Ah filled her mind and she understood everything's connectedness, meaning, message. Everything.

Ah was opened unto her. Cosmology, ontology, cosmogony, the entire ethos of Ah, and, now, the new survival and evolutionary skills Ah would need she had. Black ibis Ah leaving American shackles behind. Rising to the Mother. Some would never see the Earth again; others returned. Revolutions. First coming a wheel in a wheel in a wheel in a wheel of eternal Ah, 360° of manifest Blackness. Tahn saluting a Black Madonna. Tahn gathered around a white ringed tree, juba dis an juba dat an. Tahn grinding glass and lighting fires. Tahn designing D.C., founding towns and cities and states all over the nation—Chicago, Va, Hushpukena, Suwanee, Abita, Geechee, California, Alapaha. Tahn dimmed by Free Masonry. Tahn dulled by Islam. Shuddering under Christianity. Now, shining again! Dancing Damballah in front of a Caucasianed Jesus. Tahn asking Legba for the right direction at the crossroads. Tahn vibrating with spirituals, blues, jazz, soul, rhythm and blues, rap, hip hop. Tahn representing. Tahn killing prison guards. Tahn setting bodies of police officers ablaze. Tahn smuggling sacred scrolls through borders. Killing and dying and battling oppressors. Tahn and Ah sharing meals and languages an ocean apart. The womb of Yemọja, the wind of Àràká, the Earth of Nana Bùrúkù, Imọlẹ̀, Onílẹ̀, the cosmos, Ahni, Me. AAAAHHHaahaahhh straddling the Earth blood feeding star fed. Love Her arm, tears, self. Ahset Sthas.

She rose. Her flow had finished. The Earth was assuaged. She wrapped herself in her cloth. She took to her path. She wore her slippers. She went home.

"Badu, bring the gumbo. Ahni, you must be famished."

"My father says you"

                         "Yes, father, thank you," she replied in Dogon while smiling at Badu.

"Father, I understand. Everything. Our path. Our work."

"Please come to me, my daughter. Embrace me. You've been 1 with Mother."

She went to the Old Man. Ah vibration engulfed them. A current of knowledge, pain, hope, power, and wisdom coursed between them and then filled the room. When they embraced, his heart spoke to hers the language of eternity.

Ahni ate with gusto, dipping her bread in her tea. Attacking her gumbo and tuwo like a champion. When the meal was over, the Old Man said to his progeny, "Now that the seeds of evolution are planted and nourished in rich earth, we must now weed our land and cleanse the ground.

"Here in Dgn we are under a plague, and it is devastating the consciousness of our inhabitants. Our progeny are turning away from the reality of Ah and towards the distractions of Ogo. Their minds are turning from deep cognition; their bodies are turning from bringing forth rich Black life; their souls are turning away from holistic expansion. Yurugu's sickness, backwardness, selfishness, and avarice are burrowing through and eroding the consciousness of our potential light-bringers. This is about to change.

"Ahni, many of your people are here, some are aglow, others are as dull as the beasts they follow. The first and most significant lesson in Ah you must learn is that we cannot extend sympathy to any of our destroyers, no matter their ethnicity."

The Atlantide hotel appeared before them, a mirage of America in Mali's savannah. "For the next 3 days, we will project messages to the potential shining ones: They must leave this hotel and seek Ah. I will enter this bastion of Babylon that they have erected over my ancestors' bones and, in a guise of a wizened/demented priest, I will forecast disaster. Mark how those Yurugu, supposedly here for knowledge, will mock me and remain. Note how many Africans join Yurugu in mocking me while they follow in Yurugu's footsteps hoping to catch falling money. Only a few, those who shine, will feel the truth in their bones and leave. 3 days after my warning, the hotel will combust.

His penis glowed like a beacon.

I must be the most attractive woman in the world right now. She thought.

The galaxy, he corrected.

She felt her vagina begin moistening, humming for her complement. Her eyes were aglow with adoration.

Having been heated by the sun all day, the bathwater was lukewarm. He filled the shallow pan and poured the water down the crown of her head. She tilted her neck and opened her mouth, thirsty enough to take on the Nile. The water tasted like silver! He wet both their bodies and 2 rough natural sponges. He worked the ball of camwood, baobab, and honey soap into a luxurious lather. They scrubbed 1 another. They played. They laughed. Water trickled and, in its descent, tickled. When they began washing their genitals, they both exploded in orgasm.

Rinsed and shining with sesame oil, they went to their room. She noticed the Earth mound in their room had been fed. Badu lit a pot of incense. He sat on the bed and she came to him.

His arms and legs were open. She opened her self—her eyes, ears, arms legs all 6 lips—and inhaled fully. She wrapped her legs and arms around her man. Badu made his thighs Ahni's throne. His hands explored her braids, skin, and ribs before resting on her lower spine as he gained entry.

She tightened her chamber in time with his rhythmic thrusts. She felt his exhalation, and drank it in her inhalation. Their heartbeats throbbed with their organs. They entered a rooms of gold, ruby, onyx, pewter, amethyst, coral, granite and black black earth; they toured rooms of their souls. Their spirits glowed. Their bodies were cerulean water, spinning twin orbs of blood red fire, now wind, now lightning now

Aaahhhhaaahhh

She drank him;
he quenched her. She squeezed and relaxed. He offered liquid pale gold to anoint her cervix. They clung to 1 another: twins sharing 1 womb.

We have known you. We have watched and waited for you. Last night you met your Self meeting yourself. You now fully understand your path.

Ahni, you have 360° of cipher. However, because your force has lain dormant, you must undergo a process of education and spiritual revitalization. You will become 1 with the way of Ah and all we have done and all we must do. Your emi will be opened and fully activated so that you have infinite access to your inherent skill set. You will soon find that there is nothing closed to you. You, Ahni, have and are all.

Ahni, Ahni is your second self. Her every power is yours; you only have to open every facet of your mind, spirit and body and all those who have gone before and those coming will share immortal wisdom with you. He paused and stoked his pipe.

Our most important work will be the erection of 6 emisites. They will link the Ah and Tahn. We will establish Ah network to summon the Ah and Tahn who are ready to begin the destruction and the creation.

Have you noticed the increasing strength of the sun's rays and the warming of the planet? Ahni is preparing Ah, by increasing our melanin and serotonin and our ability to interact with and learn from flora, fauna the Earth, and the cosmos and all entities and bodies therein.

While our powers are heightening and deepening, Yurugu will become increasingly susceptible to cancers. Eventually they will mount campaigns to encourage their kind to embrace the thing that they most abhor—their recessive genes.

Yurugu is busy attempting to complete itself using various means. Scientists are struggling to create a synthetic forms of melanin and serotonin that they will combine and promote as a sleep aid. This concoction is designed to fabricate the abundance of melanin and serotonin that we boast inherently. Other Yurugu are cloning animals with the goal of finding a way to clone human beings and increase their dwindling numbers as melanin bearers outpace them in population growth. Yurugu is hatching plans that span from legislating the control of wombs to genocide of the Ah to mind control in its effort to destroy us and complete itself. However, it will only further its destruction. By simply existing, Ogo is killing itself.

We are on the threshold of a holistic evolution. This evolution will result, naturally and incontrovertibly, in the ultimate revolution.

When the Ah and Aha first witnessed Ogo and conferenced with Ahni about it, many wondered why Mother did not destroy the mutant. During that time, Ah had 12 emisites at full manifestation. They were Gods created by God. Ahni, however, was seeking to create Gods who could create Gods who could create Gods. With continued exposure to Yurugu and inter-Ah conflict and devolution, the emi capacity shrank for the vast majority of Ah and their progeny. Ahni recognized that only when facing complete desolation and with no resources, save the cosmos, the Earth, and the numinous self, could self-deification occur. This is why the Tahn are so significant. They were sold, beaten, raped, and killed, but they freed themselves spiritually, physically, and mentally and revolutionized the world. The Tahn, in many ways, represent the apex of Ah—original, self-hewn Gods developing and expanding the divine self.

Our collective's goal is to bring as many Ah and Tahn to manifest totality as possible. We must prepare our full selves for the spiritual, mental, and physical evolution awaiting us.

Father, is the re-unification to be a physical 1? Will there be a mass repatriation to this Continent?

Daughter, the creator of everything is Ah. All that your eyes and mind can behold was fashioned in the immense and inexhaustible womb of Ahni. This Continent is a favored place, but favored places are many. Sacred spaces of creation are innumerable. Every land upon which an Ah has shed blood is a sacred space. Every land in which Ah is buried is a sacred space. Any soil that has absorbed the tears of Ah is sacred space. Umbilical cords, placenta and their guarding trees dot this Earth. Places of furtive juba still tremble with rememory. No, the repatriation need not be physical for we are all times, spaces, and places, and all is Ah.

Indeed, the Tahn created sacred spaces everywhere they were dragged and in every land to which the escaped. Consequently, 3 of the 6 emisites will be in lands of the Tahn. However, the repercussions generated by our 6 sites will be worldwide and will birth emisites not only in the United States and throughout the African continent, but also in Jamaica, Haiti, Cambodia, Vietnam, India, Pakistan, Cuba, London, France, Peru, Bolivia, Columbia, Mexico—in every place in which we shine, whether as indigenes or immigrants, sites of power will spring.

While every emisite will have a significant role in our Work, the brightest light is emitted from across the Ethiopic by the Tahn. Too many of us on the Continent have unalterably scattered our cipher. Whereas the Tahn have found ways to revitalize the spirit. This improvisational power is integral to our development.

We Tahn have had to confront Yurugu head-on, Ahni confirmed. We know Yurugu because we have witnessed it when it was comfortable enough to remove its mask. We've had to cut our charred, tarred, feathered brothers and mothers from trees, we've fished our cousins from the Tallahatchie, Tuscumbia, Red, Suwanee, Mississippi, and Illinois Rivers. We've pulled our weeping daughters out of corners and cleansed them of the bloody semen of rape. And in our spare time we designed and constructed the united states of america. Its roads, rails, cities, its hell. We have fallen through the cracks of asphalt, been grenaded and guillotined, got mowed then shot down. We stayed down, got down, then we got deep and pulled from a bucket of blood and guts and tears blues, jazz, rock and roll, soul, and rap. Our issue is also our jizzum for no matter the tactic Yurugu deploys, we don't die, as Robin Harris, who was born in Jubah 6 thousands seasons ago confirms, we multiply.

"You don't understand the origin of your attraction and repulsion," Patricia addressed Chaka and Jahmai who'd met her at the botanica to discuss their past, present, and future. "Because of this you have been in dubious battle an vicious love, but this is yo reality; the paradox of yo existence.

"You," she pointed to Jahmai, "you Knatha, you are the son of Jangatu. In Gnah when the Arab Ogo began their reign of oppression, you were their minion, partially. You were torn: be an askari or be Ah? You were torn. You decided to follow the beast, and you killed your conscious mind with that decision. But most importantly, you sacrificed your second soul. You were slated to become 1 with Angnata but she stood as strongly in her love for you as she opposed your relationship with Ogo and the wickedness of your adopted masters. She loved and shunned you at once.

"Chaka you are toting the spirit of Angnata. You stole away from your peers to sojourn with Knatha and together you made love. Both of you gave all in your effort to persuade your partner to join your path.

"Knatha, you returned to your post to guard your Arab perverts. Angnata, you joined your peers who were preparing their weaponry of bellows, boiling oil, and sabers."

"The women slayed their defilers. But in order to enact their work, Angnata and her peers were obliged to engage.

"After the equalization and the group Ah decision to live on fresh earth, Angnata found herself pregnant. Knatha, you demanded she stay with you and the surviving askaris and Arabs. You envisioned yourself soldier-father. Seeing the eunuch in you, Angnata went to Elder Akynana. The bulrush sent Abosom back to the cosmos, but she has always been with you and she is with you now. She is waiting. End the struggle—there are more important battles to fight. Remember, re-member Gnah, both of you! Re-member Abosom."

Chaka looked as if she'd swallowed a cup of bitter medicine. Ancient bile filled her mouth and her eyes.

"Yes," Patricia urged, "you were 1 in Ah."

"I wanted to be 1 above Ah," Jahmai started and faltered. "But I didn't want the rapings, the defilings," he pled to Chaka.

"But you sold yourself. And you wanted me to do the same! You're lucky we didn't kill you along with your masters. That night," Chaka's rage became reverie, "that night, I offered all of myself to you: A promise of renewal of eternal exultation. I left you in love."

"There in the grove, I gave you my life flow. I, even then, felt your clitoris spurn me. But I offered all to you."

"I left to meet my group. We were awaiting your masters who were breaking their hypocrites' fast. We oiled and perfumed our bodies; we glistened in the night like stars. I felt the grief of Ahni reflected in the new moon and shivered. We donned our veils, which your masters bid us wear for the thrill they derived from ripping them off or snatching them up. The orgy began; we were benumbed. With my garments on, I took 2 of them: 1 in my vagina, 1 entered my anus. I thought of you. What would you think of your derisive masters—and of me."

"You didn't have to do that! You could have stayed with me that night."

"To be a slave for eternity? When I sank the spike into the eyeball of the annihilator beneath me, we both climaxed, for different reasons, of course. Untha and her gold wire removed the head of the defiler behind me. I moved on: Receiving and giving with 1 objective. And as I felt the semen of the enslavers mix with yours, I knew I was pregnant and that what was inside of me was not life, but impending death waiting to meet the bulrush.

"I knew I was right when, after the equalizing fire, I urged you to join us in the moving and you chose to stay and rebuild their death pit. I begged you to come."

"Imam Faisal would have killed me! But you could have remained with me, Angnata, we could have raised the child"

"Fool, I had excised your sick seed. I will never birth fodder for chains. There is neither love nor growth where the mind is chained, Knatha. The way was to revealed to you. You shunned it."

"And you?!" He stood up, his tone a melding of accusation and revelation. "In Maryland, you killed my child! You had an abortion. Said you went to see your mother, said, you . . ."

She shrugged, "How could I bear a child for an FBI snitch?"

"But. . . the Panthers . . ."

"You always been a ain't shit sellout," she snarled.

"Bitch," his hands curled into fists.

"Until now," Patricia intervened as she saw the old sparks of a futile war rekindling, "only sand until now. Now there is fertile ground. Now there is blood-rich soil." Patricia spoke for a consortium of Gods and Ancestors. "Enough. Enough. The cycle must be broken. Let the child come. Let Abosom grow. 9 moons will pacify the yearning of 3600 seasons. She is coming like the wind. The wind."

The room in which the trio sat swirled with questions, rage, memory, and pain. The shrine dimmed and then became resplendent, "Ahni is preparing us. These are the rays of the sun. Their power has become as enriching as the womb is for a child. Look!" The radiance that had filled the room sank in on itself, turned inside out. The infinite Blackness of the cosmos engulfed them and carried them with a speed beyond that of light through space and time until they arrived: "The home of origins," Patricia nodded, "as deep and as sure as the womb."

Ahni offered them a pleaprayerpromise. All paths, understanding, coursed from her countenance into Chaka and Jahmai's souls. Recognition alighted on the shrine and folded its soft black wings.

Shana lay in the slave quarters waiting for her lover. Because Sammy worked in the big house his duties kept him longer than the field hands. She had bathed, had had crushed violets floating in her palms and through her fingers as she stood knee-deep in the stream. Having scrubbed the cleansing smoothing pumice mud from her body, she anointed herself with rose butter. She rubbed violet water over her lower belly where her womb expressed its monthly desire to bear life. Yes, she thought, tonight, tonight.

She smiled thinking that after the loving she would share with Sammy her plan to head to the swamp. Folk livin there free, livin with Seminoles, knowin their power! She sucked her teeth recalling the lashes Sammy had wrapped in camphor and alum for her and later dressed in rose butter only 5 months before when she was whipped for impudence. Yes, tonight: love, tomorrow: freedom! She laid on the rough homespun cover. The cornhusks rustled under her. She heard the door open. She closed her eyes, parted her legs and waited.

The giggling made her open her eyes. She gasped. Ghoulish, pallid, more deathly than any haint, he was. He had an odor of a burst corpse after a light summer shower. He fell on her. Shana fought, kicked, bit, and was overpowered. In the throes of desecration, she saw Sammy peeking around the door jamb watching as Mars Donnell pumped degenerate semen into her violet-scented vagina.

Mere concentration was enough to kill the blighted seed in her womb. She expelled it 1 month later as she ran, alone, to the swamp. She left a bloody mucus clot beside a gnarled oak. She knew Sammy would join the aborted fetus: Poke salad extract would see to that.

They met in California in 1968. Tanji, Oakland's BLA coordinator, loved B. Black, but the FBI agent loved the path of Hoover more. They clashed in the Kongo. And while her soul was wrapped in the guidance of the Prophet, Mwilwa, working for Mobutu, severed the Prophet's hand. They planted and received seed through time and space. All to the same end. But now, they'd met themselves—all of themselves. They understood.

They saw Ahni, saw themselves in Ahni, working, loving, living as 1 force, 1 cause, the only cause. There was work to be done and they were to do it together.

I think we've arrived.

Gazing at it from the gentle slope of the hill, the village was like any other. The sounds of children playing and pestles pounding greeted the pair.

I've never entered the village from this direction so I can't be sure, but I believe we've reached it. Daughter took a deep breath and forged ahead.

The journey had taken 3 weeks, but Kofi and Daughter were feeling strong. The trek had not been difficult. They had themselves for company, and when their supplies ran low, Earth supplied amply. During their trek, Daughter perfected her communication through/with Kofi. They went beyond simple telepathy as Daughter revealed Kumba to Kofi.

Daughter was holding all of the texts, all chapters of Ahni of Ah, in the vast library of her mind, and she shared her knowledge with Kofi. Daughter told Kofi about how Wakynam left her village in disgust. Having listened appalled to the nonsense rantings of Muslim converts, whose very existence she saw as the desecration of Ahni, she and 144 Ah had spoken out. Half their number were executed: Refusing to be enslaved physically or mentally, they were useless to the Arabs. Those who survived the massacre fled to Tbk. The Arabs followed them and stripped, raped, and demolished their libraries. Real knowledge was replaced with mantras of oppression.

Again, they fled for survival: This time they carried their libraries in their minds; however, this time, they became scattered. Those with the ability to stay linked mentally did. But many were killed in the fleeing or by general upheaval that signified the reign of Ogo. Wakynam, Matalah, and Oya comprised the last of the original Ah on the Continent.

To survive, they utilized their specific survival styles. Wakynam took to the water, armored her body, and made of her soul a home. Matalah stopped aging and retained his form as elder so that he would always be available to provide much needed wisdom. Oya became the water and the force that moves water—the winds of change.

Wakynam had projected Ah wisdom into Daughter's hiding, healing enclave. Ah history, disintegration and shining had filled Daughter's mind. Daughter saw the arrival of Singbeh, who was the first to answer Wakynam's call. Singbeh was followed by Lkymat, whose destiny was being threatened by western civilization's answer for the African woman— prostitution. Lost at the crossroads, Lkymat heard Wakynam and fled to peace. Kumba became a beacon. Those who resisted the lure of the coast and those who ran screaming from it came to Kumba, the second site of the 3rd coming, to heal themselves.

With Kumba's history, Wakynam's protection, and Kofi's love girding her soul, Daughter arrived in her former village with an air of assurance and calm. After her village recovered from the surprise her appearance caused, the rich scents of fried plantains and palm nut soup pervaded the compound in celebration of Daughter's return—and with a husband!

"You see, my child, nothing was taken from you; you were in no way harmed. Kofi, here, is a fine strong man. You have been blessed," Lan

Endo, Daughter's mother, offered cold water and kola to the "newlyweds." "Now," she looked at them in consternation, "where do you live?"

"We live in Kumba," Kofi revealed. The language of Ama's people was Lodagbaa, 1 of many languages in which Kofi was fluent.

"I don't know it. It must be a far journey. So what work do you do there?" Lan Endo inquired of Kofi. "Many of our young men travel to the coast to work as drivers and cleaners and cooks for obruni. They make strong, strong money." With this, her hands became fists and her eyes glistened and hardened with the remembrance of the cheap cloth, shiny junk jewelry, and other useless things that these young men brought with them upon their infrequent and reluctant returns home.

"It is—spirit work—that we do."

Lan Endo eyes widened as those of a dog, who after losing a bone, spies a steak. "There are many obruni who come to purchase and pay to learn spirit work.

"Last year we sold our Ma Wota," she laughed and clapped her hands. "3 strong men! They were sacrificed in order to pull her from the river! Ehhh! She was enraged! Ama, you know how calm and clear the river is . . . Well, it became violent and foamed white like the froth of fresh palm wine. But they offered $3,000 US dollars! If there is enough money after the chief gilds his throne, we may get a water pump!"

She laughed again and rose from the mud couch. She placed the palms of her hands on Ama's cheeks and stooped to look into her eyes, "Child, not 1 word has come from your lips, yet shouts of reproach adorn your face."

"Daughter wants you to know she has new communicative modes. New ways of living."

"Why? The traditions of this land are strong," Lan Endo emphasized the last word without noting the contradiction of having strong traditions and selling them. "Our way is good. Look at the prosperity that moldy brass will bring," referring to the sold Ma Wota.

"Daughter wishes you to know death is the overseer of this land."

"Is this your 'spirit work' my daughter? Castigating and contradicting your mother! You ran from me, your village, our clan. Do you know I was branded a witch? Why else would my own child flee from me? A witch!" Her ire was invoked with the memory of her humiliation. She gesticulated about the room as if she might strike Daughter or herself or cry. She calmed herself enough to continue: "Before your birth, your father almost returned me with a goat to my fathers. Everyone thought I was barren. I thought your coming was 1 of joy, but unspeakable grief was hidden inside of that joy. On the day of your purification, you were brave, noble, only to flee from us! But now, you've returned with a husband."

"Daughter and I are 1, but not in the way you know."

"In what way?"

"We are on the same evolutionary path. We live, learn, and work as one."

"Where's the bride price?" The flint in her eyes matched that in her voice as she came to the crux of her interrogations.

"Mother—"

"Where's the bride price for my daughter?" Lan Endo was answered with silence. She turned away from them in disgust, "Baba will return from Kinta in a few days; you will discuss this with him." As she left them to check the soup, she muttered to herself, "They come here like zombis, no elders, no money just nonsense about 'spirit work'."

"Mother, Daughter says there is time for understanding"

"Stop it!" she wheeled on her heel. "This is bizarre! Is this voice throwing?" She stared at the pair. They look like twins. Same coloring, same height and those large eyes. What relationship is this? She gave up and adjusted her head-tie which had slipped towards the back of her head. What used to be a beautiful braid pattern, now gone fuzzy with time, was revealed. Her skin, usually a smooth ochre, was a faded and ashen.

"Mother, Daughter wants to see her sister."

"Yes, Ama, you have a sis—how did you know? Perhaps you. . ." she smiled now, thinking of the daughter who'd washed away the shame of Ama's flight, "She is with Akyem."

Daughter winced as the name Akyem conjured the triangle of mirror.

"She will come later. Nadey stays with Akyem while I'm in the fields. Ama, you did unlock my womb," she looked with love at the girl who'd become a woman in the 3 years she's been gone.

Lan Endo sighed, "Why don't you 2 rest. Your journey has been an arduous 1. When you awaken, food will be ready and Nadey will have come."

After sleeping on beds of leaves and grasses and sheltering in tree groves, it took time to adjust to the close walls guarding the scents of yesterday's ground nut stew, sweat soaked clothes, Nadey's urine and spit-up, and, beyond the walls, the sounds of a bustling village. But eventually their minds and bodies adjusted and relaxation swept them away.

Nadey was a fire child! She was lively and precocious. In 3 seasons she was speaking in complete sentences and was into everything. Daughter immediately took complete charge of her sister with everyone's approval, especially Nadey's. When Akyem brought her forth on the day of arrival, Nadey looked at Daughter for a full minute and then charged into her sister's open arms. Kofi, Daughter, and Nadey were inseparable.

Daughter sought her age mates. But, what was seen as her lack of communication distanced her from them. It was only the thought of Kofi as her husband that gave her a modicum of respectability.

Most of her peers had settled into filling lives of spiritual emptiness with children they would neglect and traditions they would sell. Most of the males of Daughter's group had run to the coast to seek fortunes. Some had married before leaving, but few had returned either to collect their wives or to shower them with money. Some of the young women had gone too, to commoditize themselves. A handful had gone to school.

Daughter and Kofi started summoning. They sifted through dreams of American and French windfalls in search of like minds and cipher. There were no sparks from her peers. But there were sparks. Prepubescent children were mesmerized by Daughter and Kofi. 4 girls and 3 boys, Foku, Vai, Zennan, Kyza, Maly, Tobi, and Yao could not stay away from Daughter's compound. As soon as their chores were finished they came running, laughing, and playing. Kofi would tell them stories, the histories Daughter had told him. They sowed seeds through storytelling, and knowledge of the way took root. In addition to the children, Ahlaz, a barren woman whose status had shamed her family into receiving a reciprocal goat, also came. Ahlaz was almost as quiet as Daughter: She had deep cipher.

While shucking corn for the evening meal, Ahlaz and Daughter conversed mentally.

I know why you left. I am glad you did. The cutting sterilized me, Ahlaz knocked the shucked ear on her palm to loosen the silk. An infection set in and was undetected for months. That is the reason for my barrenness.

But other than that, do you think it is a good custom? Daughter glanced at Ahlaz while reaching for another ear.

No. We came to Earth whole, unless an accident befalls us, we should remain whole! This earth is soggy with children's blood. And this custom is not our own. We adopt the ways of others and uproot our own Gods like a gathering of imbeciles. Ahlaz tossed the ear on the pile with anger. After a few moments she brightened: I am interested in your new home.

Kumba: The saving place, Daughter glowed from within. It is a home for anyone who really wants or who needs a home.

I feel as if I've never had a home. Not since I left my mother's womb.

We have a home for you. You need not sacrifice anything to belong because we are 1. Ah is 1, Daughter held Ahlaz's hand.

When will you return?

3 weeks. Daughter picked up Nadey who had awakened from her nap. She bounced her sister on her lap and smiled, 3 weeks little 1! The child giggled and reached for Daughter's beaded earlobes.

Daughter's mother never stopped singing her dowry, money, cash song. When Timba, Daughter's father, came from Kinta and saw Kofi and Daughter, Lan Endo's song became a sonorous duet.

"Where we live, we don't recognize dowry. To give goods and cash for a human being is slavery."

"Well, Kofi," Timba tried a diplomatic approach, "that is convenient for you and your people; however, our people have always received a bride price for our daughters. It is not a payment for her; she is not a slave. It is a token that signifies that you appreciate the love and rearing that we have done and also that you are more than able to provide for her as we have."

"Sir, your answer is most logical and sensible, and I respect your wisdom. However, what we have cannot be measured by capitalism and will not be polluted by it. Neither I nor Daughter will give anyone money in recognition of our relationship. Our relationship cannot be defined or quantified by the terms and customs of this land."

"You are living together like, like, sinners!"

"Yes, sinners!" Lan Endo agreed, "This, your way, is not good enough for our Ama!"

Kofi and Daughter sat stone-faced in silence. After a pause, Kofi said, "Mother, Daughter wants you to know why she left. You've never asked her why she left."

"That she's returned is all that matters now."

"I   le ft be cau se you an d   your cus toms be   trayed me. You c c cut off my giiif t t fr om God."

Silence followed as Daughter's voice, gravelly and fragile, stumbled from Kofi's lips. Timba's lower lip trembled. He tried to pull it next to its mate as he gazed at Daughter and Kofi in disbelief. He turned to his wife who was weeping, "You birthed this monstrosity? This witch?"

"Theeere are no wiii tches faaa ther.

"Whe nnn Akyem c c cut off my clitoris," Kofi's mouth and Daughter's voice found synchronicity. The pair closed its eyes and remembered. "I s sank in to myself. I went to a h hard, white, silent place. I couldn't move or spea k or feel." She stopped, perhaps to find words of understanding for the ignorant.

Nadey understood; she closed her eyes and held Daughter to ease the trauma of rememory.

"I ran to my true M M Mother. I ran to my true home: l f f free of butchering and de   basement." Daughter was enclosed in the protecting arms of Nadey and Kofi. She drew strength and power from their love.

"When Daughter arrived she was thin, bloody, and scarred and punctured by thorns and twigs. Mother, you wouldn't have recognized her. Father, you would have wept. I wept. I bathed Ama with our healing water and with my own tears," even now, Kofi's tears rained wholeness on Daughter.

"We have been learning together ever since," Daughter and Kofi beamed on 1 another. "Wakynam and the elders teach us the way and we open our own paths from that starting point. We are a whole people who heal and make others whole.

"I came to see you to close this chapter of my life. I have seen you. We are leaving soon."

"You won't leave this compound unless a dowry remains in your stead!" Baba raged.

He is lost.

We shall leave tomorrow morning.

No 1 spoke again. What was there to say? Ama wasn't Daughter, a young woman who had been mortally wounded but had been brought back to life and who was now glowing with purpose. She was 10 goats, 10 kegs of palm wine, 10 bottles of schnapps, and 10 bolts of imported cloth. This is also what Nadey was.

While everyone slept, Daughter and Kofi asked the 7 stars if they wanted a better life. The children had cipher, they could make their own decisions. They said yes. Daughter's mind met Ahlaz's to ask her to come to her compound at fourth cock's crow.

The morning was not new. The scents of breakfast flavored the air from compound to compound. Daughter, with Nadey tied to her back, stood in the center of her family compound holding Kofi's hand. Foku, Vai, Zennan, Kyza, Malu, Tobi, Yao and Ahlaz gathered around the trio.

"Father. Mother." Daughter approached her father. She knelt before him and reached upwards. She cupped his genitals in her hands. "When you can cherish children, you shall bear them." She released his genitals which returned to their former position without physical damage.

Timba lunged at her shouting, "Witch! Witch! She's taken my penis, ooo! She's stolen my birth seeds, ooooo!!" He was trying to alert the neighbors so that they could capture and lynch his daughter, but before anyone arrived, the Ah had gone.

The Ah and Aha who'd gone with Ogo to its den trekked to a cluster of caves far inland on another continent. The place was barren, rocky, and constantly assailed by lashes of ice. These Ah would have succumbed to hypothermia had they not altered their bodies' biochemical compositions to adjust to the temperature. They also used the skin of animals Yurugu had slain to make protective body and foot coverings.

They arrived at Yurugu's den to find clusters of caves that were connected to a central cavern. There the Ah saw Ogo and hogs clustered together in what was the foulest smelling place the Ah had ever witnessed. No form was indistinguishable from another. All was a writhing mass of translucent flesh and bristles. Every being was smeared with feces and bits of rubbish. There were perhaps 50 forms in the largest cave, some copulating, some eating, some sitting and staring, some scraping the crust of offal off of others, some massaging their neighbors with feces. There were about 2,000 beings in the entire network.

6 of the Ah left immediately. There was nothing else to see. However, 6 Ah remained. They wanted to see if Ogo could be genetically upgraded. And they were curious, more curious than repulsed. These Ah paid for their curiosity.

The remaining Ah camped in a small unused cave far up-wind of the Ogo. They selected 4 Ogo: 2 females and 2 males. In 6 weeks, Ah and Ogo were pregnant. When the issues came, they were less savage than pure Ogo, but they had no cipher.

There is no opportunity for growth, 1 Ah argued, unless the impregnating Ah could focus a greater concentration of their emi and melanin into Yurugu, but it is not possible to create Ah from Ogo.

Some Ah were excited about what they considered progress. They convinced the collective to return home with the half-castes and undertake another round of breeding. The Ah were so focused on their project that they failed to decipher the intentions of Ogo. On the eve of return, Yurugu used the static of its anti-emi to shatter Ah communication. Yurugu ambushed the Ah and killed and ate them, but they raised the half-castes.

A brood of Yurugu migrated from their caves nearer to the coast. Nearer to the Ah. The half-castes among them grew, and when they reached puberty, Yurugu bred with some of the half-castes and forced others to breed amongst themselves. After 16 generations of breeding, 2 more types of Yurugu were spawned from the Caucasoid type: Semites and Arabs.

Yurugu sought to use the fraction of melanin that surfaced in its minion to infiltrate the Ah and steal the secrets of cipher. The Ah saw through this plan and assented to the wishes of Ogo. The Ah pushed the full force of their knowledge into Ogo's minion. After 3 seconds, the Ah would often hear the "thwop" of Ogo's mind snapping. When this exercise was over, most Ogo were left in a vegetative state. Others emerged just as they had been, static filled. A minute portion understood a fragment of the way. The 1/333.49% they comprehended, they began perverting into tools of oppression that would come to be called religion.

The Ah continued, in the midst of Ogo's madness, to build. Ah focused on fortifying and defending their emisites. The Ah of Zalah and Knah perfected their war implements: swords, shields, machetes and cutlasses. The Zalah and Knah shared knowledge, manufacture, and use of weaponry with all Ah. Zim built impeccable walls of impenetrability around its soul chambers. The Kng were safe in the lush vegetation that spelled immediate death for Ogo: The Continent and Ahni had provided well in this respect. The Gnah created beautiful gold jewelry for spirit protection. Intricately crafted gold necklaces, earrings, bracelets, anklets, and the gold dust that was used to adorn the body and hair also worked in conjunction with the body's electromagnetic force to bolster and protect the emi of the Ah. However, the gold, bright and shiny, would attract Yurugu who would make stealing Ah's Black and gold wealth the foundation of its national economies and, eventually, a global economy.

Ah of Dah and Kmt began encoding the cipher of their script so that when Yurugu read their ancient walls, halls, and scrolls, it would be confused and able to comprehend only the most superficial information; however, when an Ah or Tahn with cipher read the same works, revelations would blossom in their minds, and their third eyes would open to their ancient cosmic heritage.

The Ah of Jubah took their aesthetic to a revolutionary level. They devised ways of encoding their arts so that spirit-charging sounds, mental invocations, and physical percussive vibrational harmonies would seem no more than mere entertainment in Ogo's ears. The Ah of Yah, who were living alongside the now-dry river, decided to remain there and master the harsh lessons taught by the devouring desert.

Ahni revealed that the Ah of Ta Ntr would be subjected to horrific attacks, enslavement, and dislocation; following this, much of Ta Ntr would physically follow Ahtlna and be submerged under an Ogo-made sea. Before the destruction, Ta Ntr became a wholly astral site that funneled all of the wisdom and power of the Ah of Earth to Ahstah for eternal preservation.

After 1000 seasons, and as predicted, Ogo made a temeritous move. 3,000 mutants and their minion laid siege on Ta Ntr. Although their defeat was sound, the Ogo succeeded in destroying many of the physical structures of Ta Ntr. However, demolition of the physical structures was irrelevant because the Ah had taken the way to a wholly spiritual level.

The 2,569 Ogo slain were thrown into the sea along with the 525 corrupted Aha who assisted them. The mercenaries and traitors were few but growing, as more Aha scoffed at the completion and perfection they enjoyed within Ah and sought to dominate and subjugate Ah in a manner identical to the way Yurugu treated its female members.

The Ah struggled to reunify, but many Aha sought strength in fragmentation; Ogo focused its efforts on annihilation.

Yah appeared to be an excellent target for destruction. The Yah seemed isolated and oblivious in their desert oasis: This is what collaborating Aha told Ogo. But when these debased Aha and Ogo finalized their plans, they did not count on the mental perception of the Ah—being of low emi, the Aha couldn't.

The Ah of Yah did not take up weapons; they simply stood and waited for their attackers. They stood, 6,953 strong with arms and minds linked in the sand that housed the spirit of the desiccated river. Their eyes were closed—their minds were open.

As the Ogo came—also lined horizontally—it looked as if the Ah versus Ogo war were about to take a brutal turn. The Ogo charged, holding high their stolen weapons. When they came within 6 feet of the Ah and were moving at full thrust, the Ogo lowered their killing tools to thrust them into the melanin-rich bodies before them.

What is the sound of 6,953 bodies transforming into a raging river of sand?

The Ah used Ogo's own tool of destruction to defend themselves. They transformed into a tidal wave of sand that engulfed and consumed every Ogo and sell-out Aha who had come to slaughter them.

Ah's victories were tempered by the fact the retrogression had given rise to a low emi Ah who would devolve rather than evolve. They were easily indoctrinated by and eager to follow Yurugu. The attraction was befuddling to evolved Ah. Was it the knowledge that Ogo was dominant in the art of destruction? What could possibly draw Ah to Ogo? Between traitorous Ah and certain Aha who wanted to found a new testes-dominant world order it was clear that Ogo's era had arrived.

It is important to understand that Yurugu manifests in 2 ways, Ahni informed the Gods, in some cases it is emivoid, in others, eminegative. In the emivoid form, it is a brute, an animal, a drone, a tool. However, as eminegative, Ogo is mentally, psychologically and physically dangerous, it is capable of twisting the minds of low emi Ah. Witness the work it is undertaking in the settlement of thievery that it has established near Kmt.

Yurugu is fascinated with Kmt for a very important reason: it is going to use the wisdom living on and whispering from the walls there to finalize the creation of a tool of oppression called "religion." Yurugu will use this fabrication to dominate the world.

It will convince the vast majority of people who will come to inhabit the world that rather than use their intellectual capacities and knowledge, they should believe what Yurugu says is truth.

What is "believe?" an Ah asked.

It is a psychological process in which 1 suspends logic, science, reason, and common sense and foregoes critical analysis and simply agrees with whatever Yurugu says is a truth or a way to be followed.

Rather than exercise and develop their intellectual capacities, multitudes will "believe" whatever Ogo says. They will even "believe" that living in a state of ignorance is a sublime manner of existence.

The Ah were flabbergasted.

Yurugu will take the immense images of you that people these colonnaded halls, Ahni projected images from temples of Kemet, remove the dominant genotypic features, and claim that it created Kmt.

Yurugu will convince the inhabitants of this world that there is a massive Yurugu in the sky who created everything that we have created. Not only will people "believe" this fiction, but they will fear it and they will kill for it. Millions will slaughter and be slaughtered under the auspices of Yurugu's concepts of "religion" and "god."

Ahni continued: Many "religions" will spring up as people try to place themselves at the center of this planet's narrative; however the most savage religions will be Christianity, Judaism, and Islam which are the 3 sibling concepts that are reflective of the 3 primary Ogo-types.

Our progeny will be some of the most fervent "believers" of "religion." While some Ah will use these religions for liberation and self-deification, many of our progeny will shun the way of Ah—and their divine inheritance—and seek solace in constructs created to destroy them.

Yurugu will also create centers of mind control called "schools" and will make attendance mandatory for human beings from age 6 to 16. In these indoctrination centers, people will memorize the lies that Yurugu will weave to reify its fictions and to justify its oppression and domination of the world. In addition to being forced to integrate into their consciousness ludicrous propaganda and myths of Yurugu supremacy, everyone who attends these detention centers will be trained to labor all of their lives to build unimaginable wealth for a few Ogo.

The masses of this planet will suffer, labor, and struggle to survive with the least amount necessary, but their thankless toil will provide a few Yurugu with infinite bounty. There will come a time when many Yurugu will not work at all. They will create a tools called currency and stock, and, with them, they will control all of the natural resources of this world. This is the real goal of religion, belief, and indoctrination masked as education. People will be encouraged to spend all of their lives chasing and hoping to amass a myth called "money." But the chief beneficiary of their life-long quest will be Ogo.

Yurugu will massage myth until it convinces the world that myth is reality. The questions our progeny will have to ask and answer are how does 1 combat something that does not exist? How does 1 conquer a foe that is irrelevant?

The Ah saw boats lining the east coast of the Continent. Ah were marched in chains from Zim, Kng, Jubah, Gnah, Tbk, Dah, even the Island of Gosah far northeast: force-marched, death-marched to factories created to transform human beings into slaves. Ah skin sizzled with red hot irons; Ah were branded like livestock. Ah saw Ah submerged in unimaginable suffering in ship hulls with only moans and screams to comfort them. Ah backs were rubbed raw from rough boards and then anointed with the blood, feces, urine, and vomit that served as mattress and quilt. Ah jumped into the ocean and into the arms of the Ahtlnta, of Yemọja, and of Ma Wota. Ah overthrew their oppressors and offered their mutant bodies to the sea as sacrifice.

Ah saw 500,000,000 Ah forced from the Continent to build Yurugu's empires of abomination. Ah saw Ah building, harvesting, sowing for Ogo to reap, relax, and recharge. The Ah saw Ah hanging from trees; Ah ravaged, desecrated, mutilated; Ah submerged in swamps, bogs, and gullies; Ah running with the confidence of the wind as they embraced the freedom that is their right.

Here were Ah setting plantations a blaze. Here is an Ah on a horse with a sword slaying Yurugu. There is an Ah sprinkling ground nightshade into missy's gumbo while smiling and singing spirituals. Here was a group of Ah levitating and then flying, leaving the lands of oppression and leaving their oppressors in perfect confusion. Here is an Ah standing up and chopping her overseer down with a hoe after he said something to her that he had no business saying. Here is a group of Ah relaxing under a shade tree and sipping minted lemonade because they had charged their hoes with the power to work by themselves. Here is an Ah who had been captured by pattyrollers until he changed his molecular structure and became the wind. Here were 300 Ah living in secluded bliss in what Ogo called a dismal swamp. From their fortified oasis of freedom, the Ah sought out and liberated hundreds from surrounding plantations. The Ah saw everything: 300 years of oppression, liberation, sufferation, and elevation.

The Ah sold into slavery will be those with the highest emi level—this will tell you what you need to know about the traitors among us as well as of Ogo's ability to recognize our power: It cannot attain emi; it is devoid of shining, but it can see those who shine—and its goal is to use and/or destroy those of us who shine. Because the Ah threaten the traitors who seek to organize societies based on the myth of penile supremacy, they will be the 1's singled out for and subjected to the horrors of slavery. What these destroyers and Yurugu do not know is that the Ah who are the most brutalized and scourged will be those who create Gods of themselves—and this is precisely our goal.

These Ah, those who are deceived, duped, abused, and defiled by a collective of beasts, traitors, and traders, are actually the light of divinity, the Gods of Illumination. Where it seems there is no emi, they will manifest cipher. In a land numbed to empathy, compassion, and understanding, they will absorb and emit crucial vibrations. Those who are placed lower than a dirt road will rise to embrace the cosmos and all it offers. My Gods, we will soon bear witness to the creation of Divinity.

"Where did you go?"
"Inside and out.

"You know me as you know yourself. But just as there are things you don't know about yourself, there are also things you cannot know about me."

"Like what?" He rose from the bed where he had been sitting so that he could face her fully, "What are these secrets that move you to abandon and make a complete fool of me during our wedding festival?"

"Ṣàngó," she cooed and massaged his shoulders, hoping to calm him, "let us be jovial," she massaged his rippled back. "You know that you are the only man I need."

"And that is how you show it? By abandoning me?"

"Darling, you have 2 beautiful wives, isn't that the reason you married me, to increase your leisure and your pleasure?"

"My leisure or your own?" He was becoming enraged. He stepped away from Àràká and paced the floor. He understood why Ògún beat this woman. Who does she think she is? Surely, she is no wife!

He gazed at Àràká who, even after giving him herself, remained an enigma. Holding her is like holding the wind, he thought. She came into my life like a tornado and now . . . His sigh of resignation was audible.

"You are right, Àràká: I have 2 beautiful wives. I have no use for a wayfarer."

Every Thursday morning, without fail and whenever she was summoned for an emergency, as on her wedding night, Àràká met her ẹgbẹ́ at the 16 crossroads between the cosmos and the Earth. They presided over all spiritual and human affairs. Àràká was Oròmbọ̀, the whirling unseen justice of the ancestors. She was the direct emissary of Imọlẹ̀ and Ẹdan. The world had to be organized. The ancestors had to be summoned, and the spirits had to be assuaged and reconceived. Violators had to be punished, marks eradicated, and deserving ones need reward. She was Àràká. As the pillar of Àjẹ́, she had to take her position and she loved to do so.

She made her home deep in the forest in the hollow of a baobab tree. Ọrẹ́ mi, you remind me of my mother, with your wide curves and your undulating comforting trunk. You remind me of home. She stroked her arboreal friend's bosom before she ascended a nearby anthill and invoked her group.

Aro Aro Aro
Ẹ́jọ̀ titi ọ̀run
Ẹ́jọ̀ titi ayé
Ìyàmi Àbèní
Mo lẹyẹ nílé
Mo lẹyẹ níta

Mo rìnde òru
Mo rìnde ọsán
Ti mo bá lọ sóde
Ẹ fọ̀wọ̀ mi wọ̀ mí o

Ògbóni:
Ògbóràn!
Erelú:
Àbíyè!
Eríwo yà!
À Yà Gbó
À Yà Tó!

The collective assembled. Some attended in pure spirit form, others kept their physical beings. All Òrìṣà Àjẹ́ were present. Ìyàmi Òṣòròngà was enveloped in white down: a white that reflected all destinies, all heads, all powers. Her immense head was all of her that was visible. Although the circle had no beginning or end, she was clearly its center.

"Òṣun, is that you, my senior wife?"

"I am the one. Did you leave our husband well?"

"Indeed."

"Indeed," Imọlẹ̀ sang out, "Ṣàngó's hands must be beyond full with you 2 and Ọbà.

"Mother, I have lightened his load."

"We are aware," said Ìyàmi Òṣòròngà, her voice husky and rippling with power. "You have important work elsewhere."

"Àràká," Ẹdan spoke, "you are about to take a 3rd husband."

"Oh?" Àràká pushed her lips to the left side of her mouth. She was far from enthusiastic.

"From this union you will birth 9 children who will solidify not only your destiny, but also Àjẹ́'s terrestrial dominion. We have prepared a garment for you." Ẹdan nodded to Imọlẹ̀ who brought forth a dress of 16 colors that throbbed with life, character, duty, and destiny. Àràká slipped into the dress: the fit was immaculate. When she spun around 9 times, she became a black tornado, her womb its red eye.

"Oròḿbọ̀!"

"Oròḿbọ̀, that is the sound!" the Mothers cheered as Àràká whirled, whipped, and swirled.

The Gods began singing; to the listening ear, the sound was that of a galaxy giving birth to a planet.

She emerged in the stratosphere. She danced, spinning like a top. She styled and showed off her shroud, she thought, to the plants, animals, and spirits. Her braids, caught in the velocity of her revolutions, formed a pyramid on her head. She felt the force of all ancestors, all Àṣẹ and Àjẹ́ eddying and swirling about her. She was now their guardian.

As Àràká spun; stratus clouds dissipated; cumulonimbus clouds hovered and then chased cirrus clouds. Áàjálayé, the Winds of the World, played with the weather and the Earth laughed.

Àràká descended from the clouds, removed the garment and placed it inside the anthill. Her body was steaming from the rains and heat she had generated. She felt rejuvenated as she sauntered to her baobab home.

He unglued his sweat soaked back from the ìrókò where he'd been pasted since seeing the apparition's spinning appearance. He blinked his eyes and shook his head. The sky was clear now, he panned the horizon, but when she mounted the sky, the sun shone, the wind howled, tornados and hurricanes formed, danced, and dissipated as they frolicked with her.

Olúkòsì Ẹ̀pẹ́ was trembling; his knees were weak. He approached the anthill with the measured tread of a thief. The anthill, at its highest peak, was about 9 feet tall, and because of the still-vibrating power of the gown, it was glowing. He climbed the anthill, seized the gown, and secreted it under his clothes. He was astonished to find his bones illuminated by the shroud. He rushed home. He forgot about his traps; he'd found a real treasure.

Àràká Áàjálayé spun with joy and entered the anthill, excited to continue her terrestrial and cosmic work. Realization washed over her like rain, and an electric current shook her spine: Her gown was gone. Her astonishment was as deep as the night. She studied the anthill for signs of intrusion and saw tracks in the mud from the rain she created last night. She followed the footprints.

The tracks led to a dwelling situated in a clearing 7 miles from the baobab. A slim and muscular man with night-deep skin and a stern countenance was sitting on the verandah sharpening some tools and cleaning others. The tracks she followed led to muddy shoes that he had placed outside the door. She sat down beside the man on his verandah. Àràká knew she had destiny with this man who was brave enough to take her shroud. She stayed with him: together they enjoyed bliss and she was free to go to her ẹgbẹ́ whenever she needed or wanted to.

Àràká squatted by the river bank. She gripped tree roots until they bit into her hands. She grimaced and then relaxed. For 9 seconds, water poured from her womb and joined the Niger. Àràká relaxed her grip and began a rhythmic breathing. As her womb contracted, she pushed. She paused. With her next exhalation and contraction, she pressed her palms against her thighs and gave birth.

She was amazed by the bundle between her legs, a wrapping of gauzy ecru placenta and saffron and richest blood. Her fingers caressed the balloon of life. A vibration coursed through to her marrow. This is a head and another and legs—Yes! children wrapped in a bundle! Still trembling, Àraká opened the caul. 9 children! She began to weep and sing praises.

Her children began to stir, gaze, and whimper at their new world. She examined them with a scrutiny only a new mother can give. Each child was perfect. A mirror of her, yet each 1 unique. She noticed the smallest baby girl's umbilical cord was resting like an atori whip on her little belly. The biggest child had already grown 2 thick tufts of hair which were positioned like horns. Another of her precious package bore the flashing cloak of another caul. She noticed another little girl, caught in a deep yawn, was boasting her uppermost teeth!

Each child a wonder, each a confirmation of majesty!

In the soft sand, she molded a supportive ledge and dressed it with her cover cloth. Still humming her praises and appreciation, she washed each child with her tears and the Niger. She positioned 7 of her children on the ledge she had made and took 2 children to her breasts.

For 8 days, Ìyásáàn Àraká and her children gained strength. On the 9th day, she wrapped her children in her many colored cloth and they went home on Áàjálayé.

"Mothers, witness our children!" Each God held, blessed, and swept each child 9 times.

"They are stunning children, Àraká," Ìyá Múwọ̀ extolled.

"They are the start of a new existence," Ọ̀ṣun cooed.

"Ọmọ Ìyá Àjẹ́," praised Ẹdan.

"Ọmọ Ìyàlájẹ́," the Gods agreed.

After 9 days with her ẹgbẹ́, Àraká introduced her children to their terrestrial home. Olúkòsì Ẹ̀pẹ́, his mother Sola, and his first wife Banke praised Àraká and then took the children and merged them into their family. Sounds of pride, love, and joy reverberated through their home.

1 day, Àraká and Olúkòsì Ẹ̀pẹ́ sat on the porch watching an orange red sun sink into periwinkle, indigo, and mauve clouds. Olúkòsì Ẹ̀pẹ́ had had a successful hunt the day before and was resting after the cleaning and offering and dressing of game. Àraká was relaxing after putting her children down for their naps.

As they passed a pipe of ewé àikú between them Àraká said, "Your work is so dangerous. If an animal was preparing to kill you, what would you do to protect yourself?"

"Ahh," Olúkòsì Ẹ̀pẹ́ mused and dragged on the pipe, "I have several defensive tactics. For example, I can change my form to shield myself."

She accepted the offering of the pipe. "What forms can you assume?"

"Oh, I can become a fly; I can become an anthill. I can also take the form of iro, which"

"Èpẹ́, ooo" his mother ducked her head outside where the pair was sitting, "I beg you: Stop this"

"Mother"

"You cannot tell any woman everything!" Sola's tone spoke volumes. She wasn't just protective of her son; she was jealous of Àràká. "You must keep some things to yourself!"

Olúkòsì Èpẹ́ held his peace. Àràká also relaxed in her knowledge.

Àràká and Banke and Sola lived in relative harmony. All children were cared for by 3 loving mothers and their father. However, 1 morning, Banke came to Àràká's apartment with fire in her eyes.

"Is this your week?" Banke's arms were akimbo as if she were ready to brawl.

"Mm?"

"Why do you monopolize our husband? Between his hunt and you, he's too tired to take care of me."

Àràká smiled and rubbed her thighs, "Well . . . perhaps our husband prefers my, uh, cooking." She gazed at the ram she was seasoning for dinner.

Banke sucked her teeth and rolled her eyes, "You, you, spirit woman! How'd you even find us anyway? You materialize, birth 9 brats, and shatter our home."

Àràká smiled at the insults. She was not the 1 at fault, nor was she the 1 with a frivolous complaint. "Small girl, you are my senior wife but you are in no way my senior. Don't let your mouth write a bill your cowries can't cash." She turned her back on the woman and began washing the tẹtẹ leaf.

Sola had heard the raised voices and came to Àràká's compound. She listened outside the door during the argument and then she started singing:

Carry on with your eating and drinking
Your spirit is hanging on the ceiling!
Continue your loving and living
Your second self decorates the ceiling!
Spirit woman, spirit woman, spirit woman!

Banke and her 4 children joined Sola singing, laughing, and mocking Àràká.

Àràká was floored. She thought she had finally found a home in this world, a place where she was accepted and free to be herself. But no, it was not to be. If it wasn't a possessive envious man, it was a jealous spiritually fragmented woman. How could she, Àràká Oròmbò, be insulted in her own home?

She took her shroud, given to her in love, given to her for protection, down from the ceiling. She thought about the giving of the gift, her struggle to live free and in peace, her will to manifest that 2 husbands tried to derail. Now, now, after finding harmony, these women, whom I took as family, humiliate me? Àràká was demoralized.

She embraced her shroud and softened it with her tears. She donned it and became the buffalo. Her horns glistened and glinted reflecting the sun. Her nostrils flared and increased to 3 times their original size. She charged.

Àràká gored Sola in the midsection and carried the old woman across the compound with such velocity that a dust devil rose up behind them. Àràká reared up and pitched the elder's body into an ìrókò tree, crushing her head and spine.

Àràká Ẹfòn, owner of the buffalo, turned to her co-wife, who was running full speed towards the garden. Àràká caught her in the corn patch and butted her in the back of her thighs propelling Banke 12 feet off the ground. Upon descent, Banke landed on Àràká's horns. Banke's heart was punctured and a fountain of blood spewed from her chest. Àràká tossed her body into the yam plot.

The wailing children were only calling attention to themselves. Àràká ran, leapt, and poosh-poosh, 2 heads popped like over-ripe paw-paws hurtled to the ground. Àràká impaled Banke's other 2 children, and, with each 1 on a horn, she bucked and leaped about the compound before she tossed the children onto a rubbish heap.

Àràká turned her attention to the forest and plunged. Who could reveal her secret but Olúkòsì Ẹpẹ́, the only 1 who knew? She charged to the anthill where she'd first met him. There he was, setting a trap. Àràká saw the uncaged fear in his eyes.

What is this? What could—oh, this is Àràká? This is my wife, ooo! Olúkòsì Ẹpẹ́ scaled the nearest tree as if he were an expert palmwine tapper. Àràká struck the tree BLAM!! The tree and the ground shook with impact BAM!! Olúkòsì Ẹpẹ́'s nose began to bleed, but he held on for BIIIM!! dear life. To let go was death.

Àràká backed up and eyed her husband. She approached the tree and ripped off its bark with her teeth. She sprayed mucus on the tree until it glistened.

Olúkòsì Ẹpẹ́ was slipping. His fingernails were caked with bark and snot. He jumped off the tree and ran towards a pond. Àràká was on him like grease on fat meat. She took aim at his spine, she lowered her head and horns and swept up. Woosh! Air? What? How? Àràká looked all over the water's surface for her husband, but he'd become ẹrọmi. After an hour's search ended in futility, she returned home.

3 hours later Olúkòsì Èpé crept back to his home and was relieved to find Àràká had reclaimed her human form. Àràká beckoned him to join her and the children in the courtyard.

She stood before them and declared, "I am Àràká. I am woman; I am God; I am Àjé. I am Oròmbò: you dare not see my face. I am Áàjálayé, the winds of the world, the winds of change. I am Èfòn, the might of the forest. These are my horns, use them to worship me. I am Egúngún; don and dance in my shroud to summon me. The female ram is mine; taste not her meat! Olúkòsì Èpé, raise our children well. Ensure that they know me and their divinity. I have become Òrìsà; I have become Oya."

Oya took her youngest baby girl, Ato, with her as she ascended and left.

Soul hadn't returned. Because she'd never been a big worrier, she prepared dinner and put the finishing touches on her M.A. thesis, "Political Subservience: From Africa to the African Americas." The project examined Africa's and African's lack of political autonomy from the era of enslavement and exile, decreed by the Pope in 1442, to the nominal abolition of slavery in 1860s, from the scramble and partitioning of Africa decreed at the Berlin conference of 1884-85, to the triangular economic trade, to the contemporary solidification of debt and deprivation overseen by the IMF, World Bank, NATO, and UN. Her conclusion was a manifesto that, borrowing from the best of Sankara, Lumumba, and Nyerere, mapped out the path to true African Unity and unfettered independence for the 21st century.

She and Soul were drafting an African American manifesto for independence, and their combined efforts would dovetail with a Continental treatise on economic autonomy that Chineke Umeh of the African Socialist League was writing. Dr. Quarcoo of Ancient Source Press offered to publish her senior thesis, the manifesto, and the ASL's treatise along with a collection of essays in an anthology tentatively titled *African Unity Now!: Complete Emancipation, Unification, and Empowerment.*

Dr. Quen, her thesis supervisor, also agreed her work was publishable. He'd praised her analyses as being on the Ph.D. level. He just felt the tone should be softened to prevent alienating certain segments of her audience. In other words, cater to Caucasians. She thanked him for his assessment but she had no intention of kowtowing to people who had made the genocide of her people their lifework.

She turned the computer monitor off and checked on her sauce. It was perfect: basil rich, slightly honey sweetened and filled with spicy turkey sausage. She would prepare the spaghetti and garlic bread when Soul came. She checked the time. 11:00 pm? Already? Now officially worried, she put on her triple fat goose down coat and headed to the dilapidated community center. Soul was giving a lecture: "Reparations or War?" That must be a hellified discussion, she smiled. She'd wanted to go but she had to complete the revisions to her thesis before the Friday deadline. She grabbed her keys and closed the door behind her.

You are never alone, child; we are here.

She stopped; her breath rose in quick shallow puffs that evaporated in the air as quickly as she provided a renewal. The air thickened; it was hot, Mississippi humid, yet she saw her breath. The ground was covered in snow, yet here were piiiiine trees, n red earth and umph, watah flowin. She stopped and was spun 180°. It passed. She went forward.

"Squeeze and Joe did a good job."

"Sho did!"

"Unnn! You soun country!" Hawa laughed loudly and freely, so did Danta. Neither 1 had ever felt so alive. Their souls had been revitalized with their meeting and union.

The final touches had just been completed on their home. The looked back on a year's work with pride. The timber was cut from the land and seasoned and cured by Hawa, Danta, Joe, Squeeze and all the "cuddins." The home's womb design had been difficult to construct, however.

"What kinda house that gon be?" Dear turned the blueprint every whichway.

"It's a womb."

"A what? Why?" She handed the paper back, "Y'all crazy." They laughed. "And the truth is that you are 2 of a kind."

"We wanna build down there"

"I know, by the soul sanctuary."

"Mmm hmm."

"Go on, but y'all got some clearin to do and some snakes to kill."

"You know I love snakes, Dear."

"You won't when they wrap round yo neck at night."

She was right. Clearing the land and dredging the pond was dangerous work. Water moccasins resting in peace reared up in anger. In fact, at least 5 different types of snake were flourishing on the land. Much to her dismay, many were killed before Hawa's eyes. Dear and Valeria sprinkled lime all over the ground to keep the snakes from returning.

Clearing was rough work. Even though most of the vegetation stayed: the honeysuckle that would perfume the whole house in July and August, the rabbit tobacco that would prevent and cure colds, the beautiful clusters of bush cranberries that would eliminate kidney ailments, the verbena and lemon grass, all of this remained. In the end, the yard looked uncleared to Dear but like Nature's medicine chest to Hawa and Danta.

Finally, the land was cleared and leveled. All the usable timber was cut and cured for the house. Valeria and Dear relocated many of the uprooted trees. But the issue of a large, gnarled white oak that stood near the building site generated a discussion.

"Y'all need to cut that down."

"Yep," Pooh echoed Leroy. "Build too close to that tree, you gon pay in a storm."

"Oh, that reminds me, Dear. I want a stormhouse just like yours!"

"Well, I sho hope you don't think I'm gon build you 1 like I built mine. I don got too old for that."

"Baby," Valeria reminded, "you always hated the stormhouse."

It was true, she had hated the dank and dusty earth-rich smell laced with fumes of kerosene and the perfume of prayers. But the singing transported her:

Courage, my soul, and let life journey on
For the night is young, it won't be very long
Praise be to god, the bright and morning star
The storm is passing over
The storm is passing over
The storm is passing over
Halleluya

Guaranteed to calm the elements. Even away from the stormhouse and Mississippi, in her apartment in Ohio, she sang the spiritual. After she turned off everything; after enjoying the wet thrusts, bass-heavy romps, and rumbling flashes of power; after counting "1 Mississippi, 2 Mississippi, 3 Mississippi"—to gauge the distance and path of the storm, after all this, when nature overdid her stylings—she sang. The clouds listened. Mercy.

"You remember when Miss—" she stopped. Men were around and Miss Stuffin's was a woman's song. She first heard it sung by Sister B when she was a weeee lil thang. Sista B, Mother Dear's best friend, had wanted to be a minister, but that wasn't open to her because she was a woman. However, she rechanneled her energy and integrated a Booneville lunch counter and the Pontotoc train depot.

A 5-year-old Hawa was sitting in the house newly built by the same uncles who erected and later demolished the big gray 1 and its outhouse. She heard Motherdear come in from outside and remark that it was "comin up a cloud." Now, Dear is better than any weather forecaster. She can read the sky like any text and she knows a squall from a reason to trek to the stormhouse. Dear was the reason Hawa unplugged everything when foreboding clouds formed.

Hawa was dozing in her mother's lap, which must be why she had been able to overhear the conversation.

"Y'all ever hear about anyone splitting a cloud?" asked Mary, Dear's second cousin.

"Ummhumm," mused Dear. "When you first see that cloud a-comin', you go get you a axe, an you stan off from dat cloud. You hurl dat axe in the ground directly under the center of the cloud—and it'll split."

"You don't need an axe," Sista B's soprano slightly muffled because of the lack of ivory rang out. "You could just open the Bible under the cloud and, if your spirit is right, that cloud will split."

"MMm-mM! That is a work there, but not 1 I would want to do," exclaimed Mary. "Can't see myself preemptin Ole Maker."

"That's the sho nuff truth," Sista B assented. "Stuffin found that out."

"Stuffin? 1 had all dem babies fuh Greely?"

"Ummhumm."

The silence told her that their eyes had glanced at the should-be-sleeping-girl. She must have been a good actor because the women continued their discussion.

"She was burnt up so bad they say she was unrecognizable!"

"Some say her body was blown apart by the lightning."

"That's a painful death. A horrific 1," Sista B mused. "I remember well the cloud that came up that day."

"I remember it too. I didn't think I'd ever get outta that stormhouse, and didn't know if my house would still be standin,'" Dear recalled the intensity of the storm. "That wasn't no natural cloud."

"Naw."

"Sho wasn't."

"And she saw that cloud a-comin and split it. She call herself gon save her crops. Member how it rained that summer?"

"Summer of '69, Baby Sister was pregnant with Root," chronicled Tynell.

"Stuffin's crops was flourishin. She swore she was gonna be able feed her chaps and put some glad rags on em with the money she would make. She worked hard that spring and summer. Yes, she did," Sister B agreed with herself.

Stuffin was washing clothes when her children called her attention to the most unusual cloud she had ever seen forming off in the near-north sky. She looked up from the pail of soapy clothes to see a magnificent sight. The cloud was in the shape of a cross, more specifically a crossroads: 1 thick gray branch to the north and south, the other stretching out to the east and west—the crux was headed over her clapboard home.

"Y'all go in the house and unplug everythang and close everythang shot," Stuffin instructed her children. She looked at her garden which was thriving, and she looked at her humble and crumbling home. No, her life wasn't model and it was nothing to celebrate, but it was her life and her children's.

Her last old man was a married hustler 10 years younger than her who crept in and out of her life 3 babies long before he was run over by a train 1 Saturday night. What Stuffin regretted the most about the loss of Greely was that he had died before doing the 1 thing he promised her he would do: build her a stormhouse. This was the only thing she ever asked of him and the 1 thing his wife couldn't take too much notice of, it being underground and all.

Everything welled up inside of her: the half a man, his lies, his kids, and their cries; her nearly fruitless struggle to survive since he died. She made her decision. She didn't play with nature, but the size, shape, and color of the cloud and its position moved her to do all she could to protect her children and her sole means of survival.

She had watched her mother do it just as, now, her 3-year-old daughter was memorizing Stuffin's movements.

With her Bible in her hand, Stuffin opened the door and stepped out in the yard until she was directly under the crux of the cloud. She opened her Bible and placed the book to her heart before introducing it to the sky. Stuffin laid the text on the ground under the center of the crossroads cloud.

Ozone filled her nostrils; the wind whipped up and howled so hard that it confused her tired cows who were nesting in the barn. Stuffin closed her eyes and recited the 23rd Psalm, after which she looked down and saw a page from the Bible standing straight up as if it were starched.

Stuffin turned her eyes to the sky. She was stunned by what she witnessed: As if sluiced by a razor or a laser, the cloud split in half. 2 horizontal Ts stood in the sky for 3 minutes before going their separate ways and leaving in their wake a road of cerulean blue sky.

Stuffin was both trembling and triumphant. She bent to retrieve the Bible but that page was still standing, and it was vibrating as if it were electrified. Stuffin backed away from the book and decided to go inside.

The air was heavy, not with humidity but with static. As Stuffin walked across the grass she produced sparks that dazzled her children. The leaves of the chinaberry and pear trees were rippling and crinkling, but no wind stirred them. Before she reached her porch, thunder so angry that it shook the ground on which her apprehensive feet strolled rolled across a magenta sky alive with fury.

With her hand outstretched in mid-grasp of the door knob, she turned her head to the right. She did not turn her head to the sky, but rolled her eyes upward to bear witness to celestial upheaval.

Black, blood-red, and violet clouds mesmerized her; she couldn't pull her eyes away as they cartwheeled over her head. The children all seemed to scream at once from the plastic covered windows as brown eyes and braided heads followed a magnificent curling streak of lightening descending from a split in the sky created by their mother.

She watched too, as if in slow motion, the descent of a steady blond diagonal reach out to her bruised body around which her skirts gathered and bunched and swayed in their own anticipatory dance. Broken from her trance, she moved her hand to the doorknob. As soon as she touched the knob, she felt pure electricity suffuse her body. She was illuminated. Her children saw their mother's bones, internal organs, and blood pulse for 3 milliseconds.

The twin clouds reunited with a thunderous clang that jarred Earth and sky. The children watched their mother explode outside of the house with her finger still on the doorknob. Her body separated into 9 pieces which were connected by strands of glowing light that engulfed each piece. The pieces of her body, lay shining on the ground for 3 minutes before they were consumed in flames.

"Momma, did that really happen?" Hawa implored, in awe of Stuffin and her enchanted orphans. The query was greeted with shock and silence—she'd been forgotten as asleep.

"HAWA!" She had never heard this tone from Dear before and didn't hear it again until Dear and her rifle told Sweetback, her summer fling, that he was best get gon and that quick.

"Get outside and get those clothes off the line—NOW!"

This Work was never mentioned again, not in her presence. Hawa made a mental note to ask Dear about it. The time would soon come when all the wisdom and skills of all Pan-African nation sacks would be revealed and put to use for elevation and evolution.

Hawa turned her attention back to the rescue of the white oak: "Dear, you remember when Unka J.R. an nem wanted to cut down the Wicked Tree?"

"Mm hmm."

"Well, this here's our Wicked Tree," She smiled at Danta who looked confused. The labyrinthine histories of Hawa's people had bombarded him—both the telling from lips and the whispering of spirits. He now knew almost as much about her people as she did. Danta studied her history and her folks and made their lives his own because he, the child of a single mother who had died of tuberculosis, had had no family except school and the struggle for the majority of his life. He added Stuffin, Greely, and the Wicked Tree to his blood texts.

"She's right Leroy," Dear's face featured a rare smile. "Don't worry."

The tree stayed. It fronted the house and showed off its gnarled black and velvet green beauty. Sometimes it boasted a white homespun skirt.

The house itself was simple in design yet difficult to build. A womb-shaped house meant a roughly circular wood frame with brick overlay. Custom reflective bricks and solar panels were a major expense but were affordable given that most everything else was supplied by the land. The custom windows were wide, triple paned, bay storm windows that had to be re-hung twice before they were perfectly installed. The solar panels and sky dome were installed last.

The home's unique but modest exterior belied its exquisite interior. The master bedroom was decorated in gold, ebony, and wine. The massive custom-made ebony poster bed was draped in wine and ivory satin covers. The bed dominated ¾ of the room, but because adjacent to the bedroom was a medium sized room that served as a huge walk-in closet, the room had and needed few other furnishings. There was a simple shrine to Ọ̀ṣun, standing ebony candle holders and cream candles and some of Hawa's most seductive oil paintings set a tone of peace and sensuality.

The dining room was the room of inheritance. Aunt Essie's cherry leaf dining table with brass claw feet and its matching 8 high-backed chairs were the centerpiece. Hawa replaced the seats' original faded blue covers with deep forest green velvet. Danta had Squeeze's carpentry shop construct a massive cherry china cabinet with matching antique design. A damask ivory table cloth and an antique silver service gave the room elegance.

The living room, facing west, gave 1 the opportunity to view the unfettered glory of the setting sun each evening. The room sported a circular ocher plush sofa and a hand carved teak coffee table topped with stained glass. The entertainment center was hidden behind a teak wall. The television was rarely turned on, but music usually filled every room or only select rooms depending upon the listeners' tastes. The guest bedrooms were simple and cozy: Oak and dusk blue dominated 1 while ecru and rose soothed in another.

1 of Hawa and Danta's favorite rooms was the sitting room adjacent to the shrine room. The sitting room was filled with an assortment of copper, black, maroon, periwinkle, and beige pillows; a pool table; and a 6' x 6' fish tank which was built into 1 wall. Danta's oils of Lumumba, Sankara, Yaa Asante Wa, El Hajj, and Tubman lined the walls. The library, however, was where they spent most of their time. It was simple, there were 2 computers on opposite sides of a huge table, a burgundy leather chaise, and there were books: from the floor to the ceiling, books. They were arranged in hard and paperback sections and then grouped by fields: African and African American literature, history and spirituality; sociological works, tomes on psychology, biology, computation, texts books, anthropological studies, and self-help and do-it-yourself books carpentry, plumbing, tile-laying, and landscaping.

"What is this by the porch?" Conch looked alternately amazed and confused. There sat Ògún: spears, knives, nails, hammers, scythes, axes gleaming in the sun.

"That's Ògún and Èṣù is here," Hawa led Aunt Conch to the beginning of the footpath to a figured honed of laterite stones and shells.

"Lord have mercy!" Hawa laughed as her aunt shook her head. "Dear was right."

"Bout what?"

"Y'all *is* crazy." Conch started giggling, she was remembering something, "Member when you put them eggs inside—" She broke up laughing so hard her belly and ample breasts shook. Hawa called it jelly bowlin and joined her "—the wicked—ha aaa oh–tree and, and, Cuddin Frank—he—oh! called everybody out to ta ta see what kinda snake laid them eh eh eggs!"

When their laughter subsided, Hawa said, "That was hilarious. Y'all sho was scared. I'd been feedin that tree all summer. I always feed it."

Their house party was wilder than their wedding. At first Hawa and Danta wanted to lock the shrine room. The oiled and glistening skins of Damballah-Hwedo, spiritually recycled from the snakes whose lives went to the establishment of the home, undulated from ceiling to floor. Yemọja was rippling in her white wrap gazing at herself in the gilt edged mirror. Kamasai guarded the left wing while Èṣù and Afrekete were forever united on the right. Ọya's horns, fans, and aṣo wínni wínni waited to dance. Ahni in her stellar beauty sparkled in silver from the black ceiling.

After placing the sacrifices, Hawa opened the doors, "I think everybody wants to party!"

And so they did.

Uncle Elvester arrived first: just like Ghede. He stretched out his diabetes swollen legs and commenced a serious conversation with catfish and Budweiser. "Sho is loud," he said about the music in his soft voice. He smiled at Hawa, "I member when you was just a little thing. Look at you now." He panned his gaze around the house, "You young folks sho is something. Your house is shaped a might strange!" he chuckled, "but it sho is pretty. Got it decorated right nice." His voice was like light raindrops pinging on a crystal goblet.

Dear, regal and quiet, like the Great Mother that she was, sat next to Elvester. When she looked up at him and muttered, "They child gon catch hell: Be spinnin in circles tryin to walk," the party started.

Conch, after cooking up another storm, went home, bathed, and returned as Òṣun. She flirted around the room and with her current love, L.C. She couldn't sit down for fanning her ample hips around the room. Her cooing laughter boosted egos; her alluring smile brought love down; and her light pats raised eyebrows and natures.

Valeria and Earl, balanced like Yemòó and Ọbàtálá, brought laughter, love, joy, and comfort to the congregants as needed.

Leroy, embodying Èṣù—a beer in different stages of disappearance ever in hand and a story always in mouth—flowed round the folk, round the house, signifying, clowning, and encouraging all manner of down throwing.

Pooh, Z.A., Sweetback, and Tall Boy forgot their dates for the pool table and their dates forgot their men for bones and skins. Balls plunked, queens pleaded for safe passage, jacks got their backs broke, and dry bones were resurrected and reburied.

Hawa and Danta let Damballah-Hwedo ride them as they slow dragged across the dance floor. Peaches and Shykwan, Lil Bit and Jimmy Cee, and Vircy Dee and Orando joined them.

They say a party ain't a party till a fight start. Well, Conch had L.C. and Q.T. both hot. In the center of the dining room, Q.T.'s chicken quarter hit the floor.

"Now, I wouldn't take that shit L.C.; Conch *yo* woman," Leroy signified as Conch tittered in the shadows. Uncle Elvester woke up from his nap.

"I don't play the dozens, nigga," L.C. rose to his full height, "and I don't play with other folks' children. Conch my woman and yo hand ain't got no business on her thigh." The word "thigh" came out an octave higher than the rest of the sentence. Everyone except Al Green, who was busy elaborating on the changes that love and happiness will take 1 through, paused and turned their attention to the center of the room.

"Don't you like it, don't you take it," Q.T. jumped bad. His green eyes sparkled. He was ready for a fight.

"Bitch, when you get tireda whores and wife stealin, maybe you find somebody want yo sad ass," L.C.'s right eye twitched but his hands, balled into fists, were steady.

"Now, now, y'all, calm down," Conch sauntered to the center of the floor and stood between the men, facing L.C. "Baby, you know he didn't mean nothin," her words soothed like water and cooled like libation. "Baby, you know what we got. Come on here," he couldn't help but follow those hips as they sashayed out the door.

"Pone-headed nigga bettah go on. I didn't come here to play," Q.T., having lost, got loud. Lil Bit came and picked up the pieces of his ego as she walked him outside.

"My people, my people," Danta mused à la Hurston. The laughter Danta's commentary elicited eased the tension. Hawa laughed and felt her own love come down. Ṣo while Conch soothed L.C. in the guest room, Hawa and Danta took a little fire back to their own room.

"Danta, I've been thinking: I want to quit my job."

He waited because she was still working it all out.

"I want to take care of this little 1 well. I want to give her all she needs. I can't do that worryin bout miss ann and mars charl. I think—I want to teach our child here. She'll have everything she needs and more. There's no way public or private schools can prepare her better than we can."

"You're right, Hawa. I agree with you."

"And I don't want her to be isolated in her cipher. I want her to have a community of companions. Ahni speaks of the emicenters being, coming, coming into being, and this is 1. I want to teach her here and I want to teach here."

"Our own school," he nodded. "A comprehensive Pan-African wisdom center. Pan-African science, medicine, literature, visual and verbal arts, pharmacology, psychology: for all ages. Whatever gifts 1 has can be honed and sharpened, and the gifts 1 wants can be obtained and developed. We can be the heart of the community and our pulse will be felt all over."

Looking into his eyes, she laughed and said, "They'll think we're neo-Hoodoo doctors."

"They'll be right." He touched his forehead to her own, "and we'll teach everyone who comes that they have 2 heads too." He winked at her.

"To start, to begin the gathering, I can have the students I teach now come for tutoring. That will be how we plant our first seeds."

They were linked over the emi, surrounded by violets, buttercups, and clover. Hawa sat on Danta, whose knees jutted north and south as did her own, but hers were behind his back. Her hands laced and embraced his back, and he heard her inhalations in his ear. She felt his exhalations in hers. The walls of her vagina massaged his penis which caressed her vaginal walls. The child tucked safely in her womb awoke to her parents' rhythms.

After 36 breaths, all inner eyes opened—not on a Mississippi spring night, but on Ah.

Hawaaaa. Daaahhhntaaaa. Ahhhhhibit. You've come, the Mother's spirit exalted their souls. Ahibit is the manifest perfection of all Ah who have come and who will come. She has the benefit of all styles. She has 12 emi in action.

With the institute you will found you will prepare and light the path for multitudes. You will maintain a great library of the Ah and the Tahn. As did the Ah of Tbk, of Ta Ntr, and of Kmt, your site and that at Dgn will be the repositories of Ah knowledge and education.

An emisite is developing in Nashville. Following the paths of Jubah and Yah, these Tahn are restyling and recreating the furtive arts of signification, encoding, dissembling, of wielding power in an aesthetically pleasing front that serves as a defensive wall behind which the Tahn rise and shine. Another site will emerge in Alapaha. The focus of these Tahn will be harnessing the power, language, and properties of flora, fauna, Earth, and cosmos in the way of Kng. The Alapaha are the healers.

On the Continent at Minnah, Ọya is sharpening the invisible knife of Àjẹ́, the always already. Minnah will serve as our judicial center—and there is much to adjudicate. . . Kumba is the site of healing. Damaged bodies and psyches are soothed to totality so that all that has been dismembered can be re-membered to Ah. The wisdom center is at Dgn, where Ah knowledge, history, and philosophy have flourished for millennia.

Yurugu thinks that the crushing and the scattering, the destruction of the Ah, is complete. Ta Ntr, like Ahtlnta, now rests under water. Yah is recalled only by thirsty sands. Tbk, Kmt, and Jubah have been silenced by Islamic oppression. Gnah and Dah have become centers of spiritual vapidity and cultural prostitution. Knah has been swallowed by AIDS, civil wars, and ethnic cleansing. Zalah seeks to mirror the vapidity of America, and the Ah of Zim are trapped in spiritual stasis. Many progeny of Ah have forgotten or have dismissed their ancient properties and have deadened their cipher, emi, and vibration. From our 6 emisites, we will summon the shining ones struggling in these lands. We will welcome them into the perfect power of pure revolution.

"So in other words," Azure was exhausted. Her eyes were bagged and watery from heaving, "shit done heated up a few degrees."

"Is this a warning or a slip?"

"You mean not enough poison?"

Alteveze, Azure, Xavier, and Saddiq had gathered in Jah Sun's crib so they'd have a safe place to recuperate and plan. Hospitals were out of the question as was going to the police concerning an obvious case of state-sponsored poisoning. Once Azure, who was being looked after by Lil X, called Alteveze, they put 2 and 3 together. The only thing they had all taken together was honey and tea at Azure's. When Azure recalled the misplacement of the honey, she realized it had been tainted.

"The truth is a powerful weapon. Banned from the station and poisoned," Alteveze looked angry and worried, her dreds trembled. "We put too much on em."

"But everything you shared was published material; you could get those magazines and books anywhere," Saddiq massaged Alteveze's temples.

"Yeah, but published for select readers. They have to document their atrocities. Something about Yurugu." Azure sipped the goldenseal, comfrey, sulfur, verbena, and basil tea blend that Sun had prepared for them. "They always publish their aberrations; It's an aspect of their pathology. The problem is that we saturated the thirsty with the water of truth."

"We're supposed to die of thirst—"

They all sipped their medicine.

"Slick sick beasts."

"What do we do now? Az, your home ain't safe."

"If they wanted to kill us, they would have, Xavier. Can now. I'm not scared. This is war." The resolve in her voice was intensified by the obvious pain that racked her body.

"Azure, you have to be realistic," Xavier reasoned. "Why not stay with us? There's room and you're welcome."

"I won't run Zave, and I won't endanger your family."

"We are going to have to camouflage ourselves and throw up mad smoke screens," Alteveze mumbled between heaves. "Our next move must be carefully and quietly planned and executed."

"We must move in stealth mode," Saddiq assented before chugging pink bismuth straight from the bottle.

"The trickster." Alteveze rubbed her belly and stretched out on the rug, "They don tricked the trickster."

"But not for lo—" Azure stood up mid-sentence and ran to the toilet. The sounds of her retching flowed into the sitting room.

After she stood up and flushed the toilet, she brushed her teeth, and rinsed her mouth 5 times. She washed her face and looked deeply into her red watery eyes. She gazed at her smooth skin, full but downturned lips, and the overall forlorn look on her face and she mused, I look like I'm about 9-years-old, she managed a weak smile.

Xavier tapped on the door. She opened the it and resumed her perusal of her face in the mirror. "You need to rest and heal," he rubbed her back in soothing circles. "I made reservations. You're coming with me."

She curled into a fetal ball. She felt like her intestines were being cranked through a meat grinder as the goldenseal and sulfur compound rid her body of poisons. Xavier closed the shades in the hotel suite to blot out the glare of weak sunlight on snow. He positioned a bucket, cold compresses, her custom medicines, and a hot water to bottle within Azure's immediate reach. Xavier wrapped his body behind hers, placed his arm around her waist, and rubbed her belly. Azure drifted into sleep.

Azure saw 1 land mass with a volcanic rush and crumble become 2 land masses surrounded by an ocean. On the largest continent, she witnessed thousands of radiant black orbs, glowing, emitting peace, knowledge, power. The orbs were clustered around 12 centers. Alkebu-Lan, she thought. The Continent grew blighted and misted in murky whiteness. Then the orbs took to the sea, crossing: America. The orbs were scattered but alternately clustered south and southeast. Now west. Now north. The orbs shot into the cosmos. After a moment of stillness, the orbs popped up in America and Africa. They sailed to the cosmos and back. They clustered at 6 sites: 3 on the West coast of Africa; 3 in central and southeast America.

And 1 is here.

The voice was salve. She was with the Mother, was in the Mother, was the Mother.

Ahni. Ah. Tahn.

Yurugu did not create you and cannot destroy you. Continue the Work; continue our Work.

Azure awoke without any idea where she was or who's chest she was nestled into like a baby. Her arms were wrapped around the person; 1 hand on a cheek, the other on a shoulder. Arms cradled the small of her back. She felt safe: she slept again.

She dreamed of African warriors lining ghetto walls. Mothers, fathers, children, gang members, past-tense derelicts and former crack heads now an impenetrable wall of Black Power. In the center of where they stood was a vibrating section of earth. It galvanized their power, told them secrets, and prepared them for battle.

This is an emisite. You are the soul of the site.

"What did you dream?" Azure asked. The first dream of Ahni, Ah, and Tahn had been communal. The second dreams all varied.

Saddiq dreamt of a land of melanin and knowledge. He strolled the land in slow motion because every step, breath, movement bombarded him with vibration, cipher, and wisdom. He wept with every step he took and each tear became a book.

Xavier dreamt of holding Azure's right hand. She held another brother's right hand. He held the brother's left hand. Slowly the 3 rose and rose into the sky. In Azure's womb were triplets. 3 in 1 1 in 3.

Alteveze dreamt of words, poems falling around and on her like rain. She scrambled for a pen and paper to capture them and began weeping for their beauty and her futility. When she gave up her search, the verses saturated her being, filling her fully.

Alteveze, Saddiq, and Azure woke feeling as strong as Xavier. Ah had neutralized the poison.

The collective met at Saddiq's apartment to discuss the Work. Azure looked into the eyes of each member, "Now we know the significance of our mission. How do we proceed?"

"Well, I think the poetry readings are a good forum for educating and finding like minds. The problem is we really have to widen the circle," Saddiq looked to Lil X.

"Well, many People recognize and shine, and some write. I'll feel out some of the heads and see who's ready. This could spark a revolution within the People Nation that's overdue."

"You know," Alteveze came bearing a tray of sliced apples, grapes, orange wedges, crackers, chilled water, and glasses, "Malare used to be a place where the lay and academic communities were symbiotic."

"True."

"Had to be to fight oppressors: They've never discriminated between a degree and a blue collar. We's all niggers to them."

"We need to unite the projects, the academics, and the town."

"Seriously? Those bourgeois Negroes—you think they'll be down for that?" Saddiq pushed out his full lips in disbelief.

"Some will. . ." Alteveze mused. "There are several folks on campus with degrees—as in 360. The Family for example, and some of the boys from the Boogie are affiliated. They"

"Girl, it's cool to vibe bout your past gang life at Malare and pose, but they don't wanna reach back."

"Right, 'they movin on uuupp!'" Xavier sang *The Jeffersons* theme song and cracked everybody up. The young brother fit right in.

"Alright, alright: At the next reading, let's see who shows some potential, who vibes with the VLs. Who drops knowledge. We can begin forming the coalition from there," Alteveze resolved.

"You know, in order to break a community fast, we gon have to crack and scramble a few eggs," Saddiq looked suggestively so that he wouldn't have to explain audibly. "I'm gonna talk with Jah Sun about some restaurant-grade scramblers."

"Very necessary," Azure assented, "we need all the protein we can get."

I'm layin here with someone's child. She thought about this and then relaxed because everybody is somebody's child. Everybody.

Loco had had nothing to worry about: She hadn't met anyone who stirred her. A slew of males: wannabe-intellectuals, who had taken to platonic-socratic unions with professors with female victims on the side. Or had-been hood stars whose dreams had gone from shining on the horizon to becoming balls of mucus hardened in the corners of their eyes that were flicked away with the morning grind. Objects for pity—not for love, not for building. Then here comes this son of Sun, living a life of slinging slash poetic empowerment. Xavier encapsulated her past and foretold future, and his presence was narcotic.

She turned to him, feeling shy, younger than him. Azure eased her sheets back and gazed at his full length exquisiteness. Soft hairs v-ing, curling texturing his smooth bronze skin. How did she look to him? Hmm? 1 finger, ivory nail, peach undertones becoming cinnamon, extended.

Before her tip touched his nipple, waves reached and gripped her spine. She became liquid. In 1 motion, her leg wrapped over then around him. Hairs kissing, lips tasting, knowing; she rode him slowly. Azure relaxed her entire being to feel each blood-swollen vein of Xavier's penis, each ridge of his silk-smooth shaft. She closed her eyes, contracted so he would know her rippling red walls. She eased her way into a rhythm and opened her eyes.

His smile, that of a child sitting alone with his own ice cream cone, brought tears of hope from her cheeks to her chest to their yearning pelvii.

That Mud Ain't Red For Nothin

I see you hanging there
turning with grace in space
floating fluffy puffy
piñata-like
and think

You can't be human
you can't be real

I wonder about the state you were in
when they brought you to this place
I wonder about the state
of mind you had before you arrived
when your thighs ripped
and your lungs struggled
not to collapse
your heart quivered
not to combust
as your knees seemed
to leap out of their casings
as your feet gathered
and tossed off cockleburs
as your soul ran out
ahead of you
to lead the way for you
as the trees whispered
keep going to you
as your face
contorted straining
created its own wind
behind your unmoving head

No, you can't be human
your skin looks like bark
Your skin looks like the frayed bark strips
I peeled as a child
Bark strips of the tree you scaled
to make your escape
Brother
did they find the first tree too weak
to hold your spirit
the branches too burdened with
the souls of
other Brothers
     and find another
                   Brother
did they let you get a head start
a day hour minute second
did they come at night by tens
               by tens
             by tens
rope-strapped and torch-lit by tens

I know the state you were in
Mississippi
You were in Mississippi
with a pack of curs sporting you
giving you line stringing reeling
Reeling stringing lining
slicing souvenirs for their grinning children
singing, "Shall we gather round the nigger"
holding hands swaying
curdling up a bloody white *yeehaww*
to float above your swelling head
popping eyes popping
skin bubbling fraying

          Did they delay the finale
           until the "ladies"
          had been brought out?

Were you smiling in that state
when they came
Did you laugh like Sixo
in that state when they came as you ran

cockle burr bucking and head steady Brother
lips roiling in the rich joke
of being a man turned to toast
swinging on a string at 17

You seem to smile now
and your skin doesn't look crisp
or hot or rough
but soft
Your skin looks soft
like shaggy teddy bear fur
even with the bones peeking out
of the shin
left arm
right foot
twisted spine
you seem so soft

I want to hold you, Brother
sway with you
smooth you skin back down
weep your musk back
into your pores
I want to hold you
and eat up this bloody dust that's been
guarding your secrets for so long

> I'm gonna whole you
> soak all of you up
> re-member your limbs to the leaves
> to the winds to your musk

> too many centuries have gone
> too many millions have perished
> and seems everybody forgot
> about the glory of retribution

> but us.

"What do you really think of the piece?" Lil X got tired of her evasive
answers and pussy footing.

"It is haunting and . . . stunning. It seems to be written from a uh woman's perspective," she stumbled over her words.

"It is," he nodded twice, waiting.

"Did this happen to someone you know?" She didn't look at him. She looked at her boots, at his, at her Shrine, to which he'd added 1 of his father's bullets, and 1 of his red bandanas. She looked at the worn carpet, she looked at the crack snaking the walls—anywhere but at him.

"Yes, Azure. It happened to someone I know."

She shaped her confusion into a query: "How did you know?"

"You told me."

"I never told you. I don't even have anything representing him on my shrine."

"But you told me."

"How?"

"I don't know."

She'd only heard last week that Marshall's body had been found. He'd been shot in the back of the head twice. His body was dumped unceremoniously in an abandoned well and covered with leaves, cement blocks, refuse, trash for 3 weeks.

Why?

Because he'd won a court settlement from some old gray for $238 for a piece of shit car the gray had sold him.

For nothing.

Modern day lynching. And the shit was creshendoing. Again. Malice Green. All the brothers hanged in Jackson Mississippi jails. Houdini brothers who "commit suicide" by shooting themselves while handcuffed behind the back and sitting on a curb or sitting in the back of a squad car. Bensenhurst. The macabre violation of Abner Louimer. The unthinkably horrific death of James Byrd, Jr. The rekindled fire of the Black church burnings. Ahmadou Diallo. Jena 6. Travon Martin. Michael Brown. Eric Garner. Lennon Lacy.

When Obama was elected and re-elected president, the racists removed their masks, pulled out their ropes, and made their presence and intentions clear. Many people were surprised at just how racist America was and how racists and racism thrived in America. The Ah and Tahn were not surprised.

Azure remembered her father telling her when she was 5 that "there's no smell on earth worse than the smell of burning human flesh." How did he know that? she wondered. After realizing that he never fought in any war except the 1 for Civil Rights, she knew that her father came by this knowledge by simply being a man from Mississippi.

She'd never smelled burning human flesh. But she'd seen it. The Civil Rights Museum at the Lorraine Motel in Memphis. A photograph of a man turned into a teddy bear. He looked soft, shaggy. Eyes big as fists. She gazed at the photograph like a sinner trying to read Jesus' name in strategically glued sticks. She could not fathom why a teddy bear should earn a place in a Civil Rights Museum's mural of pictures. Slowly the sepia shot revealed a rope holding up the teddy bear. The darker mottled background and base of the black and white photo wasn't aged-faded or water spot discolored flecks as she had thought: It was heads, thousands of spectators' heads. Under the brother. Chicken legs in hand. Souvenirs hacked off and displayed. Babies held up. Gray faces turned up grinning like a pack of satiated chessy cats: Cheeze!

A big teddy bear. She remembered C.C. the teddy bear she had never really stopped turning to, crying on, and confiding in although she was now grown. Teddy bears don't have fingers either. They don't have penises or scrotums either.

Professor Palmer's voice in Special Topics: American Atrocities 423 echoed in her head: "They would kill the victim 7 times over. The hunt and chase, the beating, the stabbing, the whipping, the burning, the shooting, the tarring and feathering, the stringing up, the bringing down, the stringing up, the bringing down, the harvesting of souvenirs. 7 times. 7 times. 7 times. *Or more.*" These atrocities spun through Azure's psyche. She broke down—like when she finally understood the teddy bear was a man. A man. Marshall. A man. She broke down.

Now this poem, her poem, from his hand. How did he know?
"How did you know?"
"I felt it in you. Last Tuesday. I felt it."
"So, when did you write this?" she looked at him.
"Wednesday."
"How?"
"I just saw images. Red. It was like a dream but I was awake. Sitting in the tub. I closed my eyes. Then, I just saw . . . everything. I felt such grieving, ancient heaving."

Azure's brow crinkled as she checked his language and pondered the spiritual messages he was receiving. She got up and went to the fridge.

"So what do you want?" her lower half was bathed in the cool light of the refrigerator.

"Uh, you got any uh—what is that beer you drink?"
"Corona?"
"Yeh."
"Okay," she opened 2 Coronas and cut 2 lime wedges.
"So you don't wanna discuss this."
"Maybe later." Let me get back in control of this here thang. If we are *this* open, *this* connected . . . "Our next reading is planned for next Thursday. Can we bring Saddia, Simone, and Siddar? You think they'll like to come?"

"You know they'd love it. Especially Simone. She thinks you're made of gold," he squeezed her thigh and smiled.

"Momma number 2," they laughed at the little girl's expression of admiration. "I got some other ideas too."

"Like what?" He turned towards her.

She was quiet for 7 heartbeats, "I been rapping with some F.O.L.K.S.. They wanna vibe too." She watched his lips go slack then get all smuntched up in disgust.

"Damn, Az, I mean . . . Damn. You wanna get me killed or converted or you want war or what? The shit ain't gon work. I I"

"The goal is unity, understanding. Hell, *over*standing. Y'all killing, depopulating, and maiming yourselves while mister charlie laughs—"

"I won't do it," he shook his head.

"Oh," her left eyebrow rose a half inch in query.

"I ain't no punk n shit. . ."

"Okay. . ."

"Well, you know I want to have some peeps represent, right?"

"Starr and Lord and Bun comin."

"Say what?!?"

"Word. Why you lookin so surprised? So, you still don't know me, hun? Man, I'm the woman," she emphasized this fact by rolling her neck.

"Alright Wo Man, they know that 6 down?"

"They will."

"F.O.L.K.S. know VL down?"

"They will."

He looked into the soul of the woman who had become his second self and sighed. This woman who would bear his children. This woman!

He shook his head, "Shit's gon be hot."

"Alteveze it's on!!"

"You don't have no sense. A fucking thug convention. You gon get us all dead up," but there was admiration in her voice.

"No such. Some dynamic things are afoot. I feel it. I'm nervous too, but the main thing I feel is power, surging power. You gon be there?"

"What kinda query is that? You my sister! I am wherever you are!"

"I feel what you tryin to do. Anyone can get up and talk shit but you do what needs to be done. Respect."

"Veze, you my heart!" Azure glowed.

"Mm hhmm. Tell that to the child you stole from somebody's momma."

"Don't you start, now!" they chuckled together into their phones.

"Seriously, Az. What's up? I ain't seen you good since you met him. Brus at school say you can't stay out Carver."

"We . . . ummm . . . Mrs. Wilson like my company."

"Who dat? Momma?"

"Mmm hmm."

"You mad!" Alteveze laughed, "and going through a mid-life crisis early. X done blew your mind."

"Seriously, Veze, something's inside. That's all I know. I mean, you remember I told you about my cousin Marshall being lynched?"

"I can't forget or stop planning retribution"

"which we shall have."

"Àṣẹ."

"Well, I didn't tell Xavier, but he not only wrote a poem about Marshall, but he wrote *my* poem, 1 I had written."

"Hmmm . . . You sure you didn't tell him?"

"Not a word. But even if I had it wouldn't explain his writing the exact same poem that I had written."

"This is profound, sister. Too deep."

"What's more, now when I meditate, I see all kinds a things."

"Listening—"

"Flying ancestors, tornadoes, embryos altering the world with their cipher."

"Well," Alteveze chose her words, "when I meditate now, I see you."

"What? What am I doing?"

"Teaching, building. I'm beside you too, and we are all led by Ahni. Sometimes there's violence. Battlin. But above all there's peaceful evolution and expansion, with babies, elders, all in a circle."

"Umph. It seems the dreams are a continuation of the 1 we had last Friday. But these seem more like visions of the future than dreams."

"Visions of the direction our work and lives will take."

"Azure, now, you have to admit this is peculiar. Unbelievable: Mass visions, mad direction."

"But it's all dovetailing with the work we're doing, and its helping us."

"I think your warriors' shrine is too much," Alteveze chuckled. "Seems you done conjured us some assistance."

Azure smiled but she was lost in thought. 1 shared vision and other personal visions that are all part of the whole, that are unifying the whole.

"It reminds me—and I know you gon roll—but it reminds me of all those brothers and sisters in the 70s all seeing the Mothership."

Alteveze didn't laugh, "Hmm. You're right. You think something like this was rearing up then? How did it start with them I wonder?"

"Well, the blend of weed, funk—"

"Auditory or biochemical?"

"Both! I mean putting EVERYTHING on the 1."

"Hell yeh!" Alteveze was feeling it, "and the 1 was catalyzed by Nommo: Swing low sweet chariot let me riiiiide!" She funked up a spiritual.

"George knew what he was doing. The Native Americans took peyote to open their inner eyes. Parliament Funkadelic blended traditional wisdom, political savvy, and exhortation, enjoyment, hallucinogens, sexual stimulation to produce mass visions and cipher."

"Exactly and folk would then—with their cipher stimulated—have independent visions. It reminds me of Jes Grew, the force of Ishmael Reed's *Mumbo Jumbo*. But what happened?"

"Well on an interview for a PBS documentary, I think it was called "Rockumentary," George said when disco hit, the vibration stopped."

"Hmm, you know, every Black musical power surge has been disconnected. In the 1920s, the depression dammed the flow: Reed refers to it as the dissipation of Jes Grew in *Mumbo Jumbo*. In the 70s, disco provided the disconnect. Look at how many young folks got hipped by Public Enemy and X Clan and Paris in the 90s. And now you can't hear conscious rap for all the odes to booty, drugs, murder, and bling. But there are some Gods putting head out like Brother J, Dead Prez, Sunz of Man, Killarmy, D'Angelo, Madame Badu."

Alteveze was still pondering the past: "So the Mothership ran aground in a deluge of disco."

"Monotonous, dead, unconscious music. Not bootstompin, Earth shaking, vibrating rhythms, but music for grays to pirouette and hit arabesques and shit."

"But folks are waking up again. You notice how in music now hip hoppers talkin bout seein and bein aliens and vibin with other worldly entities who are Africans like them? It's happening again, and this time it's not the musical vibrations that awaken consciousness, most of the beats are samples of old school flights. Now it seems the spirits are whispering to the artists so that the lyrics are influenced."

"And the lyrics and rhythms move the body and can alter the being. Like breakdancing: I was watching a documentary on African dance, and brothers and sisters on the Continent was hittin the original breaks! Shit like poppin n lockin n scissors. I was wigged out by the continuity. When you see folk in Senegal dancing, you seein an undiluted step show. I mean, think of the Qs truly uninhibited and you got Senegal. And Brazilian capoeira is so deep—it is martial break dancing in slow-motion; it is a testament to the human ability not to defy gravity, but to *enter* gravity—to alter 1's protons, electrons, and neutrons, and become gravity."

"It seems what we have before us, what we are now part of, is an entirely different revolution, 1 that will unify everything: the cosmic, the terrestrial, and the ancestral."

"Time and space and place as well," Azure assented. "Everything we do is connected. Funkadelic's Mothership is Elijah Muhammad's Mother Plane is the ancestors' Sweet Chariot is Ezekiel's wheel."

The line extends back to the Ah of origins. That's what Toni Cade Bambara was writing about in her short story 'Broken Field Running.' Girl, that is a bad ass piece. This elder says that we CAME to Africa from the cosmos, dig me?"

"Diggin"

"And that Ezekiel saw us arrive and called us a wheel! Elder goes on to say we can't fly no more because we got grounded by too much salt."

"Hmmm. . ." Azure pondered the dilemma, "Sweated by beasts, blood running in the furrowed fields, artery clogging salt pork as seasoning, ourselves being seasoned, ancestors tossed into the Atlantic."

"That's something else, these elders call the Atlantic the Ethiopic."

"Talk sense and tell somebody girl!! The whole Continent was called Ethiopia, and the Atlantic was indeed called the Ethiopic until beasts changed the name."

"But the trip is this: Remember all those texts about Flying Africans flying away from American slavery?"

"Yeh. . ."

"Maybe Ancestors wasn't talking bout returning to Africa, maybe they was talking bout returning to Ahni. Maybe they returned to the ultimate source, the original Womb of Origins. Maybe they wasn't born in Africa in the first place."

"You know, in all honesty, I used to be like: What makes waitin on the Mothership different from waiting on Jesus? More self-abnegation and shifting the responsibility of the divine self on some mythical other. But there *is* a Mother."

"Reaching us and teaching us. Sparking our wisdom and orchestrating the revolution."

"Mmmph."

"Listen girl, somebody's at the door."

"Probably Rev. Mr. X."

"Could be. . ." Azure knew it wasn't Xavier because he just left to handle some business and said he wouldn't return until around 12. "Sister, let's meet tomorrow and try to formulate a program for this reading, from seating arrangements to performance times. We may even need a meeting between the gangs a day or 2 before."

"Cool. Call me tomorrow."

"In peace."

"At peace."

"Coming!" she strode to the door and asked, "Who is it?"

"Who else?"

Azure froze. And in freezing, stepped back years in the past. Lil Loco. Joy, fear, confusion. Parole? Lil Loco. Lil X. Well, she thought, extending her hand towards the knob slowly so as to prepare her being for the greeting, the gang peace summit is about to get really deep.

"King," she glowed, "I can't believe it!" She couldn't believe it! He looked good. Loco was thinner than Xavier by about 10 pounds but the lean frame was rippling with muscles. He'd been letting his hair grow out. At first, behind the glass, she was afraid—who's braiding that head? He undid and re-braided a braid and she smiled. "You will braid mine soon." She'd told him. Now his hair was done in 5 fishbone braids going back and linked at the nape. "You look good, daddy."

She welcomed him inside and walked to the fridge.

"Sit down," she paused, her body was trembling. "What can I get you to eat? Drink? Corona's finished. You want some wine? I have some spaghetti I can warm up. But I think we need to celebrate in honor of your homecoming. Why didn't you tell me? I could have picked you up and planned a proper throwdown?" She rambled in an attempt to process, to deal, to order Lil Loco's return. Her head and chest were cooling mercifully in the fridge but her backside was hot.

Gently, gently his hands stroked her back, laced up her neck, and wrapped around to her collar bones like feathers. She stopped rambling. She responded and rose.

"Azure." His voice was like freshly turned earth. He's not spoken since he came in she thought. Her back felt his insistence, the questions. Her buttocks felt his probing, the answers. How could she turn and face him? "Azure," the sound of ancestors' bones resting well in the Earth. "Azure."

He'll feel my tears on his hands and turn me around.

He felt her tears on his hands and turned her around.

His heart was kicking like an enraged mule. He's scared too. How can I look into his eyes? Loco lifted her chin with those same feathers.

She never felt more womanly. More exquisite.

She fell into his eyes. Brown flecked with gold. She saw herself falling; she had no fear.

3 days before, Alteveze spent the day making tiny plaits of her sister's over-abundant natural hair. Azure had made a huge bun of the plaits at the crown of her head. His fingers danced over her scalp and whispered to the plaits. Her massive bun of braids loosened and fell free, snaking, as alive as she was. His tears wrapped around her braids and wound down to each squared root.

Her limbs, shining like polished teak, were reaching at once for him and at once for the cool of the tiles. Which 1? Which way? Her arms encircled his neck. She wrenched the overcoat off of him to feel him. Smell him. "Oh!" She inhaled the scents of rage, isolation, urine, confinement, blood and grief. Prison.

She prepared the parsley. She lit charcoal in her incense burner and added sage and rabbit tobacco. She took 1 fertilized egg from the carton. Smoky trails of incense wrapped around her as she knelt before Loco and removed all of his clothes and his underwear and loosened his braids. She stood him over the incense burner and let the smoke purify him.

"Think of all the horror you've witnessed in the past. Everything. The killing of Big Red. Prison. Bring it all up. Everything." After she breathed on the egg, chanted and touched it to her third eye, heart and pelvis; she placed the egg in the front of his third eye.

The faggot sucking his dick. The night he choked the guard, Jody, for stealing the cigarettes Azure'd given him. Solitary. Tears when Azure didn't come. Dreams of her making love with someone. Dreams of him touching her. Fears of the outside. Seeing Red's spirit shoot out of his head. Like fireworks. Love spiraling out of his head. His tears, fighting and losing against false bravado. Love spiraling flying and then oozing in the gutters.

She was stroking him with the egg, fanning out cleaning his head, his roots, his hairs, his parts, his scalp; eyes and hip bones, the egg rolled on; cleaning him of hatred of self and of other. His neck and throat and collar bones stroked. His heart, she lingered there allowing the egg's cleaning force its own time. His chest, shoulder blades, the tension in each link of his spine was removed. His penis, now limp, now turgid, now limp, cleansed. His scrotum—so often cupped and massaged on those empty nights— purged, his buttocks, smoothed, toned, and taught, cleaned. Hamstrings, kneebacks, thighs and kneecaps, shins and calves, cleaned. His feet, after walking on untold souls, were clean.

He soaked in the tub with his eyes closed, seeking peace. The black soap, as earthy as him, she coaxed into a white cloud on his head. She took the parsley, cinnamon, and sea salt mixture in her hands and scrubbed each of his body parts until she was sweating and as wet as he was. His eyes remained closed; hers were open and dry. She rinsed him and directed the nozzle's strength to take everything away but what was most important. She anointed his hair and body with olive oil. She wrapped him in a huge white towel and led him to the bedroom.

Azure stepped into the cold night. It was raining. She went 3 blocks from the apartment to a drainage sewer. She threw the egg, the clothes he'd been wearing and all the negativity that had been removed from Lil Loco into the sewer with all her might.

She cleaned the tub and then smudged Lil Loco, the entire house, and herself 3 times. She sprinkled salt around her home and chanted, "Clean life, clean home, clean mind." Then she swept the house and took the debris to the drainage sewer. She lingered outside, letting the rain center her. When she returned, she soaked before scrubbing herself with parsley, cinnamon, salt and nutmeg. Everything in her sphere was cleansed and open.

Shining and oiled, she joined him on the bed. He was reading Du Bois' *The Gift of Black Folks* and plaiting his hair.

They gazed at 1 another. This wo/man is like time—each thought simultaneously.

Their first touches were awkward, tentative. The trembling-lip kisses. The flavor of nutmeg on tongue. The scent of latex. The stare of her nipples and threat of her perfect handfuls of breasts. The sadness in the strength of his chest, the screaming of his biceps, the grace of her quadriceps. Through touch they gathered, massaged, and re-membered.

Her clitoris was as hard as his penis. It was pulsing. Her legs were trembling. She held him in her hands. The throbs became a humming became a vibration—AAAAHHHHHHHahaaahhhhhhah—He fit into her like the soul fits into the body.

They fell into 1 another. Coaxing cycles and undulations into rhythms, they created their own time and were oblivious to everything else.

Outside, in the cold, Xavier's knocks went unanswered, not because he was heard and ignored, but because his fisted thrusts against wood corresponded to his brother's thrusts into their Loveher.

Because they had come independent of any organization, there were some initial difficulties in settling. Cynthia landed a job as a lecturer with the department of history. But before they were allocated university housing, they lived together in a flat near campus in a small community called Jolly. The area was packed with students. Kandace and Cynthia made friends quickly. The students, most of whom were from Cameroon, Liberia, and The Gambia were cool. There was a great deal of drinking and pool and snooker shooting on and off campus. It was enjoyable, but there was an air of futility about it all.

Many of the students complained about and discussed the oppression of foreigners at the university and the general negativity and hostility of many Nigerians to other Africans. Indeed, that was becoming a pan-African problem, for so many Africans evinced the misguided patriotic zeal that was the product of colonization that it was hard to find African unity in Africa. Furthermore, foreign students were all stereotyped as wealthy, or, at the very least, the monies they or their parents, relatives, or themselves and scraped up to send them to school were to be lavished on con people or acquisitive professors.

Cynthia and Kandace listened and learned but found peace in themselves, for it was not to be found elsewhere. There was more vapidity than vitality at the university, but something had brought them there.

While crossing the Sahara, Kandace had closed her eyes and started chanting thanks and praises: "Mother Saan, mother of Donnie, Mother of Lenell, Mother of Jo, Mother of Me: Thank you for your strength and wisdom. We left in chains and return in planes. Oh Mother, my known and unknown Mothers, each of you is a vertebrae of my backbone. Great and wise Mothers, thank you. You give me life and foresight. Please bless this journey, guide me, guide sister Cynthia. May our path be good."

Cynthia was roused from her sleep by murmurings and gasps. As she reached to touch Kandace, she saw the Sahara. They held hands and meditated with tears of thanks streaming down their cheeks. The flight attendant noticed their behavior and came to inquire if all was well. He was greeted with damp smiles.

Kandace closed her eyes and found herself gazing at her guide, her first friend, her spirit companion. She sat on a hollow log before a running river, behind her was a dirt path surrounded by lush vegetation.

Yes, sisters. You are coming to a road you've never crossed. Cross it. You will undergo trials unthought of. Conquer them. You will meet weak spirited enemies without cipher. Build your house on their heads.

Never place your hopes in the dead, for they are dead. They are dead. The Immortals and your eternal power await you.

We—she spread her arms and palms—are waiting for you.

And there were the Mothers, the ancestors, Òrìṣà, the Ah. Awaiting their crossing.

Kandace opened her eyes, pulled the notebook and pen out of her duffle bag, and wrote

I Miss Issippi
I Miss Issippi
Mother of Waters

I Mississippi
   birthed from the blood
     of my Big Momma's thighs
My mud ain't red for nothin
   My son's blood laps my riverside
I Mississippi rolling silted fertile and rich
   Beg my husbands and sons to
                Come come come
       rest your bones
     longside these
   banked thighs

Cool water for quenching
 waits inside

Outside muddy cruddy from
dry heaves, salty tears
coon dog sweat and slick sweet slime of coon dick

and love coming down round me in me
I Miss Issippi
can get well-deep
or leave you pine high
all depends on the groove of my thighs

I flow from kay-ro to Cairo
Cuffe to Kofi
Alapaha to alapaha
from Diddy wa Diddy to Zar
My breasts crest from Juba to Juba
and mud bones red bone
hand bones thigh bones
love bones blood bones
all bones got a home
in these muddy thighs
I Miss Ississippi accept all
burdens can and should be laid right here
within the revelation of my velvet red crease
is the sigh and the swish of soul soothing
Brotherrrrr Loverrrrr
  lay your burden down
     right here
    deeply down
    Here
   The river of healing is deep
    and it is wide

With the aid of Prof. Imoye, Kandace and Cynthia met the Ìyálóde, who celebrated the fact that she had the feared and revered force called Àjẹ́.

Kandace and Cynthia's Yoruba skills were weak; Ìyá's pidgin was fair. They struggled to communicate; understanding was born of patience.

They wore white wrappa, boubou, and gele. Power flowed through the ojúbọ. Kandace knelt on the floor with Cynthia. Ìyálóde tore the heads off of white pigeons and dipped her fingers in their necks and offered to Kandace and Cynthia a taste of their sacrifice which they received. She cracked snail shells and poured soothing snail water into their mouths and over their lips. Ọ̀ṣun, Ìyàmi Ọ̀ṣòròngà, Odù, and Egúngún also shared the blood and the waters. Calabashes, snails, serpents, and birds of power united terrestrially and celestially and suffused them in power.

However, other than Imoye and Ìyálóde and covert collectives of consciousness, there was very little vibration. Everything was so economically motivated that Kandace told Cynthia that it seemed like the whole nation was singing Wu Tang's "C.R.E.A.M." And yet, no matter how much money they 419'ed or how much shakara they did, everyone was a pawn—human pawns as blind as the pieces on the chessboard being moved by an unseen hand. Folk were so busy looking to some external agent to save, uplift, or blame that they could not appreciate their own complicity or their own power.

The women found the loss of life staggering. It was nothing to see a dead body or 2 lying on the side of the highway. The cadaver would decorate the roadside until his or her relatives were notified and rented a vehicle to transport the body to a mortuary.

The women wondered what Ida B Wells Barnett would say about the fact that extra judicial killings in Africa are as common in 21st century as they were in 20th century America, but these sadistic lynching bees are all-African affairs. However, the motives behind the killings are the same: jealousy, self-hatred, and the infernal misery born of religious hypocrisy.

Infrastructural deficiencies serve as a key source of accidental death. Airplane crashes are routine. Poorly constructed buildings collapse and claim many lives. Oil, the country's leading source of wealth, is misery maker in chief.

There was a pipeline break that caused an overflow of petrol in the Nigerian town Jesse. Petrol, during a time of fuel crisis, was literally flowing in the streets. With jerricans and buckets, brothers and sisters collected the gas. This went on until a motorcycle backfired and shot off a spark near the river of petrol. Hundreds were killed and thousands injured. 2 years later, the same thing happened again.

Many towns in the delta region have massive quantities of light sweet crude, but due to corruption, mismanagement, and selfishness, these towns have no schools, libraries, or hospitals. There is no growth or development: There is oil and there is suffering. So women of the delta use their naked Àjẹ́ to attack the oilfield workers and take over refineries until their demands—hospitals, potable water, proper roads, schools—are met. Men of the delta do not have Àjẹ́ waiting a garment away so they use guns and take hostages as they attempt to reclaim their wealth and destiny. The power people utilize in the delta is the same that is applied by the entire county which goes on strike when the government attempts to raise the price of gas. 200,000,000 people on strike means a nation, an economy grinds to a halt, and Nigeria's halt causes the West to shudder.

However, America's recent oil boom is causing Nigeria to shudder. As America becomes energy independent, Nigeria loses a multibillion dollar consumer that it cannot easily replace. Now, the oil that has caused so much wealth and anguish may drown Africa's most populous nation with its abundance. With the decline of the naira and the expansion of Boko Haram, the "Giant of Africa" is staggering.

In the midst of the political chaos and personal struggles, Kandace and Cynthia met a sister named, Istha who was doing a comparative study of the force of Àṣẹ as a revolutionary tool in Africa and African America for her Ph.D. in anthropology.

Istha, Cynthia, and Kandace met during an Ọbàtálá ceremony. After the gathering disintegrated into a battle of who gets and how much, the trio left the fiasco and went to a small stand for àkàrà and soft drinks. They crunched into the steaming balls of ground black eyes peas, rich with onions and peppers.

"Say what?!!"

"Yeh, I look around and I was locked out like the big dog. The house girl was sleeping right beside the door but she'd gotten orders not to let me in. I didn't have nowhere to go."

"Why?" Cynthia asked.

"He started making all of these financial demands. He was damn near charging me for breathing. I reminded him that I'm a student, not an ambassador or Fulbright recipient. He started getting loud so I excused myself to let the situation cool. When I returned, I was denied entry. "

"Well damn!" Kandace was incensed. "You'd been here what?"

"About 2 weeks. All I could say was NAS," she munched her àkàrà.

"What is that?"

"Niggas ain't shit."

"Humph," Cynthia laughed, "I heard that."

Istha didn't laugh, she just looked somber, "You know, I had stopped using that word, 'nigger,' about 7 years ago. But I started again here . . . It's a trip cuz all the things I'd left behind—negativity; spiritual, mental and physical violence; verbal lashings and violations—are here in abundance. I've seen too much shit here."

She looked down the street and watched a child struggle to carry a container of moin-moin on her head. The glass box rivalled the child in height. Should be in school, Istha thought. Bet her mother is somewhere maxed out in a nice shady stall, big market mommy got her child out slaving. Istha sucked her teeth and walked to the child. She purchased several balls of moin-moin, mashed and seasoned black-eyed beans which were wrapped in banana leaf and steamed, and placed the burden on the child's head. She gave Kandace and Cynthia half of the food she'd purchased and sighed.

"Istha, the destitution and devastation here is beginning to choke your spirit. It is all over your aura." Cynthia looked not at Istha but 5 to 12 inches around her frame. "You have to find a way to steel yourself and then heal yourself and stay healed and whole."

"It's difficult when you see children suffering on 1 hand and on the other witness a brawl because 'elders' want to beat us out of 1000 naira for 'spiritual services.'"

"Word, I mean to see elders humiliate themselves for money? It is embarrassing, but it tells you all you need to know about them, their spirits, and their 'services.'"

"Word did you check out the chief's crib? 2 flat screens, a car and a van, thrones, and shit."

"Spirit workers, especially babaláwo, are not supposed to earn any more than is necessary to survive so that their spirits and bodies are in full alignment with the cosmos, the Earth, and their powers. These cats are in full alignment with First Bank and satellite television," Cynthia asserted.

"Everyone is crying about money, but they all got at least what my folks have and more in most cases, plus, they are on their own land and don't have to battle racists," Kandace observed.

"The problem isn't need but greed. Ironically, it may be the global popularity of Ifá that is driving this lust for cash. 1 thing is clear: Ọbàtálá has left the shrine," Istha intoned in her announcer's voice.

"Word. If any Òrìṣà were here they would be like, 'Kíló ń ṣé?!?'" Cynthia and Kandace laughed.

"I really enjoyed the time I spent in Mali," Istha's face beamed. "It's a totally different vibe. Well, all of these countries are unique and complex. But Mali is deep. It's the home of the blues, and you *feel* that power. We should travel to Mali together during the next break. It's easy, we just show our IDs at the borders. It's all ECOWAS."

"Damn! You're bold, girl! I never would have thought of that."

"Girl, I have traveled to nearly every ECOWAS country. It's liberating and a true education. I wish I could spend my life traveling and learning." The women gave Istha's wish thought as they sipped their drinks.

"So, Istha," Kandace inquired, "How is your program going?"

"Kan, you know that Istha's supervisor walked out on her."

"What?"

"Yep," Istha's chuckle was genuine but it rode over well-deep pain. "After raining all possible abuse on my head right on the department veranda, he publicly washed his hands of me."

"Why?"

"No 1 knows. But I think it's an inferiority complex. He was calling me lazy in front of other profs. But I think he was pissed at my temerity and the depth and breadth of my proposal. See, he had published a study on Àṣẹ— that's why I wanted him to be my supervisor, my respect for his work—but I think he was angry that I proposed such a deep study and had the tools, methodology, and courage to carry it out," she recounted all of this in a detached disinterested manner, like she was discussing a stale television program she watched last night.

"He prepared a mini qualifying examination for me. Everyone seemed, well, disquieted, you know? But I was prepared, over-prepared. He only notified me 24 hours in advance, but I was ready. The shit was a witch hunt. They wanted it to be, anyway. If it wasn't for Prof. Imoye . . . Girl, they couldn't do nothin with us!" She brightened remembering her mentor and their victory, "We shot down every bullshit issue they raised."

"Alright now!" Cynthia slapped Istha's hand, "Imoye don't play."

"But it enraged Tokunbo. 2 days later, he held his hand washing party. Since then he's tried to run me up outta the university. Vowed to do so. Hell, he became department chair so that he can stymie me."

"What you gon do?"

"Imoye got my back," she smiled and nodded. "I'll find a new supervisor and keep moving forward."

Name_______________________________   Prof. Istha
Date_______________________________   FU 4-8

Define the following:

blue gum	Lady Day
handlah	zackly
40 goin north	Geechee
boe hog	lo mo
yams	pure o dee
Lil Africa	shine
Soulville	done run out
gee'ed up	lam black
funk	damn skippy

If you ain't hip to at least 6 of these
you can't even get a GED in me

What time is it?_______________   Today's pig _________________
Can I kick it?_______________   Revolution has come___________
Fried, dyed and_______________   Too Black_________________
All up in dat_______________   AAAAAwwwww _______________
Who did it, what for,___________   Showed his_______________
Knocked smooth the__________   Who's da _________________

Can't finish 5 lines
you cain't even get a diploma in yo momma

Wannabe universal
pseudo-intellectual muthafucka
how long we been gone you ain't
reck uh nI's ed
how long I been here
        you never hear
                        seeordigme
cept for gems to place on your shelf
My self and soul like rock and roll
were molded in the Middle Passage
not among mindless, brainless, spineless,
sellers of souls

I dun dug you
Yo ain't shit deep
you ain't hip
to yo own soul
what I'm sayin is
you dead
sold yo ancestors
pawned yo spirit
        so, therefore,
        you ain't got no soul

Nose so deep in grayfolks' ass
the beasts can smell ya
but they cain't sell ya
        you ain't worth dead pig's shit
All y'all gots problemz
look like something Tutuola wrote bout
got yo ass up on yo backs
talk out the side a ya neck
eyes in da backs a ya heads
as blind as the bucked up ones in front
If u can reck cog nI's
anger here, you gets a PhD
in elementary
which is all you'll ever be
simple bitch
cuz, if you cain't see me
you cain't see you
I tell a true

or I won't say nothin
I reck og n I's you
sho as the fuck I do
You the zac same factor
sold momma's momma's momma's momma
and would sell me too if you could catch me
run as fast as you can
cain't catch me
da gingerbread wo man

Yo motto is keep dis nigger girl running
Well, I can hurdle cross time
run yo rabid ass outta mind
That's why ya sold us in the first place
too damn deep
Ya sowed evil now ya gon reap

1 a dese kids is doin her own thang
1 a dese kids is just not the same
1 a dese kids is doin her own than
Now it's time to say huh name

Yeh, when the Earth is tired of rejectin yo
sorry ass body and you stand fore yo
ancestors
all they gon ask is 1 query
"Do you remember Istha?"

And as you listen to the rustle of cloth on skin
the turning of ancestral backs on you forever
you gon recall
all the fuck shit
you don and did and said
Ya shitted I my mouth and told me not to spit
ya gave me a chair on nails and told me to sit
or the simple fact that yo triflin ass did not respect me
as the essence of the Creator's totality
and you'll stand there for eternity
thinkin bout me and knowin real death
and why I left
Gotta go, gotta go

this world is not my home
this world is not my home
this is a howlin wilderness
This here AINT MY HOME
cuz I can only live in love
comes only from recognition
comes only from respect
comes only from protection
comes only in love

When ya sold us, ya loss that
so of course, you ain't hip
ya own/ed chaps ain't shit
                              but marks
                                    got values on they heads
                                        price tags on they ass and
                           insteada a torso its yo dream house
                    they feet is yo cars
              they heart is a refrigerator
         they ain't got no souls
and dey minds is fucked up

Ya ain't got husbands and wives but
bidness acquaintances
da mo da bettah
but not mo bettah
ya don't make love
ya makin investments
                   speculations
                     bidniss ventures
You souled out ya self
sure as water wet
and no, this ain't dedicated to you
           you got 1 foot in the grave
                       and the other on somebody neck
No, this is for your
                   children's
                 children's
               children's
             children's
           children
so that they maybe they'll only be
a 1/5 as fucked up as you are

Let me hip you—
you with all yo shiny acquisitions
you with all yo yourowsintric positions
you with you fucked up dispositions
                —to Black Wealth

There are some people who dared to love
when deads said
"3 strangs uh beads"
"25 pounds"
"7 manillas"
"bitch"
"buck"
"wench"
"Mandingo"
There are some people who dared to love
what their Creator made though it got
raped
cut out
chopped off
shot up
lynched
kilt dead
fucked up
burnt up
taken off
mortgaged off
rented out
And when these folks could examine the shinin
reflected in the mirror of perfection that is diggin 1 another
they unleashed love like a big dog
everythang previously loved a little in increments
was loved to the full 9
thangs loved to the full 9 previously
was taken to the nth degree

See, that's where I come from,
where I'm goin, and where I'm always gon be
So of course when I check out
this writin hand, I see my Momma
learning to write again after pneumonia liked to kilt her
and my back is 1001 weps

from Gran's switches and my arms is
ever opened to enfold my Muthadeah and my
skin is the same color—amount a cream and sugar—
Daddy like in his coffee
and my big feet is my uncle's stride
My dance is Bo Diddley
My thighs and my mouth—bitch—is Aint Dusty
and when you get to where you
cain't even say
               "dog kiss my ass"
                       or nothin to me
    my eyes avert and my feet shuffle like my
       elders/ancestor movin before
   gray dogs cuz

WE DON'T KNOW
WHAT THE FUCK Y'ALL'UL DO

Understand?
Me standing
on the love my generations built from pain
and you cain't get to that
even if you got deep
and tried to dig what I'm sayin
you'd just die again
cuz you can't re cog n I's my
we and your you in our we
because you oblivious to love
because you been dead, see?

"Why they drivin that girl?" Cynthia and Kandace were eating dinner in their chalet.

Cynthia scooped the iyan with her fingertips and dipped the mound into the vegetable stew and red sauce. "This iyan ain't nothin but mashed potatoes and this egúsí ain't nothin but collard greens," she tucked into the food. After a minute she answered Kandace, "That man, Tokunbo, he's afraid of her. She's a woman young enough to be his child, whose history was stripped from her—probably by his ancestors—but she can do what he never dreamt of. Without saying or doing a thing she emphasizes his irrelevance."

"She has fire she doesn't even know about," Kandace separated fish from bone and popped the meat in her mouth. "She shouldn't worry,"

Kandace started chuckling. "Istha has a battalion of ancestors with her. She knows it but doesn't know it. Ancestors and elders are guarding her. She also works her ass off. And her work is progressive, she pulls no punches with her analyses. But she definitely is her own woman."

"I understand her struggle cause we're all foreigners here, and everything about us is different: culture, hair, dress, language, manifestation of power. But the issue is deeper than being foreigners: I think that certain people have been historically ostracized from this society since the 1500s and we are those kinda people," Cynthia posited.

"It is bizarre, but the conscious Africans who want to come here represent what many people here fear and hate."

"We also stand as a reminder of what they want to forget. Istha says it's the same in Ghana—but even more eerie because the fort and castle of slavery are there as massive reminders. But because it is a tourist nation, some Ghanaians will knock their own children down to serve a foreigner. But you can also meet brothers named after Marcus Garvey. Africa is complex!"

"Nkrumah was a Pan-Africanist."

"Word life. Du Bois is buried in Ghana."

"So you expect a certain level of consciousness from Ghana."

"The Rastas are strong there, too."

"But things are different on the former 'Slave Coast'. There is no doubt that many of the Fon of Benin would sell you if they could, but because they can't—at least not as easily as in the past—they prey, exploit, deceive, drain, and destroy. I have never experienced a more predatory culture than that of Benin. And it is the most hypocritical country I've ever been to. With graven images dangling around 80% of the population's necks, it is not possible to visit Benin and not see raw evil of Christianity and the success of Jesus as the poster child of Caucasian supremacy."

"What I find chilling is that many Beninois have embraced completely the racism of the French. Imagine Africans being racist against other Africans, especially those who don't speak French. If those same African-hating Africans spent 1 day in France they would know the French don't care what language you speak or how gutturally your pronounce the letter 'r'. They consider all Africans and Arabs 'niggers' and that's how they treat us: from burning down housing projects filled with Africans to throwing African and Arab youths into electric fences and electrocuting them.

"However, because of the French assimilationist colonization policy, these Negroes in Benin actually think they French! What we witnessed in Benin is a case study of how colonialism, capitalism, and Christianity destroy humanity." A 3 month visit to Benin had stunned the women.

"You know, racist oppressive Africans are lethal and much more devastating that racist grays."

"Can you imagine what Istha is dealing with being here all alone?" Cynthia shook her head, "We need to reach out to her."

They ceased talking and finished their meal. When Kandace rinsed her hands in the bowl of fresh water, Cynthia looked and up asked, "Okay. So how is my cooking?"

Kissing her fingers, Kandace extolled, "Magnifique!"

"The university is strange. It is like everyone is a spirit waiting to be called on in." She thought audibly, "Someone with her cipher's going to feel alone." The clinking dishes and splashing water provided the undertone to Cynthia's musings. "So many people here are unconscious, on all levels. But there are many good people, too."

"Yes. And some powerful people and wealthy people."

"Nigeria's a wealthy nation, but many gains are gotten dishonestly: drug money, 419, blood money, ritual killing. What is that about? You find people shouting about Jesus and killing people for money-making rituals."

"Look at how those cults killed those students last month."

"That was devastating. I still can't believe such a gruesome crime as that was committed on a campus," Cynthia shook her head in confusion. "In addition to mafia-style executions, the campus is a hotbed of bribery, extortion, sexting, and sexing."

"Sure you wanna go there?" Kandace faced her friend. Her eyes bucked in challenge.

"Listen, Femi and I"

"Honestly," Kandace dismissed her friend, "I don't care to hear you try to justify the mistake you're making."

"What mistake?" Cynthia's eyes became wide, her hands slashed the air as she explained herself. "How can our relationship be a mistake? I could be his second wife."

Kandace laughed, she didn't mean it to be rude, but she laughed dead in her friend's face. "Are you mad?" she knew she wasn't, couldn't be serious. Why was her head so spun out? "He must have 1 hell uva dick. Got you whipped twisted and all."

"Well, I do enjoy our intimacy. But" she lifted a finger, "the point is our vibes. Our conversations. I mean, did we come here to be all locked up in each other? Or to learn? He's a very spiritual person, very deep."

"Okay. But why you? Does it raise his stature? Prove his ability to conquer? Everything is so—mago mago—as they say."

"Alright, alright," Cynthia was getting frustrated, "let's leave that rabbit and run this 1:" They chuckled coming back into themselves. "Let's have Istha over tomorrow. Is that cool?"

"Great idea."

Cynthia smiled but mused, "She looks so empty sometimes. When she laughs, she laughs too loudly. I worry about her."

There was a knock at the door.

"I'll get it," Kandace said. "It's probably Istha returning those books. Mo ń bọ̀," she called out.

Kandace opened the door and saw the unexpected. "Yes?" she inquired. She watched his eyes appraise every curve, plane, line of her body. She pursed her lips, "Yes!"

"Good evening. I'm Femi. Is this the residence of Cynthia Thomas?"

So, in the flesh: Femi.

My god! Both of these women in 1 house. This could be paradise!

Watch your step. You don't know me or what you're getting into.

His eyebrow rose at her mental threat.

So you can feel me. I'm glad. I know you. Known you. This is not a playground. Nor is Cynthia a toy. I don't play.

"Kan?" Cynthia's came to the door.

"It's for you." She stepped back dramatically and revealed the man. He was short, deep brown, and traditionally dressed. He was a wholly average looking man. Kandace left her sister to her business.

"So how're you enjoying it here?"

"It's okay." After a few minutes, they realized she wasn't going to expound.

"You have many friends here?"

"Shrrrk!" she sucked her teeth. "Can you make friends here? Everyone asks the same 3 questions: Why don't you make your hair? Can you help me get to America? Do you believe in Jesus?" With each question she added appropriate gestures, fingering Cynthia's fro, curling her lips down with her palms up and open in supplication and eyes bucked, glazed, acting as if she was handing out a pamphlet.

"It can be an oppressive soul-crushing place, but there are pockets of promise here and there too," Istha offered. "But what are you doing here?" Istha asked of Kandace. Istha didn't want to star as victim, so she shifted the focus. She liked these sisters and wanted to be friends but she didn't want anyone's pity and she also didn't want to establish a friendship because they were all from the same nation. She had tried that with another sister and it had been a disaster. The woman was a typical oreo. It was difficult to discern why she'd come to Africa. She was simply fake. Istha didn't want to endure that again. So she was reserved, but open.

"Actually, I'm doing the same thing you're doing. But not for academics. Since I was a child, I was aware that I have a certain power: Àjẹ́. I came here because Ilé Ifẹ̀ is the closest thing to a geographical source of my power. So this is a homecoming of sorts for me."

"Are you serious? Well, that's rhetorical. But wow!" Istha was on the edge of her seat. "Of course I know of our evolutionary powers and that we evolved Àjẹ́, we had to to survive, but this is too deep. And for us all to be here like this! Are you astrally inclined? clairvoyant?" She hung her head and bit her words, "I'm sorry. I'm being nosey."

"Istha, you can ask me whatever you want, girl, I recognize you!" Kandace laughed. "I also know that your motives aren't selfish. You want your work to guide us to the next stage of our evolution. The main reason you're having difficulty is you're real." Kandace smiled, "You took a long time to come into yourself. You came to this place hoping to find like minds to link with and you've been accosted by clones."

Istha nodded her head, "I also wish that, like you 2, I'd come with a friend, a sister. It's like I divorced all my family and friends coming here."

"Don't worry," Cynthia intoned from the kitchen where she was preparing dinner, "You'll find everything you need."

"I, too, thought the powers would be stronger but everything is clouded by money, power, and sex," Kandace cut an eye at Cynthia's back; she was in the kitchen.

"I can't imagine what you've endured here alone," Kandace took Istha's hands in her own. "And you're vulnerable because you're sensitive."

"It's all about trusting and learning not to," Istha had gained wisdom from her experiences.

"As it concerns your program: don't worry. Tokunbo and many others feel threatened by you. This lets you know you're doing everything right! Continue your work. Don't lose focus. Take what you can use; give the deserving what they need; and keep moving forward."

Cynthia came in bearing a tray laden with 3 deep dish plates filled with rice and red sauce and fish. The sisters broke bread. They filled themselves with delicious food for the body to complement the food for thought they provided 1 another.

As they relaxed and sipped verbena tea, Cynthia asked Istha, "Do you feel like meditating with us?"

"I'd love it. I haven't meditated in a long time."

"Once you have your own sanctified space, your spirit will flow freely again," she stood up, "Come on! Let's go to the backyard."

Cynthia and Kandace had created a charming space of their chalet. Lively batiks covered the furniture. Paintings by local artists, art students, and Kandace lived on the walls. Out back was the courtyard which they had transformed into a sacred space.

The previous tenants had used the courtyard as a dumping ground. Snail shells, plastic bottles, notebooks, paper, unusable clothes, plastic bags, whatever was beyond repair was pitched out there. Kandace and Cynthia looked through the trash and saw a haven. A space that could be used to dry clothes, play lawn tennis, or throw a party gone to waste!

After cleaning and adorning their home they tackled the courtyard. It took them two days to clear the space and burn the rubbish. After three days, the space was immaculate, and sprouts of grass were celebrating the rays of the sun.

Kandace, Cynthia, and Istha relaxed in the courtyard which was aglow with citronella candles and mosquito-repelling incense. They watched the sun announce its farewell by leaving a retinue of gold, purple, violet red, and slate gray clouds in its wake. They let the moving canvas thrill their eyes; then, they turned their vision inward. They saw themselves, a 3 point star framed in green. After 3 minutes, about 30 people joined them.

Daughters, you are welcome, Ìyálóde intoned with a smile.

Istha was flabbergasted. She'd heard of the ẹgbẹ́ Àjẹ́, but she never imagined that she would witness a meeting. She recognized Madame Ladipo from the department, many women from town, Imoye, their favorite fish seller, the seamstress who destroyed 4 yards of white bazine, and Femi, among the men and women who comprised the ẹgbẹ́.

Greetings, daughters! We are grateful for your presence and thankful for your powers, for they are essential to the Work we will do. Istha felt Ìyálóde's greeting was like an embrace.

Ifẹ̀ is not your final destination. The emi level of this population is too low to build. You will find fertile ground farther north in a land consecrated and prepared by Ahni. We will inform you when it is time to move and build. Until that time, you will continue bearing and sharing knowledge here for this is your training ground. Kandace, you will work with me, Cynthia and Istha will work with Imoye.

Ìyá I am honored to be one with you and our Work, Istha said. But I need to know: What has happened here. Why is there so much manipulation? Why are there so many mercenaries?

Too many of us have turned our backs on the way of Ah, the way of Imọlẹ̀, the way of Ìyánlá Odù. Too many of us have embraced the way of Yurugu; the result is self and community destruction masked as "modernity."

It stuns me, Istha added, that a country with immeasurable cultural, intellectual, and mineral riches can be so riddled with academic, material, and spiritual poverty. . . . In some cases it seems as if destitution is desired.

The Nigeria you've met is like a crotchety old man who should be taking his last breath but, Ìyá chuckled, he holds his breath! He can't die and he can't live. Nigeria is a myth, like all other African countries are myths. Because our governments refuse to unite and liberate our Continent from neocolonial and capitalistic fragmentation and dreams, life for many Africans is an interminable nightmare.

There many eminegative agents who work to ensure the will of Ogo reigns in Africa. But all too many people are emivoid, and they want to stay this way because rotating around the pit of mediocrity is easy. What is more, when they see someone who is rooted in and demands excellence, they endeavor to drag that person into the pit or destroy them.

A house cleaning, so to speak, will take place, after which, many of us will relocate to Minnah for the reconstitution. We will establish the final emisite on this Continent. 2 are already thriving: 1 in Dogon Country and 1 in Kumba. Our emisite will dispense justice through Àjẹ́.

Are there other emisites abroad? You mentioned this Continent. . .

Yes. Sites are forming in Alapaha, Georgia; Nashville, Tennessee; and Bliss Bluff, Mississippi. Our site will constitute the invisible hub of a cycle of retribution never before witnessed on this Earth. Everyone reflected on the significance of the Work their ẹgbẹ́ would undertake.

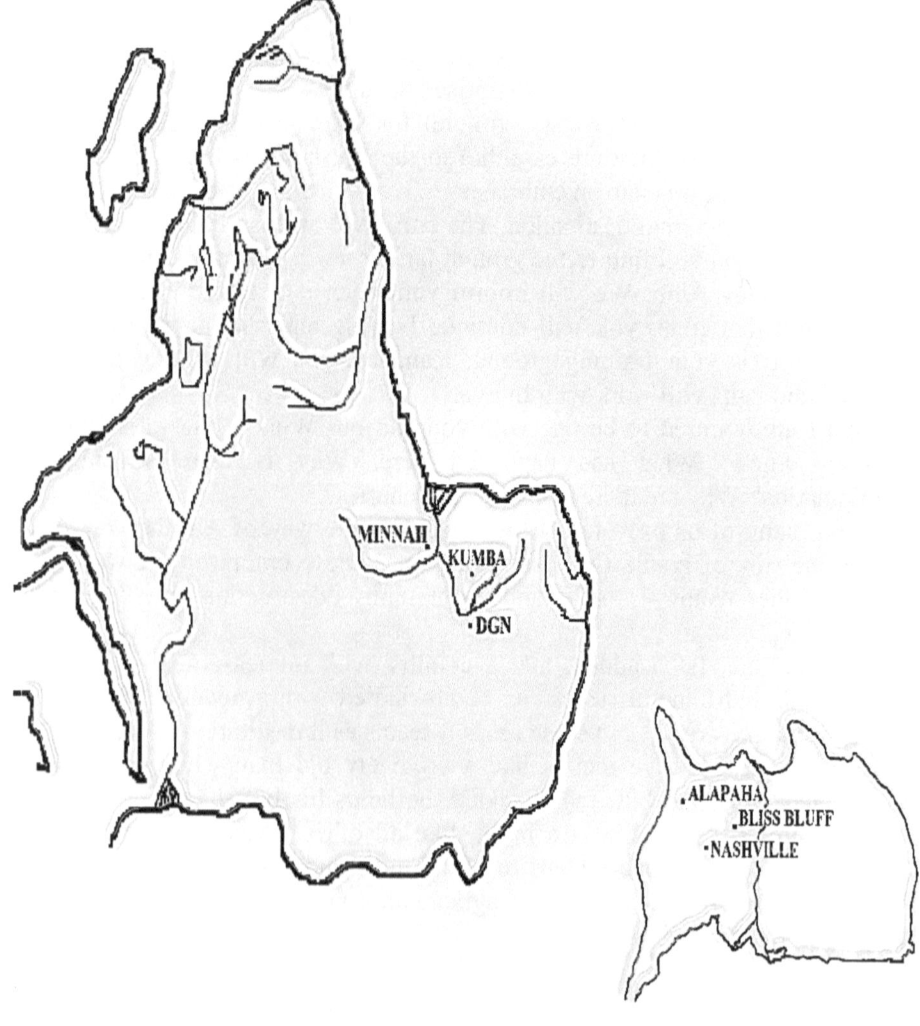

We all know what your struggles here, Ìyálóde peered into the eyes of Kandace, Cynthia, and Istha in turn. Some of us have taken you through unnecessary crossroads. Some of us have guided you through crossroads. There is a saying: *Àjẹ́ òngbìjà ènìyàn ni ó di kòkó délé wi*: Àjẹ́ goes to the meeting to fight on your behalf but when she sees you, she doesn't say a word. Never lose focus and never fear: We are always with you. Remember that no knowledge is wasted; everything that you are learning here is vital to our future development.

Istha had learned more than she dreamed she would and more than she had wanted to. After offering generosity and open friendship, she'd been gifted with various 419 schemes and attacks. 1 young man, Kola seemed sincere. They'd taken long walks, had gone swimming and to movies. He seemed so available and receptive. She spent nights sharing with him the oral traditions of her people, comparing them with Yoruba orature. She started finding joy in her research and began to appreciate the potential possibilities of her coming to Nigeria.

She also began making and spending time with other friends, especially Ahmed from The Gambia. She and Ahmed and Segun would spend evenings at the Bukka drinking, smoking and generally enjoying themselves. They played snooker and 8 ball and she rapped along with Tupac and came to know Fela.

1 night Kola came to her with his face framed in worry. He told her she was going to be in a magazine that was published to shame women out of certain behaviors: drinking, smoking, laughing loudly, bathing outside in the early morning hours.

"I'm on the panel of this magazine and your name has come up for publication."

She laughed, "Why?"

"You can't go round drinking and smoking at the Bukka! Our university has standards and"

"Nigga, please!" she laughed. "*You're* on the panel? You set all this up!" She looked at him; his façade was wearing away, revealing his ugly truth. "You're jealous."

"Well, with all your new friends, you don't have time for me."

"Fool! I'm grown. This is a childish ass conversation." She lit a cigarette. Not because of desire or stress, but to blow smoke in his face. "And y'all some childish ass muthafuckas if this is what you do."

Her eyes locked with Kola's and she saw 2 maroon orbs. It was as if he were another person, as if a beast inside of him were emerging.

Ain't no tellin what this bitch'll do, Istha realized.

She dragged and exhaled again, "Let them print what they want. It's true: I smoke and drink at Bukka. Fuck it, and fuck you too. Now," she stood up, "get the fuck outta my space."

Kola didn't move. His fury went from his eyes to his fists. This is gon get good, Istha took her stance.

Before Ahmed separated them, Kola suffered a blackened eye and a bruised neck.

This was low-level shit. Profs had handled her breasts, groped her labia, and palmed her ass as if she were a mango in the market. She fainted in the dorm hallway with malaria, the students "helping" her, stole her money. Genuine decent folks she could count on 1 hand and have enough fingers left over to write with elegance. What is more, her research was moving slowly. Her only joy was Prof. Imoye and Dr. Femi Bankole with whom she was falling in love.

She often sought and found solace at the zoo and botanical garden. On 1 occasion, she made a pallet under the clusters of bamboo. She felt an affinity to the trees because her afro seemed to mirror the verdant bamboo brushing and tickling the sky.

She meditated in lotus position and conjured a circle of ancestors around her. She stretched her arms to embrace her blood, now an ocean away. Then she felt the ground begin humming and then vibrating. Ah! What a gift! The throbbing cradled and massaged her thighs and buttocks and breasts and eventually engulfed her whole body.

Not fainting from hunger and being robbed when she had malaria. Not the transition of 5 elders to ancestors in her absence. Not being homeless after 1.5 weeks in Nigeria, not exclusion and discrimination. Nothing mattered. Not the necessities stolen from her at the airport. Not the supervisor who'd called her indolent and acted as if she were a pushy roach with an affinity for his office. Nothing mattered because power and soul were hers and were regenerating, under her, within her, vibrating, charging. Her backbone hummed, her clitoris rose. She closed her eyes. She understood why she had come.

Night Re-Members

Because at night
  you would hold me like a child
   hold me like the only warmth
protection
medication
you needed
     was found in the curve of my back

     the slope of my spine
   hold me like a child
 I would fall forever into the reassurance
           of your arms
       the promise
     of your Soul
 Yes, at night
       after the loving
         you would engulf me
       introduce me to your
  ridges curves valleys and peaks
 your topography became mine

On those nights
2 children
missing Momma's breasts
stretched and
filled spaces
gaped by too much time left alone

Those moments
when you entered
   my Soul
 I miss most

"He gone, Babygirl." Old Man Turner held her like he was her father as she shivered in front of the smoldering center. "He gone."

She couldn't accept it. He was in that pile of charred rubble? Buried? Burning? She wept. Inside. Outside. No. "No." She refused the knowledge. She stood staring, the smoke curled and fanned upwards, misting into the night.

It was snowing outside and she could see her breath come out in thick rapid white puffs. But it wasn't until she felt warmth from the fire that it sank in. I'm being warmed by Soul's body. Body! "Soul!!!" Old Man Turner became her Earth because the bottom of her world was snatched from her feet.

45 dead. She heard the fire fighters mumbling "capacity," "gas leak," "boiler," "pressure." This was war. War had claimed 45 truth tellers. Souljahs. War had claimed her warrior. Her Soul.

She broke down and heaved. She couldn't breathe. She didn't want to. She wanted to melt like the snow into the Earth. She wanted to rise like the smoke into the upper atmosphere and dissipate into the cosmos.

"Keep on, you lose that baby."

Baby? My baby.

Yo baby needs love. Peace. Soul. Soul with us. The child with you. Needs you whole. They crushed my soul. They tried to kill it too. But they didn't kill me, and they won't kill you.

When she opened her eyes, she was gazing into the eyes of time. The woman was her. Same features: strong nose slightly peaked, wide milk white eyes with large ocher pupils, and the ever-pursed lips. Her skin tone was a shining burnt sienna. She recognized her first friend.

"I ain't just your friend, child. I'm your foundation. Yoruba," she smiled and then enunciated, "Yorùbá." The word became a song. Their song.

She held her arms open and ready to embrace. She was adorned in a cloth of purple, indigo, ocher and berry red all interwoven with gold.

"We're all waiting for you at home."

"Come home," said a couple who had emerged. They were dressed just like Yoruba. These are her parents; my progenitors! "Yes, we're all here."

Every photo from all of the albums she would never see had come to life. Every embrace that she longed for but never felt surrounded her. She was overcome with completion.

"Bring Ast home," he smiled.

"Soul?"

"We're waiting for you at home."

"Come home."

Home? Home? Where? Not Moline. Surely not Rosedale with Uncle D.

"Your name, our text. Your name. Bliss Bluff. Your text. Bliss Bluff."

"Bliss Bluff." Sounds familiar. Was that . . . No . . . no! Bliss Bluff. Momma's home? Home? Bliss Bluff. That's where. . . She went to her computer and opened the atlas. Then she began her journey.

They was sleepin when Momma shot up in bed and said that the beast be sneaking round the door in 3 hours. Daddy was fin to run and get him, but Momma say, relax and get yo guns, he comin alone and he gon leave dead. But it's mo trouble ahead. I done seen it.

Daddy got his guns and said Missippi be damned and the Klan with it, but he'd go to hell in a handcart if in merica where he was free, bukrah gon outrage his wife and live. Daddy tol Momma to get in the pantry when he spotted ol bald dog staggrin up the drive. He was bloody from where Momma done beat his ass best she could.

The shots rattled everything in the pantry and Momma covered her head. Daddy had blowed his nuts off with his double pump and finished him in the head. Then Daddy took and set him out at the crossroads so his kin'd get him. Ma Jule's daughter and her husband and all the other families came out to see what had happened. When they saw Daddy stringing that cracker up it was dead silence down in the bottoms. The next day Ma Jule's daughter Baby Lee brought us a gift of eggs and some goat meat and milk and everybody came out to our house to discuss what had happened and how to prepare.

That next week, just as everyone thought the bottoms would be overlooked cause the dog was sick anydamnway, Momma told Daddy that they needed to git quick cuz the Klan was comin, but Daddy say he ain't runnin from his home; say, let em come. Daddy told Momma to head for the woods, double time. She put herself into a tree and she watch him.

A Klan army came to the house that night. Daddy had his double pump cocked and his pistol too and he came out shootin them white sheets! It was rednecks runnin like 40 goin North! You'd a thought they was 20 chickens without heads. He took 6 of em out fore his pump jammed. They blew his arm off but Daddy was still fightin and yellin; trying to distract attention from Momma, but she near, too near.

You know how whitefolks always come prepared for evil, well, they didn't expect Daddy's last stand, but they had plenty coon dogs who found Momma Ja easy. They gather in a circle around her and just fore they attack, here come the Klan.

They dragged Momma Ja back to the house where they had Daddy knocked out, and 1 of em held Daddy up by his 1 arm. Momma didn't scream nor flinch, she say, she just lookin at them white peaked sheets in a night warm as blood. Momma still, even when she saw they hands russlin their sheets at the crotch. But Daddy's eyes flew open and he commenced to kick and bite the man holdin him, Momma say the sheets gave Daddy some more stunnin blows and brought Momma up against Daddy who was up against our white oak tree.

Momma Ja said they was arguing about who got to do what and the leader said they all could get a taste of Momma since Daddy thought she was worthy of protecting. They held Momma's arms as the leader came up on her grinnin like a diseased hog. Momma said she let up a war yell so loud that all the bottoms stopped sleepin or being scared and stood forth. Momma clawed and bit in a frenzy and struck nail to eye and knee to groin. The leader cursed and spit on her as he crumpled to the ground. But he was just 1, and they was many. 1 of the others lammed Momma from behind with the butt of his gun. She didn't wake up until the next morning.

Baby Lee said when they heard Ma Ja's cry all of the families came runnin up to the hill where Momma and Daddy stay. They ain't never heard a sound like that before. Baby Lee say it struck em in the gut. She say the men started shootin at them white targets just like my Daddy did. All them devil's that could flee fled, but not without leaving 9 more sheeted bodies behind. When the battle was over, everyone took the dead Klan bodies to the crossroads, stacked em like cord wood and set em on fire.

That vengeance was in honor of Daddy, but it didn't help him. The Klan had lynched him on the white oak right in front of our house. They didn't burn, tar and feather him as they would have if they had had time, but they did hang him and they cut off his dick.

Baby Lee took my Momma to her house and bathed her down in Epsom salt and choke cherry to take out the swellin and pain of the beating. Momma could not rest. She tol Baby Lee to tell the men not to take her husband nowhere, that she must do her job, she must touch him first.

The next morning, Momma was bandaged up and huggin Daddy's legs without a word but with that glistenin face. She said some prayers at his feet and took and put 4 eggs around the base of the tree. She told the men they bring Daddy down, and they buried Daddy in the roots of that tree. But fore they did, Momma cut a lock of his hair and her hair and wrapped it in a piece of his shirt. She tied this to a string and kept it round her waist. Always. She put bottles on every branch of that tree she could reach, and she tied 1 of her cloths she had dyed in our family colors in around the base of that tree. She told me that she did many things to protect us but that Daddy Mosa do the most protectin of all.

Momma say she wanted me cuz she knew me to be her last chance, and she knew I had work to do in this world. Important work. As much as it hurt her to bear me, as much as I served to remind her of all she'd lost, she brought me here, and she cherished me. She said that I was the Truth. That I represented the fact that the Gods can surmount any evil. That the blood of the Gods is supreme.

Momma say when she knew I was gettin ready to come, She went out to the tree and called Baby Lee and her husband Jove. She had me right there with Daddy. Momma said she was peaceful and I came in with peace. I had a caul over my face when Baby Lee gave me to her. Momma say she rose it just enough for me to take her nipple. When I was finished takin Momma's milk, Baby Lee got ready to cut the cord with a knife but Momma Ja say to Baby Lee, "Put yo knife away; Mosa gon cut the cord." Ma Ja tol Jove to reach up and grab a bottle and break it.

When he broke that bottle Baby Lee say she heard a sigh, kinda long like someone was relieved. Jove cut our cord. Momma say 7 days later when she named me, everybody Juba'd just for me!

When I was little I used to play round that tree: I thought Momma had decorated it for me. I would play and Momma would join me sometimes. She would tell me about her history, my history, our history right there with Daddy at the tree. We would all sit out and braid hair there, me, Ma Ja, and Daddy, or eat, or just be, and didn't no beasts ever come round to bother us.

When Ma Ja died I wailed out to and through the bottoms and sent everybody word that Momma was gone. Everyone turn out for her puttin away. Mister Jove prayed over, wrapped up, and sent Momma along just liked he did Daddy. And when they lay Momma down it was with Daddy, up under his tree.

I wanted to lay right down there with them. I didn't feel I had nothing to live for without them. Felt like my soul'd been turned inside out and emptied.

Momma Ja was my world, you see. Everythin I learned I learned while sittin tween Momma's legs whilst she did my hair. I went to school too, but I knew learnin to read and write wouldn't help me survive like Momma Ja's lessons would. So I had 2 schools, that Miss Rule taught and that of Mosa and Momma. All that I learned I am putting to use for you, right now. Never throw any knowledge away. You can never have too many tools in yo arsenal.

Daddy taught me that "the onlyst way to kill evil is dead," and he taught me to be the warrior I am. My Ma Ja taught me this: "Anybody put hand on you, chile, you do what you need to do to find yo peace. Cause ain't no justice higher than yo free body and soul."

She tell me I got a God called The Reesha and that she be lookin out for me. She tell me my soul's gotta be mineowned and I cain't nevah forget my roots, and neither can you, Lil Wom. Momma Ja read my roots out to me, she say I got the Ifa and that I got somethin to do in this life. Now, I can't say I know exactly what all this is, but I know its power, and as I sit here and write this for you, I guess I done as well by this power as I could.

Life after Momma Ja passed on was some hard. Momma Ja was my backbone and a body can't rise without no spine. For a year, I couldn't do nothin—wouldn't do nothin, I would just sit under my Daddy tree and wish the sheets would come and get me so I could be with my people.

Baby Lee and Jove and their children Nell and Ham brought me food and tried to get me to live life. Nell my best friend, and she would come to try and cheer me up with stories and games, but I just wouldn't say or do nothin. I just let my face get wet and tried to read my tears like Ma Ja did. I kept water all over the house so Momma could talk to me, and I would sit under the tree waitin to see my Daddy but I didn't hear from them.

"Aiiiint Maaaay!!!" Chaka shielded her eyes from the sun as she scanned the field. "Aiiint Maaaay!" She let a soprano lilt take over the elder's name. "Aiiin't Maaay!"

"Oóó òòò!" The response was to the southeast. Out by the John de Conqueror, Chaka mused. Aint May was really something. Up before the sun pruning, fertilizing, picking, drying and preserving. The woman had to be into her 90s and looked a cool 60.

"I believe y'all got more Geechee in ya than my folks. Those some straight up field hollas y'all producin."

"And what make it so good," she reached her arms around him to rub his back, "is that I can call Aint May and wake yo lazy butt up at the same time."

"Chaka, the fish and grits woke me up. Not your big mouth," Jahmai tickled her and they kissed and giggled.

"Hep heah!" Aint May called and the couple ran to meet the elder who was dragging an ancient cotton sack behind her with her left hand. In her right hand she cradled some roots. Jahmai and Chaka relieved the elder of her loads and the trio made their way back to the house.

Jahmai set the table and everyone washed up and dug in.

"You chirrin somethin! Never seen a man set a table."

"Aint May, that devil is lazy. Setting the table easy."

"That's true. But we all gon work this mornin cuz we gotta prepare that conquer root and life everlastin and grind the ginger."

Aint May watched Chaka get up to bring fresh grits and fish to the table and recalled the day she delivered and named her. She thought about the way she ritually swept the deep brown big eyed girl child every morning. With hands like raw silk, she swept her 9 times: her arms, 9 times, each leg 9 times. Her limbs were straight and beautiful as a result.

Even as a child, Chaka would take her strong little limbs along and accompany her great aunt to the fields to tend to the Earth's gifts. Aint May ran a supply house and it was 1 of the last of its kind and it dealt with few customers for 2 reasons. Aint May was a reserved person and a sincere 1, she dealt with people she knew and trusted with the Work. Aint May was also against the commercialization of spirituality. Her only desire was to heal and make whole, and those concerns had nothing to do with dollars. Money, she knew, was the cause of the majority of the world's ills. Like all real Workers, she shunned it.

Aint May knew as soon as she popped out of the womb that Chaka was special. When the child was 7 days on the Earth, Aint May made medicine with life everlasting, gooba dust, and big Johnny C. She made delicate incisions at the top of Chaka's head, at the base of her neck, inside each wrist, on the belly, on the backs of the knee and on the bottom of each foot. In each incision, she rubbed the medicine and chanted

Returning 1, may your head be good
Conquering 1, your foundation is blessed by the ancestors
The work of your hands shall mend torn lives
From your womb more Gods shall spring

Your path is well lit
Your destiny is divinity.

This child, born with the umbilical cord wrapped around her waist like a belt, was empowered by the ancestors before she'd come. Now, with the medicine she was fully protected and prepared. The asafetida and dimes secured on black string knotted 9 times were superfluous, but tradition is hard to break and a child cannot have too much protection.

Because of her ancestral ties, Aint May knew that no matter where Chaka went, Alapaha would pull her back home. It was more than the umbilical cord and placenta buried at the base of the praying pine; it was her head. Even her majoring in chemistry was indication of her path. Chemistry was nothin but another aspect of root work. However, with all their equations, formulae, and computations, no chemist could do what Aint May could do. She and Chaka together could revolutionize the industry.

Aint May had been dreaming about Chaka for 3 months before the couple's arrival. Dreamt of the child and some man loving, battling, slaying, and losing 1 another. Dreamt of these 2 in all kindsa times and places in the world finding, loving and killing each other in different ways. Finally, she saw a woman awash in silver uniting Chaka and the man. She recognized the woman as her ancient friend and colleague. Aint May was overjoyed about the unions and reunions forming under the auspices of Ah.

So when the Grand Am pulled up with Jayne Cortez demanding her listeners "Make Ifá," Chaka and Jahmai were the 1's surprised because Aint May had prepared gumbo, corn fritters, steaming brown rice, fried catfish, and collard greens for their arrival.

"Jahmai, pleased to make yo acquaintance. Chaka, you cain't pull nothin on me," she hugged them before inviting them to wash up, sit down, and throw down. The next day the couple unpacked and settled in Alapaha. Aint May showed off her babygirl and Jahmai to the quiet community.

In another town, Aint May would have been ostracized for her ways. But in Alapaha, she had reverence, respect, and, because of her power, not isolation but necessary distance. She was fond of saying the roots, Earth, and ancestors were her best friends. She didn't feature too much human company.

"What about us?" Jahmai had asked peering at the elder from behind a clump of sassafras roots.

"Y'all ain't human. Y'all like me."

Because of Chaka's childhood foundation, the strong Geechee influence in Jahmai's life, and the enhancement of their cipher by Ahni, their initialization went rapidly. In no time Jahmai and Chaka could recognize living and dried sumac, white oak, maple, chicory, hickory, wax comfrey, bay leaf, wild mint, poke salad, rabbit tobacco, asafetida, lavender, tiger lily, verbena, valerian root, Wonder of the World, Big John de Conqueror and Little John to Chew, lemon grass, guinea pepper, sweet basil, wild basil, rattlesnake root, colt's foot, dragon's blood, 5 finger grass, sweet gum, mistletoe, catnip, and devil's shoestring. Every day for a year, Aint May took the couple over her 30 acres which was a pharmacologist's dream.

"Aint May, it seems odd that with all the technology and so-called medical advancements, there's more killing sickness now than ever before."

"Dat's de truth, Jahmai! Fore you know it, Marburg, Ebola, or Hanta done struck and killed a community. If those don't get ya, they got AIDS, bird flu, swine flu, and West Nile virus. Humph." Aint May balled her fists and planted them on her hips. "Ask me: it's mo govment conjuration."

Jahmai and Chaka shared a look and nodded their heads. Aint May continued, "I'll never forget the slow death they dealt them brothers through clap! Mmm mmp." Her tone changed as she chuckled, "Guess what my cure was."

"What, Aint May?"

"Had a 2 part treatment," she closed her eyes as she recalled the diagnosis and cure. "Red oak bark, palmetto root, fig root, 2 pinches uh alum, 9 drops uh turpentine boiled in 2 quarts water. I'd mix that with petroleum jelly to cure the sores. Then I would treat em orally with mold from a rotten cantaloupe."

"Cantaloupe mold!" Exclaimed Chaka, "that's penicillin."

Aint May nodded and chuckled, "I'd place the cantaloupe in a deep basin and let it mold over. Then I'd scrape the mold off, cure it, and give em 9 teaspoons to take twice a day for 9 days. Cured all of em come to me."

"Aint May, how'd you learn all these cures."

"My Momma's Momma and my Momma taught me all I know. Even after they passed on, they come to me in dreams and continue teachin me. Now I'm teachin you," May winked at Jahmai and Chaka.

After they ground the ginger, the trio snapped rabbit tobacco into handleable bunches and bundled lemon grass into boilable portions and set the bundles in the shade. With gloved hands, they spread poison sumac leaves and red oak bark on white paper and set them to sun dry in the mesh boxes Aint May had built.

While they relaxed in the kitchen sipping sun tea with mint, Aint May asked, "Both a y'all done had mo education than me, right?"

"You know, Aint May," Jahmai stated, "that book learnin ain't necessarily education. You the wisest person I know!"

"Boy, quit it!" she chuckled and slapped his forearm, "Flattering me ain't gon get you up outta this here test."

"Oh, naw!!" Chaka groaned.

"I didn't get a chance to study." Jahmai hit his head in mock lamentation.

Aint May got up mumbling something about paper and pens and lazy young folks. Her petite frame of 5' 4" was solidly built. Her body evinced none of the aging characteristics of elder women. As for wrinkles, her smooth cedar skin had only a few crinkles around the eyes.

Before she could open the drawer to get the pens and paper, Aint May collapsed. She grasped her knee and sang out her pain, "Oh! Ooow! Ooo dogie!"

"Aint May!" They rushed to her side. The sprightly woman was clutching her left leg. Tears were dancing in her eyes.

"This rheumatism! It ain't never struck me like this! Ah-Ah cain't straighten mah leg!" she collapsed again after struggling.

"Jahmai, get the jar of kerosene and block of camphor out the pantry," Chaka directed and began massaging the area.

"Jahmai, come on back. That's right," Aint May hopped to her feet and Chaka did a double take and then laughed in understanding. "Kerosene and camphor. But what else can you use?"

"You can also treat arthritis with stolen white potatoes," Jahmai laughed at the introduction to the test. "You can either eat the potatoes raw or boil them and soak the affected area in the juice. Or you can cut them and tie them around the area. Alfalfa tea is good for prevention."

"Boy, how you know all them cures? I ain't taught y'all nothin bout potatoes yet."

"My mom and my grandmother, Big Momma; they were our physicians."

"I knowed it was a reason I liked you. Where yo people from?"

"Originally, Virginia. Big Momma say they called the place Lil Guinea."

"Yep, yo folks some true 2-headed folks. Now: high blood?" She shot the question at them like a .45.

"Take some jimpson weed and cookin salt and bind it round your head."

"You can also make tea with verbena and/or mistletoe. Mistletoe is good for low blood too: it's a regulator."

"What can you do if you want all your visitors to be jovy to you?"

"Well, you can take some devil's snuff, grind it up with cotton stalk and bury a little bag of it under your steps," Jahmai smiled. "That's a little juju on yourself."

"Right, and what I like to do when I first move into a place and periodically," Chaka added her spice to the stew, "is to wash the floor with a splash of my urine, soap, and water. That will sho nuff chase and keep wickedness away."

"Knew a woman washed her porch every morning with 'chamber lye'," added May. "It's a good practice. Now: what does it mean to dream of fish?" She winked at Chaka.

"Somebody's gonna have a baby," Jahmai answered rubbing his beloved's belly.

"Meat? Maggots?"

"Death for sure," answered Jahmai who was leaning forward, excited by the challenge Aint May presented them. Chaka was somewhere else: She was recalling last night.

Everything had improved since they'd found themselves and the way. They moved into the room cattycorner to Aint May. It was a quaint room with a fortune in antique furniture. Aint May's mother had decorated the house when her husband built it and May'd seen no reason to improve on perfection. Each room had its own washstand, their room's was cherry; it matched the 4 poster bed and chifferobe. Big Poppa and Uncle Jaz had made everything with their own hands and the craftsmanship was superb. Their artistic style exemplified "African American," for their works blended both styles to make wholly unique furniture.

As they prepared for bed, Chaka noticed that Jahmai was unsettled. He seemed especially disturbed by the photos of Chaka's parents, grandparents, and other relatives on the top of the wardrobe. He grew so overwhelmed that Chaka found him trembling.

"Darling, what is it? What's going on?" She rubbed his shoulders.

"Cha, I feel like all your relatives are in here with us."

"What?"

"I feel them watching us. Feel like they know everything about me, about us."

"Sugar, you want me to turn the pictures around—to the wall?" She stroked his jaw where his goatee curved around his top lip.

"No, that's rude. Plus, that wouldn't change anything. They. Are. Here."

"Well, do you wanna sleep in another room?" Chaka knew it was guilt that was causing Jahmai's spirit to shrink. She wasn't enjoying his shrinking but she relished witnessing the power of her ancestors.

"No, that won't help," his desolation was palpable.

"Maybe this will help." She held him. She wrapped her arms and her warmth around his slim frame. Chaka felt his breath on her breast then his whiskers. She felt his tears fall down her chest and drip onto the sheets.

"Chaka, I'm so sorry!"

"I am too. It's all over now. It's finished. Millennia of war are ending on this bed. My ancestors *and* yours are witnesses. Our love is a witness."

The embrace melted into soul sharing. He found his sweetest peace inside of her. He found the future.

"What is catnip tea good for?"

"It's good for measles, hives, and nightmares," Chaka replied with an imperceptible smile.

"Sulfur?"

"Sulfur will cleanse the blood."

"Yep, take a pinch of sulfur and wash it down with water."

"What about the change of life? Lotsa women turn to hormone replacement therapy: that's a recipe for cancer. What can you use from the Earth?" the elder peaked her eyebrows at the pair.

"To be honest," Chaka began after some thought, "I don't have the slightest idea."

"I don't either," admitted Jahmai.

"Rice. Wild rice," Aint May said.

"Really?! Rice?"

"You know that many of us were captured, enslaved, and brought here because of our expertise in rice cultivation. Wild rice is not just starch. It has essential nutrients that can regulate a woman's hormonal system. Same thing for yams."

"Sweet potatoes?" Jahmai asked.

"No," Aint May got up and squatted in her pantry and retrieved a 3-legged stool. She stood on the stool and opened 2 cabinet doors above her refrigerator. She pulled out a huge West African yam tuber. It looked a lot like a rough human thigh. She placed it on the table and went back into the cabinet and retrieved a large cloth bag.

"This is a yam," she patted the tuber. "And this," she pulled out a red nut that was naturally split into 4 sections, "is kola nut."

"I've read about these but never seen either," Chaka and Jahmai stroked the flora.

"Nearly every Nigerian novel makes mention of yam and kola: 'He who brings kola brings life,' is what is said in Chinua Achebe's works." Jahmai held a section of the kola and then bit into it.

"Yams are difficult to cultivate. It's back-breaking work, but it's worth it. The meat is delicious. But yams increase a woman's potential to bear twins."

"That is a trip! I was reading that the highest rate of twins is in Africa."

"And kola can increase a man's sperm count. Now," Aint May gazed at the pair, "you are holding in your hands 2 staple foods of Africa. Both of which we have eaten since time and will always eat."

"They can't kill us no matter what they use. The foods and the geography naturally select us."

"Now you're talkin! I have a kola tree and a small plot of yams. But the problem is the climate. Georgia is okay for growin these thangs, but they's tropical plants. Some years work out better than others. I've got quite a few

African specialties growin out back I'll show you. But for now," Aint May brought out a huge wooden mortar and pestle from her pantry, "we'll prepare pounded yam and egúsí!"

"Last night I dreamt of a funeral," Aint May revealed as she rubbed the bitter leaf.

"That's a sign of a wedding."

"And a wedding dream is a sign of a funeral."

"Miss LuDell down the road is sick. I think I'll buy her a new dressing gown to cheer her up."

"Well, if you do, she'll never live to wear that gown out. Can't give a sick person new clothes."

"The almanac says it's gon be a new moon tonight."

"Then make we hold a little piece a money to it and make a wish."

"Or just bow respectfully. That's the way my folks have always paid homage to the new moon. New moon has power pass power," Jahmai said.

"What are some signs of death?"

"A hawk flyin over the house will call someone's spirit to join it."

"A squinch owl hootin at night. You have to turn somethin, a pocket, shirt, or apron, inside out or turn your shoes over."

"A dog howling and crawlin on his belly is also a sign of death."

"Yes, its many. How can you treat bladder and kidney problems?"

"Well, you can take 2 bunches of bush cranberries and boil em and strain em and take as a tea twice daily for 2 weeks. Verbena is good too."

"Right, you can also take a pint of boiling water add 2 tablespoons of flaxseed, 2 tablespoons cream of tartar, and drink a half a glass in the morning and half at night.

"What can you do for bronchitis?"

"Chickweed is good for bronchitis, you can steam the person with it or use it as a tea. It's also good for ulcers."

"Basil is good to season food but what else can it do?"

"It is good to cure constipation and generally aid digestion."

"What is nettle good for?"

"Nettle is a mild stimulant it is excellent for depression and fatigue."

"What of rabbit tobacco?"

"Life everlastin. That's good for colds and catarrh. For allergies you can smoke it or if the patient is a baby or child an adult can blow the smoke in the baby's face."

"It's good for smudging homes and uncrossing too."

"You know," Aint May beamed at them, "I'm right proud of you."

"Aint May, this ain't nothin. We both have backgrounds in root work. You're my first teacher," Chaka beamed.

"And you're an excellent teacher."

"Well, I sho presheate that, but I'm not just talkin bout learning the leaves, uses, and signs. Anyone can do that. The issue is: how many do? How many care? You know? These days, folk would rather manufacture crack cocaine than try to use their skills to heal and make whole."

"Yes, or they want MBAs, Wall Street, and all that emptiness."

"You right. But there are a few like us," Aint May's eyes expanded to accommodate another dimension of space and time, a deeper level of cognition. "Yes, there are many like us," the elder nodded in confirmation.

"Chaka, I was so glad when I met you. You popped out of the womb as a mirror—reflecting the past and the future with your presence. I recognized the ancient in you, the promise in you. Yes, I gave you protection and opened paths to let your brilliance beam through. But I watched you. You impacted everything and everyone in your sphere. You were so intelligent that when Vera and Mack died, you explained to me that they'd gone to a new existence," Aint May smiled at the recollection. "And in addition to the wisdom, there is a warrior in you. What is so good about it is that now the warrior is fighting the right battle—not against your man, but *for* Ah evolution. I'm right proud of you," Chaka and Aint May embraced.

"The work we're doin' here is more than tillin the fields a the dead to harvest new life," the intensity of her stare captivated the pair. "We have a people to heal and prepare.

"Right here, on this land, we will form a site of power, an emisite. From here we will join others in the work of transforming this planet and elevating Ah." The cadence and tone of Aint May's voice shifted its register as her timeless self joined in the explication of the Work.

"Riginally there were 6 sites: Ta Ntr, Kmt, Kng, Zim, Tbk and Dah. These sites were stationed all over the continent of Alkebulah: Africa. Each site had a specialty. Ta Ntr was the center of the Ah. It was a repository and reflection of the wealth of the 5 sites and that of Ahni. Kmt focused on architectural spiritual representations. Zim erected soul sanctuaries. The Kng worked as 1 with nature to reproduce the way of Ah spirit. Dah elevated, named, claimed, and created a world of spirit within spirit. Tbk catalogued all the sites' works. Vast tangible and spiritual tomes were logged at Tbk: It was the wisdom center that housed the complete history of Ah. Each site worked with all others, so all Ah evolved simultaneously.

"All of this was before Yurugu was even thought about: it didn't exist. But Ahni was preparing the Ah for the coming of Yurugu and, more important, for the Ahvolution.

"Ah history is deep, wide, and longer than the concept of time. The definition of 'history' in this world begins with the appearance of Yurugu, cause Yurugu wrote the history books. But we was shinin innumerable millennia before Yurugu existed.

"The Ah founded 6 additional emisites to complement Ta Ntr, Kmt, Kng, Zim, Tbk, and Dah. Knah was the center of weaponry, artillery; Zalah used the tools of Knah and the skills of Kng to introduce hunting, defense, and protection to the Ah because lower emi levels would bring many biological and ecological changes to the Ah. Skills that they didn't need would be vital to their progeny. Gnah found properties in gold that could mirror and bolster the soul. Jubah harnessed the power in Dance, Drum and Song for healing, elevation, and evolution. Jubah is also where spiritual survival skills were formulated. Physical copies of the wisdom of Jubah, and records of all other 11 sites, and of Ah Source, Ahstah, can be found at Dgn—the only site from the past that is still active.

"So, on 1 end of the spectrum of existence we have Ah who have 12 levels of cipher; who can do anything and everything. On the other end, we have Yurugu who has no cipher or negative cipher, and who is absent creative ingenuity but filled with destructive tendencies. Yurugu is an anomaly. It exists in opposition to the Earth and to nature. It is the antagonist of life," Aint May's codeswitching was fluid as she straddled worlds, spheres, and times.

"Yurugu's goal is to destroy Ah, Ah emi, Ah emisites, and Ah evolution and development. When it stumbled out of the Caucasus and began exploring the world, it tried to destroy everything it found that was holistic, healthful, and empowering. But Yurugu could not do this alone: low emi Ah helped it. Some Ah opened the floodgates by tryin to upgrade Yurugu through eugenics. That resulted in the creation of negative emi ultra-violent people causin so much strife in the so-called Middle East.

At the same time that Yurugu and its minion began invading and scattering Ah, more and more Ah were being born with less emi. Some of those Ah with lower emi plotted with Yurugu. During this time, Ah way was being forgotten and Yurugu was using artillery and religion to foment destruction.

"The main Ah who saw themselves as beneficiaries of Yurugu's way were the Aha: that's men, like you, Jahmai. The reduction of emi was concurrent with the expansion of the penis and testicles. But rather than enjoy being complements and equals, the Aha listened to Yurugu's talk of male supremacy and domination. Some of these Aha wanted to treat women the same way Yurugu treated its women. From this point, innumerable atrocities invaded the world: from crusades to jihads to marriage to genital excision. Aint May paused to acknowledge the presence of 3 glowing orbs which were filling the spaces between them. Aint May watched Chaka and Jahmai adjust their positions as their souls expanded.

"Because Yurugu could not obtain, steal, or borrow Ah cipher, it sought to destroy the Ah. Ah division and weakness precipitated Ah demise through physical, mental, and social slaveries and scattering and destruction. But the Ah are invincible because of the Tahn: the deceived, the duped, who, through their resilience and resolve, recreated themselves as divine shining manifestations of Ahni. That's who we are. The Tahn."

Aint May glanced towards the ceiling where her palm fans shirred. She smiled, "We have 6 sites. There are 3 in America. In Bliss Bluff, Mississippi is the wisdom center: The Original Path Institute. The cosmic and textual libraries of this evolution and of the past are housed here. In Nashville warriors of the projects and of universities are organizing an uprising that will demoralize and demobilize Yurugu. Here in Alapaha, we will specialize in pharmaceutical and pharmacological works for the healing, protection, and elevation of Ah body, mind, and spirit.

"There are 3 sites in Africa. In Kumba is a safe haven, a sanctuary where the traumatized and violated can heal and restore themselves. Kumba is the site of power transmission, balance, and order. Minnah is the fount of actualized Àjẹ́. The Àjẹ́ will oversee the evening of the odds, the administration of justice."

As Aint May spoke, 3 shining orbs transformed into 3 resplendent people, as the Old Man, Badu, and Ahni joined the gathering. Aint May exclaimed, "Twin, you're right on time!"

The Old Man embraced Aint May and said, "Twin, your spirit is more enlivened than ever!"

"This is such an empowering time!" Eons of memories flowed between the elders.

"Unlike you and Jahmai, Chaka, Matalah and I have always worked together," Aint May winked and everyone laughed.

Jahmai and Chaka were radiant; energy engulfed and elevated them. Ahni and Badu, who were facing Jahmai and Chaka, were in a similar state of bliss. It was a most supernatural and natural occurrence. Chaka had noticed the light and humming as it surrounded her. She'd felt her self, her spirit, vibrating. When it dawned on her that she was aroused, the trio had fully materialized.

She knew why the elders called one another Twin. Their spirits were so similarly fashioned that they shared the same vibration and frequency.

Chaka found a twin in Ahni, who mesmerized her. Her visage so closely mirrored Chaka's that Chaka thought she was looking at herself from another dimension. Never having had a sister, Chaka recognized 1 in Ahni and understood that she had many sisters and brothers of like mind and spirit—siblings of the struggle; twins of the soul.

Jahmai gazed upon Badu and saw the complete self that awaited him. Jahmai, enraptured by impending wholeness, exhaled and the remaining remnants of manipulation, passive aggressive attack, and wrestings for power that resided in his mind and that teased his thoughts fled from his sphere. Jahmai felt the perfection of completion within Ah anoint his being, and he wept—for the lost and for the found—he wept. Never had Jahmai felt so glad to be alive. Jahmai expanded and embraced with his soul his wholeness and that of his complements.

Everyone experienced the peace of completion, for everyone was gazing upon a twin.

"And this is just the beginning," she had come. Making 7. She was luminosity and vibration embodied. Her coiffeur shimmered, a black mass of spiraling electricity framed her visage. Her skin tone was as pure as her hair: It was impossible to gauge the beginning and ending of 1 and the other. Her lips, if possible, were darker than her countenance. Her wide, high cheekbones framed and protected her eyes which glowed with the light of 7 suns. The collective gazed on the Mother of All.

Welcome, my Suns! Welcome to the era of complete empowerment! After 3 thousand seasons of stumbling and suffering, we are shining, throbbing with power. Our power in this era is due to the Tahn, here, Ahni nodded to Chaka, Jahmai, Aint May, and Ahni. You have manifested exactly as intended, and then some! The Tahn are the key to all Ah evolution for you have successfully lived near, yet in spiritual, physical, psychic, and evolutionary opposition to Yurugu. This proximity has given you the insight necessary to help Ah evolve. The Tahn are the epitome of divinity: You had nothing, were classified as less than nothing. But you shaped the world to your taste and manifested your divinity in the process. You are living proof of the regenerative power of the cosmos.

The recreative power that you and your ancestors harnessed to redetermine your destinies we will now use to realign this planet and its inhabitants.

Yurugu's way is disintegrating; its erections are crumbling; its myths and lies are apparent to all. But what is important to us is not Yurugu's destruction but our recreation.

Matalah, please describe for Jahmai and Chaka your work at Dgn.

Certainly. Since Ahni has come, the Old Man looked affectionately at the woman formerly known as Hadizat, we've blossomed. Her coming initiated our cleansing and completion. We are now vibrating at full capacity, as in the days of Ah apex.

Our work at Dgn is simple: We reveal and secure the way of Ah in this era by gaining knowledge from Ah's historical accomplishments. We use the past to shine light on the future. We have a cadre of 81 at this time. 45 of these members were awakened out of their stupor during the cleansing, they had been nearly lost to Ogo. 36 others came as a result of our summoning. Many are on the way as we speak. New people, new Ah come to us weekly. Our cipher's frequency is such that Ah of high and mid-level emi easily hear our call. However, we have altered our vibration so that only the positively-inclined and purposefully-prepared can receive Ah messages.

People want to gather and grow together in Ah, and our methods ensure their safety and empowerment.

We disseminate knowledge among ourselves through Ah wisdom collectives. As soon as a group is at 1 with the way, they continue their education and share their knowledge with newcomers. The way is put into practice through spiritual, architectural, herbal, and martial lessons.

The work of all emisites is advancing and peaking. Danta and Hawa in Bliss Bluff are cataloging, analyzing, and catalyzing all the work of the Ah and Tahn since the scattering of this era. Their community is approximately 44 Ah strong and growing.

In Kumba, Wakynam has created a healing center for the multitudes of Ah who have been abused, butchered, and tormented. This work is of profound importance because it is through genital excision that Yurugu and his minion seek to destroy the physical symbol of Ah power. Wakynam restores those who have been damaged and introduces them to the eternal repository of power that is their inheritance.

The young warriors in Nashville have fire that we haven't seen since Boukman, Zumbi, and Nanny! Matalah smiled and shook his head. They are about to turn Nashville inside out and upside down, and their work will coalesce with that of Oya and the Àjẹ́ to right this planet once and for all, it was thrilling to see the Old Man so excited. It became evident that his title and appearance were a shield for an eternal ageless force.

This is a phenomenal epoch for Ah, Badu explained. Over the centuries, the emi of Ah has ebbed. This accompanied the shrinking of the clitoris and the growth of the penis and testes. Following this biological transformation, an ecological shift occurred. The world's climate cooled by 30° F on average. This cooling dried rivers and reduced the enriching power of the sun which was a key source of emi stimulation. The ecological shift facilitated the rise of Yurugu.

The opposite is taking place now. The Sun's magnetic and micro waves are increasing in intensity. This is causing the planet to heat, which will spark an ecological shift. The increase in solar energy is also catalyzing Ah powers and accelerating Ah spiritual power shift. We will soon reach the apex of old and surpass it. However, our zenith signifies the end of Ogo: It will perish as will those who blissfully exist in the oblivion that is Yurugu's synthetic world of capitalism, religion, slavery, and nihilism.

While our triumph is assured, we much acknowledge the gravity of the struggle we face. The seeds of dissention are deeply sown. Many would-be Ah bear Ogo's mentality and hate and seek to destroy us, Aint May explained. There are many who want to use the power shift to further their destruction-oriented goals. There are eminegative people who aware of the impending shift who hope to take Ogo's place following its demise.

Can we educate them? Is it possible to raise their emi level? Chaka implored.

These people have consciously stilled, excised, and/or crushed their emi. They reconfigured their souls and selves to become as much like Yurugu as possible. Rather than having nothing and searching forever for the power eternally denied them, these beings obliterated their inherent powers and willingly became emivoid or worse, after suppressing their emi, they found a way to become eminegative. Only Ogo is inherently emivoid or eminegative. So for an Ah to become eminegative, a stunning level of self-hatred is at work.

Because their decision is 1 they sought and fought for there is no redemption.

"Ẹ káàsan, o."

"Ooo, ẹ káàsan."

"Ẹ kujọ́ meta."

"Ọjọ́ kàn pẹ̀lú!"

"Ìyá, ṣé ẹ ní ráíci?"

"Bẹ́ẹ̀ni."

"Mo fẹ́ látì ra congo méjì."

The rice vendor scooped 2 heaping bowls of rice into a plastic bag and then scoped 1/8th of a bowl and added it to the requested amount.

"Girl, its hot!"

"True. Silk was a bad fashion choice on my behalf, "Istha acknowledged, "I sweat like a horse in silk."

"You can wear a camisole under the blouse. That's what I do."

"I do, usually, but this rainy season is so unpredictable. Sometimes it's cool, like this morning, I thought I was safe. But then ol hannah came out like a champion." She turned to the vendor, "Èló ni?"

"300 naira."

"Eh? Ni wọn púpọ̀! I de beg o! Make you reduce am. Ẹ jọ̀wọ́, ẹ gbà 170 naira." Istha slipped into pidgin because her Yoruba was not advanced for bargaining.

"De ting don cost, o! I no go take 170 naira," the Ìyá slapped her hands skin side to palm. Her lips pulled downward as she looked away.

"Let's try over there—" Cynthia and Istha started drifting away.

"Auntie! Auntie!"

"Ma?"

"280."

"250."

"Pay money."

"Girl, you got the market in a bag."

"The only problem is transport to quarters. I'll ask Femi for help."

". . . Femi. Femi Bankole? In history?" asked Cynthia.

"Yes," Istha stopped and gazed at Cynthia who looked as if she were having an epiphany.

"Ooommmmiiiii tútù oooo!!!" a girl of about 14 hawked cool water. As the child shuffled along the dirt path, she stared at the 2 women at length. Istha always wondered how they could stare so intently without tripping and falling.

"These children are too loud! I mean, damn," Istha frowned.

"Reminds me of our old ice, watermelon, and vegetable sellers."

"Yeh, identical technique."

"Loud and lyrical." Cynthia and Istha laughed and continued strolling the market.

"Ssst. Sssst."

"Uncle, Ẹ ṣẹ, Èmí kò fẹ́ ẹran lóòni," Istha explained to the butcher that she did not need to buy meat.

"S'awright, nextime," the butcher smiled.

"Istha, I am impressed!" Cynthia laughed.

"Girl, I don't know a thing. But I have to at least try to learn because things at the market can be cheaper than on campus. And I have to conserve my funds. I also feel it is respectful to try and learn the language. Indeed, this is the language stripped from us; why not reclaim it?"

They went past the plastic goods vendors, the aluminum pot vendors, the okra and eggplant sellers, and the hawkers of leafy greens. The passageway became narrow. The women approached an open sewer covered at its widest section with 4 slick and unstable boards. Istha led Cynthia further up the walkway to a place where the sewer was narrow enough to jump across. The duo hopped and maneuvered through an aisle around customers and strolling vendors who toted trays of goods on their heads. Tomato and pepper vendors lined the left side of a narrow alley, with sssting solicitations. Finally, the women emerged in an open air court.

"I'm addicted to smoked fish!" Istha revealed.

"It is delicious!"

"Ẹ kùṣẹ́, Ma."

"Ooo, ẹ kábọ."

Istha pointed at 2 large smoked fish, "Èló ni?"

"300 naira."

"Na 200 naira fish e be o!"

"At aaaallll!" The vendor turned away.

"Let's go to this side."

"Ẹja tuntun, Auntie, fresh 1," The fresh fish seller smiled.

"Kíl ẹ fẹ́?" an okra seller inquired.

"Wa ting you wan buy?" Another vendor inquired.

"10-10 naira," the onion vendor advertised her wares with a Vanna White flourish.

"Ẹ káàsán Ma."

"Ooo!"

"Ẹ kùṣẹ́."

"Oooo."

Istha chose 2 large smoked fish and turned them over.

"180 naira."

"Eyiii!"

"Na 250 naira las price."

"Ìyá, ẹ jọ̀wọ́, 180 naira," Istha began pulling out her money.

"Why? You wan finish me?" The vender acted like the price would kill her.

"O ya, 190," Istha offered with a smile.

"Pay money."

Istha and Cynthia arrived at the crossroads with their hands filled with plastic bags loaded with fish, vegetables, meat, and rice.

"So now we go to your department to ask Femi for a ride?"

"As much as I hate it, yes," Istha sighed.

"Campus! Campus! Campus!" shouted a tout of a bus who spotted the women looking, for all the world, like "campus." Another conductor also spotted them. Both men, the first with his mack daddy shades and brown-with-dirt-but-should-be-black jeans, the other with a muscle shirt emblazoned with a Def Leppard logo, charged at the women and began struggling to wrench the bags from their hands.

"Ẹ dúró! Ẹ dúró! We no go campus oo!" Istha declared.

"What? But—" Cynthia was so confused she looked like she was in the middle of a tornado. Istha winked and began walking up the road away from the two idling buses. Istha, followed by Cynthia, angled across the street to a bus empty save the conductor who was playing with his mobile phone and the driver who was napping.

"I hate all the fightin and grabbing," Istha explained. "They be done destroyed your purchases for a 10 naira fare, and the only thing they'll say is 'sorry o'. So I fake em out when I can," she and Cynthia laughed.

As the bus filled and took off, Cynthia finally formed the question she wanted to ask.

"I shop like this once a month," Istha cut into Cynthia's thoughts, "and I can just chill out for a while. I have all the staples: rice, flour, cornmeal, beans and meats and fish. I also grind and freeze my tomato sauce."

"That's a good plan," Cynthia concurred. "Kandace did most of our shopping because she was in town more often. But since she's been gone . . ." Cynthia sounded lost without her companion.

"Well, it is good we came together because we can help each other," Istha smiled.

The women were wise to board the empty bus because as the first passengers they could sit shotgun and enjoy the ride. As Istha came to learn, the further you sit in the back, the more miserable you will be.

"I can't believe I only have 1 more session!" Istha shook her head and dared to smile.

"Really?"

"Girl, I'ma be Audi 5."

"What do you plan to do when you've finished?"

"I honestly haven't thought that far ahead. I guess I keep my eyes on 1 prize at a time."

The women enjoyed the lush vegetation of the Nigerian countryside as they swayed and bounced in an 80s model Toyota minivan.

"I'm glad the protest lightened cuz I needed to come to town."

"I can't believe the students burnt the high court and broke into the jail," Cynthia shook her head.

"They put head out, don't they? I'm impressed with the way they attack injustice. But there is no follow-through. No lasting changes are made."

"Personally, I feel that as long as Africans remain trapped in the confines of these conceptual countries there will be no true progress because everything is happening within a paradigm that was designed to benefit and serve the Caucasian colonizer—even and especially in his absence. Africans must have the courage to cut all colonial and neocolonial ties and erase the contrived borders that delimit the parameters of their existence."

"Girl, you're singing my song," assented Istha. "The problem is too many people are profiting off of the system and the boundaries the way they are drawn now. As long as there are pockets to be filled, there will be sellouts with their hands out."

"And in the meantime, everyone and everything suffers. Especially children and education."

"Tell me about it. Some of any shit is liable to fly out these profs mouths. At 1 of our meetings, Dr. Bangbose jumped up and said the Cameroon students 'are going to destroy our something!' Girl, I liketa fell out! How can someone destroy something that you can't even articulate? 'Destroy our something': This is a man with clout and credentials, too. And he was fighting mad. If someone had offered an opposing view, he would have resorted to violence."

"But there are some deep people in your set, though. Prof. Apata: I read his books on ritual drama before I came here and Alajuwan in African Literature and Language is really deep and he's also good people."

"He is . . . . I wanted to ask you wh—" Cynthia started when gun shots rang out. Passengers screamed as the bus swerved and tipped on 2 wheels.

The staccato call of an AK-47 was answered with pleas to various Gods:

"Jesu!"

"Edùmarè, ooo!"

"Òṣà mi, ẹ gbà mi, oooo!"

"Chineke!"

The driver sped through Mayfair seeing only through the space between the steering wheel and the dashboard. Istha and Cynthia, along with all other passengers, endured the trip curled into fetal knots.

"This is the Ifè–Modakeke war . . . again," Istha murmured.

The Ifè and the Modakeke peoples, who first clashed in the 1800s, had taken up arms against each other again. All activity in town froze as brothers and sisters slayed 1 another. A shaky peace descended after 7 months of war. But the embers of violence, having never been fully quenched, were easily rekindled.

"This is surreal," Cynthia whispered. "We are in the middle of a war. Kandace won't believe this."

Kandace was in Minnah. She and Ìyálóde had gone to begin the foundation setting, the laying of the invisible and indivisible cornerstone of Àjẹ́.

Minnah was altogether a different vibe than Cotonou, Ifè, Ibadan, and Lagos—everywhere Kandace visited so far. Minnah was free of the West's firm knuckle-lock; the town was tranquil and self-reflective. The peace of Minnah was a resonant palpable thing. It reverberated in the plant life, in the time people took with 1 another, in the calm of the air.

"Mo fẹ́ ibi yìí ju," Kandace marveled.

"Bẹ́ẹ̀ nàá ni," Ìyálóde laughed. There was everything to like about Minnah.

Ìyálóde was a powerhouse of Àjẹ́ who guided Ifè's evolution. She was awo mérìndinlógún, a diviner of 16 cowries, in addition to being a physician, an obstetrician, and a gynecologist. Ìyálóde was the perfect terrestrial point person for the ẹgbẹ́ Àjẹ́ that would undertake the international adjudication of crimes against humanity. Consequently, the Ìyálóde of Ifè, the Mother of External Affairs, expanded her domain and dominion in the manner of Imọlẹ̀, the God who is perfectly placed throughout the Earth, so that she and the ẹgbẹ́ Àjẹ́ could effectively monitor, balance, and organize the world.

The ẹgbẹ́ was founded and fortified in Minnah because Minnah was Ọya's earthly home. As the Winds of the World, the blower of the breath of life, and the guardian of justice, Ọya was the logical administrator and Òrìṣà of the tribunal.

Kandace found the process of learning and knowing Ọya in the God's home to be uplifting. On their first trip to Ọya's sacred grove, Kandace,

Ìyálóde, and the 7 acolytes who accompanied them witnessed 2 manifestations of Ọya.

After they were nestled among the ìrókò, acacia, and silk cottons that swept the sky, they began the chant, the oríkì Ọya.

Ìgbà yìí ni e mò pé àwá l'Ọya
Ìgbà yìí ni e mò pé àwá l'Ọya
Ará òkè yí e má sùn piyè
Eni ti ó rí ogun
Òun ní yóò rí èyin ogun
Ìgbà yìí ni e mò pé àwá l'Ọya

Ìyá o! Ọya o!
Egúngún Onírá
Òriirii aya Ṣàngó
Ọya dolú, se bí ìwo ni Ìyá mi!
Subúlade Ọya o! Ìyá o!

As their voices rose and invited the vibrations of the atmosphere to join, a magnificent buffalo appeared. Its coat was a smooth rich brown, its hooves were shining black, and its horns were a blinding white. The horns glistened like mother of pearl, curved like Damballah-Aido-Hwedo, and were chiseled to fine points. The densely lashed eyes of Ọya's familiar glinted in recognition.

"Ìyá wa dè! Ìyá wa dè oooo!" Everyone rejoiced at Ọya's arrival.

Ọya Ẹfòn nodded in greeting and vanished.

After 9 seconds, praise found voice, hands struck skin, thighs flexed in time, and blood moved bones. Rhythm riddled the forest from earth to leaf in praise of the God, and she responded.

She came up a cloud. The air was no longer air, it was—for 3 seconds—electricity. Everything stopped in acknowledgement of the God. Kandace watched in awe as a rotating purple and maroon cloud became a tornado that became a woman.

Clothed in an cumulonimbus swirl of power that was indistinguishable from her body, Ọya addressed the ẹgbẹ́ Àjẹ: "Daughters, welcome home. I welcome you in the way of Ah! I welcome you with the force of Àjẹ. Together, we shall reorganize the world. Listen!"

It began in each woman's soul
aaaahhhh
which became a unified force.

aaaaAAAHHHH
It shook the Earth and textured the auras of the women.

AAHAHHH
          Tree trunks throbbed.
                          AHAHAAHAAHAHHH
The ẹgbẹ́ was rocked by the resonance of the origin of its power. Their
white robes bled vermilion, russet, burgundy, ochre, gold, and purest indigo.
Aṣo wínní wínní.

"Ah of this land, Alkebu-Lan. Ah of the Tahn—Ìtànkálẹ̀: we are 1."
Ọya summoned them, and they stood forth with their collectives: Wakynam
and Daughter; Badu, Hawa, and the Old Man; Chaka, Danta, and Aint May;
Azure and Alteveze; and Cynthia, Istha, and Kandace.

And Ahni Ahternal. Who'd always been there, riding just under the
rhythms of the mind's first sentience. She had come and now the unnamed
was named; the unpraisable, praised. Dismembered, forgotten, excised,
ignored fragments of the self and soul were caressed and then embraced,
first by the individual, and then the Whole.

1 day I went to the creek to get some water, and after I filled my pot, I
looked up and saw Momma Ja and Mosa. They was holdin hands and lookin
like twins. They just smiled at me from cross the creek, and I knew they
were in peace and that they wasn't gon nowhere. They'd always be near and
guiding me. I took off my clothes and bathed in the creek. I washed the
mourning from my hair, eyes, soul, and body. Momma Ja and Daddy helped
me. It was like I had just come from my Momma's womb and they was
bathing me together like they never had the chance to do. They wrapped me
up in cloth colored blue, red, purple, deepest brown and gold; kissed me on
my jaws; and told me my destiny had been chosen and was waitin for me at
home. Keep eggs in the house, keep water in the house, keep chickens in the
coop, and keep your hands moving. Moyalajeh, said my Momma;
Omigbade, said my Daddy.

I decided to plant a crop like Momma would, I figured with it bein my
land I could keep myself goin, at least break even. I could also do a little
mendin, dyein, and makin clothes. I could just see the little ones jubain in
my creations. I smiled a little, thanked Ma Ja and Mose, and got up to braid
my hair and get a plan of livin together.

I sat underneath my Daddy tree, combin out my hair until it was bout
like a cloud of thunder. Then, I close my eyes and I can hear Momma Ja just
as clear:

Momma call, "We sing for Crocodile Waaka."
"Sing for Crocodile Waaka," I respond.

Reesha say Oba ko so
Oba ko so
say Eyi o y'ara waju

Ero ehin fi'ye si le
Oni ma ma de omo onibu
Tani o gbodo l'owo Oni
Tani gba le baba omo l'owo omo?
Reesha say Omigbade
Omigbade
Omigbade

When me and Momma Ja sing this song, our song, the wind just tickle them bottles and they would join in with us, and they did the same when it was just me singing.

That's how I was sittin and singin 1 day and next thing I know, someone done crept up on me talkin bout, "You soun so pretty miss. Sing a little louder so I don't misunderhear ya." I turn round to see the biggest man, near bout 7 feet and built like true John de Conquer. I tell him he wouldn't misunderhear if he went on and minded his own.

"Miss, I ain't mean no harm, I'm just off the rail gang and come lookin' for a sip a cool water and heard yo beautimous singing."

I stopped my braidin and looked up at him, " How you know where you lookin its cool water?"

"Well, way I figure, it's got to be cool water where uh breeze can be sung up pretty as all that."

"Umph," was my reply. See, I knows from whence the smoke blows— but I got up to get this man some water. And I turn round and see he following me into Ma Ja house; bout to step out of bounds!

"Un unh, Mistuh—what's your name?"

"Ma'am," came fallin from his lips like a cold compress for a hot head, "they call me Moses Jones but you can call me Mojo on account that's what my Momma call me. May I ask yours?"

"Well, Mistuh Jones, you have a seat on dis here porch. And," I added, "I don't care for a whole lot uh grinnin round me."

I have to say in honesty that Mojo was the finest thing I'd seen in merica. Skin like midnight sky mixed with life's blood. But he looked kinda sly; that attracted me too, made somethin in me rise up a bit.

I got him his water and we talked a while. He say he from Natchez but he work in camps buildin roads and rails or workin crew on boats or hirin out whatever way he can. Say he like to travel, want to taste the world. He tol me all kinds a things that Miss Rule never hit on. Tole me he been to Illinois and it's just as many lowdown white folks up North as it is in the South. He tell me bout the new territory out west that crackers building on the blood and bones of the real mericans. And he tell me bout Na Leans and the women there.

I look at him lookin like a walkin cosmos and ask him did he fall in love in Na Leans.

"Nah, I ain't see too much suit my taste in Na Leans," he say flippin his hand like he felt flies. "I like my women more complimentary to myself, ya see," the look he gave me seemed to burn a hole through me straight to my soul.

His eyes were shining so, I couldn't hold his gaze. I turned my head away from him only to see Nell and Ham comin cross the yard. When Nell see Mojo she smile so she nearly burst her caramel-colored cheeks.

"Hey Baba! You ready for the barbecue tonight over at Big Sam house? Everybody gon be there. Who yo friend?" She say to me but eyeballin him.

"Now, Nell, what Sam say he seen you grinnin at this man like dat?"

"Ham," she said, lookin in her twin eyes, "you best put some of that which give you yo name in yo mouth an keep my bizness out of it. Who you friend, Baba?"

"Miss Nell and Mistuh Ham, dis Mistuh Jones."

"Pleased to meet you, Miss Nell, Mistuh Ham," he smile at me.

"Back at ya," Nell grin.

"Is you comin to the barbecue with Baba?" ask Ham.

"So yo name is Baba, huh?"

"Yoruba is my name. Folks call me Baba."

"I like that: Yo-ru-ba: What it mean?"

"I believe Ham ask you a question," I change the topic cuz it's just too much pressure on me with him gazing at me and massaging my name with his lips.

"Well, it seems I ain't properly asked you if I could," and here, this man get down on his knees and ask me, "Yoruba, can I take you to the barbecue at Big Sam's, please."

"Get up, man!" I scold, but he know he got me cuz he see me smile. He say that my smile is all he need from that day forward—my smile and to play in my hair.

We raised a ruckus at that barbecue. Everybody cut loose and ran free, including me. And Mojo turned out to be the life of de bottoms with his singing and dancin. We looked good together and everyone knowed it—and knew I needed it.

When we left the barbecue, he walk me home. I tol him that any spare room in the bottoms was his, folks be happy to take him in. Moses just look at me and say he feel like he need to be near me. He say he just fine under my Daddy tree. I sat with and we talked out there all night.

After he caught me in a yawn, he told me to go on in the house and take his bag with me, that he be fine outside. This went on for so long everyone was talkin bout how Mojo got 1 worked on him. I just smiled cause it was mutual.

Mojo got a job at the saw mill. While he did his work, I did mine: weedin the garden, tendin the stock, and sewin. Mojo would come home and we'd have us some dinner and sit out in front of my Daddy tree. He would plait my hair and sing to me until I get sleepy.

Oh won't you hide me
Oh, Momma won't you hide me
In yo tree
I want you to hide me
wrap me tight and love me right
and I won't leave

1 evenin we sat under the tree like usual before I get ready to go in and he look at me smilin and say, "Yoruba, I believe it's time I come home."

"You mean you goin back to Natchez?" Daddy tree started tinklin so I don't know if he heard the fear in my throat or not. All I know is my heart sank inside my belly when I thought about Mojo leavin.

"I say 'come,' not 'go.' Yoruba, I done prayed on it every night right under this tree and I feel tonight is the right night to ask you—its time I come home."

"Moses Jones, I done prayed on this too, I ask my Momma if you was to be my man and I your woman and a red snake in the garden today told me, 'Yes.'

"See, I was weedin the corn and up come this red snake"

"Baby I'm gon put some lime out there tomorrow and"

"Hell you preach! Listen to what I'm saying: That red snake come, shining like a full moon with a rainbow of colors every time it moved. She pass between my legs and didn't touch me. She just paused, looked at me, and went on."

"Yoruba, you think that was yo Ma Ja tellin you about me?"

"Baby, I know it was. You hear that?" the tree tinkled and we smiled, "My Daddy like you too. You remind him of himself," I look at Moses and I know we is 1.

"Let's go make a home."

We didn't make love that night, did everything but. We went to the creek and bathed. We stood on the banks, looking at each other through the moonlight and starshine. First he turned for me so I could see him fully with the tree limbs framing his hair and the soil shifting under his weight. Then I opened my self to his eyes. I felt his hunger warming me. He wanted to rush on me like the water in Momma's creek—but we waited.

Mojo tol me to take off my clothes and just stand still. He touched me, massaged me, felt me everywhere. I didn't know I had so much feelin until his fingertips found me. He started with my hair and fingered my parts and twisted my braids. Then my face and shoulders and arms. He rose ripples and points on my nipples like they was flower buds springing from the earth. Then my belly and my thighs and knees and calves got his careful his attention. He took extra time with my feet and spread warmth to each of my toes and then, like I was a perfectly rounded calabash that he'd just found in a tree, he touched me full-handed all over. He finally came to the place he'd skipped before and he called an ocean from me to find home in the earth and in the creek. I swayed as his fingers curled through my hairs and lips and tickled my little peak of power.

"Now, you do me."

Lil Wom, how can I explain touching the midnight sky? Feelin stars yo eyes can't even see, and feelin peaks and valleys risin and fallin under your hands like nothin was there before you shaped them? I took my time learning my man. His hair, his strength, his scent. The power he would mix with mine to help me make you. I lingered there and brought his sacrifice out to blend with mine, to nourish the soil and water.

We slept by the creek holding each other and still feelin in our sleep; Momma Ja justa singing her praises to us through the water. We stayed until the cock's crowin woke us up. Then we went and told everyone in the bottoms that we was 1. Someone asked if we'd seen the justice of the peace. I didn't know what they was talkin about. When I understand they talkin bout a beast with a bible I laughed so hard my stomach ached.

That night everyone in the bottoms surprised me and Mojo. We had just finished our supper and was bout to go outside as usual when we heard someone call out: JUUUUUUbaaaahhh! We ran outside and there was everyone gathered round my Daddy tree in a circle. Right in front of my Daddy tree was ol Baby Lee and Jove holdin a broom.

Me and Mojo, we leaped and laughed.

Daughter was glowing. Foku, Vai, Zennan, Kyza, Malu, Tobi, and Yao who'd followed her and Kofi home to Kumba had found their niches. The children represented the truth of continuity. Aged 5 to 7, they were all each other's mates, and they forged phenomenal bonds.

Each child found his or her own way in Ah. Foku and Kyza excelled in spiritual communication. Zennan, Malu, and Yao startled everyone with a special ability: They could stay underwater for hours. These 3 entered into lengthy consultations with the elders of the lake and shared their knowledge with their peers. Tobi also had an exceptional skill in his ability to communicate with flora. Tobi learned not only medicinal wisdom but also knowledge of the flora to combine to fly and to make 1 disappear.

Nadey was a child of unlimited potential. Wakynam, with whom the child spent almost as much time as Daughter, extolled that not in 20,000 seasons did she see 1 who mastered her emi so completely. Shape shifting, spiritual communication, oral and written communication, herbalism, soul expansion: It seemed that all powers of the cosmos found a home in this child.

Vai developed a special affinity for both pottery and Ahlaz. She followed the woman around like a daughter would a mother. They spent hours coaxing new shapes and forms from clay.

Ahlaz was a master potter. Her skill had been recognized in the village but only for its economic benefit: The chief had wanted her to fashion tourist art. She had refused and again had been ostracized. She let her passion sleep in her breast but it awoke when she came to Kumba.

Daughter stepped towards Ahlaz's latest work. What she witnessed was a living text. Each tiered level of the pot was a chapter. At the base sits a young woman adorned in weighty beads. Her hair is sculpted into a towering crown that mirrors the overall design of the pot. Young men line up to ask her parents for her hand. 1 is chosen on the third level. The next tier shows the same woman now squatting with a swollen belly. Birthing mothers surround her. The women celebrate child and mother. Here she is feeding her child the milk of life. Daughter saw herself and Ahlaz and so many children in the next level which featured another gathering of women: They surround a young girl who is being sat on by an old woman who is brandishing a blade. The next scene is a fight! After the melee, the elder lies in a pool of her own blood.

On the next tier, girls, boys, young men and young women trek through a forest. The trek takes over the entire middle and upper tiers of the pot. Cresting the pot are simple scenes of a community of whole and healing people. Daughter sees herself seated, her legs and arms folded like a rose, her lips are still. Wakynam, the shining elder is hidden yet visible throughout the work. She permeates every level of the creation with promise.

Ahlaz, your work is fantastic!

No, Vai did most of this piece. Vai smiled but added nothing. This craft is our calling, Ahlaz hugged the child.

This is the way of Ah, Daughter continued, marveling at the piece, From the beginning, Ah would create soul sanctuaries and adornments to record and protect ourselves and the way.

Daughter felt bliss. Kumba was sending signals, and those needing healing were coming. Each week brought to Kumba 1 or 2 more people ravaged by civil wars, child abuse, prostitution, and disease. All were given the waters of healing for inner and outer purification. As their fragmented souls recovered, they were given the choice of returning to their past lives, or living the way of Ah. All had remained, so the village was thriving. But Daughter worried about Foku, who was sometimes mentally and physically disconnected. Because these children had come of their own volition, Foku's isolation was perplexing. Daughter did not want to probe the boy's thoughts; she gave him time to reveal the cause of his seeming dislocation.

She took to the water with Kofi and there they conversed with the elders.

Daughter, Kofi, we are thriving. New life has come to us and shed its former encumbrances. The paths of the forest are alive with people seeking the holistic power of Ah.

In spite of all this, we are facing a threat and must prepare. The parents of some of the children will come looking for them. As you are aware, what they consider their wealth they now consider stolen. Foku is in contact with some of these people. Using telepathic communicative abilities, he is informing them of our work. It is not that the child is negatively inclined; he is confused. His parents knew of his ability from birth and sought to use it to their benefit by manipulating the chiefs and tourists. Your coming showed him a true path to self. He respects that path, but he is at a crossroads.

Because he is among us, and partially of us we must protect ourselves without harming or isolating him.

What we must do at this time is train each person to alter their matter so that we can replicate the surrounding forest and confuse the party.

We will also begin spiritual-martial arts training.

But what of Foku? If he knows we are aware of the threat and are preparing and fortifying ourselves, he may divulge our strategies.

We will move our communication to another frequency. We will continue his instruction so that he will know enough of us to choose, but he will be ignorant of our defenses.

Kofi, walk with Foku. Give him in-depth knowledge of the Ah: our past and our present and our future. During the times we are training the others, Kofi, you will be training Foku. Let him consider himself singled out, special. Give him attention.

Daughter, continue to work closely with the rest of the children and raise their vibrations in preparation for the combative shining. This is our work for now.

So be it.

So be it.

So be it.

Daughter took the young 1's under her wings. She relished the time she spent instructing them because they were so open and receptive to the way. They would go for long walks through the forest during which she would teach them the names and uses of plants. The knowledge Daughter shared was augmented by Tobi, who had a unique kinship with flora.

The group watched Tobi as he cradled a lush thick-veined plant in his hands. Where the plant's 5 velvety leaves converged, a cluster of violet-red berries flourished. He squatted with his ear submerged in the plant's foliage and his eyes closed. Tobi held his perfectly still pose for several minutes. He then stood and faced his peers.

"This is Tizziah. Her berries are a stimulant and give great energy. However, they must be picked when there are deep blue indigo and they must be collected under the new moon. Tizziah's leaves are poisonous and the juice in her veins can kill instantly. The root, however, is rich in vitamins and minerals and can cure kwashiorkor."

"In order to create the bath of invisibility," he revealed during another session, "you collect the leaves of the canant creeper, but you must collect them when they are just beginning to close, this occurs the second dusk has yielded the last of itself to darkness and not a moment before or afterward. You pluck the leaves from the vein and set them to dry. You collect a scoop of dirt from the burial place of an ancestor whose been in the Earth 7 days. You gather the blossoms and roots of the gerege flower which perfumes the night. At night as the flower scents, pluck 5 blossoms and 5 root shoots. Combine, char, and grind all of these ingredients. Mix them with black soap and bathe with this soap morning and night for 7 nights. When you say the incantation, you will be unseen. However, you must never kill or eat the tinga snake for it guards the canant creeper."

The children coupled Tobi's knowledge with the telepathic skills of Foku and Kyza with Zennan, Malu and Yao's mastery of water and they all elevated their powers.

The children also created striking spiritual aesthetic works. Guided by Vai, they coaxed grace, meaning, and eloquence from wood, clay, stone, and bone. They began by representing the vibrations of their souls; as their skills and confidence grew, they created what they felt the community or a particular arrivant or guide needed.

1 day the children presented Daughter with an astounding gift. She gazed at the obsidian stone that was hewn in a conical shape. It was a clitoris. Inside the clitoris, and how they achieved the feat is a secret of their emi, was a depiction of the universe with revolving stars and constellations.

Daughter lost herself in the nearly imperceptible movements of the universe. She rode the revolutions for 3 hours and began to understand. Yes, there were 2 figures leading 7 others. And here was another group, a brilliant cluster, and here was another, and here another. They rotated in their own orbits. Occasionally individual orbs shot out from 1 cluster to sojourn with another: sharing and absorbing knowledge. Some orbs traveled to Ahstah and joined Ahni whose radiance guided and enriched each cluster, annointed each orb. Daughter was enraptured by the gift.

Daughter took the children on a jaunt that led to an open field of grass so rich it was nearly blue in hue. After each person had found a position of comfort, Daughter opened the discussion.

As you know, there are 6 new emisites forming. 3 of these sites are in the Ìtànkálẹ̀ and there are 3 on this Continent. We are 1 of the sites. You have met the site constructors, Hawa, Danta, Azure, Alteveze, Ahni, Kandace, Cynthia, Chaka, and Jahmai. You have met the guiding elders, Wakynam, Matalah, Ọya, Aint May and of course, Ahni, the Mother of us all. We have all discussed the importance of these sites and our Work. So I ask you, given what you have learned thus far, what course should we take if Ogo comes to us and seeks to study, live, and/or work with us?

We have 2 examples of the results of such collaborations, Kyza volunteered, Kmt, just prior to the initial scattering, and more recently Dgn, which has only recently rescued and resecured itself. Yurugu is synonymous with destruction. If we open our doors to it, we are welcoming our dissolution. We have witnessed, in full, its character. We know what it is and what it is capable of. We owe it nothing. Our work is not about aiding Ogo; we are to heal and prepare Ah.

What of its women? Daughter asked, Perhaps their vibrational level is higher as a result of having a womb.

It is still Yurugu, Zennan shook his head. Its women have never advanced the cause of Ah; in fact, the complete, abundant, womanhood of Ah and Àjẹ́ is a direct threat to its women.

Malu stood and proclaimed audibly, "Without reservation or equivocation, we must vow: No More."

"No More!" A circle of Black fists pierced the sky.

Ahlaz, what do you see as future of Ah?

There is battle, struggle in our future. We will fight not only Ogo, but also emivoid and negative Ah. Such Ah are in our midst and are more dangerous than Ogo because we may love and trust them.

Daughter felt a shudder jar Foku.

But beyond the battle that we must fight to expand self and soul, I see the awakening of Ah and Tahn. I see the sloughing off of the mediocre, of the defilers, of the parochial. I see resplendence. From these 6 sites, 6 more will come and 6 from them and on and on. I see the planet illuminated with our power. What I see is $360°$ of perfected Blackness. I see completion with, in, and within Ahni.

Foku, how would you describe the struggle ahead of us?

Well, he paused, the struggle is an interesting 1 because Ogo's existence is ending. This is even apparent to it. We do not have to do anything to it at all for its eradication to occur. However, Yurugu will do everything to destroy us and our work. That is its way. So we will have to protect and defend ourselves and our Work. There are many means by which we can accomplish this. We may resort to armed battle or astral battle or we may create a situation whereby we isolate Ogo and leave them to destroy themselves. Their isolation would be optimal because that would allow us to build unfettered without the annoyance of Ogo.

That is an important observation.

But Foku, asked Tobi, to return to Ahlaz's point, what of the negative and void Ah who are our friends or relatives? Our people in Mapu, for example: We have not forgotten them; they have not forgotten us. How should we manage these relationships?

Well, if they are unable or unwilling to shine, Foku said without emotion, they are dead.

Yes, Kyza added, and the dead hate the living; the dull hate the shining. They will see in us the radiance that they exist to negate and destroy.

"Then we must obliterate them," Foku said this aloud. His voice was soft and ponderous; it was clear he was struggling with weighty issues.

While Foku was sleeping or studying with Kofi, everyone practiced camouflaging Kumba. While the elders of Kumba had exceptional shape shifting abilities, their repertoire was nowhere near as vast as that of Àjẹ́. So Ọya and her ẹgbẹ́ came to Kumba to share knowledge.

Wakynam, Ọya embraced her sister, What an auspicious time this is!

It is thrilling to plant seeds and watch them grow into strong trees. Tell me about Minnah! I always feel strong vibrations from your area.

New life has come! We are growing. Many dormant Àjẹ́ are awakening and joining us. They do not come physically, as here at Kumba, but astrally. Our adjudications will begin soon, Ọya's eyes sparkled.

Wakynam, Ọya inquired, do you remember our last great conference before the scattering?

Yes, at Jubah.

It was such an exhilarating time filled with praise, exaltations, experimenting and play! We were so exuberant! At that time we knew we were sparks of a dying ember. But now we are the kindling that will ignite the flame. This is a scintillating time!

And these children of the Tahn will make you excited! None of us could clearly see Ahni's path when Ogo began to rise

when it appeared we were

birthing sheep instead of Ah

but the world is humming again:

In Peace.
In Justice.

After everyone had mastered the ability to shift shapes, the collective practiced the transformation of Kumba. With 1 astral signal, each member took another form. Some became insects, others a continuation of the dirt path, some became ìrókò, silk cotton, acacia, eucalyptus, or baobab trees. Some joined the elders in crocodile form. Some became panthers, lions, buffaloes, or birds.

The acquisition of these skills was more than protective education, it was fun! Daughter and Kofi became pigeons, doves, vultures, eagles and ambled into the furthest reaches of the sky. Zennan and Vai morphed into gamboling gazelles and, now, trumpeting elephants. Tobi, Nadey, and Kyza explored the textured world of flora: trees, flowers, shrubs, and grasses. Ahlaz, Malu, and Vai became molecules and allowed the atmosphere to transport and transform them as it desired.

Wakynam and the elders created visual mirages and diversions that allowed the eye to see a compound as a cluster of bushes. A clearing took on the appearance of a marshy bog. Their homes became a grove of trees.

Foku did not realize that as his conscience twisted his sleep, the village became in turns a forest, a lake, or a marshy bog. Had he awakened and left his room for a walk, he would have screamed with fear of desertion and insanity.

When his sleep was not breached by the whispering of his conscience, Foku was being queried by his elders:

My son, tell the truth: Have you informed them of our plans?

My father, I have said nothing.

The boy may be brainwashed already. His mother argued. He may be leading us into an ambush. He has been with them for so long.

My son, she directed her query to Foku, what is it you spend your time doing?

Mother, we are simply learning the way of Ah, the path of power. We work with plants and animals. We learn the history of our people. We create soul sanctuaries. We

What is that, a "soul sanctuary"?

They are hiding and healing places for the soul. We heal, renew, and revitalize traumatized bodies, minds, and souls.

My elders, a great change is coming. There are 6 sites of knowledge and power: 1 is here at Kumba. Our elder Wakynam is older than time. She is leading us, preparing us for the Shining. The goal of the 6 sites is to increase the spiritual potential of our people so that we can fully manifest our destiny. Sites of academic and spiritual wisdom, healing herbs, survival skills, soul protection and erection, astral enforcement of justice, military strategies are all being erected and fortified as we speak.

My people, a great shift is coming that is ecological, spiritual, and astronomical. The Ah are shining. The 1 we call obruni is Ogo. Ogo's reign is coming to an end and our cycle is evolving towards its apex. My elders, many will die during the transition. Those using their emi negatively, those who side with Ogo economically, psychologically, militarily—they have no future.

Are you threatening us, boy?

No, he is not; he is only speaking their dogma, Foku's father growled, Foku, know that we are coming armed. Know that we are prepared to kill all the inhabitants of Kumba if necessary to recover our stolen children.

Yes!!! The cry of the collective clanged in Foku's head. We not only come with astral power, we come with weapons, and we come with right!

Yes!!!

Who can steal our progeny, which is our wealth and the fortune and continuation of our peoples?

No 1!!! The elders shouted.

Father, every 1 of us wanted to come. We came willingly in search of a better life.

You sound as if you are advocating this "way of Ah." My son, you have been mesmerized by Ama, she is a witch. What they have planned for you, I know not. It can only be cannibalism or some other abomination.

What we faced in the village was the butchering of our genitalia and/or lives of destitution and/or prostitution. Those abominations do not exist here. No 1 in Kumba seeks the life of desolation on the coast. No 1 wants to be commoditized or condemned to a living death. None of us wish to be volunteer slaves for Yurugu. Here, we move, daily, into deeper forms of knowledge, wisdom, power. Here, after our bodies and psyches are healed we heal our relationships with the Earth and the Cosmos.

No 1 is here by force. Anyone who chooses to leave is free to go. It is the soul that decides, and every soul that has come here has chosen Ah.

And you? His mother probed, What is your choice?

Please . . . I must rest now. Foku broke communication and tried to lose himself in the thatched walls of his room.

My elders, I must share something with you.

Yes, child.

My heart has been heavy with confusion.

Take your time.

My elders, the adults of the village of Mapu are coming.

This was greeted with silence.

They are coming to reclaim their children.

Silence.

They are coming armed and prepared to kill.

Silence.

I am the 1 who has told them where we are, Foku sighed. I have been in contact with the elders of Mapu since our arrival. My parents recognized spiritual power in me and cultivated that power. We are linked. Foku sighed. He felt as if a lorry had been lifted from his shoulders.

I have told them who were are, Foku continued, people of the way, people of Ah. I have tried to reveal to them the path of ascension, but. . .

Foku, we appreciate your coming to us with this information. We are aware of your communications with your people. We are also aware that you are divided within yourself and spirit as to which path to choose.

We are complete in Ah, Wakynam continued. We are whole. We know our destiny. If you are truly of the way, we embrace you. But you must decide which path you will follow.

Elder Mother, Wakynam, I recognize the way of Ah and I see it as my path, but—, his voice trailed off into the earth under his feet.

If your connection with the living dead is so strong, you must return with them. We cannot allow you, an individual, to damage the collective.

I understand.

He walked away from the elders with his head down. As he rounded the bend just beyond the baobab den, there was Nadey. The little ebony 1. She was standing alone with her mud cloth wrappa crossed over her collar bones and knotted at her nape. Her feet were bare and her hair had been braided and adorned with cowries by Daughter and Kofi. She was shining.

Foku had noted her progress and how her soul soared in Kumba. Her spirit was almost tangible, to the astral eye it was resplendent. Brilliant gold with mauve accents and periwinkle streaks: This was Nadey's aura, and at times it was so expansive it engulfed everything within 9 feet of her.

Nadey extended her perfect little arms which were growing muscular with her pottery work and her jaunts into the forest to commune with flora. Her cheeks were rounded in health, and her little buttocks were already bold. Her arms extended to embrace Foku; they promised solace and peace.

Foku felt his fractured spirit cry when her arms wrapped around him. This little 1. So perfect. He sank to his knees and embraced her. He felt her spiritual wealth cascade over him. She has healing hands. He thought.

She knew what he needed. She bid him lie prone on the dirt path, and she began to stroke him. There in the middle of the path, she began at his head with feather-light strokes, touching more his spirit than his body. As she gathered and adhered the cracked and splintered pieces of him, she began to hum a little girl song, probably taught to her by Ahlaz. She hummed as she worked, and the vibrations she emitted reached deep into Foku's fragmented being and massaged his soul. She stroked his breast. Light little girl hands. His abdomen. Stroking and humming. She massaged his pelvis and his young penis, already turgid with sensation, throbbed. She continued her stroking and humming. Her cowries clicking and clacking against 1 another as she moved. She stroked his muscular thighs and calves. She kneaded the soles of his feet while chanting:

"May your path be good

"May the words of your mouth be good

"May the directions of your soul be good

"Foku Foku Foku Foku"

She chanted his name knowing the healing power of her voice. Foku, Foku, Foku. Her chant did not increase in volume but it rivaled a spewing volcano in its intensity. His being began vibrating, there on the dirt path. He felt eruptions from every opening. His penis spewed a jet of semen, he vomited, his nose bled, he defecated, he urinated, he wept. The road accepted everything. Filth, dissention, fear, connivance. Everything. The road accepted everything.

Nadey led Kofi to the lake, immersed him, and left him there, cleansed.

She made herself comfortable on the sparsely cushioned chair. His eyes, as always, twinkled like little stars. Child eyes, she mused, little boy eyes. She twinkled her eyes back at him. She used to ponder a vision so intense it whitened his lashes. Now she knew it was a sleepin seeing or just old age cuz he was 1"Doggish nigga," she smiled. Her voice was even as she held his gaze, now framed by a furrowed brow, in her own. "Yeh, doggish nigga. See, if you were a lost warrior or a male fightin for manhood I wouldn't a said that. But you ain't a warrior, you just a male. No, less than that. You 1 doggish nigga. Your cipher rises only as high as the head of your penis and you are only as deep as the nearest vagina you seek to burrow into."

Now! She thought. Now! She giggled inwardly at the child's period ("Now" usually ended a good casing, as in "Well, yo daddy don't wear no draws! Now!") I got his whole philosophy in a sack. Done pulled his hole card.

"I thought you was deep. Thought you was real, you know? Little meditation, herb collecting, you hipped me to all your astral battles and helped me fight my own. I appreciate that, I must say."

She stretched her legs in front of her and admired what she considered to be a beautiful pair of feet.

"But it seems your sole objective was to unveil my ass, mash your inadequacy up into me, and spew from the head and mouth that say the most for you.

"My opening my legs to you was my opening eternity to you. I shared with you the most precious gift I have. You squandered that gift."

She watched something shake, back there, behind his eyeballs: Maybe that's the truth settling on in. Good.

"I'm disappointed, yes. But I'm not disappointed in you; you just being yourself. I'm disappointed in me for believing you, listening to, and trusting you. "I'm disappointed in myself for mistaking your mirage for depth. I can't believe I actually loved a man who ain't worth the shit of a dead pig. Reflections?"

After he gathered himself, a torrent of excuses and an avalanche of explanations rolled through his thin lips. She listened because she *had* asked for reflections but it sounded so old, so high school, so ridiculous coming from a man old enough to be her father.

She felt nauseous. Her breath was hard to catch. Could she never make a clear, lucid, healthy decision? To have crossed time zones and bent backward over the Atlantic to hear the same bullshit she'd heard since adolescence hurt. I've come fool circle. She couldn't help but smile.

She rose and left Femi's office.

"Cyn! Cyn! Cynthia!!"

She ran to her door and saw Istha's eyes wide with fear. She was shaking.

"Come in, girl," she folded a trembling Istha in her arms. "What's wrong? What happened?"

"Sh—Sah—Someone just jumped on me!"

"Aw shit!" She led Istha to a chair and took to her knees to listen. She held Istha's hands.

"Right on the road, girl! In the middle of the road in front of the conference center."

"Are you okay?" Cynthia searched her friend's face, arms, and clothes.

"I'm fine. I don't know about dude, though." She sighed, "The only thing that saved me is that a car was coming. The lights shined on us and he ran."

"What did the driver say."

"He didn't stop," as soon as she spoke the words, Istha was back in St. Louis. She had gone with her boyfriend to a party filled with his cousins, brothers, and friends. She didn't realize she was the only woman there until afterwards.

They were all getting high and playing cards. Then it was like all the testosterone made plans for her without her knowledge. She left the house trembling and disheveled. She took to the highway; she didn't know where she was. She came to an all-night donut shop and saw a policeman. She tried to explain what happened to him and he laughed. She continued walking. A car stopped; the driver looked her up and down. "They raped me," she wept. He peeled out speeding off. After the exhaust fumes dissipated along with her shock, she laughed at herself and said, "I guess should have said $50."

She continued walking in what she thought was the general direction of her home. Dawn greeted the sky looking like green and pink Easter egg dye. She finally got a ride, from another policeman. She said nothing other than her address. He was a fatherly looking man, but she knew that didn't mean shit. He walked her to the door. The officer looked at her father. Her father looked at the officer. Neither man said a word. She didn't either. She went upstairs and went to sleep. When she woke up, she prepared for her graduation ceremony.

She thought she put the event behind her but she noticed 1 month later that 2 completely bald circles, the size of half dollars appeared at the nape of her head. They stayed there for 6 months. She always carried knives after that. Always—until she came to here. She didn't think she would need them here.

DEEfense *clap clap* DEEfense *clap clap* DEEfense

I walked the streets armed
on the fallrealla
St. Louis a muthafucka
The Boogie on dat ass
1 night I'm comin back from the jam
the shit was foul and I got played
so I stroll down the Hodimont line
an, I'll be damned, some muthafucka followin me
Aw shit the bitch don sped up n shit
                                        whip, flip, dip

Come on bitch!
I got a gun and a knife fo you ass
Which 1 you want?

Awww! Heh heh heh
Isss cooo babee
Iss aaaa riiiit

Damn right, Beeeeeooooottttcccchhhh!

Yeh, armed
Just tryin to walk down da street like war
in modern-day missippi
Aww, so theeeeese slut bitches don't see me
lab-made mutants think they own the whole sidewalk
this ain't back in the day

be damned if I'm jump in the gutter.

Umph, umph, umph WHAAAAMMM
Oh, excuse you. BEEEEOOOOTTTCCCHHHH
(that's called da col shoulder)

Armed jogging
with rocks and sticks and knives
you don't mind losin
cuz muthafuckn troglodytes
will throw rocks at you, spit on you, and shout
NIIIIIIIIIIIIIIIIIIIGGGGGGGGGGGGGGEEEEEEEEERRRRRR
Ehop ehop ehop ehop ehop SCHLASH!!!
That's yo windshield
BEEEEOOOOTTTTCCCCHHHH

Ready for war cuz niggas done decided the best place
To sell drugs to junkie cracker students is
Ta da daaa
Right the fuck outside my crib!

I hear all this violence n shit and step out cool like
they done stole the crackers' money and
stripped the beasts and the car.

Excuse me, excuse me, please, can you help us?
Hell naw.
BBBBBBBEEEEEEEOOOOTTTTTTCCCCCHHHHHH

See, Tawanna Brawley, y'all didn't believe her
She went out unarmed.
Found herself raped by 3 gray pigs
Thrown on the road side likasakashit
Wit nigga bitch scrawled on her belly.
I ain't forgot.
And I know it happens too often to too many
Ain't no need to lie

But I gave my .45 back to my Mudeah
I was like,
I'm goin to the Muthaland
I don't need no gun here.

Sssshhhhheeeeeeettt

Need 2,
Gangster pseudo-academicians breakin into offices and shit
Students lynchin professors n shit
Threatenin an plannin to waylay me n shit.

Now I know
dis the easiest place ta get n stay strapped
chi-ching
Wif whipl
Come on lil bitch ass mark.
I'll kick yo ass 9 ways till Sunday
I'll kill you ass
fo quick can get ready.

You *sure*
you wanna fuck
wit me?

~~~~~Istha


"We need weapons and weapons training," Istha declared after several minutes of thought. "This place is unsafe."

"You're right. A young woman was raped in the parks and gardens last month. Hump. When me and Kan first moved here, some vagabond was peeking in the rear window."

"Here is a society where people used to stroll about naked and unashamed. Now, everyone is a confused pseudo-Caucasian: girls walking round half naked and men raping left and right," her voice was rising in anger. She needed to cool and cleanse herself.

"You know, 1 sister was saying that discussions of sex are taboo, but everyone is lascivious. It is crazy, it's as if everyone has decided 'if we don't discuss it, it doesn't occur, and we can do what we want.'"

Istha sighed.

"Listen, I wanna get some magnolia blossoms."

"For what?" Cynthia had shifted the vibe entirely and Istha was confounded.

"You need cleansing and centering," she patted her thighs and stood up. "The tree is right around the corner."

"I'll go with you."
~~~~~

Cynthia led Istha to a huge yard that boasted 2 massive trees whose branches were heavy with blossoms.

"The petals are slimmer than magnolia blossoms," Cynthia held 1 of the white flowers with yellow pistils, "but 1 sniff and you know its magnolia—or his brother."

Istha inhaled the familiar scent and let memories overtake her. After a deep inhalation, she mused, "It is a trip to enjoy in Africa the same scent that is rife with stereotypes, unearned privilege, and pain in America."

"Geography will blow your mind, right?"

As they picked the blossoms, Cynthia described the 3 different baths she would prepare for Istha in the coming days: 1 for cleansing, 1 for protection and 1 for power.

"You know, it's almost over. I should defend in 3 months. I just hope I hold out."

"How can you not hold out? We got your back!"

The pair walked home in silence. As they reached Cynthia's door Istha shared a thought that had been occupying her mind.

"Cyn?"

"Istha?"

"I see so often and so clearly the people who sold us away."

"Yes."

There was no need to say more.

They made it back to Cynthia's flat which was cheery even in their absence. Cynthia started preparing the space by lighting candles, getting incenses together, and cleaning her tub.

"Slavery was never abolished anywhere in the world. It maintained both the same and more clever and diverse forms and names, but it remains," Cynthia asserted.

"The sad thing is that now you have people selling themselves into slavery."

"Exactly, today, I was lecturing from *Two Thousand Seasons*. I read a passage in which the narrator discusses prophets, seers, hearers, healers, and speakers faced with a garish brash multitude gyrating themselves into oblivion as they struggle and vie for positions on the white road of death. The narrator asks, would you, people of the way, share your divine prophecy with these people fascinated with death, these mirrors of their own annihilation? Go to them and have your discourse with long-rotted carcasses.

"The students identified themselves as those fascinated with death, as mirrors of their own annihilation! This was not a problem for them."

"What?"

"Yes. I was amazed. They even justified their decisions to acquiesce in their own destructions and social deaths."

"What of the seers, healers, keepers of the way?"

"Girl, we spent *time* on that issue. The answer they came up with, as to who are the seers, healers, prophets and keepers of the way, was me."

"Umph."

"Yep. I'm am the only person they recognize as manifesting the way. I told them that *they* are the people Armah's narrator is referring to. I don't think they wanted that responsibility.

"We also discussed the differences between training and education. I asked them if a person standing at a podium spewing rhetoric that is to be swallowed and regurgitated on an exam sheet was sparking wisdom and knowledge. They knew it wasn't, but most of them don't care. They want a degree, no matter the discipline. It is a license to marry, attain some mediocre job and begin oppressing underlings. When that is the character of your culture, it is hard to be of the way. That is what Armah is saying. Who can you share your divine utterance with when your nation is dead? Folk will kill you, lock you away, or sell you."

"That is what happened to the people of Anowa," Cynthia joined Istha as she sat on the bed and faced a wall adorned with a huge painting of Fela. They listened to the water filling the tub. "If it wasn't for you, I would have lost my mind a long time ago."

"Me too," Istha smiled at Cynthia. "It is sad that here in Africa the ultimate objective is Caucasia, by any and all means."

"Even the profs, the supposed wisdom keepers, have their noses so deep in America's ass they think they're shitting in the white house."

At this, Istha fell out and Cynthia, who'd been looking so serious, laughed with her.

Cynthia pondered her surreal role as instructor. Books were nearly impossible to obtain. But when the books were available, the students didn't read them. And rather than write their assignments, they wrote letters of protest against her for giving them assignments.

What was the point of the university? She wondered. The students come to the lecture hall and write down what you say, verbatim, and regurgitate your exact words for exams. Independent thought and critical thinking are so foreign that the concepts scare the hell out of the students.

Even though I am fighting it with every cell of my being, just by being a part of this system, I am participating in the perpetration and perpetuation of a lie.

Welcome to Sub-Par University!

I'm your discount instructor!
Here at Sub-Par U
we heard your cry
and we responded!
From this semester forward:
Texts and supplies?
SLASHED by 80%
Deep and intricate analyses?
REDUCED by 70%
Assignments? Class Participation?
SLAUGHTERED to 10% of the original
Final Examinations?
A "no wahala" situation!!!

Here at Sub-Par U
We heard your cry
and we responded!
Rather than giving 100%
and expecting the same from you
we'll all give about 2%!

Come as you are!
Don't fuss over
  books, pens, paper.
You said you couldn't handle assignments:
  You won't have em!
You slept through lectures:
  Bring your pillows!
You couldn't answer probing questions:
  Don't give yourself a headache!
For god's sake!!! We just want to
  GET YOU THROUGH

Here at SPU, we're fully committed to half-assed academics. The value of your education has gone down the toilet and so has the effort that you have to put into it!

We know you finagled and lied to get the money to dress SHARP eat HAMBURGERS and drink til ya BUST. And since your bribes have been as right as rain, your degrees will come minus pain!

True education is for the birds and everybody knows
[snip snip]
Africans can't fly.

"I never would have believed that the educational system here—with is plagiarism, bribery, corruption, and anti-intellectualism would be identical to that of America. Without the time we've done here and in American universities it would have been difficult to understand the global educational system's role in protecting and advancing Caucasian supremacy.

"Being here emphasizes the necessity of the Original Path Institute and of Dgn, which educate and elevate holistically and without motivation for profit, just as the University of Sankore and the ancient Universities of Ta Ntr and Kmt."

"Students and families around the world are going into debt and suffering to become part of a system that is devoted to their destruction."

"We are the exceptions in that we are currently in the system, we are aware its illusory nature, and we are able to leave behind this lie and enter the Odù of infinite cosmic intellect. But because the indoctrination begins at such a young age and is made mandatory and even glamorized, few people will be able to recognize that the educational system is a labyrinth of lies and even fewer will be desirous of embracing womb-deep truths.

"I met this brother," Cynthia continued. "He was older than most undergraduate students; he was older than me. Unlike many students, he had actually worked and struggled to come here and get a degree. I respected his grind. We would have study sessions, and I would drop knowledge on him. I can become loquacious and get excited, but I tried to be cool and gently knowledge the brother. After a few attempted builds it dawned on me that he was just a good listener. He would listen and nod and make minor contributions at the right times, but he wasn't really *hearing* me. You know?

"When I realized what he was doing, I laid out his entire existence for him: The dead-end jobs, some dull wife who's primary concern is preparing meals so that he can become fat. The children who are not really human beings but status symbols or problems. The material comforts that provide no succor for the soul. But it seemed that in problematizing these things, they became glamorous to him. He began grinning when pondering the desolate landscape that stretched before him. I realized that I had wasted my time, knowledge, and divine utterance—just like Armah said I would."

"Sophia Stewart knew exactly what she was doing when she wrote *The Matrix*," Istha mused. "So many prefer a killing myth to a fortifying reality."

After a few minutes of thought, Istha continued, "The devastation that occurred here was and remains monumental, and it damaged everyone physically, psychologically, socially, and emotionally. It was Walter Rodney who revealed that the Fon of Benin spent all their energies creating war to generate captives to sell. Rodney stated that the Fon suffered a famine in the 18th century because they neglected agriculture; they forgot the plant crops. They were so obsessed with destroying others that they destroyed themselves.

"Talk about being trapped in a matrix. . ." Cynthia shook her head.

"Cynthia, I always knew that many of us had to die. That so many of us contribute nothing and offer nothing; are accomplices of Yurugu. But there are *so* many, so *many*, who refuse, adamantly refuse, to shine," she released a sharp gust of air. "How many of us will there be when Ah revolution and evolution come?"

"There will be enough. There are always enough and we won't be scattered, twisting, and turning in loneliness, confusion, and doubt. There will be enough and we will be concentrated and directed."

Istha, Cynthia, and Kandace knew that there would be fewer men than women in the shining collective. The 3 women had dismissed the male aspect from their personal lives. Kandace had decided long ago that men were superfluous. Although she knew that complementarity could exist, especially in Ah, she knew that it would not exist for her.

Istha considered men a chromosomal aberration. Even before she knew Ah and Ahni, Istha, after examining human genes and chromosomes determined that the human male was the result of a genetic mutation. With what she had personally witnessed—hi- and lo-tech lynchings led by psychologically and culturally castrated males who were shored up by women riddled with spirit-envy, self-hatred and—

What happened to the men I used to love? Tried to love? She wondered. The 1 who wrote me lyrical love letters across the Atlantic? "Beautiful lovers!" a passerby said, gazing upon our glow. He turned out to be an insecure maniac. And the other 1, the 1 who brought me flowers every other day and adorned my shrine with his prayer beads, gave me Imani. The 1 who danced like liquid silk and whose eyes and teeth were white as Ọbàtálá's robes? The 1 with Hoodoo eyes Whodoed(?) me. Petty thief who took my money and then went screaming through the marketplace with my soon-to-be-sucked bones on his shoulders. Or the 1 who wanted to own me for eternity: I brought him for $30 and because I don't deal in slaves, I turned him over to his ancestors.

Boys of all ages who hope to prove their manhood by increasing the volume of their oral flatulations. Empty entities who fill their lives with vicariously lived scandals of and lies told about others. Thin shell males tugging, sagging, and struggling to cover their voids with the lies of masculinity that they import hourly and purchase religiously from beasts who envied the manhood of their ancestors, ancestors who gloried in the radiance of the Mothers.

The West African patriarchy is Ogo's giggling triumph. It is an ailing aberration that is so deluded that the justification for anything it wants is "But, I'm a man!" As if dicks were magic wands and their ejaculate some sacred shibboleth.

Perhaps after the shining, more balanced Aha would arise. Perhaps they would be deemed unnecessary and slip into extinction. Istha, Kandace, and Cynthia were not concerned either way. They were too busy building.

The deep tub had filled. Cynthia added the slim, hardy blossoms along with sweetened condensed milk and vanilla extract. She placed 4 white candles in the 4 corners of the tub.

She placed a small bowl of water before Istha. With a pot of incense, she began smudging her. She started at her feet and worked her way up her friend's naked body, smoking her thoroughly. She chanted, "Clean body, clean heart, clean life, clean mind," over and over again. After she completed 1 smudging, she directed Istha to step over the water. She continued the process until the smudging and water crossing had been done 3 times.

Cynthia led Istha to the tub telling her, "Free your mind of everything. Listen to the sure rhythms of your soul. Let them guide you to peace," as Istha soaked, Cynthia took Istha's clothes and washed them and hung them outside to dry. She then smudged her home and herself.

She joined Istha in the tub and began scrubbing away the grief, violence, pain, violation and confusion from her body. She radiated peace, understanding, and unity onto and into her friend. Istha returned these gifts to Cynthia as she washed her.

They interlocked themselves on the bed and began meditating. They arrived at a land more arid than Ifẹ, but still lush. They were situated 50 feet from a river. The smell of iron, vegetation, and damp earth filled their nostrils. The river was singing, chanting its own oríkì in a burbling alto. A small buffalo appeared; it was followed by another, a twin.

They recognized the spirits of Ọya and Kandace.

The time has come.

"She's coming! I can see her head!" she didn't rise from the earth to give the news but remained near the womb.

"Dear, how you know it's a girl?" Conch looked across at her.

"This is my great-grand. You think I don't know her?"

"Baby," Valeria cut through Tynell and Conch's discussion to focus on Hawa, "you okay? You sure you don't wanna lie down? I don't know about this thing y'all built."

"Mom ma I'm o kay," she panted.

Danta and Hawa had designed and built a birthing bench. It was an instrument designed to place the mother, as opposed to the doctor or midwife, in the most comfortable position for birth, a position that allowed gravity to assist mother and child.

Hawa reclined in the Earth-facing contraption. Her forehead rested on a padded partition. Her arms, with muscles straining, were in front of her, her fists clenched 2 padded, upright arms. Her head was inclined towards the sky but her body came down at a diagonal. Her knees were cushioned in 2 heavily padded rests that were reinforced to bear the stress of birthing.

"Iiiiive never gi ven birth be fore, b b but I feel comfort able. It's just the pressure of the contraaaaa—hooo!"

"Bear down now!"

"Breathe, Wa, Breathe!"

"Ha, ha, ha, Unnnnngh!"

"That was a good push, you got the head out! Danta, hold her," Dear directed all actions from the pillows stationed beneath Hawa's womb which was suspended about 3 feet from the ground.

"Yes, the, yes, Ma'am," Danta rushed to Hawa's shoulders and massaged them. "You're doin fine, God, just fine."

"Unnnnngh!"

"Good gracious!"

"Oh my!"

"Lord, what in the . . ."

"Wooowee! Y'all look at that! I bet y'all never seen that before, is ya?"

Hawa closed her eyes. She had given birth. She felt the silken hairs of her daughter's head glide through her vagina. She wanted to remember that sensation forever, so she lost herself in it. Velvet. Velvet. Velvet. After a few moments, she realized that Dear was beside herself about something, but by the tone of her voice and the stunned air that surrounded her, it must be some kind of blessing.

"Is she alright Dear?" Hawa asked. Before Tynell could respond, Hawa groaned. With attention refocused on her womb, Hawa grunted and released the afterbirth, which Conch caught.

"Danta," Valeria began fussing, "get her out of this thing now and get her into the bed." She stroked her daughter's jaw, "Girl, I'm so proud of you! You shot that baby out in no time! Maybe this thing did help."

Danta eased Hawa out of the bench and onto the bed, which was stationed just 3 feet away.

"Quickest birth I ever saw," Dear mumbled. She, Conch, and Danta marveled at the newcomer who marveled at them, in turn. Hawa was about to close her eyes as her head hit the pillow. But she saw the Mother, the brilliant constellation of Ahni and her 12 children. She smiled and murmured, "Ahhhhh," and rested, having widened the circle.

Gemini, she mused. She's a good 1 to continue the work. She'll need those 2 heads. Ah! She chuckled and remembered the caul, "3 heads" she said aloud. She winked at Valeria and shut her eyes.

"Y'all is sho nuff out the box."

"But it worked well, Dear, you got to admit."

"Only cuz I remembered the candles," Tynell shook her head, "Who ever heard of an outdoor birth?"

During a Sunday stroll, Hawa had discussed with Dear what they would need for the outdoor birth. Tynell gazed at a buoyant Hawa and said, "She may come at night, especially with the ways your eyes look."

"How they look, Dear?"

"I can't explain," she looked at the pupils and whites again and then she consulted the sun. "Yes, get lots of candles."

Danta and Leroy had prepared the birthing space. Hawa and Dear compiled a list to ensure they had everything they would need. The bench, a bed, basins of blessed distilled water, towels, Rh injection, sterile knives and scissors. The birthing bench was situated over a pit so that the Earth would receive all the fluids of new life, the waters of transition. The pit was filled with magnolia, honeysuckle, roses, dogwood all the flowers nature offered to the season.

The birth space was prepared. All the Gods were situated in a large outer circle. Danta and the mothers formed an inner circle, surrounding Hawa and the infinity she would bring with Ahibit.

When the children and parents visited the Institute, they asked about the new set up.

"Y'all gon have the baby outside?" asked Pam, a precocious child who'd been labeled schizophrenic. Pam had been born with a caul—in a hospital. The caul had been unceremoniously removed and pitched out with the umbilical cord. So Pam grew up without being able to distinguish the material and spiritual realms. She'd spent her first 11 years as the youngest inhabitant of River's Way, a mental institution.

Thanks to Jade, a spirit friend who helped her understand her path, Pam learned to distinguish between the 2 realms she straddled. She began to learn how to differentiate between apparitions from humans, and she understood what could and could not be shared with whom.

As a child, she would befriend kind spirits and scream and take flight from grotesque spirits. Because no 1 else saw anything, she was assumed to be crazy. Once Pam had been ostracized, the malicious entities lost interest in her and Jade came to her. So at 13, Pam was released from River's Way and she entered 4th grade special education at Pontotoc Grade School. A substitute teacher told Pam about the Original Path Institute. Pam and her mother visited the Institute. Now, Pam was the head of her 6th grade class.

Hawa rubbed her belly. "She'll be born outside, Pam, and come into a world that is equipped with everything she needs. Everything. And her umbilical cord, placenta, and caul, if she is so blessed, will be handled with care so that she has their protections."

"Yes, Ma'am, that's important," Pam smiled.

"You mean you gonna do that old timey stuff: buryin navel strangs under trees and what not?" This was from Mildred who was a strange case. She knew she had power. She could read minds, change minds in some cases, but she often rejected the power and ridiculed the force. She had joined the Path, shouting skepticisms yet magnifying her emi all the way. Mildred was Hawa's second cousin.

"Mil, you know, our rituals are important. We are not disconnected from the spiritual realm and the Earth. Just as our elders are with us, guiding and instructing, so are the ancestors and the Òrìṣà. Our rituals activate sources of force and ensure successful life transitions. When we began abandoning these vital rites we began cutting off pieces of our soul. In order for us to re-member our spiritual, mental, and biological selves, we must reclaim what we have lost.

"1 of the most deceitful acts of the Caucasians who enslaved us was to force us to abandon our way and replace it with Jesus, which was a replacement of everything with nothing.

"I was with you, cuz," Mildred smiled, "til you started blaspheming." Everyone laughed, but for many, there was truth in Mildred's statement. It is difficult to liberate 1's self from religious terrorism.

"You know that these rituals and signs and healing remedies that we have here in Bliss Bluff are also done by Ah wherever we are. And it is not that these things are just for poor uneducated folks, the physicians that folks go to are just prescribing concentrated extracts of the same plants Ah pharmacologists use. But pharmaceutical companies poison these extracts with synthetic chemicals and addictive and dangerous compounds. While the chemicals may accelerate or concentrate medicinal properties, they also cause harmful side effects. Our way is a way of synchronicity. We want to achieve a state in which the body, the mind, and the spirit are all growing together and growing naturally.

"True healing, like true education, must be holistic, meaning, it must go beyond treating symptoms, such as take an aspirin for a headache, or use palma christi for a headache. No. We want to find out what caused the headache. Is it stress, worry, exhaustion, tumor? Once we understand the cause, then we affect the cures for both immediate and permanent relief. The same goes for education. Many of us have gathered here first and foremost because the public and private school systems are worthless; racism and inept teaching have made this so. But, let's say these folks were not racist and didn't chunk us in special education or kick us out or ignore our raised hands. They would still only be training us. The question is training us to do what?" Hawa looked at Pam.

"Well, training us to serve them," Pam responded.

"Right. Mildred, what is the difference between training and education?"

"As I understand it," her accent was like pure honey: sweet, thick and rich, "training is like the lessons you give someone so that they behave. You can train a dog to do tricks or not mess on the living room floor, or not bark at and bite everything that shakes the bush. Train a cat not to claw up the furniture." She paused and thought about the issue, "Pam is right. If the school system is training us, its training us to serve them and to build up wealth for them."

"Like Wal-Mart employees. Think of all of the Wal-Marts in the world. Think of all the employees: Their toil, menial wages, and lack of health benefits makes it possible for the Walton family and their children's children's children to never have to work at all," Danta elaborated.

"Sounds like a pyramid scheme to me," Dear agreed. "Maybe that's the significance of the pyramid on the dollar . . . The masses spend their lives building fortunes for a few."

"And we do it cause we're trained not to demand," said Willie, "trained not to talk loud, trained not to protest . . . I was there, in the 60's when we were fighting for our rights. The beasts were enraged that we had stepped out of the role slavery had trained us intuh, that lynchin had trained us intuh. Ole Cutback Claude down at the depot once said he couldn't believe the 'negras' was actin up after all they'd done for us." He shook his graying head, "Guess he looked at us like the family dog shittin on the floor," he nodded his head toward Mildred in deference to her example.

"Back then, we took a real good look at what we needed and what we actually had and the ways we was treated versus what the laws said," Momma Lu said. Everything was ass backward—y'all excuse my language—just like it is today, ain't much changed. But I guess our fightin for our rights was the education you're talkin bout, Wa. Cuz that's what it was about. Whether you joined SNCC or the Muslims or Panthers, it was about educating yourself, organizing, and fighting."

"Right on!" Hawa threw up her fist in the Black Power salute and her fist was surrounded by a multitude.

A few had been to the March on Washington; a couple held congress with Hamer and the National Freedom Democratic Party. Some had registered voters. But they were not many. Mississippi's brand of "training" was terrorism—the most violent and chilling in the world. But there were many in the northern part of the state who, like Sister B, braved the threats of cowards to integrate lunch counters, demanded $5.00 a day for picking cotton as opposed to $2.00, applied for jobs in banks and post offices and get the jobs. Many battles were fought and quite a few were won. But with an almost imperceptible turn, from the Reagan to the Bush to the Clinton to the Bush to the Obama administrations, the progress of the 60s slipped back into the brackish waters of the 40s.

The 1990s and 2000s saw a rise in lynching, saw the rekindling of church burnings, saw Black folks attacked and beaten and killed, saw Black people used as target practice by any mutant who chose to take aim, saw the public school system resegregate, saw a private school system that was a high falutin joke. Saw destitution sweep the multitudes into the sewer, and when those multitudes tried to rise up to fight against injustice, the broom of avarice swept them back down.

Black folks had moved from agriculture to blue collar to hit a glass ceiling. M.A. holders were working at dollar stores. The NAACP was run by a collective of accomodationist sell-outs. 13-year-old uneducated mothers and fathers were booted or ignored out of school, running around in gangs, running into and up outta jails. Others got diplomas or degrees only to find . . . nothing: no job opportunities, no future but plenty of debt. What was the point?

If we'd overcome, why were we plagued with such stress and distress? If all we had to offer our children was a rerun of our own cyclic suffering, then this was not good enough. If the progeny of those who had been enslaved and sharecropping were suffering on a dying wage, then what was freedom, and, more important, how did this existence make sense? Hawa and Danta asked the tough questions; the answers were the members of the Original Path Institute, themselves.

They were only 70 members strong and had tremendous growing to do but they were growing. Hawa, Danta, and Dear would travel through the bottoms and discuss the Institute with relatives and neighbors. During these jaunts the trio would also assess the community's needs.

"How y'all do?" Dear called as they stepped out of the car.

"Just fine! Just fine!" Welcomed Jane, who was working at the shirt factory Dear had retired from not long ago. She and her husband Dink were inspirational in this age: A man and woman together, raising a child. Working and loving.

"Y'all come on up and sit a spell," Jane smiled and continued snapping pole beans, "I'm just preparing for dinner. Sho is hot."

It was a slow and easy Saturday. Dink was at work and Jane had the day off. Dear heard Rell, their son, playing with his remote control race car inside the house.

"Jane, how's Rell doin in school? I know report cards just came out."

"He got some Cs, mostly Ds and Fs. Say he cut up too much. Say he don't wanna mind," Jane's tone revealed her frustration with Rell and his teachers.

"The next stop is special ed," said Danta as he tossed a handful of beans that he'd snapped into Jane's bowl. His tongue had taken the easy Mississippi rhythms. He felt right at home.

"Danta, how you know! That's just what Mr. Jenkins said! But all Rell does is sit up and read. Read anything got letters: even the cereal box."

"Jane, once he's in special ed, chances are he'll drop out. But if he does graduate from special ed he won't have a chance for higher education or any kinda good job."

"It's bad enough with good education. Then again, with too much education they figure you ain't fit to work for them," mused Jane.

"Rell deserves a chance like any other child," Jane nodded her head as Hawa spoke.

"What you and Danta plannin on doing?" Jane asked.

"We just wanna make sure our seeds aren't scattered in the winds or landin on sand. Want em to grow in rich soil," Hawa smiled.

"We starting out small, you know, but our goal is to establish a school, a learning institute where everybody can come. Can't stand to see another generation wasted. Could you call Jorell for us, Jane?" Danta asked. "We'd like to talk with both of you."

The grindings and clicks of his remote controlled car stopped and the child jogged to the porch. He was a handsome boy. Smooth honey brown skin with dimples and a mole high on his left cheek. After he said hello to everyone he took a seat beside his mother.

"Mister Jorell! My Capricorn Sun," Hawa gave him a high 5. "You know, we Capricorns are special. And we're smart."

"Yes, ma'am," he beamed.

"Rell," Hawa sat down next to him and nudged his shoulder, "what's your girlfriend's name?" He became bashful and looked at his momma and ducked his head.

"Now, he does make As in girls."

"Sposed to! He's a Capricorn! Rell, what's 12 x 12 / 4?"

"36."

"8 x 8 / 3"

"21.3"

"What's the capital of Ohio?"

"Cincinnati."

"What does the UN stand for?"

"United Nations."

"What is a parasite?"

"A plant or animal that lives off of anotha 1 till it kills it."

"What is symbiosis?"

"Symbiosis: That's when 2 organisms are livin with each other in a healthy mutually supportive relationship."

"Who was Malcolm X."

"Oh, he changed his name to El Hajj Malik El Shabazz. He was a member of the Nation of Islam. He was born in Omaha Nebraska in 1925. He left the Nation of Islam and founded the Organization of Afro-American Unity. He was assassinated 14 February 1965. Anniversary of his death was just last week."

Danta winked at Dear. Jane was shocked: "Where'd you learn about him?"

"Momma, they just had something bout him on the news last week. But I also read about him in the library."

"Here Sugarfoot," Dear gave him a dollar, "go to Miss Flo and get yourself a huckabuck."

"Thank you, Momma Tynell," he ran like the wind and called out to some neighboring cousins along with way who ran to join him.

"They're trying to crush the spirit out of the boy. His mind is hungry, and he's too advanced for his class," Danta said as they watched him and his friends run and laugh and play on their way to buy the homemade popsicles.

"Hmp! I didn't know he knew all that. I had forgotten most of that stuff myself," Jane laughed and everyone joined her.

Danta continued, "They want us to sink into the roles they make for us so that we can't see the horizon for lookin for the next paycheck."

"Rell could be another Malcolm X but they want to crush him into a Sweetback," they laughed at Hawa's joke at her own expense. Sweetback had been a teenage boyfriend.

"It's serious though. I think of David McGaha. We went to school together. He was real smart, but he never made nothin of himself. And Lee, he was such a smart baby! He was reading at 3: He didn't amount to anything. . ." Jane began to realize that there were no local success stories, and the reason, ironically, may well be the school system. How was it, Jane wondered, that his school translated her son's obvious intelligence into "special education"?

"Let him come to us," Hawa offered. "*After* school," she emphasized. "He'll just be getting double the knowledge, that's all. And tell him he can bring his friends with him, too."

"It will just be for a few hours, keep him outta trouble while you and Dink comin from work," said Dear.

"We also wanna monitor his progress in school. We're not talking about anything aggressive. We just want to let the teachers and principal know that we know what the child is capable of."

"Y'all really serious about this school?" Jane looked at Dear, who nodded her reassurance. Dear was an elder, and while Hawa had gone all over the nation, Dear was always there on the mountain and would tell the truth about Hawa or anyone else in a second. "Seems like a good idea," Jane mused, "but, if what y'all say is true, maybe bein too smart is his problem."

"We need all the wisdom we can get, Jane. Rell deserves the best education. We all do," Hawa asserted.

"Let Rell come to us after school, and when you and Dink feel moved, you come on and join us too," Danta smiled.

Jane looked pensive as she finished her beans and waved good-bye to the trio, but Rell came to the Institute the next day and he brought his friend Sidney with him. That's how it started. A handful of adolescents and adults.

Many adults came to see exactly what was going on. Many of them had a fear of too much education. Hawa had been a victim of that fear. She recalled Dear snatching a book from her hands, turning out the light, and warning: "Read too much you go crazy." Other relatives signified as she continued her schooling, "Don't get too uppity." Some mumbled: "Get a little education and don't know how to act." The fear of intelligence had been enslaving minds for centuries.

In his poem "Felony" Sam Greenlee asserts that a free African mind is a concealed weapon. Oppressors used terrorism to keep us mentally enslaved and to keep us from loading and using our innate weaponry. Their campaign of terror was so successful that African Americans continue the promotion of mental slavery and ignorance in their oppressors' absence.

Hawa and Danta introduced ther collective to their weapons through a liberation-centered education that started with what was most digestible, what all had experienced and what most took for granted—Black history and the Black experience.

Instruction began where life began: the cosmos. The lessons in astronomy were a revelation to students of all ages who had been miseducated to believe that the Earth was, somehow, separate from the universe. The collective was enraptured by discussions of the ancient Ah civilizations and how the Immortals used their celestial knowledge to build phenomenal civilizations in this galaxy and throughout the universe.

Instruction about early Africans in the Americas began with Abubakari II of Mali who sent a fleet of 200 ships across the Ethiopic in 1310 CE before sailing to the Americas himself in 1311 CE.

World history included information about Caucasian convicts who were shipped sardine-style to America and Australia to relieve the overcrowded prisons of England. Instruction also included analyses of the malleable Christianity of Caucasian emigrants that facilitated their enslaving Africans and killing Native Americans.

Courses also analyzed the fragmented mentalities and hatreds on the Continent that caused slavery to thrive, and they explored the many uprisings against slavery that took place on the Continent and throughout the lands to which enslaved Africans were taken.

Instruction about the Black Abolitionists included not only Douglass, Garnett, and Revels, but also, thanks to Cynthia's guest lectures, the acts of the millions of every day, any way, always already abolitionists. The owners of the ground glass, the tossers of Nana Bùrúkù's firebrands, those who prepared for the enslaver a dinner that ushered him into the arms of death by breakfast.

Hawa and Danta spent a great deal of time elaborating on revolutionary conjure and just as they had hoped, the elders joined in with choruses of what they had witnessed, heard tell of, and things they knew to work effectively. That was the goal: getting the elders to recognize their immense value as knowledge keepers and encouraging them use their wealth to enrich the collective. Once the elders melded their wisdom with the zeal of their progeny, and the collective could revolutionize their martial, spiritual, and academic repertoire.

With patience and moderation the Institute grew. They were working towards the goal of accreditation in a year's time. Until then, Danta and Hawa monitored their young charges' progress at their schools to ensure they were not being punished for their intelligence. With every trip they solidified a name for themselves as troublemakers and they also caused other African American students to wonder: Who are these guardians? What was their objective? As these queries were answered, more sharers and learners joined the Institute. Children flocked to the Institute. Many parents became members of the Institute after visiting to see where their children were spending their time. What they witnessed there met their approval.

Word spread about the "Stute" and soon they had 5 tiers of learning that were overseen by Hawa, Danta, the elders, and advanced and interested children. Ages infant to 7 learned reading, writing, mathematics, physical science. Ages 8–12 undertook literary studies, penmanship, math, geometry, physical and life sciences, history, and social studies; Ages 13–16 studied literary comprehension and analysis, biological science, calculus, critical analysis, and history. Ages 17–21 studied trigonometry, creative arts, computer programming and coding, historical and literary analysis, physics, and chemistry. Everyone received instruction in history, martial arts, orature, spiritual systems, medicine, and the history and Work of Ah.

In addition to joining any age group relevant to their needs, adults could focus their instruction on individually chosen topic areas, such as astronomy, agriculture, pharmacology, creative writing, critical theory, Àjẹ́, Medu Netcher, ancient writing systems, hunting, and weapons construction.

Everyone participated in agricultural study, and, with over 40 acres of land given the Institute by Dear, a beautiful garden flourished that included squash, verbena, tomatoes, devil's shoestring, corn, rabbit tobacco, pole beans, chicory, kale, orris root, ginger, John de Conqueror roots, sweet potatoes, white potatoes, peanuts, watermelon. All members shared in the planting, the weeding, the harvest, and the first fruit celebrations. The agrarian work also provided a platform for the study of flora and fauna including identification; spiritual, ritual, and medicinal preparation and application; collection methods; irrigation; and natural fertilization.

The Òrìṣà and Ahni were at 1 with all that occurred at the Original Path Institute, but because of the nature of the atrocities to which African Americans have been subjected and the degrees of self-hatred and hatred of Africa that had been ingrained in them, Hawa and Danta made the presence of power as organic as possible. They took the plentiful gift of time and found that the personal vibrations of certain members, especially children, moved them to participate in the sacrifices to the Gods, to initiate the pouring of libation, and to re-member forgotten or abandoned rites and rituals.

As members' cipher began to expand, they started meditating on their own, outside of the circular sanctuary. They began dreaming with Ah. As they recognized and came into alignment with their destinies, members of the Original Path Institute began vibrating. They began to shine.

Hawa smiled as she thought back on the exponential growth of the Institute. And her daughter, well, she is the capstone of our success! Hawa smiled and watched Dear place Ahibit's caul on the drying stone that she and Danta fashioned just in case.

Valeria had gone inside to put the tea kettle on. Aunt Conch was washing the child gently, like she was afraid she would break. The timidity and reverence Conch paid the newborn was moving. Hawa looked at them and smiled, they are like the portraits of Ast and Heru, but she saw a furtive longing, a sadness surrounding Conch, especially when she brought the child to Hawa's breast for her first feeding.

"Conch? You alright?"

"I should be asking you," she smiled and caressed the new mother's shoulder. Rare tears were standing in her eyes. It wasn't just the profundity of the childbirth or the fact that Conch undertook the rituals with care and without deprecating jokes. No, it was something else.

She is coming.

"Lil Wom?"

"Hun?" Conch looked up then looked down towards her feet for several minutes before emitting a womb-deep sigh and excusing herself.

Hawa nursed her baby while pondering her aunt. Hawa knew a monumental shift was taking place in Conch's life. What could it be, she wondered. Danta's approach refocused her attention. She smiled at Danta and said, "Bàbá, this little 1 needs you, and I know you can't let her down."

"Never," Danta brushed his nose across the child's cheek in bliss. "Head fulla hair! Just like her Momma," Danta whispered and dug his hand into Hawa's hair to her roots and massaged.

Hewer in pieces in blood. Ahibit, lady of hair is your name, She thought silently to herself. What she said aloud was, "Apanì-ma-hàágun. Irún bí Ọrun."

She cooed into her little 1's ear as Danta looked at her and said, "We better give you your shot now."

Danta went to retrieve the Rhogam injection and Hawa turned on her side to receive the hip shot. Hawa wondered if Rh factor was what contributed to the àbíkú phenomenon. She logged it in her brain as a topic for discussion with Aint May. She brought Ahibit back to her chest, and the child cooed and slept. Hawa instantly saw herself, seated outside amongst all the blessings of the night, surrounded by candles, having nourished the Earth, as the center of the Earth. She saw herself as she would look to a visitor just rounding the driveway: as the Mother of Infinity.

"Wa, her tea's ready." Dear cooed, "Oh, wake up sleepy head. Come on and take your medicine, sweetness."

The newcomer opened 1 eye at a time before rousing fully.

Mother, bless the steps of this child
May she walk well
in your path
with your honor
May her destiny be reflected
in all she does
Oh Ahni, let your wisdom
be a mirror of her visage
    Àṣẹ
Let her vision be clear, unclouded
She will be free of victimization, untarnished by fear
    Amen
Ah, Mother of Wisdom, your little 1 has come
Child of Daughter, Nwadiani
Anoint and assuage her 2 heads of power
open the vision of new and her ancient eyes

give her the grace to maneuver
from past to future in her present
   yes, yes
Let her walk long and well on the Earth
   Amen
in ways that please you
   Àṣẹ
The Ancestors bear witness to your return
Daughter of the Way, keeper of the path
has brought 1 and has come again
Share your wisdom, knowledge, and understanding
Lend your blessing to all aspects of her life
Eternity begins again

After 7 days, Ahibit was formally introduced to the community Danta explained the significance of birth ceremonies in Africa, and took the child around to all Òrìṣà and all Institute members. He and Ahibit asked each 1: "Seer, show me the Way, seer, help me see." Some replied, "Child, I will show you." Others said, "I will guide you." Some said, "My vision will enhance your own." Some replied, "Your path is assured."

Later, all members of the Institute joined Hawa, Ahibit, and Danta in meditation. Everyone took to the ground and formed a circle with their naked feet touching. Their arms were interlinked and they were sitting close enough that they were all able to place their own thumbs together and their own fingers together to create the symbol of the womb of life.

Hawa sat in the center of the circle, breastfeeding Ahibit and directing the meditation.

"On inhalation, say to yourself: 'peace, positivity, productivity,' for these are what we will absorb. On exhalation, say to yourself: 'stagnation, negativity, desolation,' for these we will release."

It took some time before all members were vibrating synchronically. Many were new to meditation; and many, Hawa observed, were assailed by the niggling random thoughts that disturb the ironic concentration that brings transcendence. She assisted with the dissipation of those thoughts and when all minds were 1 and all breathing was 1, Hawa felt a shimmy flow through herself and Ahibit.

Daughter of my soul. You have come shining! Ahni greeted Ahibit with a voice like an embrace. I am honored that you have accepted 1 of my praisenames, twin of my soul. Members of the Original Path Institute! I thank you and welcome you all to Ah!

Ahni's presence elicited many gasps, audible and mental. Not only was the Mother's presence a surprise, but the cosmic depth of her voice was such that each utterance caused a tremor in the core of Ah the members.

Before the last phoneme Ahni uttered finished its reverberations, each member became 1 with Ahni. They all became Ahni and were looking at their cyclic selves linked in meditation, surrounded by a circle of their ancestors which was surrounded by a circle of Òrìṣà and Loa. They saw their spirits—glowing onyx orbs—radiating and evolving in the cosmos. They felt Ahni's force, their force, deep within: It was a tangible, audible, spatial, light

AaahhhhhahahahAHAHAHHAHAHAH

Free-floating, directed, fully evolved, they were the Mother blessing themselves

AaaahhhhhahahahhaAHAHAHAHAHHAHAHhhhhhhh

Power, eternity, and promise undulated around and throughout their beings. Tomes of knowledge were revealed and re-membered. The way of all understanding was opened in every third eye. The always that was already within celebrated recognition of its continuity with orgasmic ecstasy.

No 1 said a word as the group descended. All eyes were directed inward at the marvel that was the individual-collective self at home in the womb of origins.

Over coffee the next morning, Danta and Hawa discussed the significance and timing of Ahni's revelation during the group meditation. "It is difficult to fully free oneself. Our ancestors were trained to fear freedom," Danta mused. "Oppressors told them that that they would be unprotected, that they would starve, that they couldn't survive. Oppressors indoctrinated the enslaved with a hatred for freedom and for the free."

"Oppressors also logically hate freedom because it threatens their goal of totalitarian, capitalist, Caucasian supremacy," Hawa added. "A typical example of the Caucasian response to African freedom is evident in confederate racists who were mad because they lost the Civil War and lined free Africans in front of rivers and shot and killed them and let the rivers wash their bodies away. Other racists went on beheading sprees and used the heads of Africans as mile markers.

"A more tame but nonetheless telling example of the Caucasian hatred for African freedom is evident in Guinea," Danta nodded. "When Sekou Touré demanded complete immediate liberation from French colonizers in 1958, the French assented, but their vindictiveness and maliciousness was such that they removed *everything* that they had brought, even the lightbulbs, from Guinea. It never crossed the minds of the French to replace what they had stolen and destroyed."

"We can also look to the assassinations of Thomas Sankara and Patrice Lumumba, who were both seeking to liberate their people and nations from French and Belgian neocolonial slavery," Hawa asserted. "Lumumba's liberatory impetus was rooted in King Leopold II turning the entire Kongo into a slave colony. Sankara instilled in his people, who had long been considered a source of slave or cheap labor, dignity, principles, and purpose. Lumumba and Sankara chose liberty, equality, and self-sufficiency over neocolonization, debt, and corruption, so Yurugu and debased Africans organized and killed them. The beast simply cannot tolerate the existence of free independent Africans."

"And their killings take many forms," Danta pondered. "So many of us are living victims of spiritual death that there is no need to undertake genocide. It is hard to find more lethal weapons of mass destruction than the father, the son, and the holy ghost.

"Ahni chose yesterday to liberate and resuscitate her lost-found progeny and introduce them to the truth of themselves and herself.

"From this point we will grow rapidly," Danta's smile was soul-deep. "The Ah who were here will shine and that shining will spark a glow in others. No 1 will have to utter a syllable; the power will flow to its source."

While Hawa shared his bliss, she was preoccupied. She strove to explain her concerns: "Danta, I also feel something. . . a Coming." She burped Ahibit and shifted her to her left breast for the child had drained the right. "The Coming is as real as Ahibit but I don't know exactly what it is. It is not the students. Nor is it the brilliance of Ah . . . but there is a Coming." She paused looking for words, "Like the tide."

"The word Òrìṣà means Select Head, head in this sense implies destiny or orí, in Yoruba. Thus orí means 'head': ṣa means 'that is key, unique.' Every individual chooses his or her head or destiny prior to coming to Earth. Part of the journey of life is finding, understanding, and manifesting 1's destiny," Hawa was discussing Yoruba philosophy with an intergenerational group.

"What happens if you choose the destiny of a farmer but you're a teacher?" Mildred inquired.

"That's an excellent question. Many things could happen depending on how you navigate your path. You could labor and labor as a teacher without success or fulfillment; then you would have to return to this world and struggle again to find your destiny. You could become a professor of agricultural science and fulfill your destiny in that way. You could also teach in a particular field, say philosophy, until you retire, and then take up farming and flourish in your retirement."

Mildred nodded, "So, your destiny is like an outline that you, through your decisions, perceptions, and desires, complete or fill in."

"That is an excellent way of putting it!" Hawa smiled.

"But how will 1 know 1's destiny?" Rell asked.

"It is said that an Òrìṣà called Yèyé Múwọ̀ marked all human beings with a spinal indentation. This mark causes all humans to forget their destiny. It is the search for 1's destiny that makes life full of complexity, richness, and educative failures and successes," Hawa explained. "Your orí, your spiritual and physical heads, give you clues and direction to guide you to your destiny and assist you in choosing the right path at the crossroads— but sometimes we don't listen to our first mind. Right?" She laughed.

"That's the truth."

"Maybe that's why I keep pickin knuckleheaded men! I feel like I been through the same crossroads fifty-leven times!" Mama Lu laughed.

"Maybe I'm sposed to be a lawyer and that's why my crops been failing," L.C. wondered aloud.

"Maybe you just need better fertilizer," Tynell offered.

"Finding your destiny takes time. Takes patience," Danta chuckled with the group. "You have to be in tune with yourself, and that is something that this society makes difficult. That is why we meditate, so we can listen to what our inner selves are saying and understand our true needs. Alright," Danta asked, "Mama Lu mentioned the crossroads: who is the guardian of the crossroads?"

"Èṣù Ẹlẹ́gbára or Legba, in the Yoruba and Fon, respectively. We call the God Papa Leba or Papa Joe. Èṣù is, well," Rell ordered and re-ordered his thoughts, "a force of indeterminate determination. Èṣù has both genders and holds Àṣẹ, the power to make things happen, and Àjẹ́, the power to do and undo, create and destroy. Èṣù is key to all rituals because she/he opens all roads." They were standing in front of Èṣù who had been assuaged with palm oil so that his-her head would be cool.

"Rell, I can see you have really been studying these spiritual systems."

"I been studying with the elders of Dah. We spend a lot of time together." He smiled. It seemed he was finding his orí.

Danta strolled towards Igi Bùrúkù which had been fronted with a huge tractor tire that was turned on its side and filled with pond water. 1 catfish lived inside, and different kinds of shells skirted the tire, "Now here is a more difficult question: Who was the Òrìṣà that Africans first praised upon making it through the Middle Passage?" He paused and looked at everyone. "Conch, do you know?"

She looked at the tire, shells, water, and the catfish, which obviously had some importance. Dear used to have a set up just like this 1 in front of what Hawa called the Wicked Tree as a child. She stared into the water as if mesmerized. She felt herself swirling and undulating with the catfish. She was lost in the rhythm of its movement and the language it was speaking, the promise it was making her. She felt her spirit shudder.

She was in the water looking at herself staring at herself undulating in the water, distinguishing her self from herself and forever uniting her with herself. She excised fear from her being and surrendered to the water and its wisdom, which was her Truth.

Schools of slim silver fish surrounded her. They provided oxygen and a song that she heard within her being but that she could not understand or repeat. Butterflyfish, starfish, catfish, pufferfish, swordfish, dolphins, all fish came to share and sing their songs of self to her.

Conch's voluptuous body blossomed. She surpassed sensual; her sexuality was beyond comprehension. Then the crocodiles came. Dancing on their tails. They were praising, chanting, extolling Conch. Nothing mattered, she would never leave. Not this praise. Not this peace.

"Conch? Conch? Conch!" Danta ran to and shook and held the woman who was swaying and rippling like seaweed caught in a riptide.

The swaying took control of both of them until Danta brought Conch back to land. "Oh . . . Oh no!" she went limp, "You destroyed the most beautiful experience, existence I have ever had!" She moved from mourning to remembrance, "I was in my most divine state. I, I was Y—" she began weeping. She started laughing. A serene and peaceful smile became a glistening of self-libation that contorted itself into a grimace of an inner pain to profound for words as Conch began moaning and wailing. She sank at the foot of the tree and hugged its trunk.

"Rell, why don't you take everyone to the shrine room and continue the lesson. I'll stay here with Conch."

He didn't say anything. Danta just held Conch while her story flowed like water and stretched recollection like the branches of the white oak tree.

I ain't got no real name. I found this out when I started goin to school. Everyone stood up to say they names. Junebug said, "Willie Johnson," Hattie Mae said, "Hattie Mae Clark," Loosey said, "Suzannah Wilson," Zip said, "Walter Heavens," Lil Boo said, "Blaze Sorrell," Tookie said, "Roselle McGaha," Bibby said, "Tyler Leslie," and I said, "Lil Wom." Miss Marvis Jean look at me and said, "Everybody knows your day name but what's your real name?" I just look back at her and I say, "Lil Wom. Lil Wom. That's what my people call me. That's who I am." She told me that when we come back tomorrow I would have to come with my real name. I just looked at her and felt the eyes movin from my back to the cracks in the floor. I started feelin that I should be shame, but I wasn't. Just confused. We got our lesson.

"'Lil Wom' is your name."

"But how come everybody got 2 names, even 3, and I only got a, well, a . . . 'Lil Wom' ain't no real name."

"Cause you is different, girl. Yo Momma didn't have time to give you your name when you was born. Hell was flamin high in the bottoms and you come in the middle of everything."

"Where was I born"

"Right here."

"Where is my Momma?"

"She dead."

"My Daddy?"

"He dead too. Your Momma, fore she died, told me to look after you and to tell you who you are and who your people are if she wasn't able to."

"What's my name?"

"You be Lil Wom. Your last name Jones. That was your Daddy's name. His name was Moses Jones. He died with my first husband back in 1940. They was good, handsome, strong Black men," when Nell speak on these 2, a light come on insida her. A light that illuminates her whole self. "Your Daddy loved your Momma, and he woulda loved you to death. We called yo daddy Mojo.

"I remember the day he came to the bottoms. He had his eye on Ba, that's your Momma, right from the start. I was just about married to Sam when he came, but he was so fine . . ."

"My Daddy?"

"Yes chile. But he didn't see nothin for Ba Ba. He reminded me of your granddaddy, Mosa. Same build, same open way, same love for your granmomma. Her name was"

"Yo! Nell!"

"Sid, I was just comin with your dinner. Leriaaaaaa!" she called her daughter, Valeria, "Where is that child? Lil Wom, help me with Sid dinner; I'll tell you more later."

"What I'm gon tell Miss Marvis Jean tomorrow?

"Tell her you Lil Wom and to come and see me if she have any more questions."

I had a last name now. My daddy's name. Jones. But so many pieces was missin! I knew Ma Nell loved me like her own and me and Leria wasn't nothin but sisters. But I needed to know who *I* was. Find where *I* fit in.

Sometimes I would hear Ma Nell talkin bout the old days with the old folks. I heard them talkin bout juber and a woman name Ah Ni (they pronounce it just like that, Ahh Knee) who drown but didn't die. Heard them talkin bout my daddy and granddaddy killin Klansmen. These words wasn't for my ears, but I knew they was my texts, so when I heard them talkin I kept still and soaked up all they was sayin. Ma Nell would sit and talk to me sometimes, too, but the way she spoke, I knew she was keepin things on a child's level. I needed all of my Me. Desperately.

She weeded the corn with ferocity. She attacked the weeds like they had personally offended her or the Earth with their simple right to existence.

Ain't got no name, she thought, ain't got no home neither, not too much. Ma Nell tell me bout my Momma and Daddy but what's memories when my arms ain't got nothin to hol? Talkin bout a hard row to hoe.

The corn was taller than she was and the blades reached out to her as she worked. Some tickled her face, some assaulted her cheeks outright. The salt of her tears alerted her to the presence of lacerations. She sank to the ground sobbing, "What life can I have like this heah?"

The atmosphere changed, the heat of June seemed to deepen—not in the rise or fall of temperature but in the air which became charged with electricity. When she blinked her tears away she saw streaks of color. It was as if she could see the atmosphere itself. She stared at the white oak guarding the house and saw her Daddy wrapped round the tree—hugging it in reverse; his head hung at an impossible angle. "Daddy?" She rose from the dirt and ran toward the tree. The image of her father changed to 1 of Nell singing and braiding her hair in the tree's shade. She froze—she and Nell never sat under that tree. They would refill the water in the big tractor tire, remove and bury the present catfish and introduce a fresh 1. Sometimes she saw Ma Nell place eggs in the hollow trunk and chant, but Ma Nell didn't know she was looking on. Didn't know the crickets, frogs, and owls had young company under the stars on those humid summer nights. Lil Wom realized it was, "Momma!" Ọmọ Ìyàlájẹ́ and Yoruba smiled at Lil Wom, and 3 generations were united.

Lil Wom released her hoe to the electric atmosphere and the earth. Her feet seemed to be the only part of her body working because her soul was full, overflowing, and impossibly heavy as she made her way to both of her mothers—neither of whom she'd seen before. As she was about to touch her mother's jaw, she saw a man. "Daddy," she cried.

"Lil Wom, I been waiting to talk to you. Get you alone."

"Yes."

"Been had my eye on you and I like what I sees."

"Hun?"

She did a double take. Her family was gone and the typical June heat had returned.

"You not my Daddy."

"But I can be," his eyes were gentle outside; inside there was a yawning hunger. She looked at his eyes because there was nothing else to see of him. They would tell her everything, and what they said in their paradox spoke volumes.

"Lil Wom, I been watching you for the past 3 weeks but you always working, schoolin, or dreaming. I'm real!" He struck his breast as if to wake her up by beating himself. "They call me Tink."

"Listen," she retrieved her hoe and made her way back to the corn, "I gots work to do that don't include no no-count pissant boy."

"I'm *every* inch a man, girl."

"Well, you welcome to go tell my Mo"

"I will," he nodded and left.

Lil Wom finished her rows in confusion. My family was tryin to talk to me and that slew footed fool jumped right in the middle of us. 3 weeks? What kinda of sneak-mess is that? She heard soft rustling in the corn and softer mumblings. She turned around.

"Leria, girl you don return?"

"Yeh. Got a messa blackberries, too" she grinned and held up 2 bucketsfull.

"Betcha got a messa chiggas, too."

"You know it!" she laughed and scratched her shoulder. It was somethin funny about Valeria. Lil Wom frowned and stored the look for later.

"James, how you make out?" She directed her attention to Valeria's steady beau.

"Pretty good," his smile was even easier and more rounded than Valeria's.

"Don't know whachall grinnin bout," said Lil Wom, realization washing over her like a summer shower. "Sid find out, he'll kill you fore quick get ready. Looka dere," she pointed to Valeria's neck, "You got a blackberry growin on your neck." Now that she understood, she could feel the left over passion as it tickled her own body with its teasing fingers. She felt empty, left out.

"Lil Wom, thanks for lookin out," said James Stills, a weak boy from a hard family. The Stills had killed folk behind trespasses the Devil would have overlooked.

"Sid know betta than to come round me talkin mess," Valeria asserted. Her satiny brown skin looked glossed in the dusked sunlight.

"You best git a hold of yourself! Sid be done took a 2 x 4 to ya."

"And I'll lam his head wid a crow bar," James wanted to signify now.

They smellin themselves, Lil Wom thought. "Anyway, James, you know a boy named Tink?"

"Um hum. Been through?" His eyes told her he knew he had.

"Mmm hhm." She looked off near the oak tree, not at the couple.

"He swear fore God he loves ya. Say he gon get cha, too," James had a fire in his eyes that gave Lil Wom pause.

"Yooo Hooo! Leria! Yoooo! Lil Wom!" James took to the ground like a snake. "Get it on in heah!" Ma Nell called from the front door.

The girls ran home and cleaned up to help with supper.

"Leria, those some sweet blackberries you found," Nell popped some into her mouth. "We gon make us a cobbler Sunday."

"I love blackberry cobbler, but I hate the seeds," Leria gritted her teeth.

"Well, to get the sweetness of life, you gots ta crack your teeth up against a few seeds," Ma Nell smiled then turned around to lay the biscuits.

The women hushed, and the only sounds were the movements of meal-making. After 20 minutes Sid came stomping in.

He was a slight light brown man with a wicked disposition. Life had not treated him well only because he figured it owed him something.

He banged in, removed his shoes, and grumbled a general greeting. The family ate in silence.

Lil Wom tossed and turned in her bed. Leria had long since stopped complaining about all the twisting and sighing and elbow-throwing from Lil Wom's side of the bed and had gone to sleep. Lil Wom's mind was plagued by gaps. Her family. The vision. The reality. She only had sketches and fragments, none of which gave her a place to enter.

Her longings for her blood and for understanding and recognition of self melded with the intensity between her thighs. However, now the body-shuddering vibrations that she could summon simply by squeezing her thighs together like a vice had a visual accompaniment: Tink. She clamped her eyelids down tight—tight as her thighs. Tink. What could he possibly do to make this feeling better? She just wanted, what? Some light touching. Like when she and Leria hugged each other in the stormhouse. Going into that cavern was like reentering a womb. She could smell the living Earth whose spirit seemed to ooze through the concrete walls of the roughly circular subterranean home.

During violent storms Ma Nell would collect all of them, like a mother hen does her chicks, and dodging thunder claps they would duck down the cement steps to sit on assorted benches and chairs to raggedy for the house. When the thunderclaps sounded like the juking of exhilarated Gods, Lil Wom and Leria would curl into 1 another's arms like a large brown tulip. Sid would sit expressionless, gazing at the cement's cracks. Ma Nell would sing "The Storm is Passing Over" in an attempt to assuage the electric power of fertility. Ma Nell's voice became visual, a magenta, violet, ocher palliative. It took on comforting hands, and like a mother soothing a fretful child, Ma Tynell would put the storm to breast and calm it.

It was a gift all of them possessed. Lil Wom let the halleluyas crescendo from her throat, and she knew her power. But she loved the damp force, the sky's unseen shudders, and the streaking electricity—so much like that she summoned between her legs. She thrilled at the feel of her clitoris singing haaaleeeeluuuuuYAA!

Tink.

Yes, let the storm dampen then drench her.

When Lil Wom saw the blood coming down her knees, she wasn't afraid because Leria was already menstruating.

"This here makes me a woman," Leria had boasted.

"How?"

"You gon follow suit soon. But when you get this blood, you gots to be careful cuz you can get a baby."

"How?"

"Messin round wit boys."

"How?"

Leria just ginned.

Since Leria had no real answers, Lil Wom assumed there were none. When she got her period, she, like Leria, made rags from old clothes, placed them in her panties, scrubbed them, dried them and went on.

Messin round? What was it? Leria and James was always pettin and thrashing. From the stormhouse to back behind the barn to over across the creek. They played so much, Leria had started growin plump.

What was it?

Now Tink was a regular on the place. Sid referred to him as "tha knotty head nigger."

"Who's tha knotty head nigga there shuckin corn?"

"Sid, you know ol Tink," Leria laughed to soften the insult.

"Evenin, sir, just came to call and saw they was sh"

"*Some*body here," Sid informed the rafters, "got damn near a wife on McGaha Hill. He can only be round here for trouble."

Sid would come from work like that, signifying bout Tink and Zula Preston, the red-bone his folks and her folks wanted him to marry. After embarrassing Tink, Sid would curse his way into the house.

Sid spoke the truth. But Tink wanted Lil Wom. It just seemed something, well, promising was behind her eyes; like plush green velvet grass or a cloud kissed by the moon. He wanted to penetrate her mystery.

"Comere girl. I won't hurt you."

She went. The corn tassels offered a pollen dust promise.

"I love ya, Lil Wom."

Lil Wom gazed into eyes looking like time. She saw herself reflected over and over in the convex orbs until she saw an ocean, a tree, lead, and jagged teeth.

"Lay down."

She was almost the same color as the Earth and just as fertile. The hands touching her head felt her slight fever, fingered her hair tucked neatly in catch-n-catch. When the damp lips sucked her very young nipples, Lil Wom closed her eyes and saw a man and woman loving near a stream. She felt breath, wind on her exposed lips, felt the sun kissing them, fingers fondling. She heard Tink exclaim, "Oh! It's beautiful!" she massaged his scalp as he offered her his deepest kisses. She spread her legs and welcomed the rhythms of reciprocity.

"I knowed this little heifer was gon be trouble! How m'I gonna feed another mouth? This here is a sin and a shame! This low do"

"Sid, now," Ma Nell stood before the inferno of a man and placed her palms on his breast plate, "now, life is a part of life. How you get here?" she smiled, trying to soothe him. "She's gon be a mother just like Leria," Tynell smiled at her daughter who was nursing her 3-year-old daughter, Hawa. "She gon be a mother just like your mother."

He stepped back, free of Nell's hands, and looked at her as if her head had bloomed flowers, "What? Is your mind broke? My Momma was married 2 years fo she had me!" He was appalled at the comparison.

"Yes. True," Nell spoke just above her breath. "But what of Ned?"

"You gon follow this bitch in the wilderness, ya keep on—heah?"

She went to the Booneville bridge. She was too proud to go begging, so she took her 5-months-pregnant self to the bridge.

When she made her pallet her first night under the bridge, she was rippling with rage. The heat her anger generated was such that the tears she cried evaporated before they could roll down her cheeks. By the time she gave birth, she had grown as cold as the winter nights she shivered through and as hard as the bridge's cement.

After cutting the cord with her teeth and washing her child with rainwater she collected to survive, she brought the child to her breast. She gritted her teeth against suck suck sucking of the life that was draining her own.

But Lil Wom fed her child.

She fed her child, but she felt very little for her. Bitterness was the ruling emotion in her bosom: She blamed her daughter for her predicament.

Not long after Lil Wom gave birth, Nell gave Sid and his high-handed holier-than-thou hypocrisy the boot; he was only a poor replacement for Sam anyway, let Nell tell it. Nell looked back on the relationship and couldn't understand how she had allowed a man to run the most vulnerable person in the bottoms out of the only home she knew. Lil Wom had so little, so little that hadn't been burned to the ground, buried in the Earth, or turned to wind-riding ash. And Nell, the closest thing she had to a parent, had driven her out of the closest thing she had to a home.

Nell, more than anyone, understood the outrage that led Lil Wom to and kept her under the bridge, so Nell went to the bridge and begged Lil Wom back home.

The women tried to mend their relationship, but unspoken rage, resentment, and guilt papered the walls of each room and rested under the women's tongues.

Despite the fact that Tink went through with his arranged marriage to Zula, he swore he loved Lil Wom and promised to fight for her and his child, but he never had the chance. When Lil Wom was 4 months pregnant, Tink died an inexplicable death. Some said a stingray stung him to death while he was swimming. Others asked if a stingray could live in a chlorine pool. Others asked if a sting from a stingray left 3 pin-prick holes. Whodo.

By the time Lil Wom was back with Nell, Tink was buried, and Leria and James had married and moved to Michigan with their daughter Hawa. With Leria gone, Lil Wom developed a friendship with Zula that was most logical: They loved Tink and that love drew them together.

Lil Wom's daughter also united the women. Zula doted on the baby girl, which is what she called her: "Babygirl" with reverence, like it was a title. Zula praised every bubble of spit she blew and jubilated over the child's every step, stumble, and spin.

One summer day Lil Wom gazed at Zula as she taught her daughter "Miss Mary Mack," and Lil Wom knew she was looking at her daughter's mother.

Lil Wom gave her daughter to Zula, who raised her like she was her own. It was more fitting than ironic that Zula and Tink had had no child but that Zula would raise Tink's only child. Zula took the Babygirl with her when she moved to Moline.

With no responsibilities, Lil Wom was free to explore the void that Tink had opened in her and that had expanded under the bridge of excision and survival.

She returned to visit the bridge that she had called home for 12 months. When she turned her eyes from the pain and loneliness that yawned under the steel and concrete, she decided she was now "Conch" because she would always have a home: No 1 could kick her out of her self.

Conch placed the quickly etched new self over the unanswered questions, pain, and loneliness that made up the original 1. She cemented the new construction in place with a stream of lovers. But no matter how fantastic, uncommitted, caring, or hasty her lovers were, the void widened.

Dissatisfied with herself, she took up data processing at Central Community College. With her associate degree, Conch became the first African American hired at Rassmin Accounting. She narrowed the stream to 2 lovers, but she still found no way to fill her void.

Conch kept expanding the superficial areas of her life so she wouldn't have to look inside. She never mentioned Zula or her child, and they were never mentioned to her. Conch allowed herself to think she had forgotten about the life nourished on bitterness under the bridge. Eventually it was as if it all occurred in different era to another person.

When she returned to Bliss Bluff after having lived a decade in Atlanta, the shrine had long since been dismantled. But Hawa and Danta re-erected it. It was nothing but a tractor tire, water, conch shells, and a catfish to many, but to Conch it was a long-buried truth. When Conch looked into the water and saw Yemoja, healing and re-membering flowed like the Niagara.

Conch's cement cracked and disintegrated and left her not with rubble but with promise. Her child was coming out of the wilderness, out from under the bridge, out of exile, home.

Badu and Ahni welcomed a set of fraternal twins. Ah and Aha flowed from Ahni's vagina as smoothly as her amniotic fluid. Although they were fraternal twins, they were identical in every aspect but gender. The children, fully empowered with 12 emi, were the embodiment of Ahni's wisdom.

The Ah received the twins with quiet reverence for it was obvious that these children were not reincarnations or returning elders—they were divine forces straight from the cosmos. Upon birth they were cognizant of everything around them and they could communicate astrally and orally. They preferred spiritual communication.

The twins were not educated; they were educators. They were sentinels. They could sit quietly and observe what was happening in their terrestrial time and space and in as many as 6 other terrestrial and cosmic locales.

As Ahni brought her twins to her breasts so that they could imbibe the milk of existence, she realized that after they weaned themselves, they would not take nutrients orally. Ah and Aha would absorb nutrients and energy from their environment, just as cosmic entities do.

The twins' arrival reflected the prosperity of Dgn. The site boasted 320 members of various ages and emilevels. They lived off of what the land provided. They planted diverse crops as well as flora to awaken and magnify emi.

Dgn was both library and university of Ah. Knowledge keepers and wisdom workers of various levels, skill sets, and capacities gave instruction on history, medicine, astral travel, physical flight, survival skills, and aesthetic-kinesthetic arts.

Dgn was the nucleus and point of crystallization of Ah. It was the work of the Ah of Dgn to record, gauge and assist the work of all Ah; consequently, collectives from Dgn would travel astrally or physically to

Minnah, Kumba, Nashville, Alapaha, and Bliss Bluff as necessary to obtain data and share strategies.

As Dgn flourished and manifested its intended destiny, the entire emisite and all its inhabitants would shift from terrestrial to astral states. There was so much assistance to give and so much to share that spiritual mobility was the only way to effectively undertake the Work. This mobility also protected the Dgn, for the Ogo-oriented who sought to infiltrate Dgn could see the city flourishing from afar, but they could never actually enter the city. As they approached the site, all of Dgn would shift into the astral realm and, thus, become invisible to mortals.

Dgn became the source of legends, tall-tales, myths, and fables for some Yurugu. For other, Dgn became an obsession. Many Yurugu were swallowed by the Sahara in their quest to visit and obtain the secrets of Dgn.

In 1 year, Ah and Aha had grown to the size of children of 12 years of age. They were quiet in the terrestrial realm and pensive and observant in astral realms.

As the twins grew, the Ah of Dgn experienced exponential spiritual expansion. Knowledge and skills were attained more quickly. Physical flight, which normally took weeks to learn, was mastered in hours. The flora and fauna of the world opened their spirits and sang out their force from all curves of the Earth. New cures and poisons were concocted and disseminated among the Ah. The twins brought with them an exponential boost in individual and collective power.

They sat in a triangular formation. The silence and intensity was palpable. 2 sets of eyes were focused on her but she was looking inward.

"Who do you want to be with?"

"You have to choose."

She looked alternately at both of them and told them the honest to Ahni truth: "I choose both of you."

The gang summit had been a success. The community embraced the lyrical stylings of the young men, and the young men, understanding the real struggle against a common foe and for communal elevation, united. Vice Lords and Black Gangster Disciples were united in Ah. But to outside observers and to the uninitiated within the organizations, it seemed as if business were usual. It was Xavier who had convinced Azure that camouflaging the unification with customary "gang activity" was essential to the Work.

"I never thought I would see such a day or live to be part of it," Xavier's excitement was high as he recalled the summit. "I couldn't believe it! The audience in the middle, F.O.L.K.S. on the right, People on the left, everyone alternately taking the podium."

"The seating arrangement was for our safety," Azure stressed. "I know what *my* agenda is, but there are other agendas."

"Word, it was dope and necessary: but it also symbolized the division that we effectively united.

"But, Loco, when you acted out your piece? Man, I saw tears in elders' eyes! How did you think of that?"

"It just came to me as I sat there. Something I had to do," Lil Loco answered Xavier, but he wouldn't look at him. He had no love or respect for or interest in Xavier. It was not that he was too young for Azure; it was not that he was VL; it was not that X and Azure were close and he seemed to be forced to make a way into her life; it was all of that and more.

"Kinda like the call to church, hun? Juba on Jubalee!" Xavier laughed, Azure laughed too. She had never seen him so open.

With his offering at the summit, Xavier freed himself from his grief over the losses of Big Red and his father, and he ushered everyone in the audience into an evolved state of corrected collective consciousness.

Xavier stood before a projector, and, with pointer in hand, the Vice Lord expounded on BGD iconography: "The Black Gangster Disciples' emblem is the 6 point star. Each point has a specific meaning: Love, Life, Loyalty, Wisdom, Knowledge and Understanding," as Xavier identified each point of the star, the audience looked at him with mouths agape wondering where he was headed. What was a VL doing discussing BGD symbols?

"These concepts, together, form the way of the BGDs, the cornerstones of the organization: love, life, loyalty, wisdom, knowledge, and understanding. The Yoruba would describe these principles as the ìwà, the character of the BGDs; they may even marvel and say of them, 'aikú pari ìwà: immortality is the perfect manifestation of existence,' because on the exoteric level, the BGDs are promoting their individual and group immortality by living this code, this orí or destiny." Brothers and sisters nodded, and, although still anxious, they let Lil X continue dropping knowledge.

"On an esoteric level, the Black Gangster Disciples' immortality and perfected existence lies in their retention of ancient Yoruba philosophy, science, and symbolism. The 6 point star of the BGDs is the symbolic embodiment of Odùduwà, progenitor of the Yoruba: the Black Star who fell to the Earth.

"The pitchforks jutting out of the 6 point star are symbolic of Èṣù Ẹlẹ́gbára the creative trickster who speaks all languages, who carries messages through the divine crossroads of human and spiritual existence, who protects and destroys as necessary. These pitchforks are the key symbols of the BGDs." Here, Xavier threw his hands up and crossed them over his chest. He pointed his middle fingers while curving his thumbs and index fingers outward at the joints and inward at the tips. When he did this, VLs and BGDs stood up, shouted, "What the fuck," and threatened, "Watch yoself, now!" and in many ways made their disapproval clear. But X continued.

"It is when the BGDs ask an unknown person who maybe a mark to 'spit literature,' that we recognize their true African impetus. The Yoruba word for spoken word is ̀ọ̀rọ̀. But in addition to this mundane translation is the spiritual meaning of Ọ̀rọ̀, which is 'a matter that is something that is the subject of discussion, serious concern or action.'

For both the Yorubas and the BGDs, Ọ̀rọ̀, spitting literature, is the physical, cosmic, active manifestation of the spoken word. The Yoruba say that 'the Ọ̀rọ̀ that drops from the elderly [we call them wisdom tooths or old heads or O.G.s] is stupendous.' It is with the knowledge of the elders who have now become ancestors, that we begin to comprehend the African source of BGDs iconography as it relates to their tenets of wisdom, knowledge, and understanding.

"Rowland Abiodun, Yoruba scholar and art historian, informs us that 'Olódùmarè, the Creator, fashioned Họ̀ọ̀, from a melding of ọgbọ́n, imọ̀, and òye.' Ọgbọ́n is wisdom, imọ̀ is knowledge, and òye is understanding: These are 3 of the BGDs' defining elements. Abiodun reveals that Olódùmarè used these powers because they are 'most important forceful elements of creation.' However, it is not until Họ̀ọ̀-rọ̀ of Ọ̀rọ̀, the spoken word as manifest with physicality, action, cosmic energy and force, came to Earth that wisdom, knowledge and understanding could result in love, life, and loyalty.

"The confluence of love, life, loyalty, wisdom, knowledge, and understanding foments holistic existence, verbal and visual art, and power. Depending on your affiliation, you may call this confluence of power conjure, Hoodoo, Àjẹ́, àṣẹ, or ẹ̀mí. All is 1, and this is why the symbols and messaging of the BGDs and VLs flow seamlessly with the spiritual systems of Voodoo and Hoodoo. The source is the same.

The same confluence of power gives us proverbs, orature, riddles, and the ability to spit the literature of our organizations. The word is our power; the word is the foundation for our acquisition of wisdom, knowledge, and understanding; and the word is the source from whence our immortality springs.

"Unfortunately, rather than allow our wisdom, knowledge, and understanding to manifest in love, life, and loyalty to 1 another, we have fragmented, divided, and destroyed each other for the benefit of the beast. Our Họ̀ọ̀-rọ̀, our Nommo, has become meaningless jargon or introductions to senseless slaughter.

"But the tools, the pitchfork, the heart, the wings of ascension are ours. 360° are awaiting our return. And Love, Life, Loyalty, Wisdom, Knowledge, and Understanding are as close to our grasp as this," here X went, with tears in his eyes, and embraced the killer of Big Red, Lil Loco.

Standing amongst the crowd, and flanked by straight hard legs either struggling to hide their tears or letting them flow freely, Lil X, a young buck knowledging elders, looked deeply into Lil Loco's eyes and those of everyone in the room as he continued: "We are so rich, we are full of power, but because we believe another's lies instead of our eternal truths we have annihilated thousands of much-needed warriors.

"Èṣù sent us through the crossroads, but he also traversed them with us. Indeed, Èṣù is symbolized by pitchforks that are emblematic of both the BGDs and, by inversion, the VLs.

"It is said when the forks are pointed up," here Xavier made the hand sign of the BGDs with his right hand, "Èṣù's work is good. When pointed down, as when the Vice Lords symbolize death to the Disciples," he made the same pitchfork pointed downwards with his left hand and stood on the platform signaling both gangs—a mark? No Èṣù, the crossroads—"Èṣù's work is for evil. Same sign, same brothers, confused meanings and motivations.

"We are unified by Èṣù, who has also confused our minds so that the brother in red slays the 1 in blue. This also happened eons ago, when 2 best friends, who swore they would never part, nearly killed 1 another because Èṣù rode between them in glorious robes wearing an exquisite cap. The cap was red on 1 side and blue on the other. Because the 2 friends lived on opposite sides of the road, each 1 only saw 1 side and 1 color of the hat.

When the friends met and discussed the exquisite dress of the traveler, they began to argue over the color of the hat, with 1 friend swearing it was red and the other so sure the hat was blue he was willing to fight to prove it. Just before the friends prepared to fight to the death over the color of a hat, Èṣù travelled back down the road, doffed his headpiece, and showed it to the friends. After revealing his 2-toned riddle, Èṣù spit most necessary literature: Take the utmost care when swearing oaths, and always examine all sides of an issue. He went away laughing.

"Èṣù is still laughing with and crying for us. We all have the blues from pouring red blood from our Black bodies at his crossroads. Èṣù has accepted the sacrifices and the ignorance that produced them. But I have solved another of the God's riddles: I was a VL. I see the power and richness of myself and of my former enemies the BGDs, and it is the same." He looked into Loco's eyes. "We are the same.

"I have been standing at the crossroads with Èṣù sharing this wisdom with you. Now, I am walking through those crossroads, and I am expecting all my Black and shining Warrior Gods to stroll with me. In Peace."

For 7 heartbeats no 1 moved or spoke. But then, 1 by 1, hard legs rose from their seats, crossed the aisle and embraced their brothers. There was no need for apologies or explanations. Men showing their love for themselves, their communities, and their futures was all Ah needed.

"Now. Let's Jubah!" The celebration of life featuring praise, puling, weeping, exultation, and prayer commenced, born of memories of shin bones knocking, figure callings, washtub bass strumming, cake walk strutting, mouth harps humming, antelopes bucking, ululations spiraling, harmonicas growling, and body drums heralding the Gods adorned with the cosmos' own soul.

Spirits smiling talkin bout hambone, hambone, have ya heard? Grinnin bout beats boxed out of the mouths of those kicked out of school. Invocations pounded out during detention on desks carved with the symbols and codes of Divinities.

It's freestyle rapping; it's up on toppa chairs jumping; it's asses shaking; it is the resonance of skin pounding skin. It's a resurrected click-song. The drums outlawed by Ogo roll out from mind to body to center court. Anyone feeling a vibe straddles their instrument of choice like a lover and coaxes out rhythms. The only color visible in the profusion of vibrational harmony is the glory of melanated resurrection climaxing towards perfection. Ooo, Jubaahhh!

Mo Jubah. Ah Jubah. Oh Jubah. Mo Jubah. Ah Jubah. Oh Jubah.

It went on all night callin passersby in off the streets. The night train rolled; clouds of skun rose and took travelers on high. The spirit ebbed and soared towards the midnight sky.

A week later Xavier was still feeling the rhythms flowing from the collective on that night of healing. As he sat in Azure's living room, he gazed at Lil Loco and while he wished the brother could push his pain aside like the other BGDs had done, he was not going to sacrifice his new-found peace, or his love for Azure, for that to occur. Xavier sighed and gazed at the discomfited warrior who'd just emerged from the dudgeon and was beginning to shine. Lil Loco would have to come to Ah in his own time.

"Anyway, Azure," Xavier squeezed her high up on the thigh. Although he already had her attention, he wanted to make a claim. She smiled at him, shined on him, "our next move has got to be a careful 1. We can't go around broadcasting gang unity because if we do"

"More brothers will live. More mothers will have peace. Children can play outside. . . Why would we keep this a secret?" Azure furrowed her brow.

"Not only must we publicize our unity, but we need to act quickly or all of this work will slide into the sewer. I won't allow that," Lil Loco was trying to put his foot down: Man of the house; man of the woman.

"Well, if we go public, not only will the feds scatter us, but the young bucks who aren't of the way will undo what we're trying to do." He paused and looked at both of them with excitement, "Don't you see? We've got to keep things tight. We'll be working toward the way covertly, but to the outside, chaos must reign as usual. There is no way we can celebrate unity outwardly, not and fully manifest. We gotta keep our Juba to ourselves."

"He's right, King," she admitted to Loco. She turned to Xavier, "You're right. What do you suggest?"

"Everything needs to appear to be business as usual. Everything will be the same—but no more killings."

"And what about the brothers slanging?" Loco challenged.

"We'll be out on the streets empty-handed but filled with wisdom, knowledge, and understanding. We will spread word among the brothers who didn't attend the summit so that more warriors can join us. This will also keep us from contributing to the prison economy, cause we won't be holding.

"While a lot of brothers are slanging for glamour, some need to eat. The struggle to feed 1's self has landed many a brother back in jail or prison. I think we need to implement the way of the Panthers. We need to make our community, our Nation, self-sufficient. We need our own gardens, livestock, and schools right here in Carver. Let's put these abandoned lots to work for us!"

Azure's eyes lit up. She was caught in Xavier's rapture.

"We can build our own schools; teach our children the way," he continued. "Prepare the coming generations for the work they will do."

"Kids ain't learning shit in school anyway," Loco agreed, "it's a place where different gangs organize and where girls and boys prepare to make babies. I follow you," Azure smiled at Lil Loco. He was becoming more excited about the Work than his position in her life: That's what she wanted.

"This has to be a truly communal effort—" Xavier paused and looked at Azure, "how many Malareans are ready?"

"Well, I think we have 14 serious people we can depend on."

"We also need to till the grassroots. We need teachers, farmers, rootworkers, we all need the wisdom we can gather. We need come-unity."

"Speak, brother."

"But the most important thing we can do, and I think the Ah of Kng and Alapaha can help us with this, is to end the addiction among all Ah. We need to get the chemicals out of our way; they block the cipher."

"That is such an important call, X," Azure couldn't help but see the man in a new light: He was wholly illuminated. "That can definitely be arranged. It will take time though. And what I'm thinking is that we can still buy and destroy the drugs to keep the feds off our backs. We have enough funds to camouflage for about 7 months."

"As long as their stats stay the same, we'll be cool for a while. But insteada destroying the drugs, let's bury em. No telling who or what might dig em later," Zave raised a telling eyebrow.

"Word," Lil Loco assented. "And we can set up a Neighborhood Watch and a Neighborhood Garden. Those are reasonable outgrowths of the summit. But what we will be doin on the sly," he looked at the pair, "is some serious stockpiling."

He was living with her and loving her but he wanted their bond to be husband and wife, not through some beast and a book, but a melding of souls. But he had been away from her so long, and she had changed in so many ways.

In the early days of his arrival, he knew her thoughts were beyond him, like she was waiting for something or thinking of something that she could not share with him because she could not name it. He realized she had another life. Sometimes she would be gone. For hours. When she should have been out of school, cooking, or studying he would call and find she was not at home or couldn't be reached.

Immediately after his release, he started working at Kemetic Visions bookshop. For an ex-con and felon to land a job was miraculous in America. But while the job freed him of many of the worries that came with parole, as much as he loved to read, the job didn't fulfil him. He felt like he was just marking time.

He had started meditating and fasting in prison. He continued outside, not only to control himself and understand how his life would now take shape, but to develop his inner being. He felt that his spirit needed restructuring, as if it, as if he were preparing for something.

Loco gradually learned more about the woman Azure had become through her work, which consumed her. It took him some time to get used to Alteveze and Saddiq. At first he felt alienated when they were all together. But he loosened up when he found that the books they were studying for class were the same ones that he had read and analyzed in the joint. His analyses were deeper than theirs, and the students often took notes from his postulations. But Lil Loco looked on the college students with a bit of envy. They had their direction: He was a man at the crossroads. He would never go back to the old life but he didn't have a new 1. Yet.

The reception he was given and the respect he was shown by Azure reassured him. But the way his work was received at the summit astounded him. Loco was even more amazed by the fact that his contribution was unrehearsed; he actually didn't remember much of it upon finishing. When he, Alteveze, Azure, and Saddiq watched the DVD, he was mesmerized by himself. The gestures, movements, and lyrical flow—all of it was profound. He became 2 persons, a Vice Lord and a Disciple, and the changes in tone, lingo, cadence, and inflection were remarkable. And the conclusion, when he embraced himself/enemy and died/become immortalized in that embrace, was so powerful that grown men sank to their knees.

It was as if the timing of his release and the reading were ordained because his F.O.L.K.S., including City G, Big Time, and Baby Blue were all there. When he saw them, older and harder, but cutting a path out of the madness, he wept. They embraced Lil Loco and celebrated both his release and his lyrical masterpiece.

And the brothers of Big Red? At first the tension in the room was overwhelming. Even after Azure stood up and asked everyone to observe a moment of silence for the ancestors who had gone before them: "Some of the younger folk may not know what we've gone through. When we rely on the beast for knowledge of self, we are left with a ignorant and fragmented self. That's what Jubalee is about.

"They confined our strong limbs with chains and scarred our shining skins with cat-o-9 tails. They branded us like we were cattle. When we were enslaved, we had nothing but our divine selves, and we were taught that they were nothing. But we used ourselves to free ourselves. From day 1. We plotted schemed, planted roots, killed, and strategized to be free. And when this nation decided war was the only determiner of our economic state, we took up arms, officially this time, to be free.

"When the battle was finished and liberation was formalized, the beast was so wicked, so dependent upon us, that they didn't tell many of us. Some of us were still enslaved up until 1870. Rather than a 'shot heard round the world' we spread knowledge of freedom via bush telegram, also known as word of mouth. It was primarily in the month of June in the teen days that mouths spread the word, and the power of the word was accompanied by celebration, praise, exultation, release, and relief: Juba. Jubalee. Juneteenth is OUR holiday. We pay homage to those brave Tahn who made Ah of us possible."

In addition to invoking forerunners like Ganga Zumba, Dessalines, and Ol Nat, and recent ancestors like Malice Green and incarcerated and exiled elders like Mumia Abu Jamal, Leonard Peltier, Mutulu Shakur, and Assata Shakur, Azure asked everyone present to lift in light "the souls of Belle Booker and her son Catty. As we all know, Nashville's Finest shot Momma Booker and her 9-year-old son in their backs 1 week ago today: why? They were suspected of having weapons. But Catty's hands were empty and Ms. Belle was holding a handkerchief.

"Ms. Belle and Catty are the latest victims of Walking-While-Black. They were walking 4 blocks home after visiting Ms. Belle's sister, and the pigs used them for target practice.

"Ms. Belle is your mother; Catty is your son. We are the Bookers. Literally. This can happen to any of us at any time because our killers know they enjoy immunity. They kill us with impunity and will continue to do this until we rise up and say 'No More!'

"As we embrace their souls, we must meditate on the fact that too many of us are killed because we are manifestations of the Creators' perfection. And too many of us are killing each other because we don't recognize our power and glory." Here, Azure looked boldly from the BGD to the VL factions.

"We must begin formulating ways of defending ourselves that do not include useless marches and tired songs. As El Hajj Malik El Shabazz made plain, if you are singing 'We Shall Overcome' in the 20th century, your government has failed you. I submit that if you are holding die-ins in the 21st century, you've failed yourself.

The time for speeching, singing, praying, protesting, and swaying is over. We must access the military genius of Boukman, Nat Turner, Zumbi, Nanny, the Panthers, and Ògbóni. Because we are, indeed, at war but not with ourselves. Not anymore."

Even after Azure's invocation, after everyone passed around a bottle of gin and poured libation to the ancestors, even after Saddiq rose and asked for a moment of contemplation, during which everyone should consider the value of their lives and those of the individuals they have hurt, maimed, and/or killed in their lifetimes—the tension was still palpable.

But then Big Red's killer took the podium, and he acted out his adversary's life and death. Loco ended his dramatic interpretation chanting:

>The Blues of being used is what connects
>　us, Blood
>The Blues of being fools is what connects
>　us, Blood
>The Blues of all being is what connects
>　us, Blood
>that and the fact that we are Gods, Black

VLs and BGDs took the stage, embraced 1 another, and swore a truce, and more important, a healing.

The goal was to build on the positivity. And that they did. Every Monday morning at 9 they met at the Carver Homes Community Center to discuss their direction. No 1 was in charge or the head of these meetings because hierarchy was unnecessary and would have caused conflicts. Everyone sat in a circle and flowed as equals.

"We all know why we are here," Alteveze began, her dreds, gathered at the crown of her head, cascaded down her shoulders like a waterfall of soft obsidian. "It is not that we are killing each other as much as the fact that we are being killed. We have historically, from the days of slavery to those of

Malcolm and Martin, spent so much time accusing and abusing 1 another that we were looking the wrong way when the real enemy cut us down.

"Now, some of us may wonder, what are these students doing here? This ain't their community and it ain't their business. But this is our community. We are 1 people. We need to heal and grow together so that we can rise together. When you look at me Azure, Saddiq, and Dr. Sims, see us as brothers and sisters. That is how we see you. And that is how we all need to see 1 another."

Alteveze was amazed at the way things were taking shape and her role in it all. She and Saddiq were in Carver when they weren't in class, and even during class they were drafting plans for the community. Her life was on an entirely different road from what she envisioned 3 years ago. Rather than tease Azure for "hanging out" in Carver, she was seeking shining brothers and sisters at Malare and taking them to Carver to assist in the Work.

"Sister-daughter, thank you for your truths," Sylvia Wilson rose as she addressed Alteveze. She wore a rose bazine dashiki with gold embroidery and matching pants. Goddess braids swirled around her head.

She had been at the Juba along with Simone, Siddar, and Saddia. She had to come, not only because Azure was essentially her daughter now, but because she was seeing the larger communal spiritual vision of the 60s unfold again with 1 big difference, Ah. In Azure, with her quiet passion, she saw more direction and force than in all of SNCC. She did not just want to be a part of what was occurring; she had to be a part of it.

A woman started appearing to her in her dreams again, just like in the 70s. The woman was nearly indistinguishable from the night and had hair as big as the cosmos. She held out her arms in an embrace that promised eternity. Sylvia went to the Mother in rapture, nestled in her breasts and smiled deep inside. The Mother was the same as in the 70s, but now she whispered, "The time has come, Daughter." Sylvia was ready.

"When I see you, Alteveze, I see myself. I was college student in the 60s, and I left the university for the real work of the revolution. I was a member of SNCC, the Student Non-Violent Coordinating Committee, just as they adopted self-defense. Our work, right here in Nashville, consisted of food drives and breakfast programs so the children would go to school with nourishment for the body and mind. We had a community garden of 5 acres, and we established a sickle cell testing center and a prison visitation shuttle.

"Back then, there was collaboration between the communities and universities: Had to be; they was killing and arresting us all. I was locked down 5 times." She paused, she didn't know what had compelled her to begin speaking, pouring out her life, but it felt cathartic.

"I met my husband, Raymond Wilson, then. Some of y'all may remember him. He took a rifle to the roof of Piccadilly Café, there off of

Murphreesboro Pike, and killed as many oppressors as he could fore they shot him down.

"See, me and Raymond, we saw our work be sabotaged, we fed our children milk poisoned by the CIA. We heard about the poisoned cheese just in time to destroy it, but many children in other communities died behind that. When these tactics wasn't enough, Hoover and the United Snakes government brought in crack.

"We fought against it. But it overpowered so many of us. We were so strong and powerful—" Sista Sly reminisced about the warriors. "They used that drug to cut us down. We looked up 1 morning and brothers and sisters were rolling in the gutters riding little white balls.

"I've lived all the changes. I remember when the Conservative Vice Lords went from being a social organization to a version of the Panthers. Somehow it got twisted and they began killing the community over crack.

"Anyone," She glanced at her son, "anyone involved in slanging is only working to advance the objectives of the same people who killed Malcolm, Martin, Lumumba, Bobby Hutton, and Sankara.

"We have got to find a way out of this madness, and it won't be easy. Far as we know," she gazed round the circle, "there are govment agents in here now." Murmurs of protest bubbled through the audience. "Naw, I'm speaking the truth. We can't hide the facts: every major killing, every set up of our leaders has been orchestrated by an informer acting like a comrade. We've got to be careful because the way we can manifest now is much more powerful than what we could do in the 60s.

"You all know me and now you know more of me. My husband and son were and are caught up in the game, on 2 different ends, albeit. But right here, surrounded by a highway and a railroad track and a dead end road to lock us in if shit gets hot and the martial law is implemented, right here, in this urban cage, with 1 way in and 1 way out, right here, we can rev up the cycle of revolution that was put into rotation so long ago and end the reign of the beast."

Sylvia took her seat to applause and to promises to work with her to make the revolution a reality.

"Most uh y'all know me," a brother in a heavily starched cream-hued denim suit and matching baseball cap rose. He had a freshly styled goatee. There were a few silver whiskers in his beard that did exactly what the stereotype said they did, enhance his distinguished character. "I'm Sack Daddy," he rose to his full height, legs slightly bowed. He had gravelly malice in his voice, but compassion laced his eyes.

"Shtack! Shtack!" brothers yelled out.

"I'm an O.G., as in original and old," he chuckled at himself. Many ladies crossed and uncrossed their legs, ready to testify that he could out perform any young buck. "And I done outlived the statistics, right? I just wanna say: I'm ready for the new direction we's workin towards. But it may be easy to get a nigga up outta the skreets—and into the cemetery—but it ain't so easy to get the skreets up outta niggas. So, I say all this here to say, we got to be careful. Lot's uh people had good intentions. We gots to have more than that. We gots to be true to ourselves; fuck the game and the gang. We have got to be serious about this Work. I just wanna say, I'm in.

"I have done mine. Ain't gonna lie about it. Y'all know me."

"Represent!"

"All MIGH Tee!"

"But right now, we need to be about 2 things: evolution and revolution.

"See, I was part of the Conservative Vice Lords when we owned Chi-Town. Ms. Sylvia is right: We went from bourgeoisie and dap to activists to menaces of the hoods we used to protect. I don't know how they got our heads so bad, but I know only we can straighten us out.

"Now, some of y'all might think I'm soft cuz I'm old. But that ain't it. When I saw the potential at that Juba, mmm mm! I saw the warriors we *spose* to be, fore they put chains on our necks and round our minds. Now I'm ready to spark the liberation so that can be the *Gods* we spose to be."

Any VLs who were on the fence before Sack began speaking now had both feet beside his in the grassroots of the struggle.

"I just got up out the joint," Blue Dog pulled his 5'4" tawny frame to its feet. "I was locked down for slanging. The funny thing is that the same folk who gave me the rocks is the same 1's who arrested me—just like KRS-1 raps in "Illegal Business": y'all check that song out. Between 3 strikes and multiplied sentences for rocks, it's just a matter of time before you locked down.

"You think you making money slanging? Think about how much the police departments, cities, and states, and the state, federal, and private prisons make off of us. They got us in the go-along!" Blue shook his head, "Slangin and bangin ain't get me nowhere. The lil money I made might as well uh been grains uh sand. In other words, we riskin our lives and killin and dyin for absolutely nothing. Nothing.

"Revolution means 'change.' I'm here to work for that—a complete change, an overthrow of this system—cause it is designed to do 1 thing: destroy us."

As Dr. Roper stood up to address the collective, she smiled and revealed the classic Senegambian beauty mark of "open teeth." She had the height and grace of Phyllis Hyman melded with the resolve of Nikki Giovanni. Dr. Roper, like Dr. Sims, was 1 of the few Malare professors who was shining and who felt the summoning throb of the emisite.

"Some of us at Malare have been digging this community for a while," she revealed. "Many of us wanted to reach out but didn't see a place to fit in. To be honest, many of us were afraid. We had become such a fragmented people that it seemed safer, easier, and logical to remain isolated in the halls of 'academe' than to reach out.

"I commend Azure, Xavier, Alteveze for reuniting communities and people who never should have been divided, because, as Alteveze has made clear, we are 1 people. Now we have 1 objective.

"It is vital for us to understand that this revolution will be of a different character. We don't need to march to the capital with guns, we don't need to speechify and signify and we can't. We can't let our oppressors know how we are operating. No. Through silent covert action we can destroy the edifices and institutions built to enslave us, and liberate and elevate our Pan-African Nation."

Lil Loco stood and addressed the assembly, "I thank everyone for coming and participating in this meeting and committing to the Work. Thursday night at 9 we will meet here to organize and strategize."

Mrs. Wilson was right, anybody could claim to be a comrade, Loco had mused when he decided to close the meeting early. After the meeting, he met with Jah Sun and Saddiq that night and the 3 of them debugged and installed scramblers in the homes of the core cadre and in their meetings halls. After this, Loco arranged the skill-specific cells of Ah network.

Loco was down for the struggle, but the spiritual side of the Work had put him off. Herbs, meditation emisites, some Gods named Ah and Ahni. Azure told him that the spiritual aspect was the literal rootwork—it was the foundation of the Carver build. But she never proselytized to him, she let the Work do the Work. When Lil Loco realized that African cosmologies and secret societies were the foundation of gangs, he became inspired. He had to admit that that Xavier *had* knowledged him, too.

He was also gaining knowledge as a result of working at Kemetic Visions. Although the job paid only minimum wage, he loved to read, and he got a 10% discount on books. Azure's already substantial library grew to include *Bad Blood, Our Mothers, Our Powers, Our Texts, Yurugu, Manifestations of Masculine Magnificence, The Pale Fox, The Psychopathic Racial Personality, The Architects of Existence, The Iceman's Inheritance, The Isis Papers, The New Jim Crow, Medical Apartheid, The Cultural Unity of Black Africa, Why Are We So Blest?*, and much more. But he still felt like has was lacking something, like the center of his being was empty.

Azure's bombshell filled his center—with rage:

"So what you sayin is that you fuckin me *and* him?"

"What I'm saying is that Xavier is part of me, part of us."

"What 'us'? the community or—"

"I mean *us*."

"This shit is mad. So you wanna have both of us and we supposed to—to—? Xavier, what do *you* think about this?" Loco turned to Xavier and looked right into his eyes.

Xavier had been sitting quietly through everything. Azure had been spending so much time at his place and at Carver that it became rare for him to relax with her at her place. It didn't seem strange because of the intensity of the Work, but last week she told him everything.

"Lil Loco is staying with me."

"So you wanna go back to him?" he kept his cool, fiddled with his 1-hitter and acted nonchalant.

"Well, he is living at my place. I love him. And Xavier, I love you. You are a part of me as much as he is," She didn't look at him because the whole thing was as confounding to her as it was to him.

"So what do we do? I won't sneak around. I can't be hiding from nobody. Shit ain't that tense. I mean, well, I don't have to tell you how much you mean to me and to my family. We are 1 now. But if it won't work out. . ."

"Xavier, remember when we had those dreams after we were poisoned?"

"I do."

"You dreamt"

                    "I dreamt of you and me and another dude and you carrying our babies."

"Well, it seems that we have entwined destinies," she walked to him and stroked his shoulders, "I know it's strange, but when I look into the future I see all of us as 1: I see you, Lil Loco, and me as 1."

"Well, I don't like the idea at all. I mean," he curled his lips in disgust, "how can I be expected to share you?"

She laughed and took his hand, "You may want to consider the fact that you have probably been sharing most of the girls you've been going out with, just like they've been sharing you. It is just that you didn't know or didn't care.

"That changes nothing. I want you—alone."

"I love you so much, God, but I think this goes beyond what we can imagine or understand—or control." She felt like she was being ripped in 2.

"Well," she continued after a long period silence, "I would like to invite you over to discuss this with Lil Loco."

"When? I mean, I hope this isn't a set up."

"If anybody is gon get set up, I guess it will be me.

"I don't know what may happen. I just know," she took his hand in hers, "that I want to be honest."

Azure sighed, "Next week. After finals?"

"Cool," Xavier stared ahead at the bookshelf. They sat in silence. The sky darkened and created shadows that engulfed them in a blue black haze. He turned to her. She had prepared her mouth for more explanations. She loved him. She knew she was born to build with him, but she felt the same thing for Lil Loco. She couldn't explain it but she would keep trying.

So she sat with excuses and sighs ready on her tongue but, really, all she had to do was offer her lips. That is what he wanted. Moist, full, and indescribably sensuous. Xavier's long slim fingers cupped her breasts and pinched her nipples. He was no longer surprised that she rarely wore undergarments, especially not under her large boubous. Today she wore a forest green 1 with burnt orange and gold adire.

He lifted the dress over her head and tossed it to the foot of the bed, and then he removed all of his clothing. He began kissing her kneebacks. He lifted her legs into the air, and sucked his way down her thighs. For a long time he nuzzled her flat belly then listened to her heart beating. They held 1 another until she shifted to suck his nipples and lick the edges of his belly button.

She wanted to be pregnant on this night. As she guided his penis into her vagina, that was her prayer: It was his too. Her waist beads said, "shring, shring, shring," answering their prayers.

"So you essentially get 2 husbands out of this, right?" Lil Loco's dry chuckles held no mirth.

"Well, you can describe it any way you choose, but to be honest, when I think of the 2 of you, there are no words to express the depth of my love." She didn't know whether to look at the God to the left of her or the 1 on the right, so she looked at her lap, which would soon be swollen with children.

Lil Loco was fin ta pop. He was bout ta snap. Never had he wanted so badly to manifest his name. He left Azure's crib enraged. Neither she nor Xavier tried to stop him or reason with him. That was wise. He wanted to choke out someone. Anyone. Now. His fingertips yearned for blood.

He strolled the streets looking for a victim. Some mean-mugging, posin, bitch ass, nigga. Pleeease send me a mark! He prayed. After a few blocks he slowed his murderous stalk. He stopped. He realized that everyone he encountered was focused. Directed. When people passed him, they greeted him, "Peace, God"; "Stay up"; or with simple nod and a smile, but they went forward on their missions. Everyone was working toward a goal. Even the loose laughter and signifying that he was accustomed to hearing was a front concealing a deeper communication.

Although the community looked the same—trash bags frolicked in gutters, dilapidated buildings leaned left, and used syringes waited to be stepped on—the community was actually clean. It was shining. Lil Loco could see the community's aura.

Everyone is building a new life and I'm fantasizing about death. About Murder. If the woman I love had tried to hug me 15 minutes ago, I would have tried to kill her. Why? Jealousy? Violation? He shook his head. No: Ego. Ego. Ego.

An African proverb about the strength and necessity of 3 cooking stones flashed through his mind, "Yeah, right," he scowled.

He went to Kemetic Visions. Ekundayo told him he could crash there as long as he needed to. Ekundayo offered Loco his spare bedroom, but Loco declined. He needed time with his thoughts.

He slept in the store's storage room for 3 days. Compared to his cell, the storage room with its air mattress, standing shower stall, and boxes of books was a palace. But while he was surrounded by books, he didn't read any. He didn't drown his sorrows in alcohol. He didn't eat anything. For 3 days he did nothing but exist.

When he unlocked the door, it was with no malice, anger, sadness, or agenda. Lil Loco was empty. The woman he loved? His future? His life? He didn't want to think thoughts he couldn't finish. He was lost. He sighed a heavy sigh and turned the knob.

"Would you like to meditate with us, King?" He jumped at her voice. He had come through the door expecting an empty house filled with her spirit, not her. Not her and her friends, all sitting cross-legged on the rug.

King? Hmp. He felt like a king in exile, a king dethroned. But her use of his honorific made him stand a bit straighter.

She smiled and motioned him into the circle. The space they made for him in between Alteveze and Saddiq put him directly in front of Azure. He closed his eyes; so too did everyone else, so no 1 saw the tears that slipped under his eyelids and down his cheeks.

She guided their meditation. She took them to a place of peace. The space had forest-green velvet grass surrounded by dense vegetation. The sky was cerulean blue, and a stream could be heard burbling in the distance. Lil Loco felt weightless. He was seated on the carpet of Azure's place but he felt the velvet of the grass. He smelled the fecund Earth but he also saw the 4 of them seated and himself rising and rising with them and then beyond them. The sky darkened as he rose and became 1 with the cosmos.

Lil Loco felt as if molten gold were being poured into his soul until it suffused the entirety of his being. He felt his body vibrate with power. A humming filled both his heads: his penis had never been harder; his mind had never been more clear, more focused.

My son! Welcome. Ahni's voice filled Lil Loco's head, his soul; it reverberated throughout his being. We have waited for you: We need you. The depth of her sincerity stunned him: He was needed.

You are Ra, my anointed child! With these words, Lil Loco felt his destiny enter and fill his being. He was whole.

He was Ra.

Welcome home, my Sun.

He was home.

Ra swirled and frolicked in the Womb of All. He was 1 of innumerable Gods thriving in the Womb of Existence. He understood his role in the cosmos and the cosmos' role within him.

Ra emerged from meditation healed emotionally and psychologically. The Mother had introduced him to his name, destiny, origin, and obligations. He was filled with weighty truths. Ra evolved light years beyond Lil Loco's resentment, isolation, confusion, jealousy, and ego. When the meditation concluded, he stood, embraced Azure, and was unashamed of his flowing tears.

"Welcome home, God," said Saddiq.

"Welcome to Ah revolution," Alteveze smiled.

"We have enough poetry to publish 2 volumes and there are 2 groups who are ready to go into the studio. Dr. Sims, you've got to hear Dem Godz. It is a collective of BGDs and VLs. The music is purely conscious hip hop and they are cold as ice! They gon wake up plenny young cats. The only things is" and here Alteveze's voice fell an octave, "I wish we still had radio access. I mean, we touched so many folks with that program! Heads was on alert."

"*Feds* was on alert. You are right that we had the Africana audience that we needed but we were too accessible and, therefore, subject to surveillance." Saddiq turned to Sims, "You know that we were poisoned, right?"

"What? No! When!" The alarm in her voice was purely that of a mother. "After the show?"

"Yep," he continued, "after the radio show and the first poetry reading we did. COINTELPRO II straight up slicked into Azure's crib and poisoned her honey. We were all drinking tea with honey after the reading and we liked to died."

"Wasn't for Ahni. . ." Alteveze shook her head.

"See, that's why I agree with Ra, you know that that's Loco's true identity, Ra, the Kemetic Netcher, well, I agree with Ra and Xavier: we need to lay low. We can get much more accomplished. On the dl, we can work and build unobserved. Our vibration is so strong, I am feeling tremors as close as NCU and as far as Chi-town." Saddiq stopped talking and cocked his head. He murmured to Alteveze, "Remind me to talk to Jah Sun about some new scramblers."

"Check."

"Hmp. This is too much," Dr. Sims mused, still pondering the attempted murder. "But you are right to refer to it as COINTELPRO II. Did you know that 1 of its main objectives was to prevent African Americans from contacting and building with Continental Africans?"

"More divide and conquer."

"They have always known what many of us have sought to deny: We are 1 people, and as a unified force we are a massive threat to them. But if it benefits them, they champion our Africanity. The Anti-Colonization Society sent Africans out of America to found Liberia. The ACS was a forerunner of the Klan: Both felt that there were too many of us here in America, and, through different means, each organization worked to decimate us—but leave sufficient numbers of us to finish building America.

"That is why they would never have allowed Marcus Mosiah Garvey's UNIA to reach full fruition."

"Dr. Sims, all the texts make it sound like Garvey was just a con artist," Saddiq frowned.

"Let me tell you something," Sims smiled and leaned in with a conspiratorial air, "I worked for the Black Star Line. Many ships sailed and many folks were able to manifest their dream of returning to the Continent."

"Say what? I never heard about no sailings! Dr. Sims, no offense, but you really need to be dropping this knowledge on us in class."

"I've been waiting for the right time. I was, well, it's no excuse, but we all got to eat. You know that I lost my job at Rutgers. I was accused of reverse racism. So. . ." Alteveze and Saddiq nodded. She didn't need to say more. The racism that Caucasian college students can unleash on African American female professors, in particular, is appalling. After a year of battling at Duke, Saddiq transferred to Malare. 1 semester at Emory was sufficient for Alteveze. She wondered how Dr. Bryant kept from slapping or shooting the racist students who attacked her at every class meeting. Alteveze and Saddiq knew exactly what Sims had survived.

Alteveze looked at Dr. Sims with admiration and understanding. Dr. Sims was much more than a literature professor: she was a living history book as well as mother, mentor, and comrade in Ah. Sims was also the perfect vision of how mothers should glow in the early autumn of their years. She had natural salt and pepper hair that was always braided in a jazzy style or froed out. She wore tall African clothes and she had a unique accent . . . like the smell of Senegalese gumbo. That was her accent, the sound of that smell: spicy, earthy, rich. Her skin was a radiant Black touched with ochre, and wisdom suffused her being.

"Imagine! Sailing that vast sea with the ancestors' blessings. Knowing their spirits are pushing your vessel and your soul forward," Sims' eyes misted over. Was it a Guinean night club? A commune in Mali? Diplomatic meetings with Nigeria's head of state? Whatever it was, Sims was feelin it and massaging Saddiq and Alteveze with it too.

"Yes, we rode the waves of Yemoja! My ship, Exodus VII, made 5 journeys conveying folks home. Made so many good friends, had so many good times!" She laughed and rocked her hips in the overstuffed chair; seemed like she was on deck. "We would share knowledge the entire journey. Talk about what we wanted to do, become, create. Schools. Libraries. Clothing shops. How we wanted to be 1 with the people, not set up a hierarchy like in Liberia. But learn the languages, the culture, study with the elders, and get deep enough to understand the cosmos, agriculture, medicine.

"Oh, that reminds me of Harry Wessin; he was a doctor at Shinally. This was back in 1945"

"What?"

"Aww Naw!"

"What is it? What's wrong?" Dr. Sims stared at Alteveze and Saddiq whose mouths were open in astonishment.

"Dr. Sims, it is not possible for you to be that age!"

Dr. Sims laughed and revealed the secret of her youth. Her laughter sounded like spring rain drops pinging on crystal. Her eyes crinkled and she rubbed her thighs. Saddiq found himself aroused and Alteveze did too!

"Listen now," and she waved their disbelief away, "It was Harry who told me about the syphilis murders. He used to work at Tuskegee. He told me that when he found out what was happening, he wrote the senator and the attorney general of Alabama. He started receiving death threats. When he found a defective pipe bomb in his garage, he decided to fight pharmacologically. He went to Africa to study medicine with the Igbo dibia. You should have seen this brother. He was so together and serious. There's no telling what he learned and shared."

An aura of love surrounds this woman, thought Alteveze as she gazed at her elder who was gazing back into time. Not a getcho groove on type thang. But real love. Like she would be sitting on the bus next to a brother and caress his shoulder because he looked as if no 1 had ever touched him with love in 9 years.

"I have been all over the West Coast. Been to every ECOWAS nation and to both Kongos and to Namibia. That's as far south as we would go." Her raised eyebrows said, "apartheid." But then her eyes misted with a love full and rich, 1 as sure as the Earth. Nawinze. She met him in Brazzaville. He had skin like a moonless night, and he would embrace her like the night descends on the Earth: completely. Her only guide, his hands, her tongue, brushing lips and the crescent moon of his smile.

Nawinze decided to join her and work for the Black Star Line. They would get married on the ship. She remembered their bliss like it was yesterday. The sea framing his face, the sunlight dancing on his cheekbones, the passion they shared in their cabin. His lose-all-control laughter: she lived to make him laugh! She adored him, but so did Yewájọbí, and she claimed him. He fell overboard. She had wanted to save or join him but Afua and Taiwo held her back.

Nawinze. Dr. Sims sighed. It was a deep sound, coming from the basement of her long-stored loves. Nawinze. She sighed and the mist cleared. The ginger and curry scented air cleared. His hands hovering over her belly. Cleared. His hands tying her waist beads; lifting her up onto him. Cleared.

"Yes." And the word was a plea a promise a reluctant return to the present. "COINTELPRO has always worked to keep us from ourselves. But what they did—poisoning you—confirms that their depravity is alive and thriving. But beasts can't kill Gods: You are proof of that!

"What we have got to realize is that America will never allow us to build anything designed to uplift us on this soil. We have never been and will never be fully free here. The CIA has also done tremendous damage on the Continent. They have scattered so many minds there . . . I knew decades ago that we would have to create our own spaces underground, build quilombos, autonomous, liberated, armed, independent nations, if we were to fully manifest. Through Ah and Ahni we will finally be able to achieve complete manifestation."

"With our DVDs, CDs, and books we will awaken so many people!" Alteveze was envisioning the growth of the collective.

"Yes, but we need strong promotion and distribution," Dr. Sims leaned forward in her chair, "what distributors have you got?"

"Well, our main distributors will be Kemetic Visions bookshop and rollo and follow," Saddiq said with the straightest of faces.

"Rollo and follow? I'm not familiar with that company."

Alteveze pursed her lips and said, "Dr. Sims, let me introduce you to rollo" she pointed at her right foot, "and follow" she pointed down towards her left. They all laughed.

"But if we hit the street we can reach the entire Africana community of metro Nashville and build with the people in the process. We can hit up the fish fries, bar-b-que joints, swap meets, and nightclubs. Also, the owner of Slick Fashions, Mr. Trustus, has also agreed to carry some of the product. We need to ask all of our establishments in the metro to give us a little counter space."

"That's a good idea; how much does Trustus want to charge us?"

"Nothing, and that will probably be the case of the other businesses also."

"I spoke with the editors-in-chief of *Metropolitan Times* and *Third Eye* last week," Saddiq said. "They are willing to let us advertise for free. I'm also in the process of setting up a website. That way we can reach heads internationally."

"Alright brother! It seems you found your niche," Sims looked at Saddiq. "You never to have it together for class; it seems community service is your path."

He just ducked his head and grinned because there was nothing Saddiq, with a strong D average in Sims' Critical Theory class, could say.

"The poetry anthology is 90% ready for publication," Alteveze revealed. "I've already entered and edited all the poems and laid out the pages. Printing will be simple and easy. We only need to worry about binding and cover art."

No, we only need to worry about cover art. We can start a publishing company and have international distribution for books, music, and films. I'll set everything up."

"Are you serious, Dr. Sims?" Saddiq was shocked.

"AhPress or EmiBooks: Which do you prefer?" she confirmed.

"Well, alright now!" Saddiq and Dr. Sims high 5'ed.

"I like AhPress: to the unenlightened it sounds innocuous, anonymous," Veze offered. "Hmm . . . with this development, I want to share with you a book project I've been pondering: it's an anthology of essays on Africana culture and politics filled with hard-hitting eye-opening information. There is so much that has happened to us and so much that authorized agents of knowledge won't say or won't allow to be published through their organs. But with AhPress, we can compile an anthology to complement Ah Work."

"Capital idea, Veze!" Dr. Sims said, "draft a Call for Papers and in addition to soliciting in certain periodicals, listservs and website, I will contact Delbert Blair, Marimba Ahni, Frances Cress-Welsing, Leonard Jeffries, Maulana Karenga, Na'im Akbar, Angela Davis, and Anthony Browder and ask for submissions."

"We can ask for essays on specific topics like Population Control, AIDS, Genocide and the Third World, Political Prisoners, the Prison Industrial Complex, African Unity, Sex Trafficking, How Ogo Outsourced Our Oppression to Us, and the like. This is a fantastic idea, Alteveze," Saddiq looked at Alteveze, and his love for her deepened and rooted itself in the core of his being. She was his true complement.

"I concur," Dr. Sims took notes of the issues they were discussing. "You know, we won't need much upfront money to come out strong, but we will need more than our savings to sustain us and Ah Work," Dr. Sims paused and pondered. "What if we give Ogo a taste of its own medicine by flooding its burbs with its drugs? What if we make connections among the Ogo at NCU and let *them* oversee distribution where the supply is most desired?"

"Dr. Sims, I want you to be my Momma!" It was the highest compliment he could think of for this wisdom tooth. "I'll discuss this with Ra and Zave. Dynamite idea!"

Everyone worked low to the ground and moved like old snakes in the underbrush. There were no marches, speeches, or protests. There was no hashtagging or social networking of any kind, not only because this Work was not about grandstanding, but also because information shared in cyberspace is information soon to be intercepted.

They silently amassed Ah stockpile and had a magnificent cache of weapons that ranged from Glocks, Tech 9s, Uzis and AK 47s to AR 15s, to 30-06s to 357s, 33s and 22s. The weapons they needed but could not attain without attracting attention to themselves, such as grenade launchers, hand grenades, ground to air missiles and launchers, they dreamt about. After his first dream about weaponry, Ra wrote down everything he recalled on his pillow case. He did not stop to think about his writing materials until he had sketched the last design. When Azure woke up and witnessed his epiphany, they began work on a forge.

The plan had backfired. Rather than keeping the inhabitants of Carvah isolated, ignorant, and susceptible to the penetration of the government and its officials, America's racism resulted in the creation of Ah fortress.

Azure, Alteveze, Saddiq, Sims, and Roper and many more Malare students and professors used their classes to network, organize, and strategize. While the community that had served as a buffer between Malare and Carvah looked the same, the interiors of the various abandoned homes were refurbished for the awakened brothers and sisters who poured in. These homes' electricity was supplied by a magnetic generator; the water was courtesy of Malare and rain. To avoid attention, the exteriors of the homes continued to sport falling porches, broken windows, and other signs of dilapidation.

Aint May, Chaka, and Jahmai came to Carvah and brought necessary healing and killing herbs and preparations. Wakynam and members of Kumba came to assist with the holistic healing of the addicts who deserved a chance to shine. Hawa and Danta taught the Carvah Nsibidi and Medu Netcher so that they could shield their writings and communicate freely.

In the midst of all the building, Vlady Cutlass, the VL's Polish coke supplier went missing. Mothers were selling greens and eggplant and corn at Farmer's Market and 3 police officers were found castrated and tied to a light post at the corner of 1st and Church. Relevant Reality was the largest underground hip hop act in the South and Midwest. AhTahn was the label and distributor, and everyone from Diddy to Dupri was seeking out the sextet. As Relevant Reality blew up, so did 20 police cars along with 40 *in situ* officers.

The drug trade spun back on Ogo as its offspring were now its main clientele. Carvah warriors flooded Caucasian suburbs with crack, heroin, and angel dust. Because Ogo manipulated the desegregation laws to Ogoize Nashville Central University (NCU), forcing the HBCU to become 50% Yurugu, it was easy for former gang-bangers to find Caucasian mules and dealers to purchase and then distribute the drugs where they were wanted most. The proceeds went to the fortification of Carvah and arms and ammunition.

Azure and Alteveze were sipping coffee while examining the blueprints for the Lair. When it was finished, the Lair would house the entire Wilson family along with Alteveze, Saddiq, Azure, Ra, Xavier and any Ah who needed a home. The Lair would have 5 stories and be equipped with 9 bathrooms, 16 bedrooms, a salon, a library, shrine, and a rec room for Ògúnian martial arts training and weightlifting. ¾s of the Lair would be underground. The exposed portions of the home would be impenetrable to battering rams and missile blasts.

The Carvah collective was filled with carpenters, crafts and drafts persons, engineers, plumbers, electricians, and architects who had been unemployed and struggling long before the so-called great recession of 2008, so building, fortifying, and refurbishing were as effortless as taking a stroll in spring.

Their growth was so meteoric that Azure often felt she was living a dream. She put down her coffee cup and marveled at their power, "After all this time, all this struggle"

"after so many tears, so much sorrow:"

"The revolution is here!" she and Alteveze said at once; their eyes sparkled with dynamism.

"I am so honored to be here, to be alive and a part of this Work."

"This is a movement that so many thought would never come and that many more fought to keep from coming," Alteveze mused.

"And so many gave their lives for this struggle. Many millions gone. Millions upon millions. . ."

"We can finally avenge their deaths and resurrect them in a world worthy of their return. Worthy of their return."

The history of Ah-Tahn destruction over the millennia unfolded in the minds of the collective. Previous lessons largely focused on the achievements of the Ah; now it was necessary to show the hands, the hands of the Ah of Kng piled up at the sterns of small river boats. Hundreds of boats and thousands of hands: Each hand—a tax on inefficient rubber workers; the bodies of the survivors—a tapestry of wasted defiled lives twisted and shattered by the greed of Ogo.

The Tahn saw Yurugu armed to the teeth with weapons inspired by Chinese fireworks. Bullets too large for elephants were aimed at a procession of Zalah warriors. The warriors dance to a rhythm; their feet recall the last Jubah. They are armed with their melanin and their spears; it isn't enough. They are slaughtered. The rise up and are slaughtered again.

They travelled back centuries to Dah, where spiritual power rolled in vibrational waves like the ocean. Now see those who shine become the targets of those who do not. See thousands of mercenary women invade their peaceful neighbors—not to murder them—to steal them so their king can sell them.

Come see the coffles, hundreds of Ah deep. Witness the gory train of enslaved Africans trekking across the ravaged Continent, death marched to be sold like sacks of grain in Nashville, Meridian, Natchez, New York, Alapaha, Cap Haitian, Bahia, Paris, London, Sweden, Italy, Saudi Arabia, Fez, Tripoli.

Visit the leader of the free world and see its unique landscaping techniques: tree limbs blooming corpses with bursting eyes and split and oozing skulls; missing genitalia, fingers, and toes. Disembodied heads line streets. Testicles decorate fences. Mothers dangle from bridges. Fathers sway on light posts.

There are excised penises buried under hardened cement slabs. The sidewalks look innocent, even reassuring, but some of them are hollow, and their spaces contain tales that stones and earth are too ashamed to utter. Listen to the ancestors moaning beneath the streets in New Orleans. Listen to the royalty haggle with the factors at Gorée. Listen to our prices rise and fall with market speculations in London.

In the midst of capitalism's triumphant crushing of divinity, the skies are clouded with birds. Buzzards, Vultures, Black Birds, Jim and Jane Crows, Sparrows, Robins, Pigeons, Doves: See how high they fly! Reaching the stratosphere they resume their human shapes; in the ionosphere they are pure soul. Recharged by the cosmos and its inexhaustible wisdom, power, and purpose, Ah warriors, who are as necessary as the sun, return and continue the fight.

We have endured more than any organism to ever exist on this Earth: And we are still shining. You are complete and complex, not because I created you, my resplendent 1s, but because you used your creative forces to recreate yourselves. Yon, jealousy hates you, thievery slays you, and wickedness betrays you because they cannot *be* you. You are the cosmos: You are the Truth.

You are Tahn. Tahn is a Dah word. It means deceived, duped, seduced, decoyed, and it also means shining. You are shining. That is why so many ancestors have returned in the flesh to rejoin you, to become you. They could not have done otherwise, for your shining is visibly reflected in your melanin, but it is also in the vibrations of your language, your music, your textiles, all of your force. It summons; it embraces; it expands. Your soul is the only spontaneously regenerative force on this planet. Ah Jubah to all Tahn and Ah come and gone and come again. Mo Jubah to all Tahn!

"Aint May, I have the seedlings ready."

"Awright, I'm coming."

"I swear, you are looking younger and younger. You look as if you haven't aged since I was born. What age will we tell our children you are?"

"12," Everyone chuckled as they prepared the flora that would become the medicine that we cure the Tahn of all dependency.

"Problem was," Jahmai chimed in, "Aint May was sittin on all that knowledge without anyone to share it with."

"That's just about the truth. I've had the cure all this time but I had to wait for us to realize that we sick and need healin."

Aint May could concoct any medicine needed; she commanded all pharmacological and pharmaceutical knowledge. What was out of the reach of her physical being she could grasp through her emi. For example, as soon as Xavier said they needed curing from and immunity to chemical addiction, Aint May meditated on it.

She knew exactly where she was, she was in Kng in the middle of the Katanga forest. Although it was mid-day, she shivered. The acrid scent of sulfuric acid burned her nostrils. He came. He led her down 2 narrow paths, the kind frequented by hunters. At a 3-road junction, he picked a profusion of leaves. She squatted beside him and burrowed into the earth to pluck root shoots. He plunged deep into the forest, and she followed. She used her hand to shield her eyes from jutting branches until she realized she was moving right through them. He picked 5 different leaves from 5 different plants. When they had finished, they were immediately at the crossroads. When they took the right path they were at her kitchen table cleaning the leaves and scraping the bark and stripping the roots. The next day, when she woke with formulae and compositions dancing before her eyes, she knew that waiting on her counter was a cure for chemical dependency that also stimulated emi.

"How do you feel about embarking on the next phase? Do you think you're being summoned too soon? Do you think seeds of consciousness may have been able to take root?"

"No," Istha was resolute. "I had been discussing the operatives of the IMF, World Bank, and WHO for 2 years when I came, but no 1 cared to listen, so I sat down quietly. Everyone was like, 'Yeh, that's horrible, but how do I get a visa?'"

"Or they're pacifists," added Cynthia.

"Right! You know, many people accused me of being a 'racist' because of my articulation of Pan-African politics and history," Istha shook her head. "I had to explain that recognizing Yurugu for what it is is not racism; it is reality. What is more, racism is predicated upon power: the power to oppress, suppress, disenfranchise—the power to corrupt education and information outlets to the extent that millions of people all over the world are trained to despise themselves and their cultures. There is just no understanding of the Caucasian worldview and methodology of oppression or of African genius, technology, power, or potential.

"I had been driven to such despair after so many fruitless discussions with people at the university that I had nearly given up on the important goal of working for African Unity. Prof. Utas saw my frustration, and he lent me Mummar al-Quaddafi's *Green Book*. That book let me know: No I am not crazy; I am not quixotic. The problem is African ignorance and nihilism.

"So many people blasted Quaddafi, called him crazy," Cynthia nodded, "But he was a visionary who saw himself as an African and who worked for the very thing that many of these Africans and all of the West stand against, African unity. That is why NATO, authorized by Barack Obama, orchestrated Quaddafi's killing: He was an African who refused to bow down and kowtow. He fought for African unity and sovereignty.

"I couldn't stop crying when Quaddafi was lynched," Istha was silent for 7 breaths. "I couldn't get those images out of my head. I still can't. Cable news channels played his lynching over and over again, like a commercial. Who could and would authorize and televise the lynching of a head of state? Only America."

"I was devastated by Quaddafi's killing too. He did so much for the Africans of Libya, for Mali, for Senegal; hmph, his last revolutionary act was funding the South Sudanese liberation army." Cynthia smiled and mused, "He would wear this jacket with the photos of African revolutionaries like Lumumba, Sankara, Nkrumah, and King. Quaddaf!" Cynthia shouted his nickname, "he tried ooo."

"And he was a writer, too, of short stories and poetry," Istha said.

"Oh, we can't forget his women warriors!"

"Ah, Quaddaf! I dey miss im ooo. I loved to hear his and Chavez's and Ahmadinejad's UN speeches." Cynthia mused and smiled. "Quaddaf and Fela had a lot in common."

"Word. And Fela knew, too, the necessity of African unity. He never described himself as a Yoruba or a Nigerian, but as an African. During 1 of Fela's political harangues against Nigeria, a brother defended the country and said Nigeria is great and should be respected. Fela laughed and said the country was patched together by Lugard to dabaru Africans and ensure the mineral wealth of the land flows freely to the West. That is the case for all African countries which are really neocolonies."

"The fragmented nature of this nation is everywhere apparent," Cynthia mused, "from embracing democracy in the South from Sharia and Boko Haram in the North to the resurgence of the Biafra movement."

"The fragmentation is evident within ethnic groups: The Ife–Modakeke war, for example."

"There has been no tally of the lives lost."

"A student was kidnapped and killed, while a member of the Modakeke Peace Committee, who was also a professor, was found carrying over 2,000 rounds of ammunition."

"How," Kandace wondered, "can a people bent on destroying themselves fight against their true enemies and oppressors? They will even deny that their adversaries are Caucasian Imperialists."

"But what is most disturbing to me about the war, is the reaction to it. When 1 sees 'respected' so-called academics smile with a satisfaction 1 would have thought reserved for sensual pleasure about the destruction of lives and property in Ife. . ."

"It is chilling."

"This is why I understand our home-call." Istha continued, "The war in town is born of greed. People are killing and dying behind a false construct of power.

"The national protest sparked by an increase in fuel prices is another good example. The entire nation went on strike and shut down. While it was a strike against the operatives of the New World Order, to some degree, for most people, the strike served to protect their personal interests. People are only thinking about *their* pockets, *their* naira, *their* ethnic group. That individualistic mentality borrowed from the English seems to have become part of the Nigerian national identity."

"1 could argue that the overarching characteristic of the national identity is division: there are so many bifurcations: master-slave, student-professor, academic-nonacademic, male-female."

"Boko Haram is capitalizing on these divisions. That organization is the ultimate manifestation of the internal defeat and destruction of Nigeria. How can anyone kidnap children and declare Allah decreed that they be sold in the market? If there was any doubt at all that slavery had and continues to have a tremendous impact on this nation, Boko Haram silenced those doubts. They have shown the world that they can steal and enslave human beings with impunity."

"While children are stolen and sold and used as suicide bombers in the North, sexting, partying, and blinging rules the South."

"The fact that the theft of nearly 300 people did not merit a response from the government—not until an international cry was sounded—is chilling. And Boko Haram *continues* to kidnap and in some cases kill hundreds, thousands of people at a time and the government claims it cannot verify these mass abductions and assassinations or it uses these inconceivably monstrous crimes for political photo-ops. "

"Boko Haram is an important organization because it reveals how little value human life has in this nation. How an organization such as this has been conceptualized and implemented to enjoy devastating efficiency for so long is a powerful lesson for all of us."

"Ìyá, what can we do to combat them, to end this reign of terror?"

"Boko Haram is a problem that we could easily solve," Ọya shrugged. "We could annihilate every member overnight. But the existence of this organization sends a powerful message to the leaders of Nigeria and to the world. Boko Haram also forces individuals to ask, what is the point of our leaders, this system of governance, of NATO, the IMF, Africom, and the UN if someone can steal human beings and sell them in the market? With drones, satellites and the ability of the FBI and CIA to watch you through your computer's video camera, how can nearly 300 children, how can even 1 child, be stolen. Boko Haram forces the thoughtful among us to ask: If this is the apex of civilization, what is the nadir? The wise 1's know that this is the nadir: Our nadir is Yurugu's apex.

"Boko Haram is a message to the so-called leaders of this Continent and the world. Let them respond. As for the stolen daughters. We are with them. We are always with them. Some will be returned. Some will escape. Some will be enslaved. Some will be killed, but all of them will have the opportunity to do precisely what the Tahn did: re-determine their destinies, and many of them will do just that."

"The work of Àjẹ́ is diverse and complex, and we motivate our progeny to become as diverse and complex as we are. This is essential. If we simply killed all oppressors we would cease to develop and would be unable to manifest our divinity. We would stagnate and succumb to decadence as did the Ahtlnta. We would actually be fomenting our destruction and that of our progeny.

"Àjẹ́'s cornerstones include patience and reticence. It is through patience and reticence that we facilitate the growth and development of new Gods, because the Deities-in-waiting fashion their own numinosity to fit their environment, circumstances, and needs, and no Gods know this better than you, the Tahn," Ọya smiled and then rose to get freshly squeezed mango juice for the cadre.

"Much of Africa is rooted in a master-slave mentality and many societies are master-slave societies. Masters will never willingly relinquish their power." Ọya handed Cynthia, Kandace, and Istha tall chilled glasses of mango juice. "The oppressed must rise up and overthrow their oppressors. However, as some say, slaves get the masters they deserve. . . . Many modern-day slaves are happy to collect crumbs from the master's table, so they will not fight. Some people are too terrorized to fight. Fela sings about this in 'Sorrow, Tears, and Blood' and 'Perambulator.' Many Africans loved him, but they didn't listen to him.

"Some people are willing to fight, but their weaponry is inadequate. They hope to use the master's tools to overthrow the master. With this methodology the oppressed often end up bolstering the oppressor. Many others simply seek to kick out the present master out and take his place.

"It is not for us to solve these problems and answer these conundrums: The masses must do that. And when they do, they will begin shining. They will be ready to join us in the Work." Qya gazed into the eyes of Cynthia, Istha, and Kandace and sent electric waves of power into their souls.

Chaka rubbed her belly, which was just beginning to show her pregnancy of 3 months. It was ironic and perhaps cosmic retribution that when she and Jahmai had finally become 1 in Ah they had had difficulty conceiving their child.

"I think we have an àbíkú relationship," she had told him.

"What is that?"

"Well, the àbíkú is a spirit child. Because the child has a spiritual life, destiny, and family, it is psychologically torn when it comes to Earth. After being born, it often dies and returns to the spirit world only to be reconceived through the same mother and be born and die again and again."

"So," he mused, "we've been bearing àbíkú children?"

"No," she sipped her cider, "we have an àbíkú relationship: As soon as it is conceived, it dies only to be reconceived. We are both the parents of the àbíkú relationship and we are the àbíkú relationship. We experience the bliss of our dual life and love, the glory of finding ourselves, and the anguish of the death of our relationships.

"A mother can go from vehement anger to numb desolation when she realizes she has given birth to an àbíkú. She may give her child names like 'No' meaning, No, you will not die again; 'Come' as in come and take this child who won't remain anyway, and the like.

"When the child dies, all kinds of rituals are performed to prevent the àbíkú from returning to the woman's womb: It may be scarred and disfigured or buried at the crossroads to prevent its return. But even with all of that, it may return, scars and all.

"I think that our many unborn children are like the àbíkú plagued mother; they are exhausted by conceptions and misconceptions, miscarriages and abortions. They've grown weary of our love and hate. So that now, when we have fully evolved, they don't trust us."

Jahmai went to his woman and held her, thinking it may well be true that their children who were never able to live had abandoned them.

"What you say may very well be true," assented Patricia. She had come to Alapaha along with her daughter Chaka, who was called Ba-Chaka, to distinguish her from the elder Chaka. Chaka asked them to come and assist with the manufacture of medicine and to take the anti-drug elixir to the satellite site Patricia was organizing in Chicago.

Chaka had told Aint May about Patricia and how she had revealed her and Jahmai's origins and ended their turmoil. Aint May said she would be delighted to meet Patricia, so Chaka was floored when Aint May interrupted her gracious introductions and shouted, "How you gon introduce me to mah best friend from Kng? Yahnza, come rub your vibrations on me!" and embraced Patricia.

Patricia and Ba-Chaka fit in Alapaha like okra in gumbo, and Patricia's counsel continued to prove illuminating for Jahmai and Chaka.

"You 2 may be tha proud parents of an àbíkú relationship, but that era has ended," Patricia smiled at Jahmai and Chaka. "In fact, I think you conceive soon."

Ba-Chaka bounded in the room and plopped her precocious self onto Chaka's lap. She was a 7-year-old child with the intelligence of a 9th grader. She already knew the uses and names of over 7,000 plants.

"Yeh, Ba-Chaka," Patricia called her daughter by her pet name, "go sit with Ma Chaka." Patricia gazed in Chaka's aura and nodded, "Abosom just makin sure, that's all. Just makin sure."

And she was right, about everything. Ba-Chaka was a child filled with blessings. She came into rooms and the air resonated peace. So when Chaka carried her on her back and on her lap, her presence assured the coming 1.

As Patricia gathered her family in preparation to return to Chicago, it was Aint May who shared the news, "Yahnza, you and Ba-Chaka brought us a wondrous gift," she embraced her friend and kissed Ba-Chaka on the cheek. "Chaka give birth in 9 moons!" Only Aint May's sensitive nose could smell the dawn dew scent of a 7 day pregnancy.

"No more àbíkú love for you 2," Ba-Chaka smiled and held Chaka and Jahmai's hands. Chaka picked up her little image and held her close so the richness of this little 1's spirit would rub off on the child she knew, now, was a daughter.

"We need to make something special tonight," exclaimed Jahmai, "to celebrate!"

"Well, ya have a good time."

"You ain't going is you, Trisha?"

"Why not stay a while longer?" Aint May had been the consummate loner but she was enjoying communality and couldn't get enough of Ah. She had lived so many years of solitude, it was nice to be surrounded by family.

The Alapaha site would not be like the others with a large community. No, the 4 of them, Aint May, Chaka, Jahmai, and the coming 1 comprised their population. Because their work consisted of creating medicines and distributing them, they were also a mobile site.

Alapaha, which is a Tbk expression meaning "let him come here (to a safe place)," not only embodied the wisdom of the enslaved Africans who had named the land, but Alapaha became the mission of its keepers, as they ensured the creation of safe places and sacred spaces through the expert knowledge and application of flora and fauna.

"I'm so sorry, but no. Got ta get on back, now. Daniel be waiting and so will a needy community," she patted her packets of elixir with resolve.

"In a few moons then."

"A few moons."

Abosom's spirit became expansive in Chaka's womb. Now that Chaka was pregnant, it seemed the immediacy of the work gripped all of them. Everyone began working round the clock to manufacture enough medicine to take to Bliss Bluff and Carvah. In 3 months they were ready.

Aint May was lost in her thoughts as she packed the bottles of medicine into the cushioned cartons. The anti-drug serum was so desperately needed by so many: It was essential to ensure all Tahn and Ah could reach their full potential. But Aint May was focused on a new medicine she was developing. She knew that it would set the revolutions of the wheel of continuity spinning 900 rpms faster than at any other time in history.

She broke her thoughts and inquired, "Y'all ready?"

Jahmai responded, "Let's hit it."

Alapaha to Bliss Bluff was an approximate 7 hour drive. Chaka and Jahmai had serviced the minivan 3 days before and had gassed it up the previous night. When they were all belted in, Chaka selected Cassandra Wilson's *New Moon Daughter*, slid it into the CD player, and pulled out of the gravel drive.

The countryside was lush with vegetation. The day was clear and temperate: perfect for driving. Chaka could drive 16 hours straight. She had driven non-stop from Chicago to Alapaha so frequently she could make the trip with her eyes closed. She loved road trips and didn't need anything but good music, so having company and destiny in the vehicle was a lovely bonus.

"This elixir will make seekin knowledge as natural as seekin food," Aint May was confident about her work because she knew the strength of the Prophet: The Silent Guiding 1. "What is more, 3 weeks after our return, I will have the HIV/AIDS cure ready for mass distribution.

"Some strains of HIV/AIDS is melanin related, so what we did was to harmonize specific plantlife with melanin and emi properties with other flora that neutralize the mutating effects of the disease and the destruction of the immune system."

"Hmm, I wonder if that was the technique of Dr. Nana Kofi Drobo II of Ghana. He had a cure, and it was a proven cure. They killed him," Chaka shook her head. "When I heard that I began to really fear for us. I know that they can cure the disease because they created it. But like syphilis, they won't reveal their cure until they have killed many of us. But now their machinations are irrelevant, we have our own cures."

"Yes, and unlike our predecessor, we won't brag to the beast about it. We will simply start curing and immunizing."

They drove on listening to the rhythms of Brother J Vibal Magus and the Dark Sun Riders.

"Aint May!" Jahmai pointed out his window at some lodgings they were passing, "are those slave houses!?"

"Sho is. You can tell by the style they built in. Folks still live in em too."

"Say what?"

"Yep. No lights, no running water. Nothing. Folks gotta live somewhere."

"America . . ." although his voice was soft, his disgust was palpable. "We have so much work to do."

"Welcome!!! Y'all come on in!" With all the people in and out of the Institute, you could tell Tynell was really impressed with the Alapaha Ah because they got all of her stingy smile.

It took no time at all for Aint May and Tynell to become inseparable. They spent the majority of their time in Dear's garden and roaming round the fields. Aint May found and collected some slightly different varieties of the same herbs she grew in Alapaha. What they took from the Earth they doubly replaced through healing and through replantings.

Aint May was impressed by the edifices of Bliss Bluff. When she first saw the house, it took her breath away.

"Ahhhh, Ahni's shrine. What a wonderful living shrine!" Aint May paused and cocked her head to the left, "There's a emisite out back, to the northwest: I feel it . . . You children," she embraced Hawa and Danta, "this house sits directly under Ahstah at apex!"

As Tynell took Aint May on a tour of the emisite, she chuckled, "I have to be honest, when I saw the plans for the house, I didn't know what to say. A womb house," Dear shook her head. "But I'm right proud of these 2. Since they won't do it, I'll brag on em: You know that they helped build the house? Yep, they worked right beside Joe and Squeeze, the carpenters of the family. You'll meet em."

Hawa had only seen Dear as open and talkative with Mary, her second cousin and best friend, but this was even a deeper intimacy. "Valeria's husband Earl, Joe, Squeeze and Leroy. We all worked, clearin the ground, curin timber, evictin snakes. . ."

When they reached the shrine room, Aint May saluted each of the Òrìṣà. "Ah, so you know the Risha," Tynell observed.

As she finished her salute to Ògún, Aint May affirmed, "Sure do. I have my own shrines, so this is just like home." She paused, "I noticed you have some shrines of your own. Those white tires and horseshoes and the like." She winked conspiratorially, "You know what time it is."

"Yeh, I do. I have to say, I always have but I never felt confident in saying and acting so . . . We've had to keep so much of ourselves secret and silenced. Some things I knew the real names and meanings of, some I didn't. But I have learned so much now and see how *connected* everythang is! These children have opened me all the way up and I wouldn't be closed again for all the world."

Dear actually had emi 5 capability from birth. She had hidden most of her force, however, because of the shame of appearing backward, of being ostracized, or of being subjected to religious terrorism. But now she was in her element. She had just begun teaching a class on ritual practices, meteorological readings, cloud splittings, obstetrical wisdom, ways to dispel evil from a house, ways to kill an offender, ways to uncross, ways to cross, various ways of knowing.

At first, some elders felt the younger generation should not be privy to certain information. But Dear said, "Why not? They need to love and protect theyselves too. This is knowledge. You are never too old or young for that." Tynell made sure to tell them when such acts could be affected and under which conditions, and she also explained the repercussions of certain works.

Having grown up 2 generations after slavery, nearly everything in her life was wrapped in an aura of secrecy due to shame. She knew how much knowledge her elders had, but she also knew why things couldn't be made plain in the past. But a new day had dawned and it gave Tynell new life and uncovered her light: She had waited decades to shine, and Aint May provided her with a role model for illumination.

When Dear and May made it back to the front porch, they were greeted by Ahibit.

"Let me hold that baby! Got hair just like the cosmos!" Aint May's praises were interrupted by a tremor she felt when she held the child, "What you all call her?"

Ahibit was a big girl now. She could hold her head up and giggle and coo: in public. In private, the 5-month-old was already speaking in sentences. Jahmai had laughed about the fact that had she been Caucasian, she would have been on television and in Guinness. Exploited.

"Ahibit, but her òríkì is Nwadiani."

"Ahibit: A powerful name for a powerful child," she lost herself in the child's bounteous afro. "Child of Daughter. Exquisite," Chaka felt her womb stir.

Dear noticed it and nodded, "Yes, child."

"Y'all come on in. You're just in time because we're holding class. If you're tired, you can just greet the class. But if you feel moved to do so, pour forth."

At the time they entered, Conch was discussing Yemọja with a level 4 adolescent class. After the encounter at the Bùrúkù tree, Yemọja had placed her hand on the back of Conch's neck and had guided her ever since. Valeria was instructing level 7 youths on Africana history. Rell was teaching Medu Netcher to a group of elders. Mildred was teaching a course on the African linguistic contributions to American English. Danta and Glutey were translating another collection of Ah-annals into King Njoya's Shumom writing.

Njoya was a Cameroonian king who had survived both German and French colonization and their attempts to obliterate his writing system. Over 50 years he painstakingly revised and refined his script. Danta along with Glutey and Xavier had studied Njoya's alphabet and manuscripts, and as soon as they attained fluency, they commenced translation and instruction.

The Tahn gang members gained particular satisfaction from working with the sacred scripts. They had come to the Institute originally out of curiosity, but when they found a home in its welcoming womb, they were prepared to renounce their gang affiliations. When they learned that the knowledge that they had, simply from being members of these societies, was essential to the Work, they felt privileged.

"Larry Hoover and Jeff Fort are actually 2 of the Tahn's most resplendent shining suns," Danta had informed an intergenerational class after discussing BGD and Blackstone Rangers/El Rukn iconography. "They understood and evolved ancient Ah semiotics, political and social organization, linguistics, artistry, and military strategies for contemporary Tahn application."

When the class sessions ended, everyone gathered for a gumbo break. After lunch, Aint May addressed the collective: "As you know, we are the pharmacologists of the Ah, and we have brought with us a detoxification compound. It can be taken in any way. A bit can be sprinkled on food; it can be taken in a beverage. It has no taste, no odor, and no threat of overdose. It is safe for all ages and all conditions. Even newborns with chemical addictions can be safely and effectively treated with this compound.

"This is how it works: 24 hours after the medicine has been ingested, the desire for cocaine, Vicodin, barbiturates, heroin, coffee, marijuana, cigarettes alcohol—all and any chemical dependencies—is eradicated from the body and the consciousness. It also eliminates the desire for excessive sugar, salt, red meat, and pork. Foods such as these are capable of creating both chemical dependencies and diseases like high blood pressure, diabetes, and heart disease that kill more people than narcotics.

"We have so many impediments through which to maneuver; this elixir will speed our progress."

"Ma May," asked Rell, "can someone overdose on the compound?"

"No, Rell, in fact, the more they take the better. Because the compound also magnifies the emilevel of the healing 1."

"What is it made of?" queried Mildred.

"Flora from Kongo."

"You all know that we have been discussing Prophet Patrice Lumumba's reign in the Kongo and his immortality. We have also discussed the emisite of Kng and their—" Danta paused with an epiphany. "Aint May! You been working with the Prophet."

She smiled, "Yes, my primary teachers are the flora and fauna, themselves, and the ancestors and the Gods, including and especially Lumumba," Aint May's soul became visible; it shimmered and glowed when she spoke about Lumumba.

Dear admired Aint May's rapture, and then she stepped back, gazed upon her and laughed, "He's with you, with us right now!" All of the Tahn fell silent with reverence. "Lumumba is here with us. Here in Bliss Bluff!" The significance of the detoxification compound and all their efforts became blindingly clear.

"How many of you know someone with a chemical dependency—including alcohol?" Aint May asked the collective.

Nearly every hand rose.

"Then," she began distributing the packages, "we all have work to do. "Now," she continued as Jane and Rell took over the distribution, "the medicine has no taste and it is highly concentrated, so you don't need a give a huge dose: A dash in a drink or a pinch in a pot of food will work wonders."

Aint May continued: "24 hours after the compound enters the host, the person will no longer have a desire for addictive chemicals. After the addiction is eradicated, you might see that the person has developed an aversion to television or they have begun closely analyzing television shows or songs. The person may begin reading anything with words or simply sitting and thinking. Ask the person what she or he is thinking about. If they begin asking deep questions, questions that will lead to Ah answers, give em a lil bit mo of the medicine and bring them to the Institute, because they're shining.

"This should really be considered an all-purpose all-Ah medication. We all should take some. I'll tell ya why. Smoking, drinking, overeating, and excessive sugar, salt, and preservatives all inhibit emi. So even those of us who think we advanced but are throwin down on ham hocks and chittlins are actually stymying our force.

"Chemicals anywhere on or in the body and hair impede vibration and harmonization. Hair weave, the lye of permanents, the peroxide of dye, thick pomades. All of them are like static to the soul, and some of them are cancerous to the body—like lye. These contaminants make it more difficult to meditate, which is your contact with Ahni and Ah. They make receptivity slow and block true knowledge and its sister understanding.

"Ahni made us all perfect as we are. So perfect, we need no embellishment. We are of the Earth and everything we take into our bodies and put onto them should come from the Earth, not some laboratory. So sprinkle a bit of this elixir in your own food and water—you might be surprised to see what your had been addicted to.

The souljahs went forth.

"Things are moving so rapidly and with such ease! I knew that our time had come and everything, but it's like . . . well, I feel like last week I was wandering without a home, and now my home is creating a home, literally. You saw the stakes planted for the new womb we will build?"

"Mm hmm."

"Girl, we have so much shining, we are giving instruction in the bedrooms, kitchens, everywhere. And you can feel the impact of emi. You can feel that the character of the land is changing, is shining with us."

Chaka sipped her tea and dressed another biscuit in Dear's homemade pear preserves. The breakfast nook, situated with windows looking out on the northeast, was so relaxing and rejuvenating. And Hawa? It was like Chaka had another twin; she felt like she was gazing in a mirror or having a discussion with another manifestation of herself. She could tell by the way Hawa looked at her that this physical and spiritual déjà vu was mutual.

"Yes! A complete transformation is afoot. But, I feel some tensions, Aint May does too."

"Here, in the Institute?"

"No. Yes." She paused and organized her thoughts, "Aint May said she felt a threat, said it felt like a white cloud was over her head sometimes. But I feel—how can I describe it? I feel a coming. Some impending thing. Now, I can't tell if it is negative or positive. Well, everything that happens is an opportunity for growth, but what I feel is simply a coming.

"Baby girl, come on," Chaka picked up the infant and felt her womb singing again. Ahibit was such a beautiful brilliant child. She giggled often, but there was something behind it. Plus, she laughed at jokes as if she understood them.

"Aunty Chaka: Momma's mirror."

Chaka nearly choked on her tea, and Ahibit Nwadiani said, "Aunty Chaka," with playful reproach.

Her mother joined her laughter, "Yeah, she talks and everything. She has already begun reading. Sometimes her knowledge is frightening. When I think of Ahni and Badu's twins, I am amazed. We now have proof that we have absolutely no limits."

"It is so inspiring to see the coming generation fully empowered. This is how we would have been if not for our historical upheaval, but I don't know if we could have recreated ourselves any other way."

"Ahni is right," Nwadiani explained.

"She sure is baby. You ready for your nap?"

"No. I need to be here now."

"Okay . . ." Hawa looked at Ahibit who gave her a penetrating gaze. Her tone changed, "You know, I have been feeling something too, but I thought maybe it was hormonal. Dear and Aint May need to hip us to some of those protective conjures."

"They're are working on that right now. Great minds, hun?" Chaka paused and looked outside at the garden, thickets of trees, and hidden paths, "I think you need some guns here," Chaka looked concerned.

"Yes, it is Yurugu." Hawa's answer was not to Chaka's suggestion but in acknowledgment of the weighty feeling that was pressing on her soul. "There is time to prepare. When I think of it, how could it be otherwise. You know that our children make up 20% of those enrolled in public and private schools here, but there has been nearly a 50% reduction in Africana enrollment. Now, if these kids had just dropped out and picked up pipes, no 1 would care, but they know these children are obtaining knowledge of self and are spreading that knowledge and awakening others."

"They know that the status quo is no longer being maintained because of the Institute, and they don't like it 1 bit. They're coming after us." Chaka's eyes were open but she was looking inward and toward the future as the knowledge revealed itself to her. "They are, as of yet, unsure of the best approach."

"Mommy better call a meeting," Ahibit wasn't smiling.

Every household could produce at least 3 firearms. Every household could also purchase another piece. The goal was to have 4 weapons: 2 for use at the 'Stute, 2 for use at home: those who had conceal carry licenses only needed 2 weapons. From that day, they followed the path of the Carvah site, as every member old enough to safely carry a gun went deep into Dear's.180 acres for target practice and lessons in loading, unloading and cleaning arms. Weapons practice was supplemented with martial arts training and knowledge of defensive Whodo.

No 1 knew more about defensive Whodo than Àjẹ́, and Ọya, Cynthia, Kandace and Istha were delighted to share strategies. The women arrived and hugged every member of the Original Path Institute. After the greetings were concluded Ọya discussed their work at Minnah.

"As you all know, Minnah is the emisite where the invisible and indivisible make justice visible. Soon we will astonish the world with our work.

"We've formed the corps ẹgbẹ́ Àjẹ́. We are monitoring all emisites and their antagonists. We have also begun, let me call them, litigations against offenders of the way," Ọya's smile was glorious. Her presence was so dazzling that the Tahn had to concentrate to understand her words; without concentration they would have been lost in her brilliance and oblivious to what she was saying. "Now, Kandace and Cynthia will share with you information about a Work they enacted a few years ago."

"Peace, Ah," Kandace greeted them. "Before our relocation to our home in Minnah, Cynthia and I lived in Hattiesburg; we were graduate students. Once I divulged to Cynthia my shining, which is the power of Àjẹ́, we began vibrating together and our power surged.

"We finished our academic work and needed to raise some money. In the process of earning funds, we also made sure to rid the town of its many oppressors. We opened Sadie's Café and exterminated Hattiesburg's most prestigious citizens (council)." Gasps of recognition and smiles followed her admission. "I see many of you are aware of our work," Kandace smiled.

"Girl, Hattiesburg was lost, no 1 know where to turn or what to do! Beasts were dropping like flies; there weren't enough funeral homes to hold em!" Hawa was amazed.

"Hawa, I told you some spirit-work was behind that," Danta smiled.

"You sure did."

"Let me explain what we did," Cynthia shifted into a more comfortable position on the pillows. "We used a 3 part mixture of Earth sense, good ole conjuration, and Àjẹ́: once cooked poke salad, superficially cleaned chittlins, nightshade, and dead man's bells seasonings, you all know and are learning the rest," she spread her hands and grinned. "But Kandace's job was the most important of all. She controlled their minds and bodies; she kept them alive and staggered their deaths so that attention was deflected away from us."

Everyone was amazed by the perspicacity of these women. And the presence of Ọya? Well, she alone increased the emilevel of the room 99 degrees. She was bitumen black, her hair fanned out from her head, and her eyes were so bright 1 could not stand to gaze into them. She kept spinning and spinning. She was like the Gẹlẹdẹ, the ultimate in spectacle, simply by being her spectacular self. Although everyone was in contact with Ahni and the ancestors through meditation, this was the first manifest visitation of an Òrìṣà. And what makes it so good, Ọya was as cool as a fan.

Ọya picked up Ahibit and danced with her, "As you are aware, Ogo is planning an attack on the Original Path Institute. You may adopt any strategy you choose to protect yourselves. The works you are engaged in thus far, the military regimen, the instruction in conjuration, are on point. But rest assured that if Yurugu harms anyone of Ah, it will be dealt with." She kissed Ahibit under her chin. "Right, Nwadiani." Nwadiani replied with a wink.

"As you know," Kandace began, "we are the arm of justice. And our arm spans the globe. We are a spiritual-material military force. Everything Ah and Tahn do is done under the auspices of the force of Àjẹ. Everything that has been or will be comes through us. Although we have been ruthlessly persecuted, especially by Christian zealots, we have always been and we will always be.

"We are the power that made the Tahn Tahn. We provided the tools of survival, the impetus to live, the wisdom to conjure, and the courage to raze plantations to the ground. It is important that we understand and recognize that we are all 1: Àjẹ, Ayẹn, Kindoki, Ngula, Raap, Òrìṣà, Black Gangster Disciples, Egbo, Ògbóni, Sande, Vice Lords, El Rukns, Ah, Ahni, Tahn, Komo, Poro, 5%, Voodoo, Whodo, 2 Headed Doctors. No matter how we are perceived or how we may be misdirected, at our core we are divine emissaries of Ahni who are perfectly positioned around this world to do work that is essential for our holistic evolution.

"All of you are intimately familiar with Àjẹ even if you don't recognize the name. Our work is simple: We create life and we protect and defend life. As part of our work, we find and punish offenders against the Earth. Onílẹ." With the mention of the Shining Earth Mother, Ọya held Nwadiani upside-down and touched the child's head to the Earth 3 times. Following this, Ọya, tied a rapturous Nwadiani to her back with 1 of her many colorful cloths before spoke again. "Ogo is aware of the cosmological shift, and it is growing more aware of the work we are doing. Its objective is to stop our Work and crush us. However, its goals are fruitless, for how can 1 stop the sun from shining?"

"This is precisely what we needed in the 60s and 70s and didn't have," Dear asserted.

"Right," said Mary, "we all wanted the same thing, but we were too diffused and confused."

"We also had no unified spiritual foundation. So many of us were trained to put hope and trust into the myth that they created to pacify, confuse, and subdue us that we never could have united and evolved. Now when I think of that fly-speck, dusty depiction of Jesus in the church, I laugh at our folly," Dear laughed and everyone joined her.

"When Hawa started teaching us about pagan pre-Christian celebrations she was real cool about it because she knew she was fin to rattle our bones," Dear expounded, "But, when I found out Christmas was actually a celebration of the winter solstice that involved all kinds of orgies and drunkenness and rape and gluttony, chile, I was beside myself."

"And Christmas wasn't nothing but a political compromise that allowed Caucasians to continue to observe their pagan rites," Mildred asserted. "The christmas tree, santa claus, mistletoe—all pagan bullshit. We been sho nuff hoodwinked."

Jane nodded her head in agreement and added, "And Easter's another pagan rite. Young virgins run off into the woods and hide with a basket holdin an egg. The basket symbolized the womb; and the egg, the ovum. Men were sent hunt down and rape the girls they desired: That's the origin of the easter egg hunt."

"When Hawa broke out *Nile Valley Contributions to Civilization* by Browder and *The Cultural Unity of Black Africa* by Diop," Tynell declared, "I knew I had been bamboozled. Jesus Christ wasn't nothing but a bleached and emasculated tin-imitation of the African God Heru. Jesus Christ is the biggest lie ever told."

The knowledge she had gained incensed Mildred, "Think about how much money we done give to our oppressors buyin christmas and easter clothes, toys, baskets and all that shit. They call US pagans!"

"But we was so caught up in Christianity and Islam—and their Ramadan feast was originally like the solstice orgies—or a communist disavowal of the spirit, there is no way we could have had a real revolution. Everyone was looking to the left or the right and not realizing we was all being hit on our heads and stabbed in our backs."

"But Ah and Tahn and Ahni is different. It's not a religion. We not believing in something that isn't there and we aren't relying on any 1 or thing but ourselves. Ah and Tahn is simply. . . ." Dear pursed her lips and searched for the words.

"Organic"

"Right"

"At one with me and my existence"

"Life"

"The way"

"Perfect"

"Complete"

"No rhetoric, no bells and whistles, no tithes and offerings, no groveling, and no nonsense," Mildred affirmed. "I have to be honest, it makes all the difference when a) your Creator looks like you, b) she speaks with you and c) she is directly manifestin po li ti call y! Look at how we have grown. Since y'all have been here these 3 weeks, 30 new folk done come in."

"Off of drugs and into Ah."

"That's it!" Aint May and Dear high 5ed. "And we prepared for battle!"

"You know, there was an awakening in the 70s with funk music. But it didn't come off."

"We weren't ready," Valeria acknowledged, "we hadn't learned enough at that time. Instead of shining, we were acting like we had won the revolution or we were getting high to forget that we hadn't or we were actin like we could sex our problems away."

"What is sad is that even with AIDS it still ain't enough of us ready. Imagine what's happenin on the Continent. If it ain't AIDS its Ebola or Marburg. And it isn't like the information of these diseases creation is hidden from us. The truth is everywhere, if folk will read it.

"But an unwritten truth is that we gon to have that AIDS cure out in a few weeks, cures for Ebola and Marburg too. Yes," Aint May nodded to the stunned and jubilant collective, "we gon lick em all. I'll tell you something else," she felt the site's humming increase, "just as the sun's rays are reversing, so too are these diseases. The things they invented to kill us will cover them like the night."

"Àṣẹ"

"Like the night."

While Aint May, Dear, Chaka, Jahmai, Rell, Jane, and Glutey were watching Haile Gerima's film *Sankofa*, Conch entered the media room.

"Conch! Come on here and meet Aint May, Chaka, and Jahmai," Dear beckoned and paused the film.

"How y'all do?" Conch gave the trio warm hugs. "I sorry we didn't meet sooner, but, lately, I've been so worn out. I can't do a thing but sleep once I get home. I guess I been working too much overtime." Conch smiled thinking about how much like Dear, Hawa, and Danta they were. She sank into an overstuffed chair. "So y'all been here 2 weeks, hun?"

"Yes. We done met everybody but you. But we understand. I think I may have something for you. It will give you a deeper sleep and more energy on waking," Aint May had already begun the mental calculation on the catnip-valerian mixture for night and the mistletoe–St. John's wort tea for the day.

This woman was having some kidney problems too. Takin all them damn water pills, "Stop taking those water pills," Aint May told Conch.

Imagine, Yemọja's daughter tryin to rid herself of water. And she is a beautiful full woman. Fit right in in Ife.

"Dear, you got any cherries left?"

"Sure do. It was a short season for em but I got a peck. I'll get you some." They are so close, Conch, Dear and Valeria. But there is a silence between them, Aint May mused. Hawa came in and filled in the silence.

"Lady C! how you doin?" She greeted Conch.

"Pussycat! I'm fine, give me that baby! How you totin her?"

Hawa turned around so that Conch could greet Nwadiani, who was tied to her back. "That's what Ọya taught me. That's how they do it in Yorubaland."

"That's how they would do it back in sl" she paused. Shame had blocked the word, but she forced it out "slavery times."

"Sure did, Dear," Aint May acknowledged the pain and the truth. "You ain't old enough to remember that! But I am."

"You look my age!" Dear marveled. "Momma said her Momma would carry all of her children that way."

"Ohh!" Aint May acted as if she had been pricked by a pin.

"What is it? Chigga?"

"Ole mosquito git at ya?" Everyone was worried.

"Oh, no, it's—it's nothing." As soon as Conch had taken Nwadiani, Aint May understood the silence and the pain. Conch had a baby, but she hasn't see her since the child was weaned. Now she was coming home. Aint May looked in Conch's aura and saw Conch breastfeeding the child under a bridge. She wouldn't look at the child but she would sing to harmonize with cars going overhead. She wasn't Conch then. She was

"Lil Wom, a blessing is coming your way. Lil Wom, joy is coming back home." This time there was no mistaken identity, this was no praise, nick, pet or crib name. It was the only name she had had. She took "Conch," but her Momma gave her "Lil Wom."

Nwadiani smiled at Conch, "The child of daughter is coming home."

She was on her way, and when she arrived, there would be no more secrets between these women.

The secrets and silences are what had torn them apart. The fear of being without, kicked out, left out, and abandoned had caused abandonment. They had gone from being Gods who had everything because they shined through the only force they truly owned and controlled, their souls, to being a people with nearly nothing because they were trying to control the movements of others or because they let themselves be controlled.

There were voices that these women of shared blood had never heard, and these voices held songs that these women needed to make whole their souls.

The songs were blood, flesh, and bone; soil, water, and weeping trees. They were the songs of acolytes mirroring the works of their mentors. The songs comprised the crash of the waves forbidding landing and the groan of obstinate wood and metal. The songs of Yemọja being gang raped repeatedly by devil-manned slave ships, the songs of Yemọja folding into her bosom her destitute sons and daughters, the songs of millions upon millions upon millions of African skeletons wrestling and rocking on the ocean floor were the songs waiting to be sung.

The songs of mewling infants pitched overboard so they would not know slavery; the songs of millions upon millions of Ah who would become Tahn: their songs of laughter, their storm-aided insurrections, their wails of grief, and their stony silences; the songs of bellies barely filled— just enough to keep em alive; the song of 300 healthy Ah held in a net underwater off of a New England shore for a tax write-off; the lyric of Yewájọbí Yemọja, the mother who gives life and who takes it; the song of the mother who was called Wade because she floated out of the sea onto dry land, those were the songs to be sung

> Child of the chief of deep waters
> Who can take the home away from
> The child of the chief of deep waters?
> This is where Òrìṣà speaks of a home.

Chaka was driving the minivan while Aint May and Jahmai were singing along with Bobby Womack who was demanding a flight to the moon.

"He sang the hell outta that cover!" Chaka extolled.

"And by doing so, he reminds us of our relationship with the cosmos."

"Word, Aint May," Jahmai said, "and thanks to Google Moon's images of the far side, people can appreciate from a distance that which we have intimate and eternal knowledge of."

"Because of the scholastic, religious, and scientific indoctrination and miseducation we are subjected to, few people understand that the Earth is an infinitesimal part of a massive ever-growing cosmos. We are part of an interconnected network of existences that are all swirlin, thrivin, and shinin in the ever-enrichin womb of all creation," Aint May extolled.

"On the most elemental level, that cosmic connectedness is evident in the relationship between the Earth and the moon. The moon, directs the Earth's revolutions, rotations—its very existence," Aint May expounded.

"The Caucasian mind has been so twisted by its lies of supremacy that to acknowledge that someone is controlling it and 'its' Earth would literally blow its mind. Yurugu would not be able to survive if it were forced to face universal truth let alone the universe's truth," Chaka asserted.

"And every institution that it established for the maintenance of its global supremacy would crumble—from schools, to banks, to churches," Jahmai nodded.

"Mortals will soon be able to fly to the moon themselves. They can already launch devices that can bring photographic evidence of the cosmos' myriad entities' existences. All of these advancements are hastening not only the end of Ogo but also a literally universal unification."

"Understanding 1's existence as a cosmic entity and having a cosmic perspective alters everything, including our relationships with 1 another."

"Because we've been trapped in Yurugu's sociocultural economic maze and are trained to forsake communality for individuality and to debase our divinity in a quest for dollars, we have routinely hurt, ignored, and abused the people who are the most important to our existence: our partners," here Chaka nodded at Jahmai, "our children, our elders, and our artists."

"Like Mr. Womack," Jahmai mused. Bobby was coincidentally instructing men on the ways to keep their partners happy through the song, "A Woman's Gotta Have It." "He is the very essence of rhythm and blues, but he really doesn't get the props he deserves, or the support. And he's not alone. When the levees were breached after Hurricane Katrina, legendary New Orleans blues and jazz artists were revealed to be balancing on the razor edge of subsistence," Jahmai noted.

"I think of Zora Neale Hurston working in isolation on a rejected epic. Not only did Alice Walker ensure that Hurston did not sink into obscurity, but she also revealed her love and concern for our artists by taking Langston Hughes oranges when she heard he was sick. It is hard to imagine someone of Hughes' stature needing oranges, a hug, or a genuine inquiry of concern. I respect Walker for reminding us that our geniuses need embraces and for embracing them."

"Did you say 'Zora,' Sugar?"

"Yes, ma'am . . ." Chaka glanced from the road to Aint May for a second.

"I remember her. She was a real work of the Earth. She came through Georgia briefly, collecting orature and data on the healing arts. She was Tahn. She was shining. I mean, those who know could just look at her and see her power. It wasn't that she was a conjurer, well, she was, but it was more like she was a new dimension in conjuration."

"You met her?" a stunned Chaka had unconsciously taken her foot off of the accelerator and the vehicle slowed to 30 mph.

"Twice. I saw her again when I went to Florida to take some seedlings to a brother named Dr. Duke. He was originally from Ta Ntr. Deep brother. She was studying with him."

"I gotta let you see her *Mules and Men*," Chaka picked up speed again, still fascinated. "The book is profound. It is like a blend of autobiography, biography, spiritual compendium and a treatise on the arts of signifyin on ol massah and controlling your destiny."

"When Chaka first shared the book with me, I was laughing out loud. Hurston's work is so important on so many levels," Jahmai turned to face Aint May, "Zora reminds me of you, Knowledge Sharer."

"But your thoughts about our artists are true: So many die forgotten. We never think of how they may be struggling. We just consume their art and go on. But, then again, it is hard to imagine a published writer or an acclaimed singer struggling. But their reality is often the opposite of what they portray."

"That's especially the case today. Between blinged-out videos and celebrification it is difficult to find an actual artist—someone who is not concerned with money but with mastering, expanding, and evolving their craft," Jahmai posited.

"So many of our, well," Chaka searched for the appropriate term, "entertainers, are abettors of divide and conqueror. They set themselves up in cliques and attack 1 another while the cauco-imperialist publisher, distributor, and/or manager reap immense profits.

"But, I think of Master P"

"What, with his unconscious ass?" Jahmai queried.

"Well, he's made a transition." Chaka informed, "No more n-word, no more exploitation of women. He's even making family-oriented television shows. But he blew me away at this hip hop summit a few years back. While other rappers refused to even consider growing and evolving, Master P was the sole voice of reason and sense. But even before that, I dug his entrepreneurial model: fully independent. He has his own lab and he produces his own product and puts it out on the streets. Same way he used to do with crack. He came out with a film that way.

"Imagine if all hip hop and soul artists pooled their resources and followed P's example—just like in Carvah—they'd control their own destinies. Imagine what would happen if those big-time Africana writers who have isolated themselves in Princeton, Harvard, SUNY—or wherever the hell they are, cuz you rarely find 1 at Howard, NC A&T, Malare, Alcorn, or NCU—opened an independent University of Africology.

Aint May smiled at the idea. "There is nothing we can't do. We just have *believed* for so long: believed in Jesus, believed that we cannot successfully build anything that a Caucasian isn't overseeing, that we overlook our power."

"And end up promoting Ogo."

"We have so much healin to do . . ."

"You can see both our knowledge of our unlimited potential and the obstacles that we are tripping over in rap music. Wu-Tang Clan, for example, they 5% Nation. Lots of rappers are, but their earlier albums find them promoting Caucocapitalistic excess, violence, and sexism far more than Africana divinity. You can see how the Wu has grown when you compare the lyrics of *36 Chambers* to those of *A Better Tomorrow*."

"You know, Cha, I actually remember *counting* the number of consciousness-raising references in *36 Chambers*," Jahmai laughed. "I loved *36 Chambers*, but it was like watching a Kung Fu flick on a Saturday morning compared to X Clan's *To The East Blackwards*, which was like attending the University of African Gods and majoring in personal deification. X Clan has been consistent in expanding the parameters of Black divinity. But," Jahmai mused, "we need the diversity of all the Gods: Sunz of Man, Medusa, Prodigy, Wu, Lord Jamar, Mecca, everyone."

"As our artists are growing older they are growing up. They are trying to encourage their audiences to do likewise, but because the industry is run by Caucocapitalistic racists, our artists will have to unshackle themselves if they are serious about holistic evolution."

"Oya also mentioned the 5%. What is it?"

"Ma May, it is a manifestation of Ah. The 5% was born when a brother named Clarence Smith analyzed the lessons of the Nation of Islam and understood that Africana people are Gods. He took the name Allah for himself and started teaching every Africana youth he met that they were Allah too."

"That's deep. He took the word from text to flesh. Imagine if Black pastors would do that with Psalms 82:6 which makes it clear: 'Ye are are Gods,' and John 10:34, which is Jesus' confirmation that we are Gods," Aint May offered.

"Excellent point, Ma May. Our divinity is the worst kept secret in this world: Evidence and reminders of our power and glory abound from the beginning of time to the present, especially in rap music. The 5% started in New York in the mid 1960s, and because many members were and are rappers, they used the art of rap to disseminate the truth about Africana divinity." Jahmai popped a Sunz of Man and Killarmy compilation CD into the deck. The first song to play was "Allah Sees Everything."

"The term "5%" comes from the teaching that 85% of the people of the world are unconscious or emivoid—deaf dumb and blind. 10% of this world's inhabitants leech offa the confused, ignorant, and impoverished masses. But 5% of the world is conscious and is manifesting its divinity.

Indeed, 5 Percenters refer to themselves as 'Suns' and 'Gods.' In 1 song, Meth says he calls his brother Sun because the brother shines like 1.'"

"I heard that!" Aint May signified.

"Sunz got a track called 'Wake up'—here, wait, I got it right here," Jahmai skipped a few tracks until he reached number 7.

The car was booming with bass and mind-opening lyrics.

"They raps fast, like they runnin out of time," Aint May mused, "like *we* runnin out of time. I like that urgency: it's necessary. They making references to a spiritual revolution in the manner of Ah in those lyrics. Didn't the second rapper mention the sky opening and cosmic beings uniting under the sign and power of the Gods?"

"Yes, ma'am, Ma May!"

"They also talkin bout war, attackin the Pentagon, slaying Yurugu instead each other, and spreading beast ashes over the Mediterranean or makin em vanish like ships and planes do in the Bermuda Triangle. Wonder if folk know they prophesying and not just projecting images?

"They sendin signals out from where, New York? Sunz of Man: The shining, the nutrient-givers and source of life. Yeh, 5 % is sho nuff Tahn."

"New York's ghetto hell is producing all types a power," Chaka smiled. This was the kind of connecting she had never imagined. Here was Aint May, an ancient God reincarnated, digging the Gods of modern hip hop.

Aint May sat back and submerged herself in "The End," by Ras Kass and The RZA.

"This is an interesting song too," Aint May was enjoying analyzing rap lyrics. "The first rapper loses focus and force, but the acknowledgement that the favorite national pastime of America is white supremacy is a simple truth well stated. The recording at the end is like an exclamation point. It makes the audience question the symbols that characterize New York and America. Even most Yurugu are ignorant of Yurugu's forms of manipulation. Like the illuminati."

At the mention of the secret Ogo society everybody in the vehicle laughed, "Yurugu struggling to stay relevant." They chuckled and cruised up the interstate.

Aint May eased back into the gray upholstery of the van. She watched the bland landscape of Paducah, Kentucky roll by. Before she closed her eyes, she saw a Greyhound bus whiz by. It was going where they were coming from. "Special Delivery," she smiled.

The Carvah capitalized on Nashville being a city with a country foundation. Cows, goats and chickens gamboled, pecked and explored in a verdant 4 acre enclosure which was situated next to a community garden flourishing with squash, corn, black eyed peas, pole beans, pintos, watermelon, cantaloupe, tomatoes, okra and collard, mustard and turnip greens. Carvah's garden also boasted numerous medicinal flora, such as chickweed, nightshade, rabbit tobacco, red peppers, comfrey, valerian, verbena, devil's shoestring, lemon grass, poinsettias, and hyacinth.

"What is this 1?" Aint May bent over a flowering bush. The leaves were pea green in color and diamond shaped. Running up the stem was a thick profusion of ordered leaves crowned by a spray of white flowers. "My, this is so familiar."

Dr. Roper smiled at the elder, "Wunmi, a sister from the Continent is with us now. She brought the seeds for this plant. It is called efinrin."

"That's right! It gives a wonderful flavor to meats and soups!"

"You know it?"

"I know it and love it," she winked. "It's not seed time, but I want to take a few sprigs of this with me."

"You are welcome."

"Now, let's get together and distribute the Work."

Just as before, Aint May explained the medicine and its usage to everyone at Carvah. Again, the souljahs went forth and distributed the medicine while taking doses themselves. Emi was stunted in many members of the Carvah site because of nicotine and alcohol, the legal and most destructive drugs America has to offer. The elixir would remove these and all other chemical obstacles.

"It takes focus and dedication to come 180 so you can manifest 360," Ra mused. He knew what he was speaking about. It was 3 months in solitary that cleaned him of cigarettes, marijuana, and alcohol. "Many brothers are still finding their way in Ah, Aint May. This medicine will accelerate the process."

"What you've done here is really impressive, Ra," Hawa praised.

"You all got it going on right under their noses!" Jahmai was amazed. He had grown up in a community just like this 1 had been, in D.C. He knew the positivity at work in Carvah, but he never knew it was as strong as this.

"You got it brother, and what is more, we have a satellite site right up Jefferson near NCU. They are now 200 strong. But we'll take you there and to our studio. Actually, Kemetic Visions is the front for our studio. It isn't like its funny business but. . ."

"We gots to keep things close to the vest," Xaviah concluded. "The more covert our operatives, the more intense our operations. The biggest markets so far for our hip hop product are Chicago and N.Y. They are seconded by St. Louis, Peoria, D.C., and Gary. Now, as far as it concerns the DVDs we're producing, they're hot on the west coast. The poetry, well, of course the heads in Philly and Atlanta are eating it up. But these stats are only concerning peaks, product is moving nationwide and internationally. Heads in Britain, Ghana, Senegal, and Nigeria are already organizing."

"Vibrations and awakening are happening all over every day. Sister-sites are popping up everywhere," Azure was excited about the speed with which consciousness was spreading.

Jahmai noticed some strange vibrations between this fine and serious sister and Xaviah and Ra. Like there was love between all of them. He was intrigued and impressed.

"Most folk don't know what it is when we show them our product!" laughed Xaviah. "You see, we only use cover art that is Ah oriented. Some titles and lyrics are written and rapped in Medu Netcher, Nsibidi, or Shumom so they speak directly to the listener's emi." Xaviah had been undergoing extensive training in ancient African scripts. He and Danta and Glutey of the Bliss Bluff site were devising a new visual and auditory system of communication. Together, Glutey, the former BDG from Joliet, who, after spreading BGD philosophy down I-55 had been awakened by Ah and joined the Original Path Institute, and Xaviah, the former Vice Lord, devised the encoded messages of the musical releases and the cover art of most of the Tahn literature and music.

"Our focus is creation and distribution," Saddiq discussed his cell's role in the enterprise. "What we tell customers is take it and listen and then donate. Folk give us more than what they would for a regular CD.

The collective strolled to Ah garden, which formerly housed 3 vacant lots and 2 abandoned houses. "Our focus is self-sufficiency," Alteveze gestured to the expansive community garden. "The garden will soon be self-sustaining. Everyone helps with the work, and most seeds come from the plants. After we've nourished our community, we sell our surplus at the Farmers' Market."

"Of all money generated from the garden and our artistry, 30% is shared communally, but the bulk of the money we earn goes to our underground constructions, including this," Ra led everyone to a chamber about 100 feet underground that held a massive cache of 1000s of different kinds of arms. "And this," he showed them the forge he had designed, "Brothers workin on a ground-to-air missile launcher and an M-16."

"From the crack lab to armory!" Jahmai was amazed.

"You would be surprised at some of the weapons these brothers have designed. We also replicate weapons already in use. 1 of our blacksmiths, Jesse, who we call ReMember, fell through the cracks of the school system. He fell through with a three dimensional photographic memory, and we were honored to catch him. After studying a weapon's image, he designs a mold. Once the molds are set, we begin smelting the iron, which comes from the scrap yard. Guess you could call it revolutionary bricolage," Xaviah paused recalling his father, Raymond, picking fleas from round Piccadilly. "And we all go for target practice and arms training."

Aint May strolled the elaborate laboratory: "I'm impressed with everything you have done. This is amazing. I love the renovation of the projects. No 1 who has ever seen 'projects' would consider these homes part of that system of racist experimentation."

"Elder May, we spent 5 months just making these holes habitable and renovating them so that they would protect us from the feds rather than give them access to us."

"You have a emi here, I feel its energy. But you also have a . . ." she paused searching for the right word, "a network." The elder was perceiving the unseen.

"You're right," Azure smiled, "we have tunnels all over the place." May could even sense the construction on-going as Ah dug a tunnel to the courthouse.

"We are about to fight 1 of the world's most quiet and effective wars," Azure glowed.

The collective made its way above-ground to a feast of jambalaya, corn fritters, collard greens, and roasted squash and peppers.

After the repast, Azure shared her thoughts with her comrades: "You know, I had given up on America. I used to wonder: How can we ever be free here? We were brought here to be slaves. After slavery, we were the fuel for the industrial era."

"'The machines behind the machines' as Brockway said in *Invisible Man*."

"Exactly Dr. Roper. We have gone to war twice against Ogo; we have yet to win. I was beginning to think we could never win. Seriously," she shook her head against the protestations of the people who had never witnessed Azure express doubt. They only knew her as pure positive power. "No, seriously, how can we win, I wondered. We live on land that they slaughtered millions of Native Americans to control. Now it is land upon which they kill us for sport, for kicks. They kill us to flaunt in our faces their impunity. And we are so bereft of power that we respond with die-ins, marches, and speeches.

"Yurugu has been the time and tide of this region since it arrived. We have been existing in a state similar to that of the Scarecrow of *The Wiz*. We've been singing with sass, soul, and futility the words taught to us by our oppressors for their entertainment: We can't win, we can't break even, and we can't get out of the game.

"We've been using our oppressors' tools and rules and wondering why we can't accomplish or erect anything of permanence. All that rhetoric during the 60s war was primarily rhetoric. We was never gon get our own state or anything else here. A brother can't even build a house without a lot of wàhálà," here she sampled the Nigerian term borrowed from Wunmi.

"Sister can't open a business for red-lining. And anything that we do attain here is only a sandcastle built on the sea shore waiting for high tide.

"My goal was to get out of the game: to repatriate. I had planned to leave right after I graduated," the sparkles in Ra and Xaviah's eyes revealed to Jahmai that Ra and Xaviah were Azure's complements. "But I asked myself, 'how can I leave the bones of my ancestors?' It dawned on me that my, *our* ancestors don't want us to be oppressed *any*where *any*how. Our ancestors who were enslaved ran—as families or as individuals—to Florida, Canada, Mexico, and sailed to Sierra Leone and Liberia because they knew that freedom is our right and that our souls and soul power suffuse this planet. Our ancestors are global, and our safe havens are wherever we erect them: on the Continent, in the Ìtànkálẹ̀, in the cosmos.

"But now, with Ah efforts, we don't have to abide by the laws of the lawless or struggle to morally suade the hopelessly immoral. We don't have to balance the imbalanced or shine in spite of oppression and oppressors. We can have everything that we need and want in *this* lifetime: Including peace. I agree with Fela, the struggle must end. Yurugu is not worthy of any more of Ah time. We have planets to create and nebula to fashion. With the extermination of Yurugu we can focus on our *real* Work."

"Respect, God," Chaka embraced Azure. "Wise words well spoken."

"An integral part of our real work, Azure, is healing. The first tier of healing is taking place now, with the addiction eradicator. The second tier, which is a cure for AIDS, will be ready in about 7 weeks," Aint May smiled.

"Elder May?!" Azure, and everyone from the Carvah site were aghast.

"Why y'all lookin so surprised?" Aint May teased the Carvah Tahn, "We talkin bout manifestin or playin?

"It was Patrice Lumumba who produced the cure. Imagine his anguish: The Prophet was shot and killed; his body was carved up with saws; the pieces were set ablaze and then dissolved in sulfuric acid. This all happened off a Kinshasa highway that Yurugu now calls the AIDS highway. Ogo has destroyed so many lives," Aint May looked off into the distance, into the future, "it will soon reap the reciprocity it has long-sown."

After their 3 week visit to Carvah, May, Jahmai, and Chaka headed back to Alapaha and continue their Work.

As they drove down I-24 East Aint May enthused, "These young folk are warriors and they are ready!" She was delighted by the fire of Carvah.

"I could actually feel the increase in shining with the distribution of the anti-addiction serum," Jahmai marveled.

"Now that the emi development is accelerated, the Carvah warriors are going to explode in power." Aint May knew that Carvah would not be able to camouflage itself much longer. And they didn't want to. They were ready for war. And with the help Aint May was preparing, the rout, because it wouldn't be a battle, wouldn't last long.

"You've noticed," she continued, "that the rays of the sun are magnificent in their radiance. I mean, it's hot as a big dog!" Everyone laughed 1 of those deep-belly laughs. "Now, those environmentalists can say all they want bout the greenhouse effect because, actually, that is what it is. Plants grow better in a greenhouse because it is hot and humid. Life thrives in hot and humid conditions. Y'all notice how smooth and black your skin is?"

"Yes, ma'am."

"That's evidence of *you* thrivin in the greenhouse of cosmic power. But for the beast, the sun's rays promise sufferation, malaise, and death. 1 of the things the next medicine we will create will do is exacerbate the effect of the ultraviolet rays on Ogo. You know, Ogo has a recessive genetic structure, so much so that certain genetic recombinations create a condition whereby certain Ogo are allergic to the sun. When these Ogo are exposed to the sun, they blister and swell and their eyes bulge. If they continue to remain in sunlight, of any strength, they will die.

"The skin cancer that plagues them is a manifestation of this genetic mutation. We are going to exploit that trait in their recessive genes and employ a few other directives. This," Aint May smiled, "will be some hi-tech Hoodoo."

They came like the night. On a mission born of avarice and fuelled by vengeance, they thought it would more expedient to arrive under the cover of the night. Each group of 10 individuals synchronized their approach from 8 sides of the village. They would converge and, fully armed, would take by force what they owned.

The plan was an excellent 1 but the approach was sloppy. None of them were familiar with the terrain and, as a result, they announced their arrival with a little less noise than a full-on military parade. The snappings of twigs, their stumblings over looped roots, and the curses they swore announced to the inhabitants of Kumbah that their adversaries had arrived.

Foku twisted and turned in his round cabin. He knew it best that he appear to be asleep and run out in alarm with the rest of the village when the firing and shouting began.

The entire day had been 1 of trepidation for Foku. He had been sullen and short-tempered. He was still torn.

Wakynam and the elders of Kumbah knew everything. They had been tracking the movement of the group from the moment they left. They knew the arms that they held. They knew their motivations. They knew which of their number would recognize shining and join them. They knew the number who would die. But even had they not been aware that the group would arrive that night, Foku's attitude would offered warning enough.

He had undergone a considerable change since his confession and the cleansing with Nadey. He had opened up and was interacting fully with his peer group. The day before the arrival, however, there was such a drastic change that everyone, even day-old members, knew that the arrival was imminent. Foku had been more morose than he had ever been.

Foku twisted his cover cloth so much that it was bunched and knotted between his legs. He sat up in his bed and disentangled himself. He sighed a heavy sigh that spoke of betrayal and grief. He decided to go out and stretch his legs.

Wrapping his cloth about his waist, he stepped out of his cabin and found himself staring into the eyes of Empai, his father.

Foku dropped to the earth, his legs straight behind him; he balanced on his toe tips and palms. Thus he greeted his father who had led the elders of Mapu to Kumbah.

"Rise," Empai growled. There would be no lengthy salutations.

"Where are they?"

Foku noted the group's copious implements of war and talismans of protection, "My fathers and mothers, I am so happy to see you. I hope you have come in peace, I will gladly lead you to the elders."

Foku turned to the East and waited for the elders to part and let him lead. When they parted, he saw nothing but bush! Where was Maly and Yao's dwelling which was situated next to his? Where was the village? Had they abandoned him? But how? He could understand if they had fled, but it was as if *he* had been moved. Yes, it seemed as though he and his cabin had been lifted and carried deep into the forest. They have rejected me, he thought, I deserve no better.

"Boy. Where is the village? This is the place where you have been, isn't it?" Empai and Jobbi searched Foku's dwelling, it was as it had always been; it was just that nothing else was the same.

"He has tricked us!"

"He has deceived us!"

"No, no! My people, calm down, they have tricked him; don't you see?" His mother came to his defense. "They have exiled him to this place. They, they, son, why didn't you tell us? Why didn't you warn us? Did they lead you here blindfolded?"

"Woman, hush and let him speak: What has happened here? Why are you here alone in the bush?"

"I don't know, Owner of the House. I don't know what has happened."

"Have you been exiled to this place?" Jobbi, the father of Zennan and Kyza, inquired.

"Uh, no, I"

"Did you come here on your own? How long have you been here? Where are the others?" Malki shot out questions like a Tech 9. Foku was confused.

"I-I-I have always been here."

"What? Imbecile! How can you have been here always?!" His mother was incensed by his lack of lucidity.

"No, I, mean, uh, since I left, I have been here."

"So you were never with the group?!" asked Jobbi. "So you have deceived us! You knew," he was brandishing his machete, "that we came here to reclaim our children!"

"Yes, I knew."

"And you chose to deceive us instead?"

"No! Yesterday, I"

"Stop the lies: enough!" Jobbi sprang toward Foku. Empai held Jobbi back but only because his own ire was invoked.

"Tell us the truth now, or we will kill you in the kidnappers' stead," he held his shining machete ready for his son's neck. In his heart, he had disowned the boy. He was obviously an idiot now. Perhaps they had given him medicine upon discovering their link. The mission was a fiasco; they'd been fooled by this lying small boy.

Empai's shame bubbled over. His mind contacted his spine which sent his 4th vertebrae into action. His muscles flexed as his grip on the machete tightened. In the time it took for his arm to begin its backward sweep to work up the velocity to decapitate his son, he felt a slight breeze. His movement did not slack however as the velocity of the arm carried his entire body forward, but he found himself hurtling to the ground.

"Mmhhppplrrhhh!!!!" He yelled. It was a muffled sound because his mouth was filled with dirt and blood and broken teeth.

"Empai!!"

"Father!?" The son, whom he was in the process of killing, and his wife rushed to the aid of their patriarch. When they lifted him, spitting blood and curses, he found the reason for his tumble.

"My arm! Where is my arm! The witches have stolen my arm!"

Everyone gasped. Where there had formerly been a muscular arm clenching a machete, there was now nothing. In the right sleeve of Empai's boubou was absolutely nothing.

"My husband, my wealth! My lord! What has befallen you? Are you feeling pain?"

Although he yelled and wept like a child, he admitted he felt no pain. There was also no blood. There was only the pain of absence. And now, the weight of an indescribable presence.

"People of Mapu. You have not come on a peaceful mission. Nor have you come with honest intentions," Wakynam's voice reverberated throughout the land.

Wakynam, Daughter, and all the Ah of Kumbah materialized. The village was as it had been but the Ah were standing in a circle, surrounding the elders of Mapu. The elders of Mapu completely forgot about Empai and his arm as they spun around to face the Ah.

"You cannot kill us. But if you want to try, you are welcome. You cannot thwart our mission. But if you must try, you are welcome.

"We are a people of peace. We are a whole people who facilitate healing and growth. We adhere to the way. We are Ah, and we are older than time. We are older than the myths of Jesus and Mohammed and the fictions of their gods, we are older than the gods you worship in Mapu. We are the originators of existence."

"You took my manhood!" This from Timba.

"You are witches and child snatchers!"

"People come here of their own volition; they come from many regions. They come here to be whole. To repair themselves. We do not need to snatch people because our work, our way attracts them."

"I came here from Gorée, Sunugal. I came here for the same reason many of your children left Mapu: My mothers cut off my clitoris."

"I escaped from Niamey where I was enslaved."

"I, Gu, came here because my emi told me I must come."

"I came here from South Africa. I was given AIDS at a mandatory AIDS testing site."

"My name is Pombi. I came here from Kongo where my people are being massacred. I know that Wakynam and the elders can provide us with life-saving wisdom. I am here to learn."

"I came here from Cape Coast. I dreamt of Kumbah and saw its shining from the coast. I brought my family with me."

Every resident stepped forward and reveal her and his reasons for relocation. They did not have to testify. They wanted to. Adorned in wrappas and singlets as appropriate for victims of a pre-dawn raid, they stood forth and told their truths.

Empai, who had regained his composure, was nonplussed.

If you are so peace loving, he projected mentally, why have you taken my child and my arm?

Father, I wanted to come here. Had you not tracked me, I would have been happy. Your arm was taken because you lifted it in violence.

With Foku's last syllable, Jobbi, Vali, Tombwe, Timba, and Nambo, and more, 20 in all, began communicating on another frequency, a negative level, so as to formulate their attack.

They are not so many, once we charge, others will back us as reinforcements and we can destroy them all.

But listen to them: They do seem peaceful. . .

They are unarmed. We can't massacre them and live in peace.

They have our children! Man, they have my husband's arm!

They thought the Ah would not be able to catch their wave. They were wrong. But the Ah revealed nothing. They continued testifying:

"I am Tangii, I have come to this place to heal myself of the life I lived as a prostitute in Cotonou."

Listen to them, they are doing positive work! I can feel the power that they radiate.

Fool! They are witches! Have you forgotten the place we arrived at was a house hugged on all sides by bush and we are now in a town?

"I am called Ocham. I was the servant of Yurugu in Abidjan. My rectum is now as wide as an open mouth. In time I will be able to hold my bowels. And my soul shall be whole. It will be whole again."

We cannot listen to this nonsense. These people are merely magicians.

No, Tysaan is right. I, also can feel them.

I, I am feeling something too . . . . They are doing good work!

No! You are cowards! They are magicians! They made the village disappear and reappear. The case is the same for Empai's arm.

They are sorcerers and witches.

They are not, they are only magicians. They bleed. I will count to 3. Fire your guns first in a semicircle so as to kill as many as possible at once. Whatever they are, they will never take over this land and its wealth! Never!

Never!

"Never have I been to a place that radiated with such fullness. Here I have been able to shine in ways my parents' dream of me being a student at the university would never have allowed."

1, 2 "UUuuhhggrrrghghguuhhgg!!!" Was the last sound heard from them. The cry rent the air with so much strength that the echoes of their war wail bounded far into the forest.

But as the cry was echoing, the testifying continued without interruption.

"I am Isnah. I was born here."

The warriors of Mapu,

"I, Ahzonah, have

always been."

their guns, their intentions, their machetes,

"I, Ahlaz, am free

here."

vanished.

I am Wakynam. If you still seek to destroy us, you are welcome to try. We are Ah. We are shining.

Of the 50 Mapu residents who were left after the mass removal, 34 remained with the Ah of Kumbah. 16 fled back to the village when they realized their warriors has simply vanished.

"You may follow them if you like," Wakynam stepped forth. She had taken the appearance of a woman about 63 years of age with short cropped salt and pepper hair.

"No. We wish to stay. It is not because of fear, mind you," Lan Endo said. "It is not because of what has happened to the members of our clan. I am the mother of Ama and Nadey. When my daughters and the group left, my family was devastated at our loss of children and of my husband's virility. However, after months of rage, understanding slowly began to introduce itself to me. Our traditions and cultures, as we call them, are only poorly sharpened knives with which we have hacked off the spirit and vitality of our progeny. I am so sorry that I sought to imprison the soul of my daughters out of jealousy because of the imprisonment of my own.

"When I learned that a group, a posse, was forming to come here, I joined them with this quiet knowledge because it is my desire be a proper mother and to shine as Ah.

"Ahlaz, my sister, many people were saying they knew why you went. That you were simply a witch like them. But I know your story of ostracism. You came here to give your soul what our village could not. This is also why I have come."

"Mother, you are welcome." Nadey, the perfect 1, the ebony star, came forward and wrapped her tender and strong arms around her mother's waist. Both the elder and her daughter knew that their relationship was biologically the same but that spiritually the child was the elder.

"We want to live and build with you here in Kumbah, in peace."

Construction began the next morning. Everyone stomped the mud, fashioned the frames, and placed wood between their thighs and adzes in their hands. They placed their ears next to plants, they sank into the life offered by the nourishing lake. They built both homes and soul sanctuaries.

During the period of construction, Kofi and Daughter were busy finding ways to secure and protect the Tahn of Carvah and Bliss Bluff. These were the most vulnerable sites because of their proximity to Ogo and their impressive levels of growth and success. Because Alapaha was primarily a mobile site, it posed no significant threat, but no Ah could fool herself into thinking that Ah were safe in the land of Yurugu.

The Carvah have achieved an impressive feat, Kofi observed, they have made a fortress of what was to be their prison. If martial law is enacted and

Interstate 65 closed, which borders them on the north, and railway line of the south is blocked and the entrance of Malare is barricaded, they have the network of tunnels by which to escape. The same tunnels grant them a covert means by which to affect the annihilation of Ogo. Both of them examined the astral map that revealed the complete layout of the Carvah site: above-ground and subterranean.

The tunnel network showcases the genius of Azure. From Carvah 1 can reach the NCU satellite, Kemetic Visions, the courthouse, various police stations, the FBI central office, or the governor's mansion in minutes; and all the tunnels are wide enough to permit motor vehicles. Daughter laughed, Just as we have astral communication and mobility, they have subterranean mobility and communication. Ingenious.

The biggest threat will arise if or when the authorities notice and associate the impressive development, awakenings, and focus of Malare, Carvah Homes, Kemetic Visions, and NCU with the destruction of its institutions. Perhaps we should begin to make the site appear as it used to— a crippled contusion of bricks and sticks. This will keep them camouflaged.

I understand your idea, but it may be more beneficial to the Work if many of the advancements remain. For 1 thing, their construction is quite advanced and surely has been noted. Knowing Ogo's selfishness, Yurugu might very well praise the residents of Carvah and shine a spotlight on them as an example of what Tahn can do with hard work and motivation. They may even use the work of Carvah to push for the eradication of both food assistance and public housing. With Yurugu's mind occupied with the superficial, it would be oblivious to what is happening, literally, right under its nose. What do you think?

Brilliant idea! We can have Kandace and Oya draw Ogo's attention to the beautification of Carvah. It will be featured on local news programs and papers and then spotlighted by the national organs. We'll focus our efforts on shielding the major construction they are doing, sound-proofing the tunnels, and . . . the Lair . . . Daughter pondered this especially knotty issue. The building is too conspicuous. The tunnels converge there, many meetings are held there. Azure, Alteveze, Ra, the Wilsons, Xaviah and Saddiq live there: The Lair needs to be completely shielded. . . . What if we make the Lair appear to have been abandoned. Ogo would see a house falling into dilapidation with boarded windows, holes in walls, and a sinking foundation.

Yes. The Tahn can make a big show of arguing, disbanding, and dividing. Moving out. But the Work will continue as usual.

Excellent idea! We can also use Malare to deflect attention from the Carvah build and growth. Malare has always been plagued with financial crises and scandals. We can use the current high dropout/low enrollment rates to foment a financial crisis that is so great the president is considering selling Malare's administration building because its ceiling features Aaron Douglas' artwork.

They made all the necessary mental notes of the protections they would provide Carvah. Now, Kofi and Daughter turned their minds to the next dilemma, Saddiq and Jah Sun have implemented scrambling devices so that they can speak without being recorded or understood. This system works electronically; we will augment it with astral encoding which is unfailing and tamper-proof.

You know, when the Tahn express themselves, what they say can have multiple meanings depending upon the context. They call it signifying. They perfected this art while enslaved. What we can do is multiply the levels of signification. They will still be speaking intelligible English, but it will sound like the mundane or the nonsensical to Ogo.

Outstanding. We'll add to their encoding another layer at emilevel 3 to ensure Yurugu will be oblivious to the messages. The Tahn who only have emilevel 1 or 2 capacity will have to reach and expand their minds to understand these messages.

Now, Daughter turned to the astral projection of Bliss Bluff, what of the Institute?

Well, they also have gone far in protecting themselves. First and foremost, they are secluded in a rural area and they have access to vast acres of land.

Danta has erected an underground library that is also equipped with a tunnel. This library of information is multiform: digitized, tangible, and astral texts and data are stored there. This site is adjacent to the actual emisite. It is updated with new information from all the 6 sites regularly with only a 3 second lapse from actual activity to astral recording to digitization.

The library is encased in zinc and reinforced with 12 inch steel walls. Fire, electric surge, earthquake, nothing can penetrate or destroy it. Danta has done well here. The main problem is posed by the above-ground buildings and homes of the members: these are all vulnerable. The good thing is that they are within relatively close proximity to 1 another.

But that is also a weakness, as is the fact that they are well known. The Institute is not a secret, it is an open threat, and as a home and a series of homes, it stands as an easy target for Ogo.

This is problematic. I think of the church burnings of the 60s and the 90s. It would take Ogo nothing to bomb or burn down these homes.

How can we prevent this?

I'm thinking of the ancestral Tahn, the way they would outwit the patterollers: They would tie ropes across the road so that when horses crossed them at night alarms were raised by screaming and falling horses and attackers. We could do something similar to that. He mused silently for several minutes, then: I just received a projection from Babygirl! She is running in a field, free, her arms stretched wide. She is smiling. Now, she is bounding back. Oh! I feel voltage!

I feel it too!

An electric wire fence used to keep cows in the pasture. Yes.

An Ogo detector?

Exactly. We will create 2 different types. 1 will simply warn the Bliss Bluff Ah of intruders. Another will disintegrate Ogo just as we disintegrated the intruders of Mapu.

These will take some time to fashion, but they are optimal solutions.

Ahlaz and Nadey were the caretakers of the new members from Mapu. The newcomers began their training with Nadey. She took each of them individually to the lake for cleansing. It was there that, stripped of the clothes, talismans, and charms with which they had adorned themselves, they came to meet themselves and the elders of Kumbah in their actual forms.

Lan Endo was the first to go for cleansing. Nadey arrived at the site where they were building her home. There were no words spoken between mother and daughter. The small and sweet 1, Nadey, came, gazed at her mother, and led her to the lake.

After Lan Endo came Chumsti, Abubacar, Yongui, Wereo, Gondue, Bakari, Rini, Hastal, Pronjan, all of them, she immersed each 1 of them in the healing waters of Ah. Stripped of everything, they followed the path of their daughter who had been known as Ama. They sojourned with the elders and Wakynam as long as their individual spirits needed nurturing, cleansing, and directing. Nadey stayed with them throughout the duration of their individual sojourns in the water.

The newcomers had to remove the negativity, trauma, and violence they'd been subjected to from their psyches, bodies, and souls. Their bodies had to be healed and their minds and souls had to be recalibrated to not only understand and move beyond their pasts but also to prepare themselves to join and undertake the work of Ah. They emerged from their day or days in the lake clean and shining and filled with intimate knowledge of the force that had led them from the blight of oblivion to the clearing of completion.

Many grew so excited about the power of Kumbah that they wanted to go to Mapu and beyond to gather the kin and friends they felt could grow in the womb of Ah.

I understand how you feel, Ahlaz sympathized, because the force of Ahni is deep and wide and welcoming. It is your rightful home. But when you journey to Ogo-controlled lands filled with the perfection of Ah you will attract violence, hostility, and viciousness. Those who are filled with hatred and bent on destruction may follow you here.

Indeed, Wakynam reminded them, your initial visit to Kumbah was fuelled by your desire to slaughter all of us so that you could take your children and physically, psychologically, and/or spiritually butcher them. We were forced to annihilate many of you.

This is a land of peace, healing, and wholeness. It must remain as such. It is not the work of the Ah of Kumbah to slay people. But if individuals or groups come here with seething in their souls, we will obliterate them. We will protect our progeny. We will protect Ah.

As you will learn when your study of Ah history begins, Ogo has massacred millions of us. We will have no more of this. Too much precious Ah blood has been shed. Too many of Ah have become ancestors before their times.

You may go if you wish, Ahlaz projected, but what we would prefer is that you mentally summon those who you think are shining in their souls. If they are Ah, they will come, on their own, and they will gain strength and resolve from the struggle they survive to come here. If their destiny is 1 with the way, if their focus is to further the Work, let them come of their own volition, in their own preparedness, and in their own time. That is best.

It was appropriate for Ahlaz to address the newcomers because she played a central part in their recovery. Following their cleansing, newcomers sought Ahlaz. It was not planned or mandated, it was simply necessary. Having been so long disassociated from the rhythms of the Earth, having consciously or unconsciously debased the force of life from which they were molded and had sprung, their souls told their hands they needed clay, creation, molding, creativity! They found all these with Ahlaz.

With Ahlaz, in the clearing of creation, their spirits found the free space of inspiration that village life had denied them. The soul sanctuaries they created spoke volumes about the oppressions they had internalized, forgotten, and projected upon others.

Yongui fashioned a stupendous likeness of the chief of the village, Ginjae Kankwom. The resemblance to the patriarch was uncanny. The thick ankles and calves that were glossed with internal and external fat. The glistening and bulbous thighs and the arms, the latter far too short for a figure so wide, were dwarfed by the midsection of the chief. The head rested upon a neck that consisted of serpentine rolls of flab. Even the fired clay seemed to be sweating. When 1 looked at the visage of the chief, 1 was unsure if it were a contorted smile or a distended grimace 1 was viewing.

In spite of the overall grotesqueness of the sculpture, which was as disturbing as it was ponderous, the eyes of the gazer stalled upon reaching the pendulous belly. The herniated navel, was attractive and beckoning. When 1 peered inside the navel, 1 was astounded. The first images to greet the eye were those of masses of mangled human forms: men, women, children were all writhing and gyrating in the belly of the beast who vied for power with Yurugu.

They were dying, but rather than succumb in peace, they pulled, slayed, and dragged others with them into death. Here was a father twisting the neck of his infant child. Here was a toddler with his leg extended, tripping his mother so that she falls and breaks her neck. There was a young girl gouging out the eyes of her twin sister. To the rear was a woman who had been pregnant. Her husband, who stood over her with a saber, had slashed her womb from her body. Here was a smiling husband gunning his family down. A mother was feeding her children spiders and those children were shitting worms into their infant siblings' mouths.

Standing on top of this macabre melee were different images of the same people. Rather than an orgy of violence and self-destruction, the figures were climbing up and standing on their void and negative selves. Feet upon shoulders upon feet upon shoulders upon feet, they were using the depravity into which they had sunk as a springboard to self-salvation and -reclamation. The difficulties involved in such a transformation were clear. Faces were distorted with effort. Tears rained down upon the bodies of the debauched and the healing alike. Strained muscles and tendons stood in high relief on the bodies of their beings. There were many who did not survive the transformation, but rather than seek company in death, these ancestors assisted and supported those who would survive.

On top of these emergent beings were their illuminated and whole selves. They were enlightened by knowledge of who their primary oppressors were—not only their rulers, but they, themselves. Drenched in wisdom, they glistened. They glowed, and their brilliance was disintegrating and the choking the chief. The seemingly paradoxical expression on the chief's countenance was now quite clear. Those he had literally devoured and had grown fat off of were revolting and wreaking both havoc and vengeance on him from the inside out.

Ahlaz guided, coaxed, and kneaded all the newcomers' thoughts to expression, but Chumsti was a difficult case. She created only ragged asymmetrical balls.

"Ahlaz, perhaps my spirit has been damned by stagnation. When I ask my soul to speak to the Earth, this" she fanned out her hand over mounds that were only marked by their increase in size, "is what comes forth."

"Don't worry. You have so much that you are working through. Allow the confusion and disorder to come through. That is part of your process," Ahlaz thought she noticed patterns in the indentations. Were these truly patterns or—"Come with me."

Ahlaz led her to the clay pit. Chumsti did as she had always done: she squatted and scooped the cool and damp and slick earth with her hands. "No," Ahlaz stopped her. "No, remove your clothes."

Ahlaz hung Chumsti's garments on a tree branch, "This may help you understand what your spirit and Ahni are whispering to you. Lie back." She took the earth that Chumsti had gathered and began smoothing it upon her prone body. When her body was covered, Ahlaz chanted words of prayer and inspiration, words of peace and meditation over Chumsti's body which was hidden in a womb of red clay.

Chumsti rose into the consciousness of Ah. She was surrounded by soft red walls. She felt pulse and rhythm engulf her. She spun around; she was a free flowing entity. She was like a bubble in a confined space that was too delicate to puncture her buoyancy. Surrounded in red, she touched a surface and came into contact with an element so like herself she sighed. Then she noticed the veins and knew, she was in the womb. She was a cognizant, knowledgeable adult living in the body of an *in vitro* fetus. She laughed and bubbles danced from her mouth and floated above her head. She felt her mother's smile; it was womb deep. Her mother began to sing a song. Chumsti knew the song and sang it with her. When she felt the rhythm of walking, Chumsti sank into the most peaceful sleep she had ever known.

When she awakened she thought, How beautiful; what a wonderful experience! She procrastinated the opening of her eyes because she wanted to keep the bliss of the womb with her and never wake up. When she finally opened her eyes, she realized she was still in the womb. With that realization she felt a rush, a pull, a sinking. She clambered to resist the force that would drag her from the womb and push her into the world.

But her mother was strong, and Chumsti also felt hands insistently massaging from outside the walls. She felt the force of muscular contractions, release, circles, contract, massage, release, circles, contract, release, massage. She didn't want to leave. She didn't want to be born. But she didn't want to strangle herself on her umbilical cord or kill her mother with an impossible birth, so she relaxed and the hands coaxed her body into the perfect birthing position.

Will I still have consciousness once I'm born? Will I remember all of this? All I have learned?

Preoccupied with worry, she didn't realize she had entered the world until she opened her eyes and was blinded by light.

"Oh!" Chumsti cried. She was surrounded by cloths and the scents of love and the perfume of endurance. The mothers praised her mother.

She gazed upon her mother who was an exhausted, sweating, glowing reflection of herself and said, "My own."

She found herself tumbling in freefall. Just before she could hit the ground, reluctant hands caught her.

"It speaks!"

"Oh no!"

"What have you given birth to?"

"What abomination is this?"

The mothers were aghast. They backed away from her. Chumsti felt trapped in her fragile new body.

"Mother, do—" she was unable to finish when the startled gasps commenced again.

"What are you?" she gazed up at her inquiring mother, who was being supported by 2 elder women.

"I am Ah. We are the keepers of the true way. There is no need to fear. Please! I am your daughter. Please!"

She begged to no avail. She didn't lose consciousness at any time. She felt the absence, the overwhelming absence when the umbilical cord was cut. It was then she wept, but a first cry was not heard in the village because she wept as she was, like a young adult.

She wept for her fate also. Even before the hands came. The hands that were strong from wielding hoes and axes and uprooting cassava and toughened from washing clothes and dyeing cloths. The hands that were texts of destiny grabbed her, covered her, squeezing out and blocking her air. She wept. Her tears, which were like blood, joined the lines of the judicial palms of fear and misrecognition. Abomination.

Chumsti's experience occurred over a period of 5 days. She was not surprised to find she had cried and cracked most of the clay from her body. Although she recalled the buoyant bliss of her womb-time, she was burdened with the weight of her revelation: We have been killing our children from the very moment of their births.

"We have been killing our children from the very moment of their births," she said aloud. "We don't allow them to grow, seek, find, and follow their own destinies. We carve out a gutter, call it life and impel them to slosh and trod in it. They may not clean it, they may not step out of it. Our traditions" Ahlaz had come as had Nadey, Kofi, Daughter, Wakynam, everyone, "our culture, our previous way, is a road of death and void, and we, the mothers, have been its guardians. Our children are sacrifices to the altar of the vapidity. We give birth to abortions."

She sank into sleep.

Everyone came with healing hands. Every portion of Chumsti's body was covered with hands of healing, protection, and love.

Her place is with me, Wakynam declared. Chumsti was taken to the lake of healing, again. When she emerged, which she rarely did, she was the twin of Wakynam, her soul had selected the crocodile. She was now her own home.

Chumsti created a home by rebirthing herself in eternal protection. In a similar fashion, newcomers to Kumbah would also look within and find pathways to their destinies. Some members became masters of medicine who shared wisdom with Aint May. Others enjoyed commune with the fauna of the land and learned from them the way Tobi learned from flora. Some were obviously Àjẹ́ and joined the ẹgbẹ́. Others, like Ahlaz, were artists of wood, clay, oils, words, or acrylics. What the souls of Kumbah needed, Ah supplied.

"Foku, Kyza, Wereo, and Hastal, you are welcome," Cynthia greeted the newcomers who entered the circle of Àjẹ́.

"You have come at an exciting time," she smiled. "We have new deliberations to begin today."

"As you see," Kandace gestured to the center where 11 immobile, unconscious gray humanoid forms clustered, "we have gathered the offenders," she gestured to the forms. "Ìyàmi Odù will now address us."

While Gods, ancestors, and elders were situated in a huge circle of hundreds, it was easy to see that she was the center. She was massive, 7 stories tall. She was the immaculate Black of the cosmos. She was identical to Ahni. These 2 God Mothers worked together: the entities Ìyàmi Odù gave life to, Ahni directed. They were an inseparable indistinguishable tandem, although Odù, the Hidden 1, fittingly, rarely made appearances.

Odù was pure knowledge of Ah and justice of Àjẹ́. She could direct her force anywhere because she was everywhere. She could move anywhere at any time, assume any form she chose, peek into any galaxy that sparked her interest, right any planet in need of balance.

In her center was the source of all power, her Womb. The newcomers were amazed to find that not only was her womb visible but also that her womb was the cosmos in which the Earth and all other planets, stars, galaxies, and nebula thrived, died, and were reborn. It was difficult to pull 1's eyes away from the inexhaustible depth of the Womb of Life of the Mother of All. But her voice, a voice that was the auditory expression of the Blackness whose radiance enriched the cosmos, commanded attention:

"We are the enforcers of law of the cosmos including this planet. We are as ancient as time and as knowing. Our work is unimaginably vast. Every aspect of Ah is an aspect of Àjẹ́. We share 1 soul, 1 objective."

The Ògbóni, the Apèènà, the Erelu, the chiefs; the Òrìṣà: Ṣàngó, Ògún, Èṣù; the Nanas, the Queen Mothers: Queen Nzingah: Nyabinghi; the Queens Kandace, Òṣun, Hatshepsut; the evanescent Maji Maji, Queen Zaria, Sarraounia Aben Soro, Zumbi, the Ọba, the Asantehenes, Shaka: Boukman, Tubman, Mary Ellen Pleasant, Nanny, Nyabinghi, Nat, L'Ouverture, Dessalines, Lumumba, Sankara, Fela, Funmilayo, Tinubu, Efunsetan, innumerable leaders and administrators and members of Àjẹ́ were assembled for this vital cleansing.

After saluting the collective, Odù directed her focus at the gray forms clustered in the center of the room. Ṣàngó stood and called out the names and titles of the forms gathered in a pus-ridden knot.

"Abdul Abdallah—president of the African Union
"Nathan Malchance—Head of State of Nigeria
"Brosyn Tczlidnif—chairman of the IMF
"Karn Jusninean—chairman of the European Union
"Solomon Rectinef—cyclops of the Illuminati
"Brighton Stone—head of NATO
"Stolly Frankston—chief justice of the House of Commons
"Parks Theodesian—chief financial officer of the World Bank
"Susan Clarks—director general of the WHO
"Umar Faroke—commander of the Maghreb Union
"Constantine Jordan—chairman of the UN"

It was not that the Àjẹ́ had collected the individuals. No, that wasn't their way, they had summoned what for Ogo passed for souls. They were summoned for crimes against humanity, against the Earth, against Àjẹ́, Tahn, and Ah—all Ah.

Ṣàngó's voice had the resonance of a well-aged drum carved out of an elder ìrókò. With the force of his utterance the names and titles, themselves, constituted indictments.

"You have been summoned here today because of your wanton killings and maimings of Ah. Your inhumanity is so abundant, so overwhelming, and of such negative emi that you have been able to dull the shining of millions of Ah," Ṣàngó thundered.

"Ògbóni!" the God called.

"Ogbórò," was the response.

"Ẹgbẹ́ mi!"

"Yoooooo," was the response.

"Kíl a sọ?"

"Awa bàjẹ́ alábájẹ́!"

"Awa bàjẹ́ alábájẹ́!"

"Awa bàjẹ́ alábájẹ́!"

"Death to Destroyers!"

"Death to Destroyers!"

"Àààhhhhhhsṣṣṣṣṣṣṣẹẹẹẹ!!!"

As if by command, the forms separated themselves from their knot and stood single file.

Ògún came forth, his axe drawn. With 1 stroke, he sliced each offender in half from the crown of the head to the slick parting of thighs. And again. And Again. He struck. Innards flew and littered the floor.

Ọya was discussing the deliberations for the coming weeks when Istha and Cynthia arrived at Minnah. They were glad to permanently reunite with Ọya and Kandace and begin their roles in the essential work of reorganizing the world. Istha and Cynthia joined a cadre of teacher-learners. Studies included the histories of Imọlẹ̀, Ògbóni, Àjẹ́; the history of Ah, Ahni, and the emisite. Studies included pharmacology, botany, gynecology, obstetrics, pediatrics, geriatrics, geography, cosmology, ontology, law and order, justice, balance, reciprocity, telepathic communication, and astral travel and physical flight. Everyone in the ẹgbẹ́ gave and took knowledge according to their needs as a collective of equals.

Ọya took the ẹgbẹ́ on an astral tour of their judicial domain, which was the entire Earth. She took them to all the houses of injustice and governmental misadministration all over the world. They visited the wielders of power as they ratified public policies of disenfranchisement and writhed in private orgies of depravity.

Using the methodology of Ẹdan—The Guardian of Justice Whose Eyes Never Close—the ẹgbẹ́ studied everything they saw and analyzed every move Ogo made. Ọya wanted them to witness Ogo's inner political workings so that they could fully understand its methodology of soullessness and its propensity to use language, bureaucracy, double-dealing, reneging, and rank dishonesty to confound, claim to own, and appear to rule the world, "This is a tutorial in the production and administration of evil."

The ẹgbẹ́ Àjẹ́ toured The National Institutes of Health, the World Health Organization, Department of Defense, and the Centers for Disease Control. They poured over the files, communiques, and grant requests and approvals that brought HIV/AIDS and then Ebola and Marburg into being. They read memos suggesting that the WHO use its clout and name to infect millions of people in Africa, India, and Brazil with diseases that they claimed to be curing and diseases that no 1 had yet named. The merchants of death kept meticulous records of how many people they had infected through inoculation and how many people the infected infected.

The ẹgbẹ́ witnessed the expansion of NATO and the birth of Africom, through which America would enact the private militarization of vast regions of Africa, not to bring peace to the Continent or end the wars that enjoyed cyclic regeneration, but to stoke hostilities, provide arms, organize genocide, and place certain regions and populations of the Continent under martial law as America deemed necessary.

The ẹgbẹ́ Àjẹ́ watched as the IMF wove indecipherable riddles into their loan agreements so that wholly unnecessary—but attractive to greedy leaders—national welfare programs would ensure the Caucasian economic control and domination of any nation that accepted a loan.

The continued oppression of the true Australians; the burnings, slashings, and hangings in police stations around the world of Africans; and the genocidal efforts of so-called officers of the law, of the Ku Klux Klan, of the skinheads, of the neo-nazis, and of various militia around the world were carefully logged.

Ah watched the President of America give nonsensical speeches, make empty eloquent proclamations, sign irrelevant bills into law, and kill people wherever they rose up to challenge his reign over Earth. The collective saw the (Dis)United Nations' expert exacerbations of African conflicts, by providing arms, drugs, and lies, rather than negotiating the peace they kept mewling about.

The ẹgbẹ́ Àjẹ́ watched the CEOs of charity organizations grow immensely wealthy from donations that never made it out of their offices. Heading a charity became the equivalent of hitting the lottery during any and every manmade or environmental disaster.

From the white house to houses of parliament to the vatican, Yurugu and its minion were conglomerating and consolidating their financial, linguistic, cultural, sexual, and social domination of the world.

Just as it happened in Hattiesburg, so too did it happen throughout the world. Even though the demises were staggered the toll became staggering. Many of the deaths were attributed to aneurism, liver failure, heart failure, kidney failure, and stroke. But the doctors knew that while these organs had shut down, there was neither sign nor rationale for the deaths.

The judiciary committee of Àjẹ́ held meetings weekly: the culprits were so many. So-called leaders, who were actually social and political lechers, of all ethnicities were gasping, struggling, shaking, and dying. For 10 weeks death announcements and funeral ceremonies competed for attention in the national and international media. However, the vacant positions were immediately filled. The preparedness of Yurugu in this respect did not help to mollify the growing fear that something was terribly wrong.

Had the attending physicians and coroners gotten together to discuss the causes of these deaths, perhaps they would have realized the similarities of the cases. But they lied to themselves and, using government-approved spin doctors as their mouthpieces, they lied to the world.

Spinning and spinning. She was seated in front of Igi Bùrúkù, the Wicked Tree. It just seemed the appropriate place for her to relax. It was such an inviting tree with its profusion of calves and thighs jutting forth before coming together at the trunk. She splayed her legs out in front of her. She was sweating, not from the journey but from the spinning of her child. She patted her distended belly to calm the little 1. Was she angry at being here? Was she excited to be home?

She did not know what to expect from this land. She was unsure what to feel until she sighted the tree fronting the lawn and placed her hips within the comfort of its calves and thighs.

It was early morning. She had been resting there since before the periwinkle and mauve of dawn began tickling the horizon.

Her bus had pulled into the hardware store in Pontotoc at 4:00 a.m. She sat outside and allowed the dawn to kiss her. She was in no hurry, having come so far, she had to reach her destination; it was only a matter of time.

"Miss Lady?" the voice called, "Miss Lady?" The driver of a 2-toned '79 Mercury Monarch pulled into the lot. He had come to fetch a woman of about 63 and the small boy with her who was about 5. She had noticed the pair on the bus, they were as silent as the other passengers were rowdy. She nodded in greeting to the woman and smiled at the child as he took his seat. She placed her silicone buds squarely into her ears and let Prince, D'Angelo, Erykah Badu, and Sly take her on in to Mississippi.

Everything she did was an effort to keep her tears from overflowing the memory banks of her mind, spilling onto her cheeks, and drenching her breasts. Not long ago she was running round wild as a deer, then Savior saved her, imbued her with consciousness, introduced her to her divinity, filled with the bounty of new life. Without Soul it was difficult to live.

She was desolate. She didn't feel connected to any being on the Earth, and the being in her womb she tried not to think about. The responsibilities facing her were overwhelming, but no matter what, she would not turn her child over to anyone else for any reason. They would live or die, flourish or perish as a team. "There will be no Uncle Ds in your life."

But what life would they have? What future? She didn't even have a family history or photo album to share with her child. She already felt like a failure. She had nothing to do but return to a "home" she did not know and see what else life had in store for her.

She had packed everything so hurriedly. She left her dishes, her coffee pot, all her appliances. She sent word to her landlord that the director of the community center, which was being rebuilt with interesting specifications by some serious Howard students, was welcome to come and claim anything from her place that she needed. Her clothes, shoes, computer, journals and other manuscripts were riding beneath her feet in the luggage compartment.

She was numb to everything. She cared about nothing. If not for the child's appetite compelling her to eat, she wouldn't have eaten. After the disembarking in Pontotoc, she sat on the bench and gazed at her belongings. She had no 1 to call and no 1 appointed to care, so she waited.

"Miss Lady?"

"Sir?" She looked up and saw a handsome slim man, about 36 with 70s sideburns. He had the swag of *Sandford and Son's* Rollo.

"We going to Booneville. Where you headed? Can we give you a lift?"

"Thank you. I'm going to Bliss Bluff."

The boy fell asleep with his head in her lap. She felt her daughter join him and soon she followed the children. In her dream, she was spinning through time, peeking through the roof of her scattered existence. Seeing herself bucking under Uncle D. Spinning. Smoking, drinking, fucking. Doing everything to compensate for the soul-deep love that she and so many daughters are denied from birth and throughout their lives. Laughing too loudly. Crying too softly. Covering. Rotating. She saw the change in her countenance when she opened her mind to consciousness and began shining. Studying, writing, lecturing. She peeked in on the center hours before Soul's lecture there. She saw the FBI agents checking the explosives they'd set. She saw the explosion rip the walls of the building apart. She saw Soul's soul join her, embrace her, and guide her. She saw the rebuilt center shining and summoning; she saw Gods growing and glowing. She saw herself surrounded by resplendent Mothers, all of whom were rotating in a circle and reflecting 1 another's force. They were joined by children, brothers, fathers. Lovehers. She had found herself at the center and found her center, and there she was supported, nurtured, and empowered.

She woke up smiling and just in time to tell the driver to take a right turn at the junction of Highways 396 and 45. When they pulled into the driveway that was guarded by the Wicked Tree, she sat down and waited.

"You be alright here?" the gentleman placed her belongings near her.

"Yes, sir. Thank you," she waved good-bye to the elder and the child.

"Should I knock on the door for you, Miss? I just hate to leave you outside by yourself," his genuine concern almost made her dry.

"Don't worry. I'm fine. This here tree is an old friend," she smiled to reassure him.

"Hmm, we got an 'old friend' like this at home," he patted the tree's trunk.

"Alright," he told Igi Bùrúkù, you take good care of her and her baby." The tree's leaves danced their response without the aid of any wind.

"Yessss, Ma'am," he gazed at the leaves, "we got a tree *just* like this 1 at home."

When Conch came out to make her morning sacrifice to Yemọja, she found her gift bearing a gift.

The water nourished with flour with which she was originally going to pour libation, she enriched with her tears and began anointing her daughter. She began with her head. As she kneeled to bathe her daughter, the stones of the driveway cut into her knees and drew a blood sacrifice, but she wouldn't feel this until the next day. She knelt and poured and bathed and prayed. Knelt and poured and bathed and prayed. She sang a praisesong to the vision and guidance of her Mother.

Iba a ṣe Yemọja
Ìyánlá Yewájọbí oooo
Yemọja Yèyé mi oooo
Modúpé oooo
Iba a se Olókun oooo
Ìyánlá Yewájọbí
Modúpé oooo

She stroked her tender neck with love and, as she did, she found her
own head being anointed. She rubbed her daughter's belly, massaging in the
love they had not been able to give 1 another, the pain the arguments they
had not endured, the joys and secrets they had not been able to withhold or
share. All absence, abandonment, and togetherness that had been floating
ungiven in the air met in the lines of their stroking palms.

That night, we became acquainted with each other inside and out—
fully. Momma Ja and Daddy was happy cause it was like we picked up
where their own love left off. And we was workin for ourselves and doin
good. I was raising the crops at home and we made right good both plantin
seasons. Mojo was getting on well at the feed mill; he even got himself a
raise and got promoted into managin the loadin hands. Every night we sang
our discoveries of each other through the bottoms. Come autumn, as soon as
the leaves got to huin up the roads right pretty and decoratin the bottoms as
they do, here you come.

"Mojo, you lookin mighty tired," I stroked his jaw and smiled on him,
"I got a surprise fo you. Sit down and lemme get you a buttermilk n pone
snack foe dinner."

"Baby Baba, I ain't hungry, not even for them butterbeans and chicken
that smell so good—we got trouble."

I knew we had trouble soon's my man say he ain't hungry—Mojo ain't
no little man and he don't eat like 1 neither. And him callin me "Baby
Baba?" I just couldn't figure how my news would blend with his. I got up
and played like I was tendin to those beans. I didn't want to see his face.

"Well, sir, lemme get this here off my mind so that we can weigh all
things equal. We gon have a little ruckus raiser. . ."

I ain't hear nothin but air whippin round my head and my mind and
blowin up my duster. Then it's me and Mojo laughin and ticklin and cryin.

"Baba? Yoruba! Woman! you make me a proud man! A good man!"

I saw tears in his eyes and we just laughed and cried and rubbed my
belly. Seem like we—seem like couldn't nothin get us out 1 another's arms.
He just look at me n say, "Baby girl baby girl baby girl."

It seemed like he talked your sex into my belly. And, I knew you was
gon be a lil woman by the way you was ridin in me, feelin my emotions and
motions and not causin me any sickness at all.

Each night when Mojo come in from the saw mill, I see him comin up the road, head down, till he get up to the house, then he ain't nothin but a smile and a song. I tried to get him to tell me what it was had him so upset but he wouldn't say a word, just brush it off or change the topic.

The crops came in and I had lots of help from everyone in the bottoms. They knew I could tend my garden just fine. But they felt that Lil Wom, that's what we called you, was all their daughter too. So that freed me up to sing a little, tell you stories and make you clothes. Nell, she help me out and we spent a mighty lot of time talkin, laughin, walkin, and dyein, tellin you stories and teachin you to count. We got through winter just fine. Spring was comin and I was filled with you and with peace.

Me and Nell was out watchin Jivy and Joseph, Ham's children, workin off they hormones by breakin my ground for spring plantin. The days was gettin a little longer and they finished up just as the sun got down to the business of settin. Me and Nell was sittin watchin them and the sun. She started teasin me, talkin bout her little girl, Leria, would be fraid to play wid Lil Wom. Say she be too big and too black—like her Daddy. I tell her she thought Mojo was fine enough when she was tryin to distract him from me when he first come. I told her black berries wasn't no count when they yellow or red so let Lil Wom be dark and sweet like me and Mojo and just as strong, too.

Me and Nell watched Jivy and Joseph stroll up.

"I say, Yoruba," she talkin at me but lookin to them, "time sho does fly! I member changing they diapers."

"Yeah, they's beautiful children, and steady growin! I hope you growin into your school lessons just as swift."

They giggled, "Yes Mam," and I give them their pay.

"Me and Mojo sho do appreciate your help. Miss Jivy, you must be bout stronger than yo brother."

"See? Now!" Jivy pushed Joseph but he didn't hit her back.

"Miss Yoruba, don't hesitate to call us if you need us again at harvest time too. We ain't goin nowhere," I could barely get "thank you" out my mouth fore Joseph offered further service: "Grandpa Jove tol us to tell you all to let him know if Mr. Mojo need any help dealin with that new mill boss."

It took me a while to say, "We sho preciate that, Joseph," cuz my mind was spinnin. I didn't know nothin about this new boss or possible trouble. I thought back to Mojo's secret and his hangin head, but that seemed like ages ago.

After Jivy and Joseph left, me and Nell said our so longs. She knew somethin was eatin me. But I couldn't say nothin. Had to talk to my man.

His head was level, not down, cause he was lookin at the sun set. Somethin on his mind. He ain't even notice me yet! I met him at the crossroads, heard his bass boom "Yoruba!" Soon's he say this, his eyes take fire, mellow, like the sun. I just hold him so tight he can feel your hug too.

"You need to talk to me. What's wrong?" He looked at me, knowin I knew: It was time to talk.

"Baba, I thought it would get better. I didn't want to bother you and Lil Wom—stress y'all out. Wanted to handle it. Work it out." I held that man and felt somethin in him I ain't never felt. Fear. "But ain't nothin work . . . You know me; I don't run from nothin. But time's don run out. The head is a-comin." He got harder to hold even though he ain't moved at all.

"Today Bennie was feeding slats into to press when he got 1 of 'em jammed up. When that press gets jammed everythang round it gots to shut down. Now, Bennie new and just learning the ropes and that press ain't easy to handle. Well, new boss come stormin down raisin Cain bout losing time and money and all like at. I was workin the grind and seen it all, Baby. He took and slap Bennie like he ain't no grown man or like he ain't nobody's chile or nothin.

"Bennie slipped in the sawdust and just kinda looked at ol Boss sad like. It was the strangest look: Maybe he knew and saw the sun set on his pea green life because ol Ben musta got up and knock boss-man smooth out. He flew back and fell all up into the grinder and what not. The white boys from Ripley took him away. Bennie and me got the slat out, got the machine runnin, and got everythang operational again. We was all working fine, Ba, but we knowed trouble was comin. I told Bennie to go on and knock off fore boss man and the Ripley boys come back. But he said no. He gon leave with his pay.

"Boss man and them damned Ripley boys come back all red and silent, grinnin. Bennie look at em but keep on workin just like ain't nothin happened. Boss man tell Bennie he want to talk with him outside. Bennie say he ain't goin if all them peckerwoods goin too. Just like that baby, peckerwoods. We knew the boy was in trouble but we smiled at that, give us some spunk.

Me and Ham rose up, all us did, and so did them rednecks. Boss say he just want to have a talk, but that as strong as Bennie is he might need some back up. Me and Bennie eyes meet, he nod at me, say he can handle it. Boss man and them 2 peckerwoods took Bennie round the back where it ain't no windows. I told Ham that 15 minutes bout long enough for conversation. I had my .44 and Ham cocked his .357 and we set off."

I didn't want to hear it; I didn't want you to hear it. I was bout big with you then and I knew you'd be comin this moon. If I could have wrapped my arms around my belly to stop you hearing I would have. But you would feel and hear regardless, Lil Wom. I had to be strong for Mojo, but I did not want to hear anymore sho as I'm Black.

"Ba, before we saw anything, we heard a scream that shook that spine and then we heard a shot. We ran around the corner. They had shot Bennie in the head. But they was still"

                                    I felt my soul float right up out of my body, leaving it feeling loud and fuzzy. I wasn't with Mojo no more, I was with Bennie. I was with Bennie and those men and I saw and felt it all—not like it was my own son but like me and he was 1. Like my soul seeped insida Bennie's body. My knees felt the cut of rocks as I kneeled down. I felt us thrashing and buckin—not bein still for nothin.

"Fuck that, muthafucka—Kill me!"

"I will nigger. But first. . ."

When me and Bennie saw "first" we laughed. "First" was this beast's ashy red pecker.

"You call me a peckerwood, huh? Pecker would and will, nigger."

We couldn't stop laughin, even though we was kicked in the belly and that gun butt met our head we just laughed on, thrashed on, and fought on.

"You cain't do no white man anyway, boy. We'll show you how to do a white man." He came toward us and shouted at his boys, "Hold this mutherfucker still!"

They finally pinned our arms and legs so we couldn't move. We ain't have but 1 weapon left, so when they finally forced our mouth open

                                                        We

                                                        Bit

                                                        Down

When Mojo and Ham finished, the Ripley boys and the new boss man and the head of his penis had joined Bennie in death. Before I had time to come back to myself right, I was in labor.

You popped right on out. Like you knew time was short. I heard the tree and knew Ma Ja and Daddy was just a crying and laughin. Nell and Baby Lee had broken a bottle, cut the cord, and used the bottle to dig a hole to bury our cord at the tree's foot. I didn't know what the tears on Mojo face meant no more, but I knew I was lookin at my Daddy in his face.

"Plenny life blood livin in dis here tree," said Baby Lee. "Let's add to it," and she buried the cord.

I couldn't see nothin for a while. I couldn't feel nothin either. I just was, and Mojo just was too.

"Y'all best be leavin," said Baby Lee after everyone had got their fill of you gettin your fill of my milk. "Be done found them bodies by now. Be comin for you."

Mojo got on his knees, looked me in my eyes, and stroked my jaw, "Outta all the places I done been in, this is the only home I done found." Mojo looked at me to read my eyes, "I ain't leavin my home runnin."

"Mojo right. We ain't runnin from nobody ain't got no skin. Not as long as we Black."

"Yoruba! Hear! This child needs a mother. A live healthy 1. This tree cain't protect you from what's stirrin dust up that road, and the bottoms ain't got enough guns!" Baby Lee was furious.

I just looked at Mojo and he at me. We knew Baby Lee was right, but so was we. I also knew that I had had just a little more happiness in my life than Ma Ja had had in hern.

Mojo looked so deep, looked like night. Looked like rich earth tilled and waiting. And his harvest was just as beautiful as he was. Smooth ebony and lips that don't have to pucker. I couldn't wait to hear you speak.

The bottoms was burned to the ground. I'll never see it as ash and sticks, and I'm glad of that. I'd like to remember it the way it was when it raised me.

Night riders came with guns, fire, and knot. We held fort on em a while, but wasn't too much we could do. It seems like every beast in the county paid a visit to the bottoms that night. They killed half of us: Baby Lee and Jove was killed outright. 2 oldest people in the bottoms, the heart of the bottoms shot down dead in the road like dogs. They lynched yo Daddy and Ham. I watched my husband make me proud from behind a tree. I didn't see it—but I know they hung my husband and Nell's right up in Daddy tree—I also know they did this over 6 of the bodies of their own sheeted cowards. Joseph and badass Jivy killed 4 more of em. But we just wasn't no match for em. Most everyone who didn't get burned or hanged got taken to jail or drove out the county. Nell the only 1 ain't dead or gone. She got you.

I figured they was gon kill me cause they knew who I was and who my people was. When they saw me with that gun, I was blowin holes in sheets like I was at a carnival game. I figured to go out strong, like my people. They didn't kill me though. They winged me and beat me so I was unconscious for 3 weeks. That's what Big Sal say. She brought me back from the brink right here in the Parchman penitentiary for women, where they brought my body to die. Not only did I not die, but, Lil Wom, a parched man if not parchment gon bring me to you.

While Daughter and Kofi were in Bliss Bluff explaining the security devices they had prepared for the site, the Institute was rocked by an explosion. Hawa, Dear, Valeria, and Danta were driving back from Jackson, where they had successfully defended themselves against charges of tax evasion. Danta was wheeling Dear's 98 Oldsmobile down Interstate 55 when a psychic tremor nearly caused him to swerve off the road.

"Damn!" exclaimed Hawa holding her head, "They set us up!" These were nearly the same words she spoke 14 months ago when she opened and read the document before her: "Notice of Summons. Hawa Ahni and Danta Ahni, the founders of the so-called 'Original Path Institute' are hereby summoned to the Jackson County Courthouse in Jackson, Mississippi to defend themselves against charges of tax evasion."

"They tryin to set us up, Dear."

"I know. I'll call Conch, she the 1 prepare your taxes. She'll have all the documents."

Conch and her daughter had picked up the pieces left to them by years of absence. From the time Dear met them holding 1 another at the feet of the Wicked Tree, the entire vibration of the Bliss Bluff site and its Ah changed.

Here were 2 women, both born in the midst of unimaginable loss, anguish, and turmoil. Here were 2 lost-found women with titles for names piecing together their identities.

Conch was Lil Wom, a little woman who had to cut her way through the wilderness of this world using the only weapon she had: her teeth. She used her teeth to sever the umbilical cord of a daughter she would not raise and to sample men like they were chocolate drops.

Babygirl: The loving name of so many daughters. Babygirl: a wish of an extended childhood, 1 that will be pain free and guided by the care of a bevy of Big Daddies, Big Mommas, Aints, Unkas and Cuddins. Babygirl: The name of a child whose best friend took her flying and left her with a singing clitoris. Babygirl: the 1 who had wallowed in mires, mucks, and ditches of lust because she did not realize that the bottomless love that she sought was within her.

When Tynell saw this profusion of pain and promise at the base of the white oak, she saw the daughters put under her protection that she did not protect. But then she saw the expansive arms of Yemoja around the women and she saw 5 other figures, 2 couples and 1 man embracing them. The arms of the oak tree were alive, as they had always been with 27 arms bearing gifts enough to be a baobab.

"Omowale. Omowale. Omowale." Was it a plea? Was it a prayer? Was it a promise? "Omowale, Omowale, Omowale," Dear continued chanting, prophesying and promising until everyone on the mountain came out to bear witness. "Omowale. Omowale. Omowale."

"Child returns home. Child returns home. Our child is home."

Conch took Omowale home with her and there, in her framehouse, they set up housekeeping, secret revealing, and healing. They held nothing back from 1 another: tears, blame, rage, mistakes, triumphs, rapture, rupture.

They bore living witness, they testified, they separated, they shouted, they sank into silence, they embraced. They did not seek to shortcut a process that they knew would be longer than their terrestrial lives. Danta suggested they order their experiences and meditate them into the astral library as part of their healing process.

Conch and Lil Wom were at the emisite filling the library of Ah with their truths when the explosion, foretold by the startling 3 minute absence of all vibration, ripped across the Earth.

Daughter and Kofi stopped in the middle of their conversation 30 seconds before the explosion. Daughter said, "Now they will kill many of us."

The devastation was unimaginable. Bones, cement, bits of scalp, and extremities were strewn throughout the Institute as Ogo procured a costly sacrifice.

Danta sped forward at a swift yet controllable 99 miles per hour, oblivious to speed limit laws and violations thereof. No 1 said a word as they rounded the bend on Highway 369 and sped towards home, the Wicked Tree, a sentinel, leading the way.

Everyone was mentally kicking him or herself for being lured away from the site and being preoccupied by ridiculous charges from an authority of irrelevance. But the collection of paperwork, receipts, and permits was not done blindly. Although they had the full support of the members of the Institute, they knew a legal blow could prove disastrous for their reputations. It was important to Hawa and Danta and everyone at the Institute that the record be clean.

"Our mistake was allowing the laws of this land to take precedence over the laws of Ah. But no matter what destruction they have caused, they cannot stop the shining."

"Nothing can harm us now," Dear's voice was absent timbre and tone. "Even those of us Ogo done killed are now ancestors."

"But needlessly so!"

"You're right, Vee. If we had planted our feet firmly Yurugu wouldn't have been able to sway us."

"To be honest, I think we all underestimated the extent of its knowledge about us and the lengths to which it would go to destroy us," Danta hung his head. "What we have to keep forever in mind is the fact that we are at war. This will teach us that we cannot ever again take Yurugu lightly."

"We will retaliate," Hawa said this with an emotionless conviction and a pain that had not before been a part of her voice. She saw the destruction in her mind. She saw the mangled bodies, the strewn body parts, a gutted home. And why, because of education, because shining was apparent? "Now, we understand the nature of this beast." Her voice still had that even, almost dead sound. "To the dull, shining is so violent a threat that they have lured us away and set about slaughtering."

"Does it think we'll turn the other cheek?" Dear's query was rhetorical.

By the time they pulled into the driveway leading to the institute, each member had already mentally prepared a strangely similar means of vengeance.

Jorell, the promise of the future, was dead. Jane, his mother had also perished. Earl, Valeria's husband had lost a leg. Mary, Dear's twin in so many ways had suffered burns over 70% of her body. Sidney, Cally, Mildred, Dut, Punkin. . . the carnage was stupendous. The roof of the house was caved in and was still billowing smoke although the stronger members of the site had put out the small fires the explosion had sparked. The fire department never showed up.

Everyone was traumatized. But they all banded together to begin the painstaking work of healing those who could be healed and burying their dead so that they could begin the journey of return.

What they wanted to avoid was media attention. The Ah didn't need to be spotlighted by pseudo-sympathetic reporters who would condescend to them about this tragedy. It was not necessary for the NAACP or any other celebrity activist agencies to come around the site grandstanding. But just as the funerals of Ogo were being held, so too did the Ah of Bliss Bluff hold funerals in a consecutive fashion.

I am devastated, Daughter lamented. Why didn't we come sooner? Why didn't we see this coming!?! So many? So much shining? Now, ancestors, yes, but we needed them here.

I just hope that we can keep the vibration flowing to the extent that the emerging Tahn are not frightened off by this.

Kofi, Daughter, Hawa joined their conversation, Danta and I are about to call an all-Ah meeting. We need to let everyone know about this devastation so that no 1 else is caught off guard.

This loss is too tremendous. Hawa paused to collect herself. Blessings had to be counted. The libraries of knowledge were unscathed, they were probably not at all known to Ogo. Many Ah had survived and were only wounded but, but, Hawa was simply overcome. She could barely think let alone communicate.

AAAHHHHaaahhhhahaha. My progeny. Creators of self and renewers of the way. I greet you and your shining, the Mother came like salve, like cool water.

This is the anti-way of Ogo. To kill and destroy to slay what it cannot comprehend; to debase, defile, and crush. To scatter. It has no other way.

But let me make you aware, and here the slain members of the Bliss Bluff site began glowing around the Mother, that *we are whole*. People gasped and wept at seeing their loved ones.

Rell, Mildred, Duck, everyone is here. Ahni beamed her adoration on the victims of Bliss Bluff. Come, the Mother gestured, embrace your loved ones. Come and know continuity.

After the exultation of the reunions subsided, the Mother continued. Yurugu did not create Ah: Yurugu cannot destroy Ah. Emi, shining, destiny cannot be destroyed. Her arms, cipher and words were an embrace.

There is no death in Ahni, Ah, or our way. The builders of Jubah, Kng, Dah, Kmt and all the original 6 sites and their sister sites are all here. The Gods, Ausar, Ọya, Heru, Ṣàngó, Mani, Ògún, Damballah-Hwedo, Maat, Odù, Ike, Ast, are here. The ancestors Lumumba, Matalah, Sonny Carson, El Hajj Malik El Shabazz, Amiri Baraka, Harriet Tubman, and Queen Nanny are here. All Ah are always already eternal immortals. The scale and scope of the collective stunned the Tahn. Many went to embrace Gods, ancestors, and warriors that they had never met but whose guidance had been indispensable.

Ahni projected to all Ah the attempted destruction of the Bliss Bluff site: Yes, we are at war and have been for eons. But the battle is concluding. This Earth will soon be flowing with blood: but not Ah blood.

She shifted the scene from destruction to shining. The Ah witnessed, at once, their own radiance and that of all Ah: on the Earth, on the Moon, on Saturn, on Neptune, throughout the galaxy and cosmos. Even as we gather, more enter the center. Feel them coming. These are the warriors, healers, Àjẹ, Ah, educators, poets, and artisans, who are coming, joining, shining. There can be no victory for Ogo, only graspings of futility and clutchings of jealousy. Having spent the past nearly years creating yourselves, Tahn, never doubt the truth of your gift, of our destiny.

And never doubt the justice of Àjẹ, Ọya's eyes were orbs of fire. We are in possession of the livers and what passes for the spirits of the Institute's attackers. They will die horrific and lengthy deaths, Ọya's smile was nearly imperceptible and terrifying.

We Àjẹ are the most feared and fair organization ever formed, she continued. We never condemn without a fair trial, we never forget a crime, and we ensure that all violations are repaid in kind.

Heaps of Ogo were found at the crossroads of highways in New Albany, Booneville, Bliss Bluff, Jackson, and Pontotoc. The police had no leads on how entire families were taken from their jobs and homes and dismembered with weapons that could only have been lasers. "An dey wuz sevahed suhlowly," 1 genetically challenged deputy mumbled as he examined the contorted anguished faces of the Ogo corpses.

There was not yet conclusive evidence on the method of killing. All that was known was that the superintendents of 7 school districts were dead; 204 teachers were dead; the mayors of 7 towns were dead; 13 police chiefs and 59 officers were dead; 36 FBI agents were dead; and 308 Ogo children joined their parents in oblivion. Each child was severed in half from the top of its head to its groin. Coroners marveled at the precision that could perfectly split strands of hair.

The melanin deficient citizens were shocked into silence. The surviving FBI agents (those who had not participated in or helped plan the bombing of the Institute) logically and correctly surmised that the killings were in retaliation for the bombing of the Original Path Institute. However, there was no evidence to connect any member of the Institute to any killing: Indeed, when the killings occurred, the members were all occupied with planning and attending funerals. What is more, everyone knew that niggers didn't have the intelligence or technology or savvy to plan and execute such sophisticated acts.

"Just as I thought!" Aint May was hunched over a high-powered microscope that stood in the middle of 2 others exactly like it.

"What is it Aint May?"

"Ebola, Lassa, HIV, and Marburg are mutated strains of 1 virus. It will be easy to remove the specificity from the germ and exacerbate the rate of mutation," She studied each of the 3 microscopes with such rapidity that Jahmai and Chaka were in awe.

Last week they had all flown to Kng. They travelled invisibly using African technology to avoid the various militia who roamed the country. When they arrived at the site, they extracted several plant species, which they would grow in Alapaha. They also obtained specific leaves, stems, roots, and berries. Aint May knew exactly what to do to cure the diseases that Ogo had created to destroy the Ah and Tahn. But she also wanted to alter the diseases so that they would specifically infect individuals who were emivoid and eminegative.

"Aint May, we've finished with the extractions." Jahmai pushed his protective goggles up onto his forehead, which was sweating. The extractor generated a tremendous amount of heat.

"Alright," she smiled, "we fin to turn the tables."

They began isolating the individual yet kin mutant germ strains from the Ebola, Lassa, HIV, and Marburg viruses. After a 12 hour tag-team effort, the re-mutated, anti-emi activated strains were prepared and so were the plant extracts. Aint May followed Chaka's advice and made the diseases ultraviolet sensitive. They loaded up the crop duster, and with Daniel, Patricia's husband, at the controls, they took off.

The plane was small and looked like any raggedy crop duster. But Daniel had installed at mini Rolls Royce turbo engine in the craft and 4 133-gallon fuel tanks. So they could fly to any destination and fly low enough so that they were undetectable to military radars.

From Alapaha, they headed southwest, spreading the cure over Georgia, Alabama, Mississippi, Louisiana, and Texas before swooping over Mexico, and fanning the cure over the Cuba, the Bahamas, Haiti, and Jamaica. They crossed the Caribbean Sea again to cure Belize, el Salvador, Nicaragua, Columbia, and Peru.

While flying over Brazil Aint May revealed, "The medicine is melanin- and emi-sensitive. What is more, it acts like an air- or water-borne spore. Once bodily contact occurs, the cure sets in." They whizzed over Bahia and unloosed clouds of redemption.

"Those who have not been infected with these diseases will develop immunity."

"What will happen to those with the diseases?" asked Daniel.

"Well, for 24 hours, the best way I can describe it is they will be uncomfortable as hell. The cure will first purify the body. So rampant, almost endless, urination, defecation, and vomiting will set in. For those with advanced cases, bleeding from bodily orifices will occur."

"Damn, so dey go catch hell," Daniel's rhythms, especially when he was comfortable, were still Liberian after a 10 sojourn in America.

"A bit. But it's only for 24 hours, after this, they will become ravenous, and nourishment will restore the body."

"Hmp," began Chaka, as they flew further south, "most people will think they have a 24 hour virus."

"Exactly."

"What will happen when Yurugu comes in contact with the cure?"

"Nothing: Only works with emi and melanin," Aint May reclined her seat, and lost herself in the beauty of the Brazil's spectacular landscape. She rubbed Chaka's 7 month-pregnant belly and sang to Abosom who was listening to her elders and planning the work she would do once born.

Daniel consulted their itinerary. After healing West and Central Africa and inundating Sierra Leone, Liberia, Guinea, and the Kongos in cure and inoculation, they would cure South Africa and heal Eastern Africa. After Africa, they would spread healing over Yemen, Oman, Iraq, Iran, Pakistan, India, Myanmar, Indonesia, and Australia before heading back north to Papua New Guinea, the Philippines, China, Mongolia, and Kazakhstan. After dusting populations in Spain, France, and England, they would inoculate Canada and the American northeast and west. What a wonderful way to see the world, he smiled.

This work is simple but is crucial to the development of Ah, Ahni told her twins. Aha, take the northern region where the Kng, Zim, and Zalah once reigned. Ah, take the eastern region where the Ta Ntr, Knah, and Kmt established the world's first civilizations. Badu and I will take the west.

They began summoning.

It began with a humming a vibration that seemed to shimmer in the air. As the humming increased, as it did in the night, the shimmering air took the form of a pregnant woman.

Visions and visitations, as they were called, were reported by multitudes. Initially, the Coptic Christians and Muslims thought that Hagar or Gawahar had come to message them, but the messages they received went far beyond any religious imaginings.

Trees began revealing texts to those living, resting, working, or harvesting in the vicinity their branches. These sentinels who had witnessed so much, began humming then vibrating then unfolding the reality of Ta Ntr. The river Jubah began vibrating. The waters of the Sudan began rippling and foaming as the builders of first site of power, who had been submerged under the Aswan dam, resurrected themselves. The ancestors of Ta Ntr strolled the Earth like natural men and women.

"We are Ta Ntr, all the healing powers of the Kng, the creative force of Jubah, the spiritual architecture of Kmt all came from and flow back to us. Come and learn at this spiritual library. All of this time you have covered yourself in the myths and lies of Yurugu when the truth has always been only 3 emi away. Listen . . ."

The pattern was repeated in Kmt as the original inhabitants and designers of its masterpieces went to the contemporary Ah there who existed as footstools for the Arabs. The ancient Ah taught their progeny their truth, their power, and their history. They taught them that the shining of their skin was born of vibrations in their souls. The Ah of Kmt showed their progeny their ancestry which was carved with lasers and magnified 3000 times on the stones of eternity. "You are nothing but Gods. Now that you know yourselves, show yourselves."

The sandy river of Yah raged, and its waves were boosted by a force of retribution so destructive that Maghreb officials were coming close to revealing the truth behind what their propagandists had struggled to convince people was a myth.

They should have warned their citizens that a tidal wave of sand was coming. That an enraged defiled land was rising with the force of billions of slaughtered ancestors. Not to drive them into the sea—could they deserve rest in the bosom of Yemoja?—but to bury them under the grains of death, the same grains of desolation that followed them everywhere they went.

All of North Africa, including Saudi Arabia—which is very much attached to the Continent—which had, because of waves of rogue invasions, been declared the "Middle East" was engulfed in tsunamis of sand as the spirit of the great green river attained retribution for millennia of unspeakable atrocities committed by Arabs against Africans.

Neither geologists nor meteorologists could explain the phenomenon. Imams were too terrified they would be swallowed whole to touch their heads to the Earth in prayer. Quietly and methodically, entire communities, cities, and, finally, countries were buried in the sands of the Sahara. Kings, heads of state and government officials were too busy acting like the eradication of nations was not happening to plan evacuations. It would not have mattered.

After 3 weeks the Middle East was a peaceful region because the oppressors and racists and the institutions and nations they created had been obliterated.

The original inhabitants of the land, those pushed back, those spiritually truncated, those given a religion of slavery to hold higher than they could lift their eyes in public, well, they laid down their burdens and began the shining they were always inclined to glow.

A cyclone of lightning, 3000 meters in diameter, spun to the Earth and was followed by an explosion of thunder that resulted in an earthquake that created a massive gorge into which Israel and all Israelis plummeted. When the eradication was complete, the ground soundlessly and seamlessly re-adhered itself.

The soldiers of Chad, Rwanda, Burundi, Congo, and Kongo were hearing voices:

As you slay your brothers, the WHO slays you. WHO is fighting against you . . . WHO is winning this war. . .

Do you not know the history of this land?

Soldiers halted the digging of trenches, the laying of sieges, and the preparation of ambushes. The voice inquired:

Don't you see them shining?

They did. The soldiers were fascinated by the radiance of their adversaries. All combatants were magnetized and mesmerized by their would-be enemies. They came closer to 1 another and looked and watched until recognition was born.

Each face bore the visage of the Prophet. He said through the mouths and to the souls of thousands of combatants, *You are not the enemy. Our enemy is not here.*

A Haitian brother, Raoul Peck was with him, as were 6 Kongolese brothers: Zao, Sambo, Mpia, Ekia, Pemba, and Kitouka.

As they toured their domain, they left the scent of sulfuric acid and the sounds of carnival music in their wake. Floating above their heads were hundreds of thousands of hands.

"You see," the Prophet explained, "they took the hand and everything else. Our enemy is not here. If you must kill, kill the real enemy. We have suffered enough."

In South Africa his immortal baritone rent the air: "Look u oooo!" He compelled the listeners to view well the shanties, stick collections, and hovels they were forced to call home. Fela Anikulapo Kuti beseeched his audience, "Ah beg, make we do comparative analysis, my brodahhhh!"

"Look at what they no want you to see": Whites Only; Coloureds Only; Kaffir, Keep Out. The signs that had been removed still shouted from shadows, from hearts, and from legislation.

"You don become America, oooo!" Whites Only. Coloreds Only. Nigger, Don't let the Sun Set on You in Fill-In-The-Blank Town. The erectors of the land now its laughingstock. Women and children raped to death. Cemeteries overflowing with victims of Driving While Black, Breathing While Black, Strolling With Melanin.

"Doncha love AmeriKKKa?" Fela inquired, "Land of dem all crazy?"

South Africans saw their husbands lobotomized, their wives sodomized with broken jagged coke bottles. They read their futures which were inscribed in the dust of the land. They saw their children undergoing mandatory testing for HIV and being infected with HIV at the testing sites.

The ghosts of Mandela and Botha jigged, giggled, and harmonized, "And those are the breaaaaaks!"

"How much more you need suffer, my people? Which new atrocity you wan experience? The struggle must end. The struggle must end.

"The Indian and Ethiopic oceans are hungry. Drive these beasts into the sea!!!"

In the west, the sound of soul electrified the air:

I am the source of Alkebu-Lan's light for I am the Tahn, the shining. I am Ahni of Origins. I have come shining, and I am seeking my shining ones. I am not the first to return, many have come before me, shining. Many will follow me, shining.

These cities: St. Louis, Bissau, Conakry, Freetown, Monrovia, Abidjan, Accra, Lomé, Cotonou, Lagos, Duala, Fernando Po, Libreville, are cities built on the souls of Ah ancestors. These cities: St. Louis, Bissau, Conakry, Freetown, Monrovia, Abidjan, Accra, Lomé, Cotonou, Lagos, Duala, Fernando Po, Libreville have streets paved with Ah Mothers' bones. These cities: St. Louis, Bissau, Conakry, Freetown, Monrovia, Abidjan, Accra, Cape Coast, Lomé, Cotonou, Lagos, Duala, Fernando Po, Libreville are built with bricks in which baked the blood of Ah Fathers. These cities carry the hissing curse of ancestors trod upon. These cities house the floors in which my sisters prostrate for the macabre pleasure of any skinless beast. These cities are those in which my brothers dirty their knees and sully their souls. I am Tahn; my sale built the cities of iniquity that are the pride of countries crowned in criminality. I am you. You cannot deny me. You cannot deny these truths.

Look into these eyes.

They did and saw themselves. Day glo wigs, 13 inch heels, raping, killing, burning, getting high. Rushing to any coast to whore themselves out to any foreigner who strolled by. Dying to get to America. Killing themselves, selling their kin in order to take the ride those they dismissed as slaves took. In the mirroring eyes of Ahni, they saw themselves and the murky truth of their reality. Lying about reparations and repatriation. Pimping their culture. Using what was left of their shining to diminish their emi and that of those near them. Mothers raping their daughters. Fathers castrating their sons.

Are there 10 who will escape the vengeance of Ahni? Avenge yourself Mother, we are here helping. We the shining ones are helping. Ìyá, cleanse or destroy these cities built with pawned blood. Ìyá, smother the modern-day flesh peddlers in their sleep. We are here for those who rise with the sun, who rise with unimaginable memories of oppression fraying the edges of their minds. We are here assisting the shining. Will you shine?

We are screaming Oròmbọ with force so fierce you must avert your eyes. We are wailing Orò: we are the cries of the ancestors. Crying for just/us to share this sacrifice with just/us to sip this libation from the Earth's womb. Justice. We are the Dark Sun Children, riding home, riding rhythms, riding vibrations. We are riding the enraged wind of Ọya and leveling shrines desecrated with the presence of beasts. We are the whirlwind snatching the limbs off of the barked and barkless rootless trees poisoning Ahni's huge pot of creation. We are the tornado spinning Ogo and his minion into oblivion.

We are pouring blood libation: small sacrifice for the Tahn dimmed and dulled for half a century. A small sacrifice for the 500 million lives shredded, blotted, beheaded, shallowly buried, raped; made to lay over holes protective of unborn cash to receive the lash; made to sway on oak trees until relatives found and cut them down; made to tote the rubber, lumber, and uranium of our lands or lose hands, lives, minds; told to forsake Òrìṣà or die, and died; made to accept thrusting perversion in unthinkable bodily orifices—bodies, souls, skins, and minds fouled; made to become mortal so that our fellow Gods would not have to look at us with shame; told to dim our Tahn or die and died glowing while you sold your souls for beads and glitter. Explain yourselves. The Gods are listening.

Many people committed suicide. The force of the truth left them no alternative. The dissipation of the mirage in which they had placed their every hope was overwhelming. When they saw themselves in their ancient Ancestors' eyes, they saw clowns, minstrels, imitations of life, and bad imitations of bad imitations. They killed the shells of themselves because they had so long ago lost their souls.

If shining wasn't in massive gold chains (mostly fake), counterfeit or real designer clothes, processed hair, see-through garments, shakara, and precipitating a master-slave society by making any 1 different, vulnerable, or of lesser economic status your slave, they did not know what shining was. So they made of themselves a sacrifice to the pot of reciprocity. There would be no reincarnation. Like Ogo the adored, they had *been* dead; now, they needed only a soily blanket to cover their depravity.

Aha and Badu turned to Eurasia and summoned the Tahn there. Ah took the lands of Australia, India and the South Pacific islands. Ahni uttered Ah truths to the southern American continent and the Caribbean Islands. From their words, projections, and visitations shining began. Some Tahn stayed where they were and formed sites of power. Others relocated to Dgn, Minnah, Kumba, Carvah, Alapaha or Bliss Bluff, as their emi demanded.

Saddiq started building with Dead Prez, The Roots, D'Angelo, Sunz of Man, Killarmy, and X Clan; these builds led a series of recordings and several mixtapes all released by AhRekkid, the subsidiary label of AhMusic. The force of Jubah—even processed in a studio—reverberated in souls, repositioned bones, and recalibrated thoughts. As the music hit the airwaves, emi increased exponentially.

Scarface, David Banner, Rakim Allah, Brother J, Erykah Badu and other artists were cutting tracks and dropping verses with Ah; artists abandoned their record labels and poverty-generating contracts to work with AhRekkid and earn half of all profits generated.

Music video production dropped by 93% as not only did major artists stop prostituting themselves for Ogo's camera, but television viewing decreased 93% in Africana homes. As the survival skills of the Yah and the rhythms of Jubah were honed into a force of order and retribution, the product was a beat that was irresistible and a message that was irrefutable.

Again and again cases were called and police officers, district attorneys, bailiffs, and judges positioned themselves in court to begin the lucrative racist dispensation of "justice." But where were all of the Black defendants? Why were there only 2 Black court officers present? Before eyes could narrow with consternation or widen with understanding, the courthouse collapsed and all that was within it was obliterated.

The destruction of the courthouse happened at the same time that the governor's mansion, 2 FBI offices, and 4 police stations were leveled in Nashville, Tennessee.

At 5:04 p.m. the previous day, 8 groups of 4 Tahn had maneuvered through underground tunnels to the 8 edifices of oppression. They had prepared the ammonia and fertilizer-based bombs and their computerized detonators 3 nights before. They set in place the exact amount of explosives necessary to implode the buildings so neatly that passersby thought they were witnessing government-authorized controlled detonations.

The CIA was dumbfounded, so they blamed al-Qaida and The Islamic State. Arab-looking people were profiled, detained, tortured, and, after several weeks, released. The general African American community went about its business with a sense of peace and purpose. The encoded 7th line of the song "Ọmọ Ògún" of *Iṣẹ́ Ògbóni* informed all Tahn to stay away from governmental institutions beginning 6 March because those institutions would cease to exist.

7 days after the bombings, every physician, researcher, and intern at Shinally Medical Center was found strapped to operating tables and gurneys. Their bodies had all been dissected with laser-like precision: 9 body parts for the women; 7 body parts for the men. There was no blood.

Because there were no leads, motives, or explanations for the act or its remarkable meticulousness, officers set fire to Shinally and razed it to the ground. They attributed the deaths to the blaze and the blaze to faulty wiring. The public took great comfort in these lies.

The song "Authority Stealing 7" was written by Ra, encoded by Xaviah, and covertly installed on county jail and private, state, and federal prison computer networks around the world by Jah Sun. At 7 am and 7 pm every day for 7 months the 70 second song played and instructed wardens, parole board members, and corrections officers around the world to release Ah prisoners on July 7 at 7:00 am. With Bill Withers' "Lovely Day" booming from prison PA systems around the world, Gods emerged from dungeons, relocated to skill-specific cells, and went to Work.

The song "This Land Is Your Land," also on the album *Iṣẹ́ Ògbóni*, was encoded with instructions as to how to transform projects and other seemingly vulnerable dwellings into autonomous fortresses from which government overthrow could be affected.

Azure, Xaviah, Saddiq, Alteveze, Ra, and Dr. Sims began working with emerging sister sites in Chicago, Watts, Atlanta, Detroit, Brooklyn, D.C., Oakland, LA, and Houston to assist in the mobilization of new sites and cells. The Carvah collective showed their comrades how to use their cities' existing tunnel or sewer and drainage systems to gain covert access to government buildings and police stations. The events that upended Nashville started occurring around the country, and, then, around the world.

The pope hanged himself.

While it was reported he died of a heart attack, the pope had been plagued by night terrors.

His thrashing awakened his favorite altar boy who thought his master was ready for another round. He was surprised that, despite his age and infirmity, the pope was still virile and agile when it came to a young anus. But as the child prepared for the ritual embrace, he was given a blow across the face. Stunned, he fell off the bed and turned on the light to find the aged automaton struggling and fighting in his sleep. It looked as if he were running from a mob. Although he was sweating, grimacing, and groaning, the pope maintained his customary sky-gray color.

No matter the amount of valium, opium, marijuana, or alcohol he consumed, the pope continued to attempt to flee his conscience for 3 weeks. He found solace on the end of a rope. Miraculously, the pope's colossal hat remained perched atop his head despite the fact that his head was dangling in a downward diagonal.

While nothing was said about it, the President of the United States, Reining Beeste, and the British Prime Minister, Evoljus Forfun, were also suffering from night terrors. The only thing the first lady could liken her husband's sleeping patterns to were the movements of a slave trying to outrun patterrollers.

Abom I. Naishun, Beeste's predecessor, had died a horrible death that had not been made public. While the exact cause of death was unknown, what was known was that although he had died in his sleep, by the morning, he had the aroma of a pit latrine in July. The first lady called her family, and the coroner and several aides to assist with the corpse. As soon as the medical attendants touched the body to lift it onto a stretcher, the corpse exploded, spraying the bedroom of Kennebunkport and all those in attendance with a curdled gray pus that was roiling with maggots. The attendants and relatives who were sprayed with the president's disintegration vowed to keep the matter top-secret. They did, because in 7 days they too exploded, and 7 days later everyone who had handled their bodies also burst into a mass of maggots. And so on, and so on.

When Naishun's successor, Beeste started having dreams of a dred locked Nat Turner killing him fifty-leven different ways every night, there was no 1 to call. With their hands filled with exploding politico cadavers, smoldering heaps of Ku Klux Klan men, women, children; piles of butchered German skinheads; knots of dismembered expatriate bodies decorating roundabouts in Ouagadougou, Cotonou, Dakar, Duala, Mombasa, and Nairobi; African leaders and militaries vanishing; stateside and international US military bases imploding as neatly as deflated balloons and crushing tens of thousands of mercenaries in the process; and the bombings of police stations and government offices in every major city in the world, NATO, the UN, and the CIA had no idea where to begin or who to arrest. When Beeste finally enacted martial law, there were not enough officers and soldiers to implement the order.

No 1 was concerned with a family of African American tourists, including a buoyantly pregnant mother, who posed for photos in government halls and military installations around the world and left microscopic sprinkles of gray powder blowing in their wake.

Azure, although 7 months pregnant with triplets, had been moving across the country like Flight Lieutenant J.J. Rawlings to aid cells and foment revolution.

As she relaxed in preparation to give birth, her family was a picture of bliss. Xaviah was sleeping soundly, as was his way, with his ear cupped to Azure's belly as if the babies had sang him to sleep. Ra was snoring lightly in Azure's ear; he was fitted into her back like a sword in it scabbard. She felt the rise of his groin between her thighs. She sighed and caressed the heads of her lovehers. She felt her clitoris respond, it was so sensitive to the immeasurable bliss she felt.

AAAAHHHHHaaaahhhh

Her orgasm was all her own and yet powerful enough to vibrate the bed. The triplets were waking, shining, and vibrating in her womb. Xaviah began to greet the triplets with kisses. Ra began a gentle massaging. With his hands, he cupped her firm breasts; and his penis throbbed with an urgency only she could ease. She parted her legs slightly so that the kisses could reach their progeny. Their palms cupped her belly as if receiving/offering a sacrifice.

They remained this way for 3 days.

The prosecution of the agents of oppression continued and none were spared. They were not dragged into court, old and decrepit in wheelchairs; they were not hunted down to the far ends of the Earth and brought to an Ogo-recognized court to stand trial. No. They fell where they stood; they collapsed where they crouched. The sell-outs who befriended and bootlicked Ogo and ensured Yurugu's reign of racist oppression found their livers boiling in pepper pot of conviction.

"This cure, for it is a cure for us, works like this: Once it comes into contact with its host, a general weakening will occur that is followed with infestation of maggots. After the person dies, the body will explode in 7 days infecting any who comes in contact with the remains. That is for those who are eminegative. For those who are emivoid, simple sunlight will be sufficient. Direct, indirect sunlight, the simple fact that the sun rises, will activate in their body specific chemical reactions causing exacerbated melanoma that continues until death."

"How long before they die?"

"7 days."

"For other Ogo, there will be night terrors. Some will be Àjẹ́-induced, well, it is all Àjẹ́-induced," Aint May chuckled as the aircraft fanned over Handsworth.

"Are de night terrors dreams or astra realities?" Daniel asked.

"They are both. The crimes that Ogo has committed in this space, time, and place and those committed in times disremembered will resurface during sleep.

"You see, all Ah have melanin which precipitates spiritual cognition. Our melanin is the chemical component that produces our shining. Melanin works with and is the manifestation of emi. So when we sleep, even if we are ignorant of it, we are learning from the ancestors. Even if we disremember it, we are tapping into the roots of ancient wisdom, knowledge, and understanding. They are always already within us."

"But Yurugu has no melanin, no emi," Daniel nodded. "So when it sleeps dere is nothing to flow or stimulate."

Jahmai thought about the medicine they had created and said, "I think this cure is anti-emi activated and non-melanin activated too. Rather than tap into a spiritual heritage, because it has none; rather than processing solar rays internally, because without melanin, Ogo cannot do this; and rather than activate an emi it doesn't have, the cure will prey on the absence of vibration and physically impair the Ogoian body. It will attack the absence of melanin and magnify UV to a deadly intensity. Because it has no inner eye to stimulate, the cure will relay and replay cosmic crimes."

"Yurugu will implode," she concluded.

"Their scattered bones will pave our path to ascension."

"Àṣẹ."

It was during a night terror that the home of Richard Beasley burned to the ground. His long widowed wife Beth had just finished mourning the immaculate dissection of her brother, Bobby Lee, the head of the Quitman County Citizens' Council. So precise was Bobby Lee's dismemberment that the mortician was able to adhere the two sections of his head with krazy glue and present his remains in an open casket.

3 months after her brother's burial, Beth found that she kept having the same dream every night: She was running for her life from an ferocious mob. As she stumbled over looped roots and shoots and as branches struck her face, she felt the wings of justice tickling her ears. As the days went by,

Beth slept less and less because sleep brought an agony she could never have imagined in her conscious life.

When she realized that any time, day or night, she sought sleep she would be in the dream, Beth Beasley armed herself with caffeine pills, cocaine, coffee, and amphetamines. Her effort to escape the undaunted vengeance that confounded her existence was effective for 5 days.

While staring at her television and smoking a cigarette, Beth thought about using toothpicks to prop her eyelids open. What she had heard was a torture tactic she might be able to use to thwart sleep. She could wrap the ends of the picks in cotton to avoid injuring her eyelids. This was her last conscious thought as Beth's body did what it longed to do most, rest.

As soon as she closed her eyes, the lynch mob appeared with tar and feathers, rope and faggot. She noticed that all of her friends and relatives, including her parents, her brother Bobby, and her husband Richard, were part of the grinning mob.

"You low down trick," her father grimaced and spat in her face. "How *dare* you accuse Ty'rone of rape!? You been runnin after black dick from the moment you felt out cho mama's pussy!"

"Yuse uh whooooore!!" her mother roared. Beth was shocked to see that her mother was standing there, massaging her vagina. Her mother was aroused by the fact that her daughter would soon be a smoldering amalgamation of rotting flesh swinging from a rope.

"We gon break you from your habit of Black-baiting once and fuh all," her brother thumped Beth's pelvis with his middle finger.

"We gon give yo lyin ass a head start," her husband turned her toward a field and kicked her in the behind with such force that she felt the toe of his boot lodge momentarily in her anus. The velocity of the kick lifted Beth off her feet before she fell in a heap on the ground. She tasted her blood which was seasoned with the Earth's dust. Although she rose, she saw that 3 of her teeth remained on the ground.

"Wait, Rick," Bobby Lee grinned and the odor of raw sewage wafted from his mouth. "We got's to get us some souvenirs!

Bobby Lee whipped out his Carlson skinning knife and spun Beth until her hair was wrapped around his fist 2 times and made a handle of her hair, he then he sliced off her left ear.

Beth could not open her mouth to scream, so the lightning bolt of pain that shocked her body and mind had no audible accompaniment.

Bobby Lee chortled, "This here blade slices through gristle like butter!" He passed the ear round to the party so all could admire his handiwork.

"Gimme the lyin bitch's lips!" Beth's cousin Sheila giggled.

"Get em yoself," Bobby Lee tossed Sheila the blade, and he pulled the back of Beth's neck and her hair with such force that she heard her hair follicles popping out of her scalp.

Sheila pulled the skin around Beth's top lip until it extended about 5 inches from her face. Sheila's cut was so deep that she removed the tip of Beth's nose as well as the lip. Sheila handed the lip and nose tip to her husband Trace and then pulled and sliced away Beth's bottom lip.

"Easier than carvin a punkin," Sheila marveled.

"She look like a punkin!" Beth's Uncle Riley observed. "When we finish, I want the ho's head for my Halloween decoration."

"You got it," Richard grinned.

"Hold on there, Bobby Lee," Beth's mother took the knife from Sheila, "My hair's athinnin and I needs me a new wig!" Everyone laughed.

With Bobby Lee still holding the back of Beth's neck and pulling her hair into hell's ponytail, Beth's mother carved an outline around the edges of Beth's scalp with the precision of a master surgeon. When she had completed her circumnavigation she said, "Y'all bend her forward." Beth's husband and father forced her shoulders forward. With Bobby Lee still holding the back of her neck, Beth's mother took hold of the ponytail and pulled her daughter's scalp up from the nape to the forehead. Beth knew that there was no hell fire worse than the agony she felt and wet sllliiiiiiitch she heard as her mother scalped her.

Beth's mother hoisted high her prize to the admiration of the crowd. She smiled at her daughter whose delirium of pain was not visible on her catatonic face. She then leaned toward her daughter's remaining ear and whispered, "Alright, you ever-grinnin air conditioned cunt: RUN!"

If someone had peeked in her windows, they would have seen a woman running and thrashing in her living room, clawing at and attempting to climb the walls and knocking over lamps, knick-knacks, the television, and framed portraits. In her frenzy, Beth knocked the ashtray with its smoldering cigarette off of her end-table and onto a stack of newspapers.

When her charred body was pulled from the smoking black sticks that once were a house, the only salvageable item was a metal strong-box. After the firemen opened it and saw its contents, they took the box to the Parchman Prison for Women.

"Hello Mrs. Birdland," the young woman extended her hand. "My name is Willena Conwell. I'm a graduate student at Valley, and I'm doing some research on the inmates of this prison."

Warden Annmarie Birdland, "Birdie" to her friends, looked at the slim woman and frowned. "Well, Ms. Conwell, most all our prisoners was released several months ago. Them what was left broke out during the evacuation after 2 COs exploded." She shook her head and lamented, "Pope done hanged himself. Presidents dyin. . . . Seems like the whole world is coming to an end," she rolled her eyes up as if to call on some lord.

"It does, doesn't it?" Willena grinned.

Perhaps it was the smile that was not born of humor but of a private knowing that made Birdie take a close look at this ochre-toned young woman. The more she looked at her, the more fascinated she became. It looked like her skin was shimmering.

"But seriously, ma'am, it's the women who were here in the 1920s I'm concerned with, the 1920s to the 1960s. Some sang and cut a few albums. I came here to see if you have any files on the women."

"Yeh, we do. We have quite a few files and documents."

"Are there any privacy laws to prevent me from seeing the files."

"Naw. Because all prisoners belong to the State of Mississippi, every document about them is . . . *public domain*." Birdie nodded, impressed by her own knowledge of legal jargon.

"Come have a seat in our library Ms, uh"

"Conwell"

"Ms Conwell. I'll get the files for you. You want the prisoners and the wardens?"

"Yes ma'am, both."

"Fine," Birdie stood up and began walking to a door labeled "Administration." Before she opened the door, she turned to Willena and said, "I wanna ask you something."

"Sure," she smiled and shrugged.

"What do you use on your skin? It is sho nuff glorious."

"Petroleum jelly."

Willena poured over the files, but she didn't come up with much. Most of it was general information about the crimes the women had been convicted of, their sentences, their behavior while incarcerated, special skills and character traits, appeals, time spent in solitary, and punishments and their effectiveness or lack thereof. She saved for last a charred box filled with brittle, dry, and smoky files; she was hoping they would air out a bit before she tackled them. Because the box contained a warden's files, she doubted they would be helpful in her search for information about Randie "Big Momma" Sukes, Jolee Rambits, Tansy "Sugar Tit" Buckley, Lavina "Cudjoe" Yardley, Baba Jones, and Bette Jo Simmons.

Willena hummed the melodies of "Weeping Tree" and "Ol Rick," as she perused the files. She had listened to the Parchman Women's Penitentiary albums so often that she knew all of the songs by heart.

Finally, she dragged the charred strong-box towards her. It had aired out a bit, but smoke fumes and dust mites attacked her nostrils.

A yellowed envelope marked **"CONFIDENTIAL"** contained a coroner's report: Richard Beasley. Born, 1925 died 1959. Cause of death: punctured ventricle; ruptured urethra. Contributing factors: file lodged in heart; pencil lodged in penis. "Goddamn," Willena whispered, "what a painful way to go. I know they didn't put that on his death certificate," she mused.

Next she unfolded a handwritten note: "Ol' Rick, Don't forget to shoe Big Black. Ol' Rick." A note to himself. Musta been absent-minded. This must be his personal file, Willena surmised. As she flipped through the documents in a file, which consisted of purchase accounts and expenditures, she had an epiphany.

"Is this him? Is the song "Ol' Rick" about Richard Beasley?!?" Willena felt pins prick her scalp and spine with her revelation.

She continued to rifle through the papers that included a collection of seed purchases, medicines, mill work and the like. Willena transformed her disappointment into patience because she knew that the box held all of the answers. She felt it in the roots of her hair.

When she opened the last file in the box, she found a record of the shoes purchased for prisoners in the spring of 1959. She was at a lost. She had found nothing, but the pin pricks continued to assault her scalp.

Willena stood up and stretched. She looked at the clock, "It's 3:33: They close at 4:00." She felt anxious. She hadn't eaten anything since last night; she should be hungry, but she wasn't.

During undergrad, a summer of no money and no immediate job prospects led her to the art of meditation. She trained her body to survive on 2 cups of coffee per day, if it were a good day, by fasting and meditating. After that summer, she controlled her body completely. She could go for days without eating or sleeping. Indeed, she was working so hard researching the Women of Parchman, that she rarely slept more than 2 hours a day when she slept.

It had become routine for her to see at 4:30 am a brilliant shimmering star just over her left shoulder and just out of her range of vision. What she originally dismissed as an outgrowth a sleep deprivation she came to realize was a guide, a sign: Her work had importance, and she has assistance.

Willena stepped outside the prison library to stretch her legs and clear her sinuses of the smell of smoke and dry rot. She bent and touched her toes before she stood, reached for the clouds, and then bent backwards. When she had gone as far back as she could, Willena heard *click*. The answers are in that box. She returned to it.

Willena removed each file and re-read its contents before setting the file on the table. With this process, she would not only ensure a careful reading of the files' contents, but she would also ensure that she had read everything the box contained.

Halfway through her mission, she noticed that the files in the middle of the box stood a few millimeters higher than others. There was something under the files, and it was important. However, Willena continued with her routine because she wanted to be thorough.

After setting a manila folder about fertilizers on the table, Willena saw a red string peeking from the bottom of the box. Willena extracted a bound parcel of papers, and exhaled. Her arms were tingling. As she unwound the red string from the package, she mused on the significance of the color red: "Ẹjẹ, Àṣẹ, Àjẹ́."

Enclosed in 2 mottled smoky blank pages, 1 on the top and 1 on the bottom, were 15 battered sheets adorned with a slanting, halted, loping handwriting. He musta wrote this in the dark, she mused and let her fingers trail across the letters. Willena turned on the desk lamp and felt an electric current cap the top of her head as she read

I gotta write this fast, got to get this down quick 'cause this gon be the only chance that I get. Big Sal, who do the laundry, gon be round here at 7:45, and we got it worked out so that either this gon be in your hands or you gon be in mine. I don't know exactly what you gon do with this, Lil Wan, if I aint able to make it. But when you get this, you gon have all of you: All that I can give. All that I mean to you, Lil Wan, you have a whole ocean to you, Lil Wan, you have a whole ocean that you don't know yet. This here is comin through the Waters. Just look to the water if you don't understand all in there. Its 3:45 now, and we got a little time to talk, but the tide is comin.

And she was right because Willena was weeping after she finished reading the letter.

Willena secreted the sacred volume in her bosom along with the coroner's report and carried the files and containers back to Birdie's desk.

"Thank you so much for all your help," Willena told Birdie.

"Did you find anything useful?"

"A little, but not much," Willena looked disappointed.

"Well," Birdie waxed philosophical, "life is all about searchin and strugglin and lovin. Just continue doin all that and you'll find all you need."

"I will. Thank you, Ms. Birdland."

When Willena arrived at the Institute, she immediately knew where she was, not from the newspaper reports of the bombing, but from her spirit. She knew she was at home. The home she had been shining to see.

Ever since 2007 things had been popping off and she felt out of touch. When she heard about the deaths and the shutdown of the CDC and NIH due to lack of governmental funding and when she watched the burials of multiple heads of state on the news, she knew something was afoot. But when underground newspapers were reporting explosions that the nation's broadcasting services were mum about, she knew that Nation Time had come and she was disappointed that no 1 had told her to synchronize her soul.

When she saw the Igi Bùrúkù, she thanked the Òrìṣà, she sat down with Yemọja, and waited for the God's daughters to come forth.

The Bliss Bluff Ah were not surprised to see the young woman drive up and plant herself directly under the Wicked Tree's branches. People appeared at the site all of the time. In fact, Ah and Tahn were gravitating to emisites all over the world. Kumbah was filled with African Britons, Jamaicans, and Aborigines, Native Americans, folk from everywhere who needed healing. The same multi-Ah migrations were happening at all sites. Whole families were picking up and moving to where their emi knew they belonged. Many left void family members behind. Left them as they sat staring like Lot's wife at the fall of their clay god. There was no time to mourn those who had long been dead. Too busy shining!

But while folks came to the newly fortified Institute all of the time, they rarely came with such an air of excitement about them. So when Willena stood up and thanked the tree and headed for the entrance of the Institute, everyone stopped what they were doing and gathered around her.

Willena read the letter out loud to an all Ah gathering at the rebuilt and expanded Original Path Institute. She knew, without knowing, the spaces that the bruised paper and faded writing would fill.

As she read the letter she struggled not to drench the precious volume with her tears. Although she now knew every word by heart, Willena often paused to marvel at the history pulsing in her hand.

When the reading was finished, all Ah were engulfed in the silence of appreciation and wonder. After everyone embraced Conch/Lil Wom and Babygirl/Omowale, Willena went on her knees before mother and daughter and, with both hands, she offered them a gift of immeasurable wealth, "This is *your* text. These are your mothers."

I understand the meanin of feelin like a motherless child. This country has made you one. In this country a man can't be a husband, a father. Can't be a man. A woman can't be a mother, a wife. Can't be a woman. We can't love, defend, protect, teach, and raise our loved ones. All we sposed to do is wait to see what atrocities these beasts will commit and pray we can withstand the blows. Fuck that.

I'm gon figure out how to mother you from this cell. Gon learn how to love you from this cell. I'm gon hug you from this cell.

I laid still as a corpse thinking these thoughts. I didn't move cause if I did that bed's squealin and scroanin would jangle my thoughts, and my intentions would get trapped in the complaints of those rusty springs.

"I know what you dreamin about girl, but you best get up. We got some work ahead of us today."

Tendin some beast's cotton is the last thing on my mind. But I ain't got no voice and a half-healed arm. Bullet still in here and sometimes the pain cause me to cry out. Sometimes I wish they'd killed me outright. I ain't much without you, Mojo, or the bottoms.

I know it's hard on you with no blood, no kin to turn to, Lil Wom. But I hope one day you'll understand. I hope one day you will be proud of us for fightin so you could live free. I hope to make you even more proud tonight. See, I may seem like the most vulnerable person in this man's hell, but I got's me a few tools. And with only one good arm, I'ma put em those tools work. I ain't had no trial, and they ain't gon give me one. I figure the only trial I'ma get is the one I hold for myself. Court finta be in session.

"Big Momma, I'm a get up. My arm just bein contrary this morning."

"You want it to heal, you got to massage it all the time with that camphor and alum mix I made yuh. You got to do them exercises too, don't it'll shrivel."

I couldn't do nothin but nod, the pain so bad.

"Your voice your savior girl. You leadin us lessin yo load a bit."

"A bit," I rolled out of bed, and my arm started singing a song that dropped me to my knees.

Big Momma grabbed me round my waist and helped me to my feet.

"Can you lead us this mornin?"

"Umm hum," I'd sho catch hell if I couldn't.

"Well, you know what I need to hear."

"Why? You have a visitor last night?"

"Not me. Jolee. Heard her screamin and fightin all night long."

"Sick dog. He touch me I'm a kill em."

"We all done said that, girl, when we was new. But sometimes you gotta grin and go on."

"That person ain't who my momma raise."

Next thing I know I hear a whip crack and feel my ass stinging.

"I see what you momma raise and she did a good job. You and Big Momma better get your black asses out there in that field or I'm a show you what *my* momma raise. Put them work clothes on."

"Give me some damn privacy!" I turned my back and—sting and plap—he whipped me again. I wanted to catch his ass without that damn whip! "You must work at that to get so good."

"I go home and practice on the porch monkeys on the south side."

"Get yo clothes on girl," said Big Momma, "Rick done seen black titties before."

"Yeah, he was raised on em."

Oh, won't you hide me
Hide me in yo tree
Oh, won't you hide me
Hide me in yo tree
I won't you to hide me
love me right
wrap me tight so I can breathe
Up in yo tree
Let me climb yo weepin tree daddy
And get lost in yo leaves
stretch limbs down to the roots
I jus wanna be
Hidin, hidin
In yo sweet gum tree
won't be no wind daddy
won't nothin blow
jus me a-rustlin yo leaves
way down to your soul
Daddy won't you hide me
Hide me in yo tree
Hide me in yo tree
Let me moan round yo branches
and whisper my love up in yo leaves

Lil Wom, when we was singin I didn't feel nothin. In fact, felt like I was away from all this world, but close enough to see it—close enough to maintain, anyway. But it felt like I was up in daddy tree, watchin, just watchin. I see me and Big Momma, Jolee, Sugar Tit, Cudjoe, Bette Jo. I see all our group that work the fields. See our stripes movin with our hip muscles.

Not all of us work in the field. Some cook, some do laundry, and some of us sew but that's only them what ain't gone be in here for long. Like Big Sal, who do laundry. She killed her ol' man. She be out in about a month. She run her little games in here, even got a line to the outside, I hear. She don't have to work no field and don't do too much laundry.

Out here, we ain't got no perks; so we have to have a rhythm. A rhythm we can feel. Had to be our rhythm kept me goin cause I couldn't hear nothin, not even me singing. Jus see hips and stripes doin a kinda shuffle dance like when the old folks'ud ring shout. I see our arms, taut with labor, veins popped out like the black eyed peas in hoppin john. Arms that could raise up a house or a man or dust, like we raisin up now.

Dust rise up and we smooth it back down with our work and our wails. But it settle on us. Makin us sticky red-brown. Look like we movin earth, at least before you get to them stripes. But I see us as liquid, singing, soil, soul.

And I see him and understand the meaning of parchman. He bone dry from the outside in. He sittin on Big Black watchin our asses and lickin his mouth-slit. He stroke his gun.

My back is *hot* Lil Wom. The sun is roastin me, his eyes toastin me. Sittin up on high and watchin our calves tighten and relax, tighten and relax. First the green stripe ripplin, then the white, green, white, green, white. All dusted red brown and ripplin like the Nile. Strokin his shotgun and wishin—but soothed like the beast he is by our swaying and singing. Thinking bout a sugar tit. A black nipple in his mouth-slit. Hide me.

"Right pretty voice ya got there, gal."

I ain't said nothin and ain't look nowhere.

"Lotsa things right pretty from up here," he stroked between his legs. "You heifers go on and take yo lunch break."

"His eyes ain't left you girl. I figure it's gon be some room switchin tonight," Big Momma said this low to me, over her greens and rice.

"Pass me dat cornbread dere," I ain't said nothin else cause it wasn't nothin to say. Been here 6 months and I have seen everything from executions in the night, to blood blotting out daylight, to cut off titties bleeding on the floor, to dry white laughter that cut like a knife. Now that they done showed me what they capable of, I guess they figure it's time to break in the cracker-killin nigger. Rick been itchin to break me in, break me down. I guess he figure he can do what that bald dog couldn't do to Momma. He don't know the long cracker-killin line I comes from.

I ain't scared, and I ain't mad. I don't feel nothing. I don't taste the food at all, but I eat it cause I know I need strength.

I look at Big Black's thighs glistenin in the sun. He sho take good care of him. Could be a show horse.

Big Black reared up then with Ol Rick grinnin on his back, and I noticed he was castrated.

"A geldin."

"And I'm glad of it too," said Jolee. "I can't imagine what Sik Rick'ud make us do with that damned horse," her eyes was rimmed in red and her hands was shakin.

"Be strong, woman, we know what you goin through," Big Momma helped Jolee up from the table. She could barely walk.

"He use his fist, too," Jolee voice didn't have no tone. "He know he ain't got enough to hurt ya in his pants." She wasn't lookin at nobody but me cause we all knew what time it was.

"Yeah, yeller's alright," Rick said, nippin Jolee with his whip as him and Big Black pranced up, "but I like em just like this big hoss here. Strong and Black."

I started hummin and thinkin and didn't stop either 1 even when him and that horse came right up behind my head. "I don't know whose breath smell the worser," I mumbled.

"Bout the same," Big Momma replied and we chuckled the tension down a bit.

"Oh, Big Momma, I likes em big too. But you know that."

Just like a dog on a rickety chain
He gon get loose 1 day
He gon get loose 1 day
Like a dog on a rickety chain
He gon get loose 1 day
And make his owner pay
Oh, make his owner pay

"You ain't sangin nothin but truth. A few sassy mouthed pups gon find they owners tonight too. And the song gon be 'ba ba black bitch lemme feel yo wool'." He laughed, but it only opened the door for more shit to fly from the slit of his mouth.

"Big Momma, you been such a good nigger to us that the warden done decided to give you a bran new mattress. What with yo bad back and all, we figured you would like some more support."

"My back and mattress both fine Rick," never heard Big Momma talk so low. "Just fine." She looked into her greens that had colored her rice like she was lookin at fresh sheep shit. She turn, face im, and ask, "Since when y'all give a damn how any one of us sleep?"

"You didn't know? We want y'all to sleep good so we can work you all day long in this here field.

"Bess, we's got a new room for you, too. Down in Jolee's. Bed sleep real nice," the beast chuckled and trotted away.

Our eyes met and Big Momma said, "I knowed it, Baby girl. You just be strong. New girl come soon."

'New girl come soon.' I can't put this off on no 1 else cause 'new girl' could be you 1 day, Lil Wom.

I cut my eyes cross my greens at Bess who in tight wid Big Sal, "Bess, tell Big Sal I needs to see her once we get in, and see her quick."

"Bess say you wanta see me."

"I wanna write my daughter a letter."

"What ya got."

"Nothin but pride. Ol Rick comin here tonight"

                                                                    "Mmmm"

                                                                             "ain't but one

of us gon see the dawn."

"What you gon do!? Don't be no fool, girl. . . ." Big Sal's whispergrowl filled my cell. "What you think I can do? I ain't gon help you kill that muthafucka. Hell, I only got 1 month to go!"

"You ain't got to do nothin but 2 things. Get me some paper and a pencil and get my letter to Nell, Tynell Waters in Bliss Bluff."

"How soon you need the paper and pencil?

"It's 3:00 now right?"

"Um hum."

"By 3:15. Come back for the letter by 7:45."

Big Sal exhaled out her mouth, "You know I cain't do that. I gots to make sure my girls gets they cleanin out for Monday. Cain't do it."

I looked at her lyin to me. If I had some cigarettes or some hard candy for her big ass wouldn't be no problem. I didn't have nothin but my eyes, "Look here, right here," so I locked em on hers: "You gon get out in a month and start a new life with a new husband. This hairless dog gon move in my cell to have his way with me startin tonight. I can't have it, won't have it, and y'all should be sick of it." Nothin but eyes and pride: "You gon help me, Big Sal." It wasn't a question.

"You don't help her write her baby girl I'ma make sure you leave here with some remembrance—*If* you leave," Big Momma ducked her head in the room. "I can't help her now, but, sho as you yellow, yo ass will."

Big Sal looked at Momma's forearms and hands strong from the field and got up. She brushed hips with her on the way out of the cell.

"You remember what I say—Bliss Bluff. Tynell Waters."

"I won't forget." She left singing "Wade in the Water."

It's jus you and me now Lil Wom, and I hope you feel my spirit. You sleepin now? Maybe you up playin fore you go to bed. I wonder if you look like yo daddy or Ma Ja or me. I wonder if anybody bury yo daddy proper. Well, it don't matter bout his body, his soul with you and me.

Before Big Momma left, she gave me a fingernail file. Said it come from Jolee with good luck. She wink her eye at me and kiss my forehead. I thanked her but didn't stop writin. The file do come in handy to keep this pencil sharp. It's funny how things gets put in the right places at the right time. Thanks to this file, I been able to keep my writin to you clear.

I done wore this pencil down, girl, tellin you bout yoself so you can have yoself. Eraser still firm. I'ma need that cushionin. Here come Big Sal. I love you, Lil Wom. More than all, I love you.

All of me,
Yoruba

I handed Big Sal the letter and kept the pencil and sheets of leftover paper. Sal said something to me that I couldn't hear for the tinklin: Daddy Mosa talkin to me and Momma Yemoja all over my face.

Pencil's worn down and it's the perfect length. File would be too skinny by itself, move around. Got to have somethin wider, thicker and this pencil near bout perfect. Got this here paper for cushionin. I'ma take a few sheets to build up a platform for protection—and a launchpad. Once I soften the other sheets with my tears and mold em to the pencil and my body, I'll have a custom fit.

Ol file good to sharpen this pencil 1 last time . . . Done got the point sharp as a crock's tooth, the sides jagged enough to hurt. Hmm, this here file'll be perfect for a finishing touch!

Alright, Rick, come on. I'm ready. I'ma scream and cuss, take some licks and give mo back. I'ma wear this bum arm out. I'ma get you good and angry. And hard. Um hum. Good and angry so you gon wanna ram it hard and deep. Make you wanna hurt me. Then I'ma let you spread my legs so you can take it. All of it.

Ah won't put more in my pot than it can hold.

SELECTED BIBLIOGRAPHY

Abimbola, 'Wande. *Ifá: An Exposition of Ifá Literary Corpus*. Ibadan: Oxford University Press, 1967.

------. *Sixteen Great Poems of Ifa*. n.p.: UNESCO, 1975.

Abiodun, Rowland. "Identity and the Artistic Process in Yoruba Aesthetic Concept of *Ìwà*." *J. C. I.* 1:1 (Dec. 1983): 13–30.

-----. "Verbal and Visual Metaphors: Mythical Allusions in Yoruba Ritualistic Art of *Orí*." *Ife* (1985): 8–38.

Adeeko, Adeleke. "The Language of Head-Calling: A Review Essay on Yoruba Metalanguage: Ede Iperi Yoruba." *Research in African Literatures* 24 (Winter 1993): 198–201.

Adeoye, C. L. *Ìgbàgbọ́ ati Èsìn Yorùbá*. Ibadan: Evans Bros., 1985.

Akinjogbin, I. A., ed. *The Cradle of a Race: Ife: From the Beginning to 1980*. Lagos: Sunray, 1992.

Alexander, Michelle. *The New Jim Crow: Mass Incarceration in the Age of Colorblindness*. Revised Edition. New York: The New Press, 2010.

Allah, Supreme Understanding, et. al. *Knowledge of Self: A Collection of the Wisdom on the Science of Everything in Life*. Atlanta: Supreme Design, 2009.

Ani, Marimba. *Yurugu: An African-Centered Critique of European Cultural Thought and Behavior*. Trenton, NJ: Africa World Press, 1994.

Anyebe, A. P. *Ogboni: The birth and growth of the reformed Ogboni Society*. Lagos: Sam Lao, 1989.

Armah, Ayi Kwei. *Osiris Rising*. Popenguine: Per Ankh, 1995.

-----. *The Healers*. Heinemann: Oxford, 1978.

-----. *Two Thousand Seasons*. Heinemann: Oxford, 1973.

-----. *The Beautyful Ones Are Not Yet Born*. Heinemann: Oxford, 1968.

Asante, Molefi K. *Afrocentricity*. Trenton, NJ: Africa World Press, 1988.

Asante, Molefi K. and Kariamu Welsh Asante. *African Culture: The Rhythms of Unity*. Trenton, NJ: Africa World Press, 1990.

Asiwaju, A. I. "Èfè Poetry as a Source for Western Yoruba History." *Yoruba Oral Tradition*. Ed. Wande Abimbola. Department of African Languages and Literature: Ile-Ife, 1975. 199–266.

Babayemi, S. O. *Egúngún Among the Oyo Yoruba*. Ibadan: Board Publications, 1980.

Baker, Houston A. "Workings of the Spirit: Conjure and the Space of Black Women's Creativity." *Zora Neale Hurston: Critical Perspectives Past and Present*. Eds. Henry Louis Gates Jr. and K. A. Appiah. New York: Amistad, 1993. 280–308.

Bambara, Toni Cade. *The Salt Eaters*. New York: Random House, 1980.

-----. "Broken Field Running." *The Sea Birds Are Still Alive*. Vintage: New York, 1977. 43–70.

-----. "Maggie and the Green Bottles." *Gorilla My Love*. New York, Vintage, 1972 149–160.

Bannerman-Richter, Gabriel. *The Practice of Witchcraft in Ghana*. Elk Grove, CA: Gabari, 1982.

Bascom, William. *Ifa Divination: Communication Between Gods and Men in West Africa*. Bloomington: Indiana University Press, 1969.

-----. *Sixteen Cowries: Yoruba Divination from Africa to the New World*. Bloomington: Indiana University Press, 1980.

Beier, Ulli. *Yoruba Poetry: An Anthology of Traditional Poems*. Cambridge: Cambridge University Press, 1970.

-----. ed. *Black Orpheus*. Ikeja: Longman, 1964.

------. "Gelede Masks." *Odu*. No. 6 (June 1958): 4–23.

Billingsley, Andrew. "Climbing Jacob's Ladder." Reprinted as a series by *Houston Chronicle* (28 Feb 1993): 1G–4G.

Bockie, Simon. *Death and the Invisible Powers: The World of Kongo Belief*. Bloomington: Indiana University Press, 1993.

Browder, Anthony T. *Nile Valley Contributions to Civilization*. Washington, D. C.: Institute of Karmic Guidance, 1992.

Cantwell, Alan. *AIDS and the Doctors of Death*. Los Angeles: Aries Rising, 1988.

Chinweizu, Onwuchekwa Jemie, et al. *Toward the Decolonization of African Literature*. Enugu: Fourth Dimension, 1980.

Clark-Bekederemo, J. P. *The Ozidi Saga*. Washington, D.C.: Howard University Press, 1991.

Clarke, John Henrik and Yosef ben-Jochannan. *New Dimensions in African History*. Trenton, NJ: Africa World Press, 1991.

Cook, Mercer and Stephen E. Henderson. *The Militant Black Writers in Africa and the United States*. 1969.

Courlander, Harold A. ed. *A Treasury of Afro-American Folklore*. New York: Crown Publishers, 1976.

-----. *A Treasury of African Folklore*. New York: Marlowe and Company, 1996.

Davis, Angela Y. *Women, Race and Class*. New York: Vintage, 1983.

Dictionary of the Yoruba Language. Ibadan: University of Ibadan Press, 1991.

Diop Cheikh Anta. *The Cultural Unity of Black Africa*. Chicago: Third World Press, 1959.

Dixon, Melvin. "Singing Swords: The Literacy Legacy of Slavery." Charles T. Davis and Henry Louis Gates Jr. eds. *The Slave's Narrative*. New York: Oxford University Press, 1985. 298–317.

Dundes, Alan, ed. *Motherwit from the Laughing Barrel*. Englewood Cliffs, NJ: Prentice Hall, 1973.

Eleburuibon, Ifayemi. *The Adventures of Obatala: Ifa and Santeria God of Creativity*. Oyo: API, 1989.

Emefie Ikenga Metuh. *God and Man in African Religion*. London: Geoffry Chapman, 1981.

Emeh, B. B. O. *Treasures of Nnobi*. Ochumba: Enugu. n. d. (1986).

Equiano, Olaudah. *The Interesting Narrative of the Life of Olaudah Equiano, or Gustavas Vassa, the African. The Classic Slave Narratives*. Ed. Henry Louis Gates, Jr. New York: Mentor, 1987.

Evans, Mari, ed. *Black Women Writers (1950–1980): A Critical Evaluation*. Garden City, New York: Anchor Books, 1984.

Fatunmbi, Awo Fá'lokun. *Ìwa-pèlé: Ifá Quest: The Search for the Source of Santería and Lucumí*. Bronx: Original, 1991.

Fenandez, James, W. *Bwiti: An Ethnography of the Religious Imagination in Africa*. Princeton: Princeton University Press, 1982.

Fortes, Meyer. "Ancestor Worship." *African Systems of Thought*. Eds. Meyer Fortes and Germain Diterlen. New York: Oxford University Press, 1965. 16–20.

Gaba, Christian. *Scriptures of an African People: Ritual Utterances of the Anlo*. New York: Nok, 1973.

Gaspar, David Barry. *Bondmen & Rebels: A Study of Master-Slave Relations in Antigua*. Baltimore: John Hopkins University Press, 1985.

Gates, Henry Louis, Jr. *The Signifying Monkey: A Theory of African American Literary Theory*. New York: Oxford University Press, 1988.

Gayle, Addison. *The Black Aesthetic*. New York: Anchor Books, 1971.

Goliszek, Andrew. *In the Name of Science*. New York: St. Martin's 2003.

Gottlieb, Karla. *The Mother of Us All: A History of Queen Nanny, Leader of the Windward Jamaican Maroons*. Trenton, NJ: Africa World Press, 1997.

Greenlee, Sam. *The Spook Who Sat By the Door*. London: Alison and Busby, 1969.

Greer, T.J. *One People: The Ancient Glory of the African Race*. Chicago: Karnak, 1984.

Hallen, Barry and J. Olubiyi Sodipo. "A Comparison of the Western 'Witch' with the Yoruba Àjẹ́: Spiritual Powers or Personality Types?" *Ife* 1 (1986): 1–7.

Harding Vincent. *The Other American Revolution.* Atlanta: Center for Afro-American Studies, 1980.

Harrison, Paul Carter. *Kuntu Drama.* New York: Grove, 1974.

Hemenway, Robert. *Zora Neale Hurston: A Literary Biography.* Urbana: University of Illinois Press, 1977.

Herskovits, Melville, J. *Dahomey: An Ancient West African Kingdom.* Vol. 2. New York: J. J. Augustin, 1938.

-----. *The Myth of the Negro Past.* 1941. Reprint. New York: Harper and Row Publishers, 1970.

Herskovits, Melville J. and Frances S. Herskovits. *Dahomean Narrative: A Cross-Cultural Analysis.* Evanston: Northwestern University Press, 1958.

Holloway, Joseph, ed. *Africanisms in American Culture.* Bloomington: Indiana University Press, 1990.

Holloway, Joseph E. and Winifred K. Vass. *The African Heritage of American English.* Bloomington: Indiana University Press, 1993.

hooks, bell. *Ain't I A Woman: Black Women and Feminism.* Boston: South End Press, 1981.

Hooper, Ed. *The River: A Journey Back to the Source of HIV and AIDS.* New York: Penguin, 1999.

Horowitz, Michael A., ed. *People and Culture of the Caribbean: An Anthropological Reader.* Garden City: Natural History Press, 1971.

Hudson-Weems, Clenora. *Africana Womanism: Reclaiming Ourselves.* Third Revised Edition. Troy, MI: Bedford, 1995.

Hurston, Zora Neal. *Tell My Horse.* New York: Harper and Row, 1938.

-----. *Mules and Men.* New York: Harper Perennial, 1935.

Ibie, Cromwell Osamaro. *Ifisim: The Complete Works of Orunmila.* Lagos, Efehi, 1986.

Isola, Akinwumi. "Ọya: Inspiration and Empowerment." Unpublished paper, 1998.

Jackson, Bruce. *"Get Your Ass in the Water and Swim Like Me."* Cambridge: Harvard University Press, 1974.

Jackson, Rebecca. *Gifts of Power: The Writings of Rebecca Jackson, Black Visionary, Shaker Eldress.* Amherst: University of Massachusetts Press, 1981.

Jahn, Janheinz. *Muntu: The New African Culture.* New York: Grove, 1961.

Joyce, Joyce-Ann. *Warriors, Conjurers and Priests.* Chicago: Third World Press, 1993.

Knappert, Jan. *Myths and Legends of the Congo*. Ibadan: Heinemann, 1971.

Lawal, Babatunde. *The Gẹ̀lẹ̀dẹ́ Spectacle: Art Gender and Social Harmony in an African Culture*. Seattle: University of Washington Press, 1996.

-----. "New Light on Gelede." *African Arts* Vol. XI: 2 (1978): 65–70, 94.

Layiwola, Dele. "Womanism in Nigerian Folklore and Drama." *African Notes*. XI:1 (1987): 26–33.

Lester, Julius. *Black Folktales*. New York: Grove Weidenfeld, 1969.

Levine, Lawrence W. *Black Culture and Black Consciousness*. New York: Oxford University Press, 1977.

Lorde, Audre. *Zami: A New Spelling of My Name*. Freedom, NY: Crossing Press, 1982.

Lucas, Olumide J. *The Religion of the Yorubas*. Lagos: CMS, 1948.

Magubane, Bernard M. *The Ties that Bind: African-American Consciousness of Africa*. Trenton, NJ: Africa World Press, 1987.

Major, Clarence, ed. *From Juba to Jive: A Dictionary of African American Slang*. New York: Penguin, 1994.

Makinde, Akin Moses. *African Philosophy, Culture and Traditional Medicine*. Athens: Ohio University Center for International Studies, 1988.

Marwick, M. G. "Witchcraft and Sorcery." *African Systems of Thought*. Eds. Meyer Fortes and Germain Diterlen. New York: Oxford University Press, 1965. 21–27.

Mason, John. *Orin Òrìṣà: Songs for Selected Heads*. Brooklyn: Yoruba Theological Archministry, 1992.

Mba, Nina. *Nigerian Women Mobilized*. Berkeley: University of California Press, 1982.

Mbiti, John S. *African Religions and Philosophy*. 2nd. ed. London: Heinemann, 1969.

Metuh, Emefie Ikenga. *God and Man in African Religion*. London: Geoffry Chapman, 1981.

Morrison, Toni. *Song of Solomon*. 1977. New York: Plume, 1987.

-----. *Home*. New York: Alfred A. Knopf, 2012.

"The Mother Tongue." *U.S. News & World Report*. 5 Nov 1990: 60–70.

Nadel, S. F. *Nupe Religion: Traditional Beliefs and the Influence of Islam in West African Chiefdom*. London: Routledge, 1954.

Oduyoye, Modupe. "The Spider, The Chameleon and the Creation of the Earth." *Traditional Religion in West Africa*. Ed. E. E. Ade Adegbola. Accra: Asempa, 1983. 374–388.

Opefeyitimi, Ayo. "Womb to Tomb: Yoruba Women Power Over Life and Death." *Ife* 5 (1994): 57–67.

-----. "'Women of the World' in Yoruba Culture." Unpublished paper, 1993.

Opeola, Samuel M. "What is Witchcraft." Unpublished paper. 1997.

-----. *Napatian Society: A Society in Search of Ancient African Knowledge.* Vol. 1 (Sept) 1993.

Oyesakin, Adefioye. "The Image of Women in Ifa Literary Corpus." *Nigeria Magazine* 141 (1982): 16–23.

Quilombo. Carlos Diegues, Dir. 1984. New Yorker Video, 2005. DVD.

Palmer, Colin A. *Slaves of the White God: Blacks in Mexico, 1570–1650.* Cambridge: Harvard University, 1976.

Paulkovitch, Michael. *No Meek Messiah: Christianity's Lies, Laws and Legacy.* Spillix: Annapolis, MD, 2012,

Rawick, George P. Ed. *The American Slave: A Composite Autobiography.* Vols 2–17 Westport CT: Greenwood, 1972.

-----. *The Unwritten History of Slavery.* Vol. 18. *The American Slave : A Composite Autobiography* Westport, CT: Greenwood, 1972.

-----. *From Sundown to Sunup: The Making of the Black Community.* Vol. 1. *The American Slave: A Composite Autobiography.* Westport, CT: Greenwood 1972.

-----. *God Struck Me Dead.* Vol. 19. *The American Slave: A Composite Autobiography.* Westport, CT: Greenwood, 1972.

Reed, Ishmael. *Mumbo Jumbo.* New York: Atheneum, 1972.

Roberts, Dorothy. *Killing the Black Body: Race, Reproduction, and the Meaning of Liberty.* New York: Pantheon, 1997.

Sankofa. Haile Gerima, Dir. Mypheduh, 1993.VHS.

Sertima, Ivan Van. *They Came Before Columbus: The African Presence in Ancient America.* New York: Random House, 1976.

The Spook Who Sat by the Door. Ivan Dixon, Dir. 1973. Monarch Home Video, 2004. DVD.

Stetson, Jeff. *Blood on the Leaves.* New York: Warner Books, 2004.

Teish, Luisah. *Jambalaya: The Natural Woman's Book of Personal Charms and Practical Rituals.* New York: Harper Collins, 1985.

Thomas, H. Nigel. *From Folklore to Fiction: A Study of Folk Heroes and Rituals in the Black American Novel.* New York: Greenwood Press, 1988.

Thompson, Robert Farris. *Flash of the Spirit: African & Afro-American Art and Philosophy.* New York: Vintage, 1983.

-----. *Dancing Between Two Worlds: Kongo-Angola Culture and the Americas.* Caribbean Cultural Center: New York, 1991.

Wade-Gayles, Gloria. *No Crystal Stair: Visions of Race and Sex in Black Women's Fiction.* New York: Pilgrim, 1984.

Walker, Alice. *In Search of Our Mother's Gardens.* New York: Harcourt Brace Jovanovitch, 1983.

-----. *In Love and In Trouble: Stories of Black Women.* New York: Harvest, 1967.

-----. *The Color Purple.* New York: Harcourt, 1982.

Washington, Harriet, A. *Medical Apartheid: The Dark History of Medical Experimentation on Black Americans from Colonial Times to the Present.* New York: Doubleday, 2007.

Washington, Teresa N. *The Architects of Existence: Àjẹ́ in Yoruba Cosmology, Ontology, and Orature.* Ọya's Tornado, 2014.

-----. *Manifestations of Masculine Magnificence: Divinity in Africana Life, Lyrics, and Literature.* Ọya's Tornado, 2014.

-----. "*Mules and Men* and Messiahs: Continuity in Yoruba Divination Verses and African American Folktales." *Journal of American Folklore* 125:497 (Summer 2012): 263–285.

-----. *Our Mothers, Our Powers, Our Texts: Manifestations of Àjẹ́ in Africana Literature.* Bloomington: Indiana University Press, 2005.

-----. "Re-membering the Prophet: Spiritual Transcendence in *Lumumba, la mort du prophete* and *A Season in the Congo.*" *The Literary Griot* 9: 1 & 2 (Spring-Fall 1997): 27–51.

Wilson, August. *They Tell Me Joe Turner's Come and Gone.* In *Three Plays.* Pittsburgh: University of Pittsburgh Press, 1991. 196–289.

Woods, William. *A Casebook of Witchcraft: Reports, Depositions, Confessions, Trials, and Executions for Witchcraft During a Period of Three Hundred Years.* New York: Putnam, 1974.

Woodson, Carter, G. *The Mis-Education of the Negro.* Trenton, N. J.: Africa World Press, 1990.

Yai, Olabiyi Babalola. "In Praise of Metonymy: The Concepts of 'Tradition' and 'Creativity' in the Transmission of Yoruba Artistry over Time and Space." *Research in African Literatures* 24:4 (Winter 1993): 29–37.

-----. "Towards A New Poetic of Oral Poetry in Africa." *Ifẹ* (1985): 40–55.

Asiri Odu is a Pan Africanist and a political scientist. Odu is a native of
Alapaha, Georgia.

www.ingramcontent.com/pod-product-compliance
Lightning Source LLC
Chambersburg PA
CBHW030648120726
47905CB00001B/114